edge
darkness

Karen Rose was introduced to suspense and horror at the tender age of eight when she accidentally read Poe's *The Pit and the Pendulum* and was afraid to go to sleep for years. She now enjoys writing books that make other people afraid to go to sleep.

Karen lives in Florida with her family, their cat, Bella, and two dogs, Loki and Freya. When she's not writing, she enjoys reading, and her new hobby – knitting.

Praise for the novels of Karen Rose:

'A high-octane thrill ride that kept me on the edge of my seat and up far too late at night!' Lisa Jackson

'Intense, complex and unforgettable' James Patterson

'Fast and furious' *Sun*

'Takes off like a house afire. There's action and chills galore in this nonstop thriller' Tess Gerritsen

'A pulse pounding tale that has it all' *Cosmopolitan*

'Rose juggles a large cast, a huge body count and a complex plot with terrifying ease' *Publishers Weekly*

'A blend of hard-edged police procedural and romance – engaging'
Irish Independent

3 0116 02063901 7

Karen ROSE

edge of darkness

HEADLINE

First published in Great Britain in 2017 by
HEADLINE PUBLISHING GROUP

First published in paperback in Great Britain in 2018 by
HEADLINE PUBLISHING GROUP

1

Cataloguing in Publication Data is available from the British Library

ISBN 978 1 4722 4585 4 (B format)
ISBN 978 1 4722 4586 1 (A format)

Typeset in Palatino by Avon DataSet Ltd, Bidford-on-Avon, Warwickshire

Printed and bound in Great Britain by Clays Ltd, St Ives plc

HEADLINE PUBLISHING GROUP
An Hachette UK Company
Carmelite House
50 Victoria Embankment
London EC4Y 0DZ

www.headline.co.uk
www.hachette.co.uk

For all my readers. Thank you for allowing me to have the job of my dreams and for loving my characters as much as I do.

As always, for Martin.

Acknowledgements

Terri Bolyard, for listening while I talked myself free of plot snarls.

Marc Conterato, for all things medical.

Caitlin Ellis, Sarah Hafer and Beth Miller, proofreaders extraordinaire.

Amy Lane for all the knitting.

Geoff Symon, for his crime scene advice.

The Starfish – Chris, Cheryl, Sheila, Susan, Kathy, and Brian – for helping me stay on track.

As always, all mistakes are my own.

Prologue

Andy's body jerked and his eyes flew open. His own shiver had woken him up. *Cold.* He was so damn cold. *So move, dammit. Get your blood—*

His memory returned and with it, a mind-blowing panic.

He couldn't move. He was tied up. Someone had tied him up and left him here. Wherever *here* was.

Scream, dammit. Scream for help. He drew a deep breath into his lungs that burned like fire, and his body shook in a fit of hoarse coughing.

No, he remembered. *Don't scream.* His head still throbbed from the last time. He'd woken once before and screamed. How long ago? It had been dark then. It was dark now.

The man had come when he'd screamed. Dressed in black. *Of course.* Didn't the bad guys always dress in black?

Because this was a bad guy. Andy had screamed for help. For anyone. But guy-in-black had kicked him in the head so hard he'd seen stars. That had shut him up quick.

That wasn't what had put him back to sleep, though. No. He fought to swallow because his fear was a living thing, filling his chest with ice, choking his throat. The man had brought a smelly rag with him and had covered Andy's face with it. He'd tried not to breathe it in, but the man had aimed a hard punch to his gut, forcing him to gasp in a breath along with whatever was on the rag.

1

Just like in the alley.

Yes, yes. Andy remembered the alley now, the one behind Pies & Fries. He'd been on his break and had gone out for a smoke. Someone had been waiting. It had been dark already and Andy hadn't seen the guy until he'd lit a match and even then he hadn't seen a face. Or a body. The sudden flare from his match and the shadow at the edge of his peripheral vision was all he'd seen.

Who did this to me? Why? He didn't have enemies. Not anymore. Not here, anyway.

He'd started over. He had.

And now he was going to die here. *Wherever here is,* he thought bitterly.

I'll miss my final exams, and I had As. Even in English Lit. He'd worked so damn hard for that A too.

Which did not matter right now. None of that mattered right now.

I need to get out of here. Before he comes back. Whoever he is.

I need to get out of here. Need to find Linnie. Never told her that I love her. Need to tell her. Need to tell her that I didn't mean it. Any of it. They'd had a fight. He'd said terrible things. She'd think he meant the things he'd said. That he'd run away. Like everyone else in her life. Like everyone in both their lives.

I made a mistake. It couldn't have been her that he'd seen that day. With another man. She'd denied it so forcefully when he'd screamed his accusations. His rage. His hurt. She'd backed away, weeping, still denying. Then she'd fled. *And I let her go.*

And then, when his temper had calmed, he'd believed her. She wouldn't do that. She couldn't. *I believe you.* But he hadn't told her. Not yet. *Unless I get out of here, I never will.*

He struggled against the ropes that bound him, wrists and ankles, but all it did was burn his flesh. He collapsed into a heap on the cold concrete, barely holding back the sob that threatened to rip him up from the inside out. It came out a whimper. A teeny little whimper.

Be a fucking man, dammit. Do something. Save yourself.

But it was no use. *I'm going to die here.*

You can't die here. You've come too far. Fought too damn hard.
For nothing. I'm going to die here.

He was so cold. He could feel the icy concrete through his thin sweater and socks. They'd taken his parka and his shoes. Both were new too. *New to me, anyway.* He'd bought them at the thrift store just last week. He'd paid his spring tuition and had just enough left over to buy some winter clothes. Because nothing from the year before fit anymore.

Because I finally grew. He'd waited for years to be big enough to fight back. Finally, he was. *And some asshole shoves a smelly rag in my face and I'm down for the fucking count.*

Who? Who could do this? *Who the fuck would* want *to?* It wasn't robbery. After he'd bought the parka and shoes at the thrift store, he'd only had twenty bucks in his pocket – and those were his tips from the dinner rush. Everything else – all one hundred forty-two dollars and six cents that he had left in the world – was in his checking account.

Nobody in his right mind would want to rob him and the one person who hated his guts was in jail.

That sick bitch was in jail, wasn't she? New panic layered over the old. The judge had sent her away for fifteen years. It had only been three.

Oh God. If she gets out, I'm dead. Andy began to pant, hyperventilating. The cops would have told him, right?

No, genius, because they don't know where you are either. You ran away, remember? Changed your name. Didn't leave a forwarding address.

The only people who knew where he was were Shane and Linnie. Linnie . . . she'd never want to see him again, he thought, closing his eyes. *The things I said . . . I'm so sorry.*

Shane would always come if Andy called. But Andy hadn't called. Hadn't returned any of Shane's calls after they'd gone their separate ways. *Because I wanted to start over.*

Just like Shane had. Shane was never afraid.

A tear spilled from his eye and trickled down Andy's face. *I'm not going to live to see the morning.*

Not if they kept him out here all night. He'd freeze to death.

3

Do something. Be a damn man. Find a way to cut these ropes before he comes back and makes you breathe from that smelly rag again.

Find a way to get free so you can find Linnie. So you can tell her.

There was nothing on the floor that he could use to get free. No metal with a sharp edge. No plastic, even. Not even one rock. Nothing.

It was just concrete with rough wooden walls. Someone had slapped some planks together to make a shack. There was no mortar or fiberglass or anything between the planks – nothing to keep out the cold. It was just going to get worse.

Andy went still when he heard the snap of a twig outside. Someone was coming.

Maybe it was help. *Maybe they've come to take me home.*

But then the door opened and his heart sank. It was the man again, still dressed in black. Without a word, the man picked him up and slung him over his shoulder in a fireman's hold.

Pain radiated through Andy's head. The rest of his body was so cold it was numb. He saw the ground pass under his feet as the man carried him across a yard covered in the thin layer of snow that had fallen two days before. His body was jostled as the man opened a door and . . .

Oh my God. Warm. It was so warm. His feet were on fire with the worst pins and needles ever as the blood began to circulate. Another whimper escaped his throat.

'Put him down there,' a voice said quietly. Male. Older. So menacing that Andy shivered again.

New pain swept over him when the guy in black dumped him face down on a sofa. An old sofa. Dusty.

A new voice cried out in distress, female and . . . familiar. *Oh God. Familiar.* 'Why?' she asked, physical pain in the single syllable. 'Why him? He had nothing to do with this.'

'Because I need him,' the man said. 'Sit him up straight.'

Guy-in-black yanked the collar of Andy's thin sweater, pulling him into a sitting position. He was in an office with old, ratty furniture. *In a garage?* He could smell the oil.

Andy stared at his captor in the dim light provided by a single lamp.

He was . . . *Nobody*. Nobody Andy had ever seen before. Not old, exactly. But not young, either. Maybe forty or fifty? It was hard to tell in the semidarkness. He appeared tall and strong, the sleeves of his starched white shirt straining around his biceps.

He was nobody Andy knew and certainly nobody he'd dare cross. But the woman . . . *Oh God, Linnie*. She knew who the man was. It was clear from the expression on her pale, pathetically thin face. Her swollen, bruised face.

'Linnie?' Andy rasped. This man was dangerous. And he had them both.

Maybe it's a mistake. Maybe we're both a mistake. He meant to take someone else.

But then Linnie shook her head. She wouldn't meet his eyes. 'I'm sorry,' she whispered. 'I'm so sorry, Andy.'

Not a mistake then. The man hadn't meant to take someone else. Or at least he'd meant to take Linnie.

This must be him. Andy had seen them going into a motel room. He'd seen them . . . together. 'Who are you?' Andy asked him, deflated and broken. 'What do you want?'

'You, Mr Gold. Specifically, your services.'

'My services?' Andy repeated stupidly. 'What services? I'm a *waiter*, for God's sake. I'm majoring in English Lit. You've got me confused with someone else.'

The man turned to Linnie. 'He doesn't know, does he, Linnea?' he asked and Andy's gut turned inside out with dread. Linnie knew why he'd been taken.

Linnie closed her eyes. 'No,' she whispered. 'He thinks you're my lover.'

The man snorted a laugh. 'Lover? As if. Tell him the truth.'

Linnie shook her head, shrinking back into the chair in which she sat, turning her face away. Her bruised and battered face.

Andy leaned forward, suddenly furious. But still tied. 'You hit her? You *hit* her?'

'I slapped the shit out of her,' the man said with a mean smile. He backhanded her again, making her yelp in pain. Like a dog. 'Tell him, *Linnie*,' he commanded mockingly.

5

'Linnie?' Andy's shaking voice jumped an octave, his heart beating so hard it was all he could hear. 'Tell me what? Who *is* this guy?'

'Tell him,' the man commanded. 'He deserves to know why he's here.'

Andy felt the bile climbing up his throat, burning. Dread now lay in his gut like rancid lard. 'Linnie, please?'

'He's my . . . pimp.' She spat the word out.

Andy's mouth fell open in shock, but he didn't say a word. Her *pimp*? Linnie was a prostitute? No, it couldn't be true. *She'd have come to me if she needed money. She would have told me. Wouldn't she?*

He'd loved her for years. They were going to get married someday. Because he would have found the courage to tell her how he felt. Eventually. He would have.

I should have told her that I loved her. His eyes stung. Because he still did.

The man's smile was pure evil. 'And?' he coaxed silkily. 'Who owns you, Linnea?'

A sob jerked from her chest. 'You do.'

'Yes, I own you.' The man shoved her away like trash. 'You're mine. Don't you ever forget it, bitch,' he snarled. 'Close your mouth, Mr Gold. It's highly unattractive.'

Unattractive. The word hung between them, suspended on the air. Vibrating like a plucked string. *Unattractive?* Andy's gulp was audible. 'I'm not doing that,' he said desperately. 'I'm not going to be attractive. I'm not going to sell myself.'

The man stared at him for a moment, then threw back his head and laughed. 'You think I'm going to sell you? Oh, kid, that's rich. You're not gonna hook. You're gonna kill.'

Andy shrank back into the sofa, horrified. 'No. I won't.'

'Yeah, you will.' The man pushed the hair away from Linnie's eyes. It would have been a tender gesture had it not been accompanied with such contempt. 'Because if you don't, I'll put a bullet in her head.' He tapped her forehead. 'Right here.'

No. No. Just . . . no. Andy's chest froze as a keening cry came from Linnie. 'No,' she moaned. 'Please. I'll do it. Let me do it instead.'

The man backhanded her again. 'Shut up!' he snarled. 'He'll do it.'

Andy's lungs unlocked and he gasped in a breath that was too fast, too sharp. 'You can't do this. You can't kill her. You just . . . You just can't.'

The man's smile curled at the corners, sending a chill down Andy's spine. 'Take her,' he said to the guy who'd tossed Andy over his shoulder like a sack of grain. 'Show him what we are capable of doing.'

'No.' Linnie moaned the word. 'Please no.'

The guy in black tossed Linnea over his shoulder just like he'd done to Andy and carried her from the room. A minute later Linnie began to scream. Horrible, horrible screams. He was hurting her. The guy in black was hurting her.

And there wasn't anything Andy could do to stop him.

He closed his eyes, unable to look at the man's grin of triumph. *Her pimp.* This man was her pimp. She'd promised she wouldn't. She'd *promised*. They'd made a pact back in foster care, the three of them – him, Linnie, and Shane. They'd promised no matter how hard it got that they'd never sell their bodies. She'd *promised*.

She'd lied. And right now, Andy wasn't sure which hurt more – the knowledge that she'd broken their pact or that she'd obviously been lost and desperate enough to do so. *Or that she didn't come to me for help first.*

The man lit up a cigarette and took a long drag, exhaling in a thin stream of smoke. 'So, Mr Gold, what's it to be? More of this? My associate can make her scream for a very long time. Or can I depend on you to save your friend's life?'

Andy opened his eyes. Forced himself to look at the man who held their lives in his hands with such casual disregard. The man tilted his head, listening to Linnie's screams.

'Well, Mr Gold? Make up your mind. My patience is growing very thin.'

Andy gritted his teeth. 'What you want me to do?'

One

Cincinnati, Ohio,
Saturday 19 December, 3.30 P.M.

'Are you sure this dress looks okay, Mer?'

Meredith Fallon sighed patiently as she turned to the younger woman walking beside her. 'It looks amazing, Mallory. *You* look amazing. Very stylish. No one will think you're any different than any other eighteen-year-old who's just signed up for her classes.'

But there was far more to Mallory Martin, who'd actually left the safe house where she'd stayed for four months, healing – which was huge. She still had so *much* healing left to do. In the ten years that Meredith had been counseling children and adolescents, she'd encountered few clients more victimized than Mallory – and even fewer with her courage.

'Yeah, but they're signing up for college. I'm just . . .' Mallory looked away. 'Dammit.'

'You're taking charge of your life. Have I told you how damn brave you are?'

'Twice. And that's only today.' A small smile was followed by a self-conscious grimace. 'I know I'm being stupid, fishing for compliments. I'm sorry.'

Meredith's sigh wasn't so patient this time. 'What did we agree about that word?'

'Stupid?'

'Well, yes. But mostly "sorry." Strike them both from your vocabulary right now.'

Mallory drew a breath and gave a hard little nod. 'Eliminated.'

'Good. Let's walk faster. It's not much further to the café, and my toes are freezing.'

They were going to celebrate. Mallory had signed up for adult classes today. Her first step toward getting the high school education she'd been denied by the monster who'd held her captive for six long years.

'You should have worn warm boots,' Mallory said archly. '*Without* four-inch heels.'

Meredith glanced at her brand-new suede knee-high boots with a happy little grin because Mallory was lecturing her, a small thing, but so *normal*. The girl had become one of Meredith's all-time favorite clients. 'But these are prettier. And they were on sale.'

Mallory shook her head with affectionate exasperation, as if Meredith was a child. 'At least you *needed* them. They can keep all the *other* suede boots with four-inch heels in your closet from getting lonely.'

Meredith's smile dimmed. Not from the criticism, because A, it was clear Mallory was teasing and B, her friends had given her shit over her overflowing shoe closet for years.

It was because she *had* needed them. Not the boots necessarily, but she'd needed *something*. The boots were an early Christmas present to herself, because it didn't look like she was going to get the one gift she really wanted. Back in the summer it had appeared that things might work out, that for the first time she'd have someone other than her family to snuggle with while watching the lights sparkle on her tree.

She'd been stupid to hope. The hours that she and Adam Kimble had spent together had been precious and few – and obviously not as important to him as they'd been to her. They'd been working the same case. The case had closed and he'd disappeared. Again.

Which took talent and forethought, because they shared a circle of friends. There had been many opportunities over the last four months for them to run into each other, purely by accident. But they hadn't. Finally, she'd had to conclude that he was purposely avoiding her. And it hurt. A lot.

Except that he hadn't avoided her entirely. She thought of the envelopes she'd found in her mailbox every few weeks. No name, no return address.

They'd been from Adam. No question. Pages torn from coloring books, the designs having been carefully filled in with crayon or colored pencils. Not a stray line on the page. Detective Adam Kimble was careful to stay inside the lines.

The early pictures were colored in shades of red, but as the weeks had passed, he'd added more colors. One of the recent pictures had been done with watercolor paint. She'd counted fifteen distinct colors. It hadn't been too bad, actually, as art went. As messages went, his was clear: *I'm working on it. I'm getting better. Don't give up on me.*

Or maybe it was just wishful thinking on her part.

'Meredith?' Mallory's voice was timid. 'I'm sorry. I was just trying to tease you.'

Meredith came to an abrupt halt in the middle of the sidewalk, realizing that Mallory had stopped in front of the café, was watching her seriously, and that they'd walked an entire city block in stony silence. Shame filled her in a rush, leaving a bitter taste in her mouth. *This is supposed to be Mallory's day, but I made it all about me.*

Meredith forced herself to smile. 'Oh, I know, honey,' she assured. 'It wasn't you or what you said. Sometimes I get caught up in my own head.'

'Good to know that it can even happen to you. Makes me feel better.'

Meredith's lips curved. 'Good to know that I can help even when I mess up.' She pointed to the café's sign. 'Let's go in. I hope you like it. They have the best pasta in town.'

'Good, because I'm hungry. But I do have one question,' Mallory said gravely.

'Only one?' Meredith had to chuckle when the girl rolled her eyes. Again, so normal. *Be thankful, Meredith. Don't pine for what you can't have.* She couldn't force Adam to want her and it was time she stopped mooning over him. 'Shoot. What's your question?'

'What happens when I get a license and start driving again?'

11

Meredith paused, her hand on the handle of the café door, puzzled. 'Please?'

One side of Mallory's mouth lifted in another teasing smirk. 'Well, if I can't say "stupid," how can I possibly drive? I mean, you said it at least three times when you were looking for a parking place. How do I drive without using that word? Or bastard? Or fuuu—' She drew the f-sound out, her dark eyes dancing. 'Fudge?'

Meredith threw back her head and laughed. 'You little stinker.'

Mallory grinned, clearly pleased with herself. 'Maybe, but I made you smile. Really smile, I mean.'

Meredith swallowed hard. 'Get inside before I turn to an ice cube.' She held the door open, her throat thick but now for a different reason. Mallory had made a joke. *To cheer me up.* That the young woman who'd been so cruelly abused had somehow managed to retain her ability to care . . . It left Meredith humbled and clearing her throat harshly.

Her voice was still raspy when she told the hostess, 'Reservation is under Fallon.'

'Right this way.' The hostess, a young woman about Mallory's age, led them to a table by the window. 'The best place to people-watch,' she said, seating them with a smile.

'And to wait for the fireworks where it's warm and comfy,' Meredith said.

Mallory's wide eyes lit up, but she waited for the hostess to leave before leaning in to whisper, 'Fireworks? Where?'

'Out on Fountain Square,' Meredith told her. 'We'll have a nice meal, linger over our coffee, then go outside and see them from the street.'

'Is that why you picked this place?'

'Oh, no.' Meredith looked around the café fondly. 'My gran and I came here after the *Nutcracker* ballet every year, just the two of us. Back then, the ballet was at Music Hall and very fancy.' It had returned to Music Hall this year after a long building renovation, and Meredith had wanted to take the girls who lived at Mariposa House, but decided against it. Most of the girls would have panic attacks around that many people. *Maybe next year.*

12

'How fancy?' Mallory asked wistfully. 'Long dresses? Gloves?'

'Not quite that fancy,' Meredith said with a smile. 'But I'd be all dressed up in my Christmas dress with a big bow in my hair and Gran would wear her best Sunday suit. And pearls. Gran always wore pearls.'

'So do you,' Mallory said. 'Your earrings. I've never seen you not wear them. Pearls' – she glanced at Meredith's hands – 'and bangles.'

Meredith gave one of her earrings a fond stroke, because her wrist bangles were not up for discussion. 'They were my gran's. You'd have liked her. She was a real pistol.'

Mallory's smile was amused. 'A pearl-wearing pistol.'

'Yes, indeed. She carried a pistol too. Gran was a pearl-wearing card shark who cursed like a sailor, packed heat in her enormous purse, and still managed to fool everyone into thinking she was just a sock-knitting granny.'

Mallory glanced up from her menu, brows lifted. 'Don't knock the sock-knitters. I know lots of knitters now and they carry too.'

Meredith snorted a laugh. Her newest friend Kate was an FBI agent, a sharpshooter, and a compulsive knitter. Kate was quickly winning knitting converts from their circle of friends. Now their monthly movie night included wine, chocolate, and yarn.

Meredith wasn't a knitter, but she'd quietly carried a gun for years, either in the pocket of her blazer or snugged up into her bra holster. As a therapist to children and adolescents, she sometimes encountered family members who threatened her with violence. She regularly trained at the range, but thankfully she'd never had cause to use the weapon.

'I miss my gran,' Meredith said wistfully. 'She was my rock after my folks died.'

Mallory tilted her head, curious. 'When did she die? Your gran?'

'Three years ago,' Meredith told her, acutely aware that she'd never divulged personal information to Mallory before. *I need to transition Mallory to another therapist. Soon.* The thought hurt. But it should have been done already. They'd grown too close over the last few months. 'She had a heart attack. But it was fast, at least. She didn't suffer. But it was a shock, even though she was in her eighties. I wasn't ready to let her go.'

Mallory's lips drooped. 'I wouldn't have been either. What about your parents?'

Meredith drew a breath, because their deaths hadn't been quick or painless. And because the anniversary of their deaths was looming over her. Another reason for her recent retail therapy. 'Plane crash,' she said quietly. 'Seven years ago.'

'Oh.' Mallory's gaze was full of trepidation. 'What about your grandfather?'

Thoughts of her grandfather made Meredith's lips twitch and she saw Mallory relax in relief. 'Oh, he's still alive and quite the troublemaker. He retired to Florida. Has a place on the beach and he fishes every day. He says he *catches* fish every day, but I'm pretty sure he lies. You might get to meet him. He'll be here for Christmas.' He never let her spend Christmas alone. 'Now, let's check out the menu. I'm going to indulge.' She went straight to the desserts. 'Otherwise, running every morning makes no sense whatsoever.'

She was trying to decide which chocolate dessert would be her reward when she heard Mallory's sharp intake of breath. Looking up, Meredith's breath did the same.

A young man stood between their table and the window. Pale and terrified, he was shaking like a leaf. Her first instinct was to *run* and she'd learned not to ignore her instincts. She didn't run, but set the menu down, forcing her lips to curve as she rose. She slipped her hands into her blazer pocket casually, releasing the snap on her holster. 'Can I help you?'

The man swallowed hard. 'I'm so sorry.' Then he reached into his pocket and pulled out a gun. 'I'm sorry,' he whispered. 'I'm so sorry.'

And then he pointed the gun at her.

Meredith drew a breath, ignoring the startled cries around her. She'd talked down gunmen before. She could do it again. 'All right,' she said calmly. 'Let's talk about this.'

He shook his head, obviously desperate. 'It's too late for that. I have to.'

14

Meredith risked a glance at Mallory from the corner of her eye. The girl was staring at the barrel of the gun, her eyes wide and glassy. She'd gone into shock.

'You don't have to,' Meredith said to the young man, keeping her voice calm. 'We can fix this. Whatever it is.'

The young man shook his head. 'Just . . . be quiet. Please.' The gun in his hand jerked as his body trembled violently.

He doesn't want to do this. He doesn't want to be here. He was being coerced.

Meredith held one hand out in supplication while her other slid the gun from its holster, keeping it in her pocket. 'Don't do this. I can help you. What's your name, honey?'

Another desperate shake of the man's head. 'Shut up! I need to think!' He flinched, his free hand flying upward to slap at his ear. 'Stop yelling at me! I can't think!'

No one was yelling. The restaurant had gone completely silent around them.

He jabbed his finger in his ear. 'I said I'd do it!' he cried.

Schizophrenia? she wondered. He was about the right age for emergence, but schizophrenics didn't generally hurt people. Except maybe when they heard voices telling them to shoot people. It was also still possible he was being coerced. She needed to figure out which was the case. Talking him down would require different approaches, depending.

Meredith didn't dare look away from him. 'Get down, Mallory,' she said levelly.

'No!' the man shouted, his eyes darting to Mallory's sheet-white face. 'Nobody moves!' He pointed the gun at Mallory, then back at Meredith. 'Do not move.'

Meredith used his momentary distraction to pull the gun from her pocket. Her hand did not shake when she pointed it at the man, whose eyes grew even wider.

The only sounds were heavy breathing from the restaurant patrons and an occasional muffled sob of terror.

'Put the gun down, honey,' Meredith said softly. 'I don't want to hurt you. I know you don't want to hurt me.'

The young man whimpered. He was barely older than Mallory. *Just a boy, really. A scared boy.* 'I can't do this,' he whispered.

'I know,' Meredith soothed. 'I know you can't. It's all right. Please drop your gun. Let me help you. I want to help you.'

'He'll kill her,' the young man whispered hoarsely.

Who? she wanted to ask, but did not. It was far more important to talk him down. 'We can help you. I know we can. Please . . . Please just drop your gun.'

Cincinnati, Ohio,
Saturday 19 December, 3.55 P.M.

'Dammit,' he hissed, watching Andy through his binoculars from inside his SUV, parked on the curb outside the little café. Fallon had a gun.

The transmitter in Andy's pocket picked up Fallon's calm voice trying to talk him down. It seemed like she was succeeding because Andy had not fired yet. It didn't really matter. Giving Andy the gun had merely been the best way to get the kid as close to their table as possible.

He'd used the radio receiver in Andy's ear to urge him closer to the table where Fallon and her young charge sat. He'd told Andy to pull the trigger, reminding him that Linnea would die. Which was going to happen anyway. The girl had seen his face.

As had Andy. The kid was never going to walk away from this either.

He shifted the SUV into drive, but kept his foot on the brake. He then tapped the CALL button on his cell phone. He'd started to lift his foot from the brake when he froze.

Nothing had happened.

Everything should have happened, but there had been *nothing*. No explosion, no shattering glass, no flying debris. *Nothing had happened.*

Throwing the SUV back into park, he grabbed his binoculars and focused on Andy once again. The kid was still pointing his gun at Meredith, who pointed hers right back. He was still alive. *Goddammit.*

16

He checked the number he'd dialed. It was correct. He dialed it again, to be sure. Still . . . nothing.

'Fuck,' he muttered. Through the radio he could barely hear the kid's whispers. *He'll kill her.* Andy was about to spill all to Meredith Fallon. *Son of a bitch.*

'Hell no.' That was not going to happen. He reached for the rifle he'd stored under the seat, ignoring Linnea's shocked gasp from the back seat.

'No!' she cried. 'You can't.'

But he could and he would. No more loose ends.

Two

'A smidge to the left. It's too far to the right.'

From his perch atop the ladder, Adam Kimble gave the shiny aluminum-foil-covered star a critical look then glared down at Wendi, the petite director of Mariposa House, where victims of sexual trafficking came to heal. Wendi looked like Tinkerbell, but Adam knew that she had a spine of steel and a will of solid titanium.

He bit back a wince of mild alarm because he knew she was hiding fierce annoyance behind a perky smile. He was a seasoned homicide detective, thirteen years with Cincinnati PD. He shouldn't be so intimidated by Tinkerbell, Adam thought sourly. Yet he was.

He hadn't asked her why she was so annoyed with him because he knew why and he really wanted to avoid that conversation. Because Wendi was right.

I'm a selfish sonofabitch, he thought wearily, and not for the first time. Not the first time that day or even the first time that hour. He thought it every time he came to this house, where he could see *her* everywhere he looked, even though she wasn't here today.

Which was why he was. He always made sure to schedule his volunteer hours at Mariposa House for whenever Meredith Fallon would be somewhere else. Anywhere else.

It hurt, not seeing her face, hearing her voice. But it hurt so much more to see the look in her green eyes. Disappointment. Regret. And shame. The last one sent a spike into his chest every damn time. She had no reason to feel ashamed. She'd done nothing wrong.

18

It was me. It's all on me. Every failure, every weakness, every regret. And he had so many. But he also had a plan to make it right. To make himself into the man she deserved.

A plan he did not intend to share with her ferociously formidable friend while he stood on a sixteen-foot ladder, adjusting the Christmas tree topper that had already covered his hands with glitter.

The girls who'd made the star had been quite liberal with the glitter. He wiped his hand on the seat of his jeans, wishing they'd been a little more liberal with the glue.

'A second ago it was a smidge to the right,' he grumbled.

'That's because a second ago it was too far to the left,' Wendi told him sharply, and Adam wondered if she was simply giving him a hard time.

His suspicions were confirmed by twin snorts from the two men preparing the trimming for the fifteen-foot Christmas tree that dominated the living room of the old house that now sheltered twenty young women in various stages of recovery and renewal. Stone O'Bannion was stringing popcorn and Diesel Kennedy was sorting through boxes of antique ornaments that had been discovered in the attic.

Both men worked for the *Ledger*, the local newspaper. A year ago, Adam would have sneered at the thought that he'd be in the same room with reporters unless he was arresting them, but it had been a crazy year and now he counted these two men among his closest friends. They'd worked together for months, swinging hammers, sanding, painting, and polishing until this old house had been transformed from a spooky old mansion harboring the memories of past victims of abuse into a shiny, warm, welcoming haven.

Adam had thrown himself into the work because it was necessary and important, because he'd needed the distraction of physical labor, but mostly he'd done it for Meredith. Because she and Wendi had devoted their lives to the residents of Mariposa House – girls and young women who weren't ready to be streamed into foster care. Victims of brutal sexual abuse or rescued from the sex trade, the girls ranged in age from nine to eighteen, but most were in their teens. This place was a halfway house, every aspect engineered to transition the residents back into society.

He could see Meredith's touch in every corner of the house. It was as homey as her own. He wanted to give her her dream, even if he couldn't give her anything else. Not yet.

He jolted back to attention at the lazy amusement in Stone's voice. 'The star itself is fine, Kimble,' he said. 'The real problem is the tree. It would look better moved by the window. What do you think, Wendi? Don't you want him to drag the tree over there?'

'No,' Adam answered firmly before Wendi could get that thought into her head.

'No,' Wendi said at the same time, distinctly unamused.

Stone laughed. 'Oh, come on. It'll be perfect! Think how it'll catch the light.'

'Shut up, O'Bannion.' But Adam's words were all for show. Stone was laughing and it looked good on him. The guy had nearly died from gunshot wounds back in the summer and still hadn't fully regained his health or stamina. His balance was unsteady at times, which was one of the reasons that Adam was on top of the ladder and not Stone.

Diesel lifted his eyes to Adam's perch. 'I think you should have listened to me before climbing the ladder to fix what ain't broken,' he said, raising one dark brow in challenge. He'd been the one to originally mount the tree-topper.

'It was crooked,' Adam insisted.

'Of course it was,' Diesel said. 'It's crooked because it was handmade by kids. It's okay that it's crooked. Not everything has to be perfect.' He eyed Wendi cautiously. 'If you want a perfect star, go buy one from the store.'

With his extensive body art, shiny bald head, and pierced ear, Diesel Kennedy looked like a sinister Mr Clean. At six-six, he towered over them, scary-looking as hell. Until he smiled. Then the small children he coached in the pee wee leagues would run to hug him. He was a good guy wrapped up in a thug's skin.

Wendi sighed. 'Not using it would hurt the younger girls' feelings. If you'd just—'

'It's fine, Wen. Leave it alone.'

The growl came from behind him and Adam looked over his shoulder to where FBI Special Agent Parrish Colby sat on the floor cross-legged, fighting to untangle a string of lights. The lights were definitely winning. The bulldog of a man seemed the least likely match for the pixie-like Wendi, but they'd been a bona fide couple since summer.

'You're not even looking at the star,' Wendi protested.

Wearing a red Santa cap and tangled up in the lights, Colby looked like a disgruntled, pugilistic elf who'd gotten into way too many fights with the other elves. The man looked up at Wendi with an exasperated eye roll. 'It's fine,' he repeated. 'The fucking star is fine.'

'Parrish,' Wendi scolded. 'Language.'

'They're not here,' Colby shot back, referring to the girls.

It was true. Through a miracle of planning, all the girls who lived at Mariposa House were somewhere else for the day, leaving the house empty so that Wendi could decorate and wrap presents. She'd recruited volunteers, both to chaperone the girls and to decorate.

Adam's cousin, Deacon, had been roped into chaperoning with his fiancée, Faith. *Better them than me.* Setting up the tree and hanging lights was far more his speed. And it allowed him to help out at a time when Meredith would definitely not be here.

Staff and the other volunteers had taken some of the girls holiday shopping. Those who weren't ready to face strangers had gone to a craft class, making holiday gifts.

And their oldest resident, Mallory Martin, was registering for GED classes. He also knew that Meredith had taken her there, because Special Agent Deacon Novak, his partner on the Major Case Enforcement Squad, had told him so.

Deacon hadn't shared this in an official capacity, however. He'd shared it as Adam's first cousin and oldest friend, having heard it from his fiancée. Deacon was engaged to Dr Faith Corcoran, who

21

was Meredith's friend and fellow therapist in the pediatric and adolescent psychology practice that Meredith had started from scratch.

They were all intertwined, Adam's friends and family. It made things awkward at times, everyone knowing everyone else's business.

Well, not everything. There were things Adam kept even from Deacon, because . . . *I don't want him to know. Because I'm ashamed.*

Secrets aside, the one thing that had united them all was the need to provide safe haven for the girls who lived here at Mariposa House. Guiding them in building a life was their ultimate goal, so the GED class was a huge personal milestone for Mallory.

And for me. Because he, Deacon, and the rest of the Major Case Enforcement Squad had taken down the vile piece of shit who'd assaulted Mallory and many others. It had been a rare win and he savored it.

For once, Adam hadn't been too late. He hadn't failed. And kids were alive who might not otherwise be. He'd held onto that truth in the months since. Sometimes he held on harder, like at three a.m. when the ones he hadn't saved haunted his nightmares and he woke drenched in sweat, his heart racing and his throat burning from his screams.

And needing a fucking drink so damn bad he thought he might die from it.

The remembered need from early that morning became urgent and present, hitting him so hard that his vision went momentarily wavy and his body trembled. He clutched the edge of the ladder, the sharp press of the metal against his skin providing just enough pain to disrupt the sudden craving that he'd nearly allowed to ruin his life.

He closed his eyes, willing his thoughts to detour away from the well-worn path lined by the faces of every victim he'd ever failed. Forced himself to see instead the faces of the victims he'd saved. There weren't as many of those. But they existed. They lived.

So no. You do not need *a drink. You might want one. But you don't* need *one.*

He drew a breath and focused on the clean pine scent of the tree he and Diesel had set up in this house. This house that was safe haven for the victims that had been rescued.

He drew another breath, his body and mind back under his control, and was relieved to find he'd only been out of it for a few seconds because Wendi was still scolding Colby.

'It doesn't matter if the girls are here or not,' she was saying. 'You leave your bad language and habits outside. You know that.'

'Sorry,' Colby grunted.

A brief silence was followed by Wendi's chuckle. 'No, you're not.'

Colby's answering chuckle sounded like a rusty saw blade. 'Maybe a little.'

Adam glanced over his shoulder, watching Wendi drop a quick kiss on Colby's mouth. 'You're going to strangle yourself,' she told him fondly, tugging at the strings of lights that wound around his arms, legs, and even his neck. The resulting smile that bent Colby's lips was startlingly sweet. Worshipful, even.

Adam abruptly turned away, ignoring the lump in his throat and denying the fact that his eyes stung. *That*, he thought, *is what I want*. That tender moment he'd just witnessed. Except he didn't want just one moment. He wanted a lifetime of them. A kiss and a smile from *the* someone who cared about only him. Even if he didn't deserve it.

Because he *didn't* deserve it. Didn't deserve *her*. Not yet.

But I will. I just need a little more time, that's all.

Adam's restless gaze swept the room, freezing on Diesel's stricken expression as he also watched Colby and Wendi. Diesel lurched to his feet, muttering that he'd left something in his truck. He was out the front door before anyone could say a word.

Well, shit. It was pretty common knowledge among their circle of friends that Diesel had a thing for Adam's cousin Dani, but hadn't done a blessed thing about it. With a sigh, Adam descended the ladder to find Stone watching him, a concerned look on his face.

'You okay?' Stone asked. 'You looked like you got dizzy or something up there.'

23

Dizzy. Yeah. It was an easy out and Adam grabbed at it. 'I think I need something to eat. It's been a long time since breakfast.' He shrugged. 'Blood sugar must have dipped.'

'Then eat, stupid.' Stone shook his head. 'I brought a ton of food.' He leaned forward conspiratorially. 'And there's beer in Diesel's truck. Just don't tell the warden.'

Adam flinched. He couldn't help it. He shoved down the voice that echoed through his mind, *It's only beer. Just one won't hurt.* But one became two then a six-pack and before he knew it he was waking up hung-over and missing hours of memory.

Adam had opened his mouth to give his standard answer – no thank you, he was on call this weekend. If a body popped up, he'd have to go to work.

But Wendi jumped back into the conversation. 'I heard you,' she snapped, still sitting on Colby's lap. 'Dammit, Stone. You can't have beer here.'

'There's no beer in *here*,' Stone said. 'It's in the truck. *Outside.*'

'It doesn't matter.' Wendi sprang to her feet, fists on her hips. 'And don't give me that look. You know the rules. You're just being an asshole.'

'I'm sorry. You're right.' Stone managed to appear contrite for all of two seconds before a smirk quirked his lips. 'But you swore.' He held up two fingers. 'Twice.'

'Ffffff . . .' Wendi stifled another swear word and lightly smacked Colby's arm when he choked back a laugh. 'Hush, you. Fine, whatever. Take a break for a snack, but no beer. And don't dawdle. It's already four o'clock, and we haven't started on the outside lights. I'd like the outside lights ready for the girls when they come home, and it'll be dark soon.'

Adam blinked. He hadn't realized it was so late. He'd specifically timed his tasks so that he could be gone before Meredith returned with Mallory. A sense of panic skittered through him. 'I . . . I can't stay much longer. I can come back later.'

Wendi frowned, her chin lifting in clear warning. 'We're not finished.'

'I told you I had to leave by three,' Adam said.

She skewered him with a glare. 'Yeah, you did. Because you're a coward.'

Adam set his jaw, bracing himself for the rebuke he deserved, but still hoping he could avoid it. 'If I am or not, it's not your business.'

From the corner of his eye, he saw Stone settle into a chair and grab the bowl of popcorn, his expression one of rapt fascination that the bastard didn't even try to hide.

Wendi's approach was quick and furious. She stopped when the toes of her shoes hit Adam's. 'You're right. It's not my business, except when it affects my friend.'

Her friend Meredith, who he'd wanted since he'd first laid eyes on her. The face he pictured when the cravings got so bad that his chest tightened until he couldn't breathe.

Colby sighed wearily. 'Wendi, honey. You promised her you wouldn't. You promised *me* you wouldn't.'

Anger flashed in Wendi's eyes. 'I know,' she said to Colby without breaking eye contact with Adam. 'But I can tell him that she's not going to be back for another two hours at least. She took Mallory for an early supper downtown so they could see the fireworks.'

Adam's panic dissipated and he drew a breath. He'd known about the supper. Had heard Wendi mention it earlier that week. Had known Meredith wouldn't be back for a while. He'd wanted a buffer, but it didn't look like he'd get as big of one as he'd hoped.

'Fine. I'll do the outside lights.' He backed up a step, but Wendi matched it, staying with him, tears abruptly filling her eyes.

'She's sad, Adam,' Wendi whispered hoarsely. 'Sad and lonely because she's waiting for you. If you don't want her, let her go. Let her have a life with someone else.'

His chest was abruptly concrete. Hard, heavy, and immovable. *No.* He wanted to say the word, but he couldn't make his mouth function. *No.* He couldn't let her go. He couldn't let her have a life with someone else. *She's mine.* Mine, *goddammit.*

Air. He needed air. He shoved his breath out, sucked in another that felt like broken glass. He spun around and stumbled through the front door, just as Diesel had minutes before. *God, aren't we fucking peas in a pod?*

The outside air was cold enough to shock him into drawing another breath, dry and cold. Bending at the waist, he braced his hands on his thighs and tried not to throw up.

Mine, mine, mine. The steady chant inside his head helped him regulate his breathing. *Panic attack.* He recognized it now that it was over. He hadn't had one in months.

Not since the last time he'd had to walk away from Meredith Fallon.

She's sad and lonely.

But I'm not ready. Not good enough. Not yet.

Cincinnati, Ohio,
Saturday 19 December, 4.00 P.M.

'Let me help you,' Meredith said once again. Sensing the boy wavering, she held her breath, waiting until his gun hand opened wide and the weapon fell to the floor. His shoulders sagged as a sob tore from his throat. Tears ran down his face.

'I'm sorry, Lin.' He fumbled with the zipper of his coat. 'He'll kill her. He'll kill her.' He looked up, his ravaged eyes meeting Meredith's. 'Get down. Run, for God's sake. *Run.*'

The glass window shattered. And the boy's head . . . exploded.

Meredith froze in shock, staring as the café erupted into screams and overturned tables. Already on the floor, Mallory grabbed Meredith's jacket and yanked her down.

Another shot rang out, followed by a shrill scream, all while Meredith stared numbly at the gun in her hand, she hadn't pulled the trigger. What the hell had just happened?

And then outside the café, the roar of an engine and the squeal of tires filled the air.

Around her, she heard the dull rumble of voices, many of them dialing 911. Shaking harder than the boy had, Meredith held on to the gun with one hand and fumbled her purse with the other. She found her phone and dialed without even pausing to wonder why she'd chosen the number she had.

Mount Carmel, Ohio,
Saturday 19 December, 4.03 P.M.

Still bent over, Adam stared at the brown grass of the mansion's front yard while he brought his breathing under control. Panic attacks sucked ass. He was seriously considering calling his AA sponsor when a pair of huge feet in steel-toed boots shuffled into his field of vision. Schooling his features, Adam straightened and lifted his eyes to Diesel's.

Diesel had also schooled his features, no surprise there. He gripped a Xerox paper box that appeared to be at least twenty years old. 'You okay?' he asked.

Adam nodded. 'What's in the box?'

'Menorah. First day of Hanukkah's coming up.'

Adam forced himself to smile. 'I didn't think of that. Are any of the girls Jewish?'

'Dunno. But it seems like we should have one as long as we've got a tree. This one belonged to my mother. I was going to put it on the mantel inside.'

Adam's smile became real. 'That's really nice, Diesel. I'm . . .' He pointed to the boxes of lights someone had stacked under one of the big oak trees. 'I'm going to hang the lights out here. I could use the help.'

Diesel looked relieved. 'I'll put the menorah on the mantel and be right back out.'

'Thanks, man.' He started to step aside so that Diesel could get to the front walk when Cyndi Lauper started singing 'True Colors' from his phone and Adam froze. He hadn't heard that ringtone since the day he'd installed it.

For Meredith. He snatched at the phone, his heart rocketing in his chest. 'Hello?' he asked cautiously because there was no freaking way Meredith would be calling him. Not unless something was wrong.

Something *was* wrong. In the background, he heard screams and loud voices and sobs. 'Meredith?' he said sharply, his imagination immediately filling in the blanks with terrifying images. 'Are you there?'

Diesel went still, his eyes on Adam's, but he said nothing. Just waited.

'Meredith?' Adam pressed, his panic returning. 'Tell me you're there.'

'Yes.' Her voice was thin and brittle. 'I . . . Can you come, please? I need you.'

'Yes. Yes, of course.' He tried to keep his voice calm, to tamp down the terror that had grabbed him by the throat. A strong hand gripped his upper arm, hard enough to hurt. Grounding him. Adam looked up at Diesel's steady gaze gratefully, then pointed to the house. 'Get Colby, please,' he said and Diesel took off at a run. 'I'm here,' he said into the phone. 'Tell me where you are, sweetheart.'

Meredith sobbed once, quickly swallowed. 'At Buon Cibo.'

Right. He knew that. He'd heard Wendi say that days ago when he'd been fixing a leaky pipe in the kitchen. He dug his keys out of his pocket as Colby, Wendi, and Diesel came running, Stone following behind more slowly.

'I know the place,' Adam said, pushing through the old mansion's wrought iron gate to his Jeep, the others following. 'I'm almost in my Jeep. Tell me that you're okay.'

Wendi's hand covered her mouth, her face gone pale. Colby had his arm around her shoulders protectively.

'I'm . . .' Meredith's swallow was audible. 'I'm okay. Mallory's okay. There was a shooting. A man is dead. I didn't fire, I swear I didn't.' Her voice broke at the end.

Adam clenched his eyes shut and made himself breathe. 'She's okay,' he told the others and climbed behind the wheel of his Jeep. 'So is Mallory, but there was a shooting at the café where they were having supper. Buon Cibo.'

'We'll follow behind you,' Colby said and urged Wendi back toward the house when she tried to run to Colby's sedan. 'You need a coat, Wen. I promise we'll hurry.'

Colby's voice seemed to calm her and Wendi sagged against him, nodding weakly.

'Call us if you need us,' Diesel yelled as Adam fired up his engine and drove away with a squeal of tires.

Adam raised his hand, then focused on Meredith. 'Have you called 911?'

'Everyone did,' she said, breath hitching. 'Other customers.'

'That's good,' he said soothingly. 'Where are you right now, honey?'

'In the café. Under the table.' Her breaths were fast and harsh. 'I had my gun out, Adam. But I didn't shoot him.'

Adam frowned, the scenario unclear. And . . . *Wait.* Meredith carried? He hadn't even known she owned a gun. 'All right. Who did shoot him?'

'I don't know.' Another swallowed sob. 'He was pointing his gun at me but I'd talked him down. He'd dropped it. And then . . .' She was crying and Adam's hands tightened on the wheel in frustration that he couldn't already be there.

I should have been there. For the millionth time, he cursed his own weakness. *If I hadn't been so fucked up, I'd have been with her, where I belong. I'd have been there, and she'd be all right.* 'And then?' he asked softly.

'His head . . . It just exploded.' She gagged a little, then dragged in a deep breath. 'I'm . . . Oh, God. I'm covered in . . . God, Adam.'

'Got it,' Adam said quietly. She was covered in a dead man's brains. He navigated the curvy back road as fast as he dared, then stepped on the gas when he hit the highway. 'I'm on my way, Meredith. Put your weapon down on the floor. They'll be able to tell it wasn't fired, but you don't want the police to have to disarm you. Did you put it down?'

'Yes,' she whispered.

'That's good,' he said smoothly. 'Where is Mallory?'

'Sitting next to me.'

'Under the table?'

'Yeah. She pulled me down after the guy's head—' Her voice broke again. 'Adam, he was just a boy.'

Mallory had acted quickly, just not quickly enough to keep Meredith from being covered in a dead boy's brains. 'But she's okay?'

'In shock, I think. The window's broken.'

'In the café?'

'Yes. I didn't know there was a second shot.'

Adam had to force his lungs to function. 'What happened?'

'The first shot, it broke the window. The big window near where we were sitting. The second shot . . . It hit a man, a customer. Sitting behind me. He's bleeding.' The whispered words were almost a whimper. 'One of the other customers is doing first aid. I can't. I'm . . . My hands are . . .'

'Got it,' he said again, unclenching his jaw. 'They may want to swab your hands, so I'm sorry, but you can't go wash them. Not just yet.'

'I know. He said he was sorry. The boy. He told me to get down, to run. Right before his head . . .' The sob took over and she didn't say any more.

'Sweetheart,' Adam said helplessly, then hardened his tone a fraction. 'Meredith.'

'Y-yes?'

His heart was pounding to beat all hell. 'Are the cops there yet?'

Her sobbing grew muted, then she was back again. 'Yes. They just got here.'

'Fine. That's good. When they get to you, give them your phone. Better yet, put it on speaker. I want to talk to them first.'

Three

*S*onofamotherfuckingbitch. He slid behind the wheel, one hand slamming his car door closed while the other crumpled the remnants of the removable vinyl decals that had covered the doors and the license plates of his SUV. Today he'd been a plumber. He pulled back into the heavy downtown traffic, then glanced in his rear-view mirror a final time.

A crowd was already gathered around the restaurant and a cruiser passed him with its lights on. In minutes the police would have the area cordoned off with crime scene tape and they might even lock down the city. He was getting out, just in time.

There should have been so much chaos that getting away shouldn't have even been an issue. Meredith Fallon and her young companion should have been dead. *Dammit.* This had been the perfect opportunity and now it was gone. He hadn't trusted anyone with this kill, not even the two men he normally trusted with his life. It was too important.

This is my livelihood. Hell. This is my life.

He'd waited and watched and had finally picked the perfect time and place . . . only to watch it all fall apart. Now both Fallon and the girl would be on guard. The cops would circle their wagons around them and he didn't know when he'd get another chance.

Dammit. He'd really believed Andy would follow through, especially given the boy's background. The kid had killed for Linnea before, after all.

31

Regardless, he hadn't planned for there to be anything left for the police to investigate. The bomb concealed beneath Andy's coat should have blown everything into smithereens. His uncle Mike had made two, side by side, as he always did. He'd tested one, as he always did, and it had detonated perfectly – as they always did.

He had no idea why the second bomb had not. He wouldn't have to wait long to find out. CSU would figure it out and someone on the inside would give him the details.

'You . . . You killed him.' Linnea captured his attention from the back seat. Her body was rigid, the bruises extra dark on her face, which had grown dangerously pale.

'He fucked up,' he said simply. 'He had to fire one shot. That's all.'

'He's not a killer.' Her emotionless words were delivered with no affect whatsoever. She was probably going into shock. Which wasn't a big deal. She wasn't going to live much longer anyway. As soon as he got out of the city, he'd put a bullet in her skull and dump her body where it wouldn't be found until spring.

'Yes, he was a killer. He didn't kill today, but he was a killer.'

'He was younger then. And scared.' Her voice trembled. Broke. 'It's not the same.'

'It's exactly the same, but it doesn't really matter, does it? Especially with him being dead,' he added, fully intending the words to be as cruel as possible.

Her only reaction was to close her eyes. Two tears slipped down her cheeks. She looked like exactly what she was – a used-up whore who'd finally given up.

Still, he'd be careful. All he needed was for her to scratch his face or do something equally annoying that he'd have to explain away when he got home. He headed south, toward the river. He'd take care of Linnea and still make it home in time for dinner.

Cincinnati, Ohio,
Saturday 19 December, 4.20 P.M.

'Get the hell out of my way,' Adam muttered to the long line of cars in front of him. He'd made good time from Mariposa House until he'd hit downtown. Everyone was coming in to see fireworks and traffic was stalled.

He was tempted to use his emergency flashers to cut through the snarl of cars, but he wasn't technically on duty – just on call – and Meredith was okay, physically, at least. The threat had been eliminated and the first responders were there, securing the scene.

She was physically okay. But her hands were covered by a young man's brains and the very thought made his foot tap the accelerator in frustration.

Fuck it. He reached for the dash flasher switch, damning the consequences. The worst that could happen was a reprimand and that was unlikely. But his phone started playing Darth Vader's theme and he checked his movement, reaching for his cell instead.

'Hey, Loo.' His lieutenant, Lynda Isenberg, had always had his back through good times and bad. His choice of ringtone was pure bullshit teasing on his part and she knew it. The list of people he trusted implicitly was very short and she was near the top.

'Detective,' she said curtly, which meant she had an audience. In the last year she'd taken to calling him by his first name. 'Have you heard about the shooting on the square today?' Her voice had the tinny quality of being on speaker, which meant she had an audience who was listening to every word.

Brass, probably, he thought. That meant this was bigger than 'just a shooter,' although it had never been a routine crime for him. That shooter had aimed at Meredith.

'I heard it was at the Buon Cibo Café,' Adam told her levelly.

'You heard right. I need you to get to the scene,' Isenberg said. 'You'll be joined by Special Agent Triplett. The two of you will co-lead this investigation.'

Permission granted. Adam flicked the flasher switch and cars began trying to pull over. Not easy with such gridlock, but a lane was slowly opening up.

That Jefferson Triplett would be his partner was a bit of a surprise. Not an unpleasant one, of course. Adam liked Trip. The rookie was young, but had seemed to be good at his job every time their paths had crossed.

'Is Zimmerman there?' he asked, inching his Jeep forward. The special agent in charge of the local FBI field office often loaned his staff to Isenberg's Major Case Enforcement Squad, the FBI/CPD joint task force that was Isenberg's baby.

'He is,' Zimmerman said. 'Hello, Detective Kimble.'

'Sir,' Adam said politely. 'What's the situation? Why is the FBI working this one?'

'Because,' Isenberg said, 'the would-be shooter, who ended up being the victim, was wearing a bomb.'

Adam sucked in a shocked breath. *Holy shit.* A bomb. In a crowded restaurant on a street filled with holiday shoppers. 'Why? Where?'

'"Why" is what we need you to find out,' Isenberg said, 'and "where" is the vest he wore under his parka. He pulled the zipper of his coat seconds before he was shot from someone outside on the street. The first cop on the scene noticed the explosives.'

Adam recalled Meredith's shaken words. *He told me to get down, to run.* Right before the young man's head exploded. 'He wanted Meredith to know. He told her to run.'

'You've heard more than we have,' Isenberg said dryly. 'Deacon and Scarlett have recused themselves as lead because of their friendship with Dr Fallon, but said they'd be able to support you. You're next in line for a new case. Should I recuse you as well?'

'No,' Adam said, hoping he hadn't snapped it out too fast. 'I'm . . . entanglement-free.' *For now.* He'd keep it that way if it meant keeping the case. He didn't trust Meredith's safety to anyone else. 'Has the restaurant been evacuated?'

'Yes, to the hotel across the street.' Isenberg sighed. 'We have a lot of very traumatized witnesses. It was . . . intense. Which I'm sure you've also *heard*.'

'Meredith told me,' Adam said honestly. 'She was as close to hysterical as I've ever heard her.'

'Why did she call you, Detective?' Zimmerman asked mildly.

Adam could picture the older man's face, his brow wrinkled in concern because he knew the answer to his question already. 'I don't know. Maybe because my name starts with A and I was the first cop in her contact list?'

Isenberg's snort held disbelief, but her words carried quiet promise. 'I'll remove you in a heartbeat, Adam. You got me? Do not become . . . entangled.'

'Yes, ma'am.' He could picture her face too, unsmiling, framed with gray hair she kept as short as his own, her sharp eyes narrowed. 'I'm nearly there.' He winced a little, knowing in his heart that the statement could be correctly interpreted more than one way. Yeah, he was nearly at the scene, but he was also very nearly entangled. 'Anything else?'

'Yes,' Zimmerman said. 'Agent Triplett is lead on anything having to do with the bomb itself. He has extensive experience with incendiary devices.'

Adam blinked. 'Trip? Where did he get bomb experience?' Arriving at the scene, he parked his Jeep behind the line of cruisers and ambulances. Trapping his cell between his ear and shoulder, he opened his back hatch and quickly suited up, shrugging into his bulletproof vest. 'He didn't serve in the military, did he? He's barely out of college.'

'Don't let his age discount his expertise,' Zimmerman advised. 'He's one of the best bomb disposal techs I've ever known. Our hazardous device team is already on the scene with Agent Triplett. They know to expect you.'

'Be careful, Adam,' Isenberg said quietly. 'The shooter outside clearly intended to kill a lot of people. We don't know who was the actual target today or why. The young man stopped at Dr Fallon's table, but he could have been instructed to pick someone at random. Based on the explosives visible in the vest, he could easily have taken out the entire café.'

Adam nodded grimly. 'He failed, so he may try again. Got it. I'll update you ASAP.' He ended the call and finished securing his bulletproof vest. Grabbing his tactical helmet and a gym bag packed with a suit jacket, a button-up shirt, and a tie, he holstered his service weapon in the vest then slammed the Jeep's hatch closed. He glanced at the hotel across the street. Meredith was probably inside. Hopefully CSU had taken whatever evidence they'd needed from her hands so she could wash them.

35

He hoped that soap and water would be enough for her to feel clean.

Soap and water had never done the trick for him. He wore the blood of too many victims on his hands, and no matter how many times he'd washed them, he never truly felt clean. He didn't want that for Meredith.

Two cops were positioned at the hotel entrance and he could see two more inside the lobby as he jogged up the line of cruisers to find Trip.

Meredith would have to wait a little longer.

Anderson Township, Ohio,
Saturday 19 December, 4.30 P.M.

He's going to kill me. There was no question in Linnea Holmes's mind. He'd killed Andy like he was . . . nothing. Andy was not nothing. He'd been . . . everything.

I'm so sorry. She wanted to scream her apology to the darkening sky, but she didn't. Because she wanted the bastard who'd killed Andy to believe he'd broken her. That she wouldn't fight. But she would fight. She wasn't going to let him kill her.

Through a hole in the pocket of her coat, she fingered the switchblade she'd hidden in the lining. Andy had given her the switchblade so that she could protect herself. She didn't know where he'd gotten it from. She figured he'd either won it in a poker game or had stolen it. She hadn't cared, but Andy had. He hated having to cheat and steal.

That was why Andy had pointedly shown her the receipt when he'd bought her the coat when the weather turned cold in November, long before he'd bought one for himself.

He always took care of me first. Always. That he'd died believing the worst of her . . .

But the worst was also the truth. Mostly. Yes, she'd whored herself out. But not for the reason he thought. She wasn't sure she ever could have told him the real reason.

Tears stung her eyes. *And now I'll never know.*

She owed Andy Gold everything. *I'm not going to let him down again.* She steeled her spine. *Revenge will happen*, she promised herself. Promised Andy.

The SUV finally stopped. They'd been driving east for twenty minutes, leaving the city behind for the countryside. She'd never been this far out in the country before. Overgrown with trees and vines, it was like no one had touched the land in years.

She'd kept her head bowed so that he'd continue to think she was in shock, but she'd been carefully observing their route so that she could find her way out. She tightened her grip on the switchblade. She'd either get away, or she'd be dead.

She lifted her chin, widening her eyes. Pretended to be surprised. 'Where are we?'

He didn't answer, just got out of the SUV. Leaving the motor running and his door open, he walked around to her side, drawing a gun from a shoulder holster.

This is it. She whispered a prayer in her mind and hoped that God would hear her.

Gripping his gun in his right hand, he reached for the collar of her coat with his left, his body bracing to yank her out of the car. *And then to shoot me and leave me here.*

I don't think so. Linnea gritted her teeth. *Not today.*

She whipped the blade from her pocket, holding it the way Andy had taught her to, releasing the blade she sharpened religiously, just as she'd promised Andy she would. *As if your life depends on it*, Andy had urged when he'd given it to her. Today it would.

She struck out, catching his right forearm as she swung her legs from the car and jerked her knee up into his groin. He bent over on a shocked gasp and she met his head halfway, butting her skull against his so hard she had to blink away stars.

'Fucking bitch,' he snarled, tightening his grip on her collar – and on his gun. *Dammit.* She hadn't cut him deep enough in his gun arm. He hadn't dropped it. Panic nearly froze her, but she pushed it away.

Again. Do it again. And again. Until he stops. Or you're dead.

She struck again, plunging the knife *hard* up into the underside

37

of his arm. With a furious cry he released her, stumbling back a step. Ignoring the searing pain from the injuries she'd sustained in last night's beating, she used both feet to shove him away, using his own momentum, then shoved the SUV door, hitting him again.

A shot cracked the air, but it hadn't hit her, so she leapt from the SUV and ran to the driver's side, not looking back. *Don't look back. Don't look. Just drive.* She yanked at the gearshift and floored it, not stopping to close his door or hers.

For a split second she saw him in her side mirror, making a desperate grab for the back door as the tires squealed, slipping on the snowy road. Then the tires gained traction and the SUV lurched forward, fishtailing.

She saw him fall to his knees, aiming his gun at the vehicle, and she ducked down as far as she dared. More shots cracked the air, so fast she lost count. One hit the back window, making her flinch, and then . . . *nothing*. No breaking glass.

She glanced into the rear-view to see a small dent in the back window, but no webbing, no fracture. She felt the hysterical laugh bubbling up and was powerless to stop it.

Bulletproof. He had bulletproof glass in his SUV. And it had worked against him.

Finally, *something* worked against him.

She raced to the end of the road, relieved when it connected to a larger one. She turned sharply onto the two-lane highway, the centrifugal force causing the back door to slam shut. *Good.* She hadn't planned for that to happen, but she'd take it.

She tapped the accelerator hard enough to make the driver's door swing close enough that she could reach it. She pulled it closed, then floored the accelerator again.

Where am I? She knew she was east of the city, but she didn't know anyone out here. She didn't have a phone. She glanced at the charging cord hanging from the USB port in the stereo. No phone was attached, so he probably had it in his pocket.

Which meant he was calling for help right now. *Shit.* She'd need to ditch the SUV quickly. He had . . . staff. Devoted staff. Linnea had no idea what he'd done to earn such loyalty, but his thugs obeyed his every command. She winced, her body protesting her sudden activity back there. His thugs especially obeyed the commands that allowed them to torture anyone smaller than they were. Which was pretty much everyone.

She wore bruises all over her body. Inside and out.

It wasn't the first time she'd been forced to 'entertain' one of his 'associates.' But last night's thug had been particularly brutal. He'd wanted her to scream, and she had. He'd counted on Andy agreeing to anything to make her torture stop, and he had. But not really.

She'd known Andy wouldn't be able to kill. She'd seen the grim line of his jaw, the sorrow in his eyes. Andy had known he would die today, but true to character, he hadn't let anyone else get hurt. That was just who he was.

Grief pierced her heart. Who he'd been. *Goddammit.* He was gone. *Forever.* He, who deserved to have every happily-ever-after in the world. Now he never would.

Linnea's eyes filled and she brushed the damned tears away impatiently. She didn't have time to grieve. She didn't *deserve* to grieve. Not until Andy got justice.

You should call the police. Tell them what you know.

She huffed bitterly. *Like they'd believe me? A whore?*

Besides, a call to the cops could get her arrested. And she wouldn't last a single night inside. He had his fingers in the jail too.

For now, the only people who knew she was involved in this morning's shooting were him and his staff. For now, she could hide. And wait for her chance to kill him herself.

Then she'd go to the cops. Then she'd take whatever she had coming. Because then Andy would be able to rest in peace. *And so will I.*

Cincinnati, Ohio,
Saturday 19 December, 4.30 P.M.

'Just a little more, Dr Fallon.' Special Agent Quincy Taylor's hands were gentle, his voice incredibly kind as he knelt on one knee in front of her. 'I'm finished scraping under the nails of your right hand. I'll finish your left and then you can wash up.'

Meredith flinched. *Wash up?* Like she'd gotten her hands dirty tending her garden or painting a bedroom wall? One *washed up* from activities like those. But not from this.

Agent Taylor had cleaned the bulk of the mess from her hands when he'd arrived, only minutes after the first cops, then he'd asked her to wait while he attended to the scene.

And then they'd been evacuated – an utter nightmare. At least Kendra Cullen had been on patrol duty in the square. Mallory knew Wendi's sister and trusted her. That Mallory was safe and being cared for was one thing Meredith didn't need to worry about.

Because there was still a bomb in Buon Cibo. The boy had been wired to blow them all sky-high. The look on his face when he'd told her to run . . . Meredith's heart *hurt*. He'd been so damn frightened.

And still he'd told her to run. *And then* . . . In her mind she heard the shot, felt the . . .

No. Not going there. Not again. She closed her eyes and swallowed hard, willing herself not to look at her hands. Not to gag. *Again.* It hadn't been pretty the first time.

She'd thrown up hard after ending her call to Adam and she'd been glad he hadn't been there to see that. But she needed him now.

The hotel's revolving door swished, indicating someone had either entered or exited. She'd lifted her eyes to that doorway each time she heard the sound, hoping to see Adam's face. Not caring if he wanted her or not. Not caring why he'd held himself so rigidly distant. Not caring if she looked pathetically needy.

She *was* pathetically needy. This time she told herself to keep her eyes closed, that it wouldn't be him, but her eyes were rebellious and looked anyway.

And then everything seemed to settle. *He's here. He came.* Just like he'd promised.

Adam came through the revolving door looking around the crowded lobby and . . . found her. His body stilled and his shoulders sagged. He carefully sized her up, then lifted one gloved finger, wordlessly asking her to wait.

She'd waited for Adam for months. 'What's a few more minutes?' she muttered.

'I'm done,' Agent Taylor announced.

'Thank God.' She lifted her eyes to find Adam again. He was talking to Agent Triplett and both men were looking at her, but she couldn't tell what they were saying.

Agent Taylor looked over his shoulder, then back at Meredith. 'They're the lead investigators. That's why he didn't come straight over. He's got to attend to the scene first.'

Meredith's cheeks heated. 'Whatever.' *Great.* She sounded like her adolescent clients. She straightened primly. 'I don't know what you're talking about, Agent Taylor.'

Agent Taylor's grin turned a little cheeky. He was really cute in a nerdy, young kind of way. 'Call me Quincy, if you want to,' he said and pulled a box of antiseptic wipes from his kit. 'Let me get your hands clean, so that you can do *whatever* when he comes over.'

'Get them clean so I can hide behind them.' She swallowed a groan. 'I know I'm not that obvious. Am I?'

Quincy bristled in mock offense. 'I'm a trained observer, Dr Fallon. I have degrees in psychology, chemistry, and forensic anthropology.' He chatted as he cleaned her hands with gentle efficiency. 'And I'm trained in deception detection. Not that I needed it,' he added, grinning again. 'If you meant not to be obvious, you should work on that. Just a little.'

She ignored his final words. 'You can't have all those degrees. You're too young.'

His brows lifted above the rims of his black horn-rimmed glasses. 'I'm thirty-four.'

Two years younger than me. I guess I just feel older. 'That is so not fair,' she grumbled, making him chuckle.

'I might have agreed with you when I was twenty-five and looked seventeen,' he said, inspecting her clean skin. 'You don't have any open cuts, so that's good news, at least.' He gathered the discarded wipes into an evidence bag before rising to his feet with a fluidity that seemed equally unfair because Meredith felt creaky.

'I've got to get back to the scene.' He gave her his card. 'Let me know if you need anything. I mean that.'

'But—' She grabbed the sleeve of his jacket. 'The bomb. Have they defused it?'

Quincy pointed to Agent Triplett, then patted her hand. 'If that big guy over there is here, the bomb is defused and on its way somewhere secure. He's the team's bomb expert.'

Forcing her fingers to let go, Meredith considered the enormous man standing next to Adam. She knew Jeff Triplett personally because he'd recently joined their circle of friends. He was a really nice guy. Smart, funny, and a great dancer. But here, on the job, he was an imposing figure, arms crossed over his broad chest and his bald head a gleaming dark umber under the lobby's bright lights. Trip dwarfed Adam, who was no slouch at six-two.

'Interesting,' she said. 'You'd think Trip's fingers would be too big to deal with those little wires.'

'You'd be wrong,' Quincy said seriously.

'Okay, fine, but he *is* young.'

Quincy smiled down at her. 'Yeah, he's disgustingly young.' His smile faded. 'I'm glad for him, you know? He's not all hard and jaded like the rest of us. Yet, anyway.'

Meredith narrowed her eyes at him, hearing a vulnerability in his voice that pushed her warning buttons. 'Are *you* all right, Quincy?'

He looked a little startled, but nodded. 'I almost forgot you're a psychologist. I guess I'm as all right as any of us,' he said with a shrug. 'Seen too much. Too many nightmares. Today is just one more. You know the drill.'

'I worry about you guys,' Meredith said, thinking of the anguish Adam had gone through nearly a year ago, when he'd reached out to her for comfort. And then again, four months before, when he'd sat at her table and colored with her. He'd used an entire colored pencil on one picture, every bit of it red. Too many of the cops she knew suffered from PTSD, but too few sought the help they so desperately needed. 'I'd be happy to—'

'I've got to be going,' Quincy interrupted. Then, with a tight smile, he was gone.

Meredith stared after him, not realizing she'd stood up, hands on her hips, until she felt a blast of warmth at her elbow. She looked left, then abruptly up, catching her breath. 'Adam.' Her heart began to thunder. Adam Kimble was, under any circumstance, the most beautiful man she'd ever known. 'Hi.'

But it was like he hadn't heard her. He was scowling. 'What did he do to you?'

Meredith blinked rapidly. 'Please?' She followed Adam's glance to the revolving door. The forensic investigator had pushed through and now stood outside, shrugging into his winter coat. 'You mean Quincy?'

Adam's dark brows lifted sarcastically. 'Quincy?'

She cocked her jaw in irritation. *Oh, for God's sake.* Was he angry? *Possibly.* Jealous? *Unlikely.* Still, this was macho posturing if ever she'd seen it. Which, of course, she had. Many times. 'Agent Taylor? You know,' she added sweetly, 'the nice guy on your *team*?'

Adam's mouth thinned and she cursed herself for thinking even *that* was sexy. 'He put his hands on you.' He all but growled the words.

Her temper bubbled. 'He was cleaning *brains* off my *hands*. He made sure I was all right, because I was a mess. *His* behavior was fine. Whatever *your* problem is, stop it.'

His swallow was audible. 'I'm sorry,' he murmured, his tone low and . . . intimate, shivering over her skin. 'I've been half out of my mind, worrying about you, but I have to stay professional or Isenberg will take me off the case. I'm sorry,' he said again. '*Are* you all right? I should have asked that first.'

She started to say that she was all right, then opened her eyes and saw his gaze fixed on her face. The lie slid away. 'No.' Her voice broke. 'I'm not. I'm not all right,' she whispered. 'I saw a boy die today, and I'm not all right.'

Four

Cincinnati, Ohio,
Saturday 19 December, 4.45 P.M.

Adam needed to touch her, so damn bad. Needed to pull her into his arms and hold her until her trembling subsided. She was pale and . . . There was brain matter in her hair. He didn't think she knew because she'd have tried to wash it out.

He let himself grip her elbow and tugged her back down to sit in the folding chair the hotel had provided. Crouching in front of her, he damned Isenberg and her warning to perdition and pulled off one of his latex gloves. Meredith's slender hand was icy cold and smelled of antiseptic. He gripped it hard and looked up into her face.

'Tell me what happened, Meredith.'

She shuddered. 'We'd just sat down, Mallory and me. We were looking at the menu and then . . . all of a sudden he was there. Staring at me.' She closed her eyes, any remaining color draining from her face, leaving her ashen.

He squeezed her hand again. 'Meredith,' he said sharply. 'Open your eyes. That's good,' he said, more softly when she obeyed.

'You have glitter in your hair,' she murmured.

Wonderful. 'It's from the star on top of the tree at Mariposa House.'

Her eyes flickered, her mouth turning down in a frown. 'You put up the tree?'

'Diesel and I.' He started to loosen his grip on her hand, but she grasped at him.

'Let me hold on,' she whispered. 'For just a little while longer. Then you can let go.'

'Whatever you need,' he said quietly.

She huffed, bitterness flickering across her face so quickly he would have missed it if he hadn't been staring. She started to speak, but stopped herself, giving her head a slight shake. 'Fine. All right. It's okay. I'm okay.' She tried to tug her hand free, but he was the one who held on this time. He wasn't ready to let her go. Nowhere close to ready.

He frowned at her. 'No, it's not okay. What were you going to say? No, tell me,' he insisted when she looked away. 'Look at me, Meredith.'

She met his eyes and he wanted to flinch at the raw misery he saw in hers, but he didn't allow himself to respond. He didn't deserve to flinch.

She cries, Wendi had said. *If you don't want her, let her go.*

I did this, he thought, feeling as miserable as Meredith appeared. *I put that pain in her eyes.* He hadn't meant to hurt her, but that was exactly what he'd done.

'Whatever I need,' she murmured. 'Right. You can't give me what I need. Or won't. I don't know which. And it doesn't matter. Not right now, anyway.' She tugged her hand again, swallowing when he still didn't let go. 'Please, Adam,' she whispered hoarsely. 'I can't do this here. I can't fall apart. Not in front of all these people. I shouldn't have asked you to come. It wasn't fair to either of us and . . . and you have a job to do. So just let me go.'

'I can't,' he whispered back. 'Don't ask me to. Not yet. Please.'

Her eyes were glistening now and she turned her head, blinking to send tears down her cheeks. 'Fine,' she said, shuddering out a sigh. But her hand went limp in his and he knew the moment he loosened his grip, she'd pull away. Emotionally, she already had.

She cleared her throat, straightened her spine, and schooled her features into the calm mask everyone else seemed to believe was her natural zen expression.

But Adam knew better. He knew what she looked like when she

45

let go. When she lost control. When she screamed his name. He shuddered out a breath of his own.

He could not be thinking about that right now. 'Later,' he murmured. 'We can talk about this later. I promise. For now, I need to get your statement. You said he was suddenly there, standing at your table, staring at you.'

She nodded, stoic now. 'I wanted to run. Just instinct, I suppose. I had my gun in my pocket, so I unsnapped the holster.'

Her gun had been taken into evidence. 'Do you always carry?'

Another nod. 'For a few years now. I've had some parents threaten me after their children revealed abuse. A few have become violent.'

Adam had to choke back his rage. *Not now*. 'I'll need their names. All of them.'

Her jaw tightened almost imperceptibly. 'I can give you names of the people who've specifically threatened me, but they're already on record. I've filed official complaints on all of them with the police.'

He frowned at her. 'Specifically? What about unspecific threats?'

She lifted a slender shoulder. 'They don't exist.'

His eyes narrowed, immediately understanding the nuance. 'They don't actually exist or you're not going to tell me who they are?'

'Legally, the first one. Pragmatically, the second.'

He closed his eyes briefly, pulling his temper back into control. 'Why not?' he asked when he thought he could speak without snapping.

'If I identify the parents, I identify my clients. I can't do that. Not if they haven't made a threat specific to their child or to me.' Her voice was level. Kind, even. He imagined she used that voice on the children she counseled, but it grated on him.

He managed to keep his own tone professional. 'But you carry a gun.'

Another half shrug. 'I'm careful, Detective.'

Detective. *Shit*. 'Has anyone given you reason to believe you need a gun, even if there was no explicit threat?'

'Yes.'

His temper broke free. 'Dammit, Meredith. Somebody nearly blew up a restaurant on a crowded street. Do you know how many people could have died?'

Her chin lifted. 'I am quite aware. I will cooperate to the best of my ability.'

'But you won't tell me who you're afraid of. For God's sake, Meredith.'

She swallowed hard. 'I will not breach the privacy of my clients. They are children, Detective Kimble. Children who've been traumatized. The ones who've come to me through the courts are on record. Anyone who has specifically said, "I'm going to make you pay, bitch," has been reported to the police. By me. The ones that just happen to be running around the high school track at the same time I do every morning at five a.m., or just happen to be shopping for veggies at my neighborhood Kroger on Saturday mornings, or just happen to catch my eye across the crowd after Sunday mass at St Germaine's for the past three weeks . . . Those I can't tell you about.'

'And they're the reason you carry a gun.'

She nodded once, her lips pursed tight. 'So. I unsnapped my holster and when he pulled his gun I tried to talk him down first. His hand was shaking.'

He'd get those names later. Now she was holding herself together by a fragile thread. 'The first cop on scene said that other diners reported the man talking to himself.'

'I don't think he was,' she said, her brow furrowing again. 'I don't know if it's even possible now' – a hard swallow – 'what with his head and all, but you might check for an earbud. He was being coerced. I'm sure of it. He kept saying he was sorry and that "He'll kill her."' Her eyes sharpened. 'Everyone has video on their phones now. Maybe someone caught him talking.'

He'd already thought of that. 'I plan to ask the other witnesses when I'm finished with you.' Except he'd never be finished with her. Not while he drew breath. 'And then?'

'And then I drew my gun. We did a standoff for what seemed like forever, but it could only have been a minute. Maybe less. He dropped his gun and told me to run. To get down and run. He

47

started to unzip his coat, but then . . .' She swallowed again, audibly. 'The shot came from outside. The window shattered and his head . . . well, you know.' She stared down at her hands. 'I was kind of in shock, you know? I just stared at my gun, thinking I hadn't shot it, wondering what the hell had happened. I hadn't put the window shattering together with everything else yet.' Her lips twisted. 'Luckily, Mallory did. She pulled me down, just in time. The next bullet hit the man sitting behind me. He'll be all right,' she added. 'The EMTs were able to stop the bleeding.'

'And then?' he nudged patiently.

'Then tires squealed.' She sighed wearily. 'And then I called you.'

'I'm glad you did.' He gave her limp hand a light squeeze. 'So damn glad, Meredith.'

Another bitter twist of her lips. 'At least it allowed you to have a head start in getting here. Agent Taylor told me that you and Agent Triplett are the lead investigators on this case.' She looked pointedly down at their joined hands. 'I imagine your boss wouldn't want you holding a witness's hand like this, Detective Kimble.'

Adam's heart clenched. She was still calling him "detective". He wanted – no, *needed* – to hear her say his name again. 'I'm sorry, Meredith. I need to explain some things to you.'

She shook her head, sadly now. 'You don't owe me any explanations. I want things that you . . . clearly don't. I'm a big girl. I can deal.' Pasting a fake smile on her face, she tugged her hand again and this time he let her go.

He needed to tell her everything. If for no other reason than because he didn't want her to hurt like this. He'd never dreamed she could be hurting like this. *Over me. I'm not worth it.* And that was the fucking understatement of the century.

'We need to talk,' he insisted, keeping his voice to a murmur that no one could overhear. '*I* need to talk. To you. I need to explain.'

Her back went rigid. 'Am I done? I need to see to Mallory. And I really want to go home.' Her voice broke. 'I'd really appreciate if I could be done now, Detective Kimble.'

No. Don't go. Please do not go. But he swallowed back those words and pushed emotion aside to consider the case. 'Where was Mallory all the time this was happening?'

She blinked, appearing surprised. 'Next to me.'

'In the chair? You said she pulled you down after the first shot was fired.'

Meredith frowned in concentration. 'I told her to get down. After he pulled the gun.'

'What did he do then?'

'Yelled at me. Told me that nobody could move.' Her head wagged slowly. 'I can't remember exactly what he said, but it was something like that.'

'When did he talk to himself – or somebody else, if that turns out to be the case?'

Her frown deepened. 'After he pulled the gun. Before I told Mallory to get down. I think. He got distracted when I pushed Mallory down. Pointed the gun at her then back at me. That's when I pulled my gun from my pocket. I think Mallory went under the table then.' She pressed fingertips to her temple. 'I'm sorry. I can't remember exactly.'

'I understand.'

She folded her hands in her lap primly. 'When can I have my gun back?'

'I don't know. It'll be held as evidence, so not anytime soon. Certainly not today.'

'It's all right. I have another. Now may I go, Detective?'

'Yes.' He came to his feet when she did. 'Can I call you? Tonight? Please,' he added when she said nothing. He dropped his voice to a desperate whisper. '*Please.*'

Her shoulders sagged. 'Okay. Whatever—' Her voice cracked. 'Whatever you need.'

She turned and walked away. He let her go, his gut churning with the urge to go after her. He let out a huge sigh, then sent a quick text to his AA sponsor. *You home tonite?*

His phone buzzed a second later. *Yup. What's up?*

Meredith Fallon was what was up. But he wasn't going to say that. John had discouraged him from seeing her before his year was up. But if she turned him away after he explained to her? Yeah. He'd need his sponsor then. *Caught a bad case*, he texted instead. *May need to talk.*

I'm here. Call me. Doesn't matter how late.

Because John Kasper was a decent man, a retired cop who knew exactly what Adam's job entailed. *Thx*, Adam typed, hit SEND, then rejoined Trip, who was watching him.

'She okay?' Trip asked.

'No.' Meredith Fallon was definitely not okay. For too many reasons.

Trip's brows lifted, his shiny bald head tilting in question. '*You* okay?'

Adam made his lips move. 'Of course. What's our status on the bomb?'

'On its way to the lab. I'm ninety-nine percent sure it's deactivated, but the removal team took all precautions, just in case.'

'How did you deactivate it?'

'I didn't,' Trip said. 'I think the victim did.'

Anderson Township, Ohio,
Saturday 19 December, 4.50 P.M.

Finally. Civilization. Linnea pulled into the parking lot of a seafood restaurant called Clyde's Place, looking around for his thugs. That she didn't see them didn't make her feel better. She was pretty sure that she wouldn't see them first. She'd realized about five minutes after leaving him in the muddy snow that he probably had a tracker on the SUV, that he'd probably already sicced his enforcers on her. But it hadn't made sense to abandon the SUV on the side of the road. She'd be on foot and she was too sore to walk very fast or very far. Her chances were better now that she was in civilization. She could hide for a while. Maybe hitch a ride.

To where? She didn't know yet. Not too far away. She needed proximity to kill him.

Pulling the hood of her coat forward to hide her face, she gingerly got out of the SUV, wincing at the blood she'd left on the seat.

50

Terrific. She'd bled through her jeans. Not a huge surprise as she'd bled off and on all through the night after his right-hand maniac had finished with her. She stared at the bloody seat for a long moment, the assault replaying in her mind. Her own screams. The laughter. His and his thug's.

He'd watched. He got off on watching.

Stop. She pushed the memory into the box inside her mind and visualized locking it tight. Along with all the other memories she couldn't seem to delete.

Go to the ER before you bleed to death. It could happen. She'd come close once before.

But she couldn't go to the ER. He had people inside the hospital too. She wasn't sure which hospital, or if he had staff in all of them. She couldn't take the chance.

There was a clinic downtown. She'd used it before, after another brutal time just like last night. The lady doctor had been so kind. She'd asked if Linnea needed help from the police, accepting her quick refusal. The doctor had merely stitched her up, given her a non-narcotic painkiller. Then she'd recommended a series of STD tests, including HIV.

There'd been no judgment in the lady doctor's oddly colored eyes when Linnea had returned for the test results. No pity. No revulsion or disapproval. Only sympathy and understanding. That had been Linnea's second time at the clinic.

Which had been six months ago. Linnea hoped the shot of antibiotic she'd been given had taken care of the gonorrhea, because she hadn't been back for a second shot or to be retested after three months as the nice doctor had recommended.

What difference did it make? The other diagnosis she'd been given was a death sentence, even though the lady doctor had insisted that it no longer was. Except Linnea had no money for medicines. No money for care.

She'd been stuck in her worst nightmare, forced to 'entertain' his 'associates' over and over again. The other girls got paid, but Linnea didn't, because he'd had leverage. Information that he'd been able to use to force her compliance.

51

Some of his associates used condoms. The others would share her fate. There was some satisfaction in that. Although she had worried about the women his associates went home to. They didn't deserve to be infected too, but she'd been powerless to stop any of it. Once he'd known she was HIV positive, she'd have become a liability. He'd have had no reason to keep her alive and once she was gone, he'd have gone after Andy.

She'd have done anything to protect Andy Gold. But none of that mattered anymore.

At least she knew to warn whoever was on duty at the clinic today. Because she would go. Get sewn up. Again. She'd live long enough to kill the man who'd done this to her.

The man who'd killed Andy like he was nothing.

She just needed a little cash. Enough to get back to the city. She looked up and down the street, relieved to see a bus stop a block away. There was also a hotel at the entrance to the interstate. It wasn't a fancy place, but she'd be able to get a cab from there. If she could find enough cash for the fare. She hoped so. It was late on a Sunday and the buses wouldn't be running that often. It was cold. *And I'm still bleeding.*

Not sure how much time she had before he or his goons arrived, she quickly lifted the lid of the center console and peered inside. Nothing. It was as clean as new. The glove box was also empty, but the pouch on the back of the front passenger seat yielded a single piece of paper, folded over and over until it was only a little bigger than a postage stamp.

Linnea shoved it in her coat pocket and continued searching for cash. Even some change would be helpful. Maybe she'd even find enough to buy some food. The smell of hamburgers made her stomach growl and she tried not to think about how long it had been since she'd eaten. *Focus. Get to the clinic first and then eat.*

She opened the ashtray, exhaling in a rush. Cash – a roll of twenties, secured by a rubber band. Which made sense, actually. Prostitution and drugs – his bread and butter – were generally cash-only businesses. There were at least ten twenties in the roll. Maybe fifteen. That would more than pay for a cab. She'd have enough left over to buy another weapon, since she'd left her switchblade in his arm.

She shoved the money into her pocket. Stepping away from the SUV, she slammed the door, locked it, and pocketed the key.

The blood she'd left on the SUV's seat was deadly. If the cops found the vehicle first, they'd have gloves on. They'd be protected. If he or his thugs found it first, they deserved whatever exposure they got.

But no one else deserved exposure to her blood. She hoped a locked door would keep them out. At least her coat was still clean. She'd sit on it once she was in a taxi.

She started walking toward the little hotel, throwing the SUV keys into the first storm sewer she came across. *Stay away from the road*, she told herself. *Stick to the shadows.* Which wasn't too hard, because that was how she'd lived for the last six months.

Cincinnati, Ohio,
Saturday 19 December, 4.50 P.M.

I need to explain something to you. Meredith sat next to Mallory on a small sofa in the hotel manager's office, her arm tight around the girl's thin shoulders, Adam's words echoing in her head so loudly that it was all she could hear. How could he explain away months of ignoring her? He wasn't interested, plain and simple.

Yes, he'd sent her pictures he'd colored – even painted – but that only meant he was letting her know he was recovering. That he was getting a hold on his PTSD.

If he even starts to say 'It's not you, it's me,' I'm going to fucking hit him in the face.

'Hey,' Wendi said from the doorway, thankfully halting her thoughts. Wendi's face was tear-streaked, her eyes red. Trembling head to toe, she rushed into the room and wrapped Mallory in her arms. 'You're both okay. I was so scared. But you're okay.'

Meredith met her friend's eyes over Mallory's shoulder and shook her head. *Not okay*, she mouthed. *At all.*

'You're unhurt,' Wendi corrected in a fierce whisper. 'All I knew was that there was a shooting. I was afraid you'd been hit.'

'I told you she was fine,' Agent Colby said in that very quiet way he had. 'That they were both fine.' He came into the room and winced when his gaze passed over Meredith's hair. 'We'll get your statements squared away and take you home. You can shower.'

Meredith clenched her eyes shut, her stomach heaving again. 'It's in my hair?'

'Not much,' Wendi said quickly – way too quickly. 'It looks like . . . like the dust bunny fuzz you pull out of your dryer filter.' She sounded so pleased with herself.

Meredith opened her eyes, her lips curving wryly at her tiny best friend. 'You are such an awful liar, Wen.'

'She really is,' Colby said, affectionately tugging a lock of Wendi's hair.

Wendi looked over her shoulder at him, frowning. 'Mer can't stay by herself in her house. That man tried to kill her today. What if he comes back?'

Mallory stiffened and Meredith sighed. 'Wendi, stop. You're scaring Mallory.'

But Colby just nodded as if Meredith hadn't said a word. 'She can stay at the big house,' he said. 'I've got some vacation saved up. I'll take a few days, stay with you too.'

Meredith rolled her eyes when Wendi made goo-goo eyes at Parrish Colby like a lovesick teenager. But the man was sweet and he absolutely doted on Wendi.

I'm just jealous, she admitted. Adam Kimble had voiced no such worry about her welfare. *Considering someone* did *just try to kill me.* And the thought brought a new wave of nausea. *God. Somebody tried to kill me . . . and a restaurant full of people.*

Who? Who could have hated her that much? Who had that much disregard for human life? Well, lots of her clients' parents. The court-referred ones, anyway. That was usually why those clients were her clients. The adults in their lives had been too selfish – or evil – to keep them safe.

'We have a free room on the third floor,' Wendi was saying. 'Mer can sleep there.'

Wendi and Colby had been discussing her living arrangements while her mind had gone wandering, so Meredith made herself smile and take back at least some control of her life. 'Thank you, Parrish. I really appreciate it, but I think it's better if I don't stay with the girls at Mariposa House. It will be disruptive to their routine.' She glanced at Mallory and swallowed hard. *She might have been killed today. Because she was with me.* 'And it might put the girls in danger. I need to keep my distance until this . . . situation is resolved.'

'You didn't cause this, Mer,' Wendi protested.

'I know.' And she did. Logically. 'Doesn't mitigate the risk I pose by staying there. Parrish, you stay with Wendi. Keep the girls safe. I'll get Kendra to stay with me.' Kendra had only been a cop a little more than a year, but the woman could take care of herself. *So can I,* Meredith thought, but she didn't want to be alone tonight.

Can I call you later? Tonight? Please? It had been the *please* that had left her undone. *Dammit.*

'Kenny's on duty today,' Meredith added quickly, because Wendi looked ready to argue. 'She'll be free tonight.' She lifted a brow. 'Oh, come on. Do you really think Kendra will let anyone in my house who shouldn't be there?'

That might even include Adam. Like Wendi, Kendra had told her to move on. Neither of the Cullen sisters wasted any love on Adam Kimble.

'No, she won't.' Wendi looked unhappy, but didn't push it. 'All right.' She looked up at Colby again. 'Can we leave now?'

'I'll find out,' Colby said. 'Trip and Kimble are here somewhere. This is their case.'

Cincinnati, Ohio,
Saturday 19 December, 5.00 P.M.

'He really did disarm it,' Adam murmured as he and Trip stood in the small meeting room that the hotel had provided for their use, watching the restaurant's security tape on Trip's laptop for the third time – but not the footage of the shooting itself. The dining room camera had only gotten a partial view of the young man's face before he'd been shot. The most revealing footage had come from the camera mounted outside, specifically the three seconds that the man had crossed the street, approaching the restaurant's front door.

'He unzips his coat right there,' Trip said, pointing at the laptop screen. 'Then . . . right there he yanks the wires.' He paused the video. 'You wouldn't notice it if you weren't watching. I missed it the first time I saw the tape. I thought he was adjusting his collar.'

'He knew someone was watching him,' Adam said. 'Meredith thinks he was talking to someone, that he was wearing an earpiece.'

'He was,' a mild voice said from behind them.

Adam looked over his shoulder and had to fight not to scowl when Agent Quincy Taylor closed the door behind himself. 'Did you find it?' Adam asked, trying to keep the anger from his voice. The man had been . . . *What, Kimble?* the voice in his head asked sarcastically. *Patting her hand to calm her? Because you weren't there to do so?*

Agent Taylor blinked at him. 'Yes,' he said, his wary tone indicating that Adam hadn't hidden his anger all that well.

Even Trip was giving Adam a strange look. 'Where was the earpiece?' Trip asked the forensic investigator.

'In a puddle of brain matter,' Agent Taylor answered flatly. 'One of the bomb disposal techs saw it there and took a photo for me, because the crime scene isn't cleared for my team yet. Did I hear you say the victim pulled the wires out of the bomb?'

Trip nodded. 'Sure looks like it. The kid must have known what he was doing, to be that bold. One false move and he could have been blown to bits.'

Adam forced himself to pull his head out of his own ass and focus on his job. 'Maybe he knew what he was doing. More likely he just didn't care. If the bomb had detonated at the door, the impact would have been a lot less serious.'

'You think he was trying to save the people in the restaurant?' Trip asked.

'He tried to save Meredith,' Adam answered. 'He told her to get down, to run, just before he was shot. That indicates to me that he was still afraid of the bomb.'

'So he wasn't sure if he had disabled the device,' Trip said thoughtfully. 'That boy knew he was gonna die either way. You can see it on his face. How he flinches right before he yanks the wire.'

Adam sighed, his chest tight with compassion for the kid. 'He said "he" was going to "kill her." We can start with the assumption that the person the kid was afraid of was the one who shot him and drove away. We've got a BOLO out on the black SUV, ads for "Plumber's Helper" on both sides.' Multiple witnesses had seen it driving away. 'But it's a fake company and nobody seems to have seen a license plate.'

'A witness caught the SUV on video,' Agent Taylor said. 'I got a partial plate and added it to the BOLO. That's the other thing I came in to tell you.'

Adam blinked in surprise, but at least Trip did too, so Agent Taylor wasn't keeping him out of the loop deliberately. 'When did you get the video?' Trip demanded.

'Just now, when I went to check on the crime scene. That was after I finished cleaning Dr Fallon's hands,' Agent Taylor added pointedly. 'And that's all I was doing, Detective Kimble.'

'I know. She was pretty freaked to have her hands covered in human remains. Thank you for making the situation easier for her, Agent Taylor.'

The man nodded once. 'Quincy.'

'Adam,' Adam returned.

'And I'm Trip,' Trip said sarcastically. 'Why didn't that witness bring the video to us when we first got here?'

Quincy seemed unruffled. 'They're kids. Brothers, ten and twelve. They were goofing off, play-interviewing their parents about what they'd find under their Christmas tree. They were two blocks away when the SUV passed through their picture. At first, they didn't know they'd gotten anything valuable. The press put the BOLO in their "breaking" report and the kids saw it. They walked up to me when I was outside, saw FBI on my jacket and showed it to me, then emailed it to me.' He tapped the screen of his phone. 'I just emailed it to you, Trip. They're waiting in the lobby with their parents.'

'Thanks,' Trip said. 'We got any leads on who might want the doc dead, Adam?'

'Or why she was carrying a gun?' Quincy added.

'Really the same answer,' Adam said. 'She had a gun because she's been stalked and/or threatened by parents of her child clients.'

Trip frowned. 'What kind of threats? Has she reported it?'

'She's reported everything that's a *specific* threat.' He scowled. 'Apparently, at least one of her clients' parents has been showing up when she runs in the morning and at the store where she shops. And whoever it is just smiles at her. There's no explicit threat.'

'But plenty of implicit,' Quincy said, his jaw going hard. 'She didn't tell you who she was afraid of, did she?'

'No,' Adam admitted, wondering if he was relieved or even more jealous that Quincy seemed to be protective of Meredith too. 'She refused to tell and I didn't push.'

'Why the hell not?' Trip exploded.

Adam gave him a bland look. Which was difficult because Jefferson Triplett was at least four inches taller than he was. 'She was protecting her clients' privacy. I didn't push because she was close to breaking. I'll get the information, one way or the other.'

Trip's returned look was more of a glare. 'I'll ask her. You treat her like spun glass. She's tougher than she looks.'

Adam's brows shot up. 'How do you know that?'

'Because I Googled her when I arrived on the scene,' Trip said. 'She's faced down some nasty-assed characters in the last five years. Any of which could have put a contract out on her. Our suspect list is goddamn long.'

'What nasty-assed characters?' And why hadn't he known this? *God, Kimble, you're a selfish, clueless bastard.*

'At least three drug dealers, two pimps, and a corporate shark who vowed he'd see her pay for getting his kids taken away.'

Adam frowned at him. 'You did *not* get all that off Google.'

Trip looked a little shamefaced. 'Fine. I also asked Kendra. Officer Cullen, I mean.'

Kendra was Wendi's sister. Both women were close to Meredith. 'How would Kendra know?' Adam asked suspiciously. 'And why would she tell you anything?'

'They run together in the morning sometimes. Kenny told me about the dealers and pimps when I got here. She was one of the first cops on the scene. She was the one who saw the bomb, actually.' Trip seemed to hear the pride in his own voice and awkwardly looked down at his enormous hands. 'We've, uh, gone out a few times. Kendra and I.'

Quincy rolled his eyes. 'Good God. Are you *all* panting after each other? Adam, you looked like you wanted to take off my damn head today and Trip's getting the low-down from her best friend's sister.' He huffed out a breath. 'Look, I'm going back to work. I just wanted to tell you about the earpiece and the video.'

'Thanks, Quince,' Trip said, embarrassed, then waited until the man was gone before continuing. 'I'm going to the lab to follow up on the bomb. The lab techs are transporting it as we speak. I want to take a look at those wires the kid pulled out. If he was able to disarm it so easily, we're not talking about a sophisticated bomb-maker.'

'How long before I can access the crime scene?'

'At least an hour. The disposal team has to make sure the threat's eliminated.'

'I'll interview witnesses, then. Deacon and Scarlett are on their way to assist.'

'Get Mallory's statement first,' Trip said, his brow creased in worry. 'She's . . . fragile. This was her first day out after all that shit that went down last summer.'

When she'd been freed from a monster who'd abused her for six years, forcing her into online child pornography by threatening to abuse her younger sister, Macy. Macy was safe now, living with a loving foster family, but Adam knew that Mallory still lived in fear. 'What happened today would rattle anyone.'

Trip hesitated. 'She still has nightmares about a cop who participated in the rapes.'

'The cop we couldn't track down,' Adam said grimly. No one doubted Mallory had been telling them the truth – as she knew it, anyway. She'd said the cop had shown up to investigate her captor, but had raped her in exchange for his silence. They'd investigated, of course, but there hadn't been any evidence that the police had even been called. No record of a visit. Internal Affairs had gotten involved, but concluded whoever had raped Mallory had been pretending to be a cop. Which had been no comfort to Mallory.

'She was nervous about leaving the house today, afraid someone would recognize her from the porn. But she wanted to sign up for classes so she forced herself to leave. I just can't believe this happened today. Poor kid. She's never going to want to leave again.'

Adam figured that Trip had probably heard about Mallory's fears from Kendra, who seemed to spend her spare time helping Wendi at Mariposa House. He himself had heard from his cousin Deacon, who'd heard it from his fiancée, Faith, who was Meredith's partner.

Adam swallowed a sigh because it always seemed to circle back to Meredith, the linchpin of their circle of friends. 'I'll get Mallory's statement so she can get back to Mariposa House. I'm sure that Wendi and Colby are in the hotel by now.'

'Good.' Another hesitation. 'Look, Adam . . . I was there the day she told what had happened to her, when she was in the hospital.' Because her captor had tried to kill her to silence her. 'I filmed her statement that day. She was so scared, but she told her story anyway. She was defiant. Full of rage. But today . . . she looked numb. Like nobody was home. Be careful with her. Not that you'd be harsh, but . . . Just be careful with her.'

'I will.' Adam took no offense because the big behemoth was clearly concerned. 'You find out who made that bomb. I hear you're the bomb wunderkind.'

Trip's smile was almost shy. 'Yeah. That's me.'

'How'd you get to be that way considering you're barely out of diapers?'

Trip snorted at that. 'Damn you guys. You're not old men. And I'm not that young.' He faked a preen. 'I just moisturize.'

'And then you buff to a shine.' And on that note, they went their separate ways, Trip back to the lab and Adam to find Mallory Martin.

Five

Anderson Township, Ohio,
Saturday 19 December, 5.10 P.M.

He grunted when the needle pierced his skin. 'Careful.' His uncle had been the one person he'd trusted to call when Linnea had raced off in his own damn SUV. Mike had arrived in his pickup truck with his first aid kit and now sat in the back seat prepping him for stitches. 'Dammit, Mike, that hurts. Be *careful*.'

His uncle gave him a disgusted look, jabbing the hypo needle harder as he pressed the plunger. 'You mean careful like you shoulda been? What were you thinking? Letting a girl get the drop on you? And then letting her get away? What the ever-lovin' fuck, boy?'

He opened his mouth to protest, then realized anything he said would only be an excuse. Mike was right. He'd fucked up royally.

Linnea had fled. Now she was out there. *And she knows my goddamn face.* He closed his mouth with an audible snap.

'Yeah, I thought so.' Mike put the hypo aside. 'This is gonna take at least ten stitches. I hope the Lidocaine numbs it long enough for me to finish. That was all I had left.'

He gritted his teeth. 'I'll be fine. Just get it done.' He'd endured worse, after all.

Mike stitched a while in silence, then asked, 'Where is the SUV?'

'By now, on its way to the garage.'

Mike glanced up. 'Which one?' he asked suspiciously. 'Your house?'

'Shit no,' he snapped. 'I'm not that stupid.'

'Dunno,' Mike muttered. 'You let a girl—'

'Shut the *fuck* up about the girl,' he exploded, then hissed in pain when Mike yanked the sterile thread much harder than was necessary.

'You watch your tone, boy,' Mike warned. 'You're the one who fucked up. Not me.'

It was true. He knew that. And it pissed him off to high heaven. 'Butch tracked the SUV and picked it up.' His assistant for over a decade, Butch never would have given him grief about losing the girl that way. Unfortunately, Butch didn't have skill with a needle and Mike did. 'He took it to the garage in Batavia.' One of three Mike owned, doing enough legit business that nobody noticed a few late-night repairs here and there. 'It's gonna need new seats. She bled all over them.'

Mike's scowl faded. 'So you cut her too? At least you gave as good as you got.'

Except that he hadn't and he'd have to fess up to that too, because Mike would find out and would never let him hear the end of it. 'Fuck it, Mike,' he hissed again, because the Lidocaine hadn't fully numbed his arm and each stitch hurt like a bitch. 'I didn't do anything to her. Butch did.' He thought about the driver's seat, covered in blood. 'He didn't cut her, though. Just banged her pretty good last night.'

Mike grunted. 'At least *he* had the right idea.'

He shuddered. 'No way I'm dippin' my wick in that cesspool. Nasty.'

'That's why condoms were invented.'

He rolled his eyes. The gaggle of 'college' hookers was one of his most profitable endeavors, but besides being *way* too old for his liking, they were for business. Not pleasure. And not one of them had seen his face. Until Linnea. *Shit*.

Mike knotted the last stitch, cut the thread, then sat back. 'Done. Let me do the other arm. It's not as deep. I can get by with a few butterfly bandages.'

He did as his uncle instructed, wincing when Mike cleaned it with peroxide. 'The SUV is on its way to the Batavia garage *now*,' Mike said. 'Where was it before?'

'The girl abandoned it at a restaurant near the Beechmont exit off 275. Place called Clyde's.'

Mike growled. 'She could have found transportation to anywhere from there.'

'Yeah. I know. Butch picked up the SUV himself. Took Jolee with him. Figured Linnea might trust her if they found her.' Jolee Cusack was the face of his college hooker business. All of the girls thought she was the boss, but Jolee knew the truth.

And now so does Linnea, goddammit.

'So she's still out there, somewhere.' Mike applied a bandage. 'She hasn't called the cops yet. Why not?'

'I don't know,' he said. 'Maybe she's dead. She was bleeding a lot.' He hoped that was the case, but deep down he knew it wasn't. 'Maybe she's getting out of town.'

'You'd better pray that's true,' Mike spat. 'She can bring you down and you are *not* taking me with you.'

He gave his uncle a cold look. 'Wouldn't dream of it.'

Mike moved from the back seat to the front, then looked over his shoulder with a scowl. 'Get your ass up here. I'm not your fucking chauffeur.'

'Never said you were,' he muttered as he obeyed. Like a five-year-old. Except he'd never been a five-year-old. He was pretty sure he'd gone from two to twelve. Mostly because he'd blocked out the ten years in between. He buckled up. 'I'm ready, *Uncle.*'

Mike huffed. 'You're a fucking asshole.'

'Had a good teacher,' he shot back.

Mike smiled at that. 'And don't you forget it. Where do you want to go?'

'To the Fairfield shop. They have an SUV that's almost identical to the one the bitch bled all over.'

Mike put his truck in gear and started down the rutted, snow-covered road. 'That way you don't have to explain anything to Rita.'

'Exactly.' Not that his wife asked too many questions. He never gave her any reason to. His businesses never spilled over into his home life. And they wouldn't start now.

Cincinnati, Ohio,
Saturday 19 December, 5.25 P.M.

Mallory's statement was basically a series of nods, head shakes, and monosyllabic responses to Adam's questions. Trip had been right. Mallory was numb, her eyes vacant in an alarming way.

She'd trailed off mid-interview, staring into space. He'd called her name a little too loudly to get her attention, and she'd flinched as if he'd struck her.

He glanced at Meredith, who sat next to Mallory, holding her hand. She appeared calm. Serene even. But she wasn't. There was a pinch to the side of her mouth that was rarely visible. He wondered how often Meredith really was serene and how often she masked her true emotions.

He wished she'd look at him, but she hadn't met his eyes since he'd entered the small office where she and Mallory had been waiting with Wendi and Colby.

'I'm going to stop now,' he told Meredith quietly. 'She's been through enough.'

'Thank you,' she said, her voice a bare whisper. The sag of her shoulders was infinitesimal. He'd have missed it had he not been watching.

What else had he missed when he hadn't been watching her?

He looked to Wendi and Colby, who leaned against the closed office door, Wendi's head pillowed on Colby's beefy upper arm. 'Take Mallory home. I'll come by Mariposa House tomorrow and try again.' The only point on which Mallory had been clear was that she'd never seen the young man before. Everything else had been disjointed or had gone completely unanswered.

'I hope Mallory doesn't regress,' Colby murmured after Wendi walked her out, arm wound protectively around the girl's waist. 'She's come so far.'

'I hope so too,' Adam replied. 'But if she does, Mariposa is the best place for her.'

Colby's nod was proud. 'Wendi will make sure she's taken care of and I'll keep them all safe.'

'You're going to stay there? In the house?' Adam was surprised. 'Is that allowed?' Wendi always made sure any male volunteers were not working anywhere they might cause the girls discomfort and that included shooing them out before the girls sat down to dinner. That, like no swearing and no booze, was a house rule.

'Doesn't matter,' Colby said gruffly. 'If I can't stay in the house, I'll sleep in my truck or in a tent in the yard. Nobody's getting in that house on my watch.'

'There's snow on the ground,' Meredith protested. 'You can't sleep in a tent.'

Colby turned to Meredith. 'I've slept on snow before. There's also a shed on the property. I can set up a cot out there if I have to.'

'Thank you,' she said earnestly. 'I'll worry a lot less knowing you're there.'

'And where will you be?' Adam asked her.

Her back visibly stiffened. 'In my home.'

Hell no. Just . . . dammit. 'Who's going to watch over you?' Adam demanded. 'You were the target, after all.'

She flinched and even Colby winced. *Way to go, Kimble. Kick her while she's down.*

'Kendra's coming to stay with me tonight,' she said. 'As soon as she's off duty.'

'That's hours from now – hours you'll be alone.'

'She won't be alone,' Colby said with satisfaction. 'Diesel Kennedy is currently waiting in your driveway, Meredith. He'll stay with you until Kendra is able to get to your place. Faith has already rearranged the schedule at your office. She'll take the clients that can't skip a session. The others have been told you're taking a few days off. You'll have someone staying with you 24/7 until this is resolved.'

'Who?' Adam asked sharply. 'Who is "someone"?'

'Everyone,' Colby answered, unperturbed. 'Faith's contacted all the ladies in their breakfast group and the wine club. Between them and their respective husbands, boyfriends, partners, whatever? You're covered for the next week.'

Meredith's circle of friends had circled the wagons, protecting her. *And I'm not included in that group*, Adam admitted. Which was entirely his own fault. He had no right to guard her. He had no rights at all. But he could have had them. He could have been a member of her circle. He could have been the one she depended on, leaned on, but he'd fucked it all up. Him and his goddamned bottle. It was a hard reality to accept.

But she called me today. Me. It wasn't too late. Not yet.

'I'm so tired, I'm not even going to fight the babysitter brigade,' she said, and, despite being tired, she stood fluidly, at ease on those ridiculously high heels that made her legs far too sexy. She started for the door, maintaining eye contact with Colby.

Not with me. She wasn't being mean or rude. Adam understood that. She was simply at her emotional breaking point. *And I'm about to push her farther.*

'Meredith, wait. I have a few more questions. Just another minute or two.'

She nodded reluctantly, lowering herself to the sofa as elegantly as she'd risen. 'All right,' she said, but she held on to her handbag with a white-knuckled grip.

'You were seated by the window.' The coincidence of which was bothering him. 'Had you requested the window?'

Her russet eyebrows scrunched. 'Yes,' she said slowly. She stared at her hands for a moment before looking back up. Still not meeting his eyes. Her gaze was fixed somewhere over his shoulder. 'I called ahead to reserve the window table, the day Mallory asked if I'd take her to register for GED classes. I wanted her to have . . .' Her voice trembled. 'A perfect day,' she whispered. She swallowed hard, and when she spoke again, it was firmly. 'But I was told they didn't reserve specific tables anymore. We'd have to take whatever was open at the time of our reservation.'

'Yet the table was available when you came in.'

She nodded, frowning. 'Yes. I figured we were just lucky.'

'Maybe,' Adam allowed. 'But we need to make sure. Who knew you were taking Mallory to Buon Cibo?'

Meredith faltered. 'The others. My friends.'

'The breakfast group,' Adam supplied. Meredith gathered the women together once a month for breakfast at her cousin Bailey's house – Wendi, Kendra, Faith, and Scarlett Bishop, who was another member of the CPD/FBI joint task force – plus a few others, including Adam's own cousin, Dani. Every woman was trustworthy. Every one would protect Meredith with her life, Adam was sure of it. 'Who else?'

'Um . . . I don't know. Maybe the other girls at Mariposa House.' Adam's gaze flicked to Colby's. 'I'll have to talk to them.'

Colby nodded. 'I'll have Wendi get them ready. When? It'll be time for them to go to sleep in a few hours. We don't want to disrupt their routine any more than we have to.'

Adam knew he had several more hours here and at the crime scene across the street. 'I'll probably come out there tomorrow morning, but I'll call you either way.' He turned back to Meredith. 'I'm sorry,' he said softly, 'but I have to ask you again for the names of anyone who's stalked you recently.'

Her jaw tightened. 'I told you. I can't tell you anything about the people who just happen to be running around the high school track at the same time I do *every morning at five a.m.*, or just happen to be shopping for veggies at my local Kroger on *Saturday mornings*, or just happen to catch my eye across the crowd after *Sunday mass at St Germaine's* for the *last three weeks*.'

He frowned. She'd used the same words that morning. The same, exact— *Shit*. Understanding hit him like a brick. She was telling him where to search. And when and for whom. He'd bet that all three of those places had surveillance cameras. 'Oh,' he said, feeling foolish. 'Got it.'

She rolled her eyes. 'Thank God,' she muttered, then sighed. 'May I be excused, Detective Kimble?'

He winced at the formality. 'Of course. But, um . . .' He dug a hotel key card from his pocket and handed it to her. 'The hotel manager said to feel free to clean up in room 1254. Use the shower. If you want.'

Staring at the card, her throat worked as she tried to swallow. 'He offered?'

'I asked.' It was the least Adam could do for her, when he wanted to do everything.

She hadn't taken the card yet. 'I don't have any clean clothes.'

'There should be some in the room. I asked Scarlett to bring you some of your things.' Scarlett and Deacon had been walking into the lobby as he and Trip had been leaving the little meeting room.

'Scarlett's here?' she asked, a hopeful note in her tone.

'Yes, but she's interviewing the other restaurant customers.'

'I see.' She took the key card with trembling fingers, careful not to touch him as she did so. She still didn't look up at him and he wanted to grab her chin and force her to, but he hadn't earned the right to do that, either. 'That was kind of you. Thank you.'

She rose again, then was through the door and gone. Colby gave him a sympathetic look. 'We'll make sure she's safe. Not okay, just safe. I'm not sure *we* can make her okay.'

Adam nodded, his throat suddenly too thick to speak. Colby's subtle nudge was right on the money. *No, she's not okay. Neither am I.* And the blame for that lay squarely on Adam's shoulders. So was the fix. Tonight. He'd fix it tonight. Or at least he'd start the process. For now, he'd make sure she stayed safe.

He sent a text to Isenberg. *May have a suspect. Stalked Dr Fallon recently. Pls obtain surveillance tape from high school running track – every am for last 3 weeks + Kroger nearest her residence – last 3 Saturday am's. Also St Germaine's, Sunday am mass, last 3 weeks.* He added Meredith's address from memory and hit SEND.

Isenberg replied immediately. *On it. Do you have a name/ description?*

No. She won't say. Confidentiality. But she told me where/when to look.

No legal protection for her. She's not MD. Make her tell you.

Adam frowned, his fingers dialing Isenberg's number before he realized that had been his intention. 'You make her tell you,' he said to his boss when she picked up.

'Is she gone?' Isenberg asked.

'Yes. She's gone to wash that boy's brains from her hair,' he said acidly.

Isenberg sighed. 'Do we have an ID on the boy?'

'No, not yet. The area hasn't been cleared by the bomb squad.

I'm about to start interviewing witnesses. Scarlett and Deacon should have already gotten started. Hopefully we can get a composite description or even photos.'

'The plates we got from the video the kids gave Agent Taylor were from a car reported stolen two years ago.'

'Figured they would be,' Adam said, but he was still disappointed.

'There's a woman in the back seat of the SUV. The windows are heavily tinted so the driver's face can't be seen, nor can the woman's, but we know she was there.'

'The "her" the boy was worried about.'

'That's my assumption, but she could be an accomplice.'

True, he thought, grateful for her objectivity. 'How long will it take you to pull the videos I asked for? I'll come to the precinct to review them.'

'I'll assign someone to retrieve and review the footage ASAP. You stick to the scene. I'll let you know when we have something solid on the stalker.'

'Thanks. I'll keep you in the loop with the questioning.'

Cincinnati, Ohio,
Saturday 19 December, 5.55 P.M.

'Miss Johnson? The doctor will see you now.'

Linnea blinked sleepily. The woman in scrubs was standing right in front of her. Calling her Miss Johnson? *Oh. Right.* She gave herself a little shake. Denise Johnson was the name on her fake ID. Useful little thing, a fake ID.

Good for hospitals, clinics, pharmacies. And the occasional arrest for prostitution. The charges hadn't stuck, of course. He'd smoothed it all out and she'd been released – with an apology, no less. He had his fingers everywhere. He had eyes everywhere. Maybe even here, in the free clinic. *So get this done and get out of here before he catches up to you.*

Linnea rose unsteadily. *So tired.* Her grip on the here-and-now had started to fracture. She needed to sleep, but every time she'd closed her eyes she'd see Andy crumpling to the ground. *Gone, gone, gone. Forever.*

'Thank you,' she managed and started to follow the nurse.

'You left your bag,' the nurse told her.

Linnea turned slowly, feeling like she moved through molasses. *Oh. Right.* The plastic bag she'd taken from the little hotel she'd walked to after abandoning his SUV. She frowned at it. *Oh. Right.* It held her bloody jeans. She looked down. She was wearing polyester pants that were way too big. She'd found them in the hotel's laundry closet.

The nurse picked up the bag. 'Come with me. We'll get you fixed up.'

'Nice,' Linnea murmured, her eyes stinging. 'You're being nice to me.' It had been so long since someone had. Someone other than Andy. *He's gone. I'm alone.*

'I try, sweetie.' The nurse touched her back lightly. 'This way.'

Linnea found herself in a room painted bright yellow with pictures of puppies and kittens. It made her smile. 'This is new,' she said, and could hear her words slur.

The nurse smiled back. 'Dr Dani wanted to brighten the place up when she took over as director.'

Linnea blinked again, harder this time, trying to focus when everything was swirly. Dr Dani was the doctor she'd seen last time. 'She's still here?'

'Yep,' the nurse said cheerfully, and started to take her blood pressure.

Linnea jerked back. 'Positive,' she said. 'I am, I mean.'

The nurse held up gloved hands. 'I know, honey. You're in our system.'

Denise Johnson was in their system. *Not me.* Not Linnea Holmes. *Nobody knows me.*

Except Shane. *Don't forget about Shane.* The third of their musketeers. Three kids, terrified in foster care, banding together. Promising to always be there for each other. Shane would help. If he knew.

But he wouldn't know, because Linnea would never tell him.

70

She'd been ashamed before, but now? She'd killed Andy. She'd all but pulled the fucking trigger. Shane would hate her forever and that she couldn't bear. Then she really *would* be all alone.

'Hmm,' the nurse hummed. 'Your blood pressure is low. Do you want to tell me what happened?'

Linnea shook her head, then realized she'd have to tell them if she wanted help. 'Rough sex,' she whispered.

The nurse nodded once, lips pursed. 'Let me get Dr Dani.'

A minute later the doctor came in. Her hair was the same, black with two bright streaks of white framing her face. Her much thinner face. 'Hello,' Dr Dani said.

'You got skinny,' Linnea blurted out. 'What happened?'

The doctor slid onto a stool, her odd eyes assessing. One blue, one brown, they seemed to see way too much. Just like the last time Linnea had been here. 'I got stabbed last summer,' Dr Dani said matter-of-factly. 'I'm better now, but still trying to regain a few pounds. What happened to you? You've lost more weight than I have.'

Linnea swallowed hard. 'I've been . . .' *Not stabbed. But messed up. Broken. Scared every damn minute of every damn day.* 'Okay,' she finally said lamely.

'All right,' Dr Dani said with a shake of her head. 'Tell me what happened, Denise.'

Denise. Linnea wondered if anyone would ever say her real name in kindness again. She pointed to the bag she'd taken from the hotel. 'My pants are bloody.'

'I'll take care of it,' Dr Dani said, not taking her eyes from Linnea's face. 'The nurse said you'd had some "rough sex." Are you still bleeding?'

'A little.' But only because she hadn't moved too much. If she had to move fast or run again like she had an hour and a half before? She might bleed out before she got to kill Andy's killer.

Dr Dani gestured to her polyester pants. 'They look a little big.'

Linnea stared down at them, backtracking in her mind. 'I got them from the hotel.'

'That hotel?' The doctor pointed to the bag, its name clearly printed. 'Did someone give them to you?' she asked when Linnea nodded.

Linnea shook her head. 'Found them. In the laundry closet.'

Dr Dani smiled and Linnea's stress receded. A little. 'How did you get to the hotel?'

'Walked.' After abandoning the SUV. She remembered following a couple into the lobby, getting on the elevator with them, like she was with them, so the people at the desk wouldn't throw her out. 'Was going to ask them to call me a cab.' From a house phone. So it would look like she'd belonged there. 'Then I saw the closet.'

'And you changed your clothes there?' Dr Dani asked gently.

'Yeah. Left money for the pants.' A few dollars. *I'm not a thief.* 'Took a taxi.'

Another kind smile. 'Well, I'm glad you're here. Let's get you taken care of.' She handed Linnea a paper drape. 'Bottoms off. Unless you're bleeding anywhere else.'

Linnea hung her head, her cheeks heating in humiliation. 'No. Just there.'

A finger tipped up her chin and Linnea found herself staring into the doctor's mismatched eyes. 'You are not to blame, Denise. Whoever did this to you is to blame. I'm going to do a rape kit.'

Linnea shook her head so hard the room began to spin. 'No. Don't want that.'

'Why not?' The question was asked gently.

'Not . . .' *Not a rape.* But she couldn't make herself say it, because it was a dirty lie. It had been. Every single time she'd been peddled to a 'client' or an 'associate,' it had been.

'Did you consent?' Dr Dani asked.

Linnea shook her head again. 'No,' she whispered, tears burning her eyes.

'Did you tell him no?'

'Yes.' Linnea's voice broke on a sob. 'Over and over. I begged him to stop. But he wouldn't.' Because Butch had liked making her scream and then *he* had laughed, egging Butch to go harder. Because he'd wanted Andy to bend. To break. To obey.

Andy hadn't. And now he was dead.

72

Dr Dani's hand was rubbing Linnea's back in slow circles. 'When did this happen?'

'Last night.'

'Then I'll do a rape kit. There will be evidence. I'll call a police officer and you can give a statement. I'll stay with you. I promise.'

Linnea lurched to her feet, terror keeping her upright. '*No*. No police.'

'Shh,' Dr Dani soothed, patting the exam table. 'Sit down, Denise. I don't want you to collapse on me.' She smiled encouragingly. 'I won't call the police if you say no. Can you at least tell me why you're so afraid? I don't want you to be afraid.'

Linnea swallowed, wondering if she could believe the doctor. Swaying on her feet, she knew that right now she didn't really have a choice. 'He . . . he'd find out.'

'The man who did this?'

'I can't . . .' She edged toward the door. 'He'll . . .' *Kill me painfully. After he tortures me just to hear me scream.* 'He wouldn't be happy.'

The doctor's lips firmed. 'All right. You have time to decide what you want to do. You might change your mind later and report him. I have to submit the rape kit, though.'

Linnea considered it. She could file the report after he paid for killing Andy. Once he was dead, his right-hand man could rot in prison for all she cared. 'All right. Do the kit. I'll think about going to the police.'

'Good.' Dr Dani touched her shoulder, lightly urging her back to the exam table. 'I can see the bruises on your face. Where else did he touch you?'

'Nowhere.' Not this time, anyway. She crossed her arms over her chest protectively. As if that could hide the scars he'd put there.

'All right. I'll be waiting outside in the hall. I'll give you a few minutes to get yourself ready. Do you have somewhere safe to spend the night?'

Linnea hesitated. She couldn't go back to the apartment she shared with Jolee. Or to Andy's place. Those would be the first places he'd look. 'No, I don't.'

'I know of a shelter for battered women. Would you like me to call them for you? It's one hundred percent confidential. Whoever you're afraid of will not find you there.'

Linnea couldn't hold back her tears any longer. She blinked, sending them down her cheeks. 'Yes, please. Thank—' Her voice broke again. 'Thank you.'

Cincinnati, Ohio,
Saturday 19 December, 6.15 P.M.

'Whose car is that?' Wendi asked from the back seat where she had her arm around Mallory's shoulders.

In the front passenger seat, Meredith roused herself in time to see a blue pickup truck in her driveway as Colby parked his sedan behind it. She blinked sleepily, her brain a fuzzy mess. She was warm. Colby's heater worked well. *And I smell better.*

It hit her then. What had happened. What she'd seen. She steeled her spine. She would not throw up again. That her hair was finally clean made it so much easier to keep that resolution. *Thank you, Adam.*

He'd been kind to secure a room for her. A change of clothes. A way to feel human again. Meredith wanted to read more into it than a gentlemanly gesture, but she couldn't allow herself to do so.

As if she had a choice. She'd spent the last two hours hoping like hell that Adam's explanation would be one that she'd want to hear. One that ended with them together.

That a happy ending was in their cards was a leap, to say the least.

'The truck is Diesel's,' Colby said, putting the car in gear.

'I know that.' Wendi craned her neck. 'I meant the other one.'

'What other one?' Meredith hadn't opened her eyes in time to see another car and Diesel's truck was so tall that it blocked their view. She felt a prickle of hope that it was Adam's Jeep, but quashed the thought. Wendi knew the Jeep and she wouldn't have passed on the opportunity to rag on Adam. Her friend's loyalty was beginning to grow irksome.

'There's a Mazda parked in front of the truck,' Colby said. 'Blue four-door. It's a rental. It has a sticker in the back window,' he added when Meredith opened her mouth to ask him how he knew. 'Were you expecting anyone else?'

'Not for a few days.' Meredith rubbed the back of her neck. She'd fallen asleep in an awkward position. 'For the holidays.'

Wendi frowned. 'Will you see who it is, Parrish?'

'Of course. You ladies stay here.'

'Wait.' Meredith's mind was slowly clicking back into gear. 'Whoever it is let Diesel in my house, because he doesn't have a key unless you gave him one.'

'We didn't,' Wendi said, but Meredith was already out of the car, running for her front door.

Her friends had keys, but none of them would have been driving a rental. Only two other people had keys – her cousin, Alex, and her grandfather.

The front door opened and a pair of burly arms caught her in a hard hug.

Meredith clung, shuddering, breathing in his scent. Old Spice and pipe smoke. It always had been his, ever since her earliest memory. 'Papa. Oh God. You're here.'

Her grandfather pulled her tighter. 'I got here about an hour ago,' he murmured into her hair, rocking her where they stood. 'I just heard about what happened downtown. I would have driven straight from the airport to bring you home myself if I'd known.'

She burrowed her face into the softness of his sweatshirt. Downy fabric softener. Her big, burly grandfather loved the scent. She loved it too, even though it totally clashed with Old Spice. Because whenever she inhaled the combination, she'd been safe. *Home.*

He gently wiped the tears from her face. She hadn't even realized she'd shed them. 'Your hair is all wet, Merry. Go inside, get warm.'

She tilted her chin up, studying his face. He looked good. Tanned and . . . himself. Still strong and standing tall at eighty-four years old. 'I need to tell my friends goodbye.' She tugged on his hands, pulling him out of the house and down the walk. 'Come on. Wendi's in the car. She'd be upset if you don't say hi.'

'Why doesn't she get out?' he asked, then stopped walking.

'Oh. That's the girl you were with? The one who pulled you out of the path of the second bullet?'

Meredith blinked up at him. 'You're remarkably well informed, Papa.'

'Your friend told me all about it.' He thumbed over his shoulder. Diesel Kennedy now stood in her open doorway.

'After he scared the bejesus out of me!' Diesel called.

Her grandfather sniffed. 'He was lurking in your driveway. He looked . . .'

'Like you?' Meredith supplied helpfully. Because it was true. Both men were mountains, both covered in tattoos. Both were bald – Diesel by choice and her grandfather due to age. Both appeared menacing until you knew them. Both had soft hearts.

He smirked. 'Exactly.' He sobered. 'I don't want to scare the girl. Sounds like she's had a hard enough day.'

Yes. A very soft heart. Meredith patted his chest. 'Just say hi to Wendi and her beau. His name is Parrish Colby. I'll gauge Mallory's reaction and give you a sign. Hurry, now. We'll both catch colds out here.'

Meredith led him to the car and Wendi popped out. 'Clarke!' she cried, launching herself into his arms. He caught her, laughing in that easy way he'd always had.

'Wendi, it's always a pleasure.' He waggled gray brows at Colby, who'd also stepped out of his car and waited, arms braced on the sedan's roof. 'Hear that you're the beau.'

Colby blushed, and it was really cute to see. 'Parrish Colby, sir.'

'I'm Clarke. Good to meet you, son. Thank you for bringing Merry home.'

Meredith glanced inside the car. Mallory's head had turned and she blinked up at the older man. She wasn't herself by a long shot – she'd retreated deep inside her mind. But she wasn't afraid either. Meredith gave her grandfather a nod and he leaned in to give Mallory his kindest smile.

'Hi, Mallory,' he said, using his gentlest voice. 'I'm Clarke.'

Meredith leaned in beside him, feeling the grizzle of his cheek on hers. 'My grandfather. Remember I told you he was coming? He surprised me.'

Mallory nodded warily.

Her grandfather cleared his throat. 'I, um, I want to thank you, Mallory.'

Mallory tilted her head slightly. 'Why?'

It was the first word Mallory had said since they'd left the hotel after talking to Adam. Meredith felt the worry in her chest loosen, just a little.

'You saved Merry's life. Pulled her down under the table, out of the line of fire.' He cleared his throat again. 'So thank you.'

Mallory's mouth curved, almost too slightly to see. 'Merry?'

Clarke kissed Meredith's cheek with a loud smack. 'Isn't she? Merry, I mean.'

Meredith rolled her eyes. 'You don't have to answer that, Mallory. I'm going to get this guy inside so he doesn't freeze.' She leaned farther into the car to squeeze Mallory's clenched hand. 'But he's right. You did save my life. Remember that, okay? When you think about the guy who died? Picture my face. You saved me. Okay?'

A single nod.

'All right.' Meredith squeezed the clenched hand again. 'I'll call you later. You can call me too, no matter what time.'

Another nod. 'Okay.'

Meredith pressed a kiss to Mallory's clammy forehead. 'Try to sleep.' She extracted herself from Colby's back seat and gave him a wave and Wendi a hug. 'Thank you both.'

'You get some sleep too,' Wendi said, then leaned up to hiss in her ear. 'After you make a list of every single motherfucker who has threatened you. Ever.'

Meredith jerked back to blink at her friend, the venom in Wendi's whisper a complete shock. Wendi had experienced horrors that would give most people nightmares for life, and every day she dealt with the aftereffects of brutal violence against the young women in her care. But Meredith had never heard her use this tone. 'Wen?'

Wendi's eyes filled with tears and it was then that Meredith noticed her friend was shaking. *Damn me.* Meredith had been so caught up in her own head, so worried about Mallory and Adam, that she hadn't thought about the impact this would have on the people who loved her. Meredith drew Wendi close.

'I'm fine,' she assured her.

'No, dammit, you're not.' Wendi's small fist landed painlessly on Meredith's back. 'How could you be? You might fool everyone else, but you're not fooling me. You'll protect your clients over yourself.'

'And you wouldn't?' Meredith pushed back. 'You wouldn't risk yourself for any one of the girls at Mariposa House?' When Wendi didn't answer, Meredith chuckled. 'So, Miss Pot, stop bossing Miss Kettle around.'

'It's not funny,' Wendi hissed on a choked sob. 'And it's not the same. I don't have assholes following me around, trying to intimidate me. Trying to shoot me or blow me sky-high. You write down every name, Meredith Fallon. Every single fucking one.'

Meredith patted Wendi's back, forcing her own tone to be lightly wry. 'It'd take me days to write down every single one.'

Wendi stepped back, swiping at her wet eyes furiously. 'I'm so mad at you!'

'Wen,' Colby said quietly.

Wendi's head whipped around to glare at Colby. 'It's true. Somebody needs to make her listen.' She whirled to turn the glare up at Meredith, nearly slipping on the icy driveway. 'You're really not going to even help the police protect you?'

Meredith gripped both of Wendi's arms to keep her from falling. *I did help them*, she started to say. But was that really true? She'd told Adam where to look, and at the moment that was all she'd been able to make herself say. To a cop, anyway.

Meredith eyed the truck in her driveway. *Diesel's here, and* he's *not a cop.* Far from it. Through his work at the *Ledger*, Diesel had demonstrated mad hacker skills, excelling at digging – and finding – dirt. The *Ledger* then ran with the info, exposing those who'd somehow wiggled through the justice system, usually after hurting a child. In Meredith's mind, Diesel was a frickin' hero.

Still, asking him to hack into her most recent stalker's life made her cringe inside. But these were extreme circumstances. And if

Diesel found nothing, the police wouldn't have to get involved. The information would go no farther.

'You're not telling the police, are you?' Wendi's shoulders sagged, her eyes sliding closed. 'Damn you. You're going to let whoever did this keep trying until they don't miss.'

Meredith heard her grandfather suck in a harsh breath.

'I absolutely am *not* going to do that,' she said calmly, giving her friend a meaningful look followed by a pointed glance at Diesel's truck. She saw the moment Wendi understood. 'I'm not interested in being shot or blown sky-high any time soon. Or letting whoever killed that boy today kill anyone else. Got it?'

Wendi let out a shuddering sigh of relief. 'Oh God. Yeah. Got it. Thank you.'

'Wen, honey,' Colby said, 'get in the car. Keeping Meredith out in the open isn't doing anything to protect her either.'

Meredith noticed Colby had been tensely watching the street, hand on his firearm. Just in case her attacker tried again. *In front of my home.* She also realized the heat at her back had been her grandfather keeping close, making himself a human shield. *Goddammit.* She risked the safety of everyone around her, simply by existing. The realization cemented her resolve to get to the bottom of this, however she needed to.

'I'm going inside now, Parrish,' Meredith said. 'Thanks for everything.' Then she put her arm through her grandfather's and led him up the walk to her house.

One person had already died today. No one else was getting shot on her behalf.

Six

Cincinnati, Ohio,
Saturday 19 December, 6.15 P.M.

Showered, bandaged, and wearing clean clothes, he pulled into his own driveway and parked the SUV he'd taken from the fleet at the Fairfield garage. That he only bought black SUVs and kept them all spotless wasn't an OCD quirk. It was by design. If one got wrecked – or bled on – he could easily change it out for another. No questions meant no denials. No denials meant no lies that he'd have to keep track of and remember later.

He got out of the SUV, locked it, then did a slow three-sixty, checking out the houses on his street with a smile. His neighbors had outdone themselves decorating, especially the Wainwrights next door. Every year Ike Wainwright's lights were the nicest on the block.

'Really nice!' he called up to Ike, who was perched on a ladder, adjusting the star atop the nativity scene in his front yard. It was populated by the three kings, shepherds, and the holy family, all fashioned from wax.

Ike owned a string of funeral homes. How he'd come by his expertise with wax was not something most of their neighbors wanted to think about, but Ike made a good living making the dead presentable. This he knew because he found out about each of his neighbors, from their income to their tax bill to how often they had sex with their respective partners. Ike and Mrs Wainwright still got busy with regularity.

That meant the old man was happy and occupied and, most importantly, not a nosy neighbor. He didn't like nosy neighbors.

80

'Thank you!' Ike called back. 'I bet Dorsey that my house wins this year.'

He turned to study the Dorsey house at the center of the cul-de-sac, six houses down. The two always competed for best decorations. 'I don't know, Ike. Dorsey has that Santa's workshop and he gives out candy canes.' He looked back up at Ike on the ladder. 'You gonna have the animals this year? Because that might tip the scales in your favor.'

Ike always had a menagerie around the nativity scene, but the homeowners' association had balked last year when he'd added a camel to the sheep and goats.

Ike scowled. 'Yeah. Had to get a special permit. Lousy bureaucrats. I have a barn erected for them in the backyard. It's not like we're bothering any neighbors back there.'

Because their houses sat at the edge of the community. Directly behind their back fences was another fifty feet of trees, then a ten-foot electric fence topped by razor wire, followed by a thirty-foot sheer drop to Columbia Parkway. They got night traffic noise, but it was worth it to have the buffer. Nobody was going to sneak up on his home from behind.

'Sometimes I think the homeowners' association sits around and makes up stuff to annoy us,' he said and Ike nodded vigorously.

'But it'll be worth it, just to see the smiles on the kids' faces when they pet the animals.' The old man's face creased in a smile. 'Stop by.'

'We will. Be careful getting down from that ladder,' he cautioned. 'Don't want a repeat of five years ago.' When Ike had fallen and broken a hip. Waving his goodbye, he made his way up the sidewalk, noting the icy patches. He'd have to salt.

Or use kitty litter. He kept forgetting that salt was now a neighborhood taboo. Either way, he didn't want anyone falling on his property. One fall could trigger a lawsuit and his entire life would be on review. *No, thank you.*

He paused to pick up a toy truck and a mini soccer ball, then opened the door. 'I'm h—' A small body launched from the middle stair, sailing through the air into his arms.

'Daddy!'

'Oof!' He bit back a curse at the pain radiating up both arms and hoped he hadn't popped any stitches. Dropping the toys, he wrapped his arms around the small bundle and made himself smile. 'I think you've gained about a hundred pounds since this morning.'

Tiny hands grasped his cheeks and big blue eyes stared into his. Like looking into a mirror, every single time. 'Santa,' Mikey pronounced seriously.

'Me?' It came out as a surprised squeak. Had he been outed already? He'd been enjoying playing Santa and hadn't wanted it to end. Not yet.

'No, Daddy.' The oh-so-mature voice came from next to his elbow, and he turned his smile down into eyes as blue as Mikey's. At seven years old, Ariel was on the cusp of figuring out the holiday myth. 'Mama said we could see Santa tonight after church. Mikey's excited, that's all.'

Dammit. Church was not going to happen tonight. He had to get out there and find Linnea. He'd only come home to fetch his notebook. It was the only place he wrote anything down. It was old-fashioned paper and ink, unable to be hacked.

But he had a few minutes for his princess who was always too damn serious. 'Only Mikey?' he teased and was rewarded with Ariel's shy grin. 'You're not excited at all?'

'Well, maybe a little,' she allowed. 'You need to hurry. Mama says dinner's ready.'

Still carrying Mikey, he followed Ariel to the kitchen where something smelled good. 'I'm starving,' he said, settling Mikey into his highchair. 'What's for supper?'

Rita turned from the stove with a smile. 'You're late. Is everything okay?'

He kissed the tip of her nose. 'Never better.'

And though he might lie to the entire world, he did not lie to his wife. He dodged the truth like a boxer dodged a flurry of fists, but he did not lie. That way the police – or his enemies – would never be able to question her. She knew absolutely nothing.

82

So he would have to ensure that 'never better' was the truth.

He'd have to silence Linnea before she could turn him in. That meant finding her first, and he had no time to waste. He'd make her come to him.

Which he knew how to do because he made it his business to know everything about everyone with whom he did business, including where they'd had dinner reservations. Except that hadn't ended so well and Fallon and her companion still breathed. He'd be fixing that too. First priority, however, was Linnea.

'Good,' Rita said. 'Sit down and eat before it gets cold. We have to be at church early tonight. For the cantata. You missed choir practice this morning, so you need to be there early tonight for a dress rehearsal.'

Christ. The fucking Christmas musical. He'd nearly forgotten. He'd been planning to ditch the service tonight, but he couldn't very well do that, could he? It would look bad. Too many people would know that he wasn't in a place he was supposed to be.

Always have an alibi was his motto, and it had worked for his entire life. So he'd go and he'd sing and then he'd make Linnea show herself.

'Right.' He smiled at his family. 'I have one small thing to do and I'll be right back.' He waited until he was locked in his home office before texting Butch. *Busy tonight. Unavoidable. Keep looking for the girl.*

Will do. U ok?

Yes. Hold for instructions. Moving a portrait of Rita, he uncovered his wall safe, twisted the dial, then retrieved his notebook. He locked the safe before moving to his desk. He *never* left the safe open. An open safe was an invitation into his deepest secrets.

The notebook itself would be useless to anyone other than himself. Every entry was written in code and the key was locked away in his brain. He flipped pages until he found the one titled 'Linnea Holmes.' Twenty years old, she'd grown up in the Indiana foster care system, her best friends Andy Gold – born Jason Coltrain – and Shane Baird. Andy had been the most useful leverage against her, but he was useless now. Shane, on the other hand . . .

Shane Baird, he texted. *Lamarr Hall. Kiesler Univ, Chicago. ASAP. Bring him to me. Alive.*

He waited thirty seonds for Buton's reply: *Will take me 5 hrs to drive. ASAP enuf?*

No, that was *not* ASAP enough, not if Linnea had contacted Shane already. Shane might run and his best leverage would disappear. *Mike knows a pilot*, he texted back. *Can get you there in 90 min out of Lunken. Call him.* The guy owned his own small jet. He's flown with him a few times and he'd always been discreet.

Will do.

It would have to be good enough. If all went well, he'd have Shane Baird in his hands by the time the canatata was finished. Shane would make good bait and Linnea would give herself up, just as she had for her precious Andy.

He also knew that finding Linnea would only snip a loose end. There was the bigger, original problem of the botched job in the restaurant. He needed to fix that, ASAP.

He washed his hands and returned to the table to find his little family waiting patiently. 'Ariel, do you want to say the blessing tonight?'

She folded her hands. 'Yes, Daddy.'

Cincinnati, Ohio,
Saturday 19 December, 6.25 P.M.

Meredith shook her head as she entered her house, her grandfather closing the door behind them. A video gaming system, complete with controllers and cords, had taken over her coffee table. 'Are you planning on moving back in, Papa?' she asked lightly.

'No way in hell. It's too cold up here.' He pointed to Diesel, who sat on her sofa reading a manual. 'Your bodyguard here is a gamer. I was showing him mine.'

Meredith gave Diesel a weary smile. 'Hey, Diesel, You didn't have to come sit with me, but I'm grateful that you did.'

'Don't even mention it,' Diesel said. 'I mean, seriously, I had to fight the others to take the first shift and I didn't even know Clarke

84

Fallon was your grandfather. He's a fucking legend.'

It was true. Clarke Fallon was a superstar among game designers. He'd created a blockbuster game 'back in the day,' as he called the 1970s, and had continued creating for decades. Now that he'd retired, he kept busy consulting and mentoring younger designers.

'Do not build his ego,' she teased, then stood on her toes to peck Clarke's cheek. 'I'm going to make some tea. You two want some?'

'Depends. You got any whiskey for it?' Clarke asked.

Diesel snickered. 'I really like him, Merry.'

'Of course you do. He's an oversized middle-schooler – just like you,' she said to Diesel, then turned back to her grandfather. 'Of course I have whiskey. I was expecting you, Papa. Just not today.'

'I found a cheaper flight,' he said. 'I thought I'd told you I'd moved my dates up.'

'If you did, I missed it. Diesel, do you want to join us for tea?'

'Do you mind if I drink it in here?' He gestured at the screen. 'He's beta-testing it. It's brand new. I've only read about it so far. I want—' He broke off, blushing.

'You want to play.' She smiled at him, genuinely charmed by his enthusiasm at a new game. He looked younger than she'd ever seen him. 'I get it.' And she did. 'Go ahead. Play is good for the soul.' She'd built her counseling practice on that belief.

And it was just as well that Diesel sit in the living room for a while. She needed time to settle, to arrange her thoughts before she asked the man to commit a felony for her.

'Smart girl,' her grandfather murmured as he followed her into the kitchen. 'I think that boy needs to play more than anyone I've met in a long, long time.'

Meredith smiled at the thought of Diesel being called a boy, then her smile dimmed. She wasn't sure what kind of childhood he'd had, but suspected it had sucked royally. 'I think you'd be right. What kind of tea . . .'

Shit. Meredith's step faltered. Her refrigerator was covered with pages carefully cut from coloring books and colored in with equal care. Adam's pictures. She always took them down when she had company, but she hadn't anticipated today's events.

Recovering, she put the kettle on. 'What kind of tea would you like?'

'Doesn't matter. It's just a prop so that I can drink the whiskey without reproach.' He sat at her kitchen table, not saying another word as she worked, but she could feel his eyes on her. Every second. Until she couldn't take it anymore. She folded her hands on the counter, staring at the kettle, willing it to whistle, her stress building faster than the pressure in the kettle. She was headed straight for a panic attack. She'd already taken one of her anti-anxiety pills, right before she'd showered in the hotel, because she'd gotten her first good look at her own face. And her soiled hair. She'd nearly lost it right then.

She was about to lose it now. Hands shaking, she reached into her cupboard for the medicine bottle she kept there. She popped another pill and prayed she wouldn't need more. She'd already taken her limit for the day. She hated taking them at all, but this time of year it got bad. That, and seeing a young man murdered in front of her, she thought bitterly.

And seeing Adam again? That hadn't helped at all.

She could still feel her grandfather watching her. 'What?' she asked petulantly.

'I didn't say anything, Merry,' was his carefully quiet reply.

'You never had to,' she muttered. 'Just like Dad.' Her father could just look at her and make her confess to whatever wrong she'd committed, from breaking a window to sneaking out after curfew. *I miss you, Dad.*

She could hear the patpatpat of her grandfather's palms on his sweatshirt and knew what he was searching for. She got his pipe and tobacco from a drawer and put it on the table. 'You forgot them the last time you were here.'

'I didn't forget them. I left them here in case I forgot to bring my kit in the future.'

She went back to preparing the tea, calmed by the pill and the scent of his pipe. Her hands didn't tremble too much when she took a pot of tea and a glass of whiskey to Diesel, then set one up for Clarke.

She placed her own teapot and cup on the table, then sighed to

86

herself. She couldn't pretend Adam's colored pictures weren't there. He'd sent them for her eyes only. He'd never said so, but Meredith knew it was true. Without a word, she pulled them off the refrigerator, one at a time, stacked them carefully, and placed them in the drawer of the desk where she clipped coupons and organized recipes.

When she sat at the kitchen table, her grandfather was sipping his whiskey, his pot of tea left untouched. 'Go ahead and ask,' she said. 'I know you want to.'

Clarke shrugged. 'Seemed remarkably well done for Hope.'

Hope was her nine-year-old niece. 'That's because she didn't do them.'

'Who is he?'

She blinked at him. 'What makes you so sure a man colored those pictures?'

'I wasn't, till just now.' He puffed on his pipe. 'He's important to you.'

Meredith's heart hurt. She'd yearned for Adam since she'd first laid eyes on him over a year ago. She dropped her gaze to her tea. 'Yes.'

'But he doesn't feel the same way.'

I have to explain some things. 'I don't think so. Can you ask me something else?'

'Fair enough,' he said mildly. 'Who tried to kill you today?'

Meredith's chin jerked up in surprise. 'I don't know.'

'But you have a very good idea. Anyone bothering you at work?'

He knew about some of the more blatant threats in the past and she knew they had worried him. But he'd never asked her to stop providing therapy to the kids who so desperately needed someone in their corner. She'd always loved that about him.

'One or two,' she admitted.

'But you didn't tell the police their names.' He lifted his shaggy gray brows. 'Wendi whispers loudly. She wanted me to hear.'

'I couldn't give names. They haven't made a specific threat to me.'

Clarke gulped the whiskey, his swallow audible. 'But you can tell *me* their names.'

Her heart stuttered in genuine fear. She didn't want him to be her human shield and she especially didn't want him going after the shooter. 'I don't want you anywhere near them. If one of them is responsible for what happened today, it's a matter for the cops.'

Clarke's eyes flashed with temper. 'Yet you've given them no leads.'

'Not true. I told Ad— Detective Kimble that a person existed. And I told him exactly where the person had followed me and when. All the places have surveillance equipment.'

Understanding lit his eyes. 'Good girl.'

'Had to tell him twice,' she grumbled. 'I wasn't obvious enough the first time.' The moment that Adam finally had understood might have been comical under other circumstances. She cast a look at the living room. 'I might give him a hand.'

'How?'

'I was going to ask Diesel for help.'

'Finally!' Diesel bellowed from around the corner. He appeared in the doorway, the mug of tea she'd given him looking like a child's cup in his huge hand. He'd tucked his laptop under his arm, his expression even more eager than it had been over the new game.

'I thought you were playing,' Meredith said.

'I was. I was going to give you time to drink your tea before offering my assistance.'

Meredith chuckled. 'Sit with us, Diesel.'

He did, casting a quick look at the fridge that made her cheeks heat. He'd seen them too. 'I liked them,' he said simply. 'Especially the waterfall picture. Who colored them?'

'Maybe we can color some,' she said, dodging the question. 'It calms me.'

'Huh,' was all he said. 'I like lions and tigers myself. I can probably download a few to color, if you've got the colored pencils. It calms me too.' He flexed his big hands. 'Kate's even teaching me to knit.' Opening his laptop, he arched one brow. 'I'm ready to investigate anybody who's bothered you. Names, please.'

Meredith was still staring at him open-mouthed. 'You knit? Really?'

Clarke's lips twitched. 'Your stereotypes are showing, Merry.'

She closed her mouth with a snap. 'You're right. I'm sorry, Diesel, that was wrong of me.' She eyed his laptop. 'This can't be traced to you or me, right?'

Diesel snorted. 'Give me some credit, *Merry*. I've poked around in other people's servers for Marcus for years and haven't gotten caught. Not because of anything I did, anyway.'

Her grandfather looked curious, so Meredith explained. 'Diesel works for Marcus O'Bannion, who owns the *Ledger*.'

'The newspaper.' Clarke nodded. 'I subscribe. Read it online every day. Good stuff. Never seen your byline, though, Diesel.'

'I stay in the background,' Diesel said uncomfortably. 'I'm IT.'

'Diesel is too modest,' Meredith said, giving the big man's hand a pat. 'The *Ledger* . . . well, let's just say they *creatively* investigate people who should have been punished but who've slipped through the legal system. They expose them on the front page. Diesel digs for the dirt. Sometimes he doesn't get permission before he starts digging.'

Clarke's eyes widened in open admiration. 'You're a hacker?'

Diesel's cheeks reddened. It was really kind of cute.

'A very good one,' Meredith confirmed, 'or so I'm led to believe. I need this to be discreet, Diesel. And I need you to forget anything you see. No telling Marcus or Scarlett.'

'Who's Scarlett?' Clarke asked.

'Detective Scarlett Bishop. You met her last time you visited. Tall cop with long, dark hair. She's partnered with Deacon Novak, the FBI guy.'

Clarke nodded. 'The one with the really cool eyes?'

'That's him,' Diesel said. 'Scarlett's cozied up with my boss, so I see her a lot. And I keep a lot of secrets from her, because she's a fuckin' cop and I don't want to go to jail. And no, *Merry*, I won't tell you which secrets and I'll deny I said it if she asks.'

Meredith had opened her mouth to ask exactly that. 'Nobody tells me anything,' she muttered instead, making Diesel chuckle.

'You don't want to know. I don't snoop on anyone who doesn't deserve it, but you're so squeaky clean, you'd feel guilty about not telling the cops.'

'What about me?' Clarke asked. 'Aren't you worried that I'll tell the cops?'

Diesel shook his head. 'You want Meredith safe. I don't see you turning me in.'

Clarke nodded. 'You're right. I won't. In fact, I'll buy you a bottle of twenty-five-year Lagavulin,' he said, but Diesel shook his head.

'You don't have to do that. I don't like bullies. Homicidal bullies are even worse.'

Meredith tapped the table, getting both men's attention. 'This can't show up in the *Ledger* or in a police report. I'm protecting the privacy of a six-year-old girl.'

Diesel grew abruptly grim. 'Got it. The little girl is safe?'

'Yes. She and her mother are living with the mother's sister, and her father is angry. Having his wife leave him was bad enough, but having his daughter taken made him look very bad in front of his company. He's the type who does not like looking bad.'

'I know that type,' Diesel muttered.

There was a raw vulnerability in his words that made Meredith's counseling radar ping, but he'd never spoken to her about such things, so she let it go. 'There's been no involvement by the police or social services, so this isn't a matter of record – public or otherwise.'

'*Should* there be police involvement?' Diesel asked.

Meredith sighed. 'My gut says yes. The little girl hasn't told me anything yet, though. She's still too scared, and I've only been seeing her for a few weeks. But I know the father's type, and I don't think he's going to allow her sessions to continue. One way or the other. So far, he's just hovering in the periphery of my life. He shows up at the running track and the grocery store. Even at church. He just smiles and looks surprised, like, wow, what a coincidence that we're in the same place at the same time, *again*.'

Clarke abruptly pushed away from the table, his chair nearly upending. He marched to the sink and tapped the bowl of his pipe against his hand, emptying the residue.

'Papa?' Meredith murmured.

He hunched forward, one hand gripping the edge of the sink. 'I'm just . . .'

'Angry as fucking hell,' Diesel supplied tightly. 'If this guy is responsible for what happened today, he needs to be . . .' He shook his head. 'To be willing to kill you is bad enough. To be willing to kill dozens of other people? Evisceration is too good for him.'

Clarke's shoulders heaved once, his chuckle bitter. 'I agree. He could have . . . I would have lost you,' he whispered.

Meredith went to him, wrapping her arms around his waist and laying her cheek against his back. 'But you didn't. I'm here. I'm sure Detective Kimble will make checking the surveillance tapes a priority. We can help him out a little, though, or Diesel can.'

Clarke nodded. 'Then get him started.'

They returned to the table. 'His name is Broderick Voss,' Meredith said.

'Where do I know that name from?' Diesel typed it into a search engine. Then his eyes widened. 'Holy shit, Meredith. He's the CEO of Buzz Boys. They're all over the finance pages. They went public a few years ago. Voss went from being a struggling nerd to uber rich.'

Meredith sighed. 'Everybody thinks only drug addicts or street thugs hurt their families. Nobody wants to believe guys who work in major corporations can too.'

'What do you want to know, specifically?' Diesel asked.

'Where was he this afternoon? Does he drive a black SUV? Does he have a military background? Has he ever worked with explosives? Does he own any guns? Specifically, a rifle like the one used to shoot . . .' She drew a deep breath. 'The young man today.'

Her grandfather's face visibly paled. 'And almost you.'

'But he missed. I don't want to give him another opportunity, do you?'

'No.' Clarke's big hand drew into a fist. 'No, I don't.'

Distract him. Now. 'Papa, I'm kind of hungry,' she lied. 'Can you make me some soup? I have packets of chicken noodle in the pantry.'

'Yeah. I can do that.' Jaw taut, he got up and got busy.

'You're a pretty good liar,' Diesel murmured. 'I'll remember that.'

'He knows I'm lying,' Meredith murmured back. 'Who do you think taught me how? Don't play poker with him. He'll tell you he's never played before and the next thing you know, he owns your favorite Billie Holiday album.'

'I also still hear very well,' Clarke called from the pantry. 'And I have an excellent memory. You made a bootlegged copy for me and kept the original for yourself.'

'And you were proud of me for creatively cheating,' Meredith called back.

'That I was, Merry. Diesel, you want soup? Seems like if I'm actually going to make some, somebody should eat it. She'll just pick at it.'

Diesel's mouth curved in an easy smile that Meredith had never seen before. 'Yes, sir. Thanks.'

Cincinnati, Ohio,
Saturday 19 December, 6.55 P.M.

Adam, Deacon, and Scarlett had spent the last hour taking statements from all the occupants of the restaurant. There weren't many people he'd trust implicitly to interview witnesses without his involvement, but Deacon and Scarlett were two of them. Deacon was his cousin and Scarlett and Adam had worked homicide together for years. The three of them made a good team and systematically took statements from patrons, staff, and anyone who'd been outside at the time of the shooting.

The restaurant's occupants had all seen the same thing. The young man with the gun, Meredith trying to talk him down, Meredith pulling her gun, the shot coming from outside, the gore, the broken window, the second shot, and the injured patron.

But they'd struck gold with a couple who'd come to the restaurant to get engaged. The groom-to-be's best friend had been hiding behind a post to videotape the entire proposal. The groom had just gotten down on one knee when the young man walked through the restaurant and stopped at Meredith's table.

They'd gotten a perfect view of his face. Hopefully the victim's fingerprints would yield an ID, but, at a minimum, they had his face. They'd provided a photo to the media and it was now being shared by every national news outlet, online and on TV. So far, no one had come forward to identify the poor bastard.

Deacon and Scarlett joined him in the meeting room the hotel had provided for their interviews, both taking their seats with deep sighs.

'Are we done?' Deacon asked wearily.

'We still have one more person to chat up,' Scarlett said.

Adam rubbed his temples. 'She still in the ladies' room?' The one person they had yet to interview had hidden herself in a bathroom stall. Officer Kendra Cullen had noticed her as soon as they'd evacuated the restaurant patrons to the hotel lobby and had been rotating watch duty with a few of the other cops outside the ladies' room door. Wendi's little sister was a damn good cop.

'Yep.' Scarlett rolled her eyes. 'Every time she peeked out of the bathroom she ducked back in. Kenny went in, asked her to come out to be interviewed, but she kept saying she was feeling sick and locked herself in the stall.'

'Is she sick?' Adam asked.

Scarlett shrugged. 'She's repeatedly refused medical attention. Kenny had to go back on patrol and there's a guy standing watch now, so I guess I'm elected to go fetch her.'

'Do we know who she is?' Deacon asked.

Adam nodded. 'Name's Colleen Martel. She's the hostess at Buon Cibo. She showed Meredith and Mallory to their table.'

'Their very conveniently placed table by the window,' Deacon murmured.

'That Meredith had been told wasn't reservable when she called ahead to ask for it,' Adam added. 'I've been waiting for a background check on Colleen. I wanted to know if she had any priors before I talked to her. It came in about five minutes ago. She's clean. Not even a parking ticket.'

'I hope she's got a good reason for hiding in the toilet, then.' Scarlett stood. 'Don't do anything fun till I get back.'

Adam propped his elbows on the table, dug his thumbs into his throbbing eye sockets, and tried to figure out what the girl could have done or seen or . . . *whatever* to make her hide for hours in a toilet so that she didn't have to talk to them. But his brain was serving up nothing. His mouth was dry and his skin felt way too tight on his bones.

Dammit, he wanted a drink so fucking bad. He was glad he'd given his sponsor the heads up because this day was only going to get worse. Fortunately, he'd be able to take in a meeting at midnight. John would meet him in the basement of St Agnes's, no matter what time of the night. The guy was a truly fucking awesome sponsor. *I'm lucky.*

I'll be luckier if I can get Meredith to listen to me tonight.

He'd also be luckier if he could get a fucking lead on this case so that he wouldn't have to worry that someone was going to kill her the next time she left her house.

'You okay?' Deacon asked quietly.

'Yeah. Just a bad headache.' Not a total lie at least.

Deacon dug into the pocket of his leather trench coat, pulled out a power bar and tossed it across the table. 'Eat something.'

'Thanks. I forgot about food.' He demolished the bar and washed it and some ibuprofen down with a bottle of water, immediately feeling a little better. He scrolled through the seventy-five texts he'd received in the last hour.

'Anything new?' Deacon asked.

Adam shook his head. 'Mostly requests from reporters, but I'm happy to leave the sound bites to the brass,' he muttered, then grimaced. 'Hell.'

'What?'

'I've got texts coming in from my old unit. They're all "worried" about me.' He blew out a breath. 'There are days I wish I'd never taken that leave.' The mental health leave that had been so very necessary, but continued to get him looks from the other cops – of pity, derision. Contempt. He got the contempt look a lot, especially from the cop who'd spawned him. *Thanks for that, Dad.*

Deacon made a sympathetic noise in his throat. 'Sorry. They just care.'

He grunted. *Not all of them.* He kept scrolling, ignoring the not-so-subtle jabs, until he came to a text that made one side of his mouth lift in as much of a smile as he was capable. 'This one does. It's from Wyatt.'

After Deacon, Wyatt Hanson was his next oldest friend. The three of them had gone to high school together, but Deacon had been a nerd while Adam and Wyatt were jocks. It had been Adam and Wyatt who'd kept Deacon from getting beaten up daily, because even then Deacon had been opinionated. And far too brilliant for his own good. It was like he painted a target on his own head every morning before school.

Deacon's smile was fond. 'How's he doing?'

'Good,' Adam said. His and Wyatt's friendship had fully cemented after high school, when Deacon had gone away to college. Wyatt had been his first partner right out of the academy and again in Personal Crimes, the year before. Wyatt was the guy who'd gotten him through the disaster that had been his former assignment. 'He says if I have another meltdown, to run to his place because he has a driveway full of snow he'd like cleared.'

Deacon's white brows lifted sharply. 'That's . . . kind of horrible.'

Adam chuckled. 'It's gallows humor and it's okay. I did have a meltdown.' His smile faded. The full details of which he'd only told one person outside of his old unit. And Meredith had kept his secret too. Only a few other people knew the whole story – Wyatt Hanson and Nash Currie, the detectives who'd been with him when it happened. Their immediate boss in Personal had also known, of course.

And, obviously, the guy who'd actually done it.

Panic, reflexive and visceral, washed through him at the memory, as it always did. *So much blood.* He still heard Paula's pathetic attempts to scream in his nightmares. He closed his eyes, shoved the memory aside.

'You okay?' Deacon asked quietly.

'Yep. Peachy.' Adam scrolled through more messages from reporters and sighed again when he saw the messages from another familiar number. 'Just fuckin' peachy.'

He skimmed multiple texts from his mother, asking if he was all right. He should have already called her. He knew how she worried.

He sent her a quick reply: *Fine. Busy. Will call later. Love u.* That would calm her for now. His mother had a heart condition and he hated to stress her. His father stressed her far enough, thank you very much.

Her return text popped up instantly, and he knew she'd been waiting, her phone in hand. *Dad and I love you too.*

That made him huff a bitter laugh. His father . . . Well, Jim Kimble would never worry. He was a cop's cop. Big, burly, and bulletproof. Nothing bothered Jim Kimble. Especially not the job. Not like it bothered his 'cowardly son.' His father's words.

Words that Adam had believed far too often and far too much, no matter how often or how much he told himself otherwise. He'd melted down. Shut down. Blocked out the details that might have brought a murderer to justice. Left the investigation to the other detectives on the team.

Some days he believed that he deserved the contempt in his father's eyes.

'What now?' Deacon asked. 'That laugh didn't sound happy.'

'Mom says "Dad and I love you."'

Deacon snorted. 'She keeps saying that to make herself feel better.'

It was true, and hearing Deacon say it made Adam feel better. Deacon had no love for Jim Kimble, either. Deacon, his sister Dani, and brother Greg had lived with Adam's parents after their parents died. Jim had been an even lousier uncle than he'd been a father.

And he'd been a very lousy father.

But, for his mother, Adam would keep his mouth shut on the matter. As did his cousin. 'I know, but as long as she stays out of the cardiac ICU, she can tell herself whatever she wants.'

Deacon rolled his eyes. 'You're a nicer person than I am.'

Which was not true at all. Adam simply had failed to stand up to his old man. Ever. It was far easier to avoid the problem. So it had been months since he and Jim had spoken. Problem solved.

A little tension seeped from his shoulders at Diesel Kennedy's texts. *With Doc Fallon. She's okay. Her gramps is here. The old man is . . . interesting.*

Adam frowned, wondering what that meant. Knowing Diesel, it could mean nearly anything. He looked up to find Deacon studying him carefully. 'Do you know Meredith's grandfather?' Adam asked, relieved when Deacon chuckled.

'Yeah. Guy's a hoot. Why?'

'Diesel says he's there with her.'

Deacon relaxed a little too. 'Good. Clarke'll be good for her.' He cocked his snow-white head. 'She's been sad lately.'

Adam wanted to groan. 'Not you too. Please.'

'Just stating the facts. Not assigning blame.' Deacon studied him for a moment longer before shrugging. 'I never met Mer's grand-mother, but I understand that she wore pearls and carried a derringer everywhere she went. Her grandfather is a biker dude. Big, hulking guy, got tats out the wazoo.'

That was surprising. Meredith always seemed so tidy. But fearless. So maybe not such a surprise after all. He kept that to him-self, though. 'No wonder Diesel is finding him interesting.' Diesel was also hulking and covered in tattoos.

'Clarke's also a retired computer geek. Was one of the first video game designers back in the day when two guys could produce a game in their garage.'

Adam chuckled. 'Then they're a match made in heaven.' Because Diesel was a computer geek too. A hacker extraordinaire. Adam envied his skills.

His phone buzzed with a new text. 'Finally,' he said. 'Trip says the bomb squad just gave the all-clear for the scene. He's on his way back here from the lab.'

'Anything on the bomb?' Deacon asked.

'Don't know. Let's get this last interview done, then hopefully he'll be here so we can find out. I also need to have a look before the ME takes the—'

He was interrupted by loud female voices in the hallway. Seconds later, Scarlett appeared in the doorway with a young woman whose clothing was covered in brown dirt and whose hands were cuffed behind her back.

Scarlett looked pissed off. 'Detective Kimble, Special Agent

Novak, this is Colleen Martel. She is the hostess of Buon Cibo. I found her either hiding or retrieving this from the heating duct in the bathroom,' Scarlett said, holding up a clear plastic evidence bag. Inside the bag was an envelope that appeared to be stuffed full of something.

'It's not mine!' Colleen exclaimed.

'Drugs?' Adam asked.

'Cash. Two hundred bucks.' Scarlett worked her jaw back and forth. 'She was half in the duct when I went into the bathroom to get her. Kicked me, trying to get away.'

'I didn't do anything wrong,' Colleen insisted through clenched teeth.

'Other than kicking a detective,' Adam said mildly.

'And carrying a concealed weapon,' Scarlett added. She took another clear evidence bag from her pocket. This one contained a sheathed stiletto knife, a can of pepper spray, and a cell phone. 'She was going for the pepper spray when I pulled her out of the duct.'

'Pepper spray is not illegal,' Colleen declared, chin up. 'Neither is the knife.'

'You can own all the *knives* you want,' Adam told her. 'But *stilettos* are considered deadly weapons and concealed carry is not legal. Unless you have a permit?'

Colleen looked away.

'Didn't think so,' Adam said. 'Detective Bishop, will you see that she's transported to the precinct? We'll conduct Ms Martel's interview there.' Where they'd get her on tape.

'Absolutely.' Scarlett gripped the woman's shoulder and maneuvered her toward the hotel lobby. 'Come along, Miss Martel.'

Panicked, the woman tried to jerk out of Scarlett's hold. 'No. Not like this.' She tugged against the restraints. 'People will see me.'

The three of them glanced at each other before fixing gazes on the hostess. 'Why does that bother you?' Adam asked.

The woman closed her eyes. 'Just because. Can you take me out the back?'

'Not without a better reason than "just because,"' Adam told her.

The woman's chin jutted up. 'I fear for my life.'

Scarlett looked unimpressed. 'Who do you fear?'

The woman shook her head. 'I plead the Fifth.'

Scarlett huffed out an irritated breath. 'Will you accompany me, Agent Novak, just in case Miss Escape Artist is in legitimate danger?'

'Of course,' Deacon said. 'You'll meet us there, Detective Kimble?'

'I'll be a few minutes behind you.' He needed to check out the crime scene first.

Seven

Adam walked into Buon Cibo and came face to face with the bar. He closed his eyes. Most days he could walk into a restaurant and ignore the bottles filled with . . .

He shuddered. Filled with everything he craved. His fingers twitched and he shoved his hands into his pockets. *No booze. You just think you want it. You don't need it.*

Clenching his teeth, he turned for the dining room to find Quincy Taylor watching him so steadily, so knowingly, that Adam nearly looked away in shame. But he didn't. Because he'd kept his hands in his pockets and had not reached for any of the bottles behind the bar. He'd take that as a small win.

Baby steps. Nearly a year of baby steps. But he was almost there. Almost to a year. And then . . . well, he'd planned to talk to Meredith then. But it looked like that conversation was going to happen sooner than he'd planned. *Tonight.* He'd tell her tonight.

Quincy had gone back to taking photographs of the overturned table closest to the shattered window. The dining room was a mess. Tables were overturned and flatware, dishes, food, and menus were strewn over the dining room floor, but the focal point was one white tablecloth, horribly askew and stained with blood.

'That's where Meredith and Mallory were sitting?' Adam asked.

Quincy lowered the camera. 'Yes.' He looked down, nodding when he saw Adam's shoes covered in booties. 'You can come over here, but be careful. There's a puddle of vomit on the floor just to the

100

right of the table there.' He lifted a brow. 'Meredith was afraid she'd contaminated the scene. Said she tried to direct it away from the remains.'

Adam swallowed hard, not wanting to visualize her crouched on the floor, terrified and covered in human remains. 'She's . . . a responsible person.'

Quincy snorted. 'Of all the adjectives, *responsible* was the best you could do?'

Embarrassed, Adam approached gingerly, watching where he placed his feet. 'I'm sorry. I was out of line when I . . .' He faltered, not sure how to describe what he was apologizing for.

'For glaring at me like I was poaching on your *territory*?' Quincy was unamused. 'I've had the chance to talk to Dr Fallon a few times in the past and I'm acquainted with her play therapy techniques. I like her. She's smart and has a kind heart. And that's all. She's nobody's *territory*. Possessiveness is not an admirable character trait.'

'You're right,' Adam said simply. 'It's not. Jealousy isn't terribly attractive either. I apologize.'

Quincy gave him a sharp look. 'Apology accepted.' He resumed photographing the scene around the table. 'And if it makes you feel better, she is *not* my type.'

The last sentence was said in a way that made Adam clearly understand. And feel even more embarrassed and stupid. But also relieved. 'Oh?'

Quincy snorted again. 'Neither are you, Detective.'

Adam laughed. 'Now I think my feelings are hurt.'

Quincy smiled wryly. 'Pretty sure you'll live.'

Adam sobered. 'She might not have. How close did the second shot come?'

'Close as I can figure without running trajectories through my computer model? If Mallory hadn't pulled her down, this scene would look very different.'

Adam's chest seized up, his breath freezing in his lungs. He forced the breath out, told himself that she was all right. That she hadn't been hit. He crossed around the table and found himself staring down at the body of the young man who'd told her to run.

Adam cleared his throat. 'One of the diners caught him on video, so we have his face.' Which was extremely fortunate as there wasn't much left of it. The victim lay on his back, arms positioned at his sides. 'I assume this isn't how the bomb squad found him?'

'No. The team used a robot to defuse the device. They had to get him into a position to safely remove the vest, but we have a 3D photographic record of the scene, including the body before anyone moved it. The victim was crumpled in a heap. The bullet came from the curb, directly opposite the window. The bullet entered the back of the victim's head, probably ricocheted inside the skull, and exited at the left temple. The ME will confirm that, of course. Dr Washington is on her way.'

'Where is the bullet?'

'Found it outside. It passed through the already broken window and was stopped by the ground outside.'

Adam looked out the window to where a numbered marker sat on the snow. 'So Meredith was lucky again. If it had gone straight through . . .' *I would have lost her before I got the chance to tell her the truth.* But the truth was that he'd had plenty of chances. Months' worth. He'd wasted all of them because of his stupid pride. *I'm an idiot.* 'Shit.'

Quincy nodded. 'She was very lucky.'

'Are we certain that the body isn't still a threat? Could whoever coerced this kid to walk in here with a bomb strapped to his chest have booby-trapped him somehow?'

'Not with anything visible. The team did a scan of the body after they removed the vest. The ME will do a CT scan of the body before beginning the autopsy.'

Gathering the tail of his coat under his arm, Adam crouched next to the body. 'Did the X-ray show any ID in his pockets?'

'Nope. Sorry. Dr Washington will take his prints when she gets him to the morgue. Hopefully, he's in the system.'

'Hopefully, he's local and someone will recognize him.' Adam noted the yellowed fingertips. 'He was a smoker.'

'Doesn't appear to have any cigarettes on him, though.'

Adam stared at the body for a long moment, willing something to show up, to tell him something more about the young man who'd told Meredith to run.

But there wasn't anything. Not yet. He stood up, backing away carefully. 'I've got an interview to do. You'll let me know if you find anything?'

'Absolutely.' Quincy hesitated. 'You have protection lined up for Dr Fallon, right?'

'I've got two unmarked cars on her street. Right now she's being guarded by Diesel Kennedy and her grandfather, who is apparently Diesel's twin.' And Adam was apparently jealous of the two men too, because he desperately wanted to be guarding her himself.

'Good. You got any suspects yet?'

'She was stalked, but she won't say by whom. She's protecting a client's privacy.'

'Damn ethics,' Quincy growled.

Adam sighed. 'Yeah, except I respect her ethics.' He truly did, especially because Meredith protected children. It was just one of the things that had drawn him to her from the very beginning. 'But I don't want her ethics to kill her, either.'

Which was why if he hadn't identified her stalker by nine p.m., he was going to press her again. Harder this time.

And will that be before or after you explain things and hope she still wants you?

He had no idea. He only knew he had to keep her alive or nothing else mattered.

Cincinnati, Ohio,
Saturday 19 December, 8.15 P.M.

Adam got off the precinct elevator and went straight to Isenberg's office. She was on the phone and held up a hand for him to wait, then pointed to the chair in front of her desk.

'Yes,' she said to whomever she was talking to, 'we have a few leads and we are following them up with all urgency. I have my best people working on this case . . .' She rolled her eyes. 'The FBI is working with us. Special Agent in Charge Zimmerman and I have been in frequent contact. This appears to have been a targeted attack against a single individual.' She listened, wincing as the caller's voice grew loud and shrill. 'I am aware that a bomb was involved, but there's no reason to believe the city is in any further danger. Look, I understand people are afraid.' Another wince and she held the phone away from her ear. 'Yes, I am aware that it's near Christmas. I'll be better able to promise the downtown business owners uninterrupted holiday sales by catching the person or persons behind this. For that, I need to get back to work. I'll keep you apprised. Goodbye.' She hung up, closed her eyes for the length of a loud sigh. 'Hell.'

'The mayor, I take it?' Adam asked.

'Yeah.' She pushed a folder across the desk to Adam. 'People are scared to shop downtown now.'

'I can understand that.' He opened the folder and went completely still. It was a photo of Meredith, a side view of her speaking to her priest in the middle of a crowd. Behind the priest stood a man, smiling at her. The priest couldn't see him, but Meredith did. It was evident in the tightness around her mouth, the narrowing of her eyes. She was pissed off. And afraid.

Adam had to close his eyes for a moment, to battle back the roar of rage. Holding on to his control, he began flipping through the photos. There were at least a dozen, taken from surveillance footage at the church, the grocery store, and the running track. All featured Meredith and the man. In each one, he hovered an arm's length away. Just close enough that she would know he was there. And in each photo, she knew.

The man was in his mid-forties, average height and weight. Handsome, with an arrogant smile that said he knew it and expected everyone else to know it too. He was well-dressed, the suit he'd worn to church fitting him like it had been made for him.

The last photo was grainier, taken by a security camera in the Kroger parking lot. The same man was getting into a Lamborghini. A fucking Lamborghini.

Adam made sure his voice was steady before he spoke. 'Do we know who he is?'

'Yes. His name is Broderick Voss.' She leaned back in her chair, waiting.

'Am I supposed to know who he is?' Adam asked.

'Probably only if you read the financial pages. He's the CEO of Buzz Boys. They went public a few years back. He orchestrated the IPO. Thus, the Lamborghini.'

'Whoa.' The company's name he knew. Buzz Boys gathered consumer preference opinions, a necessary service in a city of consumer products manufacturers. 'So someone connected to Voss is seeing Meredith for counseling. Do you know who?'

'Nope. Got the photos while I was talking to the mayor. Was going to text you, but you showed up instead. Ball's in your court, Adam.' She studied him carefully. 'Take someone with you when you question him. He's very influential in this town. He could make allegations against you that were totally false, but could still hurt your career.'

'What a prince,' Adam muttered, appreciating that his boss had his back. 'I'll take Agent Triplett with me. First I need to question the restaurant's hostess. Scarlett's got her in Interview Three. You wanna observe?'

Isenberg cocked a brow. 'This is the woman whose combat boot is responsible for that bruise on Scarlett's jaw? I think I will.'

'Good. In the meantime, do you have an address for Mr Voss? I want to put a car outside his residence. Just in case he gets wind of our impending visit and tries to leave town. He could charter a private jet and slip out of our grip.'

'He doesn't need to charter one,' Isenberg said grimly. 'He owns one.'

Adam sighed. 'Of course he does.'

Cincinnati, Ohio,
Saturday 19 December, 8.15 P.M.

'Well, shit.'

Meredith looked up from the intricate Moroccan tile design she was coloring to see Diesel scowling at his laptop screen. 'What?'

105

'Voss couldn't have been in front of the restaurant today. He was speaking to a room full of donors at a thousand-dollar-a-plate fund-raiser.'

'Well, shit,' Meredith echoed. 'What was the fund-raiser's cause?'

'Let's see . . .' He scrolled down, made a sound of disgust. 'It was for a state senator's reelection campaign. There are rumors that Voss plans to run.'

'Not a shock. He's a rich and powerful narcissistic sociopath.'

'Fancy words for "asshole,"' Diesel muttered.

Meredith put her coloring aside and checked her list. Wendi had called and nagged her until she'd finally promised to write down the names of everyone who'd threatened her. The list was two pages long. Two pages. She'd had no idea there had been so many. 'Should we mark him off and go to the next one?'

Diesel shook his bald head. 'No, not yet. Just because he wasn't there didn't mean he didn't have someone else do it.' He met her eyes over his computer screen. 'Today had professional hit written all over it. You pissed off the Mafia lately?'

'Shh,' Meredith scolded, looking at the door to her basement, where her grandfather napped in the spare bedroom. Declaring himself worn out from the travel, he'd excused himself to rest, but only because Diesel had promised not to leave Meredith's side. 'That's the last thing Papa needs to worry about.'

'That wasn't a no,' Diesel noted astutely. 'Gimme the list.'

'No. We'll work our way down. Half these people are dead or in jail, anyway.'

'Cheerful thought.' He wasn't being sarcastic.

'What are you doing now?' she asked to change the subject.

'Looking for Voss's bank account.'

Meredith's eyes popped wide. 'You can do that?'

'I'm insulted.' *Now* he was being sarcastic. He actually preened at her awe.

'I don't want to know how much money he has, when you find it.'

'Fine.' His cell phone buzzed with an incoming text. He took a second to type in a reply, then looked up with a surprising twinkle in his eyes.

'What did you do?' Meredith demanded warily, then gasped when he held up his phone. Adam had texted: *Is she ok?*

Diesel's response was more to the point than he could ever know. *Better than ok. We're @ kitchen table. Drinking tea. Coloring.*

That had been what she and Adam had done the last time he'd come to her, seeking comfort after a very difficult day at work. The night Adam had made a point of saying they wouldn't end up the way they had the first time he'd come to her for comfort – in her bed.

'Diesel,' she groaned. *He's going to think that Diesel and I* . . . 'You lied to him.'

'I did not. We have tea and you're coloring. I'm just keeping him on his toes. Can't let him get complacent. Can't let him think there's no competition, after all.'

She rolled her eyes. 'There isn't. Everyone knows you're so gone on Dani Novak that you can't see straight.' Diesel's grin abruptly vanished and Meredith wanted to kick her own ass. 'I'm sorry. That was thoughtless of me. It's your business. Yours and Dani's.'

He dropped his gaze to his keyboard. 'It's all right. Go back to your coloring. I'll tell you when I'm ready for the next name on your list.'

Meredith pinched the bridge of her nose. 'For a therapist, I am an insensitive asswipe.' She splashed a few ounces of whiskey into her empty teacup. 'You want a refill?'

He pushed his glass toward the bottle. 'Yes,' he said, his voice like gravel. 'Please.'

She obliged, then opened a new text window on her own phone. Adam would think she'd betrayed his trust. She needed him to know she hadn't. *For his sake and for mine.*

Cincinnati, Ohio,
Saturday 19 December, 8.30 P.M.

Adam and Isenberg joined Scarlett and Deacon in the observation room, where they watched Colleen Martel through the one-way

107

glass. The young woman sat handcuffed to the chair, her expression one of grim resignation.

'Her prints were on the envelope and the money,' Scarlett said. 'Two hundred dollars, in unmarked, well-worn twenties.'

'She say where it came from?' Adam asked.

Scarlett shook her head. 'She hasn't said anything, except "I plead the Fifth."'

'She hasn't asked for a lawyer?' Isenberg asked.

'Not even once,' Deacon answered. 'Not in the car and not since we've been here.'

That was interesting, Adam thought. 'Has she gone through booking yet?'

'Not completely,' Scarlett said, handing him a folder. 'We haven't filed the paperwork to get her in the system, but it's ready. She's been Mirandized.'

'We might be able to use that,' Adam said. 'She wanted to be taken away through the back. She's afraid of something. Or someone. Once she's in the system, she's visible.'

Isenberg looked pleased. 'You're going to let her believe she can wiggle out of this. You think she's that gullible?'

'She tried to escape the hotel through a heating duct,' Adam said dryly. 'What I think is that she watches way too much television. She would have broken the duct the moment she put her full weight on it.' He looked at Scarlett's jaw, where a bruise had started to darken in the pattern of the toe of Colleen's boot. 'I think I'll save you for a Hail Mary,' he said to Scarlett, because the girl would not respond to her right away. Scarlett had put her hands on Colleen already, both to yank her out of the duct and to cuff her. It could be implied that she'd do it again, even if Scarlett had no intention of doing so. He'd use her for the uber-bad cop if he couldn't get answers. 'Deacon, has she seen your eyes?'

'No.' Deacon wasn't wearing his wraparound shades at the moment. 'You want me to spook her?'

'It's your special gift,' Adam said lightly. He glanced at Isenberg. 'Any advice?'

'Don't fuck it up,' she said, making him snort a laugh.

'Thank you, O wise one.'

Scarlett pointed to a box on one of the chairs. 'Her personal effects. Including her cell phone. She received a call Thursday from an untraceable number. They talked for three minutes. She texted that same number this morning saying "Thanks."'

Adam retrieved the box. 'Good to know. Thank you.' He left the observation room and entered the interview room, followed by Deacon, who'd slid his wraparounds over his eyes. He took the seat across from Colleen and motioned Deacon into the chair next to her.

Within thirty seconds Colleen began to squirm. 'I didn't do anything wrong!'

'I suppose that's what we're here to find out,' Adam said mildly.

'I don't have to talk to you. I know my rights.'

'That's true. But I hope you'll decide to.' He made a show of checking the folder containing Scarlett's report, then let out an annoyed sigh. 'Bishop didn't file this paperwork.'

'She was distracted,' Deacon said blandly. 'Had to ice her jaw.'

Colleen glanced at Deacon, then at Adam. She said nothing, but her mouth took on a slight curve, her shoulders straightening. Instantly, she looked more hopeful. Which was exactly what Adam wanted.

'She's always distracted by something,' Adam growled.

'I'll make her file it when we're done here,' Deacon promised. 'Like I always do.'

Adam saw the flash of satisfaction in Colleen's eyes. *Good.* By putting down Scarlett, they'd become Colleen's allies. 'So you're the hostess at Buon Cibo.'

Her satisfaction dissipated. 'I was,' she muttered.

Adam walked around the table and leaned against its edge, not quite in Colleen's space, but close enough to make her cringe away. 'Why "was"? Did you quit?'

'No,' she said sullenly.

'They fired you?' Adam pressed. 'At Christmas? That's unkind.'

'They haven't fired me. Not yet.'

'I see.' Adam crossed his arms over his chest. 'Your job is to seat people, so you seated the two women today. Is that correct?'

'You mean the redhead and the skinny girl?' Colleen asked, her chin jutting out rebelliously. But her lips trembled, ruining the effect.

'You mean the two *guests* who someone tried to *murder*?' Deacon's voice was icy. He'd removed his sunglasses.

Colleen jerked her head sideways to reply, but she caught sight of Deacon's eyes and her mouth fell open, her eyes growing wide. 'You're—'

'Why did you seat the redhead at the table by the window?' Adam interrupted, taking advantage of Colleen's momentary shock at seeing his cousin's bicolored cat-like eyes, each one half blue and half brown.

'He told me to!' Colleen blurted out, then her eyes filled with sheer panic. She closed her eyes, her misery clear. 'Fuck you both. I bet those are contact lenses.'

'Who told you to?' Adam demanded, huffing impatiently when Colleen shook her head stubbornly. 'Miss Martel, I swear that I will dig so deep into your personal life that you'll be able to see China.'

'I didn't do anything wrong!' Tears were now streaming down her cheeks.

Adam shrugged. 'Maybe you did, maybe you didn't. Right now I don't care. I just need to know who told you to seat Dr Fallon and her companion at that particular table. Someone tried to blow up your place of employment today. Dozens of people could have been killed. You think he's finished? You think he won't come back?' Her teeth were still clenched so he leaned in a little closer. 'You think he won't come back *for you*?'

Colleen recoiled, swallowing audibly. 'Me? I didn't do anything! Why would he come for me?' He wondered if she thought she was anything close to convincing.

Adam kept his voice gentle. 'You communicated with him, Miss Martel. You just said "He told me to." You are a loose end.' He let that sink in. 'If we catch him, you'll be safe, so you'd be wise to tell me what you know. What you did. Otherwise, he stays out there on the street. You will be next and nobody wants that. Help us help you.'

Her shoulders sagged once again. 'He asked me to seat them at that table. Said he was going to surprise her. That he was going to stand outside the window and propose.'

'Who?' Deacon demanded coldly, maintaining his role of bad cop.

'I d-don't know,' she stuttered nervously. 'He didn't give me a name. I never saw him. I only talked to him on the phone.'

Deacon sneered. 'You expect us to believe that you did this out of the goodness of your heart?'

'No! I mean yes. I mean . . .' She closed her eyes in a long blink. 'He told me that he'd leave me an envelope with cash at the podium where I sign customers in. A tip.'

'Two hundred dollars is an awfully big tip,' Adam said, and held up his hand when she started to protest. 'Don't bother denying it. Your fingerprints were all over every bill.'

'You sold out two women for two hundred bucks.' Deacon ground out the furious words. 'There might have been a hundred people hurt or *killed* if that bomb had gone off. You would have been killed too, in case that fact missed your attention.'

Colleen began crying, but Adam didn't believe her tears any more than he believed anything she'd said. 'I didn't know what he was going to do. He said he wanted to propose.'

'Even if that's true, you didn't think two hundred dollars was a lot of money just to seat his lady love?' Deacon asked, derision dripping from every word.

'That's not my money. I found it. I was afraid you'd accuse me of something.' Colleen shrugged tearfully. 'I don't know what else you want from me.'

'We want you to tell the truth,' Adam snarled, suddenly furious. 'When did he call you? I want a time and date.'

She flinched, then pointed to the folder. 'If I tell you, will you still arrest me?'

'That depends on what you tell me,' Adam lied smoothly. Because she was *so* fucking arrested. 'Time and date.'

'Thursday night. I don't know the exact time. I was on duty at the front.'

She still hadn't demanded a lawyer. 'How did he contact you?'

She lifted a shoulder. 'Restaurant phone, of course.'

Deacon fished her cell phone from the evidence box. 'You got a call at eight thirty on Thursday.'

'That wasn't him,' Colleen said. 'I told you, he called on the restaurant's phone.'

'Along with a dozen other people legitimately asking for reservations.' Deacon tilted his head, studying the young woman. 'Clever, actually.'

Because that would be very difficult to disprove one way or the other. 'She could be telling the truth,' Adam said, reassuming the good cop role. 'Who called your cell?'

Colleen licked her lips nervously. 'My boyfriend.'

'Oh, good,' Adam said with a smile. 'Then you won't mind if Agent Novak calls your boyfriend right now. We'd like to rule him out as quickly as possible. Be sure to introduce yourself to whoever answers, Agent Novak. Use your whole title, you know, including the fact that you're with the major case joint task force, investigating a homicide.'

Colleen glared. 'Fine,' she gritted out. 'You win, all right? Don't call that number.'

'Because?' Adam asked, still playing nice.

'Because I don't want him coming back for me!' Colleen shouted, then slumped into the chair. 'Look. He did tell me that he wanted to propose. I did think it was a lot of money, but I didn't know what he really planned to do, okay? That's the truth. He didn't sound very friendly, but who am I to judge?'

'How did he sound?' Deacon asked. 'Be specific.'

'Deep and gravelly.' She shrugged, then met Adam's eyes directly. 'I did not know he was going to try to kill the redhead. And I'm sorry that the kid was killed.'

'You let the victim pass through,' Deacon said. 'You didn't walk him to a table.'

She looked uncomfortable. 'The man on the phone asked me not to.'

'So he told you to expect someone to walk into the restaurant and up to the table?' Deacon asked.

'Yes. But I thought he was part of the proposal.'

'Did he look happy when he walked in?' Adam asked, knowing the answer. He'd seen the young man's miserable expression on the tape Trip had shown him.

She hung her head. 'No. But then I thought he was still part of it – like maybe he was serving her with divorce papers or something. I've seen that happen before. The amount of money made sense then. If he wanted to get her reaction on camera to something bad . . .' She trailed off, looking truly sorry for the first time. 'I didn't expect what happened. You gotta believe me.'

Like hell I do. 'Thank you,' Adam told her formally. 'We're finished for now.'

Colleen brightened. 'Does this mean you won't arrest me?'

Not on your life. Or on Meredith's life. Or on the life of the John Doe whose body had grown cold on the floor of the crime scene. 'No.'

Her mouth fell open again. 'But you said . . . That's not fair!'

Adam shrugged. 'What can I say? Life's a bitch.'

'He'll kill me,' she said with all certainty.

Adam leaned in. 'I believe that you believe that. Tell me how you know and I'll be more likely to believe you too.'

She turned away. 'I'm a loose end, just like you said.'

'He had your personal cell phone number,' Adam commented.

Her gaze rocketed back to his. She truly seemed terrified. 'I don't know how.'

She still hadn't lawyered up, despite being terrified of spending a night in jail. 'You are entitled to an attorney, you know,' he said, testing the waters.

She blanched. 'No. I don't want one. I don't want an attorney.'

'You not having an attorney won't keep you out of court,' Deacon said quietly.

She dropped her chin to her chest with a moan, rocking in the chair to which she was cuffed. 'I'm dead, I'm dead, I'm dead.'

Adam pushed to his feet. 'I'll be back.' He went to the observation room and closed the door. 'The only truth she's told is this right here. The fear that she's going to be killed.'

'Agreed,' Isenberg said. 'She's more afraid of "him" than of us. Recommendations?'

'Let her go with a tail and let "him" find her,' Scarlett said bluntly. 'Use her as bait.'

'Or . . .' Adam said, giving Scarlett a look of mild reproach, 'we can put her in a high security lockup and monitor anyone who comes close. That way she's *protected* bait.'

Isenberg nodded. 'Do it. Scarlett and Deacon can do the paperwork.'

Adam checked his phone. 'Thanks, because I still have to meet Trip and pay a visit to Broderick Voss. I want to know if he has a deep, gravelly voice.' He handed the folder with the police report to Scarlett, who looked decidedly unhappy.

'I like my way better,' Scarlett muttered, touching her jaw gingerly. 'Goddamn bitch in combat boots.'

Adam patted her back. 'You can make up an awesome story to tell when people ask you where you got the bruise. Like you were fighting off ninjas. It's way better than admitting you got kicked by a skinny girl with combat boots.'

Her lip curled in a sneer, but then her lips twitched. 'I can get behind ninjas. But you gotta promise to back me up.'

'Deal.' Adam returned to the interview room where Colleen was still curled into herself, rocking on the chair, and he wondered if her fear was that acute or if she was trying to get a psych placement. He figured it was the second one.

'We're going to put you in protective custody, Miss Martel,' Adam told her.

The rocking abruptly stopped and Colleen looked up, eyes narrowed. 'What does that mean?'

'It means you're under arrest, but we aren't going to put you with the general population. You'll be held in a secure area. In return, we expect your cooperation.'

'Like what?'

'Like participating in a vocal lineup. We're going to want you to identify the voice you heard on the phone.'

She looked wary. 'I think I can do that.'

'Good.' Adam motioned for Deacon to follow him into the hallway. They shut the door on Colleen and Adam said, 'Scarlett's got the paperwork. You're both to escort her to a high security lockup.'

'Where are you off to?' Deacon asked.

'To see this guy.' Adam showed Deacon the surveillance photographs of Broderick Voss, and explained who he was.

'You want me to go with you?' Deacon asked.

'No, but thanks. Trip's meeting me here in a few. I'll let you know how it goes.'

Cincinnati, Ohio,
Saturday 19 December, 8.50 P.M.

'Meredith!' Kendra called from the front door. 'I found something of yours.'

Meredith and Diesel hurried from the kitchen to the living room, where Kendra and her grandfather stood glaring at one another. Kendra carried several take-out bags in her hands. Her grandfather was wearing his heavy coat and boots.

'Papa?' Meredith asked tentatively. 'I thought you were taking a nap.'

'Slippery dog,' Diesel drawled with amused respect. 'You snuck out the back.'

'Which was far too easy to do,' Clarke said. 'You have a blind spot along the back of your house, Merry. Anyone can get in the basement door.'

Kendra's eyebrows shot up her forehead. 'He really is your grandfather?'

'Yes, of course. Who did you think he was?'

'Some asshole trying to hurt you. I caught him lurking out back.'

Clarke looked at Kendra with suspicion. 'She says she's a cop.'

'She is,' Meredith said.

'Told you,' Kendra muttered to Clarke.

'Well, how was I supposed to know she was telling the truth?' Clarke said, his tone sulky. 'She also said she was Wendi's sister!'

115

'She is,' Meredith said again, then popped a light smack on Diesel's arm because he was snickering. 'Not funny.'

'Totally funny.' Diesel laughed and Meredith found herself smiling because it was a little funny. Wendi was tiny and vampirishly pale. Kendra was nearly six feet tall in her stocking feet, with ebony skin.

'They were foster sisters,' Meredith told her grandfather. 'They were adopted by the same lovely lady.' Who continued to take foster kids, giving them the best of homes.

Diesel shook his head. 'She has to be one hell of a lady to put up with you two.' He pretended to be afraid of Kendra's scowl. 'Hell, Kenny, you know it's true.'

'It's fair,' Kendra allowed, then nudged Clarke into the house. 'Freezing my ass off here. And could someone take these bags? My fingers are frozen too. Don't want my trigger finger to crack off.'

'Gross,' Meredith said, taking the bags and peeking inside. 'Yum. My favorites.' Skyline chili and Graeter's ice cream. 'Thanks, Kenny.'

'There should be enough cheese coneys for six or seven people,' Kendra said. 'So enough for the two of us and these two bruisers.' She stomped the snow off her boots on Meredith's welcome mat, then kicked them off and went into the living room. 'Glad I got the Graeter's. It was the only thing that convinced Gramps here that I really knew you.'

'Only a crazy person would buy ice cream in this weather,' Clarke declared, still a little sulky.

'Only a crazy person would go for a walk in this weather,' Kendra countered.

Pausing midway to the kitchen, Meredith looked over her shoulder. 'Why *were* you outside, Papa?'

Clarke huffed. 'I was checking the security around your house. It sucks ass, Merry. Luckily, you have two unmarked cars watching over you.'

Meredith turned, fully facing them. 'I do? Kendra, did you know about this?'

Kendra nodded. 'One car has a pair of CPD detectives. The other's got two Feds. I guess Isenberg and Zimmerman are sharing resources. Now that I know there's a blind spot in the back, I'll ask one of the cars to sit on the next street over in case your shooter tries to sneak in through the basement. Kimble set it up. Didn't he tell you?'

'No. He didn't.' She'd have to add it to the list of things he needed to explain. 'Should we at least offer the officers some hot coffee? They have to be freezing out there.'

'I offered already,' Clarke said. 'They have a thermos, but might take a refill later.'

Kendra stared at him. 'You talked to them? Really? They're unmarked for a reason.'

'Which I did not know because they were *unmarked*,' Clarke said, giving her a warning glare. 'I see two strange cars on this street, each with two guys, I'm gonna check it out. They could have been waiting for Meredith to come outside so that they could finish what they started today.'

Kendra didn't back down. 'If they had been, they would have dropped you where you stood. Whoever did this has demonstrated they have no regard for the lives of innocent bystanders.'

Meredith sucked in a pained breath, her vision going temporarily gray as the memory of the young man's exploding head filled her mind. 'Papa,' she whispered.

Her face must have shown her horror because Clarke sighed and crossed the room to pull her into a hug. 'I'm fine, Merry. It was fine.'

'But it might not have been. You can't take chances like that. Please. I can't . . . I saw that boy die today. I can't . . . You have to be more careful.'

'All right.' He patted her back. 'I won't take any more chances. I'm sorry, honey.'

She nodded, her cheek pressed into his chest. 'Okay. Thank you.'

'You're welcome. Anyway, I wasn't even the first person to talk to the cops outside. Cosmo got there first. He gave them the thermos of coffee.'

'Who is Cosmo?' Kendra asked.

Steadier now, Meredith stepped out of her grandfather's

embrace. 'He lives in the blue house across the street. He's the neighborhood watch guy. He and Papa go way back.'

'Our kids used to play together.' Sadness crossed Clarke's face. 'His daughter died recently. Now they're both gone, both our kids. You're not supposed to outlive your kids.'

Quiet melancholy filled the room. 'I'm sorry, Papa,' Meredith murmured. 'Was that why you took a walk? To visit with Cosmo?'

'Partly. He's not getting around as well as he used to.' Again the small smile, this time accompanied with pride. 'He said you make sure his refrigerator stays full and his garbage makes it to the end of the curb every week.'

Meredith shrugged uncomfortably. 'He's alone. It's no trouble.'

'It's still kind,' Diesel said gruffly and Meredith smiled up at him.

'I stock fridges, you coach pee wee soccer. Kenny helps at Mariposa. We do what we can.'

Diesel blushed. He was such a charmer. Meredith didn't know why Dani hadn't snatched him right up.

The mood needed lightening, and Kendra seemed to sense it first. 'I am starving,' she announced. 'I skipped lunch and had to smell the food all the way over here. Let's eat before the chili gets cold and the ice cream gets hot.'

'We can eat in the dining room,' Meredith said. 'Diesel's using the kitchen table.'

Diesel gestured toward his computer. 'I was kind of in the middle of something. You mind if I take my food and work some more?'

Meredith studied his face. His jaw was set and she could see his mind was already back to what he'd been doing when Kendra had opened the front door. 'Anything good?'

'Maybe. I'll let you know as soon as I do.'

Eight

Cincinnati, Ohio,
Saturday 19 December, 8.50 P.M.

Adam jogged to his Jeep, wishing he had time to squeeze in a trip to Meredith's house before going to Voss's. But Trip was meeting him in the parking lot so that they could compare notes and talk strategy before visiting the man who was their best suspect.

Glancing at his phone as he crossed the parking lot, he saw another two dozen voicemails and texts. He was only interested in one at the moment. He'd texted Diesel before he'd gone into the interview room with Colleen Martel, asking if Meredith was okay.

He found Diesel's reply as he was getting into his Jeep. *Better than ok. We're @ kitchen table. Drinking tea. Coloring.*

Adam nearly stumbled. What the fuck? Coloring at her kitchen table? Drinking tea? *Those are the things I do with her.*

Mechanically he got into his car and buckled his seat belt. His first thought was that he knew Diesel wasn't making a move on Meredith. Diesel was too hung up on Adam's cousin Dani. So Adam wasn't worried about Diesel himself.

He was worried about Meredith. Her . . . intentions. Did she color at the table with every man who visited her home? *It was supposed to be special.* It *was* special. *For me.*

Memories of his two evenings with Meredith Fallon had kept him going when he'd wanted to give up. But he also remembered the hurt in her eyes earlier that day. *I want what you can't – or won't – give.* Had she told Diesel about him? About his . . . issues? His nightmares? His utter and complete failings?

My utter and complete breakdown in her arms? It wasn't among his proudest moments, that was for damn sure. But she hadn't made him feel any less . . . of anything. She'd simply held him that night while he'd shaken apart in her arms.

And then, when his panic had passed, when he was spent, she'd kissed him so gently. Like butterfly wings. And that had been it for him. He'd fallen so hard. So damned hard.

Yeah. He'd been hard all right. Hard *everywhere*. He shuddered, unable to stop himself from reliving that night in his mind. It had been the best night of his godforsaken life. He'd let go with her. Finally just let go. *I let myself trust her.* She'd promised not to tell.

Then she didn't, came the calm voice in his mind. *She promised.*

That promise had been keeping him calm – and sober – for almost a year now. No, she hadn't told anyone. That wasn't who Meredith was. She didn't divulge secrets. Which was why she was in this mess in the first place. *If she'd reported the fucker for stalking—*

Not her fault, the calm voice broke in. *You cannot blame the victim.*

A sharp pain in his hands made him realize that he'd been sitting in his cold Jeep, clutching the steering wheel in a death grip. For several minutes, actually. Starting the car, he cranked up the heat and kept scrolling, looking for Meredith's reply. His heart started galloping a mile a minute when he saw it, sent less than five minutes after Diesel's text.

I didn't say anything abt u to D. He's being annoying. Sorry.

Knew you hadn't, he texted back. *That's not you. See u later.*

A knock on his window startled him. Trip stood outside, stomping his feet, trying to stay warm. Adam unlocked the passenger door and Trip hopped in.

'Warm,' Trip said with a little moan. 'Hate the cold.'

'Then why do you live here?' Adam asked, trying to divert his focus.

'My parents are here.' He shrugged. 'I'm the youngest. I was lucky to get a post in my hometown and my folks are getting up there in age, so I stay. For as long as I'm able.'

Adam met his gaze, surprised and touched by the confession. 'Me too. Mom's got a bad heart.' He made a face. 'So does my dad, but his is just asshole-bad.' He winced then, wishing he'd kept that truth to himself. 'What do you know about the bomb?'

'Three pipe bombs filled with TATP, taped together, simple blasting caps, with a cell phone trigger. The vest's pockets were stuffed with nails and BBs.'

'TATP, like the Paris bombers used.'

Trip nodded. 'The explosion itself would have taken out the front half of the restaurant's dining room, plus any vehicles parked immediately on the curb outside. Any person within a five-foot radius would have been killed. Anyone within twenty would have been killed or at least critically injured with the shrapnel, no question.'

Adam drew a shaky breath. Meredith and Mallory had been less than five feet away, and at least thirty other diners had been within that twenty-foot radius. 'Holy God.'

'Yeah. Might have gotten a partial print from the bomb's guts, but it may not be usable. Latent's working on it.'

Adam knew better than to get his hopes up, but still . . . 'You'll let me know?'

Trip looked a little offended. 'Of course. We're partners. Anyway, the connection to the cell phone was simple. Three wires, no dead man's switch.'

'Thank God for that. Andy would have been dead in the street and the shooter in the SUV would have still had a clear shot at Meredith. What about the cell phone?'

'It's a burner.'

'Of course it is.' Adam had a sudden thought. 'What was the number?'

'For the burner?' Trip checked his notes. 'Here.' He shined his phone's flashlight on the paper. 'Midway down, on the left, if you can read my writing. Why?'

Damn. 'I was hoping it would be the same number that called the restaurant's hostess, but it's not.' He told Trip about Colleen Martel.

'A two-hundred-buck tip,' Trip said. 'Whoever did this expected the phone to be destroyed. No loose ends. Although the hostess is a loose end, as are her cell records.'

121

'Maybe he was hoping she'd be killed in the blast. That no one would look at her cell phone. The hostess podium was about fifteen feet from Meredith's table. What about the TATP? Where did it come from?'

'Somebody's basement?' Trip shrugged. 'It's easy enough to make. Just acetone and peroxide, both legal to purchase anywhere. There was a lot of it in those pipes, though. A few grams could blow off a finger. There was close to two pounds in the pipes. It's highly unstable, so the bomber was taking a risk just working with it. For that reason alone, I'd have to say the bomb maker had experience.'

'There was no "signature fuse" or anything that would ID the bomb maker?'

'Nope. The only thing is, TATP is so unstable, only a lunatic would store it for very long. We could track any large purchases of acetone or peroxide. Quincy is figuring out how much of the raw materials the bomb maker would have needed.'

'Was there a number in the cell phone's log?' Adam asked.

'Yes. Untraceable. Another burner.' He pointed to his notes. 'That's the number.'

Adam nodded in satisfaction. 'That's the number that called the hostess.'

Trip's eyes gleamed. 'We have a link. The call time in the log is seconds before the John Doe was shot. Obviously the shooter tried to detonate and, when he failed, he shot him.'

'Then tried to shoot Meredith.'

'Hostess-girl is really lucky the guy didn't try to shoot her as he drove by.'

'Yeah, well, she's not feeling so lucky right now. I'm exploiting that to get her to do an ID of the man who called her.'

'This Voss guy?'

'I hope so. He's the only lead we have so far. I only know that he's the CEO of Buzz Boys. Nothing on his personality, other than he's a sociopathic stalking asshole.'

'Not a bad place to start. You also know he has a kid under Meredith's care.'

'Yes, that's true. I wonder what he did that he doesn't want Meredith to know.'

'If it was criminal, she'd have to tell, right? The safety of the child comes before their privacy or confidentiality.'

'True again.' He Googled *Broderick Voss* and *children*. Then swore when the search results came back. 'Fucking hell. He's got an alibi for the time of the shooting. He was speaking to a whole room of people. Political fund-raiser.' Adam scrutinized the photo of Voss smiling at the crowd. The man's suit alone had to have cost two grand. 'Although, if I was that rich, I certainly wouldn't want my hands dirty. Just because he has an alibi—'

'Doesn't mean he didn't do it,' Trip finished.

'Exactly. He certainly has the money to contract it out.'

Trip had his own phone out, Googling. 'Looks like his fund-raiser was for some state senator's reelection fund. Maybe the man has an interest in politics himself?'

Adam nodded. 'And while politicians can weather most scandals these days, any scandal involving a child is still poison.' He scrolled through the images served up by the search engine. 'Here's a picture of his family last Christmas.' He turned the phone for Trip to see. 'Pretty wife, adorable little girl. She looks about four, maybe five in this picture, which is about a year old.'

Trip was nodding. 'He and the missus had a bunch of those photos made over the years. But nothing's showing up for this year.'

'I wish we knew what Meredith knows about this little girl. Otherwise, we're walking blind into this interview with Voss. On the other hand, we can truthfully say we didn't get his name from her.'

'I say we're ready for round one with Mr Voss,' Trip said, opening the Jeep's door. 'I have the address. I'll meet you there.'

The low ring of Adam's cell startled him. The caller ID startled him more. Diesel. A text notification popped up at the same time, also from Diesel. *Answer my call.*

Shit. The man had just said Meredith was all right. Adam gave Trip a sign to wait and answered. 'Diesel. What's wrong?'

'She's fine,' Diesel said quickly, but his voice was off. Half excitement, half dread. 'I need to see you, stat.'

'What is it? Tell me, for God's sake.'

'No,' Diesel said firmly. 'In person.'

'Okay, but Trip'll be with me.'

A slight hesitation. 'Fine. Use your blue-light special and get here fast.'

Kiesler University, Chicago, Illinois,
Saturday 19 December, 8.20 P.M. CST (9.20 P.M. EST)

Shane Baird left the library, immediately shivering against the biting wind coming off Lake Michigan. He'd barely cleared the library door when his cell phone began buzzing like it was having a seizure. Hunching away from the wind, he pulled it out of his pocket and saw an explosion of texts, all from his friend Kyle.

The latest in a string of texts caught his eye.

Dude. Call me. Freaking the fuck out here.

Frowning, Shane jogged back to the library and leaned against the brick wall, out of the wind. Quickly he swiped at his phone screen down to the first of the texts.

Some guy just stopped by. Looking for you. Spidey senses off the Richter scale. Guy was all big and mean looking. Dressed cas but was packing. WTF? Why he looking 4 u? Call me! There were five other texts, all from Kyle, becoming increasingly agitated because Shane hadn't called.

Shane's breath froze in his lungs, old memories playing like a shitty movie reel. Hand shaking, he called Kyle's cell. 'I just saw your text.'

'Oh shit,' Kyle said on a relieved whoosh of breath. 'I thought you were . . . I dunno. Dead or something. Where the fuck have you been?'

'In the library basement, studying. No cell bars down there. What happened?'

'I'll *tell* you what happened. That guy scared the mother*fuck* outta me.'

'What guy?' Shane's voice pitched higher, panicked. *Was it a cop? This can't be happening again.* It just couldn't. 'Tell me exactly what happened.'

'Okay, fine.' Kyle loudly sucked in a breath and let it out. 'Okay,' he said again. 'I'm on desk duty tonight. At Lamarr.' The residential hall where Shane had lived until the beginning of this semester. The hall where they'd met and bonded over video games and a mutual love of nachos and sci-fi. Kyle had been his first friend in Illinois, when he'd been so damn lonely. 'This guy came in, about an hour ago. He was trying to look, I dunno, young or something. Like he belonged here. As if. He had to have been thirty and looked like he should have been in a boxing ring. He was no college kid, I know that. He smiled and that made him look even scarier. He said he was just visiting a friend and could I give him the dorm number? I said no, but I could call the student and say he was waiting in the lobby. He looked really pissed and for a second . . . Hell, Shane. I thought he was gonna hit me.'

Shane made himself breathe. 'You said he asked for me? Me specifically?'

'Yeah. I told him that you didn't live here anymore. He asked for your address and I told him I didn't know it. But he didn't believe me.' Kyle made a choked sound. 'He said I was lying, that he knew we were friends. He said he saw us together on Facebook. Dude, who the fuck was that guy?'

'I don't know.' Shane swallowed hard. 'Swear to God.'

'Well, he knows you. I told him that I wasn't allowed to give any information on a student and I hit the panic button under the desk. He got all mad then and I thought I was dead, right there. Seriously. I managed to tell him that the campus cops were on the way. He gave me a really long look and told me to be smart. That's all.'

'What does that mean?' Shane could hear his own panic.

'I think he meant for me not to tell the campus cops what went down.'

'Did you?'

'Hell yeah, man. He got caught on the security camera, clear as day. Any lip reader would know he asked for you. I'm just giving you heads up that the campus cops are going to try to find you. Are you . . .' Kyle hesitated. 'Are you in trouble, Shane?'

'No! I . . . I have no idea who he was or what he wants. I've never had the cops after me. Ever. I study and work and go to class. My social life is playing D&D with you. Jesus.'

But he *had* had the cops after him once. Not *him* exactly. He'd been a person of interest because his friend back then had been a wanted man. He'd lied for Jason then and he'd do it again. Even though Jason Coltrain had changed his name to Andy Gold and hadn't returned any of his texts, emails, or calls in over a year.

So much for solidarity, he thought sadly. He understood why Andy had cut him off. He hadn't agreed with Andy, but he'd understood. Of the three of them, Shane had the best opportunity for the life they'd all dreamed of while they survived foster care. Andy didn't want his own past hurting Shane, which had sounded ridiculous then.

Now? If someone dark and scary was looking for Shane . . . *Andy, what have you done?*

'Shane?' Kyle prompted. 'You still there?'

'Yeah,' Shane croaked. 'Give me a sec. Gotta check something.' He opened a browser and typed in *Cincinnati*. He hadn't gotten to the double-n before a number of hits popped up. *Shooting in Cincinnati. Bomb attack prevented in Cincinnati.*

Oh God. Andy. What the fuck have you done? Heart beating like a cannon, he clicked on the first link – an article in the *Cincinnati Ledger*.

The photo of a shot-out window made his thudding heart stutter. The photo of the victim's face made his knees go weak. He slid down the wall, barely registering the feeling of cold concrete on his ass. 'Oh no,' he moaned quietly. 'Oh God.'

'Shane?' Kyle demanded. 'What is it?'

'There was a shooting today. In Cincinnati.'

'I know,' Kyle said slowly. 'I thought you'd have seen it by now. It's been all over the news all day.'

'I was studying all day. Turned my phone off. What . . . What happened?'

'Why?'

'Just tell me, okay?'

'Okay, okay. Chill. Well, the way I heard it, some dude walked into a restaurant and pulled a gun on some lady. She's some psychologist or something. Works with kids. She was packing too, and pulled her gun. She'd gotten him to drop his gun, but then somebody shot the guy from outside in the street. Blew his head off.'

Shane's breathing was choppy and he started to see little black dots swimming in his vision. He tried to talk but he couldn't form the words.

'Shane?' Kyle asked, even more slowly. 'Did you know that guy or something?'

'Yeah. Yeah.' It was all Shane could get out. He could only stare at the photo that looked like a still pulled from a video. *Unidentified victim*, the caption read. But Shane knew him. It was Andy. 'What . . . What else did the news say?' Because he couldn't see the words anymore. They were all a blur.

'Um, okay. Let me look it up.' A few seconds of silence was followed by Kyle clearing his throat. 'Okay. This says that witnesses say the victim didn't want to be there. That he said something like "He'll kill her."'

Bile burned in Shane's throat and he rolled to his knees, throwing up. He could hear Kyle's panicked voice. 'Shane? Shane?'

Shane huffed hard, trying to get his brain to work. He spat, then rolled back to sit, closing his eyes. 'I need to get to Cincinnati. Now.'

'But . . . midterms.'

Like that mattered anymore? 'I . . . I have to get to Cincinnati. *Now.*'

'Okay, dude. Just . . . settle down, okay? Let me think a minute.'

Shane tried to stand, but his rubbery legs said *no way* and he slid back down to the concrete. 'I need a car.'

'I know. I said give me a minute.' There were a series of quick dings in the background. 'All right. This is what I need you to do. Go into the library, go to the john, and wash your face. Stay out of sight for thirty minutes. Then come back out and I'll be waiting for you at the curb.'

'But . . .' Shane was overwhelmed. 'You have midterms too.'

'Not till Tuesday. I can drive you down tonight and be back in plenty of time.'

'Your car is a piece of crap, Kyle. We'd never make it out of Illinois. I appreciate you offering, but . . .'

'I'm borrowing Tiff's car. I was texting her. She says if you puke in her car that I can never borrow it again, so make sure you're done with the puking, okay?'

Shane chuffed a stunned laugh, able to see Kyle's girlfriend saying exactly that. He shook his head, putting the logistics of travel aside to focus on what was more important. 'If that guy's looking for me and he knows we're friends? That puts you in danger too.'

'All the more reason for me to leave town for a few days,' Kyle said seriously. 'Now get your ass out of sight for thirty minutes. Tiff is meeting me at Burger King and we're doing the car switch there.'

'Thank you, Kyle. I mean it.'

'Thirty, dude. Be ready.'

Shane ended the call and forced his body to rise, locking his knees so that he remained upright. And then he did exactly what Kyle had told him to do.

Cincinnati, Ohio,
Saturday 19 December, 9.20 P.M.

Adam had to park across the street and several driveways down from Meredith's house when he arrived because there were already five vehicles parked in her driveway and on her curb. His and Trip's vehicles made seven. He got out of his Jeep, scanning the street, immediately seeing the two unmarked cars providing surveillance.

'Meredith got a party goin' on or something?' Trip asked.

Adam shrugged. 'It was pretty inevitable that the crowd would gather here.' Meredith Fallon inspired loyalty in everyone who knew her. *Including me.*

Trip eyed the cars in the driveway as they approached, a slight smile tipping his lips up. 'Kendra's here. That's her Toyota.'

'And Diesel's truck and Bailey's minivan,' Adam added, glad

Meredith's cousin had come to support her too. And then he had to smile. 'And Delores's car.' It was a hunk of junk, but Delores insisted she could get a few more miles out of it. All of Delores's money went into her animal shelter. 'That means Angel is here.' Because the giant hound accompanied Delores everywhere she went.

Trip's smile became a happy grin. 'I love that dog. I've been thinking of getting one.'

'Drinking the canine rescue Kool-Aid,' Adam said, shaking his head, because just about everyone in their circle of friends had adopted a dog or cat from Delores's shelter. At Trip's arched eyebrow, Adam chuckled. 'Me too. But not a puppy. I've watched Deacon throw away too many shoes training his.'

Trip stopped at the car parked at the top of the driveway. 'Whose car is that?'

'Probably her grandfather. Deacon says he's okay, so I'm not worried.'

Trip gave him a pointed stare. 'What's this with Diesel asking us to come?'

'I don't know. He wouldn't tell me. I called him again on the way out here and he was stubborn. He can be a little paranoid,' Adam allowed. The guy was his friend, but Adam wasn't blind to his faults.

'And a lot rogue,' Trip added with a frown. 'He's hacked something. You know it as well as I do.'

'Figured it. And?'

'And it's illegal for him to do it. It's illegal for us to know about.'

'I know. I also know that somebody tried to kill Meredith today.'

'And you're willing to break the rules to protect her?'

I'd break every rule in every goddamn book in the world to keep her safe. He returned Trip's pointed stare. The man didn't have too many nightmares to live with. Yet. 'I know there have been times – when things went to hell – that I wished for inside info before walking into a disaster.'

'So if Diesel has ill-gotten information, you'll look at it,' Trip pressed.

Adam let out a breath that temporarily fogged the air between them. 'And if I say yes? Will you report me?'

Trip hesitated a long moment. 'No. I just needed to know how things are.'

'I'll protect you from fallout,' Adam promised. 'It'll be on me.'

Trip's face hardened. 'If I walk into this with you, I'm doing it on my own and I'll take my own damn consequences. You guys treat me like "the kid." I'm not. You got me?'

'I do,' Adam said levelly, because Trip's point was fair. 'You get that everyone here will know we've talked to Diesel. Everyone will know why we're here. Kendra will know why.'

'I figured that out myself,' Trip said, as if Adam were the kid. 'It changes nothing.'

Adam nodded once, respect swelling. 'Got it.'

Trip gestured to the door. 'Then lead on.'

Meredith met them at the door, her eyes wary as she studied them both. 'Gentlemen, please come in. Pardon the noise, it's a little crowded in here.'

The sheer life of the house hit Adam squarely in the face as soon as he crossed over the threshold. Amazing scents came from the kitchen. Gingerbread maybe. Conversations were being shouted over the television where a video game battle raged between Bailey's husband, Ryan Beardsley, and an older man with a bald head and a tat peeking out of his collar. Bailey's daughter, Hope, sat in the older man's lap, but her presence wasn't impacting the old guy's performance at all, because he was clearly winning.

Adam remembered what Deacon had told him. 'The grandfather is some video game developer,' he murmured, and Trip's brows shot up.

'And Diesel isn't here playing with him? He must have something really good.'

'Papa,' Meredith called over the din. 'Can you pause it?' The noise immediately quieted, then silenced as the conversations halted.

Ryan Beardsley gave them both a wave, then tugged on his

daughter's ponytail. 'Hope, come sit with me. Let Papa meet Aunt Meredith's friends.'

Hope slid off the older man's lap, but remained standing next to him as she gave Adam and Trip a narrow-eyed perusal. 'Did you catch him yet?' she asked. 'The man who tried to kill Aunt Meredith?'

'Not yet.' Adam answered her question as gravely as she'd asked it. 'We're working on it, very hard.'

'Good,' Hope said with a frown. 'This was a bad day.'

'Yes,' Adam agreed. 'But it could have been far worse. Your aunt is okay, right?'

'Yes,' Meredith said dryly. 'She is fine and she is standing right here. Hope, can you go to the kitchen and check on the cookies? We should be able to ice them soon.'

'Yeah, yeah,' Hope said glumly. 'You just want to get rid of me.'

Bailey appeared in the doorway. 'I wonder why that is? Come on, kiddo. Let's see if we can figure out how to decorate gingerbread men with tattoos for Papa and Diesel.'

'And gingerbread *girls* with tats,' Hope said, leaning up to kiss the old man's cheek. 'Because I'm getting one as soon as I'm eighteen.'

The old man rose as Hope walked away. 'You will do no such thing, young lady.' He chuckled when Hope made a face before joining her mother in the kitchen. 'So you're the cops on Merry's case. Good. I'm her grandfather, Clarke Fallon.'

Merry. Yes, that fit Meredith to a T. 'I'm Detective Kimble.' Adam shook the old man's hand and found himself biting back a wince. There was clearly a warning there.

'Special Agent Triplett.' Trip shook hands as well. 'When did you arrive, sir?'

The old man didn't even blink. 'My itinerary,' he said, pulling a piece of paper from his pocket. 'Thank you for asking.'

He didn't sound sarcastic. He actually sounded approving. Trip reviewed the page and handed it back to him. 'Thank you, sir. We needed to check. Your arriving on the same day as an attempt is made on your granddaughter's life is . . . coincidental.'

'Providential,' Ryan corrected and Adam remembered the man had been a chaplain.

Meredith smiled indulgently up at her grandfather. 'A gift.'

Adam tore his eyes away from her face. 'Where—' He had to clear his throat, because he wanted her to look at him like that. So damn badly. 'Where is Diesel?'

'Basement,' Meredith said, pointing. 'It got too crowded up here.'

'Door's through the kitchen,' Clarke said. 'I'll show you down.'

'Adam knows the way,' Meredith said quietly.

Adam couldn't stop himself. His gaze flew back to her face, remembering the last time he'd been in her house. It had been pouring down rain and he'd stood out in the street, getting soaking wet as he fought with himself on whether or not he should go inside. She'd spied him standing there, beckoned him in. Her face had been resigned that evening. Like she knew he needed her, but that she couldn't trust him not to hurt her.

Because the first time he'd been here, he'd left her sleeping in her bed without a word. No note. No goodbye. No thank you. *Because I'm a coward.* Time to change that.

'Yes. I had gotten caught in a rain storm,' Adam said, watching her grandfather from the corner of his eye. The old man knew. Adam wasn't sure how much he knew, but he knew enough, because Clarke Fallon's eyes narrowed. 'I was dripping all over her carpet, so I changed downstairs. I know the way. Agent Triplett?'

The kitchen was filled to bursting with three women, a child, an enormous dog, trays of baked gingerbread men, and something bubbling in a pot on the stove that smelled like heaven. Adam's stomach growled, reminding him that he hadn't eaten since the power bar Deacon had given him.

Behind him, Trip groaned. 'Damn, that smells good. I could eat an entire cow.'

Bailey was pulling another tray of cookies from the oven, Delores was peeling potatoes at the sink, and Kendra chilled at the kitchen table, looking more relaxed than Adam had ever seen her. He knew the feeling. He'd found peace at Meredith's table too.

'No, Angel,' Hope scolded the dog, who was nosing the plate in her hands. Adam couldn't blame the dog because there were three un-iced gingerbread men on the plate. 'They're for the detectives.' She crossed the kitchen with her offering. 'They're warm.' Her eyes twinkled with mischief. 'But naked. Sorry.'

Trip couldn't control his laugh this time, and it came snorting out. 'Naked cookies? Miss Kendra told you to say that, didn't she?'

Kendra grinned up at Trip. 'Not gonna lie.'

Bailey just shook her head. 'Hope,' she said, exasperated.

Hope waggled her brows. 'I'm going to get punished later, but it was worth it. One is for Mr Diesel, okay?'

Adam took the plate. 'I'll make sure he gets it,' he promised with a smile. 'Thanks.'

Hope gave him a long, long look, her smile fading. 'Please find the shooter soon.'

'I'll do my very best,' Adam promised again, far more gravely, because she looked so worried and because she'd said *the shooter* – a term no nine-year-old should ever know.

'Have you guys eaten?' Delores asked them.

'No,' Trip said before Adam could get out a word.

'But we can't stay,' Adam said, wishing it weren't so.

Delores waved them toward the stairs with a smile. 'Then I'll fix you both a plate to take with you.'

Thanking her, they went down the stairs that Adam remembered so damn well. The wall was paneled in light wood, giving the narrow stairwell a much larger feel. It opened to a great room, paneled the same way. There was a comfortable sofa and two loveseats arranged like a smile, all facing the giant flat screen on the wall. This was where Meredith and her girlfriends watched movies once a month. It was cozy. Welcoming. Just like her.

'Finally,' Diesel said, looking up from his laptop, sitting behind a desk in the far corner of the room. 'Took you long enough to get here. Hurry up. I smell food upstairs.'

Adam crossed the room. 'What did you find out?'

Diesel lifted a dark brow. 'You have a chance to view footage of the school track, church, and grocery store?'

133

'Yes,' Adam said. 'I know who I'm looking for. Obviously, you do too.'

'She could tell me,' Diesel said quietly, responding more to Adam's arch tone than his words. 'I'm not a cop.'

Adam sighed. 'I'm sorry. You're right.'

'Nah. I'm sorry. Shouldn't have sent that text. That was asshole-ish of me.'

Noting Trip's curious gaze, Adam huffed a chuckle. 'Yes, it was. So, tell us what you found before Trip grows old and I grow older.'

Diesel grew abruptly grim. 'Voss is being blackmailed.'

'By whom?' Trip asked.

'Dunno. But it's a hefty sum. I mean, the bastard can afford it, but still. It has to rankle to pay fifty grand. A month.'

Trip sucked in a surprised breath. 'Holy shit. A month?'

'Wow,' Adam said, blinking. 'That's some chunk of change. Where's it going?'

Diesel turned his laptop so that it faced them. 'Voss keeps PDFs of his bank statements. This is his computer's hard drive, not his bank account, but the information is the same.' He'd highlighted several transactions. 'Money's going to an offshore account. Turks and Caicos.'

'Of course,' Adam murmured. He didn't ask how Diesel had gained access to Voss's hard drive. He did not want to know. 'When did the payments start?'

'Six months ago,' Diesel said.

'When did Meredith start seeing his kid?' Trip asked.

'About three weeks ago,' Diesel said. 'I had to ask Faith. Meredith wouldn't tell me.'

'Faith did?' Trip asked, clearly surprised. 'Isn't she a therapist too? I thought she'd follow the same rules.'

Adam shrugged, not nearly as surprised. 'Faith was stalked by a murderer a year ago. It's how she and Deacon met. I think the experience made her a little more pragmatic about bending the rules.' He frowned, thinking. 'Was Meredith the child's first therapist?'

'Damn, you boys are smart,' Diesel drawled. 'Nope. Merry's her third therapist.'

Adam scowled at him. 'Merry?'

Diesel attempted an innocent look, but didn't come close to pulling it off. The ass was just yanking Adam's chain. 'That's what her gramps calls her.'

'Yeah,' Adam said. 'Whatever. Her third therapist, huh. Where does Mrs Voss fit?'

'Dunno. Didn't ask. I mean, hell, do I have to do all your work for you?'

Adam found himself chuckling. 'I'll ask Faith myself. Does, uh, does Meredith know about any of this?'

'No,' Diesel said flatly. 'She showed me a photograph of him on her cell phone. She took it when he was getting into his Lamborghini after following her around the grocery store. The photo got his license plate too. Vanity tag. Not like there are a million Lambos out there, but you can prove Voss's was there.'

She's smart. Adam had to school his face so that he didn't smile with grim pride. Grim, because she shouldn't have had to be smart in that way. That asshole should never have tried to intimidate her. 'And nobody will know you've hacked in?'

'Nope. Nobody ever knows when I do.'

'God,' Trip muttered. 'Remind me to never piss you off.'

'You wouldn't be worth my trouble,' Diesel said. 'You don't break the law.'

'Pffft.' Trip looked pretty grim himself. 'I'm here, talking to you.' Then he shrugged. 'At least we know what evidence we need to get legally.'

A muscle twitched in Diesel's cheek. 'Innocents suffer because the bad guys have no qualms about breaking the law. Think of me as a middleman. A confidential informant.'

'A CI who's an evil genius,' Trip said, and Diesel seemed to relax.

Adam sorted through the details in his mind. 'At least we know where to start.'

'The wife?' Trip asked.

'Living with her sister,' Diesel commented.

135

Adam remembered the plate of cookies he held. 'You earned all of these.'

'Not all of them.' Trip snatched one of the gingerbread men from the plate. 'Give him yours if you want to. I'm starving.'

Adam broke the head off his cookie and popped it in his mouth. 'That's really good.' He handed the plate to Diesel. 'Thanks, man. I owe you one. I mean it.'

'Don't mention it. I'm one of Meredith's fans. She does good work for kids.' A shadow passed over his face. 'Wish I'd had someone like her when I was a kid.' He pointed to the stairs. 'Go put Voss away. Please.'

'Yeah,' Adam said gruffly. 'We will.'

Nine

The phone call had come during the last stanza of 'O Holy Night', his solo in the Christmas cantata. He'd had his ringer on mute, but he'd felt the vibration in his pocket and had to fight the urge to stop mid-note and answer it. He'd set up an individual ringtone and vibration pattern for Butch, because he only communicated when it was necessary.

He made nice with the hand-shaking and smiling at all the church members for as long as he could before bolting outside in the freezing cold, still wearing his choir robe. He redialed Butch as he walked. 'What?' he asked.

'I couldn't find Shane Baird.'

The third in Linnea's little trio. 'Where did you look?'

'Started with the dorm address you gave me. The guy at the desk is his friend. Kid gave me lip and pushed the panic button.'

His heart sank. 'Tell me you weren't captured on security footage.'

'Of course not. And even if the kid does talk to the cops, I was wearing my face.'

His facial prosthetics. Without them, Butch looked even more frightening, his face destroyed in the fire that had brought them together, actually. Meth lab fires, unfortunately for Butch, burned hot.

'All right,' he said. 'What happened then?'

'I left the dorm, but stuck around the campus. Figured Shane's

137

friend had to leave sometime and he did. Drove his car to a Burger King off campus. I waited till he came out, but he didn't. A girl did. They must have done a key switch because she drove his junk heap away. I'm following her now. What do you want me to do?'

'Find out who she is,' he snapped. 'Then find her damn car.'

Butch grunted. 'I knew that part. I meant, how far am I allowed to go?'

'Do whatever you want. Just don't leave any loose ends.' Because he had enough of those right now, thank you very much.

'Sure, boss. I'll let you know what I find out. Oh, wait. You still there?'

'Yes,' he asked, forcing patience. 'What else?'

'Uh, have you seen the Internet since you been in the church?'

'No. Why?'

'They got a photo of the Gold kid. Somebody got him on video, real clear, right before his head exploded. It's all over the news.'

'Fuck,' he muttered. It would only be a matter of time before Andy was identified and he didn't know what the kid had in his apartment that could connect to Linnea. He did not want the cops to find her first. 'I'll take care of it. You just bring me Shane Baird.'

Ending the call, he drew a breath and reset his own face, his expression smiling and beatific. He knew this because he practiced in the mirror every single day.

Cincinnati, Ohio,
Saturday 19 December, 9.35 P.M.

Adam and Trip silently climbed the stairs to Meredith's kitchen where Kendra waited by the door, a large brown paper sack in each hand. She studied Trip's face first, smiling at whatever she saw there. 'Food,' she said, handing Trip his bag. 'Roast beef on Bailey's homemade bread. There's a bowl of stew, some cookies, and a slice of pumpkin pie.' She patted his stomach fondly. 'It ought to keep you going for an hour. Maybe two.'

Trip grunted his thanks, then pecked her cheek. 'Thank you. I'll call you later.'

'You do that.' She turned to Adam, her smile disappearing completely. She was all cop, stern to the point of almost-hostile. 'Your bag's got the same. I was tempted to put ipecac in your stew, but Bailey reminded me that was not legal.'

Okay, no almost about it. Totally hostile. Adam's gaze flew across the kitchen to where Bailey and Delores were quietly working. Bailey was kneading a lump of dough with her fists and Delores was decorating gingerbread men, deftly squeezing icing from a bag. Bailey gave him a silent nod, as if affirming she'd stepped in to avert his being poisoned.

'Thank you?' Adam said, making it a question, which made Bailey smile.

'I did it more for me,' Bailey said. 'I'd prefer Hope not having to go caroling at jail because Kenny's behind bars.'

'Well, as long as your motivation is pure,' he said dryly and she chuckled.

Kendra was not amused. She shoved the bag into his hands. 'Do not hurt Meredith,' she hissed. 'She is ready to break and it is scaring us to pieces.'

He deserved the warning, felt the shame wash over his face. But he knew the truth. 'She's stronger than you think.' Meredith would survive if he walked away. *But I would not.* He swallowed hard. 'But she shouldn't have to be so strong.'

Kendra's expression softened minutely. 'What are you gonna do about that?'

'Kenny,' Bailey admonished. 'Not our business. Let him go. He has a job to do.'

'I'm going to try to fix it,' he answered nonetheless.

Kendra didn't look convinced, but she also didn't look homicidal anymore either. 'When?' She held up a hand when Bailey started to admonish her again. 'I just need to know when I need to be here to pick up the pieces if he fucks it up.'

Shaking her head, Delores put the bag of icing aside and brought Adam the cookie she'd been decorating. The gingerbread man had a small star on the left side of his chest, what looked like a gun at his waist, and a square box drawn over where his heart should be. The star and the gun he understood, but the box with the little clump of icing in its middle was a mystery. 'What is that?' he asked, pointing.

'It's supposed to be a keyhole,' Delores said.

'Why?' he asked. 'I mean, why a keyhole?'

Her smile was guileless. 'You've got a heart, Adam, but you keep it locked away most of the time. Except I've seen it,' she added in a stage whisper.

'When?' Kendra's genuine surprise was another well-deserved kick in Adam's gut.

Delores continued to smile up at him. 'Do you think I don't know who comes to clean out the cages in my animal shelter before you think I'm awake?'

Adam's cheeks heated again, this time in embarrassment. *Busted.* 'I have no idea what you're talking about.'

Delores just laughed, a happy sound like bells. 'I have security cameras outside my house, in the shelter, even outside in the puppy pens. Stone installed them. It lets him sleep at night, without standing guard on my front porch.' She pressed her index finger to Adam's chin, closing his mouth, which had fallen open.

He shouldn't have been so surprised. Stone O'Bannion was head over heels for Delores and the man was no fool. He and Diesel worked closely on those *Ledger* articles exposing child-harming lowlifes. Diesel did the digging and Stone did the writing – and neither of them ever got caught. They were careful.

I should have looked for cameras, dammit.

Delores patted his shoulder. 'Stone says thank you, by the way. Saves him from having to clean the cages all the time. Between you, Stone, and Diesel, I haven't cleaned a cage in months.' Her gaze flicked over his shoulder. 'And I suddenly need to do something in the other room. Bailey? Kendra? I need your help.'

He didn't need to be a detective to know that Meredith stood behind him in the doorway. Bailey cleaned dough from her hands with a smirk and, still scowling, Kendra gave him the 'I'm watching you' sign as they dutifully filed from the room, Delores's giant dog trailing faithfully after them.

For a long moment he stood frozen, bag of food clutched in his hands, unable to face her. Then he turned in place and looked at her. Really looked at her. She looked . . . shocked, her zen veneer nowhere to be seen. Her green eyes were wide, her lips slightly parted, her brows crunched in question. She clasped her hands together in a white-knuckled grip.

But he couldn't move. He could barely breathe. *Don't fuck this up.*

'I . . .' She blew out a breath. 'You clean cages at the shelter for Delores?'

He winced, because he could hear the hurt in her voice. 'I have. Before. A few—' He stopped the lie before it passed his lips. It hadn't been a few times. It had been at least twice a week. Every week. 'I wanted to help.'

Her slender throat worked as she fought to swallow. 'And you volunteer at Mariposa House.' Her green eyes grew abruptly shiny. 'When I'm not there.'

Oh shit. Not tears. He could not deal with tears. He didn't have time to figure out tears. He took a step forward. 'Meredith.'

She shook her head, holding up a hand to ward him off. 'No, it's okay. I'm getting the picture, Adam.' Her chin came up and in a fluid motion she blinked and dashed the tears off her cheeks with impatient fingers. 'You want to be part of the group. Of the circle. Just . . . not with me.' Her smile reappeared, that zen smile he was growing to despise. 'And that's okay. They're your friends and family too. It doesn't have to be awkward. I won't make this hard for you.'

His mouth went dry, words dying on his tongue. Once again, she'd misunderstood. *Because she doesn't know the truth. Tell her the goddamn truth.*

He closed his eyes for the span of one heartbeat, opened them to find her returning to the living room. Over her shoulder he could see Kendra standing by the front window like a fucking sentry, arms crossed over her chest, motioning to the door with her head.

Oh, for God's sake. Do something. Now.

'Wait,' he ground out, reaching to grab Meredith's arm. He pulled her into the kitchen, dragging her past the doorway, away from the prying eyes in the next room.

'Adam,' she protested as he backed her against the refrigerator. 'What the—'

He silenced her with his mouth, taking her lips with a desperate ferocity that had him trembling. He hadn't planned this. He hadn't wanted to do it this way. But . . . *Go big or go home.*

He dropped the bag, not caring where it fell, and dug his fingers into her hair, lifting her face to perfect their fit. She was unresponsive, stunned into immobility. At first. Then she made a noise in the back of her throat, a hungry little moan, and he was lost.

This. This was what he'd needed, what he'd craved. More than the booze. More than anything else. Everything else faded away, the noise in his mind fading as he kissed her and kissed her and . . . drank her in. Like air. She was *necessary.*

Her hands cradled his face, so gently he wanted to cry. His chest hurt with the need to weep. From relief that she was letting him touch her. From sorrow that he'd hurt her. From regret at the time he'd wasted.

Not wasted, he told himself as he drew back, only far enough to breathe. It wasn't wasted. It was important that he'd taken the time. Reclaimed himself. So that he could now tell her why he'd stayed away. He hoped she'd understand.

Her eyes were closed, her russet lashes dark against the cream of her skin.

'Everything you thought . . .' He trailed off, words failing him. 'You were wrong.'

Her breasts brushed his chest with the breath she drew. 'About?'

'I was not avoiding being with you.' Her eyes opened, clearly disbelieving. She started to retreat, to twist away, but he stopped her, sliding one hand from her hair down her back, holding her in place. 'Wait. I mean—' He jerked his gaze to the ceiling, cursing under his breath before dropping his eyes to meet hers again. 'I mean I was avoiding you, but not for the reasons you're thinking.'

God. He wanted a drink. Needed a drink. He was shaking.

'Shh,' she soothed, relaxing against the refrigerator, no longer trying to run. 'What were your reasons?'

He glanced over his shoulder to the open doorway that led to her living room. 'I can't tell you right now. I have to do an interview and there are way too many people in your house.' Closing his eyes, he leaned his forehead against hers, sighing when her fingers raked through his hair, petting him. Gentling him. 'I'll be back. I promise.'

'All right,' she murmured. 'I've waited this long.'

His shoulders sagged, relieved. 'You may still throw me out when I'm done, but I want it to be for the right reasons.'

Her fingers stilled. 'Um, was that supposed to make me feel better?' she asked. ''Cause it didn't.'

Gripping the soft folds of the back of her sweater, he forced himself to look at her when he said, 'I'm clumsy with words. Around you, anyway. Meredith, I . . .' He shuddered out a breath. 'I want you so much, I can't think straight.'

Her breath hitched, eyes growing shiny once again, even as her mouth curved. 'Then I'll be patient.'

'Thank you. I have to go now.' He groaned. 'And I'm going to have to brave the gauntlet in there.' He was raw inside. He wasn't looking forward to the looks of interest, pity, and suspicion, depending on whose face he saw.

'Then go down the stairs and out the back,' she said softly. 'You'll only see Diesel and he's clumsy with words too.'

He found himself laughing. 'Maybe that's why we get along so well. We don't say much when we're working at Mariposa.' It was with great regret that he pulled her hands from his hair. 'I will come back. Tonight if I can. Tomorrow for sure.'

'I'll be here.'

He sobered abruptly. 'Please do be. I won't be able to do my job if I'm worrying about you getting hurt because you're out somewhere.'

Her brows lifted. 'You think I'm going anywhere? The horde may be here to keep me company, but they're also here to keep me *here*.'

'I'm glad.' He took a few steps back, dropping her hands only when the distance between them necessitated it. He made a break for the basement door, like the coward he was, and was halfway down the stairs when she called his name.

143

She stood in the doorway, holding the bag of food. 'Your dinner.'

He ran back up, unable to keep himself from taking another hard kiss. 'Thanks,' he said, and nearly stumbled when his foot hit only air. He kept himself from falling only by gripping the handrail. Rolling his eyes at the smile she tried to bite back, he turned and jogged down the rest of the stairs without looking back.

Diesel lifted his eyes when Adam approached. 'Back so soon?'

'Don't be an asshole,' Adam said without heat. 'Where's the back door?'

Diesel pointed to a hallway. 'Through there. Lock's a fucking joke.'

'I'll fix it.'

Diesel waved him off. 'Her grandpa already plans to. It'll keep him occupied for part of tomorrow so he doesn't drive her fucking crazy, hovering.' He tilted his bald head. 'Did you fix things with her?'

'Not all the way, but I'll be back. Tell her grandfather not to shoot me when I do. It may be really late.'

'Text me. I'll be up. I'll let you in through the back if the house is still full of people. Right now you are persona non grata with the ladies.'

Adam nodded, relieved. 'Thanks, man. You gonna keep searching?'

'Always. I'll let you know if I find anything else.'

'Thanks, man. Later.'

'Adam.'

Diesel's uncertain tone had Adam pausing mid-step. 'Yeah?'

'I'm . . . I'm available,' he said uncomfortably. 'If you need to go a round in the ring or just run till you run off the need.'

Adam blinked at him. 'Excuse me?'

Diesel sighed. 'You know Stone went through rehab, right?'

Adam nodded, wary beyond words. He knew that Stone had been addicted to heroin, but he didn't know what Diesel's role had been in Stone's recovery. 'Yeah. And?'

'I was . . . I was there for him. We lifted weights or ran together, at the track, in the park. So that he stayed sober. Until he could do it on his own.'

Adam sucked in a lungful of air, let it out slowly while he contemplated his reply. 'You checked me out?' he asked, pointing to the laptop again.

Diesel shook his head hard. 'No. Absolutely no. I can just tell. I see your eyes go glassy sometimes, when someone around you has a beer. And, man, the volunteering? That's a total giveaway. You've been making amends all over the damn place. I just wanted to tell you that you don't have to do it alone. That's all.'

Adam exhaled in a rush, sudden fear and gratitude warring with one another. 'Did you tell anyone?'

'No. And I don't think anyone else has noticed. If they have, nobody's gossiping about it. I didn't want to tell you that I knew, but today's been rough for you. The kind of day a man can fall off the wagon and it would be hard to blame him. But you'd blame yourself. That's why you've stayed away, isn't it? From Meredith?'

Adam nodded once, unwilling to talk about it until he'd talked to her. 'Thank you.' He held up his fist and Diesel bumped it. 'I mean that, Diesel. See you later.'

Cincinnati, Ohio,
Saturday 19 December, 9.45 P.M.

Linnea's eyes darted side to side, taking in the neighborhood, as Dr Dani pulled her car onto a side street. 'What is this place?' she murmured.

Dr Dani looked over at her with a slight frown. 'I'm sorry, you're sitting on my deaf side. I didn't hear your question.'

Linnea frowned back. 'You have a deaf side?'

Dr Dani's frown became a smile. 'I do.' She tapped her right ear. 'I have a type of hearing aid, but my battery is running low. Are you worried about the neighborhood?'

Linnea shrugged. 'A little.'

'It can be dicey after dark, but you'll be perfectly safe inside. I called ahead and they saved some supper for you.'

145

Linnea nearly slumped in relief. The clinic had given her a few protein bars and some juice, but they hadn't been nearly enough to fill her hungry stomach. 'Thank you.'

The doctor parallel parked her car expertly, reminding Linnea of Andy. Which made her eyes sting. *Not yet. Not here.* Not until she was alone. Then she could cry. Until then, she didn't want anyone to ask questions because she wasn't sure she'd be able to keep from spilling her secrets to anyone kind enough to listen. And that would be the end of kindness. She'd be hauled off to jail and they'd throw away the key.

'We're here,' Dr Dani announced. 'This is a shelter run by St Ambrose's. The head nun is a friend. Her name is Sister Jeanette. She's a retired nurse with a lot of experience with your kind of injury. And your medical condition.'

Linnea stiffened. 'You told her I'm positive?'

The doctor frowned. 'No. Of course I didn't. I'm not allowed to tell her that, but I know that she's had many women come through her shelter who were positive, just like you.' Her frown had faded and she was smiling gently once again. 'I should have the results of your viral load tests in a few days. I'll call Sister Jeanette and she'll have you call me. I will never tell her anything about your condition without your written consent.'

'Thank you.'

'You shouldn't thank me. That's your legal right. I'm merely obeying the law. Once we know what your viral loads are, we can get you the medication you need.'

Linnea nodded, having no intention of taking the medication. She'd sell it as soon as she got it. It was of no use to her now. She was a dead woman walking. 'Okay.'

'Good. Now, let's discuss what to expect. There will be a locked door that we'll be buzzed into. It's not a prison. You are there voluntarily. You can leave at any time. But someone will need to buzz you out. Whoever is on duty will do so with no questions asked, but you won't be allowed to return until the shelter opens its doors again tomorrow at five p.m. We're only coming in late because I called ahead to get permission. Okay?'

Linnea didn't like that, but she nodded again. If the door was locked, he couldn't get in. 'Will they make me leave tomorrow?'

'I'm not sure. Policy is that residents don't stay during the day, but they make exceptions for the ill and injured. So you will probably be allowed to stay tomorrow if you wish. But not if you leave. What else? Oh, they'll have clothes in your size. I did give that info to Sister Jeanette. They'll also have a coat for you to keep. I'll need to take the one you're wearing back with me.'

Linnea had never expected to be allowed to keep the coat. It was too nice. 'I understand. Someone else will need to use it.'

Dr Dani's smile was so kind that it almost hurt. 'It's actually my coat,' she said.

Linnea gasped. 'I took your coat?'

'No, I loaned you my coat. And it's all right. I'll need it back, but I'm okay for now. My car's heater works really well. I would have been overheated in my coat.'

Linnea's eyes blurred with sudden tears. She'd thought it odd that the doctor only wore a cardigan. 'Th—' She shuddered out a breath, unable to speak her thanks.

'You're welcome. Now, about the coat you were wearing.'

Linnea squeezed her eyes shut, willing herself not to dissolve into sobs. She'd already cried too much tonight and she had a headache. But it was so hard not to cry at the memory of the doctor putting her coat in a red biohazard bag because she'd bled on it while sitting on it in the cab.

'It was important to you?' Dr Dani asked.

Linnea managed a nod. 'It . . . it was a gift. From someone who l-loved me.' From Andy. It was the only thing she had left from him since she'd left the switchblade embedded in *his* arm. *Hope he gets gangrene and dies. But not before I can kill him myself.*

Which made no sense. *I'm so tired.*

She'd have to get another knife as soon as she got out of the shelter. Or maybe even a gun. Something especially deadly because she might not get more than one chance to kill him. She needed to make the most of the opportunity. But she could think about that later.

147

The doctor bit her lip thoughtfully. 'Tell you what. I'm going to submit your coat to the police along with the rape kit, the clothes you . . . appropriated from the hotel, and the clothes you brought in the plastic bag.'

The clothes she'd bled on. 'I understand,' she whispered.

'But if they don't need the coat as evidence, I'll see if we can get it cleaned for you.'

Linnea's eyes spilled over. 'Why? Why would you do that for me?'

'Because I understand the sentimental value it has for you. My brother has a coat that our stepfather gave him, right before our stepfather and mother died in a car accident. Deacon has other coats, but that one is really important to him.' She sighed. 'And because someone needs to be kind to you, Denise.'

Denise. Linnea kept having to remind herself that was her name now. For as long as she stayed alive. 'I . . . never expected any of this. I would have been happy to have a safe place to sleep.'

'You should expect more,' Dr Dani said simply. 'Let's go. I need to get back to the clinic. My dinner break is nearly over.'

She'd . . . Linnea shook her head numbly. The doctor had given up her dinner break too. *For me.* She had the sudden need to do something . . . honorable. To pay the woman back for her kindness.

I need to use a phone. I need to tell the police about the SUV. She could do that much.

She followed Dr Dani from the car to an old building with a heavy wooden door. It pulled open with a small creak and Linnea found herself . . .

Oh God. A church. Linnea scuttled backward, unwilling to move another step. Dr Dani turned to search her face, the woman's own expression questioning. 'We need to walk through the sanctuary to get to the shelter. It's downstairs. That's where they'll buzz us in.' She tugged Linnea farther inside, then pulled the heavy door closed with a thud that had her flinching.

'I can't be in a church.' Not after the things she'd done.

'Of course you can.' The doctor's voice was, once again, too kind.

'No.' She could feel herself begin to hyperventilate. 'I've done too much.'

148

'You've survived. Come with me. You can come up with other options besides a shelter beneath a church once you've had a good night's sleep.'

Linnea reluctantly followed until they came to another set of doors. On this door the doctor knocked, then stood back, pointing to the peephole. 'So Jeanette will know it's us,' she explained.

A few seconds later Linnea heard a beep and the door opened to a hallway lit with wall sconces that flickered like natural candlelight, but they were all electric. A sweet-faced older lady with a white blouse and black skirt stood there, a smile of welcome on her face.

'Dr Dani,' the woman said, hugging the doctor after closing the door behind them. Linnea heard the lock quietly click. She was trapped. She looked side to side, all around, panic building until the doctor touched her back for the briefest of moments.

'Denise,' she said. 'You're safe here. Remember? You can leave at any time.'

Denise. Yeah. She wished she'd at least gotten a fake ID with an L name. She was going to give herself away by forgetting her own damn name. Wordlessly, Linnea nodded.

'This is Sister Jeanette,' the doctor continued. 'She's one of the good guys. She's got a bed for you to sleep in tonight.'

'And a warm coat,' the sister added with a smile.

Linnea removed the doctor's coat and gave it back to her. 'I didn't bleed on it,' she whispered, hoping the old nun had bad hearing.

Dr Dani's lips quirked up. 'I know. I'm the one who bandaged you all up. I'm an expert bandage-upper.' Quickly she searched the pockets. 'There's something here for you. I found it in your other coat but forgot to tell you that I put it in this pocket. Ah, here it is.' A small white square of paper lay on her palm.

That's mine? Linnea stared, having trouble remembering where she'd gotten it. *Oh. Right.* Now she remembered. The piece of paper she'd found in the SUV when she'd been searching for cash. She took it from the doctor's outstretched hand. 'Thank you.'

'If you'll follow me,' the nun said, 'I'll warm up your supper and then you can shower and go to sleep.'

149

Dr Dani gave her arm another one of those feather-light touches. 'You have my number at the clinic now. Call if you have any issues. Even if I'm not there, I'll get the message.'

'Thank you,' Linnea said once again. 'I won't forget you, as long as I live.' *So, like, for another week. Max.*

'Sister Jeanette, it's always a pleasure,' Dr Dani said to the nun and then she was gone, buzzed through the locked door, back into the sanctuary.

'Come with me,' the nun said. 'I'll show you to the kitchen.' She started walking, her step heavy. 'Our priest is Father Bishop. He's a very kind man and a trained therapist, if you're needing to talk with anyone.'

Linnea found herself truly smiling for the first time in days. 'Father Bishop?'

'He likes to be called Father Trace, his first name, but I like to tease him,' the nun confided. 'It's about all the fun I get these days.'

She opened another door, this one to a large, industrial-style kitchen with gleaming stainless steel fixtures, appliances and countertops. The table was old, but homey-looking. 'Sit, child. I'll bring your plate to you. I hope you like chicken.'

'I'd like anything, ma'am,' Linnea said truthfully. 'I'm very hungry.'

The nun paused. 'How long since you've had a normal meal?'

Since before she'd been grabbed from Jolee's apartment Thursday night. She'd fled to Jolee's after Andy had seen her with *him* at that motel, and had accused her of sleeping with him. That Andy had died believing she'd willingly sold herself was a dull blade in her heart. 'Two days. I think. The doctor gave me two protein bars and some juice.'

'That'll keep you from keeling over, but it's not a proper meal,' the sister said, clucking her tongue.

'Can . . . can I use your bathroom?'

The nun pointed to a door just beyond the kitchen. 'In there.'

'Thank you.' Linnea shut the door behind her and searched the walls and ceilings for cameras. Because she still trusted no one. Not even Dr Dani or the sweet-faced nun. But there were no cameras

150

visible and Linnea sat on the toilet seat and unfolded the little square of paper. For a long moment she stared at it, unsure of what she was looking at.

It was actually just a fragment, the edges ragged. It was kind of rectangular in shape, but had obviously been part of a larger piece of paper. Linnea squinted at the print. It was smudged in places, like it had gotten wet. With drops.

Tears? Maybe. But she could still read the words.

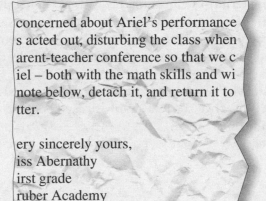

concerned about Ariel's performance
s acted out, disturbing the class when
arent-teacher conference so that we c
iel – both with the math skills and wi
note below, detach it, and return it to
tter.

ery sincerely yours,
iss Abernathy
irst grade
ruber Academy

Below the note was a dotted line and below that, an aborted attempt at a signature. The best Linnea could tell, someone had started to write *Mrs*.

Well, it seemed a first-grader named Ariel was not doing well in school. A school that contained the letters – *ruber*. The fragment of the signature was done in a childish printed scrawl. A child trying to forge her parent's signature perhaps? God only knew that Linnea had done the same when she'd been in trouble at school. But she needn't have bothered. Her own mother had never cared a whit about Linnea's schooling. It was free babysitting in her mother's eyes.

But the 'signature' on the page? That was no legit signature for sure.

The big question was, who was Ariel and had she dropped the fragment of the note into the seat pocket of the SUV or had someone else? If it had been Ariel, what the fuck had a first grader been doing in *his* SUV?

Linnea needed to find out, because this was a clue she could chase down when she left this place. Folding the paper back up, she hid it in the socks she'd been given at the clinic. Then she flushed the toilet so that the nun wouldn't wonder what she was doing in the bathroom, washed her hands, and went back to the table where a bowl of wonderful-smelling soup had been set at her place, steaming hot, a plate of brown bread next to it.

The first bite brought new tears to her eyes. She cried quietly as she ate, unsurprised when the nun slid a box of tissues onto the table next to her.

'Can I touch your hair?' Sister Jeanette asked and Linnea nodded, her tears becoming sobs when the nun simply stroked her hair.

Like Andy used to do.

I'm so sorry, Andy. I'm so damn sorry. I will make this up to you. I promise.

Ten

Meredith's scent still filling his head, Adam met Trip in Candace Voss's driveway. He was grateful for the cold air tonight, a needed smack in the face to help him to focus on his job and not the kiss that he'd relived over and over as he'd driven across town.

To interview Candace Voss. Because her husband was their best suspect. *So focus.*

The house at the top of the driveway belonged to Mrs Voss's sister, with whom she and her daughter had been staying for the past few months. It was a normal-sized house in a normal neighborhood. Nothing fancy. Certainly nothing like the house Candace had called home with Broderick Voss.

'Did Faith tell you why Mrs Voss left her husband?' Trip murmured.

Adam had called Deacon's fiancée on his way over. 'Infidelity was the only thing the wife told them when she sought Meredith for counseling. The little girl's name is Penny.'

Trip's brows shot up. 'As in money?'

'As in Penelope. The sister is Dianne Glenn. She's single and has lived here for ten years. Works for one of the law firms downtown.'

'Any trouble or reports from either the sister or the wife?'

'Nope. At this point, I'd be happy knowing why his wife left him. I don't expect her to spill her guts about any abuse – if it happened – on this first visit.'

'But,' Trip said with a frown, 'if she left him because of infidelity,

153

it means she knows about the infidelity, so it's unlikely that it's connected to the blackmail.'

'Maybe. If he's contemplating politics, the blackmail might be to keep other people from finding out. Or it could be something darker than garden-variety cheating.'

'It was enough for the wife to take the child,' Trip noted.

'And enough for the husband not to file for joint custody, even. We're not going to find out anything by standing here, that's for damn sure. Let's go.'

Trip followed him up the walk that was only wide enough for them to walk single file. Adam knocked and waited. A porch light came on above them and he could see shadows moving in the hallway through the filmy curtains that covered the slim windows on either side of the front door. Adam held out his badge and beside him, Trip did the same.

The door opened a crack, the chain still attached. 'Yes?' a woman asked.

'I'm sorry to bother you at this hour, ma'am. My name is Detective Kimble. I'm with the Cincinnati Police Department. This is my partner, Special Agent Triplett, with the FBI.'

'Ma'am,' Trip said politely.

The eye visible through the crack in the doorway widened. 'Police? FBI? Why?'

'We'd like to speak to Mrs Voss. We understand she lives here.'

'I'm her sister. What do you want with her?'

Adam made his stance as non-threatening as possible. 'Just to ask her a few questions. I'm happy to give you our badge numbers so that you can check us out before letting us into your home.'

The woman nodded, still wary, but her sudden relief was unmistakable. 'Yes, please. Do you have a card?'

Adam passed one through the opening and the woman closed the door with an abrupt snap. Adam looked over at Trip. 'We rattled her,' he said, and was surprised to see the other man's forehead bunch in a frown.

'We or me?' Trip asked quietly, his jaw going taut.

It was Adam's turn to frown until he realized what Trip was

really asking. Adam blew out a breath. 'Shit, man. I didn't mean what you think I meant. It's not because you're big or black or a cop or whatever. I meant *we*. Because we're *here*. She opened that door expecting us to be someone else. She was relieved that we were cops.'

Trip visibly relaxed. 'I wonder if Broderick has sent anyone else over to harass them. He's stalked the doc, after all. I wouldn't put it past him.'

'Yeah. Me, either.' He studied Trip's profile. 'We good?'

'Yeah.' Trip's sigh was brooding and almost bitter. 'But I do scare people. Sometimes that comes in handy. But sometimes it really sucks.'

Adam hesitated, then decided to speak, since they were apparently sharing. 'When Isenberg told me that you were my partner, I was happy to hear it. Number one, having you watching my back is one less stress. But mostly . . .' He shrugged uncomfortably. 'You've always been decent to me. Not all the cops are. Feds either.' Some had been great, like Deacon and Isenberg and Wyatt. Some had not. The cops who'd served with his dad? They *really* had not. He deliberately lightened his tone. 'I mean, a guy takes one mental health break and never hears the end of it.'

Trip huffed. 'I knew about the leave,' he said gruffly. 'But you came back, y'know? And you're still here. Still on the job. Still doing for others. So that's the important thing.'

Having spoken their piece, they fell silent, the only sounds the stomping of their feet as they kept warm. Finally, the door opened and Mrs Voss's sister gestured them in.

'I'm sorry you had to stand in the cold for so long.'

'It's quite all right. The last thing we want is to frighten anyone.' Adam smiled. 'Our records show that you are Dianne Glenn. Is that correct?'

The woman looked startled. 'I have no criminal record.'

'Property records, ma'am,' Trip clarified with a smile that seemed to put the woman at ease. 'That's all. Is your sister here?'

'She's getting dressed.' Dianne directed them to a sunken living room, decorated in modern, sleek lines. Which equalled fucking uncomfortable in Adam's experience. 'Please have a seat. Can I get you some coffee?'

'Only if it's no trouble,' Adam said. Dianne disappeared into the kitchen, while he and Trip chose two chairs that looked sturdy enough to hold them. Trip winced when the chair he'd chosen let out an ominous creak.

'Did you break it?' The concerned voice came from a tiny girl who'd slipped down the stairs undetected. Her little face stared at them through the balusters, fascinated.

Trip looked taken aback. 'I don't think so.'

'Are you cops?' the girl asked.

'Yes,' Adam told her. 'Are you Penny?'

Her face scrunched up in displeasure. 'How did you know that?'

A woman came down the stairs then, wearing a silk dress. Her jewelry was classy and understated, her face made up, but subtly so. 'I'd like to know that too. Go on back to bed, sweetheart. I'll be up soon to tuck you back in.'

'Do I have to say my prayers again?'

The woman smiled at her daughter, but the smile was strained. 'No, baby. I think God heard them just fine the first time.' She waited, staring up to the second floor until a door closed. Then she walked toward them, her gait runway-model smooth.

He and Trip stood when she descended the two stairs into the living room. 'I'm Detective Kimble. This is Agent Triplett.'

'Yes, I heard. Please sit down.'

They did, Trip's chair creaking ominously once again. Mrs Voss smiled wanly. 'Don't worry, Agent Triplett. It's just a chair. If you break it, I'll buy my sister another one and we'll have a great story to tell someday.'

Trip didn't look terribly pleased with that, but he nodded anyway.

Adam cleared his throat. 'We're here to talk to you about your husband, Mrs Voss.'

Her brows lifted. 'What has he done?'

'You don't seem surprised,' Adam said.

'I'm not. Now, anyway. My husband has . . . predilections that

156

were unknown to me up until three months ago. I wouldn't have believed you if you'd come to me before then.'

'What kind of predilections, Mrs Voss?' Trip asked.

She looked away, a flush spreading across her face. 'He cheated on me.'

That is not a predilection, Adam thought. Not the way she'd said the word, as if it tasted foul. 'Is that why you left him and took Penny with you?'

Candace inclined her head in a single nod.

Adam leaned forward, lowering his voice, conscious of the child upstairs. 'With all due respect, ma'am, cheating on its own isn't something that would make a visit from law enforcement unsurprising. Was there something specific that he did?' He caught the tightening of her jaw and his stomach gave a lurch. 'Or perhaps who he did it with?'

God. Please don't let it be the little girl. Please.

She gasped. '*No.* Not . . .' She leaned closer. 'Not Penny. Thank God she was a little older than my six-year-old.'

Adam steeled his spine. 'How old, ma'am?'

'Eighteen, or so the one I talked to claimed. I had my doubts. She looked twenty-five, but some of the others looked fifteen. They were college students, though, so . . .' She trailed off with a shrug.

Adam drew a breath that was slightly easier. 'All right. So you're saying that your husband had an affair with a college student?'

Her lips twisted bitterly. 'If by "affair"' – she used air quotes – 'you mean "orgy" and by "college student" you mean "prostitutes," then yes.'

Okay. That *might* explain the blackmail, but the attempted murder of a restaurant full of people? No, that didn't fit. And Adam still wondered how Penny fit into the equation. The child was in therapy. It might be simply because her parents had split up. He hoped so, but he didn't think so. Were that the case, Broderick Voss wouldn't be trying to intimidate Meredith away from treating his daughter.

Unless . . . unless the daughter knew something and he thought she'd told Meredith. 'How is your daughter handling the separation?'

'Not terribly well.' Her eyes narrowed. 'Why? Why are you asking questions about my daughter?'

Adam shrugged slightly. 'She's a sweet-looking kid. I was hoping she didn't know what her father had done.'

Her eyes narrowed further to slits. 'Bullshit,' she said flatly, startling him. He hadn't expected her vocabulary to include that word for some reason. 'What's this got to do with my daughter?'

Adam met Trip's gaze, his own brows lifted, and the younger man nodded.

Adam hoped he was not ruining Meredith's career. 'Okay, we're going to tell you how we got to this point, okay? Because we need you to understand how we came to be here, both here in our investigation and here in your living room.'

Candace leaned back in her chair. 'All right,' she said slowly.

'Have you seen the news today?'

She shook her head. 'No. I have made it a point not to watch the news. Why?'

'There was a shooting in a restaurant on Fountain Square this afternoon. One man was killed, another wounded. An explosive device was disabled.'

'What does this have to do with my husband?' Candace demanded. 'And my child?'

Adam held up his hand, hoping to calm her. 'I promise I'll tell you.' Everything but the hacked bank records. 'The target of the attack was shot at, but not hit. I believe you know her. Dr Meredith Fallon.'

Candace's hand flew to her mouth. 'What? But . . . You think Broderick was responsible? He's a pervert, but he's not violent.'

'Um, not true, Candy.' The sister came out of the kitchen, her arms folded tightly over her chest. 'He's hit you.'

Candace flinched. 'But . . . he wouldn't shoot . . .'

Dianne was angry. 'Fallon told you to come here? She promised us confidentiality.'

Adam held up his hand again. 'That's just it. She did *not* tell us to come here. That's why I was leading you up to this moment. She wouldn't tell us who had threatened her.'

'She outright refused,' Trip added quietly, his voice a deep soothing rumble. The two women seemed to settle. Hell, Adam even felt calmer.

'Then why are you here?' Dianne demanded.

'Wait,' Candace interrupted when Trip attempted to answer. 'Are you saying Broderick threatened Dr Fallon?'

Trip held up a finger, wordlessly asking for their patience. 'She would not tell us the names of any of the parents who'd threatened her because it violated her clients' privacy,' he continued, 'but she *did* tell us where she'd been.'

'Dr Fallon gave us a detailed account of her activities over the last three weeks,' Adam said. 'We obtained footage from surveillance cameras and studied her movements.' He pulled the photographs from his pocket and unfolded them, handing them to Candace.

Her sister stood behind her, viewing the photos over her shoulder.

'Oh my God,' Candace whispered. 'How long has this been going on?'

'About three weeks,' Adam answered. 'Your husband will show up and just smile at her. There is no overt threat, which is why she hasn't reported it.'

'That's why the other two . . .' Dianne murmured, and Candace nodded numbly.

'The other two what?' Trip prompted.

'Penny saw two therapists before Dr Fallon,' Candace murmured. 'Both told us that they were cutting back their hours and would no longer have the available slots for Penny. Do you think he threatened them too?'

'If you give us their names,' Trip said, 'we'll ask them.'

Candace nodded, still looking stunned. 'Of course. Whatever will help.'

'This still doesn't answer why you were asking about Penny,' Dianne said.

Trip's smile was mildly apologetic. 'We figured a child entered into this somehow, because Dr Fallon's clientele is exclusively pediatric and adolescent. We found photos of you, Mrs Voss, with your husband and your daughter online with very little trouble.'

159

'Because Broderick is a fucking attention whore,' Dianne muttered.

'But . . .' Candace shook her head helplessly. 'It doesn't make sense that he'd have Dr Fallon *shot*. Or that he'd kill a lot of other innocent people. And with a bomb?'

Adam had to admit that was true, if only to himself. 'Does he plan to go into politics?'

Candace nodded. 'That's why he got so angry when I walked out.'

Trip lowered his voice again. 'Does he know that you know about the multiple prostitutes?'

'No.' Candace shook her head firmly. 'He believes that I believe it was "only an affair."' Again she used air quotes. 'I didn't want to voice it aloud with him. He'd just find a way to wriggle out of it. Nothing is ever his fault. I decided to cut my losses and get out while I still could.'

Adam studied her. 'Do you believe he would have resorted to violence to stop you?'

'He did,' Dianne insisted. She pulled her phone from her pocket, batting Candace's hands away when she reached for it. 'I'm going to show them. I wanted to report the fucking bastard three months ago. I took pictures the night Candy got here.' She handed her phone to Trip, whose chair was closer.

Trip frowned, then passed the phone to Adam, who had to bite back a wince. Candace Voss sported a dark shiner in the photo, the bruise covering her eye and most of her cheek.

'Were there any other injuries?' Adam managed to ask levelly.

'No.' Candace looked away again. 'Penny saw my face. I told her that I'd fallen down, but she didn't believe me. She told me that she knew it was her daddy who'd done it. I couldn't bear that she knew. That she was so certain. I was so ashamed that I let him hurt me like that. And scared he'd do it again. Or hurt Penny.'

'Is that why she's in therapy?' Trip asked gently.

'No. Well, yes, that too,' she amended. 'Also because I found out about the party because Penny heard it going on and saw . . . something.'

Adam couldn't control his blink of shock. 'He had prostitutes in your home with your daughter present?'

160

Candace shrugged, her shoulders rigid. 'He thought she was asleep.'

'Fucker,' Dianne added under her breath.

Adam fully agreed with that statement. *Poor kid.* 'What exactly did she see?'

'We're not sure,' Dianne said. 'She won't talk about it, but she did tell Candy that there was a naked lady with pink hair in the bathroom when she got up to pee that night.'

'Pink hair?' Adam asked.

'Pink hair and ponytails.' Dianne shrugged. 'That's all we could get out of her.'

'I was away for the evening,' Candace said, her feelings of guilt still apparent. 'I'd gone to a bachelorette party and we were all staying the night so that we could have wine. I was stunned when I got home the next day. Penny said she'd asked her daddy who the lady was once she was gone, but Broderick wouldn't wake up. He was in a drunken stupor.'

And the mental picture of that was enough to banish any of Adam's own need for a drink. For now, at least. *One day at a time. One moment at a time.*

Adam took his notebook from his pocket. 'When was this?'

'September thirteenth,' Dianne said without hesitation. 'Not a day I'll ever forget.'

Candace sighed. 'Me, either. Nor will Penny. I grabbed her and ran from the house. Came straight here because—' Her voice cracked. 'I didn't know where else to go.'

Dianne leaned over Candace's chair to wrap her arms around her sister. 'It's okay. You are always welcome here. You know that. Whatever stupid things we argue about, I love you. Like a sister,' she added teasingly, but both women were close to tears.

Trip cleared his throat. 'You said that you talked to one of the prostitutes, who said she was eighteen,' he said, bringing the women back to the reason for the interview. 'How did you know who to talk to and where to find her?'

Candace's lips curved in a mirthless smile. 'After I brought Penny here, I went back to the house. My plan was to get our things,

161

but as I was coming up to the gate, I saw a bunch of cars going in and realized he was having another party. So I pulled out of security camera range and waited. Just before dawn, three cars emerged. One of the drivers had pink hair. I followed them back to the college campus, but could only follow one of the three cars when they split up to park. I picked Pink Hair. I . . . Well, I may have been a little threatening myself. I told the girl that I'd report her to the university police if she didn't tell me what I wanted to know.'

'Which was?' Adam prompted.

'First, how old were they? Second, how much had he paid them? Third, had he used condoms and, fourth, were they disease free? She swore they were all over eighteen, all students. He'd been hosting a party with some friends and the girls were the "entertainment."' More air quotes. 'She said the men were all pretty high.' Her mouth twisted. 'There had been *drugs* in my *home*. She swore they hadn't had drugs the night before, but I didn't believe her. My baby was exposed to that.' Her voice hoarsened, then broke. She blinked and tears ran down her cheeks.

'How much had he paid them?' Adam asked quietly.

'A thousand each for the night. He's been a regular big-time spender since Buzz Boys went IPO. He was always a prick, but once he got really rich? It was hell. So I left.'

'Did you get this young woman's name?' Trip's voice soothed once more.

Candace laughed bitterly. 'She said it was Kandy – with a K. Kandy Kane.'

'For God's sake,' Dianne muttered.

Again, Adam fully agreed. 'Do you remember what kind of car she drove?'

Candace's lips curved, this time with satisfaction. 'I'll do you one better. I got photos of the license plates for all three hooker-mobiles. I can email you the photos. Some are better quality than others.' Her satisfied smile faded. 'My hands were shaking.'

'When did he hit you?' Trip asked.

'Later that morning. When I'd finished talking to the prostitute, I went back to the house to get our things, mine and Penny's. It was almost dawn and all the cars were gone, so I figured the party was over. I was quiet, because he was drunk and wasted. Again. I just wanted to get our things before he woke up, because he could be vile when he was drunk.'

Yeah. I know all about that. His own father had been that way. Adam was working so hard to ensure he never became like his father. 'But he woke up?'

Candace nodded. 'I was loading the car when he caught me. He did that to my face.' She gestured at her sister's phone. 'He was hauling back to hit me again, so I hit him. I just grabbed a bottle and hit him upside the head. He staggered enough for me to run. I got in the car and he was right behind me.' She shuddered out a breath, shaken. 'I barely got the door closed and got out of there.'

'It was a good thing I unloaded her car as soon as she got here,' her sister said, trembling with fury. 'Because he had it taken away the next day. Towed right out of my driveway. Said it was his car and she wasn't keeping it.'

'But that was okay. Dianne's leased a car for me.' Candace rubbed her forehead fitfully. 'I'm going to have to find a new therapist for Penny. I can't imagine Dr Fallon will keep seeing her after this.'

'I can't imagine she'd turn Penny away,' Adam said firmly. 'That's not who she is. Have you considered filing charges against your husband?'

Dianne arched her brows in an I-told-you-so look and Candace sighed.

'Only a million times, but I'm afraid of him. And before you ask, I've also considered a restraining order, but that would be pointless. He'd just have one of his flunkies do his dirty work. I have consulted with a divorce attorney. We're almost ready to file.'

'And then?' Adam tempered his tone because she seemed to grow more fragile with every word she spoke.

'I haven't thought that far out,' she admitted. 'I need to find a job first. But I'm afraid to leave the house without Dianne. I've been homeschooling Penny because I'm afraid to let her go to school.' She looked up, her expression bleak. 'We're trapped.'

Adam leaned forward. 'Okay, one thing at a time. Even if you

163

feel a restraining order is pointless, you should still file one so that the situation can be documented.' And her old house was under surveillance, so if her husband attempted to leave, he'd be followed. But he wasn't going to tell her that on the off chance that she wasn't as innocent as she claimed. Broderick Voss likely knew he was being watched, but Adam didn't want to spell it out in the event he was unaware. 'We can't provide full-time security, but I can ask for drive-bys. In the meantime, if he does send a flunky, do you have an alarm system?'

'Yes, we do,' Dianne said.

Trip rose, giving the creaky chair a backward glance of relief. 'I'd like to check it before we leave.'

'Please come with me,' Dianne said. 'I'll show you.'

Candace exhaled wearily as Trip left the room with her sister. 'We've been talking about getting a dog. Penny loves that idea, as you might imagine.'

'That was my next recommendation. I have the perfect place for you to go for a dog.' Adam wrote Delores's contact information on the back of his card. 'This woman is a dog whisperer. Many of my friends have adopted dogs from her shelter. Give her a call.'

Candace smiled back, the first true smile she'd shown since he and Trip had arrived. 'I just might do that.'

'Good. My cell's on there too. And my email. If you could send me the photos you took of those license plates, we'd appreciate it.'

'I will. Please, tell Dr Fallon how sorry I am next time you see her.'

'Absolutely.' He hoped his expression remained professional because, inside, the memory of those few minutes against her refrigerator were hitting him hard. 'I'll make sure she knows.' Because he planned to see Dr Fallon very, very soon.

Cincinnati, Ohio,
Saturday 19 December, 10.15 P.M.

'Meredith? You okay in there?'

Meredith sighed at the bathroom door and sank a little deeper into the tub. She'd had twenty minutes of quiet privacy, the most she'd had all day long. This time it was her friend FBI Special Agent Kate Coppola, who was likely armed with several guns and at least one pair of knitting needles. 'I'm fine. Really.'

'I thought I heard you talking to yourself.'

Meredith rolled her eyes. 'If you wanted to know who I was talking to *on the phone*, you could have just asked.'

'Sorry,' Kate said sheepishly. 'I didn't want to seem nosy.'

'That train's already left the station.' It was nice to have people worried about her, but it was exhausting too. 'I was talking to my cousin Alex in Atlanta. Bailey called her and got her all twitterpated. Alex and her husband were going to drop everything and drive here tonight, but I told her that I had plenty of bodyguards and they should leave on Monday like they'd planned.' Because, like Papa, Alex never let her spend Christmas alone. It was Meredith's trigger holiday and her family knew it passed more easily when she was surrounded by their support.

'Yeah . . .' More sheepishness. 'It was pretty crowded downstairs. I can go.'

'Oh, stop,' Meredith said fondly. 'You know I don't want you to go. But I am surprised. I thought you had plans with Decker. I didn't think you were coming today.'

'I wasn't supposed to, but . . .' Kate's self-conscious laugh came through the door. 'I needed to be sure you were all right. I've stayed away for hours, but I couldn't sleep and . . .'

Meredith had to smile. For all her badassery, Kate was a softie who mothered almost as much as Meredith did. 'I'll be out in a few minutes. I've got to rinse my hair.' Because she'd washed it again. It had smelled like the shampoo at the hotel where she'd washed away the remnants of . . . She swallowed, pushing the memory away. She had to stop remembering the shot that had destroyed the young man's head. She'd drive herself crazy.

She'd had to take her anti-anxiety meds twice today. They'd helped, but she didn't want to take any more. Shampooing her hair would let her smell familiar scents. Calming scents. She hoped.

A few minutes later she found Kate sitting in the armchair in the corner of her bedroom, knitting needles clacking rhythmically as a big old dog rested at her feet. 'Hey, Cap,' Meredith crooned, stooping to pet the dog's white muzzle. 'How's he doing?'

'Really well.' Kate gave the dog a fond look. 'We had a scare last week, but it was just a little infection. A round of antibiotics and he seems good as new. The vet says he's got a few years left. Decker and I want to make them good years.' She and her fiancé had adopted the oldest dog in Delores's shelter because the dog had been passed over so many times. 'He's a good dog and he hasn't eaten a single shoe.' She pretended to scowl. 'Unlike Loki. I swear . . .'

Chuckling, Meredith sat on the floor and petted Cap's head when he put it in her lap with a huff of pleasure. 'Puppies are hard work. Delores told you that.'

'I know. Decker's doing most of the training and he's loving it. Don't get him started talking about obedience class. You'd think Loki had just graduated from Harvard or something.' But she was smiling. And then she wasn't, sobering abruptly. 'I stopped by Mariposa before I came here.'

Meredith sighed. 'How is Mallory?'

Kate shrugged. 'Sitting and staring straight ahead. I don't know what to do for her.'

'For now, we just love her.'

'I know, but I don't know how to do that. I was going to stand guard there, but between Colby and Stone, they have things sorted. Nobody needed me. Mallory wouldn't even say hi to me.'

'She had a horrible shock today. Try not to take it personally. She loves you, you know that.' Because the monster who'd held Mallory captive for six long years had tried to kill her when she'd finally escaped, putting her in the hospital with a concussion and a badly broken leg. Meredith and Kate had held her hand in the hospital and had been her first protectors as she'd transitioned into the real world. 'She may just need space.'

Kate winced guiltily. 'Like you do. Like I'm not giving you. Decker told me not to come. That you'd be overrun with people.'

Meredith patted her friend's knee. 'I was earlier, but I think everyone's planning on going home soon except for Kendra and maybe Diesel. And my grandfather, of course.'

'I met him. He's pretty . . . well, like no grandpa I've ever met.'

Meredith chuckled. 'That's the truth. How long can you stay?'

'Depends. How much ice cream you got in your freezer?' She smiled proudly when Meredith laughed. 'Seriously, how long do you need me to stay?'

'Depends. You think you can convince Kendra to go home?'

Kate put down her knitting. 'Why? What did she do?'

'Nothing yet.' Meredith focused on petting Cap's soft coat. 'Adam may come by later and I don't want Kenny to make things awkward.'

'Oh. Well.' The clacking resumed. 'Why is Adam coming by?'

Meredith fought the urge to press her fingers to her lips. They still tingled from that kiss. Hell, her entire body still tingled from that kiss. 'He's going to explain some things.'

Kate grunted. 'That sounds ominous.'

'No, I don't think so.'

'Oh?' Kate's voice became slyly smug. 'Tell me. Tell me everything.'

Meredith laughed again. 'Now I feel like we're at one of Hope's slumber parties.'

'I'll paint your toenails if you tell me everything.'

Cap rolled to his back and Meredith scratched his belly. 'Not yet, okay?'

Again the clacking stopped, but this time Kate gently lifted Meredith's chin. 'I'm just teasing you. You tell me when you're good and ready. I'll always be here to listen. Hell, you listen to me spout off often enough. Somebody needs to be your confidante.'

Meredith's eyes pricked with tears. 'I'm not sure what's happening, but I *am* a little scared to hear what he has to say.' She swallowed, uncomfortable with sharing what little she knew of Adam's secrets, but needing to talk to someone. 'He's stayed away from me for months.'

'I know.' Kate's thumb stroked her cheek just like Meredith's mother used to do. 'We all know. None of us knows why, though.'

'Something's wrong.' Meredith drew a breath, straightened her spine. 'Did you know he's been sneaking into Delores's shelter to clean cages?'

Kate blinked. 'Really? No, I didn't know that. Huh. But I don't really know him that well. We've only worked together a few times. I know he's a good cop and I know he's had some issues in the past.'

'He also spends hours at Mariposa every week. But never when I'm there. He goes out of his way not to be in any space where I am.'

Kate winced. 'That's . . . not promising, hon. Gotta say.'

'Maybe? That's just it. That's what I thought, but tonight he said I thought wrong. So I stepped back and tried to look at it from another direction. I made a few calls and found out he not only volunteers at Mariposa and Delores's, but he routinely works at Dani's clinic and does repairs at Father Trace's shelter. He even assistant coaches a pee wee team that has deaf kids from all over the county. I got that from Faith. Adam spends every free minute helping other people. Plus his actual job.'

'Huh,' Kate said again. 'It's almost like he's trying to atone for something.'

'I thought the same thing.'

'Did Dani have any insight? They grew up together, right?'

'Yeah. Dani said she knew he was fighting demons, but she'd never been able to get him to tell her specifics. I even called Deacon.'

'He'd know better than anyone. They're besties, right?'

'Well, if he knows, he's not saying. Which I can respect. But I don't think he knew either.' Meredith suspected she might be the only one who knew the particular nightmare that haunted Adam, the devastating murder of a child that he'd been unable to stop. But even Meredith didn't know all the details. She only knew that there had been a lot of blood. And that he'd witnessed it happen.

So much blood. He'd said it over and over the night he'd fallen apart in her arms, more than a year ago now. She'd expected him to cry, but he hadn't shed a single tear.

She wondered if he'd managed to do so since.

She glanced at her bed. They'd ended up there that night. Nothing had ever been the same after that. *Not for me.*

She'd assumed it hadn't meant anything to him, but now . . . She gave in to the urge and pressed her fingertips to her lips. That . . . in the kitchen tonight? That was not a pity kiss. She'd had pity kisses before and that was definitely not one.

'Mer?' Kate said softly.

Meredith looked up with a jerk. 'Um . . . sorry. Did you say something?'

'Just your name. Have the two of you . . . Is there anything you want to tell me?'

Meredith smiled ruefully. 'Not particularly. But . . .' She sighed. 'Yes. Once. A year ago. I thought we had something. But he's shut me out ever since.'

'And he's coming by tonight to let you in?'

And if you want me to leave afterward, I will, he'd said. What the hell did that mean?

'Maybe. Sounded like it.'

'Then I'll ensure Kendra is properly occupied because she doesn't trust him at all.'

No, Kendra didn't. 'Thanks, Kate.'

'My pleasure.' She gathered her knitting and shoved it in a bag with kittens printed on the side. 'Now, we were discussing ice cream earlier.'

'It's freezing outside,' Meredith said. 'You really want ice cream?'

'Kenny said she brought you some. Are you holding out on me, Dr Fallon?'

'Never.' Meredith gave the dog a final pat, then rose. 'Let's go eat ice cream. And gingerbread men. And I think there's some pumpkin pie left. We can find a movie and open a bottle of red.'

'Now you're talking. Come on, Cap.'

Cincinnati, Ohio,
Saturday 19 December, 11.15 P.M.

He turned onto the street where Andy Gold had rented a basement apartment, pleased that most of the houses were already dark. It was a Saturday night, but this neighborhood was mostly populated with either old people or families with small kids who had bedtimes. There was nobody out to notice – and importantly – to remember him.

He was actually shocked that no one had identified Andy Gold yet. The kid's picture had been online for hours, clear as day. Gold had a job and went to classes, so somebody was going to know who he was.

He'd planned to have Butch eliminate all trace of Andy Gold, including photos or notes or anything that would lead the cops to Linnea Holmes, but nothing had gone right today. Butch was in Chicago tracking Shane Baird, and this couldn't wait until he got back.

So I'm going to have to deal with Andy Gold's belongings myself.

At least he had the cover of darkness. He wouldn't dream of conducting an op like this in the daylight. He parked on the next street over from Andy's basement apartment and checked the contents of his backpack.

Glass cutters, a fuse, matches, and two jars of a jellied mix of gasoline and soap powder – easy to make and very flammable. He grabbed the large gas can from the back seat, made sure his ski mask was completely covering his face, and made his way into the shadows, moving from the house nearest his SUV, through the backyard, over the four-foot chain-link fence, and up to the rear of Andy's house.

Cutting the glass from the window of Andy's basement apartment, he removed the lids from the jars of homemade napalm and tossed the jars through the window. He then threw one end of the fuse through the window, landing it in the sticky mess and dragging it through until the fuse became submerged. He poured the contents of the gas can on the ground along the back of the house, then lit the fuse and hightailed it out of there.

By the time he reached his car, he could already see the blaze flickering through the basement windows. He'd be safely away before the smoke detectors in the house went off.

Hopefully the residents of the home's upper floors were light sleepers. They'd still be able to get out in plenty of time to call the fire department and most of their house would be saved. He didn't need to burn the whole house down, just Andy's portion of it. By the time the first fire truck arrived, the basement apartment would be no more.

Once he'd left the neighborhood, he pulled into an alleyway, once again changing the plates on the SUV. Just in case one of the neighbors had a security camera. He removed the ski mask and bagged it and the coat he was wearing.

He'd made it to his driveway when his business cell rang with a number that was vaguely familiar. 'Yeah?' he barked, pitching his voice lower than normal.

'You sonofabitch,' a man snarled.

So it would be one of those calls. He activated the voice-changing app he'd installed on his phone, his voice instantly gravelly and unidentifiable as his own. 'Who is this?'

'It's Voss, and you're a fucking asshole. I paid you what you asked.'

Voss. He wanted to sigh. The last thing he needed tonight was the pathetic whining of an arrogant prick. 'Yes, you did. And I've honored my end of the agreement.'

'No, you didn't because the cops were at my bitch sister-in-law's house tonight, talking to my wife.'

He blinked, caught unaware. 'Why would they be talking to your wife at your sister-in-law's house?'

'That's what I'm asking you! And now there are unmarked cars sitting outside my front gate! Cops outside *my* house!'

'Okay, calm down. We have not told a soul. Let's figure this out. Okay?'

'I'll drag you down with me. I'll bury you. I swear it.'

'Calm down. First, how do you know cops talked to your wife?'

'Because I have someone watching the bitch's house. I know when she arrives and when she leaves and I know where my kid is. All the time. My man saw them. One was black and big as a tank. Easily six-six. The other guy was six-two, black hair, wore a black wool coat. They showed badges to my sister-in-law. They stayed for over thirty minutes.'

171

Voss's wife had left him, then. It made no difference financially because it wasn't his wife that Voss was afraid of. It was his potential electorate. *That his wife has left him might look bad.* Depending on the reason she'd left. But first things first.

'What would your wife be able to tell them?' A long silence followed that started to piss him off. 'Voss? What would your wife know that would be damaging to you?'

'That my kid saw one of the girls at the house.' It was a grudging admission.

And a detail that had never come up in their negotiations. *You had hookers in your house when your kid was home?* Voss had no fucking sense.

'So your wife has left you?' *And taken your child? Good for her.* He'd *never* let his own kids see the underbelly of his business. Voss's kid was *six*, for Christ's sake. 'When?'

'Three months ago, but she'll be back,' Voss said, sounding like a petulant child. 'She'll beg me to take her back when her money runs out.'

It was possible, of course. It was also possible the wife was holding out for a settlement of her own. He needed to know what exactly Mrs Voss knew. 'If your wife was aware of your indiscretions, why did you continue paying me to keep your secret?' he asked mildly.

'She doesn't know about the parties. She thinks it was just one hooker, one time. And *she* doesn't have pictures,' Voss added bitterly.

It was a fair point. He had more than just pictures of Voss with more than just one slightly underage hooker. He had video and photos that Voss knew nothing about, video and photos that he'd reveal to Voss when the man announced a bid for the state senate seat he'd been not-so-surreptitiously ogling. Keeping those images from the media would be worth far more to Voss – *and to me* – than the comparatively tame party photos he was paying to keep secret now.

'Mr Voss, I did not tell anyone about our agreement. Tell me more about the cops that visited your wife tonight. Did they have any distinguishing marks? Scars?'

'The black guy was bald, drove a Chevy SUV. The white guy drove a Jeep. My guy got the license plate numbers. He has a buddy on the force who ran them. The Jeep belongs to a detective named Kimble. First name Adam. The SUV is registered to the FBI.'

His gut clenched. *Kimble? With a big black guy built like a tank? Oh, fuck. Just . . . fuck. Goddammit.* He fought to maintain a tone of mild confusion. 'I think I know the officers you mean.' Because the reporters had tried to get statements from both men while they processed the Buon Cibo crime scene earlier that afternoon. Detective Adam Kimble and Special Agent Jefferson Triplett. *Goddammit.* 'If I'm right,' which he knew he was, 'they're the ones who are investigating the shooting that happened downtown today.'

'But . . . what could they possibly want with Candace?' Voss asked, echoing his own thoughts. 'That shooting today was a college kid who tried to shoot some woman. Give me a minute.' A keyboard clacked in the background, then momentary silence. 'Oh shit,' Voss whispered. 'That's insane. *Fallon?* She was the target?'

His gut clenched even harder. 'How do you know Meredith Fallon?'

'She's my kid's shrink. Do they think I'm involved? Am I a *suspect*?' His voice became shrill. 'I had nothing to do with that.'

'Obviously they think you do. Have you had contact with the target?'

Another long silence. 'No,' he said.

But he was lying. *I can always tell.* 'Why does your kid need a shrink? Because she saw a hooker?'

'Yeah.'

'And?' He inserted a harsh edge into the question. 'What else did she see?'

'I don't know.' And that sounded like the truth. If the child was in the house at the time of one of Voss's parties . . . well, there was no telling what the kid had seen.

'Voss, don't push my patience. Have you had contact with Meredith Fallon?' he asked again, much more sharply. 'I'll find out. I have resources in CPD.'

'You have resources everywhere,' Voss said with disgust.

Yes, I do, he thought with a satisfied smile. 'So? Fallon?'

'I might have seen her around. A few times.'

'You mean you stalked her,' he said flatly.

'No. I just showed up in places where I knew she'd be. I just wanted to scare her, make it so that she'd stop badgering my kid.'

And how'd that work out for you? he wanted to ask. 'I have not disclosed to anyone the terms of our agreement, but the cops sticking their nose in your business could cause a major problem for you.' *And for me, but I won't let it get that far.*

'I have an alibi. I was speaking in front of a hundred people at a luncheon.'

'Of course. Then you have nothing to worry about. Except . . .'

'Except what?'

'Well, you're rich. You wouldn't actually take care of something like that yourself.'

'Oh my God,' Voss whispered. 'This is a nightmare.'

Indeed. 'What are you going to do about it?'

'I don't know.' He sounded defiant now, but it was a farce. 'I'll think of something.'

Too late. I already have. That the cops were sitting outside his house made it slightly more difficult and a good bit riskier, but if Voss was pressed by the police and spilled the beans about his being blackmailed . . .

That cannot happen. Especially with both CPD and the FBI involved in the investigation. Voss had to be silenced.

'You do that. And when you've thought of something, let me know what you've got planned. We'll coordinate,' he lied and ended the call.

He immediately dialed his uncle Mike, rolling his eyes at the curses that spewed from his uncle's mouth. 'Shut it, Mike. I need you.'

Bedclothes rustled in the background. 'For what?' Mike snarled. 'I was asleep.'

'I need you to take care of Broderick Voss.'

'Why?' Mike yawned. 'He stop paying? That could have waited till morning, kid.'

'He's a suspect in this afternoon's shooting.'

A beat of silence. 'Huh. How'd that happen?'

He explained Voss's stalking of Meredith Fallon and Mike snorted.

'Little shit. He was an idiot before he made a zillion bucks. Still an idiot. Okay, so how do you want it to go down?'

He considered the options. 'I think by his own hand, partying a little too hard.'

'Okay, so take some quality H with me. No problemo.'

'A little problemo. He's got cops outside his front gate. He's under surveillance.'

Mike chuckled. 'Just makes it more fun, kid. What's my timeline on this?'

'You have a few hours. Kimble and his Fed partner are about to become very busy with a house fire.'

'Wait. Kimble's investigating?' He laughed. 'We don't have to worry then. The guy is fragile as a little snowflake. He'll fold under the pressure.'

'I'm not so sure. It's been a while since his breakdown. I'm not going to underestimate him, that's for damn sure. Plus, this is bigger than one fragile snowflake. If Kimble folds, there are plenty of cops to take his place. And Feds.'

A pause. 'Are you *afraid* of Kimble?' Mike asked mockingly.

He frowned. 'Of course not. If he gets too close, we'll take him out. For now, focus on taking care of Voss.'

'Okay. I'll let you know when it's done.'

'Thanks.'

Eleven

*S*o much for getting to Meredith very, very soon, Adam thought as he parked in front of Pies & Fries, a hole-in-the-wall pizza joint near the college. Because Isenberg had called Adam as he and Trip had been leaving Candace Voss's sister's house. The owner of Pies & Fries had contacted Isenberg's office to identify the shooting victim.

The young man's name was Andy Gold. He'd been twenty years old and had waited tables at Pies & Fries. *Hell, he might have even waited on me.* Adam was no stranger to this pizza dive.

Adam got out of his Jeep, his heavy sigh lingering in the air. Trip met him on the sidewalk, his sigh equally heavy.

'Andy Gold got any priors?' Trip asked.

'Not even a parking ticket. Let's see if we can find out why he's dead.'

Trip breathed deeply when they were inside. 'You ever eat here?'

'Had my eighth birthday here and I've been a fan ever since. I recommend the meat lovers.' Adam pointed to the back corner where the owner was coming through the kitchen door. 'Shorty Redman. Been the boss since I was in high school. It was his dad's place before his. They're good folk. Active in the community. He's a good boss.'

Trip looked surprised. 'You worked here, Kimble?'

'I did.' He smiled fondly at Shorty. 'I washed dishes for three summers to earn the money for my first car.' He waved and Shorty gestured them toward another door in the back. It was the office and

176

looked just like it did when Adam had been in high school, down to the supersized cans of tomatoes that were stacked against one wall.

He shook Shorty's hand, slapping the man's back when he pulled him into a fast hug.

Shorty swallowed hard. 'I didn't expect it would be you to show up for this. But I'm really glad you did.'

Adam pointed to Trip. 'Special Agent Triplett, FBI.'

'Sit, sit.' Shorty gestured to the folding chairs, grabbing one for himself so that he sat with them rather than sitting behind the desk. 'I still can't believe this. I didn't see the news until after the dinner rush was finished. I'd heard about what happened, but I didn't see the report. And then . . .' His eyes closed and his throat worked. 'God. That poor kid.'

'Andy Gold,' Adam said. 'What can you tell us about him?'

'He wouldn't hurt a fly, that's what I can tell you. Real nice kid, working hard to put himself through college. Wanted to be somebody.' His eyes welled up and he looked away until he'd regained control. 'He was the skinniest kid, but never asked for food. One day he nearly passed out. He finally admitted that he hadn't eaten in two days. Dammit, Adam. A kid starving here? In my place? I never would have let that happen.'

'I know, Shorty,' Adam said quietly. 'You fed him.' It wasn't even a question.

'Yeah. Tried to fatten him up. Kid was finally looking healthy. I saw him on that video clip. He was . . .' A strangled sob tried to escape, but Shorty pushed it back with a visible effort. 'He was so damn scared in that video,' he whispered. 'He didn't want to hurt anyone. Ever. He was a gentle kid.'

'We believe that,' Adam said. 'We're trying to reconstruct his movements leading up to what happened today. Somebody killed him and we want to find that person.'

'Good,' Shorty said roughly. 'Hope you put him away in a dark pit. A bomb? God. He strapped a bomb to that sweet kid. Sent Andy in to do his own dirty work.'

'How do you know that?' Trip asked.

Shorty's angry gaze jerked to Trip's face. 'Because that kid did not want to be there. Any fool could see that from the picture you guys gave the media.' He sucked in a breath, pursed his lips hard. 'I'm sorry, Agent Triplett. I'm not saying you guys are fools. It's just that Andy Gold worked for me for a year and he was always on time, always respectful, honest, good-hearted. All the things you want to see. I saw his photo on the news – the one the couple getting engaged got on their video. He was pale, shaking. That wasn't Andy.'

'I understand,' Trip rumbled and the immediate drop in Shorty's tension was palpable. 'I thought maybe you knew someone who'd be able to force him. Who'd have that kind of control over him.'

'No,' Shorty said, shaking his head. 'I didn't know much more than that he had no family. He lived in a shitty apartment in somebody's basement. I'll get you the address.'

'He mentioned concern over a girl,' Adam said. 'Do you know who that could be?'

'Ah. Could have been Linnie.' Shorty frowned, thinking. 'If I ever heard her last name, I can't remember it. I only saw her a few times. Seemed shy. Half the time Andy'd use his meal allowance for her. Took care of her.'

'Did she live with him?' Trip asked.

'No. He said that she went to a different school than him. Lived in the dorm.' He made a sad sound. 'I think he was into her more than she was into him, if you know what I mean. She was . . . touchy. No, that's the wrong word. Skittish, that's it. Like if you touched her, she'd bolt.'

Trip's mouth tightened. 'Like someone had hurt her in the past?'

'Maybe. I don't know. I only saw her a few times. But . . . yeah. I think it's fair.'

Trip took out his notepad. 'Can you describe her?'

'Dark hair. Dark eyes with dark shadows under them. Her hair was shaved to the skin on one side and kind of uneven on the other, like she'd taken shears to it herself. Once she came in with a lot of makeup on. Looked a little . . . hard. She had a really quiet voice. Husky, as I recall. She looked young. Andy swore they were the same age, but she looked sixteen.'

178

Trip wrote it all down. 'Height? Weight? Clothing style?'

'Um . . . well she was about five-four, maybe. Skinny as a bean-pole, just like Andy was when he first started working for me. She wore jeans and combat boots every time I saw her. One of her ears was pierced all the way up and around.'

'Where did she and Andy meet?' Adam asked.

'He said they knew each other in high school. That's how he knew she was his age.'

'Where was that?' Trip asked.

'He never said where he grew up or anything about his family except that he didn't have any. Andy was kind of tight-lipped about his past.' Another sad shake of his head. 'I got the impression it hadn't been so good.'

'When did you last see Andy?' Trip asked.

'Friday, about nine? He took a break to smoke out back.' He met Adam's eyes. 'You know, out on the loading dock.'

Adam nodded ruefully. 'Oh, I know.'

'You smoked?' Trip asked in surprise.

'Only once. Thought I'd choke to death.' Although he'd nearly tried again more times than he could count over the last year. So many of the folks he knew at AA smoked to fight the cravings. Adam just chewed gum. He'd chewed a buttload of gum this year. 'Of course Shorty caught me that one time.' Adam returned his gaze to the older man. 'And you never told my dad. Thanks for that, by the way.'

'That's because he's an as—' Shorty broke off, shaking his head. 'Never mind.'

Adam knew exactly what he'd been about to say. *He's an asshole.* And Shorty would be right. 'So Andy was smoking. And then what?'

'He never came back. I called his phone, but he never answered. I even sent somebody to his apartment in case he'd gotten sick, but he wasn't there either.'

Adam grimaced at the prospect of getting anything decent from the loading dock. 'It's been over twenty-four hours. We'll need to get a forensic team to the dock, but . . .'

'How many deliveries did you take today?' Trip asked.

Shorty looked miserable. 'Three. And it's where all my employees take breaks. Anything usable will be destroyed, won't it?'

'We've got really good forensic guys,' Adam told him. 'Do you know what brand he smoked? We can at least separate his butts from all the others.'

'No,' Shorty said sadly.

'We'll need a list of everyone who was working last night,' Trip said. 'Names and addresses, please. And anyone who got along with Andy.'

'Everyone got along with Andy, but he didn't have any close friends. He used to joke that he'd have time for friends when he graduated.'

'What was he studying?' Adam asked.

Shorty's eye roll was sadly fond. 'English Lit. He wanted to be a teacher or a writer. Kid loved poetry.' He got up and went to the door. 'Johnny! Need you in here.' He looked over his shoulder at Adam and Trip. 'Johnny is our other smoker. Sometimes he and Andy would take breaks together. I'm going to get Andy's address and the other employees on shift last night. They're in my computer.' He pointed at his desk. 'Should I leave while you talk to Johnny? I can take my laptop out into the dining room.'

'If you would,' Adam said. 'I can't visualize you on a laptop, Shorty.'

A snort. 'I never said I was good with it, but my daughter-in-law made it about as foolproof as possible. She's got everything backed up so I can't do anything irreversible.'

He was leaving with his laptop when a young man came in, wiping his hands nervously on the rag hanging from the apron tie that wound around his waist. 'You rang, boss?'

'Yeah. These detectives want to talk to you about Andy.'

A shaky nod. 'I figured.'

Shorty gave the guy's shoulder a supportive squeeze. 'This is Johnny. He's real smart, but talks slow. Give him space and let him get the words out. Nothing wrong with that, son,' he murmured to the boy. 'Just smoothing your way.'

'Thanks.' Johnny pointed to the door once Shorty was gone. 'Should I close it?'

'Please,' Adam said. 'I'm Detective Kimble. This is Special Agent Triplett. Have a seat and try to relax. We're just asking questions.'

The boy sat nervously. 'I know. I . . . can't believe this. Andy was a good guy, honest.'

Adam's smile was sad. 'That's what we hear from Shorty.'

'And that man don't lie,' Johnny declared.

'I know. I used to work here, a million years ago.' It certainly felt like it.

Johnny nodded. 'I seen you here before, eatin'. Shorty said you had my job once, but now you're a cop.'

'That I am,' Adam said. 'You and Andy were friends?'

Johnny shrugged. 'We were friendly, but we didn't hang out. We asked him a bunch of times, me and the other guys, but Andy always was studying. He was smart, but he never treated the rest of us like we weren't, you know?'

Adam nodded. 'Were you working with him last night?'

'No. Shorty let me go home early. It was my girl's birthday.'

'Did you ever meet Andy's girl?' Trip asked. 'Linnie?'

'Twice, maybe three times. She was pretty enough. But . . . off. Like . . .' He frowned again and went silent for a full minute. 'Like a prickly porcupine. They've got cute faces, but you don't want to touch. She had this stay-away vibe going on. Some of the guys would give Andy a hard time about her. Nothin' mean, y'understand, just teasing. Andy would always insist they were just friends, but he wasn't foolin' us. He had it bad for the girl.'

Adam felt bad for the boy he'd never met. The boy who'd told Meredith to run. 'Did he ever mention anyone else besides Linnie?'

Johnny went still, the frown of concentration reappearing. 'Once he mentioned a guy named Shane. Said he and Linnie and Shane were friends before.'

'Before what?' Trip asked.

Johnny shrugged. 'Just before. I'd said my dad would kick my ass if he found me smoking and Andy said he had to answer to nobody. Then he changed his mind. "Maybe Shane," was what he

181

said. When I asked, he said they were in high school together, but his friend got a full ride to some school up north. Andy said it was a good one. Said they hadn't talked much since Shane left. He sounded really sad about that, so I let him be. Sorry. Wish I'd pried more now.'

'Don't blame yourself,' Trip said. 'Did Andy ever say Shane's last name?'

Johnny considered it for several seconds. 'No. Sorry. Wish I'd asked.'

Adam gave him an encouraging smile. 'You couldn't have known to. Agent Triplett is right. You shouldn't blame yourself. Can you tell us what brand of cigarettes he smoked?'

Johnny relaxed a little. 'Camels.'

'Great, thank you.' Adam said, then he and Trip gave him their cards. 'You've been a big help. If you remember anything more, please call.'

The door suddenly flew open, revealing a stunned Shorty. 'Come here.' He led them to the TV over the bar where the news was reporting a fire. 'That's the house Andy was living in.' He showed them his laptop, Andy Gold's employee information filling the screen. 'It's the same place.'

Fucking shit! Adam wanted to scream, but he kept his calm. 'Thanks, Shorty. We'll check it out.' He gave him one of his cards. 'Can you email me the addresses of the staff who were last working with Andy? We gotta run.'

'Sure. Hey, Adam,' Shorty called when he and Trip had turned for the door. 'Be careful, okay? Just . . . be careful.'

The tremble in Shorty's voice had Adam walking back to his old boss, clasping his shoulder. 'Absolutely. I have a lot to live for, Shorty.'

Shorty shuddered. 'I'm so glad to hear that. I was afraid for a long time that . . . Well. I'm glad to hear you say that now.'

Adam gave Shorty's shoulder a hard squeeze. 'Thanks. See you tomorrow.'

'Shit,' Trip said when they were outside. 'A bomb attempt and now a fire? Somebody doesn't want any trace of this kid to remain.'

'You're right,' Adam agreed. 'It also means Voss is either not connected or he had someone else set the fire.'

Trip's nod was grim. 'Because he's trapped in his house.'

'Yeah.' Adam bit back his frustration. Voss was connected to Meredith, but he might not be who they were looking for. He needed to keep his mind open. 'See you there.'

But first . . . He climbed in his Jeep and started it to get the heater going. Then texted Meredith. *Something came up. B another hour. Maybe 2. Can come tmw if u r tired.*

Her reply buzzed seconds later. *Am awake. Waiting to talk to u.* He drew an easier breath, but his next hitched in his chest at her next text. *Be careful. Be safe. I'm waiting.*

He wanted to whoop even as his eyes stung. She was waiting. He didn't deserve it, but he was thankful just the same. Blinking hard, he pulled out of the Pies & Fries lot and headed for the house currently burning down.

Chicago, Illinois,
Sunday 20 December, 12.35 A.M. CST (1.35 A.M. EST)

Tiffany Curtis checked her cell phone when it buzzed, sighing in relief. A text from Kyle. Finally. She'd been frantic since handing him her keys at the Burger King.

Actually, the text wasn't from Kyle, but from Shane. *K driving now. We r ok. He says we r abt 2 hr away from Cinci. He will call you when we stop. Snowing hard now. Needs to focus on road.* Eye-roll emoji. *Srsly.*

Tiffany had to roll her own eyes at the 'seriously' addition because Kyle was an awful driver. She'd thought twice about lending him her car, but he'd sounded so unnerved, so worried about Shane, that she'd agreed.

A second text had her sighing again, this time in pity. *Thank you. Srsly. U don't know what this means to me. – SB*

Shane Baird was always so serious. It had become Kyle's mission to make the guy smile and Tiffany was on board with that. She made a mental note to ask her mother to pack an extra box of Christmas

183

cookies for her to take back to campus for Shane. His friend was dead – killed in that shooting, which had to be the worst thing ever. Cookies wouldn't make it better, but it would at least show him that he wasn't alone.

Because in all her life, she'd never met anyone as alone as Shane Baird.

NP, she texted back. *Here for u. Hugs.* She added a heart emoji and hit SEND.

A creak in the floorboard was the only warning she got before strong hands grabbed her from behind. Her phone clattered to the floor.

No! She opened her mouth to scream it, but a rag was shoved into her mouth and it came out a muffled . . . nothing.

Nothing her mom could hear, especially with her CPAP machine going.

Fight. Tiffany twisted wildly, catching her foot on a hard knee, but he didn't even make a grunt. She continued to twist, trying not to sob, not to panic, but he yanked her to her bed and forced her face into her pillow, shoved his hard knee into her lower back.

Breathe. She couldn't breathe. He was suffocating her on the pillow. She struggled, lashing one arm back to grab him, grab something. *Scream.* But her protests were barely a whimper.

He caught her wrists in one of his hands, dug his other into her hair, yanking her head back. 'Fight me,' he taunted in a low voice. 'I like it.'

He flipped her to her back, one wrist in each hand now, trapping her hands on either side of her head. A sob caught in her throat and her eyes filled with tears, blurring the dark form now hovering above her.

She blinked hard. *Keep it together. Be able to describe him.* He wore a ski mask that showed his mouth and his eyes. His eyes . . . Even in the dark they scared her shitless too.

'I'm going to ask you a few questions,' he said and she flinched back. His breath was foul. 'How you answer me will determine how bad it will be for you. Tell me what I want to know and I promise not to hurt you. Much. Blink if you understand.'

She blinked, too terrified to do anything else. More tears filled her eyes, replacing the ones she'd blinked away.

Catching her wrists in one hand again, he plucked the rag from her mouth, making her cough loudly. *Mama, please hear me.*

But don't come! she wanted to scream. *Just call 911. Don't come. He'll hurt you too.*

'Where did your boyfriend go?'

She blinked rapidly, the answer on the tip of her tongue. Something kept the words frozen there. 'I don't know,' she said, pushing the words out loudly with a great huff of air. *Hear me, Mom. Please.*

She cried out when his fist slammed into her face.

'Don't you lie to me, bitch,' he growled, yanking her hair hard and shaking her head until she thought she'd vomit.

Vomit. Yes. That's what you were supposed to do. Vomit on them and they'd leave you alone. But he held her hands. She couldn't get her fingers near her mouth.

Help me. Somebody. She sucked in a breath and let out a loud scream, but he cut it off by clamping his hand over her mouth. Latex. He was wearing gloves.

'Shut up,' he hissed, smashing his palm into her teeth until she whimpered again, 'or I will permanently shut you up.' His eyes suddenly gleamed, his mouth curving cruelly. 'Your mama can't hear you.' He leaned in closer. 'Because Mama is dead.'

Her breaths grew shallow. Faster. Until her vision swam. He'd killed her mother.

No. She shook her head, denying it. He was lying. He had to be lying.

'Oh, it's true,' he mocked. 'Found her sleeping in her bed, that mask over her face. She didn't wake up when I slit her throat. She didn't suffer. But if you don't start telling me the truth, you will. Where did your boyfriend go?'

Fury blazed through her, giving her strength. Baring her teeth, she sank them into his hand and he roared, trying to yank his hand free, but she bit down harder. He jerked his hand free and flicked it, trying to shake off the pain.

185

'You fucking cunt.' But she'd tuned out his words because she'd felt the pressure on her wrists lessen. He was going to hit her again.

She jerked out of his grasp in the moment he let her go. She tried to roll out from under him, but he grabbed her by the throat with the hand she'd bitten. She grabbed for his wrist, trying to pull him off her, the pressure on her windpipe cutting off her air.

All she did was manage to rip the glove. He flung it aside.

Then he smiled and she knew. She was going to die.

'Yeah,' he muttered. 'You're gonna die. And it's gonna hurt.'

He abruptly went rigidly still, head cocked, listening.

A police siren. Getting louder. *Help. Someone is coming to help.* His hand tightened on her throat and black spots began to speckle her vision. Getting bigger until blackness was all she could see.

Hurry, she wanted to scream. *Please hurry.*

'Fuck,' he snarled and pulled his hand away.

Leaving. She gasped, the air scraping her lungs as she took it in. *He's leaving.* She heard a rustle, felt the bed give as he got off. *It's going to be okay. I'm going to be okay.*

She started to roll, to get to her mother. *Mama.* Opening her eyes, she looked up in time to see the knife in his hand.

Cincinnati, Ohio,
Sunday 20 December, 3.15 A.M.

He's coming. He's coming. The words beat in Meredith's mind in time to the racing of her heart. Adam had texted he was on his way. She stared down at her phone again, checking the time. It was less than a minute later than the last time she'd looked.

'Try to relax,' Kate murmured from the living room sofa where she sat knitting, the old dog at her feet. But Meredith knew that Kate was aware of every creak of the house. Fully armed, she was ready to defend. 'Adam will be here when he gets here. Go clean something. That always calms you down.'

Meredith did as she was told, but Bailey and Delores had done a thorough job earlier and there was nothing left to be done. With a sigh, she put on the kettle and sat down to wait.

At least her house was relatively empty. Diesel was sleeping in the basement bedroom and her grandfather was upstairs in the room that had once been her father's.

They'd sent Kendra to stay with Wendi at Mariposa House. The old mansion was far bigger and required more eyes and ears than Meredith's little house. That had been Kate's idea and Meredith was grateful.

She loved Kendra like a sister, but the woman did not like Adam Kimble. Kate, on the other hand, seemed to know something that made her softer toward him, but all she'd tell Meredith was that she knew he was 'working shit out' and that he was stressed. Which made him no different than any of the law enforcement officers she knew.

The stress and strain of their jobs was more wearing than any of them let on.

She jumped when her phone buzzed in the pocket of her jeans, reading the incoming text with a calmness she did not feel. *At the door downstairs. U awake?*

Her fingers trembled as she typed her reply. *Yes. Coming down now.*

She turned off the stove, stuck her head in the living room to let Kate know that she was going downstairs, then took the stairs two at a time to let him in.

To hear his explanation. And hopefully to kiss him again.

He was standing with his back to the door when she got there, studying the backyard and the houses surrounding hers. *Always vigilant*, she thought.

She tapped the window, her breath catching when he turned. In the moonlight he was utterly beautiful, hard jaw, soft mouth, and dark eyes that made her desperate to know all his secrets. Quietly she opened the outside door, her finger over her lips.

'Diesel's asleep,' she whispered, pointing at the closed bedroom door. She stepped back to let him in, all six-feet-two-inches of broad-shouldered . . . *mine*. He closed the door behind him and she caught the scent on his coat.

'Fire?' she whispered. Gripping his shoulders, she turned him so that she could study his face. He was grim. 'What happened?'

He pointed down the hall to the TV room where she and her friends gathered for their wine and movie nights. 'Let's talk there.'

He took her elbow and walked her forward as her brain scrambled to make sense of his mood shift. There was no tenderness. No want. Just hard . . . business.

Once they were in the TV room and away from the room where Diesel slept, she switched on the overhead light. The shoulders of his black wool overcoat were covered in a light layer of snow. She brushed it off, then reached for the top button of his coat.

Then stopped, her hands stilling. 'Are you staying?'

He nodded once. Swallowed hard. 'Yeah. For a little while.'

Frowning, she unbuttoned his coat and slipped it from his shoulders while he stood like a statue. She sniffed at his coat and blinked hard, her eyes watering at the harsh burnt odor. 'What happened?'

He'd tugged at his tie at some point, loosening it enough to undo the top button of his shirt. He looked exhausted.

Warily she lifted her hands to his face, cupping his cheeks. 'Adam?'

He shuddered out a harsh breath and dragged her against him, his arms tightening so hard that it almost hurt. But relief kept her from protesting. This was where she'd wanted to be. *Right here, in his arms.*

Lifting on her toes, she wrapped her arms around his neck and stroked his hair, not saying a word. He buried his face against her neck, his breaths ragged. He was shaking.

Just like the last time he'd come to her.

Finally, he loosened his arms enough for her to catch her breath. Then he took it away again when his mouth took hers in a kiss that was nothing like the one in the kitchen. It was hard. Bruising. Almost punishing. Full of anger? *No*, she realized. *Not anger.*

It was fear. *What the hell happened, Adam?*

Abruptly he pulled away. 'Dammit. I'm sorry. I didn't want to hurt you.'

'You didn't,' she murmured, brushing her fingertips over his lips. 'You wouldn't.'

He closed his eyes. 'I'd die first.'

'Adam.' She pressed her palms to his cheeks, his stubble prickling her skin. 'What happened? You have to talk to me, baby.'

He stiffened, then dropped his head to her shoulder, his body sagging. 'I like that.'

She frowned, but then realized what he meant. 'When I call you baby?' It made her smile. Gently she went back to stroking his hair.

'When you call me anything other than a selfish jerk.'

She kissed his ear. 'Sit down before you fall down. You look exhausted.' He obeyed, dropping onto the sofa like he was a puppet whose strings had just been cut. She was happy she'd purchased well-made furniture for this room, because the man was as solid as a rock. 'Can I make you some tea?'

He grabbed her hand and tugged her to sit beside him. 'No. I need to tell you some things before I get called away again. I'm going to do case stuff first because I need you to understand what's happening there. So you'll keep yourself safe. If I have time, I'll tell you what I'd originally planned to discuss.'

'All right.' Still holding his hand, she twisted so that she could see his face. 'I'm listening.'

'The boy. We know his name now. Andy Gold.'

Meredith's heart hurt for the boy whose last act was to try to save her life. 'Oh. Poor Andy.'

'He worked at Pies & Fries.'

'I love that place,' she said. 'Shorty's a good man. He must be devastated.'

Adam's forehead creased in a frown. 'You know Shorty?'

'I grew up here too, Adam. My dad absolutely *loved* Shorty's pizza. We went there every chance we got. What did Shorty say about Andy Gold?'

'That he was a good person. Hard working. What we kind of figured, considering he told you to run and pulled the wires on the bomb before he even walked into the restaurant.'

Meredith blinked. 'He did? I didn't know that. Wasn't that dangerous?'

Adam nodded. 'He might have blown himself up. But I'm guessing he didn't want anyone else to get hurt. We got a lead on the woman he was worried about, but that's less important to your safety at the moment.' He took a deep breath. 'While we were talking to Shorty's staff, he got us Andy's address.'

A piece of the puzzle fell into place in Meredith's mind with an almost audible clink. 'His house was burned down.'

He stared at her for a few seconds. 'I always forget how smart you are because you're so damn pretty.' He pursed his lips. 'Dammit. I wasn't supposed to say it that way.'

She smiled at him. 'I still liked hearing it, so thank you.' She lifted his hand to her lips for a soft kiss, then held it on her knee. 'It was arson?' she asked, stroking his hand.

He nodded. 'Andy rented a basement apartment from a family.' He rubbed his free hand over his eyes. 'It was a bad fire. The firefighters ran into a house that nobody should have entered, but . . .' He shrugged. 'Those guys are insane.'

'I know. I'm glad you're not a firefighter. Cop is bad enough.'

He shook his head hard. 'No. I mean . . . Shit, Meredith.'

She slid her hand over his cheek and turned his head so that he looked at her. 'Adam, this is just me. Take your time. I'm not going anywhere.' She smiled ruefully. 'First, because I live here, and second, because none of you will let me leave.'

'That's the goddamn truth.' He let his head drop to the sofa back, the picture of weariness. 'I'm not saying this right.' He turned his head so that he met her gaze head on, and what she saw there made her heart break. *So much pain.* 'Trip and I got there as they . . .' Another deep breath. 'We got there as they were bringing out the bodies. The family died, Meredith. All of them. Mother, father.' He swallowed hard. 'And two children. One was a baby in a crib.'

Her lungs went suddenly flat, as if she'd been hit by a truck. She shoved the heel of her hand to her breastbone, trying to relieve the pressure on her chest. 'Oh God. Adam. I'm so sorry. How horrible for them. How horrible for you to have to see.' More horror that he'd never be able to unsee.

'Goddammit, Meredith.' He jerked his gaze to the ceiling, then back at her. His eyes were so dark they bored into her. '*Listen to me.* He tried to get Andy Gold to kill you and then Andy was supposed to blow up. There would have been nothing left. No evidence.'

Her lungs froze again. 'And now Andy's home is gone.'

'Nothing's left. It was intense and fast-burning. Use of an accelerant was clear. Whoever killed Andy today does not want any ties back to him. And you were his target. He's killed five innocent people now, Meredith. *Five.*'

Meredith stared back at him, horrified. 'To get to me?'

'Yes.' His voice dropped, grew gruffer. 'I am so fucking terrified right now. If anything happened to you . . . I can't . . . I just *can't*. Do you understand now?'

She covered her mouth. 'My God. Five people. *Five people.*'

'Their deaths are not your fault.'

'I know that,' she snapped. 'It doesn't matter. They're still dead. Because somebody hates me enough to kill me.' *Five people. God. Dear God.*

Adam lifted her chin with his forefinger. 'Don't cry,' he whispered. 'Please.'

I'm not, she started to say, but he was wiping tears from her cheeks. And then he was lifting her to his lap, his arms tight around her, rocking her where they sat.

She slid her hand to the back of his neck, turned her face into his chest, and wept.

He held her close, murmuring comfort into her ear, stroking her hair, her back, all while rocking her like she was a baby. 'Sweetheart, it's not your fault,' he kept saying.

Somewhere behind her she heard Diesel's voice, sounding pissed and sleepy. 'What did you do to her, Kimble?'

Meredith shook her head and continued to cry. 'Nothing.'

She heard Adam tell Diesel about Andy Gold and the fire and the big man swore like a sailor. 'Did you get anywhere with Voss?'

'Yes, but we need more information before we bring him in. We have him under surveillance, so he's not going anywhere. Don't worry.'

'Sonofa*bitch*.' Kate's voice came from the top of the stairs, where she'd apparently heard it all. Meredith should have known Kate wouldn't have let her come downstairs all alone. Kate told Cap to stay, then came down far enough to lean on the banister to see them. 'Mer needs a safe house.'

Meredith jerked back, looking at Adam with panic. 'No. Please don't shut me away from everyone.' *Not now. I can't do this now. I need you. All of you.*

He stroked her face, his sigh pained. 'Your poor eyes are swollen. Kate, can you get her some ice or something?'

'Sure thing.'

'You didn't promise me,' Meredith said, hearing her voice go shrill, but unable to stop herself. 'I can't . . . I can't go to a place where I can't leave. I can't. *I won't.*'

'Shhh,' Adam soothed. 'We're not going to make any decisions right now.'

Nodding, Meredith relaxed a fraction. 'Okay.'

Diesel was not convinced. 'Bullshit, Adam. What's to stop Voss or whoever's behind this from setting *this* place on fire?'

'We've got the place under surveillance,' Adam said sharply. 'He's got to know that.'

Diesel's indrawn breath was loud in the ensuing silence. 'And if his plan is to blow her up? Or start a fire and wait with a high-powered rifle so that he can pick her off when she runs out of a burning house?'

Adam's jaw was hard as granite. 'Don't you think I haven't thought of that already?'

Diesel sighed. 'I'm sorry. I know you're good at your job.'

'It's okay,' Adam said. 'I know that you're good at yours too. And I do appreciate your fear, because it's well founded. I'm thinking the condo. That's no stuffy one-room safe house. Would you go there? Until we find this asshole?'

The condo was the penthouse of a very secure building in Eden Park. Meredith had never been there, but she knew about it because

Faith had used it last year, as had Kate's fiancé, Decker, over the summer. She had no idea who it belonged to or why CPD was allowed to use it as a safe house, but it seemed like an ideal solution. 'My grandfather too?'

Adam's nod was definite. 'Yes. Absolutely.'

'And people can . . . visit me?' Because Christmas was coming and Alex was coming and Meredith did not want to be alone.

Adam was studying her face, his eyes narrowed thoughtfully. 'Of course.'

Diesel's laugh scraped out of him. 'You had that already set up, didn't you?'

Adam's lips tilted. 'Well, yeah.' He held Meredith's gaze. 'You okay with that?'

She let out a breath. Felt her calm return. 'Which, that you made the decision when you said we didn't have to make a decision, or that you cared enough to give me an option that would keep me and my grandfather safe without giving me a panic attack?'

'Both. I think. But I'm way too tired to parse what you just said.'

'Take the bed, man,' Diesel offered. 'You really look like shit. Smell like it too.'

Adam let go of her long enough to flip Diesel the bird. 'But thank you for the kind offer,' he added graciously. 'I will take a shower. Do you have any more of your cousin's husband's clothes, Meredith?'

'Yes, but I also have the suit you were wearing when you were here the last time. I had it cleaned. It's hanging in the closet in the room where Diesel was sleeping.'

Adam's expression softened. 'Thank you.'

She ran her thumb over his lower lip. 'It was no trouble.'

'It was still kind,' he said quietly.

Diesel cleared his throat loudly. 'I am obviously in the way here. Give me a second to pull my shit together and I'll go . . . Well, where do you want me to go? I can stay with them until you're ready to take them to the condo.'

Adam lifted his gaze to Diesel. 'If you can, I'd really appreciate it.'

'Me too,' Kate said, returning from upstairs with a cold pack. She winced when she got close enough to see Meredith's face. 'Oh, honey. You look awful.'

She laughed, but it was a hollow sound. 'Adam and I both look like shit then.'

Kate's smile was satisfied. 'But you laughed, so my job is done. I'll stay with you, Diesel. Decker's out of town for the weekend and I'm not on call.'

'Where did he go?' Diesel asked, because he and Kate's fiancé had become strong friends since the summer.

Kate flitted her hand. 'Seminar. Florida.'

Meredith turned on Adam's lap so that she could study Kate's face, things making sense now. 'You were with him. You were in Florida and you came home because of me.'

Kate gave her a wide-eyed look of innocence. '*Moi*? No way.'

Adam leaned in to whisper in her ear. 'She's got sunburn on her nose.'

The tickle of breath on her ear made her shiver. She tried to ignore it, narrowing her eyes at her friend. Adam was right. The tip of Kate's nose was a red brighter than the woman's sunrise-red hair. She'd noticed it earlier, but thought Kate had been cold. The red nose had not subsided. 'You're so busted, Kate.'

Kate put the ice on Meredith's face, then kissed the top of her head. 'We were scared, Decker and me. We saw the shooting on the news and . . . I had to make sure you were all right. Decker had to stay, but I didn't, so I came home. You take care of us all the time, Mer. It's your turn. Let us take care of you.'

She went back up the stairs, leaving Meredith staring after her.

'She's right,' Adam murmured. 'Let us take care of you.' His shoulders relaxed a fraction when she nodded. 'I need to tell you about Broderick Voss. Trip and I interviewed his wife tonight and met his daughter.'

'Penny.'

'Yeah. We want to question Voss, but we want more information before we bring him in. We need to know what Penny saw that her father doesn't want her to tell you.'

'You think Penny knows something that her father finds damaging enough to try to kill me? That sounds so . . . paranoid.'

'It's not paranoid if they're really trying to kill you,' he said dryly.

True. 'Did Candace agree to allow Penny to continue seeing me? If not, we can find another therapist for her.'

'She was afraid you'd turn Penny away. I told her that's not who you were.'

A flood of tenderness had her eyes filling again. 'Thank you,' she whispered.

'It's true.' He leaned closer until their foreheads touched. 'If you could talk to her, it could give us a clue as to why he's so keen on keeping her away from therapists. You're apparently number three. The other two quit.'

Meredith frowned. 'I know. Fuckers.'

Adam snorted a laugh, then smiled down at her. 'Did you really just curse?'

She shrugged. 'I curse. A lot. I'm just selective where and when I let go.'

He really smiled then, a dimple appearing in his cheek, and Meredith realized she'd never really seen him smile like that before. 'That makes me happy,' he said, but then he was back to business once again. 'Can you be ready to leave in an hour or so? I want to close my eyes for a bit and then I'll escort you to the condo.'

'So . . . when Faith hid there, Deacon hid with her. And when Decker hid there, Kate hid with him. Are you going to hide with me?'

'Yes. As much as I can anyway. But when I'm not there, I'll make sure you're safe.'

Twelve

He roused when his cell buzzed. Rolling over quietly, so as not to wake Rita, he pressed his fingerprint to his phone and opened Butch's text.

Shane's headed to Cinci.

Fuck, he wanted to snarl, but he breathed carefully through his nose, keeping his temper under control. Grabbing his phone, he slid out of bed. Of course Rita stirred.

'What's wrong?' she whispered. She always assumed something was wrong. She was usually right, but he'd never let her know that. She was the best camouflage he could ever hope for. She was respectability and normality personified.

And she was a good cook. All in all, not a bad reason for a marriage.

'Nothing,' he soothed. 'Gotta pee. Go back to sleep.'

'Oh. Okay.' She obeyed and minutes later she was breathing rhythmically again.

When he'd shut the bathroom door, he texted Butch back. *What happened?*

Girl is resolved. Got her phone. Sending you pics of convos.

Did anyone see u?

Pls, came the reply and he had to smile. Butch could sound insulted even over text.

His phone buzzed several more times as photos came through. Butch had issues with many things, but he was remarkably savvy

196

about not leaving a trail. He'd taken photos of the girl's phone with his own, versus sending from the girl's phone.

That the new phones could be unlocked with a fingerprint made their jobs so much easier. Butch had probably removed the girl's finger and taken it with him to unlock her phone, so 'resolved' most likely meant 'dead.'

He scanned the texts that had flown between Shane's friend Kyle and Kyle's girlfriend Tiffany. Kyle had written that Shane was freaked because his old friend was dead. He needed to get Shane to Cincinnati and asked to borrow Tiffany's car.

She'd agreed, poor thing. If she'd said no, she might be alive right now. Shane himself had texted from Kyle's phone at one thirty-five Cinci time, saying they were two hours away, so they should be arriving soon, if they weren't already here.

He wondered where they'd go. Probably to the house where Andy Gold had lived, which was now crawling with firefighters, including an arson investigator. Well, he hadn't been very subtle, after all. He'd doused that house with enough accelerant for three houses.

He was sure it was crawling with cops by now too. Probably including Agent Triplett and Detective Kimble, since they were leads on the case.

Fucking Kimble. Their paths had crossed in the past and he'd always managed to slip around the guy, but a few times it had been damn close. *I really need to get rid of him.*

But that would have to wait.

Where r u? he typed to Butch and hit SEND.

Stopped for gas in Indy. Snowing here. Flights grounded. Have to drive home. Slow driving.

Make/model of car? I'll wait near Gold's house. Luckily, there was only one entrance into Gold's neighborhood. He could park there and keep watch for the borrowed car without being noticed.

White Toyota Prius. 2dr htchbk. 2014. IL plates. The plate number came through. *Gotta hit the road. Call if u need me, can't text w/snow.*

No, they couldn't risk an accident. Accidents meant cops and Butch had successfully flown under the radar for a decade. He wouldn't surface now if it wasn't life or death.

B safe, he replied. Because good right-hands were hard to come by. Especially ones he could trust implicitly. In his life there had been only two – Butch and his uncle Mike.

Otherwise, he was on his own and always had been. He liked it that way too.

Cincinnati, Ohio,
Sunday 20 December, 3.55 A.M.

Adam switched off the shower in Meredith's basement, feeling human once more. It was a very nice shower nestled in the corner of a very nice bathroom. Meredith certainly didn't do things halfway. The tile was done in a pattern of frothing waves that . . . soothed.

Everything about her soothed. Even the shampoos and soaps in neatly labeled dispensers on the shower wall. Sandalwood, lavender, forest, mountain spring. There was an earthiness, a groundedness in every scent, every color.

It was very zen. Very Meredith.

He wondered why she was so careful to surround herself with such soothing images and scents. He'd known from the beginning that she surrounded herself with a group of friends that were closer knit than most families.

Certainly more than his own family – his parents anyway. He, Deacon, and Dani had made a life for themselves and for Greg, the youngest Novak.

Meredith had drawn them in too. She was like a sun, acquiring planets that revolved around her, coming closer and orbiting away as they went about their own lives. All while Meredith remained in the center. Alone.

Adam thought she might be the most alone person he'd ever met, despite the friendships she'd so carefully and consistently nurtured. *And I didn't help her not be alone anymore.* He'd left her, expecting she'd carry on while he dealt with his mountain of shit.

But she had her own shit too. She had to. Why else would she have ever felt the need to develop that zen mask that seemed to fool everyone into thinking she was just fine? He'd seen past that mask and he knew she was unhappy.

And he now knew he could fix it. Buoyed by a confidence he wasn't sure he'd ever felt before, he stepped out of the shower and dried himself with a fluffy towel that . . . He buried his face in the towel and inhaled. That smelled like her.

Instantly he was harder than any rock. He'd have to be careful when he zipped his trousers. The trousers of the suit she'd hung in the closet. His own suit, cleaned and left hanging. Waiting for him to return and reclaim it.

Just as she'd waited for him to return and reclaim her. Which he wanted to do right now, but knew he needed to wait until she was in a safe place.

A soft knock on the door had his pulse scrambling. Diesel wouldn't have knocked so lightly. Had to be her. He wrapped the towel around his waist and knotted it, conscious this would be the first time she'd seen this much of his skin since that night a year ago. And for the first time, he was grateful that all the work he'd done hauling and fixing things over the past year had given him muscle definition he hadn't seen since playing ball in college.

'Adam?' she called through the door. 'Your phone played Darth Vader, twice. I didn't answer, but someone wants to talk to you. I'm leaving now, putting your phone on the nightstand. I just wanted you to—'

He opened the door to find Meredith standing there uncertainly, his phone in her hand. A second later though, her uncertainty was gone, replaced by momentary shock which quickly became an expression of open lust. She looked him up, then down, her nostrils flaring slightly at the deep breath she drew.

He shuddered. Hard. *Best ego boost ever.* He wanted to reach for her, but he was afraid he wouldn't be able to stop and he still had to tell her the truth. Dammit. So he reached above him with both hands, gripping the doorframe, his knuckles bone-white.

'Oh,' she said on a sigh, her hand slowly lifting to his chest like it was being pulled by a magnet. She trailed her fingertips through the droplets clinging to the hair there, her touch a bare whisper against his skin. Her gaze dropped to the towel and she worried her lower lip with her teeth, making him want to take a bite.

He heard a low growl, realized it had come from his own throat.

Her gaze jerked up, colliding with his, and she started to pull her hand away, but he caught her wrist, flattening her fingers against him. She shifted her palm to cover his heart and she had to be able to feel it because it was slamming against his ribcage like a hammer.

Then she pressed her lips to his chest and undid him. His fingers released the doorframe and drove into her hair, lifting her face, her mouth.

And he was kissing her again. Finally. Finally. It was . . . everything. She was everything. He nipped at the lip she'd bitten and she moaned, opening for him. He licked into her mouth, forcing himself to slow down. To explore.

To treasure. Because this . . . this was more than he'd ever hoped for.

She hummed her pleasure, the hand over his heart sliding up his chest and around his neck and the kiss became a sweet hello. She tasted like gingerbread. And home.

Keeping one hand in her hair, he let the other drop to her shoulder, then hesitantly brushed the back of his fingers over the swell of her breast.

She hummed again, this time in anticipation. He dragged his mouth away, resting his forehead on hers as he cupped her breast with a hand that trembled. She closed her eyes on an almost silent whimper, her body melting into his.

'God, I missed you,' he whispered.

'I was right here,' she whispered back. 'Waiting for you.'

He opened his mouth to tell her then, he really did. But Darth Vader's theme belted out of his phone, startling them apart. Meredith stared down at the phone in her hand as if it was something she'd never seen before.

'It's Isenberg,' he said quietly. 'I have to take it.'

She handed him the phone and took a step back, but he grabbed her hand and pressed it back to his heart. 'Sorry,' he said to his boss after accepting the call. 'Had to shower off the fire stink. Did we get Zimmerman to kick in a few guards for Meredith and her grandfather?'

Meredith's eyes held his. Her lips mouthed *thank you*.

Isenberg's voice was a buzzing in his ear. An annoyance. Gritting his teeth, he forced himself to pay attention to what she was saying. 'Yes, but that's not why I was calling,' she snapped. 'You need to get down to the station. We have a visitor. He says his name is Shane Baird. And he says he was Andy Gold's best friend.'

Adam sucked in a surprised breath. 'Shane. Just like Andy told Johnny at Pies & Fries. Andy told him that Shane was going to college somewhere up north.'

'Kiesler University. He and his friend drove down as soon as Shane saw the news.'

'I'll be there in fifteen minutes.' Adam hesitated, then figured *fuck it*. 'I will have Meredith with me. I'm here now. I'd come to take her to the safe house.'

A hesitation on Isenberg's end. 'And you're cleaning up there?'

'She's packing her things. I've always been a multi-tasker.' He pointed at Meredith, then upstairs, then held up five fingers. Nodding, she moved to do as he asked. 'I had to get the smell off my skin, Loo,' he murmured with all seriousness, once Meredith had left, closing the door behind her. 'It wasn't just the fire.' His stomach clenched. 'The victims . . . Burned flesh.' He could say no more, but Isenberg seemed to understand.

Isenberg's sigh was quiet. 'It's a trigger for you.'

'Yeah.' It was the only word he had to answer her.

'Okay then. Who else is there in her house?' Isenberg asked suspiciously.

Adam wanted to snap, but remembered her warning when she'd assigned him to this case. If she suspected he was in too deep – which he was – she'd yank him off this case and assign someone else to keep Meredith safe. 'Kate Coppola, Diesel Kennedy, and Meredith's grandfather. But she needs to see this Shane. We don't know why Voss – or whoever's behind this – picked Andy Gold to shoot her. We need to know if there is a connection.'

'Well, yes,' Isenberg allowed. 'But why does she need to see Shane?'

'I don't know. There might be no connection at all, but what if there is? Hell, she might know this guy, or he might know her.'

'That's a long shot,' Isenberg muttered. 'But bring her in. She observes only, Adam.'

'Got it. She can't be the team shrink on this one.'

'Good. Now get yourself in here. This kid is definitely not telling me something. I want you to figure out what that is.'

'Will do.' Ending the call, Adam whipped off the towel and finished drying off. Meredith had left boxer briefs, still in the package, a pair of black socks, and his suit and shirt, covered in the dry-cleaner's plastic, on the bed. He had to smile. She'd even laid out a tie that went with the suit. She was something, for sure.

He dressed quickly, then looked around for his shoes, only to find a pair at his feet. But they weren't his. *What the— How did she—* She'd even found shoes that looked to be his size. Cleaned and buffed to a mirror-like shine. He slid one foot into the first shoe and laughed incredulously. They fit. Perfectly. *Of course they do.*

He was staring at his shoe-clad feet when he heard the soft knock at the bedroom door. 'Come in,' he called, turning to see her standing hesitantly in the doorway, a blush staining her cheeks. 'How did you happen to have shoes that fit me perfectly?' he asked, when he really wanted to grab her and pull her in for another kiss.

But he didn't, because once he started he wouldn't want to stop. And the bed was too damned close. Too damn tempting.

She was too damned tempting.

'You're lucky,' she said with a shrug. 'You're the same size as Daniel.'

'Daniel. Your cousin's husband.'

She nodded. 'He left them here the last time he and Alex visited. Your shoes were pretty disgusting. I bagged them.' She held a white plastic trash bag for him to see.

His lips quirked up. 'You didn't clean them too?' he teased, then tensed, hoping she wouldn't think he really meant it.

Russet brows arched. 'No,' she said crisply, but she smiled, so it was okay. Her smile faltered then. 'Isenberg . . . is she upset with you for being here?'

He considered lying, but went for straight truth. 'She's warned me off any romantic entanglement with you, since you're the principal target of a killer,' he said and was rewarded when disappointment made her lips droop sadly.

'Oh.'

The single word said everything he'd hoped to hear. He closed the space between them, gripping her upper arms possessively, but gently. She was so fair, her skin would bruise easily. *As easily as her heart.* His chest tightened then, because she was staring up at him, naked yearning in her eyes. *I do not deserve this. I do not deserve her.*

He kissed her lightly this time. Tenderly, because that was what she deserved. Tenderness and care. He lifted his head and had to grit his teeth against an almost feral need to take more, because she was licking her lips. Savoring the taste of him.

'I need you,' he whispered and groaned quietly when she closed her eyes on a relieved little sigh. Because his mind was conjuring image after image of making her sigh like that in the bed behind them. 'I need you, just like this. No mask. No serene smile. I need to see *you*.'

Her lashes lifted, revealing a knowing that hit him like a brick. 'I need you like this. Talking to me. Being honest with me. No more hiding, Adam.'

'Okay,' he managed to say, then dragged his mind back to the clock ticking in his head. 'But for the next hour or so I need you to wear that mask for Isenberg. I want you to take a look at this kid from Chicago who says he was Andy Gold's friend. We need to know if there is any connection between you and Andy Gold.'

'And if there's not?'

'Then at least I'm keeping you safe until I can get you to the condo. I just need you not to look at me like you're looking at me right now. If Isenberg senses that I'm . . . emotionally involved, she'll put someone else on your case. And I don't want to give anyone else that . . .' He trailed off, looking for the right word.

'Responsibility?' she supplied.

He shook his head. 'No. The privilege.' He struggled for the perfect word, but she was watching him with those green eyes that always seemed to see right through him. *Tell her. Tell her the truth.* 'And the opportunity.' He drew a breath. 'To make amends.'

She frowned abruptly, startling him because he thought he'd said it right. 'I'm not your atonement, Adam,' she bit out. 'I'm not a cage to be cleaned or a house to be fixed or a team to be coached or a shelter to be' – she fluttered a hand impatiently – 'whatever you did at St Ambrose's.'

'Handyman stuff,' he murmured, stunned. She knew. 'How did you know?'

'Because I'm not stupid?' she snapped, then stepped back, out of his arms. Rubbing her forehead, she sighed, this time in resignation. 'Or maybe I am. Let's just go. I'll observe the kid from Chicago and then I'll go to the safe house so you don't have to worry about me. What's his name?'

His brain refused to spark. 'What? Whose name?'

She rolled her eyes. 'The kid from Chicago.'

'Shane. Shane Baird.'

'Okay, then. Let's go look at Mr Baird.' She disappeared for a few seconds, returning wearing her coat and an overnight bag slung over her shoulder. In one hand she held a parka, in the other another plastic bag, filled with something large and bulky. His coat, he realized. And probably his suit, because he'd just realized it was not piled on the floor where he'd discarded it before his shower. All that would have to be cleaned too.

'The parka is Papa's. He says to use it because he has another. It'll do until you can get home to change.' She shoved it at him. 'There are gloves in the pocket.'

Of course there are, he thought numbly, staring at the coat in his hands.

'Let's go out upstairs,' she continued. 'The sidewalk is shoveled, so we won't have to walk through snow.' Turning on her heel, she was gone.

And suddenly her words clicked. *I'm not your atonement.*

'Meredith, wait.' He ran after her, catching up in the TV room.

204

Grabbing her shoulder, he spun her around. She glared up at him, but there were tears in her eyes. *Shit.* He'd done it again. Made her cry even when he was trying to do the right thing. 'You think that I've done all this as part of my *atonement*? That I kissed you because you're a . . .' He sputtered wishing he had the words. 'God, I don't even know what.' She said nothing, but her lip trembled. 'Dammit, Meredith, you are not an *atonement*. You are not some charity case or a project. You are . . .' He closed his eyes, trying to slow his racing heart. 'You are what's kept me going for the last godawful year.'

He opened his eyes to see hers narrowing in confusion. In disbelief. 'I don't know what that even means,' she said tightly, her jaw rigid, tears balancing on her lower lashes.

Frustrated, he released his hold on her and raked his shaking hands through his hair. He held them there, clenching, pulling his hair hard enough to make himself wince. But the pain centered him. Helped him find the words in the chaos of his mind.

'It *means* that I'm an alcoholic.'

He'd gritted out the words from behind clenched teeth, he realized belatedly. Not the way he'd wanted them to come out.

But at least they were out, he thought as he dropped his hands to his sides. He felt relieved . . . yet defeated. But mostly honest. Finally. And now he just waited.

Her mouth fell open, her expression one of bald shock. A single blink sent those tears racing down her cheeks. 'What?' she whispered.

'Yeah.' He wanted to look away. He wanted to bolt. To run so far that no one would ever be able to find him.

God. His mouth was as dry as it had ever been. He wanted a drink so goddamn bad that he was shaking, head to toe. But he forced himself to remain where he stood. Forced himself to breathe. *In. Out. In. And out.* He forced himself to wait for her reaction, no matter what it was. At least she knew the truth.

'But . . .' She shook her head, still stunned. 'How long?'

He swallowed hard. 'How long what? How long have I been an alcoholic or how long have I been sober?'

'How long have you been sober?' she whispered.

'Eleven months,' he heard himself say, voice like gravel. 'And fourteen days.'

She opened her mouth, but no more words came out.

Huh. He'd never expected her to be wordless too. She always knew the right thing to say. They stood in silence, staring at each other.

And then Darth Vader screamed out of his phone, shattering that silence. Isenberg. Again. Adam answered it, never looking away from Meredith's shocked face. 'Yeah, Loo?'

'I've got Mr Baird in Interview Three. What's your ETA?'

'Ten.'

'Hurry, Adam. This kid looks like he'll break into pieces any minute.'

Join the motherfucking club. 'On my way.' He ended the call, dropped the phone in his pocket, and gathered the plastic bags with his clothing and shoes. 'We'll have to finish this later. You need to wait a minute while I get a vest for you out of my Jeep. Once you're protected, we need to go.'

Cincinnati, Ohio,
Sunday 20 December, 4.15 A.M.

Sitting a block away from the burned-out house, he sipped bad coffee and tried to stay awake. Shane and his friend would have to drive this way to get to Andy Gold's former residence.

Which was gutted. He blew out a breath that hung in the cold air of his car. Four people had died. Which sucked, because now the cops would be even *more* dedicated to finding the arsonist.

The family should have had plenty of time to get out. That they hadn't . . . well, he couldn't be blamed for that. He hadn't meant for them to die too.

At least anything that might have given a hint into Andy's background – including photos of Linnea – was gone. Nothing had survived the blaze. And once he had Shane, Linnea would come to heel. He'd get rid of them both and those ends would be snipped.

Then he could refocus his efforts on his original goal. *Fuck*

Meredith Fallon and her concealed weapon. He growled quietly. *Fuck Mike's bomb that hadn't fucking worked.*

He frowned, wondering why that was. It should have worked. Mike's devices had never let him down. He'd have to use his resources to get at the results of the Feds' investigation, since they'd been the one to remove the device from Andy's body.

As if summoned, his cell buzzed with a text from his uncle. *Done.*

A photo followed, Voss sprawled in a chair, rubber strap still tied around his arm, the needle still in his vein. *TOD 2.50am*, Mike's next text read.

What about cops outside the gate? he replied.

Sleeping. Offering from St Mickey.

It was a simple ploy, but it worked almost every time. The cops would know they'd been slipped a Mickey when they woke up, but Mike had already finished by then. Mike had shown him how to use the technique on his father during his teens, except they'd slipped the Mickey into his evening whiskey so that he'd go to sleep earlier and sleep soundly through the night. Those had been the hours Mike tutored him. Showed him the ropes. Taught him how to take whatever he wanted from whoever happened to have it without getting caught. All in all, hours well spent. And his dad had never been the wiser.

Good, he texted. *Thx.*

Going home to sleep. Don't bother me again.

He chuckled. *Sweet dreams old man.* He added an emoji of a happy face with z's.

A photo of his uncle's middle finger popped up on his screen.

Smiling, he went back to sipping his coffee. One thread snipped. A few more to go.

Cincinnati, Ohio,
Sunday 20 December, 4.20 A.M.

Oh my God. Oh my God. It was all Meredith could think as Adam sped across town. He was using his flashers to cut through what little traffic there was at this time of night.

How did I not see this? What is wrong with me that I didn't see?

All those months. All the pictures he'd colored. That first picture, the stained glass window, solid red. Then those that followed, becoming progressively balanced as the weeks and months passed. Progressively more beautiful.

Eleven months and fourteen days sober. She focused on doing the calendar math in her head, if only for the temporary respite for her aching heart.

'January sixth,' she murmured and heard the sharp intake of his breath in the otherwise silent Jeep. 'What happened on January sixth?' Because that the date was just a few days after her birthday seemed too much of a coincidence.

When he said nothing, she turned to study his profile. His jaw was like rock, his lips were pursed in a straight, hard line. His hands gripped the steering wheel, his knuckles white. He wasn't wearing gloves. Or the parka her grandfather had loaned him.

He slowed the Jeep and turned in to the parking garage under the police station. He parked, then closed his eyes. 'I can't talk about this right now,' he finally said. 'I have to talk to Shane Baird, who, according to my boss, is minutes away from losing his shit.'

But he didn't move, his hands maintaining their death grip on the steering wheel.

You are what's kept me going for the last godawful year.

She'd known what those colored pictures meant. She'd known he was asking for more time, for her patience. She'd known that.

But she'd let her emotions tangle her up. Loneliness, regret, and depression were bitter bedmates. She'd let her focus wander and . . . she'd missed seeing his pain. *God. I'm the worst therapist ever.*

She gave her head a hard shake. *I am* not *his therapist. And this is* not *about me.*

Operating on instinct, she pulled off her glove and reached across the console to cover one of his white-knuckled hands with hers. Carefully she peeled his fingers off the wheel and brought his hand to her lips.

He still didn't look at her, but his throat worked convulsively as he tried to swallow. She kissed each of his fingers, then pressed the back of his hand to her cheek. His stiff shoulders relaxed a fraction as he exhaled on a shudder. 'When you're ready to tell me, I'll be ready to listen,' she said quietly. 'For now, let me take a look at Mr Baird.'

She followed him into the police department's headquarters, a building she'd visited too many times in her role as a therapist, but never as a victim.

A potential target. That's what I am.

'You said to Isenberg that Johnny at Pies & Fries had mentioned Shane,' she said as Adam led her into the elevator and pushed the button for his floor. 'In what context?'

He was back in detective mode, his movements spare, his eyes coldly unreadable. 'According to Johnny, Andy Gold said he and Shane went to high school together, but that Shane got a full ride to a university up north and he moved away. Andy also brought a young woman into Pies & Fries from time to time. He called her Linnie.'

'Oh,' Meredith breathed, recalling the devastation on Andy Gold's face moments before his death. 'The "her" he was afraid would be killed. He said, "I'm sorry, Lin." I forgot about that until just now.'

His nod was brisk. 'A fair assumption then, but let's see what Mr Baird has to say.'

Adam took her straight to the observation side of the interview room where Lieutenant Isenberg waited in front of the mirror, arms folded over her chest. She was frowning, troubled.

She glanced up, greeted them with a nod, then returned her gaze to the two young men sitting at the table on the other side of the glass. 'The blond is Shane Baird. The ginger is his best friend, Kyle Davis. Both sophomores at Kiesler University. Kyle borrowed his girlfriend's car to get Shane here because Shane doesn't have a car and was "super rattled" when he saw Andy's picture in an article online. Kyle has apparently taken on the role of Shane's mouthpiece. The Baird kid's said only eight words since he got here. Kyle's been demanding to speak to the detective working Andy Gold's murder.'

'What were the eight words Shane said?' Meredith asked.

Isenberg gave her a considering glance. '"Who was the woman Andy tried to shoot?" He's repeated that question a dozen times. Have you seen either of them before?'

'So there *is* a connection between Andy Gold and Meredith,' Adam said with grim satisfaction.

Isenberg shrugged. 'Better than a long shot at least.'

Meredith studied the young men at the table. Both were pale, their clothing rumpled. Shane's blond hair was shaggy, but it had been cut conservatively at some point. He kept running a shaking hand through it. Kyle's shoulder-length red hair looked like he cut it himself whenever it got in his eyes. He must wear it in a ponytail, she thought, because he kept pulling at a lime-green scrunchie on his wrist and snapping it back. Every few seconds, he'd glance at his phone, precisely arranged on the table in front of him, then murmur something soundlessly. It looked like *please, please, please.*

Shane's knee kept bouncing under the table, stilling only when Kyle squeezed his shoulder.

'No,' Meredith said with certainty. 'I've never seen either of them before. I would have expected Mr Baird to be upset, but they both look like they're about to jump out of their skin. They're terrified.'

'And wired,' Adam commented. 'I don't want to spook them, although Kyle looks like he's more in control.'

Isenberg nodded. 'That's been the cycle since they got here. Every few minutes Kyle will squeeze Shane's shoulder and calm him down.' She handed Adam the file. 'The first thing Kyle will ask is if we've heard from Tiffany. She's Kyle's girlfriend and the one who loaned him her car for this trip. She hasn't responded to any of his texts since one thirty-five our time this morning.'

Adam frowned. 'She could be asleep.'

'I suggested that,' Isenberg said, 'but for whatever reason he didn't accept it. He was really worried when I got downstairs to meet them. He's upset that he doesn't get any cell signal down here, in case she's tried to reach him. I promised him I'd call the Chicago precinct near the girl's mother's house, which was where she was supposed to be staying for the weekend.' She shook her head and sighed. 'Turns out Kyle was right to be worried. Chicago PD confirmed a 911 call from that address at one thirty-seven a.m. They're sending a message to the detectives on the case to call us.'

'Shit,' Adam muttered, a muscle in his cheek twitching.

Meredith had to grip her hands together to keep from trying to soothe that twitching muscle with her thumb. He'd requested she'd stay professional, wear her zen mask. At least she could do that for him.

'How did Kyle know to be worried?' Adam asked.

Isenberg shrugged again. 'Don't know. That's what I want you to find out.'

Meredith watched the young man's mouth moving again. 'That's why Kyle's checking his phone and saying *please, please, please*.'

Isenberg nodded. 'Yeah. For now, Adam, just tell them we haven't heard anything. I won't add to their tension until I know facts. Dr Fallon can stay with me.'

'Right. I texted Trip after your call. He got called to the lab after we left the fire. They'd finished processing the internal components of the bomb and found something. He said he'd meet me here when he was done. We can debrief when I'm finished.'

Without a backward look, Adam left the observation room, emerging seconds later on the other side of the glass. Taking a seat across from the two, he smoothed his tie. 'Hi. I'm Detective Kimble. I'm investigating the incident that took place in the restaurant this afternoon. The file here' – he tapped the folder – 'says you're Shane Baird and Kyle Davis.'

'Has the lieutenant heard from my girlfriend yet?' Kyle demanded.

'She's called the precinct. We're still waiting to hear back from them. You'll know as soon as we do,' Adam promised. 'Why are you so worried about her?'

Kyle looked at Shane from the corner of his eye. Shane swallowed audibly and lifted his gaze to Adam's face. 'Who is the woman Andy tried to shoot?'

'Why do you need to know?' Adam countered coolly, and Shane erupted before their eyes, his clenched fists pounding the table in one sudden burst of fury.

'Don't answer my question with a goddamn question!' he shouted. 'My friend is dead. The woman he tried to shoot is the last person to talk to him. I want to know who she is.' He slumped back in his chair, as if the rage had taken all his reserves. 'I'm sorry.' He rubbed his hands over his face. 'But I won't tell you anything until I get an answer.'

Kyle's chin came up, but it trembled, spoiling his attempt at bravado. 'And we're not under arrest, so we can leave. We'll get the answer our own way.'

Meredith frowned at them. 'Lieutenant, I thought all the news reports on the shooting included my name.'

'They did,' Isenberg said. 'Baird has to have seen it. His insistence doesn't make sense.' She paused a moment. 'I want to see his reaction to you. Are you willing to go in there? We've searched them for weapons and Kimble and I will stay in there with you.'

'Of course,' Meredith replied. 'Whatever you need me to do.'

Cincinnati, Ohio,
Sunday 20 December, 4.30 A.M.

Shane Baird was, Adam thought, truly minutes away from losing his shit. He was debating asking Isenberg to bring Meredith into the interview when there was a light knock at the door and his boss stuck her head in. 'Detective? A word? Sorry, Mr Davis,' she said as Kyle opened his mouth. 'I'm still waiting for a call back. I promise I will let you know.'

She stood back to let Adam through the door where Meredith stood in the hall, just out of the boys' view.

'Great minds,' Adam murmured. 'I was about to ask you to send her in.'

'We'll all go in,' Isenberg said. 'Two of them, three of us.' She gave Meredith a stern look. 'If I tell you to leave, you leave without an argument.'

'I've already had a gun pointed at me once in the last twenty-four hours,' Meredith said seriously. 'I will not argue. I promise.'

Adam suspected the promise was more for him than for Isenberg and he wanted to kiss Meredith for making it, but kept his nod brusquely professional. 'Follow me, please.'

The young men started to stand when he returned, looking ready to bombard him with questions, but Adam gestured them to stay where they were. 'Mr Baird, you asked about the woman your friend tried to shoot. Here she is.' He stepped aside so that Meredith could come through the door. Isenberg brought up the rear and closed the door behind her. 'This is Dr Fallon. Dr Fallon, Shane Baird and Kyle Davis.'

'I'm so sorry for your loss,' Meredith said gently.

Shane came to his feet unsteadily and Adam got between him and Meredith. 'Mr Baird, please sit down.'

'I need . . .' Shane closed his eyes, weariness etched deep into his young face. 'I need to see her face. Please.'

'He had to take his contacts out,' Kyle explained. 'He wasn't able to get his glasses from his apartment before we left.'

Meredith took a few steps closer to the table, Adam staying no more than a step behind her. She leaned in much closer than Adam wanted and he had to bite back a growl.

'I don't know you,' she said softly to Shane. 'Do you know me?'

His gaze moved an inch at a time, cataloguing her face. 'No. You're not the one.' He dropped into his chair and buried his face in his hands. 'God.'

Meredith pulled out a chair and sat down across from the two. 'Who were you hoping I'd be, Mr Baird?'

Hands remaining in place over his face, he shook his head. 'I didn't hope you'd be. I was afraid you'd be. Why did Andy try to kill you?'

'I don't know,' she said. 'I'd never seen him before.'

Kyle looked suspicious. 'What kind of doctor are you?'

'I'm a child psychologist. I work with kids and teenagers. But I'd never met Andy before. I would have remembered him.' Her sigh was almost silent. 'I remember them all.'

'Then why did he pull a gun on you?' Shane demanded brokenly. 'It doesn't make sense. I can't even think anymore.'

'I think you're tired,' Meredith murmured soothingly. 'And

213

so am I. I will tell you the same thing I told the police. I do not believe your friend intended to hurt me. I think he was there against his will.'

Shane's hands dropped to the table, his expression one of abject misery. 'You told them that?'

'Of course.' She tentatively reached across the table, tilting her head, asking for permission to touch. Shane nodded and she covered his hands with her own. 'Your friend's last words were to tell me to run. I think he was a good person who was being forced. And now, here you are, and you know something that could maybe help Detective Kimble catch who did this. You have no reason to trust me, but I hope you'll trust Detective Kimble and Lieutenant Isenberg with what you know. I want the person who hurt Andy to pay.'

Shane's head fell forward slowly, his forehead resting on one of Meredith's hands. 'Somebody came looking for me tonight,' he whispered.

Adam took the seat next to Meredith. 'Who?' he asked, watching Isenberg take a guard position behind the two young men.

'I don't know,' Shane mumbled. 'Kyle?'

Kyle rubbed his mouth with the back of his hand. 'I work the desk at the dorm. Tonight, Saturday night I mean, this guy came in, pretending to be a friend of Shane's. Asked for his room. I told him that he didn't live there anymore – which he doesn't. He moved into an apartment in August. This guy got mad and mean and insistent. I pressed the panic button, which calls campus police. The guy left, but warned me to "be smart."'

'Did you tell the police what happened?' Adam asked.

'Yes. It was all caught on security camera, anyway. I called Shane, to warn him that some guy was looking for him.'

'Can you describe this guy?' Isenberg asked.

'Huge,' Kyle said with a shudder. 'Dark hair. His face was . . . odd. Tight, like he'd had plastic surgery or something. I told all of this to the campus cops. The camera is brand new so they got a clear view of his face and what he was saying.'

'So what happened when you called Shane?' Adam asked.

'He said he needed to go to Cincinnati, that the guy who died

214

was his friend. He'd just looked it up online and saw the news. I texted my girlfriend and arranged to borrow her car. It's newer than mine and has better tires.'

With her free hand, Meredith stroked Shane's hair and Adam felt the hard slam of jealousy. *Stupid*, he told himself. *Put that shit away. She's keeping him calm.*

Just like she keeps me calm.

'Shane, how did you know Andy?' she asked.

Shane's reply was muffled. 'From foster care.'

Meredith's shoulders stiffened almost imperceptibly. Bracing herself, Adam thought. 'I see,' she murmured. 'All right. How did you know to look up Cincinnati?'

Shane lifted his head, staring at her helplessly. 'Andy was a good person.'

'I know,' she said simply.

'But once, he did something . . . necessary.'

Kyle hadn't heard this story, it was obvious. His gaze was fixed on his friend. 'What did he do, Shane?' Kyle asked him sharply.

Shane blew out a breath. 'He killed someone. The foster father.'

'Why?' Meredith asked, so gently it made Adam's chest hurt.

'Andy was protecting Linnie. The bastard was bigger than us and he tried . . .' Another shuddered exhale. 'He did things. To Linnie. Over and over and over.'

'He raped Linnie,' Meredith said, giving the crime a name when Shane could not.

Tears filled Shane's eyes and he nodded. 'She didn't tell us at first. She was afraid that Andy would . . . do exactly what he did. But Andy heard them. Heard Linnie crying. Caught the bastard *hurting* her. And Andy made it stop. But she was so—' His voice cracked. 'Ashamed. And broken. After that she was broken.' He blinked, sending the tears down his face. 'I never should have left them. I should have stayed.'

Meredith squeezed the fist she still held. 'What happened today was not your fault, Shane, any more than it was mine. Let's figure this out so we can make the bastard who did it pay.'

He blinked and nodded. 'Okay,' he said hoarsely. 'The police came looking for Andy. Back then. We'd just graduated from high school, the three of us.'

'You lived in the same foster home?' Meredith asked.

Shane nodded. 'We had a pact. We'd always be there for each other. But I left.'

'Andy was proud of you,' Adam said quietly. 'He told a guy where he worked that you were going to make it. He was happy about that. He didn't blame you.'

Shane choked on a sob. 'That makes it worse.'

Kyle squeezed Shane's shoulder. 'What happened when the police came looking for Andy back then?'

'He wasn't Andy then. He was Jason Coltrain. He changed his name when he and Linnie ended up in Cincinnati. They hitchhiked. I gave them all the money I had saved up, but Andy used it to buy a new ID. Linnie called me, told me they'd caught a ride with a trucker and that they were okay. That Jason was now Andy and he'd got into college here.'

'Was he charged with the murder of the foster father?' Adam asked.

'No. He was arrested, but never charged. Because . . .' Shane dropped his gaze to Meredith's hand covering his. He shook his head and said no more.

'Because you lied for him?' Adam asked.

Shane lifted his gaze and started to answer, but Kyle interrupted him. 'Don't say anything about that, man.' He skewered Adam with a glare of his own. 'I'm pre-law. He's going to lawyer up if you ask questions like that.'

Pre-law, Adam thought wearily. *Of course he is.*

But they really didn't need a verbal confession at this point. Shane looked so miserably guilty that the answer was obvious. Meredith patted his hand. 'So when people came looking for you, you assumed it was because Andy was in trouble again?'

Shane nodded. 'He hadn't answered any of my phone calls for months. Neither had Linnie.' He frowned. 'I need to find her.'

'We want to find her too,' Adam said, then met Meredith's questioning eyes. She was asking permission to tell Shane what

Andy had said. Adam nodded.

Shane's frown grew sharper at their exchange. 'What? What's happened to Linnie?'

'We don't know,' Adam said truthfully. 'Do you know her last name?'

'Holmes,' Shane said without hesitation. 'Linnea Holmes. What happened?'

'I told you that Andy didn't want to hurt me,' Meredith said. 'I was calming him down, getting him to drop the gun, and he said "He'll kill her."'

Shane's eyes closed, his body sagging once more. 'He had to mean Linnie. She was it for him. He wanted to marry her, but he was too shy to tell her. And then she was . . . raped.' He spat the word. 'As if we hadn't all been through enough hell. We just wanted to make it to eighteen so we could be free. But that happened and Linnie was so broken then that Andy was afraid to tell her how he felt. Afraid she'd run away if she knew what he really wanted. She probably would have.'

'Andy took care of her, according to his boss,' Adam told Shane. 'Used his meal credit from the pizza place where he worked to take food to her.'

Shane's shoulders shook in a sob he couldn't hold back. 'That was Andy. I told you he was a good guy. He'd do anything for you. Go hungry so you could eat. Be cold because he gave you the coat off his fucking back. *Goddammit*.' He dropped his forehead back to Meredith's hand and she stroked his hair again. His hands moved, and suddenly he was clutching one of Meredith's hands with both of his, shuddering as she continued the gentle stroking of his hair with the other. 'He was good and they *killed* him.'

'I know,' she whispered. 'I'm so sorry.'

Adam lifted his eyes to meet Isenberg's. 'At least we can start looking for Linnie.'

Isenberg nodded. 'I'll put Bishop and Novak on the search.'

Shane looked up, his eyes red and swollen, tears still flowing. 'Where is she?'

'We heard she was a student. That's all we know. Honest,' Adam added when neither Shane nor Kyle looked convinced. 'Andy never gave his boss or coworkers many details about her.'

Shane nodded slowly. 'Yeah. That sounds about right.'

Good. At least he was gaining the kid's trust. Adam wondered if Shane was even aware that he held Meredith's hand so tightly. It had to be uncomfortable for Meredith, maybe even hurting her. But she hadn't flinched, so Adam didn't make an issue of it. 'Where was the foster home and when did the rape and murder occur?' he asked.

Hate flickered in Shane's wet eyes, his hands clenching reflexively on Meredith's. 'Indianapolis,' he spat. 'It will be three years on June twentieth. The rapist was Cody Walton.'

'If Andy wasn't charged for the crime, was someone else?' Isenberg asked.

Shane nodded. 'The fucker's wife,' he said with grim satisfaction. Meredith opened her mouth, then closed it purposefully. But Shane saw and his lip curled. 'You're worried that I'm not sorry that an innocent woman went to jail. I'm not. The day that the cops took Andy away in cuffs, she turned on Linnie. Blamed Linnie for "seducing her husband."' The young man's mouth twisted in bitter rage. 'But she *knew*. She knew what her husband had done. Over and over again. She looked the other way. Over and over again. She told the social worker that the girls were liars and troublemakers and the social worker believed her. As soon as the cops left with Andy, she was on the phone with the social worker, telling lies about Linnie, but that wasn't enough. She came after Linnie with a frying pan. Tried to hit her. Tried to beat her. I heard Linnie scream and ran upstairs to see why. One of the other kids was with me and we both saw Linnie cowering in a corner, trying to protect her head. We saw the bitch beating her. I gave the other kid my phone, told him to record everything and he did while I pulled the bitch off Linnie. Andy—' Shane cut himself off, shaking his head. 'Her bastard husband had been killed by a blow to the head with a frying pan, so when the cops saw the footage, they assumed she'd killed her husband in a rage because he was cheating. We had her on tape accusing Linnie of being a whore and seducing him.' He shrugged, his expressive face grown stone cold. 'Dots connected.'

Adam couldn't – wouldn't – blame the boy for lying to the police to save his friend. He couldn't verbally endorse it, but he wouldn't speak up to condemn it either. He couldn't stay silent, not forever anyway, but clearing that crime wasn't his priority at the moment. 'Do the Indianapolis police still have the video?'

Another cold shrug. 'I assume so. His wife got fifteen years, because all the kids came forward with all the stories they'd been too scared to tell. Linnie had a broken arm and a concussion from the bitch's attack.'

Shane's expression had gone cold when he started the story and now it stayed that way. The personality change was noteworthy, Adam thought. Didn't mean any of what the boy said was a lie, but he had not escaped his youth undamaged, that was for damn sure.

In fact, the kid reminded Adam of himself and wasn't *that* a kick in the head.

'Anything else?' Shane asked, his chin lifting, his eyes narrowing slightly. But he still held Meredith's hands like a lifeline.

'I have a question,' Meredith said. 'Who did you think I was?'

The stone-cold rage on his face receded, enough that he again looked like the young man he'd been when Adam had first entered the room. 'I was afraid you were Bethany Row, the social worker,' Shane admitted. 'I saw your photo online, but it was grainy. I couldn't see your face, but she had red hair like yours. Looked a little like you too. We hated her. She was the only person – other than the foster bitch – that Andy would have tried to kill, and Walton's wife is still in jail.' Fear flickered through his eyes. 'I think. Can you make sure?'

'I promise I will make sure,' Adam said levelly. 'Do you have any photos of Linnie? We can get one from Indy's children's services, but if you have one, that would let us start searching sooner.'

Finally releasing Meredith's hand, Shane pulled his phone from his pocket and found a photo, new tears filling his eyes. 'The three of us,' he said hoarsely, showing them a photo of three young people arm-in-arm, smiling. 'This was before. You know. Before Linnie was hurt. I need to find her. She might be hurt. Or cold . . .' His voice broke.

219

'Let the police search,' Meredith said softly. 'They know this town. If they can't find her at the colleges, they know all the places she might hide. You need to rest.'

Kyle looked worried. 'I don't know where we can go. We don't know anyone here and we used all our cash for gas.' He twisted in his chair to look back at Isenberg. 'Haven't you heard anything about Tiff? It's not like her to not answer my texts.'

'I'll call Chicago PD again right now,' Isenberg said. 'We'll also find you a safe place to sleep. Stay here for a little while and we'll be back. Detective? Dr Fallon?'

Meredith pushed away from the table, but gave Shane's messy hair one last stroke. 'Do you have anyone back in Chicago to help you?'

'Me,' Kyle declared and Meredith smiled at him.

'You're a great friend, but I was talking about a counselor.'

'The school has resources. He can see the shrink there.' Kyle waved the question away. 'Please, please, go find out about Tiff,' he begged.

Meredith stood up. 'Of course. We can talk more later.'

Shane gripped Meredith's hand as she stepped away, but once again there was no danger. Just a kid, grateful for her kindness. 'Thank you,' Shane said gruffly. 'For telling me about Andy and for believing he was good.'

She gave Shane's hand a final squeeze before following Adam and Isenberg out of the room. When the three of them were in the hall, a safe distance from the interview room, Meredith turned to Isenberg, ignoring Adam.

Just as you asked her to, he told himself, shoving back his irritation.

'You got news from Chicago?' Meredith asked Isenberg.

Isenberg's brows lifted in question. 'How did you know?'

'You looked sad after checking your phone. The girlfriend. Tiffany. Is she dead?'

Isenberg nodded grimly. 'I got the text along with a number to call. The lead investigator's a Detective Reagan. We'll call him from my office.'

Thirteen

Cincinnati, Ohio,
Sunday 20 December, 4.50 A.M.

Don't look. Don't touch. Don't lean. Meredith chanted to herself as she walked to the lieutenant's office between Adam and Isenberg. He was close enough that she could smell the soap he'd used in her shower.

Soap she'd smelled up close and personal as she'd finally touched all that beautiful skin, soft, warm, and wet. *And you are not going to think about that now.* She needed to think about serious things. Sober things.

It means that I'm an alcoholic. Her breath caught in her throat and she had to force herself to inhale. *Yes. Serious things like that.* She exhaled quietly and turned her attention to Isenberg, whose jaw was set in an angry line.

'Did you believe Shane?' she asked. 'About the murder that Andy Gold committed?'

'Yes,' Isenberg said. 'I'll check the details, but my gut says Shane's telling the truth.'

'And you have to report this to the Indianapolis DA,' Meredith said sadly.

'Yes,' Isenberg bit out. She said nothing for thirty seconds, continuing her ground-eating pace that had Meredith nearly skipping to keep up. 'And I don't want to.'

Meredith could feel furious regret pulsing off the older woman in waves. She knew Lynda Isenberg had a good, loyal heart under the armor – physical and emotional – that she wore. The woman's reluctance to see Shane punished further underscored her opinion and she was glad that Isenberg was Adam's boss.

Did Isenberg know about Adam's alcoholism? Did anyone know? If any of their friends did, they'd been incredibly discreet, and that was not a normal trait of their group.

'Will Shane face any charges?' she asked Isenberg.

'I don't know. I hope not. I'll do my best to keep that from happening.' The lieutenant unlocked her office door, blocking the path when Meredith started to follow them inside. 'Kimble and I are going to Skype with Chicago. You'll need to wait out here.'

Meredith blinked. 'Oh, right,' she murmured, her cheeks heating. 'I forgot that I'm the target.' *And the reason that Andy Gold is dead.* 'I'm so used to being the consultant.'

'Thanks,' Isenberg said, her expression softening.

'Sit there.' Adam pointed at the desk closest to the window that allowed Isenberg to see the bullpen, the blinds currently drawn. 'Where we can see you.'

There was no softness in his expression. No indication that an hour before he'd kissed her so tenderly she'd wanted to weep.

He's a very good actor. He had to have been, to keep his struggle for sobriety a secret among their circle of nosy friends. She'd do well to remember that.

'Meredith?'

Meredith looked up to see Jeff Triplett striding across the room. He was wearing the same suit he'd had on when he'd stopped by her house the evening before. 'Hey, Trip,' she said wearily. 'You didn't get to go home either?'

'Unfortunately, no. Got a call from the lab. What are you doing here?'

Meredith looked around. There were a few detectives at their desks and she wasn't sure what she was allowed to say in front of them. 'You should probably ask Adam and the lieutenant.' She pointed to the office window. 'They're making a call.'

He hesitated a moment, hooking a finger under her chin, lifting her gaze to his. She had to tilt her head way back because the man was huge. 'You get any sleep at all today?'

'A little,' she lied.

He let her go with a snort. 'You are an amazing liar.'

'It's my X-Man skill,' she said lightly. 'I'll sleep later. They're taking me to a safe house. My grandfather too.'

'I know. Zimmerman emailed your guard roster to everyone on the case.'

Meredith was caught between being touched and freaked. 'I have a guard roster?' She should have known she'd be under guard at a safe house, but still. A roster? 'Really?'

'Until we figure out how all the pieces connect, you're the key right now.' He flashed a smile that made women swoon. Especially Kendra, she thought dryly. 'Kate is on tonight and Troy is on tomorrow. They made it known that they really wanted the duty.'

Meredith smiled back at him, relieved. 'That's good to know. I'll be able to sleep with them on watch.' Kate had become one of her very best friends in the short time they'd known each other, and Kate's partner, Agent Luther Troy, was a very kind man. Older than the rest of them, he tended to skirt the edge of their circle. 'Troy always seems lonely. I'll have to use this opportunity to work on him, so he starts accepting our invitations.'

Trip's smile became sweet, making her heart melt a little. *Oh, Kenny, you are going to have your hands full with this one.*

'You do that,' he said. 'He's all like Uncle Luther this and that, and acting like a cross between Yoda and Charles Xavier, but he's too alone.' He looked over at the window, where Adam still stood, watching them. 'I need to get in there. I'll see you in a bit.'

'I'm not leaving this chair. His highness in there has commanded it so.' She thought he'd laugh, but he nodded with all seriousness.

'Good. We need to be able to watch over you.'

He went into the office and Meredith sighed. She didn't want to be watched over like the children she treated, but these circumstances were not normal by any stretch of the imagination and she did not consider herself to be a foolish woman. So sit she would.

She pulled out her phone and fiddled with it, wishing she could knit like Kate. Wishing she'd brought something to read or even to color. Her hands were fidgety.

Her whole body was fidgety. *I'm tired.* But way too wired to sleep. It was a bad combination, she knew. *Especially when you forget your meds. Idiot.*

She'd been so rattled as she'd packed. She'd tried to look calm for Adam's sake, but . . . *God.* Four people had died in that fire. A family. A baby in a crib. *Dead because someone wants to kill me.* She'd thought she'd been efficient, focusing on packing, but she'd obviously failed. She never forgot her meds and now was *not* the time to miss a dose.

Maybe Adam will take me back to my house so I can get . . . No, she thought. She wouldn't ask him to do that. He was exhausted and would need to sleep, at least a little. Going straight to the safe house made the most sense.

Meredith desperately wanted to be sensible, even when everything else was upside down and crazy, so she sent a text to Kate. *Did you leave my house yet?*

The reply came less than a second later. *Yes. Arrived @ SH. Why?*

They'd already arrived at the safe house. Meredith sighed. *I forgot something.* She was considering asking Kate to go back when her phone buzzed with a reply.

I cleaned out ur medicine cabinet. Dumped it all in a bag. Was in a rush so I didn't bother to check all the labels. Some of the stuff might be expired. Okay?

Meredith breathed out a sigh of relief. *Thx. Hoping to be there soon. Papa ok?*

Fine. Playing games w/Diesel who doesn't want to leave. Think u have a new cousin cuz Clarke has adopted him.

That settled something within her and she let out the first easy breath in hours. Diesel needed her grandfather. *Maybe as much as I do,* she thought.

Her phone buzzed again. *Also . . . got your . . . * stuff * from ur safe.*

Meredith's eyes widened. Her guns. Shit. Now she was wondering what exactly she *had* packed. Hopefully her toothbrush, at least. *How did you know code?*

Clarke. He says you must change code ASAP.

She sighed. Of course Papa would know. Her combination had been her parents' wedding anniversary. *Tell him I will. Thx for all. See u soon.*

A throat clearing above her had her looking up. A man in his late thirties, early forties was alternating between looking at her and looking through the window at Adam, his expression worried. He wore a dark blue suit, slightly rumpled, his tie tugged away from his collar, the top few buttons of his shirt undone. His blond hair was silver at the tips, his eyes accented with faded crow's feet, as if he laughed a lot.

A prickle of alarm skittered down her spine, and she felt the urge to bolt for Isenberg's office door, but she shoved it away. She was going to have to be prepared for fear when she met new people for a while. The last new person who'd walked up to her had pulled a gun and then gotten killed in front of her.

She knew her fear now was unfounded. She was in the middle of the police station, for goodness' sake. But she also knew PTSD happened in cases like hers. She didn't plan to be one of those therapists who ignored her own symptoms. She met new people every damn day, so she was going to have to deal.

'I don't work here,' she said, conjuring a polite smile. 'But I'm sure someone else here can help you.'

'It's okay. *I* work here. Well, not here on Isenberg's task force. Or in Homicide.' He stuck out his hand, revealing the shoulder holster he wore, complete with service weapon. 'Detective Hanson, Narcotics Division.'

Meredith shook his hand, still smiling politely even though she still wanted to run. 'Do I know you?' Because she felt like she should.

'We've never met, no. I'm a friend of Detective Kimble's.' He pointed to the window where Adam, Trip, and Isenberg had gathered around Isenberg's laptop. Adam looked up at that moment, his gaze landing first on Meredith before noticing Detective Hanson and his eyes widened, his mouth curving into a rueful smile. He held up his right hand, flexing four fingers in a 'come-here' gesture, followed by his index finger ticking like a clock.

Sign language, Meredith realized, and searched her memory for the meaning. She knew a few signs because Deacon and Dani's younger brother was deaf and they signed to him. She'd practiced hard the few times Greg had joined their group for a barbecue or party, but what she'd learned seemed to seep out of her head as soon as the young man said goodbye. Languages had never been her forte and sign wasn't looking to be any different.

Adam, she knew, was fluent, as were Dani and Deacon. Even Faith was learning, since Greg Novak was soon to become her brother-in-law.

'Fifteen,' Hanson supplied, startling her. 'He said he'd be done in fifteen minutes.'

Meredith regarded the man with curiosity. 'You know sign language?'

'A little. Adam and I have been friends since high school. He taught me a few signs.' He indicated the chair at the next desk. 'May I?'

She shrugged. 'Like I said, I don't work here.'

He eased himself into the desk's chair. 'I was also Adam's first partner, when he was fresh out of the academy. I was a few years ahead experience-wise because he went to college first. He taught me some sign back then because it came in handy when we needed to silently communicate. I kept it up.'

'Really?' Meredith wondered exactly how much of Adam's personal information this man planned to tell – for all he knew – a complete and total stranger.

He smiled at her, his eyes crinkling at the corners. 'I know who you are, Dr Fallon.'

Busted, she thought. Her poker face was not fully functional when she hadn't properly slept. 'How?'

'You're all over the newspapers, for one. Also, I used to work Personal Crimes. Several of the victims whose cases I worked were referred to you afterward.'

'Oh. That's how I know your name.' She grimaced. 'Saying thank you seems wrong for this occasion. Those were hard cases. When did you leave Personal Crimes?'

'Just a few months ago. It just got to be too much. I also worked

226

ICAC, but I had to get out of that department too. Wears on you after a while.'

Meredith controlled her shudder, but just barely. The officers in the Internet Crimes Against Children department had to view photos she couldn't stomach even thinking about.

'I'm sure it does,' she murmured. Providing therapy to the victims wore on her and she was only hearing about it after the fact.

'I figured you'd understand.' Hanson shifted his gaze back to Adam, eyeing him through the window. 'How's he doing?'

She couldn't hide her surprise. 'Please?'

'Adam. I know you're friends. He's mentioned you before. You've helped in the past. Helped him find his center.'

She said nothing and he glanced back at her. 'Sorry,' he said shortly. 'I didn't mean to overstep. I just worry about him every time he gets on a . . . messy case.'

She continued to regard him steadily. 'I don't understand.'

He shrugged uncomfortably. 'I was his partner again fifteen months ago. Right before he took his medical leave. I watched him fall apart once. I'm not keen on seeing it happen again.' He met Meredith's gaze. 'I don't want details. I just want to be sure that he's all right. I've known Adam since we were kids. Our dads are close. He has people who care about him, even if he doesn't want us to.'

That, at least, made sense, she thought. 'Well, he'll be out soon, so you can ask him.'

The detective gave her a considering look that bordered on admiration. 'Well, good. I'm glad he has you in his corner, Dr Fallon. A lesser person might have blabbed. Thank you for keeping his secrets.'

She smiled at him serenely. She'd been around enough cops to recognize backhanded interrogation techniques and there was no way she was spilling any of what she knew. Mostly because she never would share Adam's secrets, but partly because she wasn't sure exactly what those secrets were.

It means that I'm an alcoholic.

She swallowed back the sigh and inclined her head. 'Again, saying thank you doesn't seem appropriate here. But . . . thank you.'

Chuckling, he twisted in the chair, pulling his wallet from his back pocket, taking out a plastic photo keeper that was stuffed full of photos. He searched each little pocket until he made a satisfied sound. He rolled the chair closer to Meredith's, holding out one of the photos. 'That's us. I'm the one on the left,' he added.

Meredith took the picture, her mouth curving of its own volition. Two boys in baseball uniforms stood, arms over each other's shoulders. One dark, one light. The boy on the right was clearly Adam Kimble. He had boyish good looks even then. Both wore grass stains on their knees and huge smiles on their faces. 'How old were you?'

'He was sixteen. I was almost eighteen. We were only a grade apart, though. Adam was a fair student, but I'd been held back a year in middle school, which I basically hated the world for, but it turned out okay. If I hadn't been kept back, I would've graduated two years ahead of him and we wouldn't have played for the same team in high school. Those were good days.'

She smiled fondly at the photo. 'Did you win?'

'Went to the state playoffs, but lost in the quarter finals. Adam played another year. That year they went on to win the state championship. Adam ended up getting a baseball scholarship to college, which was good because with his grades? Well, let's just say it was good he could hit a home run like nobody else, because he was never gonna ace math.'

'Hm,' she said, torn between annoyance at his criticism of Adam and temptation to ask for more details. But she really wanted to hear Adam's story from Adam, so she handed Hanson back the picture.

'I ran track in high school. Couldn't hit a ball to save my life,' Meredith admitted. It wasn't entirely true, but close enough. 'I wasn't good enough for a scholarship, though.'

'Neither was I,' Hanson said ruefully. He put the photo back in his wallet, then returned his gaze to the window with a quiet sigh. 'You don't have to answer this, but . . .' He sighed again. 'If he starts to . . . need anyone, can you call me?' He patted his pockets, then rolled his eyes. 'I don't have any cards with me. Do you have any paper?'

She wanted to say no, but Adam had smiled at this man, had looked happy to see him. As happy as Adam ever looked anyway. If Hanson could be a resource for Adam, far be it from her to deny them. Digging in her purse, she found a small spiral notebook, pulled out a page and handed it to him, along with the tactical pen she always carried.

It was a stainless steel pen that could puncture a man's windpipe if it was applied with enough force. Meredith had practiced on dummies at the gym. The weapon doubled as a real pen, camouflaged by its shiny pink color, its surface covered with engraved hearts. It was her favorite pen because she could bring it into controlled environments – like on a plane, or into a courthouse or a police department – without having it taken by security.

Hanson, however, recognized its purpose immediately. He took the pen with another deep chuckle. 'I need to get my wife one of these. Where'd you get it?'

Meredith considered denying it, then shrugged. 'Amazon.'

'Of course. My number,' he said, handing her the paper and her pen.

She folded the paper and put it, the notebook, and her pen back in her purse, then changed her mind, pulling them back out. Tearing out a clean sheet of paper, she proceeded to sketch a geometric design she could color in, hoping it would be a signal to the man not to ask her anything more.

Cincinnati, Ohio,
Sunday 20 December, 5.15 A.M.

'Got 'em back,' Isenberg said, nodding at her laptop with a self-satisfaction that Adam thought would have been almost cute under other circumstances. Not that he would have ever called his boss cute under *any* circumstances. A straight arrow, both her wit and her tongue were sharper than any blade. Occasionally the humanity she held so closely in check peeked through the crusty shield she showed the world.

Like her pride when she figured out something on the computer that any five-year-old could accomplish blindfolded, like how to reestablish the Skype connection with the Chicago detectives after their call had been inexplicably interrupted.

Or when she viewed the photos and videos Chicago had taken of the crime scene and her first response had been to glance at Adam, to be sure he was all right. Because those photos were . . . difficult to look at. For anyone.

But for me? The slash across Tiffany Curtis's throat was a definite trigger for him. And all the blood? Both in her room and in her mother's? There was so much of it, soaking the bed, splattered on the headboard, the nightstand, the carpet. The phone that had slipped from the mother's hand to land in a pool of her own blood?

He drew a harsh breath. Keeping his mind from drifting back to that day Paula's throat was slit was taking all the strength he possessed. And knowing that Tiffany and her mother had been killed simply because someone wanted access to Shane Baird because Shane was connected to Andy Gold who was somehow connected to Meredith?

'Kimble?' Trip rumbled softly, bumping his shoulder. Trip had come in while Isenberg had still been muttering curses at her computer. 'We're live again.'

Adam jerked his attention back to the screen, which showed only a close-up of the knot of a man's tie. That would be Detective Abe Reagan, nine years with Chicago Homicide. Adam had looked him up while Isenberg had been setting her laptop up for the initial call. Reagan was highly decorated, according to the articles Adam had skimmed. And most of the time the articles used his first and last names because he apparently had a brother who was also a decorated homicide detective, and whose name also started with A.

Reagan backed away from the camera, revealing a woman's boots propped up on the table. Just visible over the boot tips was the top of his partner's blond head with its tumbled, tangled curls and the edge of what looked like one of the crime scene photos.

'Sorry,' Isenberg said. 'My laptop must have lost the connection, but we're back.' She gestured to Trip. 'This is Special Agent Jefferson Triplett. He's on our joint task force.'

'I'm Detective Reagan.' Reagan sat in his chair and elbowed his partner who abruptly swung her boots off the table. 'This is Detective Mitchell.'

Mitchell was small, sturdy and, according to Adam's Google search, also highly decorated, having received a Distinguished Service citation for bringing down a serial arsonist seven years ago. 'Hey,' she said. 'What do you know, Triplett?'

'About your scene? Not much. Do you mind repeating the high points?'

'No, of course not,' she said so politely, that her irritation was clear. 'Although we're still waiting for your connection to our case.'

'Mia,' Reagan murmured.

Mitchell rolled her eyes. 'I know, I know. We play nice, they tell us stuff.'

Reagan's lips twitched, making Adam's do the same. 'That's how it works,' Reagan said seriously, then ruined the effect by rolling his eyes.

'Fine,' Mitchell huffed, then sighed heavily. 'Okay. The victims are Tiffany Curtis, twenty, and her mother, Ailene Curtis, forty-five. The intruder appeared to come in through the mother's bedroom window.' Mitchell's face disappeared from the screen, a photo of a broken window appearing in its place. 'The glass was smashed and the lock forced.' The window photo was replaced by the scene of the mother's body in the bloody bed.

Adam wanted to look away from the hand limply hanging over the bed, the phone in that puddle of blood on the floor. The slit throat. The disemboweled torso. But he forced himself to stare at the screen.

To not think about how that *had* been Paula. Who'd only been a child. A child he'd been too late to save. He could feel himself mentally scrabbling for purchase. Just thinking about Paula sent him over the edge. *So stop it.*

He forced himself to focus on this woman who'd lost her life simply because her daughter loaned her car to Kyle Davis, friend of Shane, friend of Andy. Who'd been coerced into attempting to kill Meredith. *Shit,* he thought viciously.

Trip sighed. 'Shit.'

'Yeah,' Mitchell said, echoing Trip's weary tone. 'It was a real mess. The mother had a CPAP machine going.'

'She probably didn't hear her killer break the glass,' Adam said. He'd missed that the first time because he'd been fighting to keep his control. He was listening now, and didn't miss the relief in Isenberg's eyes. He gave her a slight nod. *Yeah, yeah, I'm back.* 'Those machines are loud.'

'Exactly,' Reagan said. The wide-angled photo of the bed changed to a close-up of the body and Adam steeled himself, forcing his gaze not to flick away. To look.

He maintained his focus until Trip sucked in a breath through his nose. 'Shit,' Trip said again, this time in a sad whisper.

Adam broke away, finding Meredith through the window. Drinking her in. She was safe and unharmed. He kept telling himself that, over and over until the wave of panic receded. A movement caught his eye, a figure standing by the desk where she sat and he had to smile. Wyatt Hanson.

Wyatt was his oldest friend that was not related to him, by red blood anyway. Adam's mother and Deacon and Dani's mother had been sisters, but he and Wyatt were related through blue blood. Their fathers had been patrol partners, once upon a time, and he and Hanson had carried the tradition to the next generation.

Isenberg caught Adam's stare and leaned around her laptop to follow his gaze. 'Ah, Detective Hanson is here. Good.'

'He's here to see you?' Adam asked, oddly disappointed.

'I asked Narcotics for someone to work with you on the Voss angle. I'll talk to him when I'm finished with you.'

'Oh.' That made sense, because the Narcotics umbrella covered prostitution and drugs. They might have information on the apparent prostitution ring at the college. He signed to Hanson that he'd be another fifteen minutes and asked him to wait.

The photo on screen disappeared and the two Chicago detectives were eyeing them with interest. 'Voss?' Reagan asked. 'Who is this?'

'Broderick Voss,' Isenberg said. 'We'll explain when you're finished. Apologies for the interruption.'

Mitchell rapidly typed on her phone, then looked up, wide-eyed. 'Voss, huh?' She tilted her photo so that her partner could see and he whistled softly.

'This just got even more interesting,' he said.

You have no idea, Adam thought grimly.

'Let's finish with the crime scene first,' Trip said. 'What happened after he slit the mother's throat?'

Mitchell continued. 'We believe the killer thought she was dead and went on to the daughter's room. We found earbuds still plugged into Tiffany's laptop, so she didn't hear him. She'd just been texting to her boyfriend's phone. The texts were actually between Tiffany and her boyfriend's friend, Shane Baird. He told her that they were "an hour away" and thanked her for the use of her car. Said she couldn't know what it meant to him.'

'We've talked to Shane Baird and Kyle Davis,' Isenberg said.

The Chicago cops' faces registered surprise. 'When?'

'Right before we called you,' Adam said. 'We were talking to them when we got the text from you. If you could go over the girl's murder again for Trip first, we'll fill you in.'

Mitchell looked irritated once again at the delay. 'Looks like he pushed her to the bed and climbed on top of her. He left bloody boot prints on the bed spread.'

'The mother's blood?' Adam asked tightly, visualizing it.

'Yeah,' Reagan confirmed with a nod. 'It appears that Tiffany fought back, biting his hand in the process. We found a latex glove with faint impressions of teeth that look like hers. They're the right size anyway. Lab's checking it.'

This hadn't been shared in the first version, Adam was certain. 'So he entered the house wearing gloves, but left without one at least? Did you find any prints?'

Mitchell gave Reagan a side-eyed glance. Reagan shrugged. 'Go ahead,' he said. 'It might end up being nothing.'

Mitchell leaned forward, her eyes sharp. 'So this is the thing. At some point she bit his hand and his glove got ripped and slung off. Either on purpose or by accident, but it landed across the room. He continued strangling her bare-handed with the one hand.'

233

Adam sucked in a breath at the same time that Isenberg and Trip did the same. 'Did you get prints?' Adam asked again.

Mitchell shrugged. 'Our CSI leader is working it now. Jack Unger is one of the best, so if it can be done, he'll do it. We'll keep you up to speed.'

'That would be huge,' Trip said.

Isenberg looked up at Trip, narrow-eyed. 'Did you find a print on the bomb?'

'Yes. That's what the lab wanted to see me about. They found a print, but it belonged to the victim, Andy Gold.'

There was more, Adam thought. The lab could have told him that over the phone.

'Andy Gold,' Reagan said. 'That's the young man who pulled a gun in that restaurant yesterday. Gold was the friend of Baird's who died?'

'Yes,' Isenberg said. 'How did you know that?'

'Tiffany had been texting with her boyfriend, Kyle. He asked to borrow her car because Shane's friend in Cincinnati had died and they needed to get there ASAP.'

Adam frowned, a detail catching in his mind. 'Can you show us the photo of Tiffany's body again?' Chicago complied and Adam's gaze lingered on the slash in the woman's throat for a few seconds before moving to her right hand. Which was missing the forefinger. 'I assumed you hadn't found her phone,' he said. 'Her killer took her finger.'

Because that would be the way to unlock the girl's phone and get whatever information he'd come for. Like where her car – carrying Shane and Kyle – had gone.

Reagan gave him a nod. 'You're right, her killer did take her phone. But he didn't take her iPad, which, luckily for us, wasn't locked down. It was buzzing like crazy in her nightstand drawer.'

'Thank goodness for iMessage, I guess,' Isenberg murmured.

Reagan nodded again. 'She had her messages set to sync up on all her devices, including her laptop, but that was password protected. Kyle kept texting, begging her to call him. And then your office called, Lieutenant, to ask us to check on Tiffany Curtis.'

'I got confirmation that there had been a 911 call made from the Curtis home tonight,' Isenberg said.

'Yes,' Mitchell said. 'At one thirty-seven, about two minutes after Tiffany's final text to Shane.'

Adam thought of the phone in the puddle of the mother's blood. 'The mother managed to dial 911?'

A sad nod from both Chicago detectives. 'She never said a word,' Mitchell said. 'But the operator could hear crashes and other noises in the background. The killer must have heard the sirens because he stopped strangling Tiffany, slit her throat, sliced her torso, cut off her finger, took her phone, then exited through the mother's bedroom window.'

'After taking a few seconds to rip his knife through the mother's abdominal cavity,' Reagan finished, his jaw taut. 'He was very angry. The ME says the mother was already dead at the time of the final assault.'

'He has a temper,' Adam murmured. 'Might work to our advantage. Since the iPad was unlocked, could you track Tiffany's phone with the Find-My-Phone app?'

Mitchell's nod was grim. 'Yeah. He tossed it in the trash can at a gas station in Indiana. We requested local PD get the phone and the security tapes from the gas station. The phone's on its way to us, but they've already sent us a copy of the video file. Unfortunately, the guy kept his body hunched and his collar up to cover the lower half of his face. Baseball cap hid everything else. He looks big, but we can't give you a specific description.'

'He's headed this way,' Trip said quietly.

'Yeah.' Adam glanced at Isenberg and raised a brow in question. 'Kyle?' he asked. She nodded, so he continued. 'Kyle works the desk at Lamarr dorm at Kiesler University. He said a man came looking for Shane tonight. He was very big and threatening, and Kyle hit the panic button under the desk. The campus police have a photo of this guy from the security cameras.'

'Give me a minute to call the university police,' Mitchell said, and rolled her chair out of camera range.

'What else did Kyle and Shane say?' Reagan asked, while his partner made the call.

Isenberg quickly relayed most of what Shane had shared, holding back the murder that Andy had committed and that Shane had covered for. 'There might be a third person, a young woman, who was in their tight little circle of friends. We've put her photo out on the wire as a person of interest, possibly missing.'

Mitchell rolled her chair back into view. 'The university police are sending us their surveillance video. I was listening about the missing girl, so let's move on. What's this have to do with Broderick Voss?'

'Voss has been stalking the target of today's attack,' Isenberg told them.

'And Voss connects to Narcotics?' Mitchell pushed.

'Maybe,' Isenberg said. 'His wife says she caught him with illegal drugs and barely legal prostitutes in their home, when their six-year-old daughter was present. The wife got slapped around when she confronted him, so she took their daughter and went to live with her sister.'

'Mrs Voss has tried to get her daughter psychological therapy,' Trip added, 'but we believe Voss scared off the first two therapists and wants to scare off Dr Fallon – today's target. Mrs Voss told us that her daughter's been seeing Dr Fallon for the last few weeks.'

Both Chicago cops' faces had darkened. 'If it's true, that child has to be keeping one hell of a secret that Mr Voss doesn't want getting out,' Mitchell said, her eyes gone narrow and steely. 'He was willing to kill a restaurant full of people today and he did kill two innocent people tonight.'

'Seven actually, including Andy Gold,' Adam said, his stomach giving a nasty lurch as he remembered the scene of the fire. 'The house where Andy rented a room was burned to the ground earlier tonight. The family of four who lived there didn't make it.' He swallowed hard. 'Mother, father, two kids. One still in a crib.'

Beside him, Trip sighed heavily. 'I'll never forget that sight,' he said quietly.

Adam gave Trip's shoulder a hard squeeze. 'I'd be worried if you could. But, um, make sure you deal, okay?' he added in a nearly soundless whisper. 'Don't do what I did.'

One side of Trip's mouth quirked up and he nodded once, sadly. 'Understood.'

On the screen, a muscle ticked in Reagan's cheek, grown taut with unhidden fury. 'This Voss needs to be put down.'

'Easy,' Mitchell murmured, patting Reagan's clenched fist with unmistakable affection. 'Papa Bear here has three daughters of his own. His youngest is still in a crib.' Her tone was mild, but her eyes remained as angry as Reagan's. 'My son Jeremy's fourteen, but he witnessed his birth mother being abused before she was murdered. It took years of therapy before he was . . . healed, at least. I hope this Dr Fallon can help Voss's little girl.'

'Fallon's good,' Adam said simply. 'She's helped a lot of kids.'

'How does she connect to yesterday's victim?' Reagan asked, flattening his hands on the table, palms down. His eyes remained angry. 'To Andy Gold, I mean.'

Adam was glad to see that Reagan's anger hadn't subsided, because neither had his own. 'We don't know.' He lifted his eyes to look out the window again, found her smiling at Hanson, who'd taken the seat next to her. She was giving him back something small and square, something that Hanson put back into his wallet. A photo. Adam thought he knew which one. He had the other copy in an album in his apartment. He returned his gaze to the two detectives on the screen. 'But I think it's safe to assume that our cases are connected. We'll keep you up to date as we investigate.'

Mitchell rubbed her eyes. 'I read Tiffany's texts on her iPad. She'd told her best friend – we assumed they were best friends from their text history, anyway – that Kyle told her that he'd bought her something special for Christmas. That he had an important question for her. She'd written "Tiffany Davis" over and over on a notepad on her desk.'

'Oh no.' Adam slumped, as did Isenberg and Trip. 'She was expecting a proposal.'

'That was our take,' Mitchell said sadly. 'We thought you should know.'

Adam rubbed his tired eyes. 'Thanks. Dammit, this day has sucked ass.'

Isenberg gave his knee a quick pat. 'Maybe have Dr Fallon ready. Just in case.'

Both Reagan and Mitchell straightened. 'Your target?' Reagan asked. 'Why?'

Recognizing her slip, Isenberg winced a little, but answered. 'Dr Fallon is one of our consulting psychologists. Highly respected by anyone who's worked with her. Our plan was to keep her far from this investigation, for obvious reasons, but Shane demanded to meet the woman who his friend had tried to shoot. She was willing and established an instant rapport. Her specialty is children and adolescents who've suffered emotional trauma. Shane shared more with her than we would have anticipated.'

Mitchell's eyes narrowed once again. 'What have you not told us?'

Isenberg sighed. 'It might not be related to this case. There was a crime committed in the foster home where the three kids lived. It was integral to their becoming . . . family. He was a minor at the time.' She looked at the Chicago cops directly. 'I don't know you. I don't want to risk this kid's future when it may have nothing to do with this case.'

Reagan and Mitchell gave each other a long, long look, communicating the way longstanding partners often did. 'All right,' Reagan finally said. 'We don't know you either, so . . . I'm not going to say we'll trust you. But we'll work the case based on what we currently have. For now. You'll share this information if it becomes germane?'

'The very next second,' Isenberg said soberly.

Trip cleared his throat. 'I suppose this might be a bad time to ask if you'll send us your crime scene photos,' he said with his aw-shucks grin.

Reagan's chuckle was deep and rich. 'Well, yeah, your timing is pretty bad, but I'll tell you the same thing I would have told you before you admitted to withholding information.' He sounded genuine. Adam wanted to believe the two cops were as genuine as they seemed. His gut said they were.

'Which is?' Adam prompted.

'That we have to run it by our boss,' Mitchell said. 'If Lieutenant Murphy okays it, then you'll have them' – her lips curved into a reluctant smile – 'the very next second.'

Isenberg smiled and it changed her whole face. Made her look years younger. Made Adam wonder how old she actually was. Made him wonder what had happened in her life to make her look so . . . well, *old* the rest of the time. 'Fair enough,' she said. 'Thank you.'

Mitchell nodded. 'My husband was raised in foster care. He was one of the lucky ones. He got a good family first thing, and they adopted him. I take it that Shane Baird's experience was not as good.'

'You take correctly,' Adam told her. 'Thanks. We'll be in touch.'

Ending the call, Isenberg turned to Trip. 'What did you *really* find at the lab?'

'Andy Gold's fingerprints came up in AFIS,' Trip said. 'His legal name was Jason Coltrain. He was born in Indianapolis. Was arrested for the murder of Cody Walton. Never charged. The victim's wife was found guilty and is serving a fifteen-year sentence.'

'That's consistent with what Shane told us,' Adam said, and told Trip the rest of Shane's story of the murder, Linnie's rape, and how Andy had been set free and made his escape with Linnie Holmes.

Trip's eyes widened and he looked at Meredith, who was intent on whatever she was writing. *No*, Adam thought, *she's coloring.* Shading whatever she'd drawn with the pink pen in her hand.

Of course she's coloring. But Adam kept his smile inside, because it would have been too fond and Isenberg would have known he was compromised in a hot second.

'She got Shane to confess to covering up a murder?' Trip asked, wide-eyed.

'She did,' Isenberg said. 'I think Shane wanted to tell, but she made it easier for him. What else do you know, Triplett? Because the lab could have just called you with the fingerprint results.'

'We took the bomb apart.'

'When?' Adam asked, surprised.

'When you were questioning the restaurant hostess.'

'The team did?' Adam pressed, wondering how extensive Trip's skills really were. 'Or you did?'

Trip shrugged. 'I did,' he said, adding quickly, 'but I told you it was a simple device. Anyway, Latent got a partial print. So far it doesn't match anything in AFIS.'

'But if Chicago comes up with something at their new crime scene . . .' Isenberg said.

Trip grinned. 'Exactly.'

She rubbed her hands together. 'What else you got?'

'Finally,' Trip drawled, 'saving the best for last, we got a ballistic match on the bullet that killed Andy Gold. The same rifle was used in a robbery in 1988.'

Isenberg's expectant glee became a frown. 'That was thirty years ago.'

'But we may be able to trace the rifle's ownership,' Adam said. 'It's possible.'

'Zimmerman's already got someone on it,' Trip said. 'That's all I got.'

'Me too.' Adam checked the time on his phone and inwardly groaned. 'I'm going to drop Meredith at the safe house, then I'll grab some sleep myself.'

'Gather back here by noon,' Isenberg told him. 'We need to figure out what we have and where we go from there.'

'Oh shit,' Adam said, the sudden burden of dread stopping him in his tracks. 'Kyle. We need to tell him about Tiffany and then we need to find a safe place for them to stay. Whoever killed Tiffany and her mother is clearly looking for Shane. And he's on his way back to Cincinnati. I think we can assume he'd kill Kyle to get to Shane. Neither are safe.'

Isenberg sighed. 'I'll find them a place.'

'What about the condo?' Trip asked. 'Can't they stay there too? At least for tonight. We've already got a duty roster set. We can take precautions. Maybe get an additional guard for their door and make sure they don't know where we're taking them so they can't share the condo's location.'

Adam considered it. 'They got no priors. They don't seem dangerous, but I'm not taking chances. Kate's on inside duty tonight.' He would be too, right outside Meredith's room, but if he needed to leave for any reason, he wanted the young men contained should they be more than they appeared. 'Lynda, if you can get me a uniform to stand outside their bedroom door, it'll work.'

Isenberg nodded wearily. 'I'll take care of it.' She checked her watch. 'Given that you have to get Kyle and Shane settled—'

'And eat,' Trip inserted.

Isenberg looked amused. 'And eat,' she allowed. 'Be back by three. Get some sleep, gentlemen.' She glanced at the window where Hanson and Meredith still sat at side-by-side desks. Hanson was fiddling with his phone and Meredith continued to color with a focus Adam both envied and hated. He hated that she'd needed the solace of her coloring tonight, wishing Meredith was home in her soft bed, safe and happy. *With me.*

'Adam?' Isenberg's voice broke into his thoughts and he looked at her with lifted brows, hoping his eyes hid the truth of his feelings.

'Boss?' he replied.

'Tell Detective Hanson to give me a minute or two. I'll get that extra guard before I brief him on Broderick Voss and the college hookers.'

'Will do.'

'And please tell Kyle how very sorry I am.'

He nodded briskly, swallowing the sudden lump in his throat. 'Yeah. I will.'

Fourteen

Cincinnati, Ohio,
Sunday 20 December, 6.00 A.M.

'Do you want me to go in with you?' Meredith asked Adam as she walked between him and Trip toward the interview room where Kyle and Shane waited.

'Not at first. Watch from the observation room. I'll motion to you if I need you.'

He said the last words gruffly and all she could think of was that moment in her TV room. *You are what's kept me going for the last godawful year.*

God. All these months he'd suffered. Alone.

I didn't know. I hate that you're hurting. I'm mad that you stayed away, that you needed me but didn't trust me enough to tell me. I needed you too.

'How much are we going to tell them about how Tiffany and her mother died?' Trip asked, his deep voice a quiet rumble in the deserted hallway.

'That it was quick,' Adam said grimly. 'That she didn't suffer.'

Trip sighed. 'So we lie?'

Because from what little the two had told her, Meredith knew the mother had lived long enough to dial 911. Bleeding out and in agony, her last act had been to get help for her daughter.

'Yeah.' Adam bit the words out. 'We lie like fucking rugs.'

'For now,' Meredith said softly. 'Go light on the details. They'll ask for more when they're ready.'

'Will they ever be ready?' Trip whispered and Meredith's heart broke a little more.

She patted his massive shoulder. 'Some people never are. And that's okay. These guys . . . God. They're so young.' Something in the set of his mouth set off an alarm in her mind. 'Trip? Is this your first notification?'

He kept his gaze stoically forward. 'Yeah.'

Adam's sigh bounced off the walls. 'God, Trip. I'm sorry. They're never easy, but this one's . . .' He sighed again. 'I'll do the talking. You be ready if either of them detonates.'

'Emotionally,' Meredith added when Trip's spine went abruptly stiff. 'Not like with a real bomb. They're both wound super tight.'

They'd arrived at the interview room where a uniformed officer stood guard beside the closed door. The officer took one look at their faces and his own fell.

'They've been asking,' the officer said. 'Every three minutes. Kyle tried to make a break for it once. Said he needed to get outside to get an Internet signal.'

'How did you get him to stay put?' Adam asked.

'I didn't. Shane did. Dragged him bodily, but Kyle let him.'

With a nod, Adam opened the observation room door for Meredith. On the other side of the glass, Kyle paced frantically. Shane sat on the floor, his back to the wall, knees to his chest, his expression one of exhausted, quiet anguish.

'Jesus,' Adam whispered, his throat working convulsively, his hands fisted at his sides. Letting her instincts guide, she leaned into him, resting her forehead against his upper arm, his muscle so tight it felt like she leaned against stone.

He shuddered out a breath, tilting his head so that his cheek rested on the top of her head. 'I do not want to do this.'

'I'll go in with you. For you.' She found his hand, gave it a brief squeeze. 'It's all right to need someone, Adam. It's all right to need me.'

He stiffened for a second, then drew a huge breath. 'I have to do this now. I can't keep those kids waiting any longer.'

She stepped back and followed the two into the room where Kyle froze mid-pace, then spun on his heel to face them, his face registering instant understanding. And horror. 'No.' He staggered back a few steps, shaking his head. 'No. *No.*'

Shane lifted his head from his knees in a slow motion. His gaze locked with Meredith's, then his eyes closed in weary acceptance.

Adam took a breath. 'This is my partner, Special Agent Triplett. I'm sorry. Tiffany is dead.'

Kyle was still shaking his head. 'She went to her mother's house. She was safe.'

Adam squared his shoulders. 'Her mother is also dead.'

'No.' Kyle backed up until he hit the wall, then lunged at Adam, fists swinging. '*No.*'

Trip started to intervene, but Adam caught Kyle and dragged the young man close, wrapping his arms around him, holding him upright when Kyle's knees buckled. Kyle's fists banged against Adam's back weakly, his tortured sobs the only sound in the room.

Adam held on tight, his hand visibly shaking as he smoothed it over Kyle's hair, then cupped the back of the younger man's head, holding him against his shoulder. His own shoulders sagging, he tipped his head up so that he stared at the ceiling. 'I'm so sorry,' he said quietly. 'So damn sorry.'

'She was supposed to be safe,' Kyle sobbed. 'Safe.'

'I know,' Adam murmured. 'I know. It's not your fault this happened.'

Shane's head hit the wall hard, the crack audible. 'It's mine.'

Trip went to him, kneeling at his side. 'No,' he said firmly. 'Not your fault either.'

'Why?' The single word exploded from Kyle, but was muffled by Adam's shoulder. 'She was sweet. Tiny. Did he hurt her?' His voice dropped to a whimper. 'Please tell me he didn't hurt her.'

'It was quick,' Adam said roughly. 'She would have felt no pain.'

Kyle choked on another sob, his body shaking pathetically, his fists now clenching Adam's suit coat. Adam continued to hold him, letting him cry.

Shane covered his face with his hands. 'It was that guy,' he said so quietly that Meredith almost didn't hear him.

'Which guy, Shane?' Trip asked.

Shane's hands slid off his face, his gaze finding Meredith again. 'The guy looking for me tonight. It was him, wasn't it?'

244

'Maybe,' Trip answered for her. 'We're working with Chicago PD.'

'Why?' Shane whispered hoarsely, still directing his questions at Meredith.

Meredith slid down the wall to sit on the floor next to Shane. 'Why us? Why is . . . whoever is doing it . . . killing people to get to us – you and me? I don't know. But I know these two guys.' She gestured to Trip and Adam. 'And I trust them to find out. I trust them with my life. At least we know that we're . . .' She hesitated.

'Targets?' Shane supplied bitterly.

Meredith shrugged, understanding his bitterness all too well. 'Yeah, for lack of a better word. Now the police can protect us, and everyone we love will know to be careful.' Because the thought of anyone she loved ending up like Tiffany and her mother . . .

She had to do some serious yoga breathing to keep her panic from taking over. *Papa's in a safe house. Under guard.* Her friends were mostly cops or married to cops. She'd have to warn them. They couldn't be caught alone. Nobody was safe right now.

'Like Linnie.' Shane aimed a furtive glance at Kyle, whose sobs were losing steam, but who still clung to Adam like a life preserver. Meredith knew the feeling. She wanted to cling to Adam and absorb his strength, because her panic still pushed at the edges of her control.

Shane bit his upper lip. 'Did they . . .' He looked at Kyle again, then back at Meredith to mouth the rest of his question. 'Was Tiff raped?'

Meredith looked at Trip who shook his head. 'No indication of that,' he said.

Shane slumped against the wall. 'Thank God,' he whispered, in relief.

For several long moments no one said anything. Kyle's sobs had become shudders. Shane fixed his gaze on Meredith. 'What happens next?' he asked.

Kyle pushed away from Adam, sinking into one of the chairs at the table, his face ravaged. 'I have to go home. I have to be with her.'

'We'll work with Chicago PD to make that happen,' Adam said.

'When we're sure it's safe. Until then, we'll find a place for you here. We have a place lined up for the night. We should get over there. It's almost dawn.' He sat next to Kyle, laid a hand on his back. Even from where she sat on the floor, Meredith could sense the gentleness in the gesture and somehow that made her panic recede until she was no longer shaking inside.

'Is there anyone we can call for you, Kyle?' Adam asked.

Kyle shook his head, but Shane said, 'His parents are in Michigan. I have their number.'

'Did they know Tiffany?' Meredith asked.

'Yeah. We were going there for Christmas, Kyle and I. Tiff was coming up the day after. Tiff and Kyle . . .' He sighed heavily. 'I was gonna be best man.'

Meredith's eyes stung. 'Shit.'

Shane's laugh was bitter. 'No kidding.' With a huff, he rolled to his knees, but his movement stalled there. 'I don't think I've ever been so tired. Not in my whole life.'

Trip extended his hand. 'You just need to find a little more juice. We'll get you settled and you can sleep. Maybe eat something.'

Shane took Trip's hand and slowly came to his feet. Trip then helped Meredith up and she met Adam's eyes. *You okay?* she wanted to ask, but didn't. He'd been a pillar of strength for the young man who'd needed him. Now, he looked completely spent, but she knew how important it was that he maintain the illusion. She was doing the same.

Adam gave her a small nod and stood up, back ramrod straight. He extended his hand to Kyle, who sat at the table, head bent. 'Kyle,' he said quietly.

Kyle took his hand and allowed himself to be pulled to his feet. 'They should have taken me,' he muttered. 'It should have been me.'

'No,' Shane said, exhaustion weighing his words. 'It should have been me. I should never have let you get involved.'

'No,' Adam said, his voice strong and clear. 'It shouldn't have been *anyone*. And we're going to do everything we can to make sure it's not anyone else.'

Meredith curved her lips in a smile just for him, her heart swelling with pride even though it physically ached. He'd been magnificent. She'd make sure he knew it as soon as she was able.

Cincinnati, Ohio,
Sunday 20 December, 7.15 A.M.

'Kyle and Shane are as settled as they're going to be,' Kate said, joining them at the condo's kitchen table where Adam and Diesel sipped coffee from sturdy mugs. The scent of fresh coffee had welcomed them as they'd staggered into the condo half an hour earlier.

Adam was grateful to whoever had made it because it was really strong. Not strong enough to offset the overwhelming craving for the 'something stronger' that still clawed at his gut, but it would have to do.

The bar had been conspicuously emptied of anything remotely resembling booze. It had to have been Diesel, Adam thought, beyond grateful, because – God help him – the bar was the first corner of the room his eyes had sought.

Because . . . shit. This has been a godawful night. Holding Kyle as he'd sobbed his horrified, guilt-stricken grief . . . Adam had been shaken, inside and out. He might have fallen apart without the smile Meredith had given him at the end. It was pride and Adam drank it in because he finally felt like he might actually deserve it. Still . . . if there had been whiskey at the bar he wasn't sure he would have been able to stop himself.

'Papa must have been tired,' Meredith said as she followed Kate in. 'He slept through all that. He's snoring away.' She didn't sit with them, though. Pouring a cup of coffee, she took it to the officer standing watch outside the door to the room the two young men shared.

Small kindnesses, Adam thought. Even running on the autopilot of exhaustion, Meredith had a seemingly unlimited well of kindness. *I want her kindness. I want her.*

They'd all been exhausted by the time Adam had gotten them to the condo. He and Trip had loaded Shane, Kyle, and Meredith in the back of a windowless CPD van, pulling the curtain separating the front seat from the back, and taking an extremely circuitous route so that the boys would not know exactly where they were going.

Kyle and Shane had been fine with that. They had, however, balked when Adam had taken their phones, to be stored at the police station. Once again, Meredith had smoothed the waters, reminding them that they were in danger and that their phones could be used to track them. She promised she'd get them disposable phones as soon as she could.

Luckily, Diesel was at the condo. And luckily, he always carried burner phones. Which made Trip sigh with a muttered, 'Of course he does,' but made the young men calm down, the cell phones their tether to reality.

But the most calming factor had been Cap, Kate's old dog. He'd immediately latched onto the boys, pressing his big, hairy body against their legs, one, then the other. Neither could resist him, even in their zombie state.

'Where's Cap?' Adam now asked.

'In bed with Kyle,' Kate said, her smile sad. 'Cap's clean, but I'll wash the sheets.'

'Don't worry about it,' Adam said. 'The owner of the condo has a laundry service.'

Meredith returned from her coffee errand and busied herself making tea instead. 'Did Trip leave?'

'He took the van back,' Adam said. Isenberg would be having a department car brought over that Adam would be driving later today. 'He said he was going home, but I heard him calling Kendra. I think he may be headed her way.'

'Good. I was worried about him,' Meredith said as she reached for the bright blue kettle on the stove, then faltered. 'My kettle from home?' she asked, her voice small.

Kate nodded. 'I know you like to have your things, so I packed your favorites. Your teacups and pots are in the cupboard. Your loose teas too. The chocolate one smells good.'

Meredith cleared her throat, clearly overcome at the gesture. *Interesting.* She did similar things for everyone around her every day, but was surprised to be the recipient. *That's gonna change.*

'Because it *is* good.' Meredith set the kettle to boil, then got down a teapot and cup, a matching set, both very fragile looking.

I'd break them, Adam thought dolefully. Because he tended to be as clumsy with things as he was with people.

Diesel got up to refill his mug and ushered Meredith to the chair he'd vacated, his movements so smooth that Meredith wasn't even aware she'd been manipulated into sitting. That Diesel had been sitting next to Adam was an additional benefit, because she was now close enough that Adam could detect the sweet scent of her hair.

Meredith always smelled like delicate flowers. Yet the woman sitting next to him had proven over and over again how strong she was.

He hoped she'd be strong enough to deal with what he still needed to tell her. He'd blurted out the whole 'I'm an alcoholic' thing, but there was so much more, and every time Adam thought about confessing, it made him sick. And then he'd remember that Tiffany and her mother were dead, along with five others, and he sent up a prayer of thanks that she was still alive to hear his sorry story.

'Adam?'

He blinked to find Kate snapping her fingers under his nose.

'What?'

'Diesel asked you a question,' Kate said. 'You zoned out.'

'Sorry, Diesel. What was the question?'

'It's okay,' Diesel said, pouring tea from the pot into the dainty cup, making Adam wonder just how long he'd zoned out. 'I just asked who owns this place and why you get to use it whenever someone needs a hidey-hole.' He brought the cup and pot to Meredith, the items looking like toys in his big paws. He was, however, surprisingly deft as he placed them in front of her. He waved off Meredith's thanks with a bashful blush. 'But you can tell the story some other time. You're tired.'

'I can tell it,' Adam said. 'It's not long, but it's a good one. It was a win, anyway.'

'We need one of those,' Kate said, motioning him to continue.

Meredith smiled at him. 'A story with a happy ending would be very nice.'

He hoped his cheeks weren't turning as red as Diesel's had, but having her smile at him like that was a heady thrill. 'Well, the guy who owns this place used to live in an upscale community with gates and a guardhouse, but his daughter was kidnapped one night – taken from her bed while everyone was asleep. The guard dog had been drugged, the security system deactivated, her window broken.'

'I remember that case,' Meredith said thoughtfully. 'It was at least ten years ago. Her name was Skye, right? Her face was all over the news and posters all over town. I was still in grad school and one of the profs used the case to discuss the therapy needs of the child after she was returned to her parents, safe and sound.' Eyes widening comically, she slapped her hand to her mouth, dropping it low enough to say, 'I spoiled the ending. I'm sorry.' But her wide eyes were teasing.

'I did say it was a win,' he said, grinning at her, 'so you're okay.'

'Good. I hate people who spoil the ending. Go on.' She twirled her finger like a queen giving commands. 'She was kidnapped out of her bed, and . . . ?'

'Yes,' Kate said, looking amused. 'Go on. Were you the detective on the case?'

Adam shook his head. 'Oh, no. I was still on patrol at the time. Hanson – the guy you met tonight, Meredith – was my partner. Two days after the kidnapping, the detectives working the case had nothing except the make of a car spotted lurking around the neighborhood and reported by a nosy neighbor. We spotted the car and gave chase. Finally, the kidnappers ditched the car, grabbed Skye out of the back seat, and ran on foot. There were two of them. I caught up to the one carrying Skye and grabbed her. She'd been drugged unconscious, and was barely breathing.'

'Bastards,' Kate muttered.

'Yes, but they had *some* conscience, apparently. They were taking her to the ER because they couldn't get her to wake up and her breathing had become erratic. I think they'd planned to drop her off and then run like hell. They were after the ransom. They didn't want to kill her and that was lucky for us.'

'Was she okay?' Diesel asked.

'Yes, but it was touch and go there for a while. We got her to the ER and they pumped her stomach. She didn't have much memory of the entire experience. They kept her drugged up the whole time.'

'What happened to the kidnappers?' Kate asked.

'They split up when they started running on foot. The one my partner was chasing pulled a gun, so Hanson shot him. The other one also pulled a gun. Got me in the leg.'

Meredith put her cup down with a clatter. 'You were shot?'

'Just that once and it wasn't serious. I turned to shoot back, but he'd just dropped like a rock. Hanson had stopped him too. Saved my life, because Hanson said the guy had been aiming for my head. I got Skye to our cruiser and Hanson drove us to the ER, because we were only two minutes from the hospital. Raymond, her father, was very grateful, but also very paranoid about his home security afterward.'

'Understandable,' Diesel grunted.

Adam nodded. 'He bought this place and basically turned it into a fortress. It's the only apartment here at the top of the building. And the only access is by one elevator and one set of stairs. He's got all kinds of crazy security on both of those. It was the only way any of them could sleep at night. I kept up with them, you know, on Skye's birthday and the anniversary of the crime, just to see how she was. How they all were.'

'And how were they?' Meredith asked, her voice warm, like a soft blanket.

Adam had to fight the need to shiver. 'Doing really well, all of them. Skye had nightmares for a while, like you'd expect, but she had a great counselor and gradually she healed. She started high school this year.' He chuckled. 'Raymond says she wants to be a cop. He's not crazy about that, but he's smart enough not to fight her.'

'Where are they now?' Kate asked. 'Obviously not here.'

'Japan. He got transferred by his company on a four-year assignment. He gave me the keys. Said it was mine to use when I wanted.'

'To like, live here?' Diesel asked. 'I could get used to this place.'

'*I* couldn't.' Adam laughed, startling himself. He hadn't heard himself laugh in such a long time. 'I mean, look at it. It's too perfect. I'd track mud in or break something or spill spaghetti sauce on the carpet.' He shook his head. 'Not that I could have taken him up on it even if I'd wanted to. It would be such a breach of policy. But when Faith needed a place to hide last year, I asked for permission. Raymond was happy for us to use it as a safe house.'

Meredith grew abruptly still at his mention of last year and he felt the laughter seep away, because he knew exactly what she was remembering. A pathetic mess, he'd left Deacon and Faith in the condo, then had driven straight to Meredith's house and stumbled into her arms for comfort. She'd been like a beacon, cutting through the darkness that had all but consumed him.

She still was.

But after taking her comfort, he'd left her bed the next morning like a thief. Without a word of explanation. *God, I was an asshole.* And down deep, had he really changed?

Suddenly exhausted, he got up, dumped what was left of his coffee, and washed the cup. Intensely aware of the silence behind him, he turned to face the table. 'I'm beat. Kate, are you staying awake to watch?'

Kate studied him with a compassion that made his eyes absurdly sting. 'Yeah,' she said. 'Grab some sleep while you can.'

Diesel checked the clock on the wall with a wince. 'I gotta go. I'm late for work.'

'It's Sunday,' Kate said with a frown.

'Newspapers have no weekends, and I took yesterday off. But I can come back later. If you want,' he added uncertainly, his eyes on Adam's, clearly asking for permission.

Adam thought of the booze that no longer cluttered the bar, tempting him. 'Any time. You're always welcome here and anywhere we are. You know that.'

Diesel's mouth tipped up, uncertainty giving way to relief. 'Good. Didn't want to overstep.'

Yeah, they were both talking about the booze. 'You didn't. Thanks, man.'

Meredith carefully set the fragile teacup on the table, frowning at both of them. 'You've been awake all night, Diesel. Surely there's room for you here. This place is huge.'

252

'Nah.' He pulled his keys from the pocket of his jeans. 'I don't sleep much anyway. Tell your grandpa I'll be back when I get off work. I want a rematch.'

That made Meredith smile. 'I will.' She stood and stayed him with a hand to his arm. 'Thank you. For everything. You've been a godsend today. And a really good friend.' She leaned up to kiss his cheek, making him blush again.

'That is definitely my cue to leave,' he said. 'Before I fuck up and erase whatever good thing I did. Later, guys.'

They heard him say goodnight to the officer on watch before the front door closed.

'Mer, I put your things in that bedroom,' Kate said, pointing.

'Thank you,' Meredith said, her weariness showing through. 'I'm about to fall off my feet. I'll get the grand tour later.' She started to rinse her cup, but Kate stopped her.

'I'll do it. You go to sleep.' Together, she and Adam watched her disappear into the bedroom. Kate lifted a brow. 'The adjoining room is yours.'

Adam lifted both brows. He knew those rooms were connected by a shared bathroom – or a secret pathway, however you wanted to look at it. 'Thank you?'

'You should be thanking me. It's the only way you two are going to get any privacy in the midst of all this chaos.' She looked around fondly. 'Decker and I have some nice memories of this place. I'm glad you're finally going to get to use it. Not,' she added hastily, 'that I'm glad any of this ever happened, of course.' She patted his arm. 'But it has happened and you need to grab the good moments to get you through the bad.'

Adam smiled down at her. 'That sounds very Dr Lane-ish.'

Kate's grin was confirmation that he'd guessed right. They both saw the same shrink, who specialized in treating PTSD. 'She's knitting now,' she said conspiratorially.

Adam had to cover his mouth to keep the laugh from bolting free. 'You crack me up.'

Kate looked satisfied. 'I can teach you and Meredith too. Give you something to do together. A common hobby?'

'That's okay.' He had plenty ideas about what he and Meredith could do together. From the look on Kate's face, he could see that she knew exactly what he was thinking. 'Look, if either Kyle or Shane wakes up, wake me. Let Meredith sleep.'

'I will.' Kate's expression became searching. 'I'm not going to ask if you're okay, because I can see that you're not. But if you need anything, someone to talk to . . . You'll come to me, right?'

'Yeah,' he said gruffly.

'And tell Mer about . . . everything. You know. Sobriety? She thinks you don't care.'

He sighed. 'You know too?'

'Diesel moved the booze. He never said a word, but I'm not stupid.'

'I know you're not.' And that made it easier somehow, because Kate also had major issues with PTSD from the things she'd seen on and off the job. It made him feel not stupid too. 'It's . . . hard. Every day. But tonight was . . . God.'

'There was a reason I adopted Cap,' she said, her topic change surprising him.

'Yeah? Other than you're a softy underneath all that mean?'

Kate smirked. 'Tell anyone and I'll show you what a knitting needle really can do. But seriously, yeah. When he was a puppy, Cap was in training to be a service dog, you know, for a veteran. PTSD. Cap flunked out of his certification because they found out he has some health issues, but one of the vets took him anyway. Older guy. Vietnam. He died last year, and somehow Cap got moved from person to person until he ended up in Delores's shelter without a collar or a name. She ran his chip through the system, traced his history while he was just sitting there, nobody taking him home because he's older and a little sick. When she found out what he'd been for the old soldier, she called me right away. Decker and I fell in love with him from the first minute, of course, but Decker always wanted to train a dog too. Cap had made friends with one of the younger dogs, so we took them both. Loki's not totally trained yet, so I left him with the neighbor kid until Decker gets back from Florida tomorrow. Unless I'm on the job, Cap's with me.'

Adam was certain there was a point in there somewhere, but he'd lost it. 'And?'

'And . . . you should consider a dog.'

'I'm not a vet.'

She rolled her eyes. 'Like cops don't get PTSD. I thought you were smart, Kimble. Think about it, okay? A dog might give you . . . I don't know.' She looked embarrassed, as she did when her soft side was left unprotected for too long. 'Purpose and shit.'

His lips twitched. 'And shit.'

She poked him in the chest. 'Do not think I'm bluffing about the knitting needles.'

'I wouldn't dare.' He caught her hand, squeezed it briefly. 'Thank you. I'll look into it. You were right about the PTSD shrink.' It was on Kate's recommendation that he'd stowed his cowardice long enough to call Dr Lane.

Kate tilted her head in the direction of Meredith's bedroom door. 'She was the one who suggested her to me.'

Adam sighed. 'Of course she was.' It always came back to Meredith. She was like a sun and he was just one of the planets in her orbit. He couldn't have escaped her pull if he'd wanted to. And he did not want to. 'The shrink has helped. And maybe the origami.'

Kate's grin was back. 'And knitting?'

'Don't push your luck, Coppola. My hands aren't as nimble as Diesel's.'

'Hey, Diesel's knitting *lace* already.'

Adam had to laugh. 'I'll see you in a few hours.'

'Sweet dreams, Kimble,' she said as he turned for his assigned bedroom, her voice gone serious again.

'I hope so.' It had been so long since he'd had any dream that wasn't a nightmare.

Cincinnati, Ohio,
Sunday 20 December, 8.00 A.M.

Meredith sat on the edge of the bed, listening to the water running in the adjoining bathroom. She'd finished changing into her favorite

255

purple silk pajamas Kate had packed for her when she'd heard Adam in the adjoining bathroom.

Clever, that adjoining bathroom. Accessible from both bedrooms, it also created a secret passageway between the two.

Clever of Kate to assign the bedrooms the way she had. Her friend's agenda was not-so-secret. Meredith was going to have to thank her later. That Deacon and Faith *and* Kate and Decker had grown closer in these very rooms . . . It was hard not to yearn for a happily-ever-after of her own. She and Adam could . . . well, they could do all kinds of things and no one would ever know.

But at the moment, Meredith wasn't doing anything except listening to Adam take another shower. Stuck between lust and indecision, she'd listened for the telltale click, indicating that he'd locked the door on his side, but it had never come.

She didn't know if it had been simple forgetfulness or an invitation.

She could open that door and watch him. Or join him.

But, on the off chance that it had been forgetfulness, she waited, giving him his privacy. And hoped for a knock on her door, asking for entry. Even if it was just to say goodnight. Or good morning. He didn't have to spill his guts about his alcoholism right now.

He'd been wrecked tonight, but he'd kept it together. He'd been exactly what Kyle had needed. She wanted to tell him that she'd been proud of him and she wasn't sure when they'd get another opportunity to be alone.

The water shut off and there was quiet. No knock. He wasn't coming to her tonight. Disappointment washed over her in a huge wave, leaving her staring at the door.

Those doors open both ways, you know.

True. Each time she'd waited for him to come to her. She'd known his address all these months. *I could have gotten in my car and driven to his house, knocked on his door, and demanded to know why he'd disappeared.*

Why hadn't she? *Now* that *is a damn good question.* Right now she didn't even have to get into her car. She could just walk through the bathroom and knock on his door.

Rising before she could talk herself out of it, she opened the bathroom door and had to smile at the near military precision with which he'd hung his wet towels to dry. The chrome shone and the shower tile had been dried. The only evidence that he'd actually used the shower was the steam still fogging the mirror.

Sucking in a breath, she tapped lightly. 'Adam?'

A long moment of silence. Then a sigh that sounded resigned. 'It's not locked.'

That sigh didn't bode well, but she opened the door enough to see him sitting on the bed facing the door, his pose the mirror image of what hers had been, except that his knees were spread wide where she'd sat like a lady.

I'm a little tired of being a lady, she thought, lifting her chin.

His hair was tousled, sticking up all over his head in short, wet spikes and she could visualize him rubbing it dry with a towel, not caring how it looked, and that was endearing. He wore only a thin pair of gray sweatpants, his chest bare, and that was so damn sexy. Almost unbearably tempting. Except that his head hung low and his hands were loosely clasped between his knees. He looked like a man waiting to be sentenced to prison.

So . . . lust was not on the menu. Swallowing back her disappointment, she squared her shoulders. Comfort it would have to be. 'Can I come in?' she whispered.

He nodded so she did, not stopping until she stood between his knees. He looked up, but not far enough to meet her eyes. His breathing grew rapid, his gaze fixed on the deep V of her pajama top, which wasn't boudoir sexy, but it was . . . intimate.

His exhale warmed her exposed skin, sending shivers rippling over every square inch of skin still covered. She lifted a tentative hand to his hair, smoothing the spikes, settling at the back of his head, cradling him when he leaned into her, resting his cheek against her breasts.

'Is this all right?' she asked and his arms came around her waist, pulling her closer. She kissed the top of his head. 'That's a good answer.'

He huffed a laugh. 'I was going to let you sleep.'

'I'm . . . wired. Happens when my sleep cycle gets disrupted. I just wanted to tell you good night and that I thought you were wonderful with Kyle tonight.'

His shoulders relaxed a degree or two, but he shook his head. 'It wasn't enough.'

'It won't ever be. But when it's all over and he's healing, he'll remember the detective who made those horrible moments a little more bearable.' She stroked his hair, as she'd done to Shane, but the context was so very different. So very intimate. 'And that's got to be enough for you, Adam. That and doing our best to catch the man who killed her.'

He shuddered out a breath. 'I'm sorry,' he whispered. 'I should have told you.'

She just waited, stroking his hair.

'You couldn't be my reason,' he finally said roughly.

'For your sobriety?'

'Yeah. And for my sanity.'

Her heart hurt, thinking of him fighting his battles alone. 'Did you have anyone?'

'My sponsor. My shrink.' His chuckle was self-deprecating. 'My crayons.'

'I kept them all. All the pictures you left in my mailbox. Every last one of them.' She brushed a kiss across his ear. 'I'd run to the mailbox every day, hoping for a new one. My favorites go on my refrigerator when I'm alone. I . . . take them down when I have company.'

'I understand.'

'Do you?' she asked, because the defeated way he said it made her think that he didn't. 'I wasn't ashamed of them, Adam. I . . . They were mine. Just mine. I didn't want to share them with anyone because I was greedy for any connection to you.'

She felt him swallow. 'I didn't want you to forget about me.'

'I know. I think I got a little sidetracked recently and probably overreacted to you staying away. It's the holidays. They always make me . . .' She hesitated, searching for the right word. Depressed was accurate, but not complete. Vulnerable was also true, but not complete either. 'Raw.' Yes, that worked. 'And lonely. For what it's worth, I understand why I couldn't be the reason for your sobriety.

Not so sure I get the sanity part, but I do get that I couldn't be your new addiction.'

'I wanted to come to you . . . whole.'

'I get that.'

'And I didn't want you to know. About the drinking.'

She sighed. 'Did you believe I'd think less of you?'

'I didn't know. I didn't care. And that was selfish, because you didn't know why I stayed away. I'd cut off my own hand before I hurt you.'

'Well, let's not get drastic,' she said dryly, making him chuckle. 'Besides, I'm not as perfect as you seem to think I am.'

His head came up abruptly. 'I don't believe that,' he said.

'You already know I wear . . . what did you call it? My zen mask?'

'Yes,' he said slowly. Carefully. 'Why?'

'Oh,' she breathed. 'I guess it's time to lay all the cards on the table, huh?'

His brows rose. 'Yeah. I showed you mine.'

She found herself smiling at him, even as she shook her head. 'I don't think you have. As long as we're still talking about cards.'

'For now.' He tilted his head, his expression thoughtful. 'What are you hiding behind your zen mask, Meredith?'

'Depression,' she said simply, and found it hadn't been as hard as she'd expected to show that particular card. 'There have been times in my life when it's been really bad.'

He considered that, his eyes filling with a combination of worry, understanding, and compassion. 'How bad?'

She had to look away. 'Bad.'

He cleared his throat. 'Did you try to . . .' He trailed off.

'Hurt myself? Yes.' She hesitated. 'End myself? Yes, I tried that too.'

He leaned back, gently drawing her arms from where they rested on his shoulders, and pushed back one sleeve, then the other. Closing her eyes, she held herself perfectly still, barely breathing as he found what he was looking for. She waited for . . . what? Surprise? Disgust? Pity? She couldn't blame him. She'd certainly felt all of the above too many times to even attempt to count.

She shuddered out a sob when his lips brushed the first scar. Her bangles hid the worst ones, but the rest were faded now, barely even visible unless someone was looking and no one ever did. No one ever thought to.

Pursing her lips to keep the sobs locked down, she let the tears fall silently as he kissed every single scar, large and small, shallow and deep. When he'd found them all, he kissed the pulse point at each of her wrists, then resettled her arms on his shoulders. He wiped her cheeks with his thumbs, cupping her face in his palms.

'Not perfect,' he whispered. 'Better. Like tempered steel.'

She hiccupped a startled laugh. 'What?'

His lips tipped up. 'You know. Metal gets superheated then quenched, but that only hardens it. Leaves it brittle. That's not you. Tempering is a second step.'

'Which makes what?'

His smile grew, tender and sweet. 'Something tough, but not brittle. That's you.'

Meredith pursed her lips again, harder this time, because this thing in her chest was not going to stay down. Her gaze shot to the door, panic rising like floodwaters, tangling with all of the other emotions that threatened to break through the wall she maintained so fastidiously.

Understanding flickered in his eyes and he stood up, pulling her to his side and urging her into the bathroom where he sat on the side of the decadent garden tub and turned both faucets on full blast. He tugged her to sit on his lap, wrapped his arms around her, and gruffly whispered in her ear, 'Nobody can hear. Just let go, sweetheart.'

She wasn't sure if it was the tone of his voice, the way he held her, the endearment, or the words themselves, and it really didn't matter. Turning her face into his chest, she let the wall crumble into dust, took the comfort he offered, and started to cry.

Fifteen

Adam hadn't known it was humanly possible to cry that much, but he'd held Meredith on his lap through it all, whispering whatever soothing words he could think of as she ripped his heart apart. She'd clung to him, arms around his neck, her tears soaking his chest. But eventually her sobs stilled and he turned the water off.

That he'd contributed to the pain she'd so obviously stored up and shoved down ... it shamed him. He pressed his lips to her temple. 'I'm sorry. I'm so damned sorry.'

Her sigh echoed in the quiet of the bathroom. 'It wasn't just you. It's been building for a while.' She loosened her hold on his neck, her hands sliding down to flatten against his chest, and she began petting the soft hair there, just like she had earlier, when she'd caught him wearing nothing but a towel. The memory, combined with her soft touch, made him wish for more. A lot more. Now that the memory of her hands on his wet chest and her eyes on that towel was in his head, it wasn't going anywhere, tormenting him with all the things he shouldn't be wanting a few seconds after she'd finished crying her eyes out.

This was far from the best time. And what kind of man was he to be wanting her now? He shifted beneath her, moving her closer to his knees and farther from his groin because he was getting very hard, very quickly. *I am the goddamn worst.*

She was spent. *And I still haven't told her what she needs to know about me.* But even though his brain knew these things to be true, his cock wasn't on board. At all.

Her next words had him scrambling for focus. 'I'm sorry too,' she said. 'I could have come to you. I *should* have come to you.' She pulled back to meet his gaze, and even with swollen eyes and a red nose, hers was the prettiest face he'd ever seen. 'Because you were hurting too.'

'There were times I wished you would,' he confessed. 'Then I could say that it wasn't my fault that I broke my promise to you.'

Her eyes widened. 'But you . . . you never promised me anything.'

'Not that I told you about. Out loud anyway. But to myself, yeah. Every goddamn day. One year sober and I'd be knocking on your door.'

'You were planning to come back?' she asked in that same small voice she'd used earlier when asking Kate about the kettle and his chest grew painfully tight.

Because now he understood. He could still see all those small scars on her arms, and the two bigger ones at her wrists. He wondered how he'd never noticed them before. He wondered if any of her friends knew they existed.

He'd known her serenity was a mask, but he'd had no clue what it had actually hidden. The truth was almost too much to bear, so he set it aside to answer her question.

'*Yes*,' he said fiercely. 'I told myself that I needed to be sober for one year and then I would have earned the right and I was *coming back*.' He hesitated. 'And then, if you'd have me, I was never leaving again.'

For a long, long moment she only stared at him and he didn't know what she was thinking or feeling or planning to say. Then her smile – her real smile, not the zen one – bloomed, her green eyes growing dark with purpose. And desire.

He knew this look. He'd seen it once before, that very first night. He'd imagined it on the hundreds of nights that followed, nights he'd lain alone in his bed, missing her. Wanting her. He wanted her now. *Right now.* He wanted to pick her up and toss her on the bed and . . . have her. Give her everything he'd denied them both for the last year.

262

But he remained as he was, frozen, silent, because she was regarding him intently, her confidence back with a vengeance, and he couldn't control the shiver that raced across his skin. Her hands came up to cup his jaws, her thumbs caressing his cheeks.

'I'll have you, Adam,' she murmured, her gaze locked with his, filling him with bubbling warmth. It was joy and relief and contentment and . . . too many other feelings to parse. He didn't think he'd ever felt so *valued*, in . . . *God. Maybe never.*

It had been worth it, he thought. Every damn day he'd said *no* to the cravings. Because he'd been saying *yes* to this. Yes to her. He could never tell her no.

Her hands slid up into his hair, a smile curving her mouth, sweet and provocative all at once. As if she knew exactly what she was doing to him. That she'd rendered him speechless. That she understood the power she had over him and would never use it to hurt him. 'I'll have you in my life.'

His chest hurt. But it was good hurt. The best kind of hurt.

She tugged his face down, gently brushing her lips over his and . . . *God.* He'd been hard before but now . . . *God.* It was all he could do not to buck his hips up into her like a savage. He balanced them on the edge of the tub, not daring to move because once he did, he didn't think he'd be able to stop.

'I'll have you in my heart,' she whispered against his mouth, humbling him.

'Meredith.' It came out fervently. Like a prayer. Which it was. 'I—'

She pressed her finger to his lips, which relieved him, because he was about to beg her for things he still had no right to. But then she licked her lower lip, then his, and his control shattered. 'In my bed,' she whispered. 'Please.'

He couldn't have halted the upward surge of his hips or the groan that broke free from his throat, not if he'd tried. His fingers flexing, he dug into the softness of her curvy butt to keep her from sliding off his lap. He shoved his other hand into her hair, crushing his mouth to hers. *Mine. Mine. She's mine.*

She moaned quietly, startling him by swinging one of her legs across his lap so that she straddled him. He rocked backward, nearly tumbling them both into the empty tub. He caught himself at the last second, propelling himself forward and up, gripping her thighs to keep from dropping her as he came to his feet.

Her arms wound around his neck and she hummed against his mouth. 'Please,' she whispered and he knew he should say no, knew he still had things to say, things she needed to hear, but God help him, he had no defense against the sweetness of her voice or the soft kisses she was pressing all over his face. 'Please.'

Panting hard, he hefted her higher so that her legs wound around his hips, his erection finding a home between her thighs. She ground against him, her head falling back, her lower lip caught between her teeth. 'Please,' she whispered again.

'Please what?' he asked, his voice tight with strain because he wanted to back her against the door and plunge deep into her heat. 'What do you want?'

'You. Please. It's been so long and I've missed you. I need you.' She ground against him again and any blood remaining in his head fled south. '*Please.*'

Then she was kissing him again, breaking down his inhibitions, making him want. He staggered into the bedroom and ripped his mouth away from hers. 'I need to be inside you,' he said roughly, his voice sounding foreign to his own ears. Rough and gruff and vulnerable. But he trusted her not to hurt him. 'If that's not what you want, tell me now.'

She met his eyes in the semi-darkness. 'Yes. You. Inside me. That's what I want.'

Thank you, God.

But she needs to know. She needs to know! He must have some conscience left because it was screaming at him, its words just barely breaking through his haze of want. He shook his head to clear it. 'I need to tell you things.'

She tugged his hair, kissing him hard. 'I know. But after. I need you now.'

I need you now too. Telling her his secrets was going to hurt. He'd take this moment of respite. He'd take it and hoard it and draw on it for strength when he turned himself inside out with confessions. His conscience bowing out gracefully, he carried her to the bed, pulled back the blankets, and gently laid her down, arranging her hair on the pillow.

'I dreamed of this,' he whispered. 'Dreamed of you.'

Her smile was like sunlight, filling him up, driving away the shadows. Most of them, anyway. A few stubborn shadows lingered and he'd deal with them. After.

'I dreamed of you too.' She splayed one hand over his chest, slowly fanning her fingers back and forth, dropping lower with each pass. 'Dreamed of this.' Her gaze dropped to follow the path her hand had taken, focusing on the bulge that his sweats didn't do a thing to hide. 'And this.' Her finger traced his length and he shuddered violently. She took the drawstring in her pretty fingers and gave it a slight tug. 'Can I?'

'Please,' he rasped, his voice gravelly and breathless.

She pulled at the string, releasing the neat bow he'd tied, then hooked a finger in the waistband and pulled at the sweats, freeing his cock. She sucked in an appreciative breath, lifting hungry eyes to his for a split second before returning to stare at his erection which bobbed toward her like she was its true north. Because it wasn't stupid.

His body wanted Meredith Fallon. His heart wanted her even more. That she wanted him too? It was almost too good to be true.

Her hand wrapped around him, giving a quick slide up and down, making him gasp.

'Stop thinking,' she ordered with a squeeze that had his eyes rolling back in his head. 'Start doing. Please.'

Smothering a laugh at her impatience, he kicked the sweats aside and climbed in beside her. 'Yes, ma'am,' he said, then groaned when her hand found him again.

'We have to be quiet,' she whispered. 'You weren't the last time.'

He smiled now, because the memory had changed from bittersweet to just sweet. And hot. She'd been uninhibited in bed and he'd greedily relived every moment they'd shared. 'You were louder.'

'But I can be quiet.' She lifted a brow. 'Especially if you finally start kissing me.'

He obliged, taking her mouth in a kiss that was more warm welcome than sizzling passion, but it must have been the right thing to do because she hummed against his lips, opening her mouth and her arms. It started out sweet, a tentative tasting. Relearning.

He freed the buttons of her silky pajama top, one by one, until there were no more buttons. He pulled away from her mouth to slip the top from her shoulders, letting himself stare at her beautiful breasts for a long, long moment. 'You're perfect,' he whispered, then cupped one breast reverently.

She hummed again but it sounded more like a growl as she undulated, pressing her flesh harder into his palm. 'I won't break, Adam.'

'I know. That's why you're perfect.'

She gave him another one of those lust-filled stares, then hooked an arm around his neck and pulled him down to her, kissing him with all the passion he remembered and the intense heat was back, burning him from the inside out. He'd gladly go down in flames.

'Want you,' he gritted out, pulling at the pajama bottoms that were in his way.

'Good,' she gritted back and kicked free of the pants.

He wanted to take a minute, to look his fill, but her hips were arching and his heart was pounding in his head. *Pretty. So pretty. So mine.* He palmed her between her legs and she bit her lip, releasing a muffled cry, grinding up into him. 'Goddammit, Adam. *Please.*'

He slid a finger up into her and had to press his face into the curve of her neck, muffling his own groan. 'God. You're so wet. I can't wait to be inside you.'

'Then don't wait.' It was close to a snarl and he chuckled into her neck.

Then froze. 'I didn't bring anything. *Fuck.*'

Blindly she slapped at the nightstand until she found the drawer pull. 'In there.'

He lifted up on his elbow to stare over her body into the drawer. Which was *full* of condoms. What the . . . ? *Never mind. Doesn't matter.* Pushing the question aside for later, he grabbed one of the packets and ripped it open.

She took it from his hand, muttering under her breath. 'What part of *need you now* are you missing, Adam?' She sheathed him, then gave his cock a hard squeeze and he almost came right there.

'Fuck,' was all he could say and she laughed breathlessly.

'Yes. *Please.* For all that's holy, *please.*'

So they were smiling at each other when he pushed inside her with one thrust.

God. Oh God. Perfect. She was hot and tight and absolutely perfect.

Planting his elbows into the mattress, he let them take his weight as he hung his head and shuddered. 'I missed this. Missed you.' *Love you*, he wanted to say but held the words in. He knew they were true, but it was too soon to say them.

She gripped his shoulders, digging her nails into his skin and he welcomed the burn. She rolled her hips, graceful and mercilessly seductive at the same time. 'Feels good. So good. More. *Move.*'

He obeyed, finding her eyes in the dim light as he moved, as they moved together. He found her hands, one then the other, twining their fingers. Which he hadn't done the first time. He'd been so overwhelmed by her, by everything about her, so wrapped up in his own miserable head, that he'd forgotten. He wasn't making that mistake again.

He moved slowly, steadily, and she dug her ankles into the backs of his thighs, meeting him thrust for thrust. Until she pressed her head into the pillow, closing her eyes. Arching her throat. Silently chanting his name.

Incinerating his every good intention of making this last forever, making him curse when the orgasm began to build at the base of his spine.

'Meredith. Look at me. Please.' It was with difficulty that she opened her eyes, but he immediately saw everything he'd needed to see. She was with him, body and mind and heart. His hips jacked up the tempo as he took her mouth in a ravaging kiss, all tongues and teeth, raw need with none of their earlier tenderness.

Her arms tightened around his neck. 'Adam.' It was a quiet little moan.

He let go of her hands to grip her hips, tilting her up so that he could drive deeper and she covered her mouth with her hand, muffling a little scream.

Yes. He remembered her screams. Remembered her screaming his name. 'Let me see you come,' he ordered. 'Now.'

And she did, giving herself up to him as she had that first night. As she would for nights to come if his wishes came true. Eyes slamming closed, she bit the back of her hand, and convulsed around him, her groan muted, but far from silenced.

Hearing her, seeing her, feeling her . . . *God.* He shuddered again and let go, let the orgasm take him, throwing his head back, only vaguely aware that her hand now covered his mouth.

He dropped his head, burying his face in the curve of her shoulder. Shaking. He was shaking. And so was she. Her arms wound around him, her hands rubbing big circles on his back, soothing him. Bringing him back.

She'd brought him back in more ways than one.

Gratitude swelled inside him. *Thank you. Thank you.*

She pressed an open-mouthed kiss to his shoulder, then licked the skin. 'Mmmm.' She fell back onto the pillow, smiling like a cat in cream. 'Well?'

He had to laugh. 'Well, what?'

Her smile faltered. 'Was it what you remembered?' she asked and there was a thread of vulnerability in her words. Which was fucking unbelievable to him.

'Better,' he said and watched the vulnerability disappear. 'Better than better.'

'For me too,' she whispered and two tears leaked out of her eyes and down her face. 'I was a little afraid it wouldn't be. I'm so glad it was.'

He kissed her forehead, her eyes, the tracks of her tears. Her gorgeous, generous mouth. 'Better than better, Meredith. You're perfect.'

'I'm not, but I'm glad you think so.'

'Perfect for *me*.' He closed his eyes, dread stealing over him. 'I still have things to tell you.'

'Then let's clean up and you can tell me whatever you think I need to know.' Her thumb caressed his lips. 'But I doubt anything you tell me will change how I feel.'

He didn't open his eyes. He couldn't. 'Which is how?'

'That you're perfect too. Perfect for me.'

Cincinnati, Ohio,
Sunday 20 December, 9.25 A.M.

Meredith's body was confused – half-sated and half-tensed with dread. They'd cleaned up and were back in bed – clothed as they'd been before making love. And making love was exactly what it had been.

He hadn't said anything more as he'd pulled his sweats back on, so she'd followed suit, sensing the clothing was like armor for him, allowing him to tell his story outside of the intimacy they'd created. Because now was the time for him to bare his soul and she hoped she was strong enough to hear it. She'd meant what she'd said – she didn't expect anything he was about to tell her to change how she saw him, how she felt about him, around him or under him, for that matter. But she knew her reaction would matter to him.

Please let me say the right things.

He was stiff as a board beside her, and not in a good way. She cuddled up to him, laying her head on his shoulder, relaxing a little when his arm came around her to pull her closer. She slid her hand across his chest, resting it over his heart.

It was pounding to beat all hell. She pressed a kiss to his collarbone. 'So. We were talking about the fact that you promised to come back to me when your year is up.'

His chest rose and fell with the breath he drew. 'Yeah. January sixth.'

'You'll be my birthday present. A little belated, but that's okay.'

'What?' he asked, but she had the feeling he knew exactly what she meant.

'My birthday's on the fourth.' She hesitated. 'Why did you go sober two days later?'

He dropped his head back into the pillow, staring up at the ceiling. 'God, I do not want to tell you any of this. But I owe you this much at least.'

She touched her fingertips to his lips. 'You don't owe me anything, Adam.'

He held her hand in place and kissed her fingers. 'Yeah, I do. So let me tell you now.' He took a deep breadth. 'I started drinking when I was about twelve.'

She reared up to stare at him. 'Twelve? Why?'

'My dad drinks. Always has. My friends knew we had a well-stocked bar and that my dad's friends came over sometimes. If we were careful how much we took, he'd just think it was his friends. I stopped when I was in high school – during baseball season anyway. Told myself I didn't have a problem, because I could stop whenever I wanted.'

She slid her hand down his arm, twining their fingers together. 'I heard you were really good at baseball. Your friend told me.'

'Did Hanson show you that picture of us?'

'Yes. You were very cute.'

He snorted softly. 'Thank you.'

'And now you're the most beautiful man I've ever seen,' she added quietly. 'I just wanted you to know.'

Heat filled his cheeks, charming her. 'The first time I saw you I thought you should be in a painting,' he said, charming her even more.

'The first time you saw me, I was fussing at you.'

'Because I'd brought Faith to the ICU ward covered in a victim's blood.' The victim had been an FBI agent who'd been killed protecting Faith from a serial killer the year before. 'You were mad because I hadn't given her time to change. You were right, of course. I was not . . . okay that day.' He winced. 'I almost said "not myself," but I *was* that person then – an asshole to just about anyone unlucky enough to cross my path.'

'Yeah, you were,' she agreed, because she respected him too

much to lie to him. 'Were you drinking that day?'

'No.' He huffed a bitter laugh. 'That's why I was such an asshole. I hadn't had anything to drink because I was working with Deacon. I didn't want him to smell it on me, but goddamn I needed a buzz. I kept telling myself that Deacon would "tell on me" or some such juvenile bullshit, but I think I really just didn't want him to be disappointed in me. And that just pissed me off even more. As soon as I was done that night, I hit the bar.'

'You were hurting.'

'Because of Paula.' There was pain in his voice as he said the girl's name. 'I still don't know what her last name was.' And that hurt worse, because Paula hadn't known it either, not for sure. 'What kind of person doesn't tell their child her last name?'

'One who'd cage an eleven-year-old like an animal,' Meredith said.

He flinched. 'I told you that?' he asked, stunned.

'Yes. That first time you came to me. You don't remember?' she added carefully.

'No,' he admitted. 'I was on the edge of totally losing it. I wasn't even sure I knew how I'd gotten to your house that night.' When he'd ended up in her bed. 'I'd overheard you talking to one of your patients, the victim we were guarding, and all I could think was that I needed to hear your voice again. I'm not sure how I knew your address.'

'Well, if it makes you feel better, you didn't stalk me or anything. We'd spoken on the phone about that victim earlier that day, so you had my number. You called me that night, sounding so sad. I told you that I'd listen. I gave you my address, so if you've been worried about stalking me, then don't.'

'I was, actually.' He rested his cheek on the top of her head. 'Thank you.'

'What *do* you remember about that night?' she asked even more carefully.

'Touching you. Watching you come apart. Falling asleep in your arms.'

'All very good answers,' she said lightly. 'What else do you remember?'

'I remember that I'd been here, at this condo. Scarlett and I were waiting for Deacon and Faith. Deacon and I had a big argument and he was pissed at me. He had a right to be. We hadn't been getting along and it was my fault. All my fault.'

'What happened? I mean, why were you not getting along?'

'I was a shithead. And jealous of him. I helped him get the job with Isenberg, when she was setting up the joint task force. I'd left Homicide to work Personal Crimes and there was an opening. Deacon had been on a joint force back in Baltimore and he needed to come home because Greg was out of control at school and needed him. It was a perfect fit. D was coming off a high-profile case – a serial killer who'd buried his victims in West Virginia. He was golden. I gave his name to Isenberg and she jumped at the chance to bring him in. I was happy for him. Really. Until it all fell apart.'

'Paula,' she murmured.

'Yeah. I'd been working Personal Crimes for three months. That's as long as I lasted,' he said bitterly.

'Hey,' she chided. 'Don't criticize yourself. That's a hard assignment. Lots of cops transfer out. Even your old partner did. He told me so.'

'Yeah, Hanson did transfer, partly because of me. He watched me lose it after Paula was killed. Had to put me back together. After that, I think it was harder for him to compartmentalize the way he'd done before. I feel bad about that, because he was good at that job. Lasted a helluva lot longer than I did, that's for damn sure. But now he's back in Narcotics and I'm back in Homicide, so it's like we both stepped back to our comfort zones.'

'No shame in that.'

'Maybe.' He shrugged and she knew he hadn't believed her. 'Anyway, Hanson put me back together after I watched Paula get killed, but he didn't use a strong enough glue. I came back to Homicide . . . not the same. And then Deacon was there, running the show.'

'You resented him?' she asked and he hesitated.

'Not Deacon himself. But his success? The respect he got? Yeah. I resented that.'

'Respect from whom? Not Isenberg. She gets you. Not Deacon or Scarlett. And not Faith, although you caused trouble for her at the beginning.'

'I know.' He'd been sure that Faith was in cahoots with a murderer when in reality she'd been a target, much like Meredith, her life threatened over and over again. 'I regret that more than you know. I was jealous of Deacon for that too. At the time it felt like he was taking it all – the job, the respect of my boss, and he got the girl.'

She blinked at that. 'You wanted Faith?'

'Oh no.' He shook his head. 'She's not my type at all.'

She arched a brow, only half-teasing. 'She's a redheaded, gun-carrying, opinionated child psychologist.'

He tilted her chin so that his gaze locked with hers. 'But she isn't you.'

Meredith's lips curved. 'That was another really good thing to say.' She snuggled against his shoulder. 'So what happened the night you came to me? The first time?'

'Deacon thought I'd put Faith in danger. She was safe, surrounded by cops – including me, but Deacon was livid. He'd just come from a gruesome crime scene and he was so upset. But he was moving on the case too slowly, at least in my mind. At the time I thought that he was so worried about keeping Faith safe that he didn't care that the killer was holding an eleven-year-old girl hostage.'

'Roza,' Meredith murmured. She knew the girl well, had treated her after her rescue. And then she gasped softly. 'Oh. Oh, Adam. Roza was eleven last year when all that happened to her. Just like Paula.'

'Yeah,' he said gruffly. 'Nobody else made that connection.'

She pressed a kiss over his stuttering heart, her lips warm against his skin. 'To be fair, I don't think you'd told anyone about Paula, except maybe your boss at the time.'

'No, I hadn't. I couldn't. Hanson knew, and Nash Currie knew, but only because they was standing next to me when it happened.'

'Who is Nash Currie?'

'One of Personal Crimes' IT guys. He was trying to track her computer's IP signal. But I couldn't tell anyone else about it. I tried, but it was like there was this disconnect in my mind. I'd think of her and my words would . . . I don't know. They'd just disappear.'

PTSD, she thought sadly. He'd suffered all alone. 'But you can talk about her now?'

'A little. My shrink has helped. I still . . . react when I think about her, but it's not that raw, debilitating panic anymore. It's just garden-variety panic.'

'I get that too. Everyone has their public face. Most people never look past mine. Even my friends.'

'Because you wear it so well. I didn't. I was a pathetic mess. I accused Deacon of ignoring what was happening to Roza, that she'd die because he was moving too slowly. He said he knew what was happening to her. He'd been to the morgue, *seen* the victims.'

'But you saw Paula *actually die* and that's different than attending to the aftermath.'

He frowned. 'I told you that too?'

'Yes. You were sketchy on the details. You kept saying, "So much blood."'

'Yeah,' he grunted. 'There was that.'

'Who was Paula? I mean, who was she to you?'

He swallowed hard. 'A little girl who asked me for help. But I couldn't save her.'

She brought his hand to her lips. 'You don't have to tell me any more.'

'I do. Because even though I started drinking when I was a kid, I could always stop. After Paula, I couldn't stop. I didn't want to. I was awful to my family and my friends. I pushed Hanson away. His dad too, even though he'd always been there for me. Always the good dad that mine never was.'

She felt a sliver of relief. 'I'm glad you had someone who was good to you.'

'Dale Hanson, Wyatt's dad, was that guy. Coached me in Little League, was always encouraging me. Went to father-son events with me when my own dad was too busy or too drunk. Dale kept trying, even after I pushed him away. But I pushed everyone away – Isenberg, Deacon, and Dani . . . I even pushed my mother away because she wouldn't see me without bringing my father and he kept calling me a sniveling coward.' She stiffened in his arms, so he tipped her chin up and kissed her mouth softly. 'And I shouldn't have even brought him up because he's nowhere close to the most important person I pushed away.'

'I want to kick his ass,' she whispered fiercely, hating Jim Kimble.

'That actually helps. The most important person was you, by the way.'

She smiled at him. 'I was hoping so.'

'But back to my point. I was an asshole. It's a wonder anyone still talks to me.'

'Detective Hanson said I should make sure you knew that you had people who cared about you, even if you didn't want to accept it.'

'I do now. But it's hard to see the support around you when you're mired in shit.'

'I know,' she soothed. She laid her head on his shoulder, her fingertips softly petting the hair on his chest. 'How did Paula die, Adam?'

She felt his body bracing itself. 'Her throat was slit. On Skype.'

Inhaling sharply, she held the breath for a long, long moment. 'Oh,' she finally breathed mournfully. 'And you saw that?'

'Yeah. She'd been kept in a cage. Not a small one. More a cell.'

'By whom?'

'She didn't know his name. He only locked her up at night. Or when she was "bad." Her word. Other times she was left to roam the house freely, but the doors were locked and the windows made of hurricane glass. She'd tried to break out, but was never able to. One day, she emailed me, out of the blue. She'd seen a news report on TV about the youth baseball team I was coaching. There were deaf kids and hearing kids on the team. The report showed me signing to them. Gave my email at the bottom of the screen in case other deaf kids wanted to join. She saw me signing and knew I'd understand her.'

'Oh.' Comprehension filled the single syllable. 'She was deaf?'

'Yes. She'd watched her captor send emails, but when she'd tried in the past, the computer was always locked. One day it was left unlocked and she contacted me.'

'From whose account?'

'Her captor's. We checked it out thoroughly, but we never turned up an owner.'

'What did she say in the email?'

'That she was scared, begged me to help. But she didn't know where she was, just that she was out in the country. That when she looked out the window, she didn't see anyone or anything.'

'You couldn't track the email to an IP address?'

'No, and we tried. So hard. It had been bounced off of so many proxies by the time it got to us that Nash couldn't track it.'

'What was Paula's situation?'

'Kept locked away. Isolated from the world, she had access to a TV and a computer. Of course it was being monitored. We knew that. That the computer was left unlocked right after she saw me on the TV news was too coincidental.'

'Of course.' She sighed. 'So Paula signed?'

'Enough that I could get the general gist. She remembered having a family once. A nice one, she said. But I never knew if that was her imagination or those memories were real. Anyway, I told her how to use Skype because her signing was better than her typing and because I was afraid her email was being monitored. That made everything more urgent, like we had to find her before he came back and punished her for reaching out.'

'Even though he might have set her up to be caught.'

'Exactly. She talked to us three times over Skype, for just a little while each time. Nash Currie tried to trace the signal, but he couldn't. I kept looking for clues as to where she was. I had ICAC examine the recordings I made of each call. They had all the experience on what to look for, but they were at a loss too. There was nothing to give us her location.'

Meredith kissed his jaw. 'And the fourth call?'

'It started out like the others. Then I heard a door slam on her end. She didn't hear it and I told her to hide, to disconnect, but it was too late.' He buried his face in her hair. 'He wore a mask. Only showed his eyes and his mouth. He was big. And she was small. Frail. Poor nutrition. She didn't have a chance.'

'She was just a little girl,' she murmured.

He swallowed audibly. 'I wanted to help her. So much. She was so alone. And then . . .' His voice broke. 'He started slicing at her skin and she was screaming, but it was . . . rusty screams, because she didn't use her voice.' His breathing became shallow and rapid. 'He kept smiling at the screen. Like he knew I was there. Then he'd cut her again.'

'And you were helpless.'

'I just stood there. And watched. And then I started hoping he'd just . . . finish so she wouldn't suffer anymore. Which made me feel like a monster,' he confessed, 'wishing for the death of a child so that I didn't have to hear her suffering.'

Meredith's sigh was shaky. 'Adam . . . You can't feel guilty about hoping that. She *was* suffering. Whoever killed her wanted to hurt you too. Maybe not you specifically, but whichever cop had the bad fortune to be her lifeline. He could have dragged her away. He could have cut the connection. He didn't. He was playing with you, like a cat with a mouse.'

He stilled against her. 'But why? What would he have gained?'

'That's a damn good question, don't you think? Whoever killed her wanted her to pay for trying to get help. But he also wanted to send CPD a message.'

'Don't fuck with me,' he murmured. 'Well, he didn't have to worry about CPD. We never did find out where she'd been held. Where she died.'

'You never found her body?'

A laugh broke free, bitter and cold. 'Yeah. I found her.'

Again she shifted to see his face. 'Where?' She wanted to look away, to avoid the misery in his eyes, but couldn't make herself do so.

'Trunk of my car,' he whispered.

New horror filled her and she framed his face with trembling hands. 'He left her for you to find?'

He nodded. 'We'd gotten a tip that someone might be being held against their will in this house out in the country. On a farm.'

'You thought you'd found her.'

'Yes, but it wasn't the same place. We checked the place from top to bottom, but it was a false tip. When we got back to the car, the trunk had been forced open.'

'She was there?'

He nodded. Cleared his throat, but could say nothing.

'And?' Meredith prodded gently. 'There's more, isn't there?'

He nodded again. Closed his eyes, then opened them, latching onto her like she was his lifeline. 'He'd . . . burned her,' he whispered.

'How do you mean?' she asked so very quietly.

He looked away. 'Gasoline. She was . . . unidentifiable.'

She couldn't control her flinch. 'Then how did you know it was her?'

'She had a bunny, a stuffed toy. It was the only toy she had. That she'd ever remembered having. It had been placed on her. Or what was left of her.'

'Oh my God. You still see her, don't you? How could you not?'

'Yeah,' he said grimly. 'I had to get rid of the car. That's when I got the Jeep. But I'd still see her, every time I went to sleep. I'd wake up screaming. Unless I got drunk first. That was the only way I could get any sleep.'

She lifted her hand to his cheek, cupped it. 'I understand. I really do.'

Nodding, he sighed heavily. 'I really hope you do. But I have to tell you the rest.'

So this would be it, she thought. They were finally getting to the part for which he'd been making amends all over town. She settled herself against his side once more and prayed again that she'd say the right things.

Sixteen

Linnea finished the oatmeal and eggs served by Sister Angela. This nun didn't have Sister Jeanette's kind smile. In fact, her face seemed to be set in a permanent scowl.

'More toast?' Sister Angela asked, hovering over the toaster.

'No, ma'am.' She was full, like she hadn't been in so long. She'd always lied to Andy when he'd brought her food from Pies & Fries, telling him she wasn't hungry because she knew he was going hungry to feed her. 'But thank you.'

They were alone in the shelter. There were masses being said in the church upstairs, the loud blast of the organ shaking the ceiling above her head from time to time. Linnea had been spared attendance when she begged off, citing her own battered appearance. The bruises from Friday night had bloomed, covering half her face in a dark purple that could never be covered by any makeup known to man. Or God, for that matter.

Sister Angela sat at the table. 'What are your plans today, Denise?'

Denise. 'I need to make a phone call. But not from here.'

Sister Angela nodded soberly. 'You don't want to be traced here. I know where you can make the call. Would you like me to take you?'

Linnea's mouth fell open in shock. 'You would do that?'

A small smile bent the nun's severe mouth. 'Why wouldn't I?'

Her gaze dropped to the bowl she'd all but licked clean. 'I'm not a nice person.'

The nun's hand, gnarled and twisted with arthritis, came to rest atop hers. 'We kind of deal in second chances here,' she said. 'Would you *like* to be a nice person, Denise?'

Linnea nodded. She knew it would never happen, that she'd never have the kind of respectability she'd always craved, but if she was gonna die soon – and she knew she was – she wanted to go out doing something good. 'That's why I have to make the phone call.'

'All right. I know where there's a pay phone.' The nun dug into her pocket, then dropped two quarters on the table. 'Although I think calls to 911 are free,' she said. 'Do you want me to walk with you?'

Yes. Please. But Linnea shook her head. 'I'm . . . grateful. I am. But if I'm seen, anyone around me could be hurt. And I don't want you to get hurt, ma'am.'

Sister Angela's eyes softened. 'Those are the words of a nice person, Denise.'

Huh. 'Maybe you're right. If I had more time—' She cut herself off. *Dammit.*

The nun frowned. 'What do you mean, more time? You're young. You have your whole life ahead of you.'

And that's not much time. But Linnea made herself smile. 'You're right. I do.' She slid the quarters off the table and put them in her own pocket, feeling the scrap of paper already there. 'Is there a library nearby? I need to use the computer.' Because she needed to find the '–ruber Academy' and little Ariel's teacher, Miss Abernathy.

It was possible that Ariel's paper had been left in the SUV's door pocket by a child belonging to someone other than him or his thug. But it was also possible that the kid could lead Linnea to his true identity and his address.

'There's a library a few blocks away. You'll need to show your ID to use a computer.'

'That's okay.'

'Because Denise isn't your real name,' the nun said softly, with no accusation.

Linnea shook her head sadly. She could give the woman this much. 'No, ma'am.'

'Will you tell me what it is?'

'Yes. When I've done what I need to do.' Somebody needed to know. Linnea wanted someone to remember her name. Maybe someone could get word to Shane.

She started to stand, but Sister Angela grabbed her wrist. 'Will you come back?'

'Yes, ma'am. I'll try, anyway.'

Frowning, the nun took out her cell phone and, grasping a stylus in her twisted hand, poked madly at the screen. 'It's Sunday. Library doesn't open until one o'clock.'

'If I leave to make a phone call, can I come back inside until the library opens?'

'Yes,' Sister Angela said. 'And I *will* walk with you. I'll give you privacy to make your call, but you don't have to walk alone.'

Linnea opened her mouth to say thank you, but no words would come.

The nun just patted her hand. 'You're welcome.'

Cincinnati, Ohio,
Sunday 20 December, 9.35 A.M.

Meredith was trembling in Adam's arms, her gaze still full of shock, horror, and sorrow. Adam pulled her close, wishing the ugliness in him had never touched her. It was bad enough that he had to remember Paula – her murder and finding her charred body. Now Meredith would have the pictures in her head too.

He sighed. 'A few weeks after I found her body, I asked Isenberg to take me back, to reinstate me to Homicide, and she did. That's when the drinking began to get really bad.'

Meredith flattened her hand over his still-racing heart. When she spoke, her voice was controlled. Calm. But her body still trembled like a leaf in the wind.

'When we're faced with trauma, we often fall back into the patterns that are most ingrained, usually during childhood. Yours was drinking. Part of dealing – and healing – is learning new behaviors and practicing them until they become the new fallback position.'

281

'That's what my shrink says.'

Her nod against his chest was shaky. 'Then he's smart.'

'She. I see Kate's doc.'

He felt her smile against his skin, far preferable to her tears, although those had not stopped their constant flow. 'Dr Lane? She'll do you right.' A hesitation. 'So why did you decide to go sober on January sixth?'

'You're tenacious,' he said mildly, but he kissed her forehead so that she wouldn't take offense. 'Don't you want to go to sleep now?'

She pulled back to glare at him through her tears. 'Yes. My head feels like it's a soccer ball in play, but I want this done, Adam.'

'Right.' He urged her to snuggle against him again, not wanting eye contact. She complied and he wrapped his arms tight around her. 'The morning after that first night when we . . . You know.'

'When we slept together? Yes. I do know. I was there,' she added dryly.

Yes, she had been. There. *For me.* 'I woke up and you were still asleep and so pretty. I just watched you sleep for the longest time, wanting you. *You,* I mean. Not for sex. Well, yes for sex, because that was amazing, but—' He stopped himself, his cheeks burning hot.

She patted his chest, taking pity on his rambling. 'You wanted something more?'

'I wanted everything – to hear your voice telling me it would be okay and to believe that was true. I wanted to deserve it, because I was so messed up, I couldn't find my way back on my own. But even messed up, I knew that I couldn't depend on you for my mental health. That's not fair to you. And it's not . . . sustainable.'

'Good word.'

'Dr Lane's,' he said. 'I needed to get my shit together, so I left your bed and went right to Isenberg, took a leave of absence. Which went over real well with my family.'

'Deacon and Dani criticized you?' she asked disbelievingly.

'No. Oh no. They were great. They've always been there for me. I meant my father. He, um, was not supportive.'

'Hmm,' she growled. 'I see.'

He wasn't sure she did, but that wasn't important now. *Just get through this.* So they could hopefully go on. 'I tried to get it together, but I kept seeing Paula, kept hearing her.'

'Not surprising,' she said gently.

He shrugged. 'She was always there. In my sleep, when I was awake. I was useless. I hung around my apartment and . . .' He shrugged again.

'And drank,' she supplied, still gentle.

'Yeah. I missed the holidays. I didn't even go to my parents' house on Christmas last year. I was too drunk. And I know it worried my mother and she has a heart condition, so that made me feel guilty. So I drank more. Which made me deserve you even less. It was bad. A vicious cycle. I saw the department shrink and he didn't help. I couldn't ask you for any more help. It wasn't fair to you. You can't be my therapist or my crutch.'

'No, I can't,' she agreed. 'But I can support you. I can *care* about you.'

He hoped so. 'I got invited to your birthday party by Dani and Deacon, but I couldn't face them. I'd been horrible to Deacon and . . .' He drew a breath and took the first plunge. 'I made Faith lose her job with the bank because I called her boss, introduced myself as a homicide detective, then insinuated she was a suspect. I didn't think she could forgive me.'

'But she did. She told me all about it.'

It was his turn to rear back in surprise. 'She did?'

'Yes. You suspected her of being involved in multiple murders and called her boss at the bank to verify her employment. That was standard operating procedure, wasn't it?'

He blinked. 'Yes, but I thought you'd be mad about the way I did it.'

'Maybe, but I'm not, because we all knew you were hurting then. We didn't know why, but Adam, you were obviously the walking wounded. Besides, Faith had two job offers by the end of the following week. I'm glad she picked me. She's an amazing therapist.'

'I thought you offered her a job because . . .' He frowned. 'This isn't gonna come out right. But I figured you felt sorry for her.'

She actually laughed. 'I didn't know she'd been fired when I asked her to work with me. I only had to watch her with the victims. Plus, you know, redhead solidarity.' She sobered. 'What else are you afraid I'll be mad at?'

He squared his jaw. *Next plunge.* 'I drove drunk.'

She met his eyes. 'Okay. That's really bad. Was that the night we slept together?'

'No. That was on your birthday. I'd driven by your house and there were cars parked all over the block because of your party. I almost parked and went in. Almost. I was so stressed out at the thought of seeing everyone who knew I was on mental health leave . . . I got a little buzzed before I got there. Just to take off the edge. I drove around the block a couple times, then my cell rang. If it had been my mom's number, I wouldn't have answered. She'd texted and called a few times that day, but I was avoiding her too.'

'Because she would have known you were buzzed.'

'Yeah. She'd seen my dad that way for years, after all. But it wasn't my mom's number and I guess I was looking for an excuse not to go to your party, so I answered.'

Her expression had grown grave as he'd talked. 'Who was it?'

'The hospital. Mom had been texting and calling because she needed me to come over and fix a light bulb. I figured my dad could do that just as easily, so I let it go. But my father had gone duck hunting and so she'd climbed on a chair and . . .' His throat closed.

'Fell and ended up in the hospital. How badly was she hurt?'

He cleared his throat. 'She sprained her arm and needed stitches in her head. The real damage was from a heart attack she had when she fell. I drove right to the hospital, but they'd called my father and he'd just gotten there too. He chased me out of her room. Said all the things he always did, but that time . . . He was right on point. I *was* a loser and I *was* a mental case. More than that, I was a bad son. I didn't want to upset my mom with a hallway brawl, so I left.' Tail between his legs. He sighed heavily. 'I went straight from the hospital to a bar and drank myself stupid. And then I drove home.'

She frowned at him. 'The bartender didn't take your keys?'

'Nope. I'm a functional drunk, apparently. He'd just come on shift. Didn't know how much I'd already had. I'm also a pretty decent liar when I'm drunk. He never suspected. On the way home I . . .' He closed his eyes, willing the panic away. *Next plunge. Just tell her.* 'I hit a kid on a bike. A teenager.'

'Oh my God,' she whispered. 'Was he okay?'

'Yeah. Because I'm apparently the luckiest bastard alive. When I hit him, he went off the road and tumbled down a hill. He broke his arm.' He let out a slow breath. 'I could have killed him, Meredith.'

She gripped his chin, tugging until he opened his eyes and looked at her. 'But you didn't, right?'

'No, I didn't.' *Thank God.* He still shuddered at the dread of what might have happened. 'I knew the kid. He lives in my neighborhood. Ironically enough, he was as drunk as I was. He grabbed his bike, begged me not to tell his mother he'd been drinking. I was kind of stupefied, you know? In shock and reeling. I said okay and put his bike in the back of my Jeep and drove him home. He said he was just going to tell his mom he fell off his bike. When I got home, I collapsed in my bed and didn't wake up for almost twenty-four hours.' He'd been a physical mess. His own stench had woken him. And *that* lovely little detail he was keeping to himself. 'I was completely sober, for the first time since Paula. I looked in the mirror and realized what I'd become. My mother might have died. And that kid . . . God. So I gathered all my bottles and poured them all out. Then I found an AA meeting.'

'I'm so glad you did. Shh,' she soothed. 'It's all right.'

Because he was shaking and hadn't even realized it. 'You shouldn't be looking at me like that.' Softly. With compassion.

Her lips curved sadly. 'Then how should I look at you?'

'With contempt.' *Like I look at me.*

She shook her head. 'Adam, you saw something horrific and you self-medicated your trauma. It's not an unusual reaction. But it wasn't good for you. You realized that, and now you're not doing it anymore. You shouldn't be ashamed. You should be proud. You know how few people can bring themselves back like that.'

'And if I fall off the wagon?'

'Then you get back on. Do you plan to fall off?'

'No.' He shuddered at the pictures his mind always conjured, his

285

mother, on the floor, having died alone. And that kid dead on the side of the road, his bike wheels spinning. That wasn't what had happened. The kid was just fine.

His mother though . . . Her arm and head had healed, but her heart was even weaker than it had been. Her next heart attack might be her last. And whenever that happened, he was going to have to live with the fact that he'd hastened it.

'I can't be that person again,' he whispered hoarsely. 'I'm *not* that person.'

And maybe, just maybe, he might believe that someday.

A brush of her thumb over his lips. 'Good. I'm glad.'

And that was the worst of it, he realized, briefly stunned. Those were the worst secrets and she was still here, her words, her touch still gentle. 'That night last summer, when I came to see you? When we colored?'

'I remember.'

He did too. He remembered every single second, because he'd been sober as a judge. Leaving her that night had been one of the hardest things he'd ever done and that included giving up the booze. 'I left your house and called my sponsor. Found a midnight meeting even though I'd just gone to one that morning. I sat in that midnight meeting and promised myself I wouldn't have any more contact with you until I'd earned my year coin.'

Her hand cupped his cheek and he turned into her touch. 'Were you ever going to tell me all of this?' she asked.

'Yes.' He winced. 'Maybe? I don't know. Sorry.'

'Don't be sorry. I might not have believed the "yes."' She was quiet for a long moment. 'If you need to walk away from me until you get that coin, I'll understand.'

'I don't know if I can,' he whispered. 'I need you too much.'

She sagged into him, shuddering out a relieved breath. 'Good. Because I need you too. I mean, I can get through the next few weeks without you if I must. Papa is here and my cousin Alex is coming from Atlanta for Christmas. Bailey, Hope, and Ryan will be with me too. I wouldn't be completely alone.'

And why her family was about to gather ranks around her was a question he wanted answered. But that could wait, at least until they'd slept.

She rubbed her cheek against his chest. 'It's so much nicer to have you, though.'

And suddenly it was that simple. He could get through the next two weeks without her too. He'd made it eleven months and fourteen days on his own. If he had to, he could finish out the year. But for the next few hours, at least, he wasn't leaving her alone.

Because she needed him too.

Cincinnati, Ohio,
Sunday 20 December, 9.45 A.M.

Heart thundering, Linnea tugged at the scarf that Sister Angela had wound around her head and face, allowing her to hide in plain sight. The pay phone was outside an old corner store with bars on the windows, but the neighborhood wasn't all that scary. Linnea had seen far, far worse. Having a nun at her back certainly didn't hurt.

She lifted the receiver and frowned. 'No dial tone,' she said to Sister Angela.

'Try putting a quarter in first. You should get it back once you hang up.'

Linnea obeyed, but wiped the quarter clean first. She'd have to wipe the whole phone clean when she was finished. Inserting the quarter, she was relieved to hear the dial tone. Fingers trembling, she dialed 911.

'This is 911. What is the nature of your emergency?' the operator asked.

Linnea's throat closed.

'Hello? Are you there?' the operator said.

Linnea's breath wheezed out of her chest and then she felt a hand on her back. Sister Angela, patting her gently. 'You want me to talk to them, child?'

'No,' Linnea managed. 'I can do it. I *need* to do it.' *I need to be a nice person.* She waited until the nun had stepped far enough away that her whispered words couldn't be overheard. 'I'm, um . . . Can I talk to somebody about the shooting yesterday? The one downtown? I have . . . information.'

'I see.' The operator's voice gentled. 'Let me transfer you.'

'No,' Linnea cried out. That would take a while and she didn't want to stand out here, a sitting duck if the wrong person saw her. She knew her fear was illogical. He couldn't be everywhere, but . . . he always seemed to be. She dropped her voice back to a whisper. 'Just tell them that the SUV used in the shooting can be found at Clyde's Place, at 275 and Beechmont. Tell them . . . to be careful. The person who left it there . . . they bled and they're positive. For, you know, HIV. Tell the cops to wear gloves. That's all.'

'Wait!' the operator insisted, but Linnea replaced the receiver. The quarter came jingling down and she removed it.

She used her sleeve to wipe down all the parts of the phone that she'd touched, then returned to the nun and handed her the quarter. 'Thank you.'

'You're welcome, child.' The nun's smile was . . . sweet. Linnea hadn't seen sweetness there at first.

But I was wrong. I was wrong about so many things. I have to make them right. 'Can we go back now?' She had cramps from hell and all she wanted was to lie down and curl into a fetal position.

'Of course.' In an unexpected move, Sister Angela crooked her elbow, like she wanted Linnea to take it. So she did. And she and the nun walked back to the shelter arm-in-arm. It was . . . nice. And when they got to the church she didn't feel quite as much panic as she had the night before. In fact, she felt a spurt of something that felt remarkably like hope. Like maybe, just maybe she'd be able to sit in one of those pews. Someday.

It was a nice dream anyway.

Cincinnati, Ohio,
Sunday 20 December, 9.45 A.M.

Butch rubbed his huge hands over his face. 'Tell me again why we're doin' this?' He dropped into the shabby hotel chair. 'The girls make us a shit-ton of money. None of them has even seen you. None of the ones still alive, anyway.'

No, none of them had except for Linnea, and it was really eating at him that she was still out there somewhere, presumably alive. It was like she'd vanished into nowhere.

Even if she were dead somewhere, she was still a major liability.

'Because Linnea's face is all over the news,' he snapped. Luckily, it was her old face, before she'd arrived in Cincinnati. A teenager's face, round and young. She'd been about fifteen in the photo that the cops had posted all over the Internet as a person of interest.

They couldn't have gotten the photo from Andy because everything he'd owned was gone, obliterated by the fire. The picture had to have been supplied by Shane Baird. Who, according to his resources inside CPD, had been interviewed, then whisked away to a safe house. Which meant that until he either figured out where that was or until Shane was moved elsewhere, he couldn't get his hands on the kid either. Which meant he had nothing with which to draw Linnea out.

Butch shrugged. 'She don't look like that picture no more. She's used up. Gone hard.' He grimaced. 'Haggard. She was comin' up on her ex date anyway.'

'Which was why I picked Andy for the job yesterday. He cared for her enough to want to save her, but nobody else wanted her.' Even with her rates drastically discounted. So Linnea had become a liability. 'Which doesn't really matter anymore. Eventually somebody's going to recognize her and call the cops.'

Butch heaved a sigh. 'And if whoever calls in remembers seeing her with any of the girls, the cops will focus in on them as a connection. I get it. But do we have to get rid of them *all*? Can't we keep one or two?'

Butch had issues getting women because he was a cruel SOB – but that had been true even before the meth lab fire that had left him with a face only a mother could love. Actually, Butch's mother hadn't loved him, either, so that left nobody. Their girls had been . . . unwillingly cooperative partners. If they didn't cooperate, they experienced Butch's cruelty firsthand. Just as Linnea had on Friday night.

He drew a breath and tried to be patient, because when Butch got his feelings hurt, he tended to pout. Not an attractive look for him and not a productive mode for either of them. He needed to get this job done. 'We'll get you more, Butch. Don't worry.'

Butch appeared unhappy nevertheless. 'Can I at least do the deed once more with 'em, before I, uh, do the deed?'

He aborted a laugh, snorting instead. 'No. You'll have to make it fast. Three of them are due in' – he checked his watch – 'right about now.'

'And then?'

'And then we go to the next hotel and do it again.'

Butch rolled his eyes. 'What a waste. Just sayin'.'

'We never keep them long. You know that.' The half-dozen girls who worked the university circuit never lasted more than a year. One or two of them were actual college kids. Most were simply hookers who had looked fresh-faced enough when they started.

Most of them quit on their own. Those who got old and haggard but wouldn't quit were cut loose by his business manager, Jolee. Most of them hit the streets solo. He didn't care. None of them had seen him and if they ever threatened Jolee with either violence or exposure, Butch took care of them and nobody was ever the wiser.

But having Linnea's face all over the news changed that. Somebody was going to recognize her sooner or later.

And with Voss's account ledgers falling under the microscope of Kimble and Triplett's murder investigation, it was only a matter of time before his blackmail payments were exposed. Voss wouldn't have stood up to the strain of interrogation. He liked to beat up women, but sitting under the lights in an interview room? He'd spill details in a hot minute. Which was no longer a problem, thanks to Uncle Mike.

Still, having six women disappear all at once was going to be tricky.

He pulled three capped syringes from his pocket. 'You ready, Butch?'

Butch scowled. 'Yeah. Let's do it. Still say it's a fucking waste.'

His patience splintered. 'Yes,' he bit out. 'But *necessary*. Hurry up. I have to be at church by eleven.'

Butch's expression was the same as when he ate Brussels sprouts. 'Why? You did the cantina thing last night.'

He snorted again, his impatience evaporating because Butch could always make him laugh. 'Can*tata*, not can*tina*. A cantina is that bar in *Star Wars* where Han Solo first met Luke and Obi Wan. Today's just a normal choir thing.' And an alibi. 'Get in the closet.'

Butch obeyed, just as the knock came at the door.

He opened the door, smiling at the three women standing on the other side. He didn't know their names. They matched the photographs sent to him by Jolee.

Jolee recruited new employees, made sure they were trained and showed up where and when they were supposed to. She managed the website through which their clients booked appointments and paid, and she handed out the cash to the girls on payday.

He paid her well and she never seemed to regret selling her body or selling out her fellow classmates. Older than the women she managed, she didn't hit the field as often anymore. Still, she was a team player when needed. She was to be joining the group they were to meet at the second hotel, taking up the slack left by the disappearance of Linnea.

He was going to miss Jolee. She'd been damn good at her job.

'You were sent by Jolee?' he asked. Three nods. One girl smiled back, but the other two looked bored. Well, the two bored ones would have been tagged to be terminated anyway. Employing bored hookers was no way to run a business. 'Please come in.'

They did, sitting on the edge of the bed when he motioned them to it. The smiling girl appeared to be their spokesperson. 'We were told you'd be hosting a party?' She looked around doubtfully. 'Are we early?'

'No, not at all.' With a nod aimed over their heads, he slipped his hand into his pocket and removed the cap from the syringe needle. Butch crept out of the closet, an uncapped syringe in both hands.

Ambidexterity was just another one of Butch's lesser known skills. He could also move surprisingly soundlessly for a huge guy.

Butch jabbed the syringes in the necks of the two bored girls while he took care of the smiling one. Quickly stuffing gags in their mouths, it wasn't too difficult to hold them down until the sedative took effect.

They searched them, checking their cell phones to be sure they hadn't told anyone outside their little group where they were going. The hotel was one of the seedy ones where nobody watched what you carried in or out because they did not care, but he wasn't taking any chances on being captured by surveillance cameras from the local businesses.

'Let's load 'em up,' he said and Butch unzipped the three suitcases they'd brought with them. They hefted the women into the suitcases, Butch manipulating their bodies so that they fit. Butch had seen a six-foot-three college kid stuff himself into a suitcase on YouTube a few years back and this was now one of his favorite tricks.

'This never gets old,' Butch said, zipping up the third girl. 'Like doin' a puzzle.'

'So glad I could entertain you,' he said dryly. 'Mike'll be by later to pick up the cars.'

'Is he gonna need me to ride shotgun?'

'Probably. Here, give me a hand with this one.' He grabbed the handle of the largest bag with his right hand as his left arm still throbbed, courtesy of Linnea's blade. He'd make sure she knew pain before he killed her. 'This one's heavy,' he warned as he and Butch pulled the suitcases from the hotel room to their waiting SUV.

'Jolee's been feedin' 'em too good,' Butch grunted as he loaded the suitcases into the cargo bay. Once they picked up the other three, it would be Butch's job to dispose of all six.

By the time the women were dead, he'd be suited up in a choir robe singing Handel's *Messiah*. As alibis went, it was a good one. *Hallelujah*.

Seventeen

Cincinnati, Ohio,
Sunday 20 December, 12.30 P.M.

'Thank you,' he said for the hundredth time as the hundredth person shook his hand. 'I'm glad you enjoyed it. Merry Christmas to you too.'

People were so much chattier at Christmas. Took for-fucking-ever to get out of the church and into the parking lot. But he had been especially good that morning, he had to admit. The choir behind him hadn't been that bad either. A few of the members had been a little off-key, but on the whole, they worked well together.

'Daddy, look!' Ariel cried, tugging at the hem of his suit coat.

'Whatcha got, Princess?' He slipped his left hand into his pocket, then hefted her up to his hip using his uninjured right arm. It would keep the other parishioners from trying to shake his hand and maybe help him get out of there faster.

'I made this for you in children's church. It's a design.'

'I can see that.' Giant loops and whorls and big gobs of glue dotted the red construction paper, cut into the shape of a bell.

'Smell it!' she commanded.

He complied dutifully. 'It smells like Christmas.' Because she'd sprinkled cinnamon and nutmeg on the glue. It did smell good, if you could sniff past the glue. But it was a terrible mess. He already had cinnamon all over his suit. 'Thank you. I love it.'

Ariel beamed and smacked a kiss on his cheek. 'Good.'

'Let's go to the car and get it warm for Mommy and Mikey.' He carried her out, put her in her booster seat because she was tiny for

293

her age, and slid behind the wheel. Cranking up the heat, he checked his cell phone for any recent developments.

Like that a bone-skinny hooker had been found dead in a gutter, having frozen to death overnight. *I could only be so lucky.* But there was no mention of a dead Linnea, or a live one for that matter. He swiped through a few more news stories and . . .

'*Oh my God*,' he muttered. His blood ran cold and it had nothing to do with the outside temps.

'What's wrong, Daddy?' Ariel asked with concern.

'Oh, nothing, honey,' he managed. 'Just one of the Bengals players got hurt.'

'Goddammit,' she said with a hard nod, but he was too absorbed in what he was looking at to scold her for swearing.

Butch's face looked up at him from the phone screen. Butch, who'd stayed under the radar for years. It was a slightly grainy photo, taken from a camera overhead. A security camera. It was a bulletin out of Chicago PD, a BOLO for the man wanted for the murder of two Chicago women late the night before.

Goddammit, Butch, he thought viciously. Because now Butch had an ex date too. He was past due, in fact. He'd signed his own death warrant the moment he'd allowed his face to be photographed, even with the facial prosthetics. It's not like he'd ever be seen without them, so that was his face. If he went without the prosthetics he was instantly memorable.

He brought up a text screen and typed one out to Mike, double-time, before Rita got in the car and asked what he was doing. *Need you to do a job for me.*

The reply was instant. *OK. What?*

Will let u know when I know. Be ready.

Mike sent him a thumbs-up emoticon. And just in time. The back passenger door opened, letting in a gust of frigid air. Rita buckled Mikey into his car seat and hurried to buckle herself in.

'Mercy, it's cold,' she shivered. 'Oh, the heater's going. Thank you, dear.'

'No problem, sweetheart.' He pasted on a smile. 'Let's go home.'

Cincinnati, Ohio,
Sunday 20 December, 1.45 P.M.

Lucky kids, Linnea thought, searching the Gruber Academy's Facebook page on the public library's computer. Each grade's teacher had posted photos of their students doing fun, creative activities.

None of these kids looked hungry or afraid. She'd bet none of them had addicts for mothers and their fathers probably treated them like princesses.

Except that one of the kids – Ariel – had a father who was a killer. Among his other sins. Ariel, featured in several of the first grade pictures, was almost certainly his daughter. They had the same blue eyes. Linnea remembered his eyes with a shudder.

She wondered about the woman who'd married him, who'd given him children.

Could Ariel's mother know? If so, how did she live with herself? Unfortunately, none of the kids had last names on the school's Facebook page, so Linnea was no closer to knowing the name of the girl's father.

But tomorrow would be a special day at the Gruber Academy, their holiday pageant scheduled for early afternoon. Ariel's class would be reindeer. There were photos of earnest-faced little kids making their own costumes with antlers and red noses.

One of Ariel's parents was sure to come to see her on stage, playing reindeer games with the other kids. And if Ariel's daddy brought her to school? Could she kill a man in front of his daughter? *He killed Andy in front of me.*

But Linnea wasn't like him. She couldn't make the child suffer for what the father had done. She would kill him, though. She'd promised Andy revenge. She owed it to him. She owed it to herself. *Hell, I owe it to the whole damn world.*

She memorized the address of the school and found it on a map, then closed the browser on the library's computer. Then she went back out into the cold.

She needed a weapon – a gun this time, because she didn't want

295

to get close enough to him again to use a knife. She was pretty sure she knew where to buy one. Working the streets had taught her a thing or two, after all.

Cincinnati, Ohio,
Sunday 20 December, 2.45 P.M.

'Meredith. Meredith, wake up, honey.'

Coming slowly awake, Meredith breathed in the most delicious scent she could imagine. *Adam.* He sat next to her, smelling better than any man had a right to smell. And calling her honey. She liked that. She liked everything he'd done to her. With her. For her.

She hadn't liked everything he'd told her, necessarily, because telling her had hurt him, but he'd trusted her with his secrets. That was everything.

'Why?' she asked without opening her eyes.

'Because I have to go into work.'

Blinking hard, she squinted against the bedside light he'd turned on. The rest of the room was still dark, courtesy of the heavy drapes, but she could see that he was dressed in the suit he'd taken from her house . . . How many hours ago?

'What time is it?' she murmured.

'Almost three.'

She blinked again. 'Morning or afternoon?'

He laughed. 'Afternoon. I need to go in.' He ran a hand up her arm to caress her cheek. 'I should have let you sleep, but I didn't want you to wake up and find me gone.'

Again. The word he'd left unspoken hovered between them until she dashed it away with a shy smile. 'I appreciate it.' Her smile faded as it all rushed back at her – the shooting, poor Andy, poor Tiffany, both dead. Kyle and Shane, grieving. And Adam. *My God. Adam.* The things he'd seen. That he'd pulled himself back from the edge was testament to his strength. It was a wonder he hadn't fallen completely, irreparably apart. 'Has anything new happened?'

'Not sure. I'm going in for a briefing and to take Kyle to meet his parents. They're supposed to arrive from Michigan in the next hour or so. Shane wanted to see them too.'

Swallowing a yawn, Meredith sat up. Which was a mistake because her head pounded, like it always did when her sleep cycle got altered. She pushed the pain aside, making herself smile. 'I need to set up time to talk to Penny Voss, get the details of what she saw. Should I have them come to the precinct or here?'

'Not here. Tell Mrs Voss we'll send someone to bring her and Penny downtown. I can have Agent Troy bring you to meet them later.'

'Kate's gone?'

'Yeah, gone home to sleep, then she was going to Mariposa House with Cap. She thought letting the girls pet him might calm the tension.'

Meredith sighed. 'Wendi said the girls were afraid. I wish I could have been there to help get everyone settled, but I'd just make them targets too.'

'Wendi's got it all under control.' He frowned, lifting her chin to study her face. 'You've got a headache. I can see it in your eyes.'

That he could see what she was normally able to hide should not make her as happy as it did. 'Not too bad. Nothing some ibuprofen and a double espresso can't cure.'

He winced. 'Double espresso? I thought you drank tea.'

'At night. I need my caffeine in the morning, especially when morning happens in the afternoon.' She leaned her forehead against his shoulder, gratified when his arms came around her without hesitation, moaning quietly when he threaded his fingers through her hair and began massaging her scalp.

'Better?'

'Umm. Not sure. Need you to do it a little longer.'

He chuckled and kept it up. 'Just another minute or two. I need to go.'

With another sigh, she sat back. She could get used to massages like that. Except that it made her want his hands all over her bare skin. 'If you can wait twenty minutes, I can go with you. That way you won't have to make Agent Troy stay here babysitting me when he could be helping you guard Shane and Kyle while you transport them.' She pulled the blanket aside, but paused before sliding around him to get out of bed. 'If Papa wants to stay, can the officer stay with him? The one who was guarding Shane and Kyle?'

Adam's gaze dropped to the collar of her pajama top and Meredith was suddenly conscious that several of the buttons had slipped free while she'd slept and her breasts were very nearly completely bared. He drew a deep breath, twin flags of color staining his cheeks. Her own cheeks heating, she began to refasten the buttons, wondering how they'd come loose on their own. They never had before.

Maybe they had help. And I slept through the whole thing? Dammit.

'No need to do that on my account,' he murmured thickly.

Her hands paused, her heart beating against her chest like a hummingbird's wings. She glanced up, almost whimpering at the sight of his slightly parted lips and the hungry set of his jaw. 'You' – she swallowed hard – '*are* in a hurry, aren't you?'

He jerked his gaze away. 'Yes. Dammit.'

Somehow that made her feel better, as did his scowl when she resumed the task.

'Adam?' she said softly when she'd finished. 'Can the officer stay here with Papa?'

He met her eyes, the raw desire in his sending shivers all over her skin. He banked the desire, but slowly, by degrees, taking several lungfuls of air along the way. 'No,' he finally said. 'First, the officer went off shift and since I was awake, we didn't replace him. Second, your grandfather's going downtown with Kyle and Shane.'

'Why?'

'Apparently, he and Shane bonded over video games while the rest of us were asleep. Between Shane and Diesel, you're picking up adopted cousins all over the place. Except for me,' he added glumly. 'I got the cold shoulder when I went out there to get coffee.'

'That's because of me. He's . . .' She had to look away. 'Protective.'

'Why?' Adam asked, then hooked a finger under her chin, turning her face back to his when she didn't answer. 'Why?' he asked again, his voice going deep and soft.

She opened her mouth, but no words came out because she never had any when it came time to telling that part of her story. She was saved from the effort by the ringing of his cell phone – an eerie flute tune that was vaguely familiar.

'It's Deacon,' he said, pressing a kiss to her forehead. 'I'm going to take this outside on the balcony because I get a shitty signal in here.' He hesitated, then took her mouth in a hard, fast kiss that left her stunned and breathless. He rose from the bed and walked toward the door, but backward so that he continued to face her. 'It'll be better if you go with us, so get dressed. I'll wait.'

She heard him say hello to Deacon as he closed the bedroom door. Carefully she touched her lips and let out the breath she'd been holding. 'Wow.' Then she laughed, remembering where she'd heard Deacon's ringtone. It was the theme song for an old Clint Eastwood spaghetti western. Perfect for Deacon, who marched to his own drummer. Kind of a rogue superhero. At least Faith thought so, which was exactly as it should be.

Meredith wondered if she had a ringtone in Adam's phone, and if so, what was it?

Twenty minutes. Get dressed. She went into the bedroom she'd been assigned to get some clean clothes, only to find a cup on the nightstand. Hot cocoa, she realized.

She touched the cup. Cold cocoa, actually. The cup had been sitting for at least an hour, a candy cane placed on the saucer. Her grandfather's offering. He'd been making her hot cocoa with a candy cane every year at Christmastime since she'd been small.

That he'd left it here in her empty bedroom was a message, for sure. *Busted.* No wonder he'd given Adam the cold shoulder. But it was totally worth it. And her grandfather would come around. He just needed to see what she saw. Adam's heart.

Shaking herself into action, she collected a clean outfit from the bag Kate had packed for her and wished she had her phone, but she'd surrendered it to Adam and Trip last night, just as Shane and Kyle had been required to do. There was a landline on the nightstand, but nobody had told her it was okay to use.

She needed her art supplies if she was to work with Penny. She opened the door to the rest of the condo and stuck her head out. 'Agent Troy?'

'Dr Fallon,' Troy said warmly, ambling up to the crack in the door. 'How are you?'

'Okay. And you?' He looked wonderful, actually. Healthier. He'd looked spent and sad and haggard when she'd met him last summer, but today he had a spring to his step and a light in his eyes. She frowned slightly. 'You look different. Did you change something?'

Troy ran a self-conscious hand over his smooth head. Which was now quite bald when his hair had been thinning before. 'Took a page out of Trip's book.'

Meredith smiled at him. 'I like it. You look like Jean-Luc Picard.'

Troy rolled his eyes. 'If I had a nickel for everyone who's said that.'

'You should be happy. Patrick Stewart's like . . . still really hot. I think he has a painting aging in his attic.'

Troy chuckled. 'I think you're right. So thank you. What can I do for you?'

'I need to make a few calls. Can I use the phone over there?'

'Can I ask who you're calling?'

'First, Voss's wife. Soon-to-be ex-wife, I hope. Adam wants me to talk to her daughter, see if she can tell us any more about what her father was doing. If she can bring her to the station, I'll need my art supplies, so I was going to call my assistant. Actually, I need to call her first, because I don't know Mrs Voss's phone number. It's in my files.'

'Tell you what,' Troy said. 'I'll make the calls for you on my cell while you get ready to go. Adam says we're waiting for you. And my cell is secure. If I run into any trouble with either Voss or your assistant, I'll knock on the door and let you know.'

'Okay. My assistant's name is Corinne Longstreet. And her cell's . . .' Meredith blew out a breath. 'I have no idea. It's in my phone. But Faith will know. Can you call her first?'

'Of course. Do you want something you can eat on the way downtown?'

Meredith sniffed the air. 'What did everybody else get? Because it smells good.'

'Grilled cheese and tomato soup.' He smiled sadly. 'Comfort food for the boys.'

Meredith smiled back at him, just as sadly. 'You're a nice man, Agent Troy. Yes, a grilled cheese would be amazing. I'll take a rain check on the soup. I'll be ready in ten.'

Cincinnati, Ohio,
Sunday 20 December, 3.00 P.M.

'Hey, D,' Adam said, stepping onto the balcony and closing the sliding glass door. He shivered, his suit coat no protection from the cold. At least the wind was being blocked by the bulletproof glass that ran the perimeter of the balcony. 'What do you have?'

'Several things. When are you coming in?'

'As soon as Meredith is ready. She's setting up a session with Penny Voss and her mother in one of the interview rooms. She said she'd be ready in a few minutes. We're bringing Kyle Davis in to meet up with his parents. They're taking him home.'

'Does Chicago PD know Kyle's coming back?'

'Yes. I spoke with them a half hour ago.' Right before he'd gone in to wake Meredith. 'Why? What's going on?'

'We got an anonymous 911 at nine forty-seven this morning from a young woman telling us where to find the SUV used in the shooting.'

Adam stood up straighter. 'Where? Was it there?'

'Not anymore. We got surveillance footage from the restaurant where the SUV had been parked, near 275 and Beechmont. We saw a young woman get out, search for something, then lock up the SUV and set off on foot. Not ten minutes later, a big guy came to pick it up. He had a different woman with him. That woman walked away and he got in the SUV, but cleaned the seat first, which is consistent with the 911 caller who told us to use gloves, that the person who ditched the SUV was HIV positive and had bled on the seat.'

'Linnie,' Adam breathed. 'At least we know she's alive. As of nine forty-seven, at least.' But bleeding. And positive. He wanted to sigh, then realized Deacon had gone silent. 'What?'

'You didn't demand to know why we didn't call you already.'

301

'You let me sleep. I appreciate it. If you'd needed me, you would have called.'

Another pause. 'Okay,' Deacon said warily. 'Good to know.'

Adam sighed. That Deacon was shocked at being thanked spoke volumes about how badly Adam had fucked things up between them. He never should have put it off so long. But he'd wanted that year. Wanted to prove to himself that he'd changed before he'd told anyone else. Because he'd been so damn ashamed. And, if he was honest, afraid of what his cousin would say when the truth was finally told. 'I need to talk to you at some point. Not on the phone. But I'm sorry, Deacon. I'm sorry I was a dick. I'm sorry I hurt you. Please know that.'

'It's okay.' There was warmth in his cousin's tone. And caring. 'Are you back now, Adam?' His voice cracked. 'Because we've missed the hell out of you.'

Adam cleared his throat harshly. 'Yeah. I think I finally am.' He changed the subject before they both started bawling. 'Were you able to trace the 911 call?'

'Yeah,' Deacon said, back to business. He'd asked no questions and, for the most part, had taken everything Adam had dished out in those early months. Without knowing about the drinking or the quitting drinking.

I'm a lucky asshole. I don't deserve him.

'We traced it to a pay phone downtown,' Deacon went on. 'We dusted, took all the coins, still processing the prints. The exterior of the machine was wiped down. So far nothing off the coins is popping up in AFIS.'

'Were you able to get a photo of the girl's face? Either the one who dropped off the SUV or picked it up?'

'The drop-off girl, yes. Partial, anyway.'

'Is it Linnie?'

Deacon made an uncertain noise. 'Maybe? If so, she's a lot thinner now than she was in the photo Shane gave you. I've sent the footage to the lab to see if they can clean it up. We've got uniforms canvassing up and down Beechmont, looking for where she went after she dropped off the van.'

'What about the guy who picked it up and the woman with him? Was she Linnie?'

'No. The woman with him was at least four inches taller. We didn't get their faces because they had scarves wrapped around them. Only their eyes showed. But, the man? He had the same body type as the guy who went looking for Shane Baird last night at the Kiesler dorm. Your pals in Chicago sent the university's video along with their crime scene photos. He has the right height, weight, and stride.'

Excitement prickled up Adam's spine. Things were connecting. 'Let's have Shane listen to the 911 call. He might be able to recognize Linnie's voice.'

'Good idea. I'll have it set up for him when you get him down here.'

'Thanks. What do we know about Voss?'

'Nothing yet. You knew that Isenberg borrowed Hanson from Narcotics, right?'

'Yeah,' Adam said, 'he got there when we were talking to the Chicago detectives. Isenberg was going to have him investigate the college hookers and Voss's drug source.'

'Well, Hanson's been knocking on Voss's door, but Voss isn't answering. We're going to go for a warrant, but we need more info. Hate to drag Mer down here, but we need her.' Deacon made a disgusted sound. 'I hate that we're putting such a burden on a six-year-old's shoulders. If Mer can't get anything more from Penny Voss, we got nothing.'

Adam sighed. 'My confidential informant found something.'

'Oh?' The single syllable was rife with meaning. 'Like?'

'Voss may be being blackmailed, for fifty grand a month. That's all I know.'

'Then tell Diesel to dig deeper,' Deacon said dryly.

Adam had to laugh. 'I will. Listen, I need to make another call or two and then we'll be leaving here. I'll text you when Troy and I get to the parking garage at the station. We'll bypass the lobby and bring everyone directly up in the elevator.'

'I'll meet you in the station's parking garage, then.'

'Thanks, man.' It was always good to have another set of eyes and another gun. He ended the call, then called Trip and brought him up to speed, including the photo Chicago PD had sent of the big bruiser who'd likely killed Tiffany and her mother.

'I'm at Mariposa House,' Trip told him, 'talking to the girls to see who knew Mallory and Meredith were going to be at Buon Cibo yesterday.'

'Thanks. Pass around Andy's photo too. And Linnea's. Hell, show them Bruiser's photo too. Chicago said they'd put out a BOLO so you can pull up the bulletin to show them. Maybe one of the girls will recognize them.'

He ended the call to Trip and checked his messages. And sighed. He'd gotten fifteen texts from his sponsor. Who he was supposed to have called last night. He hit redial and braced himself for the explosion. John's texts had grown steadily more worried. He'd even gone by Adam's apartment to check on him. Poor guy hadn't slept all night.

'So you actually live?' John barked without a greeting.

'Yeah,' Adam said. 'I'm sorry, John. I got busy.'

'You could have sent a goddamn text. I was pulling my fucking hair out, worrying about you, asshole.'

'You don't have any hair to spare,' Adam told him.

John sputtered. 'You do *not* get to make jokes. Not after I've been worrying all night long. What the fuck happened?'

'I got pulled into a case. It got complicated.'

John's sigh sounded exasperated. 'I know. I've been, uh, reading the updates.'

'And listening to BOLOs on your scanner?'

'Maybe,' John groused, because of course he did. He'd been a career cop. A man like him did not simply retire and fish all day. 'I heard enough to know there were multiple triggers for you in this case.' He sighed again, exhausted this time. 'You still good?'

'Yep. Still on the wagon and still on track for my shiny gold coin.'

'Yeah, well, I read that Meredith Fallon is involved, that she was the target at the restaurant downtown yesterday. She's the biggest trigger you got, boy.'

And wasn't *that* the truth? 'I know. I, um, told her. Everything.'

A shocked silence. 'You did? When?'

Adam frowned because John didn't sound as supportive as he'd expected. 'This morning, when we got a break.'

'You're with her? Right now?'

'Yes.' Adam snapped it out, then turned around to lean on the bulletproof glass. His eyes searched the interior of the condo, looking for Meredith, but she hadn't left the bedroom yet. 'Look, John, I know what you're going to say. Just . . . don't. I can't right now.'

'That's why it's bad for you to be around her right now. Dammit, Adam. You're at a vulnerable point. Too many triggers without adding *wuv-twoo-wuv* into the mix.'

That John was a *Princess Bride* fan had always boggled Adam's mind. And then the movie got shoved to the side, his mind now boggling at the gorgeous redhead leaving the bedroom, looking professional and . . . *mine*. 'Look, I'm heading out to the office, so I gotta go. I'll try to text you with updates. And I promise I'll hit a meeting.'

'When?'

'As soon as I get a break in this case or tomorrow morning, whichever comes first.'

'Fine. Let me know when and where. I'll meet you there.'

For the second time in ten minutes, Adam was all choked up. 'Thanks, John.'

'You're welcome, kid. Just . . . focus on staying sober, okay? Even if that means handing this case off to someone else. This is difficult shit.'

'Don't I know it.' Adam ended the call, drew a breath. And froze. Because on the air was a scent that hadn't been there thirty seconds before. *Pipe smoke.* Slowly he turned and walked the length of the L-shaped balcony. Clarke Fallon sat on a lounge chair, bundled up in a coat, hat, scarf, and gloves, calmly puffing on his pipe. *Sonofabitch.* The man had been eavesdropping and wanted Adam to know it.

Adam rewound his conversations and groaned inwardly. Lots of personal shit had come out of his mouth. Wagons, gold coins, and

305

meetings. *Shit.* 'You should have told me you were out here. It wasn't your business.'

Fallon returned his gaze levelly. 'I considered revealing myself. Then I thought about the fact that Merry didn't sleep in her bed last night. So I made you my business.'

Adam's cheeks went hot, despite the blustery cold. 'She's a grown woman. Sir.'

Fallon shrugged. 'I'm her grandfather. I'm allowed. So . . . Gold coins and meetings? Staying on wagons? You told her about AA?'

Adam's teeth clenched. 'Not your business. Sir.'

'But you did.'

Adam closed his eyes. *Goddammit.* 'Yes. I did.'

'Good. You're the one who colored all the pictures, I take it.'

Adam's eyes flew open. 'Yes. How do you know that?'

'Because I saw them. She kept them all.'

'You snooped?'

'Not entirely. She had half a dozen stuck to her fridge door. She put them in a drawer with the others when people started coming into her house.'

'Diesel saw them.' *That's how he knew to rib me about it yesterday.*

'He did. We liked them, for what it's worth. Especially the painting.' He puffed on the pipe for a minute that felt like a day. 'Look, Adam. She thinks you're worth waiting for. I'm willing to give you the benefit of the doubt, especially now that I know what your story is. Or part of it anyway.'

'Big of you,' Adam said sarcastically.

Fallon laughed. 'I know.' He stood up, emptying his pipe into a little wooden box which went into his coat pocket. 'That was your sponsor? That last call?'

Adam gritted his teeth. 'It was. He's a good guy. Retired cop.'

'Good. I imagine he can relate to everything you've seen.' He crossed his arms over his burly chest. 'I'll be honest, a recovering alcoholic isn't who I would have chosen for my Merry. But it's not my choice. Just . . . don't hurt her. Any more than you already have.'

Adam winced, because that dig was completely deserved. 'I'll do my best. I know she's not impervious to hurt, not like everyone thinks she is. She's got everyone fooled.'

'But not you.'

'Well, I knew there was something going on, but I didn't expect what she's revealed to me. And that's all I'm going to say.'

Fallon nodded. 'Fair enough. Let's talk later. I want to know you.' Adam must have looked horrified because Fallon laughed again. 'You don't have to look so worried, son. I'm not a bad man. I just love Meredith. If you do too, or come to over time, and you treat her right? We'll be the best of friends.'

'Okay.' Adam turned to look into the condo and saw Meredith accepting a wrapped sandwich from Agent Troy. Which made Adam smile for no good reason.

'This might actually be okay,' Fallon murmured. 'If what I see on your face is real.'

Adam just nodded. 'Time to go.'

Cincinnati, Ohio,
Sunday 20 December, 3.40 P.M.

The back of the van was arranged like a military transport plane, with jump seats along each wall that faced one another. Meredith, her grandfather, Shane, and Kyle resembled paratroopers ready to jump because Agent Troy had brought them bulky bulletproof vests.

The windowless CPD van was probably five minutes from downtown, if Troy was taking a direct route. It was impossible to know as Adam had pulled the curtain separating the front seats from the back, cutting off their view – and cutting them off from view, which was more important.

But Meredith wished she had just one window, so she could stare out of it. Or glare out of it, which was more accurate. In the absence of a window, she focused her irritation fully on her grandfather. She didn't need to be a shrink to see that he and Adam had had words on the balcony. Adam had been tense, her grandfather uncharacteristically broody.

'You can look at me like that all you want to, young lady,' her

307

grandfather said, breaking into the heavy silence. 'It won't change one little thing.'

Her grandfather sat opposite her, Kyle next to him. Shane sat next to Meredith, silent except for an occasional sigh, but at the sound of Clarke's voice, Shane's chin came up, his gaze bouncing between Meredith and her grandfather. 'What's going on?' he asked.

Clarke started to answer, but Meredith shot him a warning look. 'Sometimes,' she said to Shane, but kept her gaze on Clarke, 'folks can love you a little too much. Sometimes they forget you are all grown up and not five years old any longer.'

Shane shrugged. 'He *is* eighty-four. Which he *claims* allows him to give unsolicited advice. On video games and life.'

Clarke snorted. 'He's a smart kid, Merry.'

'Yeah, he is. He said *claims*.' She glanced at Shane. 'What advice did he give you?'

Shane's expression softened. 'That I shouldn't feel guilty that I laughed at his jokes when I'm supposed to be grieving. That laughter is basically my heart taking a break.'

Meredith's heart clenched, because Clarke had said the same thing to her when her parents had died and her life as she knew it was imploding. 'He's right about that,' she murmured. She sighed and met Clarke's gaze. 'Just . . . don't push, okay, Papa?'

'Okay.' Clarke rolled his eyes. 'I'll try, anyway.'

'Thanks,' Meredith said dryly, then looked at Shane. 'How are you doing, Shane?'

He shrugged. 'Detective Kimble asked me if I'd listen to a recording of a 911 call.'

'I know. I overheard him talking to you.' It had been as they were putting on their coats and bulletproof vests. Meredith figured that Adam had intended for her to overhear, since he'd talked to Shane while she stood only a few feet away. 'Are you okay with that?'

Shane bit at his lip. 'He thinks it might be Linnie. But what if it is?'

'Well, I guess first and foremost, if it is her, then we know she's alive.'

'Or was this morning,' Shane said gruffly.

'What are you afraid of, hon?'

'That it *is* Linnie.' He dropped his head, his shoulders sagging. 'And that she had something to do with Andy getting killed. Because if she didn't, why didn't she go to the police? Why call anonymously? I mean, I thought I knew her. I thought she'd do anything for Andy, because he would've done anything for her.' He looked at her, his eyes narrowed and red from tears, fear, and a mostly sleepless night. 'He *died* to keep her safe.'

'All good questions,' Meredith admitted. 'Ones I wish I could answer. I can ask Detective Kimble if I can sit in there with you, if you want. For support.'

His lips trembled, then firmed when he pursed them. 'That would be good, I think.'

The curtain whipped open and Adam's face appeared. But instead of agreeing to her sitting in with Shane, his jaw was taut and he held a rifle in his hands.

'Get down!' he shouted. 'Everyone on the floor.' Then he was gone and the van took a hard turn, brakes squealing.

After a single blink, Meredith sprang into action, unbuckling her seatbelt, but Shane was fumbling with his. She batted his hands away and released the catch, grabbing him by the shirt and pulling him off the seat just as the van careened again, throwing them both to the floor. Meredith's head hit the floor hard and she blinked to clear her vision of the bright flashing stars, vaguely aware of her grandfather and Kyle falling to the floor beside her.

Just as the windshield shattered and bullets sprayed the top half of the van's walls, on the side where Meredith and Shane had been sitting.

Cincinnati, Ohio,
Sunday 20 December, 3.43 P.M.

Crouching as low as he could, Adam grabbed the radio. 'Detective Kimble,' he barked when Dispatch acknowledged his call. 'Shots fired during transport of witnesses. We were shot at. We did not return fire.'

'Injuries?' the operator asked.

Troy's right arm was bleeding, but it appeared to be a slow bleed. He'd slid down so that he could see through the stripe of undamaged glass at the base of the windshield. 'Special Agent Troy has been shot in the arm. Hold on.' He looked over his shoulder, his heart stuttering at the sight of Meredith's green eyes looking up at him from the floor. *Thank God.* 'Is anybody hit back there?'

'No,' Meredith called back. 'We're just shaken up.'

Troy pulled into a small city park and stopped the van behind a thick copse of evergreens. 'We're out of range,' he muttered. With his left hand, he pulled his service weapon from its holster, wincing. 'The trees will provide cover if the sniper tries again.'

'No injuries other than Agent Troy,' Adam told the operator. 'Send backup. We're one block north of Linn and Ezzard Charles, out of range of the shooter.'

'Backup is on the way,' the operator informed him.

'Send officers to the school nearest the corner of Linn and Ezzard Charles. The shots came from the roof. Then send another van or several cars to our location. Five of us to continue to the precinct. Agent Troy will need an ambulance.'

'I can go in one of the squad cars,' Troy gritted out.

Adam didn't argue. He figured Troy knew his own body and how badly he was hurt. Besides, EMTs wouldn't approach a hot zone until it was declared safe. 'Did you copy that?' he asked the operator.

'Yes, Detective,' she said. 'Officers on their way.'

'All right.' Adam took stock of the damage. The windshield was a mess of fractures, but it had held. Both he and Troy were covered in glass because Adam's side window had not. 'Keep your heads down,' Adam said to Meredith and the others in the back. 'I'm going to take a look,' he murmured to Troy, 'in case he decides to approach on foot.'

Because if he did, they might not see him until it was too late. The sniper would likely try again to take out Adam and Troy, leaving the passengers unprotected.

Adam slipped out of the van and took a three-sixty look, holding his rifle against his chest. It was quiet today, too cold for anyone to be enjoying the small park. It was so peaceful, it was hard to believe

310

they'd been shot at only minutes before. Not wanting to drop his gaze to his phone, he called Isenberg using a voice command.

'Detective Kimble?' Isenberg answered when she picked up the call. 'We expected you already.'

'We hit a snag,' Adam said, walking around the van, his eyes on the trees, looking for any movement. Until he saw the passenger side of the van, riddled with bullets. *Holy shit.* He'd heard the bullets hitting the van but hadn't had any idea . . . *We were lucky. So damn lucky.* He jerked his gaze away from the van and back to the trees. 'We were shot at.'

'Explain,' Isenberg said sharply.

'Both boys are all right, as are Meredith and her grandfather. Shaken, but unhurt.'

'Hold on.' Isenberg relayed this to the Davises and Adam heard a small sob. Then Deacon's voice, asking Isenberg's clerk to find the parents a conference room in which to wait. 'Deacon is here. I'm putting you on speaker. *Explain.*'

'Are you and Troy all right?' Deacon asked.

'Troy's hit in the arm. Not a gusher, but he's losing some blood. We'd just gotten off the highway. Troy was driving. I was shotgun. Or rifle.'

'You're the sharpshooter,' Isenberg said practically. 'Did you return fire?'

'No. I saw the glint of the rifle on the school rooftop as we approached from the west. I warned Troy and he hit the gas, but the shooter got some shots in as we took evasive action. The windshield was hit with' – he counted bullet holes –'four bullets. Passenger side window was destroyed and there are five bullet holes on the passenger side of the van, all at the top.' He frowned as he came around to inspect them again. 'All inches from the roof. None would have hit anyone in the back unless they'd ricocheted.'

Adam heard sirens. 'I'd be shocked if the shooter stuck around, but I had dispatch send officers to the rooftop anyway. CSU should check for the casings. We're going to move the four passengers to squad cars ASAP and continue to your office. Troy will have one of the squad cars take him to the hospital.'

'All right,' Isenberg said wearily. 'How did they know where you'd be, Adam?'

'I don't know,' he admitted. 'And I've been wondering the same thing. Who knew we were on our way in?'

'My clerk, who called Kyle's parents.' She sighed. 'And anyone who was in the lobby when they arrived, asking for me. Which was at least a dozen people.'

'Someone might have heard and assumed we'd be bringing both Shane and Kyle in, but how they knew where our vehicle would be at that exact moment is still unknown.'

'They'd have to have known your route, which means they'd have to have at least suspected where you'd be coming from.' She sighed again. 'Come on in and we'll figure it out. Be careful.'

'I will.' Ending the call, Adam studied the bullet holes on the passenger side once again and took photos with his phone. Either the shooter had been rattled, or he hadn't intended to kill any of the four passengers.

He frowned again. The only one who'd been actually shot at . . . *was me.* He did another walk around the van, watching for any movement through the trees. Hugging the van for cover, he didn't relax his watch until backup arrived.

He directed two of the officers to help Troy, then opened the back door of the van and took his first easy breath. Meredith sat on the floor of the van, her arm around Shane, whose eyes were closed, his face unnaturally pale.

Kyle hadn't looked good before. Now . . . he was all but catatonic.

Meredith's gaze shot to Adam's. Eyes filling with tears, she huffed out a breath that sounded like a sob, letting go of Shane to slide to the open door. 'Are you hurt?'

'No,' he said, then staggered back when she threw her arms around his neck. She was trembling now and he couldn't stop himself from wrapping his arms around her. To hell with Isenberg's 'no getting involved' bullshit. Meredith needed him now and he wasn't going to turn her away.

He smoothed a hand down her back. Then frowned when

something hard poked him in the sternum. 'Meredith?' he murmured cautiously. 'Are you carrying?'

'Duh,' she whispered unsteadily. 'I'll check it at CPD security. I do that every time I visit anyway.'

He found himself chuckling. 'Okay.'

'You're sure you're not hurt? I saw your window. It's gone.'

'Just glass in my hair, which is going to be all over you now.'

'I don't care.'

Was it ridiculous how good that made him feel? 'I think me leaning back to warn you guys kept me from being hit. Unfortunately, Troy was.'

'I'm *fine*,' Troy snapped from the front seat.

'I'm *glad*,' Adam called back, then bent his head to whisper in Meredith's ear. 'You gonna be okay if I step back?'

Her arms tightened for a few heartbeats, then she nodded and let him go. 'Yes.'

'Good. We need to get you all out of here. I haven't seen any activity in the trees and I think if the shooter had wanted to try again he would have already. But let's not take that chance.' He took a step back, then unapologetically met her grandfather's sharp stare. 'Mr Fallon, do you need to be checked out?'

The old man looked insulted. 'You mean did I have a coronary? No, son. I did not.'

Meredith turned to face her grandfather, shaking her head. 'Papa. You promised.'

Fallon huffed. 'He's implying I have a weak constitution.'

'You *are* eighty-four,' Meredith said affectionately. 'He doesn't know you well enough to know you're a tough old coot. He's being professional. Cut him some slack.'

Then Shane sobered the mood. 'Were they shooting at me, Detective Kimble?'

'Or me?' Meredith asked.

Or me? 'I don't know,' Adam said honestly. 'We're going to find out.'

Eighteen

His cell rang, startling him. It was Mike. Hopefully with good news. Taking a look around to make sure no one was paying him attention, he hit ACCEPT. 'Well?'

A beat of hesitation. 'I missed.'

He closed his eyes, fury pounding through him. 'You're a fucking sharpshooter. How did you fucking miss?'

'They must have seen something. Seen me. Took evasive action.'

'Was *anyone* hit?'

'Just the driver. The Fed. Troy, I think is his name.'

Well, at least one of the asswipes was out of commission. 'What about passengers?'

'Unhurt. I continued to fire, aiming for the top of the van, so none of the passengers were hit.'

'Why the hell did you do that?'

'Because you said you wanted the boy *alive*, dumbass. I'll follow them, try again.'

He seethed, wanting to put Mike in his place. 'I have another job for you first.'

'Do tell.'

He rolled his eyes. 'I'll message you. Don't hesitate when you get my signal.'

'Doesn't sound positive. I'm not gonna like it, am I?'

'Probably not.'

Mike huffed a sigh. 'Fuck. This just keeps getting worse.'

314

'Taking out Kimble and Troy would have been a big step forward,' he said sarcastically. 'You could have grabbed Shane, who is still our ticket to Linnea. Maybe you should hit the target range while you're waiting for the next job.'

'Fuck you,' Mike said angrily. 'I taught you everything you know. If I couldn't hit Kimble in the van, then you never could.'

Not true, but he wasn't going to argue. 'Fine. Just wait for my message.'

He ended the call. He had places to be.

Cincinnati, Ohio,
Sunday 20 December, 4.25 P.M.

They were a ragtag bunch, Meredith thought as they exited the elevator onto Isenberg's floor. They began shedding the vests as soon as the elevator closed behind them.

A middle-aged couple rushed forward, then stumbled to a stop when they saw Kyle. 'What's happened?' Mr Davis asked loudly. He twisted to glare at Isenberg. 'You said he was okay! He's like a walking zombie!'

'He is physically unharmed,' Meredith said quietly. Damn, her head hurt. Especially now that the adrenaline was wearing off. She'd hit her head harder than she thought when she'd fallen in the van. Unbuttoning her coat, she approached the Davises, who were well and truly terrified. And tired. *Join the club.* 'Kyle is grieving and he's just had another shock. He's withdrawn into himself, which can happen in these situations. He'll need rest and quiet and most probably some grief counseling. When you take him home, can you make sure he has the support of a therapist or a grief therapy group?'

Mrs Davis put her arms around her son. 'Of course.'

Mr Davis's shoulders sagged. 'Who are you, exactly, miss?'

'This is Dr Fallon,' Shane supplied. 'She was at the restaurant yesterday when Andy—' He broke off. 'She's nice, Mr Davis. She made things easier for us. Kyle and me.'

Mr Davis put his arm around Shane's shoulders, pulling him in for a hug, but he looked directly at Meredith. 'Thank you. I'm sorry. This has just been . . .' He looked overwhelmed.

'I know,' Meredith said. 'I'm not used to being on this side of it. It's horrible.'

'I'm Detective Kimble,' Adam said from behind her. 'I'm the lead investigator on this case, but we're working with Chicago PD. What are your plans? Do you want to take Kyle back to school or return to Michigan?'

'We're going home. We want to leave within the hour,' Mr Davis said. 'Why?'

'Given what's just happened,' Isenberg said, 'and I will give you a complete accounting of it, we'd like you to wait to leave until we're sure it's safe.'

The Davises' eyes widened. 'You think Kyle is in danger?' Mrs Davis asked, a thread of panic in her voice. 'Even if we take him home and not back to Chicago?'

'We don't know,' Adam told her. 'But because of what happened to Tiffany and her mother – and adding in what just happened to us on the way over here – we think he could be. Whoever wants Shane won't hesitate to hurt the people around him to get their hands on him. We want you all to make it home safely.'

Shane dropped his chin to his chest. 'I'm so sorry.'

Adam gripped Shane's shoulder. 'This is *not* your fault.'

Mr Davis pulled Shane close for another one-armed hug. 'Hush, Shane. We'll figure this out.' He gave his son a sad look before turning to Adam. 'We want you to know that we appreciate the precautions you and the other guy took. What was his name again?'

'Special Agent Troy,' Adam said.

Davis nodded. 'Yes, him. He said that if you hadn't seen the rifle, that he couldn't have reacted in time and it might have been worse. And you had them in vests, you told them to get down . . . You took every precaution.'

Adam blinked. 'How did Troy . . . ?'

'He called on his way to the ER,' Isenberg said. 'Gave me his statement. Mr and Mrs Davis, we need Shane to listen to a recording for us. I'll have my clerk show you to a quiet room and get you some coffee while we do that. Okay?' She waited until the Davises had led Kyle away before pinching the bridge of her nose. 'Shane, you okay with this?'

Shane nodded. 'Yes, ma'am, but can I get it over with? Please?'

Isenberg nodded. 'Of course. Come on. Agent Novak has it all cued up.'

Shane tugged Meredith's sleeve. 'Please?' he murmured.

Meredith threw another look over her shoulder at Adam. 'He'd like me to sit with him while you play the 911 call.'

Adam motioned her forward. 'Not a problem.'

Isenberg's briefing room was already half filled. Deacon and Scarlett sat with Detective Hanson and a fifty-ish man Meredith didn't recognize. Adam knew him, though, and approached, hand outstretched.

'Nash,' he said with a genuine smile. 'It's been a while.'

The man stood, returning the smile and pumping Adam's hand enthusiastically. 'Too long. I'm temporarily on your team, working with Hanson. I'm in Narcotics now too. Have been for a few months.'

Glancing over at Hanson, something flickered across Adam's face. Regret maybe? Or guilt? But it was gone too quickly for Meredith to be certain, his smile back in place. 'Like old home week, then. Good to have you on board.' He turned to Meredith. 'This is Detective Nash Currie, one of the cyber crimes experts. He, Hanson, and I worked together in Personal Crimes. This is Dr Fallon.'

She inclined her head to the new guy, remembering that Adam had mentioned him when telling his story. Currie and Hanson had been standing with him, had watched helplessly along with him as Paula was murdered. 'It's nice to meet you, Detective Currie. Please excuse us if we're a little ragged. We've had an eventful afternoon.'

Currie nodded sympathetically. 'So I've heard. I'm glad you're all okay.'

Adam gestured to Shane. 'This is Shane Baird. Shane, Detectives Hanson and Currie are also working this case.'

Shane only nodded.

'I've got it all cued up,' Deacon said. 'I'm Agent Novak, this is Detective Bishop. We work for Lieutenant Isenberg, along with Detective Kimble. We were out looking for your friend, Linnie. Here, have a seat.'

Shane sat and Meredith sat next to him, Adam moving to stand behind her, close enough for her to feel the warmth of his body, but not close enough to touch. Which was ideal, because her job for the next few minutes was to give Shane strength, not to pay attention to the big, beautiful man behind her. And then she realized that by positioning himself as he had, Adam was quietly offering his strength to her. It was sweet.

'You didn't find her.' Shane searched Deacon and Scarlett's faces. 'What *did* you find, besides the 911 call?'

'She's not a student at any of the colleges in town,' Scarlett said. She was crisp and professional and that seemed to help Shane, because he nodded, assuming Scarlett's posture. 'Andy had told people at his work that she was.'

'She wanted to be a teacher, but that was a long time ago.' Shane looked down at the table for a few beats, then back up. 'What else?'

Scarlett held his gaze levelly. 'We found a few people who thought they knew her, but only when we showed them the more recent picture.'

Shane visibly steeled himself. 'Which picture?'

Deacon told him about the 911 call and the still they were able to get from the surveillance photo in the parking lot of the restaurant. 'If this is Linnie, she doesn't look like the same girl you knew. Just know that, okay?'

Deacon slid the photo across the table and Shane gasped.

'Oh my God. Linnie?' He shuddered, his words thick with tears.

Meredith laid her hand on his back, felt him trembling. 'Is it her, Shane?'

'I . . .' He choked, then turned to look at Meredith, devastation in his eyes. 'Yeah. It's her. I know her eyes. But . . . My God. She's like a skeleton.'

Deacon reached across the table to put the older photo Shane had provided next to the one that had him so distressed. 'Her eyes don't look that similar,' Deacon said gently. 'Are you sure?'

Shane jerked a nod. 'That's because in this picture' – angry now, he poked at the older photo of a laughing, happy Linnie – 'she hadn't been raped yet. These eyes?' He picked up the newer photo and it shook in his hands. 'Yeah. This is what we saw afterward. Me and Andy. God. It killed him to see her like that.'

Meredith kept a steady pressure on his back. 'Okay,' she murmured. 'But she's alive, Shane. Don't lose that fact, okay?'

He nodded and put the photo down with a precision that broke Meredith's heart. He was trying so hard not to fall apart. 'Can I listen—' He cut himself off, his gaze darting back to Scarlett. 'Wait. Who knew her like this?' he demanded. 'How did they know her if she wasn't a student?'

Scarlett met Shane's eyes directly once again. 'This is hearsay only, but we found four men who said they "had friends" who'd hired this woman for sexual services.'

Shane's mouth fell open. 'Prostitution? You're saying Linnie is a *prostitute*?'

For a moment no one said a word, then Detective Hanson spoke. 'That's why we're here, Mr Baird. We got a tip about a prostitution ring operating on the college campus. We've got a few names and we're tracking down leads. Including this young woman.'

Shane covered his hand with his mouth and shook his head. 'She promised. We made a pact, her and Andy and me. No drugs and no . . . selling ourselves. We promised each other.' He blinked and tears streaked down his face. 'This is why she called anonymously. She doesn't want to be arrested.'

This was most probably true. 'Shane,' Meredith said quietly, but firmly. 'She is alive. That's the most important thing. Andy was afraid that whoever was forcing him to point that gun at me yesterday would kill her, but she's alive. We work from there, okay?'

He nodded, then squared his shoulders. 'Can you play the 911 call now?'

Deacon tapped the keyboard of his computer and a raspy whisper came from the speaker. '*Just . . . tell them that the SUV used in the shooting can be found at Clyde's Place, at 275 and Beechmont.'* The clip abruptly ended. 'Well?' Deacon asked.

Shane's head dipped low. 'Yeah. That's her.'

'You seem certain,' Adam said from behind them.

Shane twisted in his chair to look up at Adam. 'I am. She, um, had nightmares after . . . you know. Back in the foster house. She screamed a lot. That's how she sounded after. She had that raspy edge. It's like the bastard who hurt her even broke her voice.' He slumped in his chair. 'If you find her, will the fact that she made this call help her?'

'We don't know,' Scarlett said. 'But it can't hurt.'

'But you'll keep looking for her?' Shane asked, sounding so young and lost.

'Yes,' Adam assured him. 'If she was in that SUV, she can probably tell us who shot Andy. Besides, we think she may have been injured. She may need medical help.'

Shane went still, his eyes narrowing. He twisted again to stare up at Adam. 'Why? Why do you think that?' He pivoted, glaring at Deacon and Scarlett. 'What aren't you telling me?' he demanded. *'Tell me.'*

'She left a lot of blood in the SUV,' Deacon said simply and Shane frowned.

'And? You can't know it's hers. Even if you could test the DNA that fast, you couldn't prove it was hers because you don't have anything to compare it to. Do you?'

Scarlett's black brows arched and Deacon's head tilted in that way he had when he was puzzling something out. Shane huffed an impatient breath and waved his hand. 'Kyle's pre-law. We watch a lot of crime movies. Just answer the question.'

Meredith gave both Deacon and Scarlett an imploring look on Shane's behalf. 'If you can't answer, he needs to understand why you can't. You owe him that much.'

Deacon sighed. 'We didn't find the blood or the SUV. But she told us she bled in the car when she made the 911 call. Told us to be careful.' He leaned closer, resting his forearm on the table. 'She told us that she was HIV positive, *which is not the death sentence it used to*

320

be.' He added the final phrase because Shane had thrown himself back in his chair, stunned and growing so pale that Meredith worried he'd pass out.

'*Bullshit,*' Shane shouted, pointing at the recent photo. 'Look at her. She's sick. Oh my God.' He broke then, choking on a sob. 'What happened to them? Andy and Linnie? I shouldn't have left them. I never should have left them.'

'You don't know what her condition is and why she's so thin,' Deacon said calmly. 'Let's find her and then you'll know more.'

Shane nodded unsteadily. 'Okay. Am I done?'

'Yes,' Isenberg told him. 'Thank you, Mr Baird. You can go join the Davises now.' She turned to Meredith. 'Dr Fallon,' she added, not impolitely, but it was clear that Meredith needed to leave as well.

She was okay with that. She needed to go crash somewhere and let herself have a minor meltdown. *But first, I need to pop some ibuprofen for this headache. Maybe find a bag of ice.* She started to rise, then smiled inside when Adam offered her a hand. She allowed him to help her up, then gave a shaky laugh. 'Thanks. I'm still a little wobbly from our adventure,' she said lightly, noting that he was studying her carefully. 'But I'm okay.'

'At least you've got color in your face again.' He glanced at Shane, who was shuffling toward the door. 'But he doesn't,' he added in a worried whisper.

'Don't worry. I'll see to him.' Meredith followed Shane, but paused at the door when she remembered the reason she'd been coming downtown to begin with. 'Do we know when Mrs Voss is coming in? Agent Troy said he'd talked to her and set it up.'

'She got here a few minutes ago,' Isenberg said. 'I had her and her daughter escorted to one of the interview rooms. If you can wait for us by my office, please?'

'Of course. Come on, Shane. Let's find the Davises.'

She found Kyle and his parents in one of the smaller meeting rooms and dropped Shane off with them, then went in search of her grandfather. She spied him standing at one of the windows, a sad, pensive look on his face. She'd seen that look before, always when he thought no one was watching. And most always at this time of year.

For all his bluster, Clarke Fallon carried holes in his soul. But no one would ever know unless they caught him like this. Unaware.

I learned to wear a mask at the feet of a master, she thought. She'd started toward him when the elevator behind her dinged. Startled, she turned, and because the elevator opened directly into the bullpen, she didn't have to wait to see who it was.

'Meredith!' Dani Novak rushed out of the elevator, a small box in one hand and a green garbage bag in the other.

Meredith met her halfway. 'Dani? What's wrong?' Because clearly something was.

'I need either Adam or Deacon. Now.'

'I'll take you.' Meredith led her to Isenberg's briefing room. 'Are you all right?'

'I'm fine. This is case related.' Dani stopped suddenly and stared at Meredith. 'Your case, actually. What are you doing here? You're supposed to be in a safe house.'

'Well, things are a little upside down right now,' Meredith said wryly. 'I'll explain later. What do you have?'

Dani sighed. 'Evidence.'

Meredith pointed to the door. 'They're in there. Isenberg, Scarlett, Adam, Deacon, and two detectives from Narcotics. I'm not supposed to be in there, so I'll just wait for the scoop when you're done.'

Cincinnati, Ohio,
Sunday 20 December, 4.50 P.M.

Adam stood back and stared at the white board where he'd taped photos of all the victims, near victims – his gut had twisted as he'd taped Meredith's photo to the board – and the suspects to date, which had to include Linnie Holmes until they knew differently.

Kiesler University's campus PD had sent them both a still and a copy of the surveillance video showing the huge thug of a man who'd asked for Shane last night. This photo was placed squarely in the suspects column.

'His face . . . He looks off,' Adam said thoughtfully as he studied the photo. 'More than the broken nose. He's trying to smile in this picture so that Kyle will tell him where to find Shane, but his face doesn't move.'

'It's his cheeks,' Isenberg said. 'They don't move, nor do they match his face. His nose is red from the cold, but his cheeks aren't.'

'Prosthetics,' Nash said. 'Gonna make it hard to get an ID out of facial recognition software.' And if anyone would know, it would be Nash Currie. He was what Diesel would have been if he'd joined the police force instead of working at the *Ledger*.

'You'll still try?' Hanson asked and Nash nodded.

'Of course. The girl will be difficult too, unless she's looked that sick for a long time. Although I can't imagine anyone surviving for long looking *that* sick.'

'What about the license plates Candace Voss photographed last night?' Adam asked, getting the discussion back on track. He taped those three photos on the white board.

'I ran them,' Hanson said. 'They're registered to Jolee Cusack, Sylvia Hyland, and Theresa Romer. The last two names are deceased, but someone has been paying to keep the registrations active.'

Isenberg huffed. 'Naturally. But to be expected if they're using the cars in a crime.'

'Which car was the one driven by the pink-haired girl that Candace Voss followed back to the university parking lot?' Adam asked.

'That car was registered to Jolee Cusack.' Hanson held up a piece of paper, printed with a Facebook page. 'Jolee is, according to her Facebook page, very much alive. She's a grad student. She rents an apartment about a block off campus. According to her Facebook and Instagram posts, she turned in her final paper and is skiing in Vermont. I sent a request to the local PD to check resorts and hotels. Her neighbors here say she keeps to herself. They hardly ever see her. Nobody can remember seeing her in the last three days.'

Adam studied the Facebook picture. 'No pink hair. So even though she was driving Jolee's car back from Voss's party the night

Candace followed her, Jolee was probably not the woman that Penny Voss saw or that Candace spoke to.'

'Could be a pink rinse,' Scarlett said. 'Or a wig. She might use it when she's hooking. Just because she doesn't have pink hair in these photos doesn't mean she's not the woman who Penny saw that night.'

Deacon narrowed his eyes at the printout. 'Let me see it a sec.' He put it on the table, side-by-side with the photo from the restaurant's surveillance video of the woman who'd accompanied the man when he'd picked up the SUV. 'Look at the eyes.'

It was the only thing they could look at, because the woman's face was almost completely covered by a scarf. Only her eyes were visible. But the eyes were damn similar.

'Could be her,' Adam said.

'And if it is, it means she was not skiing in Vermont as of yesterday.' Scarlett bumped Deacon's shoulder with her own. 'Good eye, D.'

Deacon shrugged off the compliment. 'Now we just have to find her.'

'I've put out a BOLO for her vehicle,' Hanson said. 'Her apartment was unoccupied and her luggage was gone.' He shook his head in disgust. 'Her Facebook location says she's in Vermont. Can't believe I fell for that.'

'She doesn't want to be found,' Adam said. 'But now I'm wondering at the connection between this woman and Linnie.' He tapped the photo provided by Kiesler University. 'Bruiser took Jolee with him when he went to pick up the SUV. Linnie didn't know he had picked it up already, because she called to tell us where to find it.'

'How did Linnie get the SUV to Clyde's Place?' Deacon asked. 'She pulls into the parking lot alone. Andy was afraid whoever had coerced him would hurt Linnie, so it's unlikely she would have been handed the keys and allowed to drive away.'

'She got away somehow,' Scarlett mused. 'Good on her. Bruiser and Jolee don't drive up to the restaurant's lot. They walk. Bruiser cleans up the SUV's driver's seat while Jolee walks away. We need to find her on area surveillance footage. I assume they parked whatever vehicle they used to get there somewhere else and that Jolee drove it back. I assume her car isn't in the campus lot anymore?'

'No,' Hanson said. 'And it wasn't in front of her apartment either. It could be parked somewhere off campus. I requested some uniforms to canvass the lots to find the car, but we should add more officers to the search. The campus cops can help.'

Scarlett leaned forward, looking around Deacon to see Nash. 'Have you accessed data from the license plate readers? I mean, they're all over town.'

Little cameras that did nothing except capture the images of cars that drove by and store them in databases. Which was great for law enforcement, but always left Adam feeling a little strange as a private citizen.

'We have,' Nash said. 'But not in the Beechmont area. That's where you were going next, right? You want us to see if Jolee drove Bruiser in her own vehicle yesterday.'

Scarlett nodded. 'And if she did that yesterday and *is* on the slopes in Vermont today? She had to either drive all night or fly out first thing this morning.'

'So we check Beechmont, I-71 north, and the area around the airport.' Nash wrote it down in his notebook. 'We can do that.'

'Thanks,' Adam said, going back to stare at the photos on the board. 'So according to some of the men on campus, Linnie is a working girl and according to Mrs Voss, at least Jolee's *car* was at Broderick Voss's house the night Candace followed it back to campus, even if Jolee herself wasn't there. Bruiser trusts Jolee enough to take her with him to get the SUV used in a murder hours before. So let's assume Jolee and Linnie work in the same ring. And that Bruiser is also involved. Maybe even the guy who pulled the trigger on Andy.'

'That's sounds fair,' Hanson said. 'So then, how is Andy Gold connected to Meredith Fallon? Or was he merely a pawn because he was friends with Linnie?'

'I'm thinking he was a pawn. I mean, Shane was targeted because Bruiser lost track of Linnie,' Scarlett said sadly. 'And Tiffany was killed by association to Shane. It keeps coming back to Linnie, who's out there somewhere on her own.'

'Bruiser either figured Linnie would run to Shane or that Shane would know where she would hide,' Hanson said.

'Makes sense,' Adam agreed, but something wasn't right. He studied the timeline and saw the logic hole. 'Bruiser was in Chicago when Andy Gold's place burned down. We're dealing with more than one person.'

'You're right,' Isenberg said. 'The suspect was in Chicago at eight thirty last night, our time, looking for Shane. He didn't leave until at least one forty-five a.m., after he'd killed Tiffany and her mother. So who's the other person? Voss?'

'Maybe,' Hanson said. 'We'll know once we get a search warrant for his house.'

Continuing to stare at the timeline, Adam grimaced. The restaurant hostess. Colleen Martel. *Can't believe I forgot about her.* 'Whoever killed Andy – whether it was Bruiser, Voss or whoever – had to have known that Meredith would be taking Mallory to Buon Cibo yesterday afternoon. We know a man called the restaurant hostess on her cell phone and asked her to seat Meredith at that specific table, but we still don't know who that was.'

'Did any of the girls at Mariposa know where Meredith and Mallory were going?' Scarlett asked.

Adam shook his head. 'I talked to Trip right before we left the condo. He's been at Mariposa House all afternoon talking to the girls and they all told him no. Mallory didn't know the name of the place until she and Meredith arrived. So it comes back to Meredith.'

'And Voss,' Hanson said. 'We can see if the hostess recognizes his voice once we pick him up. We need that warrant, Lieutenant.'

Isenberg's reply was cut off when the briefing room door swung open. Adam gaped at his cousin Dani who stood in the doorway, uncharacteristically upset. Adam slowly capped the marker he'd been using and warily approached her. 'Dani? What's wrong?'

Isenberg frowned, clearly unhappy at the interruption. 'Dr Novak, this is not appropriate behavior. You can't just—'

'I've seen the girl you're looking for,' Dani interrupted.

Everyone else stood then and Isenberg's expression smoothed. 'Then come in, please,' she said. 'Close the door behind you.'

Dani obeyed and took the chair Adam offered, putting a small box on the table.

A rape kit. Adam had seen too many in his career not to recognize one on sight. 'Is that hers?' he asked. 'Linnie Holmes's?'

'She didn't call herself that. Her ID said Denise Johnson.'

Adam leaned against the table nearest her. 'Relax,' he said quietly. 'You're all wound up.' And that wasn't like her at all. 'What happened?'

Dani drew a long breath through her nose. 'First, why are you looking for her?'

'She's a person of interest,' Isenberg said, and Dani shot her an irritated look.

'I'm not stupid, Lieutenant. She's a victim, but you've got her face plastered all over the Internet. I saw it as soon as I turned on my laptop this afternoon. So, since I called CPD about her *rape kit* last night, but nobody'd come to collect it, I decided to bring it myself. And because I did a *rape kit* and then stitched her up and found her a safe bed to sleep in, I'm invested. I need to be sure she is going to be treated properly when she's found.'

'Wait.' Hanson leaned forward, his eyes lighting up. 'You know where she is?'

Adam felt the same thrill, because this was the lead they'd been hoping for.

Dani blinked, as if just realizing he was there. 'Oh, hi, Wyatt.' She and Deacon had been a fixture at their baseball games, back in the day. She and Hanson had even tried dating once, long before Hanson was married, but both agreed they were better friends. She gave him a distracted smile now. 'I didn't see you. I'm sorry. Who's this?'

'I'm Detective Currie,' Nash said with a smile. He had a way of putting people at ease that Adam had always envied. 'I work with Hanson.'

'Nice to meet you.' She turned back to Adam. 'Why do you want the girl?'

Adam sighed. 'Dani.'

'A-dam,' she replied. 'I'm serious. What's she wanted for?'

Adam shook his head. 'Nothing yet. She was in the SUV with the shooter yesterday. She called 911 anonymously this morning to tell us where to find the SUV, but it had already been moved.'

Dani closed her eyes. 'I was afraid of something like that.' She looked up, first at Adam, then at Deacon, then shook her head. 'She came to the clinic last night.'

'Because she'd been raped,' Adam supplied, because Dani was not easily shaken, except today she was.

'Brutally. It . . .' Dani pursed her lips. 'It wasn't the first time.'

'She may be involved in a prostitution ring at the college,' Hanson said.

Dani flinched. 'God, I hope not,' she said fervently.

'Because she's HIV positive?' Isenberg asked.

Dani covered her surprise with a slow blink. 'I can't—'

'Linnie told us,' Adam interrupted. 'In the 911 call, so we'd be careful with the SUV.'

'Where is she, Dani?' Hanson asked, but gently this time.

Dani sighed again. 'I took her to a shelter last night. Look, if she's involved in something, I don't think it's voluntarily. I think she's being coerced.'

'Dani,' Adam said, hunkering down so that he met her eyes, one brown and one blue. 'She can identify the person who's killed seven people in the last thirty-six hours and who shot up our van when we were driving here today. Meredith, her grandfather, and two innocent young men were riding in the back. Agent Troy was hit. He's in the ER.'

Dani's eyes widened. 'Will he be okay?'

'Yes, but we were lucky. Dani, honey, you know me. Know us. We'll be careful and we will do our best to bring her in unhurt. You know that.'

Dani nodded. 'I know. It's just that she's so afraid of the man who hurt her. When you go, let Scarlett lead. You guys will terrify her. Plus, they won't let you all into the shelter. It's supposed to be a *secret* shelter.'

'We'll be discreet,' Adam said, trying to be patient. 'Please, Dani?'

She blew out a breath. 'Fine. I took her to St Ambrose's shelter.'

'Under my uncle Trace's church?' Scarlett asked, her brows shooting up. 'You left her with seventy-year-old *nuns*?'

Dani frowned. 'She's not violent, Scarlett. She didn't have any weapons and she was so weak from blood loss, fatigue, and hunger that she wasn't a threat. Besides,' she added with total seriousness, 'Sister Angela is only sixty. And Sister Jeanette kickboxes.'

Adam heard Nash cover a laugh with a cough.

Scarlett's lips twitched. 'Fair enough. They are tough old birds.'

Isenberg cleared her throat. 'Next steps, Adam?'

'Scarlett and I will go to get Linnie,' he said. 'Gently,' he added when Dani opened her mouth. 'We'll bring her in and Hanson and Nash can observe her in interview.' He sped on when Hanson and Nash opened their mouths. 'We're not going to send a delegation. But we will take backup. How many exits out of the church?' he asked Scarlett.

'At least five,' Scarlett said. 'You need a delegation just to cover all the exits.'

'All right,' Adam muttered. 'Hanson and Deacon take the back exits, but only Scarlett and I approach the door. Nash, can you stay and search for Jolee's car?'

Nash looked up from his laptop. 'Already on it.'

Dani stood up. 'I'm going too.'

'You think she'll trust you?' Isenberg asked incredulously.

'No way in hell, not after you guys show up. But she's my patient, so I'm going.'

Isenberg shook her head, displeased. 'I can't stop you, but stay out of their way.'

Dani nodded. 'Understood.'

Adam hesitated. 'What about Mrs Voss? Penny's only six. She's not going to be cooperative in a counseling session for much longer.'

'I'll observe while you're gone.' Isenberg raised a gray brow. 'I'm still capable.'

Adam inclined his head, acknowledging her point. 'Okay, boss. Video it for me?'

'You got it. Now go and get Linnie.'

Adam started for the door, going through the things they hadn't yet covered in his mind, the biggest of which was the shooting of their van. 'CSU is collecting the bullets that hit our van. If I'm not back by the time they're done, have them check ballistics against the bullet that killed Andy Gold.'

'I will,' Isenberg said. 'Go.'

Nineteen

'I'm sorry,' Meredith murmured, closing her hand over her grandfather's. After leaving Dani in the conference room, she'd come back to find him staring out of the same window, the same lost expression on his face. Looking every one of his eighty-four years.

Because next week, it would be seven years since Meredith had lost her parents and he'd lost his only son. But it wasn't anything they ever spoke about. Not since it had happened. The grief had been palpable. And he and Gran had been so worried about her.

Which she'd given them so much reason to be. At least she could make sure that he didn't worry about her any longer. She could give him that much.

She led him to the chair where Hanson had sat the night before and pulled another chair close for herself. And then she just rested her head against his shoulder and they sat together in silence until Meredith couldn't take it any longer.

'I'm so sorry,' she whispered.

He nuzzled her hair with his grizzled cheek. 'Why?'

'Because you're sad. And because you've had to put on your brave face this weekend so that nobody knows you're sad.'

He kissed her temple. 'Well, I won't deny that it would have been more convenient if all this had happened a month from now, but . . . Hey, you can't schedule shit like this.'

331

She hiccupped a surprised laugh. 'No, you can't.' She sighed. 'I miss them too.'

'I know you do, baby. Your folks would have been proud of you. I know I am.' His gaze was clear and full of purpose. 'You've been clearheaded and courageous through all this. Most people would be curled up, crying under their covers.'

'I might have been, but I haven't had the time,' she said wryly and he chuckled.

'It has been busy. I think that's helped. I mean, it's horrible, but just now, when you were in that meeting? It was the first time I'd had a chance to be all alone. To think. It all kind of hit me at once, you know?'

She did know. 'That's why I keep busy.'

'Except you have to be able to deal with the quiet times too.'

Yes, he was still worried about her. About what she might do. To herself. And that shamed her as much as it saddened her. 'I am. I'm better. For real,' she added when he continued to look uncertain. 'That's what I need you to hear. And believe.'

'Because of Kimble?'

She smiled at him. 'His name is Adam. And . . . no. Not really. I was okay before him. If he stays, I'll be more okay. I can't lie about that.'

'All right,' he said glumly.

She laughed. 'Try not to look so happy about it.'

He shook his head, not laughing with her. 'I'm sorry. It's just . . . I overheard him talking on the phone. When we were out on his balcony. He was talking to his' – he dropped his voice – 'sponsor.'

Meredith's smile died. 'Oh. Well, that was rude of you, Papa. That was private.'

'I know. But he hurt you and I needed to understand why. You haven't been, you know, with anyone since Chris.'

'That's not true,' Meredith protested. 'Just no one that I introduced to you.'

He blinked, stunned. 'Who?'

'None of your business. All you need to know is that I haven't exactly been a nun.'

He winced. 'Merry.'

'You went there, old man. Don't blame me if you learn stuff that you didn't want to know.'

He grunted. 'Fair enough. But Kimble did hurt you.'

'And I now understand why and I'm okay with it. That needs to be good enough.'

'It's not. Not when I have to pick up the pieces.'

She frowned at him. 'That's not fair.'

He looked away. 'You're right. It's not. But it's how I feel. And my shrink says that I'm allowed to tell you how I feel.'

'You have a shrink?' she asked, more loudly than she'd intended.

He looked around, annoyed. 'You want to say that louder, child?'

'Sorry,' she stage-whispered. 'You have a shrink?'

That made him laugh. 'Yes. Kind of.' Then he blushed. 'She's a retired shrink.'

'Papa,' Meredith said, delighted. 'You have a girlfriend?'

He shrugged, then preened. 'I do. I want you to meet her after all this is done.'

She linked her arm through his and hugged it. 'Tell me about her. I want to know it all. How did you meet? What's her name? Do you go on moonlight walks on the beach?'

He rolled his eyes. 'Her name is Sharon and she's a retired psychologist. We met in a grief group. It was after your gran passed and I was . . . at loose ends.'

Meredith's smile faltered. 'She was the leader?' Because that was not cool.

'No. She was a group member. She'd just lost her husband. That was a few years ago. We started . . . you know. Dating. About a year ago.'

Meredith's smile was cheeky. 'Dating? *That's* what you senior citizens are calling it?'

He blushed furiously. 'Merry. That's none of your business.'

She laughed. 'You are! You're having a . . .' She cleared her throat. 'A *relationship*.'

He shook his head, but his mouth curved. 'Yeah, I guess we are. I want you to meet her. She's a lot like you. Fearless.'

Meredith's eyes abruptly stung. 'Papa.'

'It's true. She's helped me. Said we need to talk through this stuff. That I shouldn't just come up here like I do every year and pretend like I'm not watching you like a hawk to be sure nothing bad happens.'

It was like a stab to the heart, but one she'd earned. Or that he'd earned, at least. 'You told her about me?' she asked, surprised to hear that her voice had grown small.

'Yeah. I'm sorry, but . . . It all came out one night and . . .' He sighed. 'I'm sorry.'

'Don't be. You needed to tell someone and Gran's gone. I understand.'

'Thank you.' He drew a breath. 'I texted her, when you were in your meeting. Told her what I'd learned about Kimble. Told her that he said he knew you weren't as . . . how did he put it? As impervious to hurt as everyone thought. And that he'd do his best not to hurt you any more. But I'm afraid, Merry. Honestly. He has issues that could exacerbate yours.'

She wanted to snap at him. Wanted to be angry that he'd shared Adam's secrets with a person she'd never even met. But his face was so open, so vulnerable in a way she hadn't seen in so many years. So she drew a breath of her own. 'What did she say?'

'That I shouldn't assume. That I should tell you that I'm afraid. And . . .' He sighed heavily. 'That I should trust you. That you sounded like you had a firm grip on things.'

Good of her, Meredith thought irritably, then swept the irritation away. This woman had given him what he'd needed. 'Papa, listen to me, because I'm only going to say this once. Imagine what would have happened if I'd had to go through all that horrible stuff back then alone. If I hadn't had you and Gran and Alex.'

He shuddered. 'I don't want to imagine.'

'I know. Think about Adam going through something just as awful, but all alone.'

He frowned. 'He has family.'

'Yes, and some of them would have been as supportive as you. But not all. And the ones who weren't? *Theirs* were the voices he

334

heard. He tried to deal with something truly horrific on his own. He's dealing, and I'm okay with how he's done so. You need to be too.'

Her grandfather closed his eyes. 'Okay,' he said and sounded like he meant it.

'Papa?' She waited until he opened his eyes. 'I'm fine. I really am. And I have a shrink too.'

His eyes widened. 'You do?'

She smiled at him. 'Yes. Someone I can talk to when things get shitty.'

'Your friend, Faith?'

'No, because she's my friend. My shrink is an official shrink. A psychiatrist. I mean, I like her, but we don't socialize. I've been seeing her for a few years now and she monitors my meds. She's good. Just wanted you to know that.'

He smiled. 'That settles my mind more than anything else you've said.'

She hugged his arm again. 'Give Adam a chance. He wears a mask too. But under it is a . . . really nice heart.'

He kissed her temple. 'For you. I'd do almost anything for you, you know.'

'Then I'm going for broke. I have videos of Mom and Dad. I haven't been able to watch them. Not in all this time. Will you watch them with me? Next week? On the day?'

On the anniversary of the day their lives changed.

His chest expanded, held, then fell. 'Yes. But, um, maybe not with Kimble around. I don't think I can without a stiff drink and I don't want to drink in front of him.'

'Okay,' she whispered, understanding.

Behind them, a voice cleared. They whipped around to find the man in question standing there awkwardly.

'Sorry to interrupt,' Adam said gruffly. 'I need to leave. We know where Linnie is. I wanted to make sure you were okay before I went to get her.'

Meredith released her grandfather, standing uncertainly. He'd clearly overheard something, although she wasn't sure how much. 'Can I talk to you for a minute?'

'Just a minute,' he said. 'We don't want her to leave where she is.'

Together, they went to stand by Isenberg's office window. 'Are you all right?' she asked. 'I don't know how much you heard, but Papa means well.'

'I don't care that you were talking about me. Are *you* all right?'

She stared up at him. 'Yes. Why?'

'Your parents died, right?'

She swallowed. 'Yes. It'll be seven years next week.'

'Is that why everyone comes to . . . support you at the holidays?'

'Partly yes. But that's not a conversation I want to have here, if that's okay. Later?'

'Yes.' He leaned a little closer. 'Wish it was later already. I really need to hold you.'

'I wouldn't mind it either. But I'm okay. Are you?'

'I am. Isenberg says she's going to observe you when you interview Penny Voss. She has some photos that I'd like Penny to see, just to see if any of them look familiar.'

'Of course.'

'Okay. I have to go. I'll be back soon.' He started walking backward, toward the elevator. 'Kate and Trip are on their way in from Mariposa House. They'll figure out how to get you all back to the safe house.'

'Thank you. Adam,' she called when he turned to go. 'Be careful.'

His smile was blinding. 'I will. Because, you know. Later.'

He disappeared into the elevator and not even her grandfather's arched brows could wipe away her own smile.

Cincinnati, Ohio,
Sunday 20 December, 5.45 P.M.

Linnea had stayed out far longer than she'd planned. Getting a weapon was harder than she'd thought it would be. Andy had given her the switchblade that she'd left in *his* arm. *Wish I'd stabbed him in the heart.*

Andy had made everything look so easy. It had taken her hours to find someone to sell her a gun on the street and had suffered near heart failure when the dealer she'd chosen had pointed the gun at her.

But he'd just been 'kidding.' Or so he said. More likely that he didn't want to have to explain why the dead girl on his street corner had keeled over from a heart attack.

Which didn't sound like a bad way to go. It would be over with. No muss, no fuss. Because she was in for a shitload of that if she did manage to survive the next few days.

Not that her body would withstand too much suffering. She was too weak and she knew it. And now, she was exhausted and cold. She hoped the nuns would still let her in. She had no idea what time it was, but it had to be close to six. It was dark already and—

She turned the corner and stopped abruptly, her mouth falling open in shock. *What the actual fuck?* The church was surrounded with cops. Four squad cars lined up on the street. *Busted. But how?* She'd been so careful not to show her face. Then she saw a familiar face and had her answer.

Dr Dani stood off to the side, her arms crossed over her chest. A woman and a man, both in black wool coats, stood on the stoop, having a conversation with Sister Jeanette, whose posture mirrored Dr Dani's. The nun was shaking her head no, very emphatically.

Dr Dani had given her up, but Sister Jeanette was preventing the cops from entering. *Thank you, Sister. But fuck you, Dr Dani. How stupid was I to trust you?*

Linnea took a step back. She'd have to find somewhere else to sleep. Hopefully somewhere warm because it was going to drop into single digits tonight. She'd prefer not to freeze to death before she killed him.

She spun around and slammed into a brick wall. Except it wasn't brick. It was solid muscle. Her heart stopped. Just . . . stopped. She looked up. And up.

She couldn't breathe. Just . . . couldn't breathe. Her hand, still shoved in her pocket, found the gun all on its own.

Butch smiled down at her, terrifyingly. 'Well, hello there,' he drawled. 'We've been looking for you all over the place. The boss is going to be so happy to have you safe and sound.' His grin broadened, showing off his crooked teeth . . . and suddenly it was Friday night again and he was hurting her and she couldn't make him *stop*.

Except now she could. She didn't break eye contact as she drew the gun from her pocket and pulled the trigger. Again. And again. And once more because he was *still fucking standing*.

He reached for her but she shoved him hard and he went down, landing on his knees. She edged back, her ears ringing because the gun was loud.

People were screaming. She could hear them . . . barely. She took another step back, staring at Butch who looked . . . pissed. And he wasn't *staying down*. He was getting *back up*.

The gun she held in both hands was shaking. Because her hands were shaking. *She* was shaking, head to toe. As she watched in horror, he gritted his teeth and was lurching to his feet when a sharp crack penetrated the fog in her brain. Then Butch's head exploded.

Just like Andy's.

More screams. People were running.

You should too. The cops will come. They'll take you away. Run.

Shoving the gun in her pocket, Linnea turned and fled.

Cincinnati, Ohio,
Sunday 20 December, 5.48 P.M.

The phone in his pocket buzzed with Mike's text alert. He'd better have good news. Surreptitiously, he checked the incoming text. *Finished off Butch, just like u told me to do. Girl got away.*

'Fuck, fuck, fuck,' he muttered. He'd told Butch where to look for Linnea and then he'd told Mike where to look for Butch. Butch should have killed Linnea and Mike should have shot Butch from the rooftop where he'd told his uncle to lie in wait.

At least Butch was no longer a liability. But Linnea was still out there, dammit.

A second set of texts came through from Mike. *She was armed. She shot him before I could. Had a bead on her, but Butch decided to be a hero and stand up to grab her one more time. Hit him first instead of her and she took off.*

Find her, he typed back, his thumbs like hammers on his screen. Mike's reply was fast and terse. *On it.*

Cincinnati, Ohio,
Sunday 20 December, 5.48 P.M.

Fuck, fuck, fuck. One minute Adam and Scarlett had been arguing with Sister Jeanette. The next, they were running toward gunfire at the end of the block.

What they found was not pretty. And too damn familiar.

A man was lying on his back on the sidewalk, legs bent awkwardly beneath him. Blood pooled on the concrete, was spattered against the dirty snow piled against the curb.

'Shit,' Adam muttered under his breath to Scarlett. 'Just like Andy Gold.' Because the victim's head was partially gone, shot from behind. 'Except for that.' He pointed at the blood darkening the victim's chest and abdomen. 'Andy didn't have that.'

He crouched down, shined his Maglite on the man's face, and swore again as recognition hit him. 'Goddammit. It's Bruiser.'

'You're right.' Scarlett huffed a frustrated sigh, then crouched on the other side of the victim, the two of them shielding the body from the small group of people behind them.

Fortunately, they'd brought four squad cars' worth of backup in their quest to retrieve Linnie, and those officers were quick to establish a perimeter and string the crime scene tape. The cameras continued flashing, but at least the photos would be grainy and less valuable to the media. Adam had to take satisfaction where he could find it.

Scarlett tilted Adam's Maglite so that the beam hit the victim's chest. 'Four shots to the chest and abdomen, fired from in front of him. One shot to the head, fired from behind.'

'Two different shooters. The head wound came from a rifle.'

'Large caliber to the head. Holes in his shirt aren't that big. Location of the rifle?'

For the second time that day Adam found himself doing a slow three-sixty, searching for the glint of a rifle, nearly impossible now that darkness had fallen. Not that the shooter was still there, not in the same place anyway. The bastard was good at getting away fast.

'Based on the spatter, he was facing east.' Adam scanned the windows and rooftops to the west. He pointed to the most likely building. 'Shooter was up there.'

'We need to get Forensics here, to get us a trajectory.' Scarlett swore under her breath. 'If that's even possible now. He's been moved. Rolled over.'

She was right. Bruiser's right cheek had an even coating of blood that could have only come from resting in the pool of blood currently on the left side of his body. 'Shit. It only took us a minute to get here.'

Most of the people gathered around them were wide-eyed and shocked, though a few appeared avid and greedy. A few wore coats, but a handful were shivering in their shirtsleeves. They must have come out of the various businesses still open along the block.

'Who moved him?' Adam asked. Nobody answered. He managed to keep his temper. 'Did anyone here see anything?'

'I did.' An older woman came forward, her phone in her hand, but as an offering. 'I took a picture when he went down.' She looked at the people behind her with an irate frown. 'Because somebody did roll him over, but they ran after taking the picture of . . . his face. I thought you'd need to see how he fell.'

Sometimes TV crime shows did work in their favor. 'That was good thinking, ma'am. I'm Detective Kimble, that's Detective Bishop over there. You are?'

'Erinn Brinton, Missus. Two n's in Erinn,' she said. 'I work at the coffee shop.' She indicated the storefront with her head. 'I came out to take my smoking break, so I saw it. The one who shot him was a skinny girl. Really skinny, like I wanted to take her home and feed her. But *he* started it. She was minding her own business and he tried to grab her. I was about to call 911, because she looked scared and he looked mean. But she had a gun in her pocket. Pulled it out and shot him. Sorry, I didn't think to video it. It happened so fast.'

'That's okay,' Adam said and gave her a nod of encouragement, because despite her rapid speech, she was alarmingly pale and trembling. 'What happened then?'

She shook her head in disbelief. 'He tried to get up. It was crazy. He was bleeding out of his stomach and . . . But he got up like a robot or a monster or something.' She swayed on her feet and Adam grabbed her elbow to keep her upright.

He looked over at one of the uniforms. 'Can you get this lady a chair, please?' Because Mrs Brinton did not look good at all. A man in the crowd offered a water bottle.

'Give it to her,' the man said. 'It's not been opened.'

'Thank you.' Adam saw the unbroken seal and opened it. Sliding his arm around the old woman to hold her up, he put the bottle in her hands. 'Drink, ma'am. Try to breathe.'

She nodded and visibly got hold of herself. Her adrenaline rush was clearly wearing off, plus the reality of what she'd just witnessed was sinking in. 'I'm okay,' she said, more like she was trying to convince herself. 'Anyway, the girl, she got this look of horror on her face and I thought she'd shoot him again. But then he got to his feet, and then, *boom*.'

'The last shot,' Adam said.

'Yeah. Knocked him forward.' She flicked at her phone and a photo appeared – the man lying on his stomach, right cheek to the pavement, one arm outstretched.

'Did you see where the skinny girl went?' Adam asked gently.

'She ran towards that corner.' She pointed. 'I think she knew him. I'm thinking abusive spouse, and that she got a restraining order, but he ignored it. I seen it happen before.' Her eyes filled with tears. 'Why won't they just *listen* when the lady says *no*?'

'I don't know, ma'am,' he told her truthfully as an officer brought her a folding chair.

'I called for an ambulance,' the officer said to Adam quietly. His nametag said Khan. 'Coffee shop owner says she's got a bad heart.'

'Thanks.' Adam lowered the woman into the chair. 'Look, Mrs Brinton, I've got to go now, but stay here, okay?'

'Okay,' she said, clutching the water bottle.

'Officer Khan is going to stand nearby. Tell him if you feel worse. I'll be back, but if the EMTs get here first, you go with them.'

That she nodded without argument spoke volumes. 'What if you need to ask me more questions?'

'Officer Khan will tell me where to find you. For now, let him help you call a family member or a friend. Then afterward, if you can, I'd like to have that photo.' He gave her his card. 'My email and my phone numbers are on here. Call me if you remember anything else.' He patted the woman's hand, then moved to where Scarlett was just finishing a conversation with one of the uniforms.

Deacon and Hanson ran up to join them. 'What the hell happened?' Deacon asked, frowning at the scene. 'Shit. That looks like Bruiser.'

'It is.' Adam told them what the woman had said. 'The really skinny girl sounds like Linnie.'

Scarlett sighed. 'She was on her way back to the shelter, but we got there first.'

'And scared her away,' Hanson added grimly. 'It'll be harder than ever to find her.'

'It's super cold tonight,' Scarlett said. 'She'll have to find shelter somewhere. We'll check all the usual places.'

Deacon gave Adam a pitying look. 'Isenberg needs to know we lost her.'

Adam did not look forward to that call. 'So does Trip. He's going to be escorting Shane and the Davises to a safe house. He needs to know that a gunman is still active.'

'Are Shane and the Davises staying in the condo?' Deacon asked.

'No. There's room for Kyle and Shane, but not for the Davises once Meredith and her grandfather go back there tonight. We want to keep Shane and the Davises together. I'll call Isenberg and Trip. We'll lock the area down, do a door-to-door search.'

'I'll get the search started,' Hanson offered.

'I'll call Quincy to do the forensics since he did the Gold scene,' Scarlett said.

'Thanks.' Stepping away from the scene, Adam dialed Trip.

'What's up?' Trip answered. 'You bring her in?'

'No.' Adam told him what happened.

Trip swore. 'So Linnie wounded him, but somebody else killed Tiffany's killer?'

'Basically. The head shot was just like Andy Gold's.'

'You got the bullet yet?'

'Not yet. Scarlett's calling Quincy. Look, if this is the shooter who killed Andy and shot at the van today, you need to make sure you're covered when you transport Shane and the Davises to that safe house.'

'I'll make sure. How's Troy?'

'I'm not sure, but he may still be at the ER. I'll let you know if I hear anything and you do the same for me.'

'Where is Meredith?'

'I left her with Isenberg. They were going to interview little Penny Voss.'

'Poor kid,' Trip said sadly. 'When I've got Shane and the Davises settled, I'll meet you at Isenberg's. Hopefully we'll have a warrant for Voss's house by then.'

Adam ended the call, drew a breath and dialed his boss. *This ain't gonna be fun.*

Cincinnati, Ohio,
Sunday 20 December, 6.05 P.M.

'I'm sorry it took me so long to get here,' Corinne apologized as she exited the elevator to Isenberg's floor. 'I brought a little of everything.'

'It wasn't your fault,' Meredith told her assistant, taking one of the boxes of art supplies from Corinne's arms. 'I wish I'd known you'd been sitting outside our office for so long. I would have told Isenberg sooner.'

'Hey, I'm just glad you're okay.' Corinne's face lit up when she saw Meredith's grandfather sitting at the unoccupied desk. 'Mr Fallon! Merry Christmas!'

Clarke smiled. 'Corinne. How are you?'

'Better now that I know you guys are okay. I got that call from Agent Troy a few hours ago asking me to get the art supplies. He

343

said he'd meet me at the office after he drove you all here to the police station. But then I didn't hear back, so I called Lieutenant Isenberg and she sent a van for me.' She smiled. 'It was Trip, Kate, and Mallory. Oh, and Cap. They're on their way here from Mariposa House.' Where Corinne also volunteered. 'They got held up in the lobby talking to Lieutenant Isenberg. They should be coming up.'

At that moment the elevator door dinged and Lynda Isenberg strode out, a cellophane-covered piece of pie from the cafeteria in her hand. She was accompanied by Trip, Kate, a tail-wagging Cap, and Mallory.

Isenberg, Trip, and Kate looked grim, but Meredith didn't get the chance to ask why because Mallory ran to hug her so tightly that Meredith couldn't quite breathe.

'Hey,' she soothed, looking at the others over Mallory's shoulder. 'What's all this?'

Because Mallory was crying.

'I think she just needed to see that you're okay,' Kate said softly. 'I'll take her back to Mariposa House later.'

'I *am* okay. But, Mallory, honey, you're going to crack my ribs if you don't let me go.'

Sniffling, Mallory immediately let go. 'Why is someone trying to kill you? *You?*' she added, as if the notion was incomprehensible to her. Which was sweet, actually.

'I don't know. But Detective Kimble and the team will find out.'

Isenberg cleared her throat meaningfully. 'Dr Fallon, the Vosses are waiting.'

'I know. I have my supplies now.' Meredith gave Mallory's cheek a light caress. 'Have a seat and wait for me. You remember my grandfather from yesterday?'

Clarke gave her his most cheerful smile. 'Come on, Mallory. Let's get some coffee and cake from the cafeteria. You gonna join us, Kate?'

'I can always eat cake. But first I want to check in on Shane and the Davises. We've found them a place where they can all stay together. Agent Triplett will be escorting them.'

Trip nodded. 'And I've got a lot of backup, this time, just in case.'

'That's good to hear,' Meredith said fervently.

Kate petted the dog's head. 'Cap, with me. You too, Clarke, if you want to come along and say goodbye to Kyle and Shane.'

Meredith watched them go, then turned to Isenberg. 'Can you have an officer escort Corinne home?'

'Absolutely. I'll take care of it after we get this interview rolling. Here are the pictures we'd like you to show the child.' Isenberg gave her three photos, then took one of the boxes of art supplies and started walking.

Meredith flipped through the pictures. There was one of a large man with dead eyes. Probably the Neanderthal who was looking for Shane, she thought. One was the grainy surveillance photo of Linnie. And the third was a laughing young woman from her Facebook page. Her name was cut away.

Meredith looked up to see Isenberg was already halfway down the hall to the interview rooms. Grabbing the other box, she rushed to catch up.

Cincinnati, Ohio,
Sunday 20 December, 6.10 P.M.

Adam was waiting for CSU to begin processing Bruiser's murder scene when his cell chimed with a generic ringtone. But this call he'd take because the caller ID showed him it was from Chicago PD. Adam had been trying to reach Detectives Reagan or Mitchell since he'd finished updating Isenberg. 'This is Kimble.'

'Abe Reagan, here. I have Detective Mitchell with me on speaker. Our CSU guy was able to get blood prints off Tiffany Curtis's clothing. Her killer left them when he grabbed her pajama top to . . . well, when he gutted her. We sent you a copy of the prints.'

The image of Tiffany's body flashed into Adam's mind, making him glad he hadn't eaten recently. 'Anything pop on AFIS?'

'Not a thing,' Mitchell said with disgust. 'But there's no way this was his first kill.'

Adam sighed, frustrated. *An ID would have been too easy.* 'Your suspect is dead.'

A beat of silence. 'Well, can't say I'm sad to hear that,' Mitchell said dryly.

'Are you sure?' Reagan asked.

'I'm looking down at his body right now. He was shot by a sniper. May be the same one who tried to take out a van in which Shane Baird, his friend Kyle, and the original target – our child psychologist – were being transported this afternoon.'

'So he was taken out by one of his own?' Mitchell asked. 'This is a cold crew.'

'Looks that way. One of the Feds on loan to our task force was hit, but he'll be okay. A few hours later, Bruiser here was trying to snatch the only witness who can describe the shooter. She shot him, then the sniper took him out. Thought you'd want to know.'

'Do you have a name for him other than Bruiser?' Mitchell asked tartly.

'Not yet. We'll pass it on to you when we do. In the meantime, we'll send you photos once CSU's taken them.' He spotted Quincy Taylor making his way from the CSU van. 'Which should be soon. Our CSU guy just arrived. I need to go.'

He ended the call as Quincy set his forensic kit next to Bruiser's body. 'Trouble just finds you, Adam.'

'Ain't that the truth,' Scarlett drawled.

Adam started to roll his eyes, but there was something in Quincy's tone that had him frowning. 'What do you mean by that?'

'I just finished processing the van. The only part of the van that appears to have been purposely targeted by gunfire was the front passenger door and window.' Quincy narrowed his eyes. 'This doesn't surprise you.'

Adam shook his head. 'Not really, no.'

Scarlett froze. 'You didn't tell us that, Adam.'

'I didn't get a chance. Dani came in with Linnie's location before I got to that point.'

'Bullshit. You were leading the damn meeting. You could have covered that first.'

'You were waiting to see what I found out, weren't you?' Quincy asked.

'Yeah,' Adam admitted. 'I mean, I thought the same thing. That the only one who should have died in that attack was me, but that doesn't make any sense.'

'Not yet,' Quincy said. 'Let me get to work here. I need to find the bullet. I'm betting it'll match Andy's and the van's.'

'Shit,' Scarlett muttered. 'Why would you be the target, Adam?'

'I don't know. I mean, Troy was the one who got hit.'

'He says that's because you leaned back to tell the people in the back to get down,' Quincy said.

Adam pinched the bridge of his nose. 'How is Troy?'

'He was admitted to the hospital,' Quincy said curtly. He sounded almost angry.

Adam stared. 'What? He said it was a flesh wound.'

'And you *believed* him?' Quincy snapped.

'Well, yes,' Adam said. 'I didn't see any other wounds.'

Quincy pinned him with a glare. 'Did he let you *look*?'

Adam tried to remember. 'No. I don't think he did. I took him at his word. Why was he admitted? He should have needed just a few stitches in the ER.'

'He took two bullets. One in the arm and one in the side. He'll be okay, but it was much worse than he let on.' Quincy huffed out a breath. 'Sorry. Not your fault. You should be able to take the word of a federal agent as truth.'

'Why did he lie?'

Quincy rolled his eyes. 'He doesn't like ambulances.'

'Holy fuck,' Adam grumbled. 'He could have just said so.'

Quincy gave him an oddly knowing look. 'Would you have admitted a weakness?' Adam remembered Quincy watching him as he'd turned from Buon Cibo's bar yesterday. *He knows. Or at least suspects.* But he couldn't worry about that now. 'No.'

'Didn't think so. Troy only told me because I found the bullet embedded in the driver's seat. I matched its trajectory to the first bullet hole put in the windshield.'

'Which was on my side of the car,' Adam said quietly.

Quincy nodded. 'The shooter was aiming for you. It didn't hit you because Troy swerved.'

'Because I warned him,' Adam said grimly.

'Which was a good thing,' Quincy insisted. 'Troy swerved and the bullet hit the windshield at an angle instead of front-on. It was the difference in a moderate wound for Troy and a fatal one for you. Troy seems to think it was worth it.'

Adam shook his head. 'When he's recovered, I'm gonna kick his ass. Idiot.'

'We're agreed on that. I would have wasted valuable time testing the blood for DNA only to find it belonged to him.' Quincy paused then. 'There is another odd thing.'

Adam rubbed his stiff neck. 'Of course there is. Please go on.'

'You've had a rough day too,' Quincy said, 'so sorry to dump this on you, but I think the shooter purposely altered his aim to hit the top of the van. You were right about where he was, by the way. I found where he waited. No cigarette butts or anything actually helpful, but he cleared an area of snow. It looks like he used a tripod for the rifle. He started firing straight and low, and as you passed by his location, Troy sped up. The bullets that hit the side should have hit low.'

'They all hit high,' Adam said. 'I wondered about that too. It was like he wasn't trying to hit anyone in the back.'

Quincy nodded. 'That's my take.'

'So he – whoever he is – tries to kill Meredith at Buon Cibo, but when he gets the chance today, intentionally misses. Shane was with her today. That's the difference.'

Scarlett pointed to the body. 'And we think Bruiser tried to find Shane in Chicago, because he wanted Linnie. Shane can't tell him where Linnie is if Shane is dead.'

Adam grunted his agreement. 'And then Linnie shoots him. Ironic.'

'Bruiser?' Quincy shrugged. 'Good a name as any, I guess. Why would his cohorts kill him?'

'My best guess is because his photo's all over the Internet,' Adam said. 'Chicago PD sent it out as a person of interest. Whoever killed Bruiser is snipping off loose ends.'

'But how are *you* a loose end?' Scarlett pressed. 'I mean, I can see if they tried to take out Troy, because the van would stop and they could get Shane. Why shoot at you?'

'If they'd taken out Troy, Adam still would have been armed and dangerous,' Quincy said, his voice very quiet. 'Maybe they figured that Troy would stop if Adam was shot.'

'Troy would have been armed and dangerous,' Scarlett argued.

'Troy's not a sharpshooter,' Quincy replied, then quirked a lip at Adam's surprise. 'I make it a point to know who I'm working with. Their skills *and* their weaknesses. Adam could have taken out the sniper before he got close enough to take Shane.'

'And if they'd shot Troy, we might have crashed,' Adam added. 'And then no Shane.'

'How did they know you were coming?' Scarlett demanded. 'This was planned.'

Adam shrugged. 'The Davises were here. Whoever planned this must not have known where we took Shane, but knew we'd be bringing him to the station.'

Scarlett didn't look convinced. 'But you could have gone different ways.'

'They might have more than one gunman, Scar,' Adam said. 'They may have had snipers posted on multiple roofs.'

Quincy sighed. 'And who knows? Maybe the shooter was trying for Troy and is just a bad shot.'

'But you don't think so,' Adam said.

Quincy shook his head. 'No, I don't.'

Twenty

Candace Voss and Penny looked up from the movie they'd been watching on Candace's phone when Meredith and Isenberg walked in with the boxes of art supplies.

Penny ignored Isenberg, studying Meredith with wide eyes. 'You got shot at.'

Meredith stifled her surprise. 'You heard about that?'

'I heard my mama and Aunt Dianne talking about it. What's in the boxes?'

Unsurprised by the little girl's quick change of topic or curiosity, Meredith replied, 'Crayons, coloring books and . . .' She opened one of the boxes. 'Play-Doh! It's the twenty-pack. And the Fun Factory. What do you want to play with? Crayons or Play-Doh?'

Penny regarded her owlishly. 'Why?'

Meredith sat down at the table. 'Fair question. Why what, specifically?'

'Why am I here? Mama won't tell me anything. Like I'm a baby.'

'You're six,' Candace said.

'And a *half*,' Penny insisted. 'Well?'

Meredith set the cans of Play-Doh on the table. 'First things first. What color?'

'Red.' Penny took the blob of dough from the can and gave it a good, long sniff.

'I used to do that when I was a kid,' Meredith told her. 'But it doesn't taste good.'

'I know,' Penny said. 'But it says non-toxic. That means it won't kill you.'

'You're right.' Meredith picked the cream-colored dough. 'So, to answer your question, we're here to talk about that night when your father had a party.'

Penny pinched off a hunk and started to roll it into a snake. 'I don't wanna talk about that,' she said sullenly. 'You can't make me. The other ladies tried.'

'You're right. I can't make you. I think I saw a rolling pin and cookie cutters in here.' Meredith emptied the contents of the box onto the table with a clatter. 'Aha! I was right!'

'You're trying to trick me into talking to you,' Penny grumbled.

'You're too smart for me to do that,' Meredith said, rolling out her dough.

'Yep,' Penny said with a hard nod.

That Penny was too smart was the reason it had taken this long to get her to open up. And having two therapists already didn't help. Penny was wise to Meredith's moves.

'These things must be done *delicately*,' Meredith murmured as she cut shapes, assembling them into a face as she surreptitiously watched Penny, who was poking her finger into the dough, a frown bending her lips.

'The witch said that. In that movie.' Penny's brow scrunched. 'The Lizard of Oz.'

'Wizard, Penny,' Candace said quietly from the other end of the table. 'Wizard.'

Penny shrugged. 'I like lizard better.'

Meredith's mouth quirked up. 'So do I. Can I borrow some red?'

'Why?' Penny asked.

'I want to make her hair.'

Grudgingly, Penny gave her some red dough. 'Your hair is red.'

'It is indeed.'

'I like red hair,' Penny said, then went back to poking holes in her dough.

'I'm glad. There were times that I didn't like it and tried to dye it. Didn't end well.'

351

Penny looked up. 'What color?'

'What color did I dye it? Purple once. Pink once. That worked better.' She put the red dough through the Fun Factory and used the spaghetti shapes for hair. 'How's that?'

Penny gave her an intense look. 'Not bad. She needs eyes.'

'True.' Meredith added green circles for eyes. 'I think she should also have jewelry.' Meredith added white dots to the dough girl's ears. 'Pearls.'

'That's you,' Penny said, no longer poking her lump of dough.

Meredith smiled, pleased. 'That's what I was going for. Should we do you?'

'Yes.'

Meredith rolled dough for two more dough girls, gave half to Penny, then proceeded to quietly make a pink-haired dough girl. Following her lead, Penny made her own face, adding brown hair and black eyes. 'No earrings,' she said glumly, glancing at her mother.

'I was eighteen when I got my ears pierced,' Meredith confided.

'See?' her mother said.

'Sucks,' Penny grumbled. 'Sorry, Mama. I know you don't like that word.'

Meredith pulled some pink dough from its can and put it through the Fun Factory, arranging the hair on her second dough girl, giving her long locks. 'What do you think?'

Penny's mouth tightened. 'It should be shorter. You're doing it wrong.'

But you're talking to me. Meredith gave a subtle shake of the head to Candace Voss when she opened her mouth to reprimand her daughter for rudeness.

'Okay,' Meredith said mildly. 'Can you show me?'

Jaw compressed, Penny chopped at the pink noodles with the plastic knife that came with the kit, making the cuttings into ponytails. Throwing Meredith a glare, she added dark eyes and red dots for earrings. Surveying her work, the child shook her head, removed the red dots and flattened them. When she reapplied them, they were bigger than the ears.

Gauges. And Meredith had seen those. Recently. From her bag, she drew the Facebook photo that Isenberg had given her. No pink hair. *But gauges in the ears. Red ones.*

Saying nothing, Meredith watched as Penny, biting at her lip, put a small white dot on the dough-girl's nose. 'Should be silver,' Penny muttered.

And one silver nose stud on the Facebook photo. *Check.*

Still saying nothing, Meredith sat back and observed. Penny took more of the cream-colored dough and rolled two fat cigar shapes and pressed them at angles to the girl's chin. *Arms. So far so good.* Then she rolled some white dough in the shape of a cigarette.

Meredith glanced up at Candace, giving her another subtle shake of the head.

Penny continued to work, focused on whatever she was constructing. She rolled a toothpick shape from the white dough, pressed it to the middle of the arm and then pressed the cigarette shape to it.

A needle.

Penny glanced up at Meredith defiantly. 'She told me not to tell.'

'I understand,' Meredith said calmly, but inside fury was roiling. 'What else did she tell you?'

'That I was cute.' Penny looked away. 'And did I want some?'

Candace sucked in a breath, covering her mouth with her hand.

Penny looked at her mother with a seriousness no child should ever experience. 'I said no, Mama. Then I ran to my room and locked the door.'

'What did the pink-haired lady do?' Meredith asked, fighting like hell to keep her voice level and soothing.

'She laughed. I could hear her when I ran.' Penny's eyes filled with an abrupt, intense fear. 'She knocked on my door. Laughing. I hid under my bed.' She looked down at the table. 'I needed to use the potty, but the lady was still out there. So I . . . I had an accident. On the floor.' Her little cheeks reddened with shame. 'I cleaned it. I tried.'

Meredith smoothed a hand over Penny's hair. 'It's all right. You were very brave. Nobody's angry with you, Penny.'

'Daddy was,' she whispered, and the color drained from Candace's face.

'What happened, Penny?' Meredith asked softly.

'He yelled at the pink-haired lady.' She took her hand and smashed the face of the figure she'd made, grinding her palm into the dough, ruining it.

'He did that?' Meredith asked.

Penny nodded, but then shook her head. 'Not to this girl. To the other one.'

'You want us to make her?'

'No. I—I . . .'

'All right,' Meredith said. 'You don't have to do anything, sweetheart.'

Penny looked up, panicked. 'I don't know *how*. She was . . . sick. Skinny and sick. I don't know *how* to make her.'

Candace was drawing slow steady breaths through her nose. Meredith gave her a smile of encouragement, before turning back to Penny. 'It's all right. You're doing great. You and your mama.' She smoothed her hand over Penny's hair again. 'Did the sick, skinny lady say anything?'

Penny nodded. 'She said *no*. But . . .' Her eyes closed. 'They made her pray.'

Oh God, Meredith thought. Candace made a choked noise, but continued to sit like a statue. 'They made her pray to God?' Meredith asked carefully. 'Like in church?'

'On her knees. They kept saying that.'

Meredith drew in a breath, held it, then eased it back out. 'They?' she asked, with only the mildest of curiosity. Inside she was cursing Broderick Voss to a fiery hell.

'Men. My daddy's friends. I didn't like them. They used mean voices.'

'You heard them? Did you also see them?'

She wagged her head slowly. 'No,' she said earnestly. 'I was hiding under the bed. I was scared. I didn't come out until they all went home.'

Meredith smiled, hiding her relief. 'And then what happened?'

'I was hungry and Mama was gone. Just for one night,' she added quickly. 'Mama didn't leave me before that. Or after.'

'I understand,' Meredith assured her. 'Your daddy? Did he leave you?'

'Lots of times,' Penny said with a shrug that Meredith was sure she intended to be careless. But it wasn't. 'He don't like me.'

Candace's eyes filled with tears, but she remained silent.

'Why do you think that, Penny?' Meredith asked her.

'I just do. He was busy. Always. He didn't want to play or even watch TV or DVDs. He told the men that night that they had to be quiet. That I'd tell on him and then they'd never be able to have a party again. That I had a big mouth. He said I was a little . . . a bad name. Like a witch. I'm not allowed to say that name.' Her chin trembled and her eyes welled, like her mama's. 'So I didn't want to tell. Because then . . .' She trailed off.

'Because then it would be true?' Meredith supplied and Penny nodded miserably. 'Penny, if I tell you something, will you believe me?'

Penny sniffled. 'Depends.'

'See? That means you are smart. And you did everything right. Can I hug you?'

Penny nodded, tears streaking down her cheeks. 'I want him to like me.' A sob broke free. 'Why don't he like me?'

Meredith hated this part of her job – when babies grew up too damn fast. She wrapped her arms around the sobbing child. 'I don't know.'

'My daddy's hateful!' Penny yelled. 'And I hate him!'

And that was an issue for another day. Meredith pulled Penny to her lap, rocked her through until the sobs became sniffles, then hiccups.

'I hate him,' Penny whispered.

'That's okay.'

Penny looked up suspiciously. 'I'm not s'posed to hate. The other lady said that.'

'The other therapist?'

Penny nodded. 'She wasn't nice. She didn't have Play-Doh, either.'

'Well, that's important, having Play-Doh.' Meredith took tissues from her bag and dried Penny's cheeks. 'You can hate, Penny. That's okay. For a little while. Not forever.'

'Because it's not nice,' Penny said glumly. 'I know.'

'Not what I was gonna say,' Meredith chided gently. 'I was gonna say that hate uses up part of your soul. That's the thing that makes you Penny and not somebody else. Your soul is kind of like your stuffed animals. You can only fit so many on your bed, right?'

'Right,' Penny said warily.

'Are you going to waste valuable space on your bed with toys you don't like?'

Penny considered it. 'No,' she decided. 'That would be dumb. I'd put the ones I don't like in my closet, like the stuffed bear my daddy got me in Germany. It was hard like a rock. So I put it in the closet. My soul has a closet where I put the hate and mean things?'

Meredith smiled at her, then pulled her tight for a hug. 'You are so very smart, Penny Voss. That is exactly right.'

'What happens when the closet fills up?'

'See, another very smart question. What do you do when your real closet fills up?'

'We give the toys to poor kids. But I don't think other kids want all my hate.'

'Maybe you could just throw it away.'

She looked anxious. 'I don't know how.'

'That's why I'm here. I'm going to show you how. But not today, because I think you've worked pretty hard today already. Now I have a few more questions to ask you, and then it'll be time for you to take your mama home, okay?'

Penny's little face drooped. 'I'm sorry, Mama. Don't be sad.'

'You have nothing to be sorry for, baby,' Candace said, her smile clearly forced. She held herself so rigidly that Meredith was afraid she'd shatter. 'I'm so proud of you, that you are my daughter. I'm sorry you had to see all that when I wasn't home.'

'It's okay, Mama.' Penny let out a heavy sigh. 'But I have bad dreams.'

'I know,' Candace said. 'We'll keep seeing Dr Fallon and maybe soon you won't.'

Penny didn't look convinced. 'Maybe,' she said with a shake of her head.

Meredith put the Facebook photo on the table. 'Have you ever seen this lady?'

Penny ran her finger down the woman's nose and over her ears. 'Can I color on it?'

'Of course. You'll have to hop off my lap so I can get the crayons.' Penny obliged and Meredith dug out her trusty Crayola 64. She bought these boxes by the case because kids loved them. She thought of Adam. *Kids of all ages.* She flipped the lid. 'There you go.'

Penny picked a pink crayon, which was no surprise. She colored over the woman's dark hair, then nodded. 'Yes. That's the pink-haired lady.'

'Thank you. Now, two more.' She showed her the grainy photo of Linnie.

Penny's face fell. 'That's the sick lady who prayed. Did it make her better?'

'I hope she gets better,' Meredith said sincerely. 'One more.' She showed her the photo of the big man with the dead eyes.

Penny shook her head, but shivered. 'He doesn't look nice.'

No, he does not. 'But you haven't seen him before?'

'No.' She looked up. 'Can I go now?'

'Yes, Penny. You can go.'

She ran to her mother who gathered her close. 'Can we stop for hot chocolate?'

Candace kissed the top of her head. 'We have to go straight home, but I will make you the best hot chocolate you have ever tasted.'

'Cookies too?'

Candace choked on something between a sob and a laugh. 'Yes. Anything else?'

Penny snuggled close. 'No, Mama. That's good. For now.'

Cincinnati, Ohio,
Sunday 20 December, 7.10 P.M.

After Meredith had wrapped up the session with Penny, summarized her notes for CPD's file, and finally found some ibuprofen for her headache, she returned to the bullpen to find her grandfather and Mallory knitting with Kate.

Of course they are. 'You just keep sucking people into your weird cult,' Meredith said, making herself smile past the pounding in her skull. She was starting to wonder how hard she'd actually hit her head. If the ibuprofen didn't help she was going to have to see a doctor, and she hated the very thought of that.

Kate looked up with a grin. 'You're always welcome in our cult.'

'Look what I made,' Clarke said proudly, holding up the scarf that was his debut project. It was perfect, of course, but Meredith didn't tell him so because the elevator dinged and her gaze swung toward the doors.

Isenberg had filled her in on both the murder of 'Bruiser' and Quincy's conclusion that Adam had been the target of the van shooting, and Meredith hadn't breathed properly since. All she could think was that Adam was out there, working the crime scene, a sitting duck for anyone who really wanted to hurt him. But now he was back. *Safe.*

He, Trip, Scarlett, and Deacon walked toward them, every face grim. Isenberg came out of her office to greet them. 'So?' she asked her team.

'We can't find Linnie,' Adam said flatly. 'Hanson's got the area locked down and he's got uniforms going door to door and checking every alley. She's gone under.'

'Oh no,' Meredith murmured. 'I hope she doesn't freeze. She's got to be so scared.'

'But she's armed,' Isenberg said.

'Eyewitnesses say she shot Bruiser in self-defense,' Scarlett said, then noticed Mallory sitting there. 'Hey, kid. You okay?'

Mallory nodded. '*I'm* not being shot at.'

Meredith ruffled her hair. 'Good. That's how it's supposed to be.'

'You,' Isenberg said to the four cops. 'Briefing room, please.' She turned to Meredith, brows arched. 'You've seen that he's all right. Now you can go. And Agent Coppola, that goes double for you. And triple for the dog. He's going to shed all over the carpet.' Without another word, she walked away.

Biting back rueful smiles, Deacon and Scarlett followed.

Trip shook his head. 'I don't get that woman.'

'She's been very nice today,' Meredith said. 'I think she's hit her quota.'

'And she's got a rep to protect,' Kate added. 'Once you achieve rank of Badass, you can't just skate.'

'Whatever,' Trip muttered. 'Why didn't she order you into the briefing room?' he asked Kate. 'I thought Zimmerman gave us to her for the case.'

'Because I'm technically on vacation. I'm just here for the knitting.' Kate glanced at Meredith. 'And for her. I don't want to trust just anyone to keep her safe.'

'Ah. Got it.' He turned to Meredith. 'Just wanted to let you know that Shane and the Davises are settled. The agents with them were handpicked by Zimmerman.'

'Thank you,' Meredith said. 'I'll sleep better knowing they're safe too.'

Still shaking his head over Isenberg, Trip went into her office.

'I'll just be a minute,' Adam called after Trip, then took Meredith's elbow and led her into a small meeting room and shut the door.

'What's wrong?' she asked, frowning.

He didn't answer, just cupped her face in his hands and kissed her. Hard. At first, anyway. Starting as what felt like a stamp of possession, it quickly softened into something tender and so sweet it made her sigh. When he raised his head, she could only stare at him, her headache nearly forgotten.

'Nothing's wrong,' he murmured, nuzzling her neck. 'I just needed to.'

She stroked his hair, kissed his temple. 'Isenberg will pull you from the case.'

'I don't think so.' He lifted his head, his expression wry. 'It wasn't like she didn't know from the beginning. The woman knows everything.'

Meredith caressed his face, loving the rasp of his stubble against her fingertips. 'I'm glad she has your back.'

'She always has. She called to tell me that you were good with Penny Voss. Actually, she said you were "impressive." That's high praise.'

'It was a good session.' She traced the worry lines around his mouth, not liking them at all, but understanding why they were there. 'What happened to Linnie?'

'We don't know. I wish she'd trust us, but we blew any chance of that tonight.'

'At least Kyle will have closure. The man who killed Tiffany won't hurt anyone else.'

He kissed her forehead. 'You know, I hadn't thought of that.'

'You've been a little busy.'

'Too busy. I can't take you to the safe house. How will you get back?'

'Kate's taking me and Papa, then she'll take Mallory home. Don't buy her vacation routine. She's barely slept. She's working. She'll recruit some help and I'll be fine.' She frowned up at him. 'I'm more worried about *you*. You were the target this afternoon and you can't hide away in a safe house.'

'You know about the van.' He sighed when she nodded. 'I wish you didn't know, but know that I will be careful, I promise.'

'But why? Why would they shoot at you? They're after me and Shane, right?'

'We think they want Shane alive, because they believe he can lead them to Linnie. It's likely they tried to take me out so that Troy would stop. Then they could have grabbed Shane alive and . . .' He closed his eyes and shook his head.

'Killed the rest of us,' she finished quietly. 'Got it. So we're all targets. Wonderful.'

He met her eyes. 'So we *all* have to be careful. We were lucky today. Except for Troy. He's been admitted to the hospital. He underrepresented his injuries.'

Her eyes widened. 'He lied?'

'Big-time, the asshole.' But his tone wasn't angry. It was actually almost fond, and that made her smile. 'Make sure Kate knows, okay? I don't think he told her, either.' He pressed another hard kiss to her mouth. 'Get some rest. I'll call you when I can.'

But he didn't let her go. He stood there staring at her with such need that she wrapped her arms around his neck, holding him close when he dropped his head on her shoulder. She could feel his erection, hard against her abdomen, but he wasn't insistent. He didn't push, didn't thrust. This wasn't about passion or sex. This was about comfort.

So that was what she gave him. Stroking his hair, she held him. It was just the two of them. No work, no boss, no murder.

Finally, he stepped back, his eyes calmer. 'Thank you. I needed that.'

She smiled up at him. 'So did I.'

He cupped her chin, brushed his thumb over her lips. 'You look exhausted. Get some sleep. I'll come to you as soon as I can.'

'If I'm asleep, please wake me up.'

His lips curled, his dark eyes sparkling with something wicked. 'Count on it.' He took a final kiss, smoothed his tie, then left with a wink that was so playful that she laughed. He jogged to the briefing room, but she kept her pace more sedate. The kisses had been lovely, but now her head hurt again and she was starting to feel a little sick.

Kate wore an irrepressible grin and puckered her lips teasingly when Meredith got back to where she, Clarke, and Mallory waited. Until Meredith told her that Troy had been admitted to the hospital.

Kate's grin became a scowl. 'I think I need to visit my *partner* in the hospital and let him know that he was supposed to have informed me – his *partner* – that he'd been injured. I mean, it's not like he's my *partner* or anything.' Cap whined at her distress and she sighed, giving the old boy a scratch behind the ears. 'It's okay, boy. But I can't take Cap into the hospital without all kinds of special fuss and I have to get you back to the condo and then drive Mallory to Mariposa House. I'll have to rip Troy a new one tomorrow.'

She paused to stare at Meredith. 'What's wrong with you? You look . . . off.'

'I have a headache,' Meredith confessed.

Her grandfather stood, sobering quickly. 'Since when?'

'Since the van this afternoon. My head hit the floor kind of hard. I figured it would go away, but it hasn't.' She touched the back of her head. 'Right here.'

'Meredith!' Clarke's tone was scolding, but his hands were gentle as he lifted her hair away from where it hurt. 'You've got a goose egg, all right. Dammit, girl, I thought you had sense. We could have been icing it. You should have been resting.'

'Clarke,' Kate said quietly. 'Not helping.'

'You're right.' He drew a breath and let go of Meredith's hair. 'You're probably fine, but we're not taking any chances. Let's go to the ER and get you checked out.'

She turned to protest, but his jaw was hard, his eyes determined. She knew that look. It was no use arguing. She sighed. 'All right, Papa.'

'I'll tell Adam where we're going,' Kate said, then shook her head. 'No, he'll just worry. I'll text Isenberg and let her decide if she tells him or not.'

'Don't I get a say in that?' Meredith asked, knowing she sounded petulant.

'No,' Kate said flatly. 'He'll just worry and then he won't be paying attention. You want that to happen?'

'No,' Meredith muttered.

'Thought not.' Kate sent one text, then another. 'That takes care of Isenberg and I just told our FBI escort, also handpicked by my boss, that we're heading downstairs and that we have a change in plans. Mallory, you're just gonna have to hang tight till we figure this out. I'll get you back to Mariposa, I'm just not sure when.'

Mallory bit her lip. 'I'm sorry, Kate. I should have just stayed at the house. I wouldn't have caused you to have to make the trip back out there tonight.'

'Nonsense,' Kate said briskly. 'You saw Meredith nearly killed yesterday. Today you needed to see that she was okay. And she is . . . mostly. You were all hunkered into yourself, and now you're not. So it's all good.' She grinned at them. 'And it's about to get even better.' She lifted her knitting bag, a larger tote than usual, and pulled out three wigs.

Meredith gaped. 'I'm not wearing one of those.'

'Never say never,' Kate rebuked mildly. 'I planned on disguising us on the way back to the condo. You and me? Our hair stands out. Let's make it a little bit harder for the bad guys to figure that you've left the building.'

Meredith winced. 'You think they're watching for me to leave?'

Kate gave her a look. 'How hard did you hit your head, girl? Have you forgotten that you're a target?'

Meredith grimaced. 'No.'

'Then hush and put on the damn wig. I've got blondes and brunettes.'

Meredith sighed. 'Blondes have more fun, right? Let me be a blonde.'

The wig wasn't really so bad. It felt like real hair, not like the cheap Halloween wigs. She turned to ask her grandfather how she looked, but the words never left her mouth because he was staring at her, his eyes wide and suspiciously bright. 'What, Papa?'

'You look just like your gran,' he murmured. 'I was just surprised.' He drew a breath, shook his head slightly, then focused on Mallory. 'You look lovely. As do you, Kate.'

Kate had chosen to be a brunette and Mallory had gone with blonde.

Mallory studied her reflection in Kate's little mirror. 'Nobody's after me, but I'm wearing one too. I've been wanting to change my look. I think I like it.'

Meredith instantly understood. Mallory had once been a victim of child pornography, her abuse streamed worldwide by pedophiles for years. And it was all still out there because nothing was ever truly deleted from the Internet. She constantly worried that she'd be recognized by a pervert who'd seen her online, because she had been in the past. Looking different might give her the confidence she so desperately needed.

Kate's expression softened as well. 'I think we all look *mahvelous*. Clarke, you're gonna have to just be you. I don't have anything in my bag that wouldn't draw too much attention to you. Let's get your noggin checked out, Mer, then you can be you again.'

Cincinnati, Ohio,
Sunday 20 December, 7.20 P.M.

Adam ignored Isenberg's glare when he got to the briefing room. He'd taken five minutes for himself. Five minutes of respite that he'd desperately needed. He hadn't known how much until he'd let himself be held. Trip, Deacon, and Scarlett were already seated and Nash Currie sat in the same place they'd left him, hours before, still bent over his laptop, typing furiously.

'So glad you could find the time to join us, Detective Kimble,' Isenberg said sarcastically.

Without apology, Adam sat next to Trip and smoothed his tie. He tilted his head in Nash's direction and Trip nodded, indicating that they'd already met. 'Do we have a warrant?' Adam asked Isenberg.

She checked her phone and frowned. 'Not yet,' she muttered. 'Should be soon.'

'Meredith talked to Penny?' Trip asked. 'I just met Adam and the others coming up the elevator,' he told Isenberg when she arched her brows in question. 'We were talking about the latest body, but didn't discuss the Voss girl.'

'Do we have time to see the video of Meredith talking to Penny?' Adam asked.

Isenberg glared at her phone a few seconds more. 'Where is Hanson? Bringing in Broderick Voss is why he was brought onto this team.'

'He must still be searching for Linnie,' Deacon said. 'We told him we were coming back. Thought he was with us.'

Isenberg dialed her cell, then held it to her ear. 'Detective Hanson, this is Lieutenant Isenberg,' she said crisply. 'We are planning the Voss operation. Please join us.' Her lips tightened. 'I've already sent one of my detectives to take over the search. He should be there by now. I *said*, please join us. As soon as possible.'

Adam bit back a wince and saw Deacon and Scarlett doing the same. Nobody defied Isenberg when she got impatient like this. Hanson wasn't being very smart.

Ending the call, Isenberg pointed a remote at the flatscreen on the wall. 'It seems we have time. I've forwarded to the relevant parts.' She hit play and Adam found himself in awe of Meredith's way of making the child feel comfortable enough to talk while pushing her to reveal her secrets. Her very painful secrets. *Poor Penny.*

Adam swallowed a sigh when Penny started to cry. He startled a little when Isenberg fast-forwarded the video a minute or two.

'She cried a lot,' Isenberg said flatly, but Adam had known her long enough to know that the acerbic attitude disguised a burdened heart. A glance at Trip showed that the younger man was figuring that out for himself. She hit play to resume normal speed.

Just in time to see Penny positively identify both Jolee and Linnie as having been in Broderick Voss's home.

Isenberg ended the video. 'The DA's got this file. He's tracking down the judge on call to sign the warrant.'

'Good,' Adam said, pushing back from the table. He went to the whiteboard and moved Bruiser's photo into the deceased column next to his victims. 'Just because Penny didn't see him at her house doesn't mean he's not involved with Voss.'

'Do we have a name yet?' Isenberg asked.

'No,' Adam told her. 'But we can say that his prints match those that Chicago PD found on Tiffany Curtis's clothing. Nothing pops in AFIS.'

'Which,' Scarlett said, 'is hard to friggin' believe. How can a guy this violent go through life without getting caught for something?'

'Good question,' Deacon muttered.

Adam's phone buzzed in his pocket and he checked the incoming text. 'It's from Quincy. He says the bullet he found at tonight's scene is a ballistics match to both the one that killed Andy Gold and those pulled from the van this afternoon.'

'Which matches one found at the scene of a thirty-year-old robbery,' Isenberg said. 'Have you made any progress on tracking that weapon's ownership, Agent Triplett?'

'No, ma'am. That far back, some of the records aren't online. Zimmerman put several clerks on it. They're searching.'

'Keep me posted.' She ran her gaze down the list on the whiteboard. 'What else?'

'I've got something,' Nash called from the end of the table.

They all turned to stare at him, like they'd forgotten he was here, Adam thought.

'A guy could get a complex,' Nash complained. 'Nobody even asked me.'

'Just tell us,' Adam said with an exasperated laugh. Nash had always been able to make him laugh when they'd been on Personal Crimes. Until Paula was murdered in front of them all. It had broken Adam and Nash, just in different ways. And it had damaged Hanson, who'd eventually just focused on keeping them from melting down on the job.

Now they'd all taken a few steps back. At least Adam was happy where he was. He hoped Hanson and Nash were too.

'I found Jolee Cusack's car,' Nash said. 'She did drive it out to Beechmont yesterday to take the big gorilla to pick up the SUV used in the shooting at Buon Cibo. She parked it in the empty lot of a business a block from Clyde's Place. She drove it back to her apartment and parked out front. I found it on the college's security cams. She drove away at ten this morning. Hasn't been back since.'

'Do you know where she drove to?' Trip asked.

'No, but I know where the car is now.' Nash turned his laptop around so that they could see the map on his screen. 'In a used car lot off Route 4, up in Fairfield.'

'Which is nowhere near the university or Beechmont Avenue,' Deacon said.

'Nor the ski slopes in Vermont.' Isenberg picked up her phone and tapped out a text. 'I'm having CSU pick it up and bring it in. Thank you, Detective Currie.'

'You're gonna need a bigger truck,' Nash deadpanned. 'Because

366

there's more. The other two license plates that Mrs Voss photographed the night they left her husband's home? Those cars are there too. Not the same plates. All the plates have been changed out. But all three vehicles are in that same used car lot.'

'How did you track them if the plates have been changed?' Isenberg asked, clearly – if reluctantly – impressed.

'Got the VINs from the registration. They're all new cars. I can track them through the manufacturer.'

'That is fucking awesome,' Scarlett declared. 'I like your friend, Adam.'

Nash chuckled. 'That's all I have. I'd like to go with you to Broderick Voss's place as soon as you have the warrant. Like Hanson, bringing Voss in is why I'm here too.'

Isenberg's phone buzzed on the table. She checked and waved them toward the door. 'And there you are, folks. You have a warrant.' She pulled a set of keys from her pocket. 'Mrs Voss gave me these. The silver one is for the front door. I've got six units standing ready to back you up. Go get the sonofabitch.'

As a group – minus Hanson, who really should have been there by now, Adam thought with an inner frown – they headed for the briefing room door, spilling into the open office area. Which was empty.

Disappointment was his first reaction. Kate must have taken Meredith back to the safe house because the women, the dog, and the grandfather were gone.

Isenberg hesitated, then drew Adam aside, making him frown. 'What's wrong?' he asked, his gut suddenly unsettled.

'Remember when I mentioned entanglements? And that I'd boot you off this case?'

He gritted his teeth. She was going to bust his chops because he took five fucking minutes for himself? But, he told himself, he'd known the risk. 'Yes, ma'am.'

She sighed. 'Meredith apparently hit her head on the van's floor this afternoon.'

His gut went from unsettled to twisted in a heartbeat. 'She said she was fine.'

'She may have thought she was. She may still be. Kate said she has a bump on her head. She's taking her to the ER to get it checked out as a precaution.' Isenberg looked him square in the eye. 'Can you do your job, Detective?'

He closed his eyes briefly. He trusted Kate. Jerking a nod, he met Isenberg's gaze. 'You'll text me as soon as you know anything?'

Approval filled her eyes. 'Of course.'

'All right. I'll text Hanson to meet us at Voss's. If you see him, send him our way.'

'Oh, I will,' Isenberg declared. 'Don't you worry about that.'

Adam nudged his worry over Meredith to the side. Not completely out of his mind, because that wasn't possible. But far enough away that he could focus on his job.

'Wouldn't wanna be Hanson,' Nash murmured as they got into the elevator.

'Truth,' Adam agreed. 'I hope he's okay. It's not like him not to at least check in.'

'Well, if he's not bleeding out somewhere,' Nash said dryly, 'he will be once your lieutenant uses that sharp tongue of hers on him. Not that I'd blame her in the least.'

Adam opened his mouth to defend his boss, then saw the genuine admiration in Nash's eyes. 'Me, either,' he said.

Twenty-one

Cincinnati, Ohio,
Sunday 20 December, 8.15 P.M.

'Shit,' Adam muttered, because Voss was not answering his intercom and both the front and back gates were closed and locked.

Adam hoped Voss was actually inside. The four cops who'd been watching the front and the back gate swore no one had gone in or out since they'd established surveillance the evening before, but Voss was smart. He couldn't have built a successful business otherwise. He was also a sick, perverted asshole and Adam wanted to see him broken and humiliated and afraid, much like his victims had been.

'There's a keypad,' Trip said. 'I can call Mrs Voss and ask her for the code.'

'Do you have her number?' Nash asked. 'I can look it up if you don't.'

'I do,' Trip told him. 'Her sister gave me all of their phone numbers when I checked their security alarm system last night.'

Adam exhaled. Calling Candace Voss was much more logical than the images flitting through Adam's mind – specifically those of him crashing one of the department vehicles through the gates and shoving Voss's fucking head through a fucking wall. Because Voss had stalked Meredith and had maybe tried to have her killed yesterday and quite possibly tried to have them *all* killed that afternoon. Now Meredith was hurt and Adam wanted Voss to hurt much worse.

Shit. I'm losing it. And I can't do that. He needed a few minutes to chill. And maybe to eat something. That usually helped. 'That sounds like a plan,' he said, his voice far calmer and saner than he felt. 'I need to get something from my car.'

Both Trip and Nash gave him sympathetic nods because he'd told them about Meredith. 'Go,' Trip said. 'I'll let you know when we have the codes.'

Grateful, Adam headed back to the car he'd signed out of the department fleet, feeling a bit too vulnerable to drive his own vehicle after being shot at. If he was a target, for whatever reason, a department car lent a small measure of anonymity.

He slid behind the wheel and found one of the power bars Deacon had shoved in his coat pocket, telling him that Faith made sure he never left the house without them. It was thick and stuck in his throat, but ultimately it was fuel and that's what he needed.

Fuel and sleep. *Damn, I'm tired.* The amazing sex at the condo had renewed him, but the few hours' sleep that had followed were not enough, especially since he'd had a sleepless night the night before. And most of the nights before that for the past year. Falling asleep had been so much easier with the booze, and a sudden craving hit him, his mouth gone dry. *I just want to be able to sleep again.*

Which was a dirty lie. One that he'd often told himself during the months he'd crawled into the bottle. *Just enough to sleep.* But the sleep had never been restful. He'd woken up sick and even more tired. He didn't need booze. He just needed peace.

Which he'd felt in Meredith's arms. Soon, he told himself. Soon, he'd fall asleep in her arms and sleep all night. Until then, he had a warrant to serve. A vile snake to arrest.

A snake who threatened what's mine. His chest tightened with a combination of fear and rage that stole his breath. Because Meredith was hurting. *In the hospital. Without me.* Because someone – either Voss or someone connected to him – wanted them dead.

And he needed to put that rage away right now or he really would end up shoving Voss's head through a wall. Then the bastard would get his lawyers to sue and somehow the snake would slither free. *So cool your jets, Kimble. Stay calm.*

At least he knew Meredith was feeling well enough to text. He read the message she'd sent him. *Isenberg told me that you know about the ER. Don't want you to worry. I'm fine. They're prepping me for a CT scan so they can be sure. JUST A PRECAUTION.* Followed by three emojis – a heart, a smiley, and a kiss.

Jesus. He made himself breathe. *A precaution. Just a precaution.*

His pulse was almost back to normal when Hanson's car pulled up behind him with a squeal of brakes. Hanson jumped out and approached so aggressively that Adam got out of his car to see what was wrong.

'Your boss is a fucking piece of work,' Hanson spat. 'Calling me on the phone and summoning me like a fucking kid to the principal's office.'

Adam did not have the time nor the patience for Hanson's tantrum. 'She can be brusque at times, but she's a damn good cop and an even better boss. More importantly, she was right. Get over yourself, Wyatt,' he snapped. 'We're here to do a goddamn job.' And the sooner Adam finished it, the sooner he could be with Meredith.

Hanson was visibly taken aback. 'Who the fuck shitted in your Wheaties?'

Adam pushed the rage back down. He was angry with Voss, not Wyatt Hanson. He *really* needed to get hold of himself. 'Look, Wyatt, I'm sorry. I'm worried right now and . . .' He shook his head. *Focus on the job.* 'I need your help on this. We need to be smart because Voss is a rich sonofabitch with slippery lawyers. This has to be textbook. Neither of us can go in there angry and make a mistake.'

Hanson's expression softened. 'What's wrong? Is it your mom again?'

'No.' Although he owed his mother a phone call, just so she could hear his voice and know he was okay. 'It's Meredith. Dr Fallon, I mean.' He told him about the ER visit. 'I know she's okay, but I'm worried.'

'I understand. I'd feel the same way in your shoes.' His brow furrowed. 'She didn't go alone, did she?'

'No. Kate's got her. Her grandfather and Mallory went with her.'

He smiled ruefully. 'Meredith always has an entourage. I'd probably be in the way.'

Hanson's eyes glinted with humor. 'I doubt that very much,' he said kindly.

The air between them was suddenly calmed and cleared. 'What happened?' Adam asked. 'Where were you all this time?'

Hanson huffed out a breath that hung between them for a second or two. 'I thought I'd seen her. The girl, I mean. But your LT picked that moment to call and give me a ration of shit, and I lost her. Did we get an ID on the victim? Bruiser?'

'Not yet.' Adam frowned. 'Where was Linnie when you lost her?'

'Outside Music Hall. They'd just let out one of the *Nutcracker* performances and there were people everywhere, taking pictures and shit.' Hanson shook his head. 'The crowd spilled into Washington Park and that's where I lost her, because your boss called and demanded I return. I looked down at my phone for the Caller ID and that's when she disappeared. I told the search team where to keep looking, but by then she was long gone.'

Adam sighed. 'That whole area is congested this time of year.' The gentrification of Over-The-Rhine had brought in dozens of restaurants and bars. This time of year they were hopping with revelers and holiday work parties.

'Hey, Adam!' Trip called. 'I got the codes.'

'The gate codes,' Adam explained to Hanson. 'Trip had to get them from Mrs Voss because Mr Voss isn't answering his intercom. Come on. We've got a warrant to serve.'

'What does the warrant cover?' Hanson asked.

'Everything,' Adam said with satisfaction. 'His little girl told us enough to get us unlimited access to his house, office, car, and bank records.'

'Then I'm right behind you,' Hanson said. 'Good job, Adam.'

'Wasn't me. Meredith Fallon got the goods.'

'Hope he didn't change the codes,' Trip said when Adam and Hanson got to the gate.

Trip radioed Deacon, who was with Scarlett at the back gate. 'Back gate code is 0915.'

'Got it,' Deacon replied. 'Let's do it.'

'Front gate code is 0713.' Trip punched it in, and everyone breathed in relief when it began to swing open. Having to call for an armored truck to push through the gates would have taken time.

Adam radioed Deacon. 'We're open here.'

'Us too,' Deacon said. 'We're driving through right now.'

Adam got back in his car and followed the team through the front gate to the wide, circular driveway. On the porch, Adam tapped his radio. 'Going in,' he said. He knocked hard and waited. Nothing. He knocked harder. 'Mr Voss! Police. We need to talk to you.'

Nothing.

'Now what?' Hanson asked.

Adam pulled the house keys from his pocket. 'We go in.'

Hanson blinked. 'Where did you get the keys?'

'His wife gave them to Isenberg.' *Which you'd have known if you'd been at the briefing.* He opened the door and was immediately hit with a blast of heat. And then . . .

'Oh God.' Adam immediately regretted having eaten the power bar because the smell . . . 'Shit.'

Trip grunted his agreement, loosening his tie. 'Makes my eyes fuckin' water.'

The radio crackled. 'Adam?' Deacon asked.

'Somebody or something is very dead,' Adam said. Covering his mouth with a handkerchief, he entered the house and checked the thermostat. 'Heat's on eighty-eight.' He looked around the corner into the living room. 'And there is the master of the house.'

Sprawled on a leather chair was Broderick Voss, a tourniquet still tied to his left arm, the needle still in his vein. 'Fucking hell,' Adam muttered. 'Voss is dead,' he said into the radio. 'Come on in. We need to search for anyone else who might be here, living or not.'

'Coming around to the front,' Deacon said and the radio went quiet.

Trip had crouched next to Voss's body, studying the fingers of his right hand, which were drawn into a claw where they dangled off the arm of the chair. 'Full rigor, so he's been dead at least twelve hours. We know he was alive as of yesterday afternoon because he spoke in front of a room full of political donors.' He turned to look at the gas fireplace behind him, where the flame burned strong. 'The heat being on high and a fire in the fireplace is gonna fuck with the time of death.'

Adam nodded. 'I know. I hope Dr Washington will be able to get us something close.' The ME was damn good, so if anyone could, it was Carrie Washington. 'We can't assume he's the only body in the house,' he added, 'especially since he's had all these parties lately. Trip and Nash, take the upstairs. Hanson, you and I can search this floor. Deacon and Scarlett will take the basement. I've got to make some calls.'

Walking outside, Adam pulled the front door closed behind him and motioned to two of the uniformed officers. 'Each of you stand watch at one of the gates. Nobody comes in unless I clear it, okay? Thanks.' The two cops nodded and took off at a jog.

His first call was to Carrie Washington's office. Carrie herself answered, surprising him, and when he'd informed her that they'd found at least one body and the circumstances, she said she'd be there personally.

'Make sure you keep all doors and windows closed, okay?'

He gave the closed front door a scowl. 'Hurry, please. We'd like to open some windows. It's foul.'

'I understand,' she said. 'See you soon.'

His next call was to Quincy, who sounded out of breath when he answered. 'Need you here at Voss's house,' Adam said. 'He's dead.'

'Fuck,' Quincy said. 'How? For how long?'

'Looks like he OD'd and I don't know yet. Long enough to smell really bad. But the heat's cranked up and the fireplace is going. What's your ETA?'

'Fuck,' Quincy said again, frustrated. 'I took a break to grab a bite. You've kept me running today.'

'Sorry?' Adam said sarcastically, then sighed. 'Look, I really am sorry, but I would appreciate you getting here ASAP.'

'Fine,' Quincy said wearily. 'As soon as I can.'

'Tha—' Adam started, but Quincy had already ended the call, so he dialed Isenberg.

'Well?' she demanded.

'Voss is dead,' he told her, giving her what they knew. 'Carrie's on her way. Hopefully we'll get a decent TOD.'

She sighed heavily. 'I was kind of hoping that you wouldn't find him at home.'

Adam understood. 'I hoped the same because we hadn't heard from him, even after sticking cops in front of his house. I figured if he was home, he'd be pulling the strings somehow. But that's not the case. He's been dead since this morning. At least.'

'So he didn't shoot at you.'

'And he didn't kill Bruiser,' Adam added. 'He is connected, though. Jolee and Linnie were here. And he's connected to Meredith.' Voss had threatened Meredith, terrified his child, and assaulted his wife. 'And . . . I get the feeling he was hiding something big. Hopefully his financials will tell the story.'

Another pregnant silence. 'Do you have something you want to tell me, Adam?'

That I know Voss was being blackmailed? 'That I *want* to? Nope.'

She actually growled at him. 'That you're *going* to tell me?'

'Whatever it was won't help at this point, but his financials will.'

'That's why you wanted them on the warrant? You knew we'd find something?'

'I had a strong hunch.'

She growled again. 'I have a headache,' she said, sounding cranky.

Adam took a look around him to make sure no one was within hearing distance. 'Lynda,' he said quietly. 'I did get a tip. But it just confirmed what we knew – that Voss was hiding something so big that he tried to scare Meredith away from his daughter.'

'I get that. I do. But . . .' Another sigh. 'You just got your head on straight and things are going so well for you. I don't want to see you torpedo your own career because you fucked up and took information you didn't have a warrant to see.'

She'd always had his back. 'I won't fuck it up,' he promised. 'You have my word. Even if I didn't have my head on straight, I wouldn't do that to you.'

Again the silence. Then another sigh. 'Okay. I'll let it go. For now.'

'Thank you.'

'Get those financials, Adam.'

'Yes, ma'am. Gotta go.'

He ended the call and drew in a last breath of fresh air. *Time to deal with Voss.*

Cincinnati, Ohio,
Sunday 20 December, 8.20 P.M.

He quickly texted Mike. *Where r u?*

Downtown. Searching for ur runaway hooker.

Your runaway hooker. The jab irritated the fuck out of him. He and Mike needed to come to an understanding about who was the boss. And it wasn't Mike. *Have a job for you.*

The reply was quick and flippant. *I live to serve.*

He rolled his eyes. For a guy who'd already fucked up twice today, Mike was being an arrogant asshole. *Use a rifle. Take night goggles. Stay far away. Sending you descriptions of targets.* He typed furiously for a minute, then hit SEND.

A slight pause. *Thot u didn't trust me w/that one.*

He didn't, but he didn't have much choice. *Am busy. Don't fuck it up. Here is location.* He pasted a map link, then hit SEND and waited for Mike to assess the map.

The reply took about a minute this time. *Why rifle? Will b difficult shot.*

He smirked. *U r the best. U said so urself. Too hard?*

Fuck u. Why rifle?

He considered his answer. *Because targets r accompanied by a shot better than u and me together*, he finally typed. *Stay back and have escape ready.*

OK fine, Mike replied, the huff of irritation nearly audible in the text.

376

He shook his head. Hopefully Mike would get the job done this time.

Cincinnati, Ohio,
Sunday 20 December, 8.20 P.M.

'I *told* you that I was fine,' Meredith said as Kate pushed her in a wheelchair through the hospital hallway, Mallory trailing behind. Since they were already in the hospital – and they'd re-donned their wigs – they'd decided to visit Agent Troy. 'I do not have a concussion, just a damn bump. I can walk perfectly fine.'

'Hush,' Kate said. 'You're lucky they didn't keep you overnight for observation.' She looked over her shoulder. 'You okay back there, Mal? You look a little green.'

Kate stopped them outside Troy's room and Meredith drew Mallory around the chair so that she could see her face. Mallory's face was pale, panic filling her eyes. 'You having trouble being in a hospital again, honey?' Meredith asked her.

Mallory swallowed hard. 'I thought I'd be all right, but this is bringing back a lot of very bad memories.' Because the monster who'd held Mallory captive for six long years, forcing her into online child pornography, had tried to kill her when she finally escaped. She'd spent several days in this very hospital last summer, recovering.

Kate bit her lip. 'I'm sorry, honey. I should have sent you back out with Clarke.'

Meredith's grandfather had refused to budge from her side until the doctor said she was okay, but once that happened, he'd hightailed it out the door, saying he'd smoke his pipe while walking Cap. He didn't like hospitals any more than the rest of them.

Meredith knew that Mallory would not have been comfortable leaving her and Kate, even though she seemed to like Clarke very much. It was still too soon for her to be comfortable alone with strangers, but that would come in time.

Meredith squeezed Mallory's hand. 'Papa and Cap are turning into popsicles out there. Let's just say hi to Agent Troy and then we'll go.'

Kate knocked lightly, then pushed open the door and— 'Oh, I'm sorry.'

Quincy Taylor stood next to Troy's bed and he looked . . . furious. So did Troy, actually. Both men blinked hard when they saw them in the doorway.

'Can I help you?' Troy asked.

'You have the wrong room,' Quincy snapped at the same time.

Meredith looked from Quincy to Troy. It didn't take a shrink to know the two had been arguing. 'It's Meredith.' She pointed to the fake hair. 'This is just a wig.'

Kate leaned over her shoulder. 'Kate and Mallory too. We just came to say hi, but we can come back.'

'We didn't mean to interrupt anything,' Meredith added awkwardly.

'You didn't.' Troy forced a smile. 'Come in. Why are you in a wheelchair, Meredith?'

'Bumped my head.' She glared over her shoulder at Kate. 'But I'm *fine*.'

Quincy grabbed his backpack and slung it over his shoulder. 'That's good to hear. If you'll excuse me, I was just leaving anyway. I have to get back to work.'

Kate pulled the wheelchair out of the doorway and they gave him room to leave. Then Kate pushed Meredith into the room and marched straight to Troy's bed, where she began giving him a stern lecture. But Mallory stopped only a foot inside the room and rested against the wall, eyes closed. Trembling. She was fighting a panic attack.

'Hey,' Meredith whispered. 'You're doing great.'

'I'm a coward,' Mallory said from behind clenched teeth.

'You are the farthest thing from a coward on this planet,' Meredith declared.

'I can't even look at the hospital bed.'

'Well, this isn't exactly anybody's happy place,' Meredith said dryly, relieved when Mallory's lips twitched. 'Before I interrupted you, what were you thinking about?'

'Oh.' She looked away, embarrassed. 'I was thinking about Cap.

Sometimes I just pretend I'm petting him. Which sounds dumb, I know.'

'No, it doesn't. It sounds very smart. Mallory, look at me.' Meredith waited until the girl's dark eyes were open and focused. 'You know what PTSD is, right?'

She nodded. 'It's what happens to soldiers.'

'It also happens to victims of crime.' They'd discussed this in therapy so many times in the past, but Mallory never remembered. 'It doesn't matter what caused the trauma. When it happens to you, your brain gets locked there. The emotions you felt at the time, they return and then—'

'I'm *there*,' Mallory interrupted in a small voice. 'I'm back *there*. And I always tell myself that I'll never go back there, that I'm strong. That I survived.'

'You are,' Meredith said fiercely. 'You did.'

'But I keep going back there,' Mallory said, her voice pitching higher.

'You know that today is the first time you've acknowledged that?' Mallory grimaced. 'Because I'm a coward.'

'No, because you're smart.'

Dark eyes flew open. 'What?'

'Look, if you know a stove is hot, are you going to touch it?'

'Well, maybe once,' Mallory allowed.

'Right?' Meredith smiled at her. 'That stove is gonna hurt. And what smart person wants to hurt? Thinking of yourself as being a victim hurts, because you have to give that thing that happened to you a name. Makes it more real.'

'Doesn't matter if I give it a name or not. I can't make it un-happen.'

'True. But what if you could get to a place where thinking about it didn't throw you back? What if you could tell your story like it happened to someone else?'

'I do!'

'Not really, honey. If you did, it wouldn't hurt so much.' She cupped Mallory's cheek. 'If petting Cap makes you happy, why haven't you asked for a dog of your own?'

Mallory blinked, as if the thought had never occurred to her. 'I could have a dog?'

'You'd have to ask Wendi, of course, but . . . why not?'

'I can't feed a dog. I don't have any money. I can't even feed myself.' Again her voice pitched up, and once again she clamped her lips together and began to breathe.

'I think we can find a way for you to afford a dog.'

'I'm not taking any more charity,' Mallory said through her teeth. 'Especially not from you. I take from you. Everybody takes from you. And you just keep giving.'

Oh, mercy, Meredith thought. *I really need to get this girl a new therapist. I'm way too close.* She'd never suspected Mallory hid all those emotions. 'Okay. Wow.'

'And now I've hurt your feelings,' Mallory said wearily. 'I'm sorry.'

'No, you didn't hurt my feelings. But you did surprise me. How about we figure this out once we get out of the hospital that was giving you hives five minutes ago.'

Mallory's eyes widened comically. 'I forgot. I forgot I hated this place.'

Meredith's lips curved. 'I know.'

Mallory glanced to her right, where Kate and Troy waited silently. Her cheeks darkened with sudden shame. 'I forgot about them too. They heard everything.'

It was true, and Meredith considered saying that Kate and Troy wouldn't think less of her, which was also true, but probably no more helpful. Briefly she considered admitting to her own insecurities, but that wasn't appropriate, either. Until she transitioned Mallory to another therapist, there were still professional proprieties.

Plus, Meredith had never experienced what Mallory had. None of them had. The girl's abuse had been broadcasted over the Internet, her privacy stolen along with her innocence and sense of self. Now, her healing had been witnessed as well.

Way to go, Fallon. Nice job. She opened her mouth to reply, but was saved by Troy.

'Mallory, would you come over here, please?' he asked.

Slowly Mallory complied, stopping when she got close enough to grip the bed rails.

Troy caught Mallory's gaze and held it. 'I did hear what you were saying. But there's no shame in it. What you're feeling isn't different than anyone else would feel after what you went through. You think none of us are scared, that we don't have to deal with our pasts and our panic? Just because we're cops doesn't mean we don't suffer from it too.'

Mallory lifted her chin. 'It's not the same as mine.'

'You're right, but it's never the same. The crimes aren't the same and the way we deal – and heal – isn't the same.'

Mallory started to protest, but stopped, narrowing her eyes. 'We?'

'Do you think I'm a coward, Mallory?' he asked, holding her gaze.

'No,' Mallory replied without hesitation.

Troy smiled a little. 'I'm betting you're thinking, fine, none of these guys really understand, because they've never been a real victim of a violent crime. Is that fair?'

'Yes. Well, maybe except for Faith. She has a scar.' She pointed to her throat. 'Here.'

Faith had been a victim of a violent crime. Meredith knew all the details. She knew that Faith still had nightmares, some that she didn't even tell Deacon about, because she knew it would hurt him. Meredith also knew that Faith wasn't the only one of their group to have been victimized. And from the expression on Troy's face, it was also true for him.

'Not everyone wears their scars where you can see them, Mallory,' he said. 'Do you know what gay bashing is?'

Mallory nodded, but when he said no more, her eyes widened. 'That happened to you?'

Gay bashing? Oh no. Poor Troy. Meredith couldn't stand the thought that someone had hurt him like that. Kate must not have known about his assault either, because she was shocked into silence.

Troy wasn't paying attention to Meredith or Kate. His focus was on Mallory. 'When I was fifteen. They didn't call it that back then, of course. I spent a month in the hospital. My injuries were . . . extensive. And when I got out of the hospital, I really didn't want to think about it. I just wanted to go forward and never think about it again, but I couldn't because I had doctors and physical therapy and follow-up visits. And because the entire town knew. It had been written up in the local paper and everyone knew. They knew everything that had happened to me. A lot of them laughed about it. It was . . . humiliating, to say the least.'

'How did you deal?' Mallory asked, subdued now.

'I didn't, not for years. Therapy wasn't really a thing back then, not for sons of blue-collar guys who worked in a steel mill. You sucked it up and kept it in. And every time I saw one of the people who'd attacked me, I'd get physically ill. Every time I had to walk by the place it happened, I'd throw up. So I decided that no one would ever be able to hurt me again. I worked out, bulked up. Studied hard, went to college. Joined the FBI. Thought I'd made it, that I'd dealt. But every now and then something happens. I see something or hear something, and it takes me back. Just like you.'

'How do you deal with it now?'

He smiled at her. 'Went to therapy twenty years too late, but I went. And I learned how to tell that story like it happened to somebody else.' He chuckled at her expression. 'You don't believe me, do you? Look at the blood pressure monitor. It's normal and it has been this entire time. Do I like to talk about this? No. I've never even told Kate and I'm gonna take another ration of shit for that on top of the one she just gave me because I didn't tell her about this.' He gestured to his most recent injuries.

'There,' he said kindly when Mallory grinned. 'There's the smile I was fishing for. Mallory, there is no shame in being a victim. By definition, you didn't do anything wrong. Now you've got to deal the best way you can. You've got an amazing support structure, so use it. Use us. We want you to succeed and be happy.'

'Okay.' Mallory leaned down to kiss his cheek. 'Thank you. For telling me.'

'Yeah,' Meredith echoed. 'Thank you. You should be the shrink.'

Troy snorted. 'I'm not *that* nice.' He glanced up at Kate. 'I'm sorry I didn't call you about this thing today. I was freaked out about going into a hospital, because I don't like them either. I've learned to deal with visiting other people, because I can leave whenever I want, but ambulances and these damn beds? They make me cranky.'

'I understand,' Kate said. 'I was just worried about you.'

'Don't be. I'm fine. And visiting hours are over. You guys need to get your asses out of here and somewhere safe.'

Meredith got out of the chair and nudged Kate out of the way so that she could kiss Troy's other cheek. 'I wanted to thank you. You saved our lives today. You're a hero. Bona fide.'

His cheeks grew charmingly rosy, even as he looked away. 'Just doing my job.'

Her lipstick had left a smudge on Troy's cheek, so Meredith leaned forward and planted a harder kiss on the top of his newly bald head. 'There.'

Troy scowled. 'You did not just put a lip print on my head, did you?'

'I did,' Meredith said. 'What are you gonna do about it?'

He rolled his eyes. 'Get outta here, all of you.'

They obeyed, Meredith returning to the chair as they said their goodbyes. When they stopped at the elevator, Kate typed a text into her phone. 'Van's waiting downstairs.' The elevator opened and it was thankfully empty. Meredith didn't want to deal with any more people tonight.

I'm tired, she thought as the elevator opened and they made their way through the lobby toward the sliding glass doors. And her head still hurt. All she wanted to do was go back to the condo and go to sleep in the bed that hopefully still smelled like Adam. He'd eventually finish his work and he'd come to her and then they would—

Kate stopped short as soon as they got outside. 'The van is supposed to be here. I just texted them that we were coming down and they texted back that they were here.' She pulled Meredith out of the wheelchair and shoved her back toward the glass doors. 'Get inside and get down. *Now!*'

Meredith's feet refused to move, frozen in panic. *Papa.* Papa was in the van.

'Now, Meredith!' Kate roared. 'Get inside.'

Meredith turned to grab Mallory, but . . . 'Where's Mallory? She was right behind us.'

'Get *inside*,' Kate gritted, then went still. 'Where *is* Mallory?'

The two of them looked at each other in horror. 'Mallory!' Meredith shouted.

'*Inside*,' Kate ordered, taking off at a run toward the front parking lot. 'I'll find her.'

No. No way was Meredith hiding. 'Mallory!' Running in the direction opposite the one Kate had taken, she ran over the grass and around the piles of snow until she turned the building's corner. And her heart stopped.

Mallory, whiter than a ghost, was being dragged away by a man wearing a ski mask.

He had one arm over Mallory's throat and held a gun to her head.

Meredith's brain turned off and her feet moved.

Cincinnati, Ohio,
Sunday 20 December, 8.45 P.M.

'No!' Meredith shouted at the man. 'You can't have her!'

She continued to run, ignoring the pounding in her head and the even harder pounding of her heart. Where was everyone? No one walked around and many of the cars had inches of snow built up over their windshields, like they hadn't been moved in weeks.

Overflow parking, she realized. This lot was much farther from the entrance than the other lots. Nobody wanted to walk that far, especially in the cold. And so this back parking lot was nearly empty, the man's SUV parked away from the few other cars.

The SUV was black. *Just like the one from yesterday.*

'Wait!' Panting, she slowed down when she was about ten feet away, her hands up, palms up. 'You don't want her. Take me instead. *Please.*'

The man laughed as he reached behind him to open the back passenger door. 'But I don't want you.' He threw Mallory to the floorboard where she curled into a ball. Meredith took a few steps forward then froze when he turned to face her, his gun now pointed at her. 'Or maybe I do,' he said salaciously. 'Hands up where I can see them.'

Swallowing, Meredith made herself breathe. And think. Because everything had just fallen into place, her ears ringing with the thunderous bang of a mental gavel.

We all thought they wanted me yesterday. But it was Mallory all along. I'm so stupid.

She had been stupid, but she wasn't going to be now. She still had her gun. Adam had never taken it from her as they'd come up from the parking garage in an elevator that required a key, bypassing the CPD lobby with its normal security checks. She'd excused herself to an ER restroom, transferring it from her bra holster to her coat pocket before they'd taken her back to an exam room. But she couldn't get to it now. He'd shoot her before she could get her hand into her pocket.

'I said *hands up*,' the man growled. 'Or I will kill you where you stand.'

Meredith did as he'd demanded. *Kate, where the fuck are you?* She glanced into the car to where Mallory lay, unmoving. 'Let her go. She's been through enough.'

The man didn't answer. Just reached for the collar of Meredith's coat.

'Freeze. FBI. Drop the gun. Now.'

Thank God. Meredith's knees buckled, hitting the asphalt before she could stop her fall. *Finally.* Kate came around the SUV to stand behind him, shoving her gun into his back.

'I *said* drop the fucking gun,' Kate commanded.

Wishing she could close her eyes, but unable to look away, Meredith watched as the man's gloved hand opened and the gun clattered to the asphalt.

Kate kicked it under the SUV. 'Very good. Now, on your knees. Mer, you okay?' she asked when the man had dropped to his knees.

'Yeah,' Meredith said, but it came out a hoarse grunt. She tried to moisten her mouth but every last drop of spit had dried up. 'I'm all right.'

'Good. I want you to get Mallory out of the SUV, and the two of you to start walking.'

Meredith obeyed, giving Mallory a little shake when she didn't immediately respond. 'Come on, honey. We're getting out of here.'

Mallory stirred, but didn't get out of the car. Meredith shoved her shoulder under the girl's arm and wound the arm around her own neck. Half lifting, half dragging, she pulled Mallory from the SUV and started walking toward a cluster of parked cars. *Cover.*

Meredith glanced around, fearing the man was not alone. Quickly she pulled her gun from her pocket. 'Mallory, baby, you have to walk. I can't carry you the whole way. You have to help me.'

Mallory's back straightened a few degrees and her feet began to shuffle. It wasn't a full walk, but it was enough to allow Meredith to pick up their pace.

'Are you hurt? Did he shoot you?' Meredith tried to see if there was any blood on Mallory's clothes, but it was too dark. Finally reaching the parked cars, she dragged her behind a minivan and gently guided her to the ground.

Just in time to hear a shot followed by a nauseating crunching sound.

Kate. Meredith inched toward the rear of the minivan until she could see around it. *Oh no. God no.* Kate lay in a heap on the asphalt near the SUV.

And the man was charging Meredith like a bull. Not letting herself think, Meredith racked her gun, bringing it into position as she'd practiced hundreds of times. And she pulled the trigger.

The man staggered back a few steps, staring down at his chest in disbelief, but he didn't bleed. *A vest*, she realized. *He's wearing a vest. Dammit.*

He raised his gaze, eyes narrowing in fury. He took a few more determined steps toward her, so she pulled the trigger again, hitting his thigh. He stumbled, his mouth opening on a cry she couldn't hear because her ears were ringing from the gunfire. But she'd hit him! She felt keen satisfaction until he disappeared between two of the vehicles.

Shit. Mallory. Meredith hurried back to her, crouching over her seconds before the man reappeared from behind the boxy Scion parked just beyond the minivan.

'You can't have her!' Meredith snarled and fired at his head, but her hand was shaking so badly that the shot went wild. Instantly she dropped her aim, firing again at his chest. Then his legs. *One* bullet had to hit. *Just one. Please God.*

But nothing did because he kept coming and she kept firing until— *Click click.* Meredith pulled the trigger and . . . nothing.

She'd emptied the magazine and he was still approaching. Except now he'd straightened – and was coming faster.

'You're gonna be sorry you fucked with me,' he said, his words barely audible because all the shots had dulled her hearing. 'I'll play with you a while before I kill you. But first, you'll watch me play with her.'

Meredith wanted to run. Wanted to flee. But she didn't because Mallory was lying on the ground, so very still.

'Then you'll have to kill me,' she shouted, 'because I'm not letting you take her.'

Meredith hunched down over Mallory, making herself dead weight when she felt his hand clench in the back of her coat, so that when he tossed her, she rolled instead of flying through the air.

'No!' she yelled, crawling back toward Mallory, because he was reaching for her.

Meredith halted when Mallory suddenly moved, her hand rising to his face, silver glinting in the light of the parking lot lamps. *A knife.* Mallory had a knife.

The knife sliced through the man's mask and even through the dull roar in her ears, Meredith could hear his scream. He reared up, staggering backward.

Another shot rang out and the man jerked to the side, his right hand instantly reaching to clamp his left upper arm.

Two more shots fired in rapid succession. 'Step away from the women! Now!'

Meredith knew that voice, even muffled and muted. *Kate. She's not dead. Oh God, she's not dead.* On her hands and knees, Meredith collapsed, her arms no longer supporting her weight. Her cheek scraped against the asphalt, but she didn't care. The voice sounded far away, but it was Kate.

He ran, the man. He backed up and fled, dragging his injured leg behind him.

Sirens filtered through the roaring in her ears and Meredith burst into tears. *Help. Help was coming.*

Shaking arms gathered her close. When she looked up, it was Mallory's dark eyes that looked down at her. Mallory's arms that held her.

But Meredith couldn't stop crying. She tried, she really tried. Two more arms encircled her and Meredith could smell Kate's perfume and it made her cry even harder.

The three of them huddled together until another thought penetrated the haze of her mind. 'Papa.' Meredith lurched away, looking around wildly. 'Where's Papa?'

'He's okay. He got hit on the head, but he's okay. I'm not lying to you.' Kate held out a hand, like she was calming a feral animal. Which was probably fair. With her heart slamming against her ribs and a bad case of the shakes, Meredith felt like a skittish deer.

Then Meredith noticed the slice in Kate's sleeve and that the fabric was dark and shiny. 'You're hurt,' she said numbly.

'I've had worse.' Kate leaned back against the minivan and closed her eyes as people began to rush to their sides. 'The cavalry is here.'

Cincinnati, Ohio,
Sunday 20 December, 9.25 P.M.

The Gruber Academy. Linnea looked up at the sign with grim determination. It had taken her almost three hours to walk the two miles from downtown to the proper-looking school in the tony neighborhood, because she'd had to stop to hide and rest. And wash Butch's blood and brains from her face and hair with water from a garden hose she'd found hooked up next to a loading dock behind a bar. The water had been icy, but being clean had been worth the discomfort. Plus she no longer was as noticeable. People covered in blood tended to draw stares.

Now she needed shelter. The school was surrounded by a chain-link fence that was taller than she was, but secured with a chain that was a foot too long, so there was a gap between the gates. Her sucky appetite was going to work in her favor for once. She slipped through, determined to find somewhere to hide while she waited to see if she saw *him* arrive to pick up or drop off his daughter, Ariel. It didn't have to be warm. Just not exposed.

She found what she'd been searching for in the minibus parked behind the school. It was a converted van. Older, but freshly painted. Older was good, in this case. Less likely to have an alarm. Getting the door open wouldn't be a problem. She'd lived on the street for a few years before being sucked into the system and had stolen her share of stuff to survive. She wasn't proud of that fact, but hoped she hadn't lost her touch.

She gripped the bus's antenna and twisted, relieved when it unscrewed. She didn't want to actually break it. If her years with Andy had taught her anything, it was that she was as respectable as the respect she gave others.

Andy. The wave of unexpected grief nearly cut her at the knees. *I miss you, Andy. So much.* She'd avenge the man who'd loved her unconditionally if it was the last thing she did. The vow gave her the strength to continue. She removed the antenna and surveyed the door locks through the bus's windows.

Then laughed out loud. The bus was unlocked. *Only in a rich neighborhood*, she thought. People thought fences and gates made them safer. They were lucky that all she wanted was a place to sleep. She started to replace the antenna, then reconsidered. It would make a decent weapon if she were attacked up close.

At least Butch wouldn't be coming for her again. She climbed in, closing the door behind her and hoping like hell there were no cameras announcing her presence. She moved to the back of the van and wanted to cry.

Blankets. Stacks of blankets. And bottles of water. And protein bars.

It wasn't a real bed in a warm shelter, but it was more than enough. Fashioning a bed and pillow from the blankets, she took her gun from her pocket and slid it under the pillow. Just in case. Then she let herself sleep.

Twenty-two

Cincinnati, Ohio,
Sunday 20 December, 9.30 P.M.

Adam shoved through the crowd, muttering 'Excuse me' when he earned a dirty look, but he really didn't care. He went through the electric doors and headed straight to the ER, flashing his shield when a staff member tried to stop him from entering the area.

Meredith is alive. She is okay. She is not harmed. Mallory was the target all along, but she is okay. She is not harmed either. And I'm going to kill Kate. Except she is *hurt.*

The words had been cycling through his mind from the moment he heard the call go out over the radio. *Shots fired. Possible hostage situation. Casualties.* He and Deacon had dropped everything, leaving the Voss crime scene in the capable hands of Trip and Scarlett.

Of course, Adam knew he'd just proven Isenberg right. He couldn't lead this case, not with the way he felt about Meredith. But he'd fight that battle later. Now, he needed to see her. To touch her so that he could know she was all right.

At least Deacon had his head on straight. Adam had left his cousin in the parking lot, managing their newest crime scene. He'd barely listened to anything he'd been told.

I need to see her. He looked in the small windows in the door of each ER bay until he found Meredith, her dark red hair in striking contrast to the white of her pillow, and his knees actually buckled. He straightened them immediately, locking them in place. He couldn't fall apart. Not yet. Not until he got her back to safety and he was alone.

391

Then he'd fucking fall apart.

He stood by her closed door, looking in the window, getting a grip on himself. Meredith lay in the bed, her eyes closed. She wore a pair of faded blue hospital scrubs. Mallory sat at her side, also dressed in scrubs, clutching her hand. Both of them were alarmingly pale and Meredith had a raw scrape on her cheek that was starting to bruise.

A growl rose in his throat. Sonofabitch had hurt her. *Again.*

But she's alive. He kept telling himself that. *She's alive.*

The two Feds who'd been on guard duty hadn't fared as well. One was in serious condition, the other critical. Both had been shot with a silenced gun and handcuffed. Their radios, phones, and service weapons had been stolen.

The shooter was in the wind, having made his escape in a stolen car. This time, though, he'd left things behind – his SUV, which Kate had disabled, his rifle, which Kate had thankfully stolen, and most importantly, his DNA. There was blood all over the asphalt, most of it his. Some of it was Kate's. None of it was Mallory's or Meredith's.

Adam leaned against the door, resting his forehead on the wood, trying to gather his composure. *Three times. Three times now I've almost lost her.*

'Adam?'

He rolled his head sideways to see Dani coming out of the ER bay next door. He frowned. 'What are you doing here?'

'I'm Kate's secondary emergency contact,' she said. 'I've already called Decker.'

'How's he doing?' Adam asked, now feeling totally numb.

Dani rubbed his back, her touch so soothing that his eyes stung for no good reason. 'Like you'd expect. He's frantic, but she's talked to him on the phone, so he knows she's *physically* okay. Mostly. Her arm's a mess. The guy had a knife. It took eighteen stitches to close the wound, but there doesn't appear to be any permanent damage.'

Adam blinked hard, his forehead still resting on the door. It was like his head weighed four hundred pounds. He couldn't seem to hold it up. 'Physically?'

'Emotionally, she's a wreck,' Dani said quietly. 'This happened on her watch and . . . well, I've never seen her like this.'

'What exactly *did* happen?' Adam asked.

'You need to ask her. I'm just here to give back rubs,' she said, then kissed his cheek. 'Convince yourself that Mer's okay, then talk to Kate. And be gentle with her.'

A wave of guilt crashed over him. 'I'm sorry, Dani,' he whispered. 'I'm so sorry.'

Her smile was sweet. 'For what?'

'For being such an asshole this past year that you'd think you had to tell me that.'

She rubbed her cheek against his upper arm, like a cat nuzzling its human. 'I accept your apology. You were in pain. I only hope that one day you'll tell me why.'

'I will. But I can't right now.'

'I know, honey. Go on in and see Mer. You'll both feel better.'

'Okay.' He pushed himself off the door. 'Wait. Where's Clarke?'

'Two doors down. They want to check him out before they release him. He might have a concussion, and at his age they're going to proceed cautiously.' Her cheeks grew abruptly flushed. 'Diesel's in with him, so he's not alone.'

'But Diesel hates hospitals.'

Dani winced. 'I know. Poor guy. But he's managing.'

Because he's needed. Adam understood that all too well. 'Mallory's sitting in there with Meredith, so I assume she's unhurt.'

'Again, physically unhurt. At the end of it all, Mallory saved Meredith by slashing the shooter's face, but she's not really *there* right now. Close as we can figure it, she was kind of catatonic with Meredith standing between her and the shooter. He threw Meredith off her – that's where the contusion on Meredith's face came from – and that apparently shocked Mallory into action.' Dani sighed. 'But she's crawled back into herself again. Hasn't said another word.'

'Dammit.' He blinked hard to clear his head. *Mallory is the target.* He was furious with himself for missing it, for not even considering it after the restaurant shooting. But Andy had pointed his gun at *Meredith* and the second shot was aimed at *Meredith*. And Voss had been involved, somehow. And he'd been stalking *Meredith*.

Still, I should have at least considered it. Goddammit.

Dani patted his shoulder. 'Why are you still standing here?'

He opened his mouth, but no words came out because Dani was right. He'd sped to the hospital like a bat out of hell, his only objective to see her, to touch her. But now that he was here? He stood outside her door, unable to push it open.

He closed his eyes, shuddering out a breath. 'I almost lost her. Again. And . . . I don't know what to say to her.'

'You don't have to say anything. Just hold her. Let her know you're there.'

He shook his head miserably. 'She's there for everyone. How do I be there for her?' He opened his eyes, met Dani's as she smiled at him kindly. 'I don't know if I can.'

'You don't know if you can, or you don't know if you can without breaking down?'

'The second one,' he admitted. 'She's been through enough tonight without watching me cry like a . . .' He cut himself off before he said 'like a girl.'

'Like a *person* who cares about another *person*?' she asked. 'Adam, your father was *wrong*. It's okay to have feelings. And it's okay to cry. If you go in there and break down, hell, if you cry like Niagara-freaking-Falls, that's okay. The world continues to spin. Now get your ass in there. Don't make me tell you again,' she added in a mock-scolding tone.

He nodded, squaring his shoulders. He could do this. He could be Meredith's strength tonight. Except for the Niagara-freaking-Falls part. He didn't cry. He just . . . didn't.

Drawing a breath, he pushed the door open and stepped into the tiny little room. Tongue-tied for several hard beats of his heart, he settled for a soft, 'Hey.'

Meredith opened her eyes with a start. 'Adam.' Her eyes welled, her voice breaking. 'I'm sorry. I'm so sorry.'

He wasn't aware of moving, but he must have because he was sitting on the bed, dragging her into his arms, burying his face in her hair. Whispering words he couldn't hear over the pounding in his ears. 'Not your fault, baby. Not your fault. Why are you sorry?'

She was shaking her head. Her whole body was shaking, so he held her tighter. 'I shouldn't have come here. I knew it was just a headache. We never should have come.'

'Sweetheart.' He rocked her where they sat. 'You're hurt and you're scared, so I'm going to give you a pass on that very ridiculous thing you just said. Of course you should have come. This is a hospital, and you were hurt. Unless you're a soothsayer, you could not have predicted any of this. So stop blaming *you* and start listening to *me*.' He pulled back, tugging her chin up so that she looked at him, her eyes wild with regret and residual fear. 'You're all right. Mallory's all right and Kate and your grandfather both got a little banged up, but they'll be all right too.'

'The Feds?' Meredith challenged. 'They might die.'

Adam wondered how the shooter had gotten the jump on two Feds, but kept the question to himself for now. 'But they're not dead yet.' He swiped under her eyes with his thumbs, taking care with her scraped cheek. He kissed her mouth tenderly. 'You did not invite a sociopath to grab Mallory any more than you invited Andy Gold to try to kill the two of you yesterday. Okay?'

He waited until she nodded, then gave her another soft kiss. 'Okay,' he said. He glanced at Mallory, who stared at him with the disconcerting intensity of one of the *Children of the Corn*. 'We have learned one extremely valuable fact tonight. You weren't the target at Buon Cibo yesterday, Meredith. Mallory was.'

Meredith nodded, sniffling. 'I know. I begged him to take me instead, but he told me he didn't want me.'

Adam's blood ran cold. He could see her offering herself in trade all too clearly. 'Start at the beginning. Tell me what happened.'

Cincinnati, Ohio,
Sunday 20 December, 9.40 P.M.

Meredith finished relaying everything that she knew, deleting anything she'd said that remotely resembled an offer to sacrifice herself. Adam had gone so very still when she'd told him that she'd begged the gunman to take her instead. He'd backed away then, his

395

expression carefully blank, so very controlled. Like if he let himself go, he'd shatter.

So she didn't tell him about any of the other things she'd said.

'I kept shooting,' she finished. 'I know I hit him at least twice in the chest, but my shots may have gone wide there at the end. My hands were shaking,' she admitted. 'He just kept coming. He wouldn't stop.' Her voice had trembled, so she paused and dug deep for her composure. 'I either missed completely, or he was that determined. Maybe both.'

'And then?' he asked brusquely, but he took her hand and held it between his.

That helped. So much. She drew a breath. 'And then I was out of bullets so I just . . . waited.' He shuddered, but didn't break eye contact. 'He pushed me aside and that's when Mallory cut him with her knife. He was . . . demented. Screaming at us.'

'But still wearing his mask?' he asked.

'Yes. I never saw his face. Just his eyes, but it was dark and I couldn't tell you what color they were. Well,' she frowned, thinking. 'I did see his jaw, because Mallory got him with the knife. Part of the mask was ripped back and he was bleeding. He didn't have any noticeable markings, though. No beard or scars or anything.'

'Did you see his skin?'

'Yes. It was pale. He was definitely Caucasian. Anyway, he reared up, yelling, and that's when Kate shot him in the arm. I . . .' She closed her eyes, the emotions rushing back. 'I'd thought Kate was dead. She was crumpled on the ground and I'd heard a shot and then a crunching noise. I thought he'd thrown her against the SUV. I don't know what happened.'

'I'll talk to her when we're done,' he said evenly. 'But she's going to be okay. Dani said she needed a lot of stitches, but there didn't seem to be any permanent damage.'

'Oh God,' Meredith breathed. 'That's so good to hear. Is Decker coming?'

'Dani's called him. I'm sure he is.' He squeezed her hand. 'Then Kate shot the attacker?'

'Yeah. His arm was kind of hanging there and he made a run for it. Then I heard the sirens and, I mean, it was like . . . I lost it then.' She looked at Mallory. 'And then Mallory was holding me and I knew she was okay, and then Kate came and we just . . . We were done.'

He drew a breath through his nose, his nostrils flaring. His jaw was clamped so tight that it was a wonder she didn't hear his teeth cracking. He blinked slowly, several times. Gathering his control, his composure, much like she had.

Finally, he turned to Mallory. 'Do you have anything to add, honey?' he asked, his tone so gentle that Meredith had to shove back a sudden sob that took her by surprise.

Meredith didn't expect Mallory to say a word. She hadn't during the entire ordeal. But Mallory nodded.

'They saved me,' she whispered. 'Mer and Kate. Mer wouldn't let him have me. She did beg him to take her instead. And I was so scared that I couldn't tell her to stop. I just lay there, like a useless slug.' Self-contempt dripped from her barely audible words.

'Mallory—' Meredith started, but Mallory whipped her hand up. 'My turn,' she gritted out. 'It is my turn to talk.'

Meredith pressed back into the pillow, startled. 'Okay.'

'She ran after me and offered to trade herself. And when Kate came and held her gun to the man's head, Meredith grabbed me out of the SUV and carried me for . . . I don't know how far. I kept telling myself to move. *Move. Help.* But it was like I was frozen.'

'But you did move,' Meredith said softly. 'You did help.'

'Not enough.' Mallory turned so that she spoke to the wall. 'What she's not telling you is that she told him that he'd have to kill her first. I thought he was going to.'

Adam's eyes darted to Meredith's face and there was no disguising his anguish. He swallowed hard. Then he drew a breath and the anguish tempered, morphed. Became something like pride. The pressure on her hand increased until it was almost painful.

'Any of us would have done the same, Mallory,' he said, still so gentle.

Oh God. This is the man I knew a year ago. This is the man I've waited for. Meredith's eyes welled and she blinked quickly to clear them.

Mallory's lips trembled. 'Why?'

His smile was so damn sweet it nearly broke her heart. 'Because you're ours now,' he said. 'And we take care of what's ours.'

And that, Meredith thought, was that. Her heart he'd nearly broken . . . it belonged to him, cracks and all. To take care of and to keep. She'd never really had any choice.

Bowing her head, Mallory wrapped her arms around herself, her sobs quiet, yet forceful. 'I thought he was going to kill you.'

Meredith smoothed Mallory's hair. 'But he didn't. Because *you* saved *me*.'

'That was remarkably brave,' Adam added. 'And we're all grateful.' He cleared his throat. '*I'm* grateful,' he added gruffly.

Locking eyes with his, Meredith brought their joined hands to her cheek and held them there. His eyes were no longer remote and expressionless, no longer filled with anguish or even pride. They burned with something far more. He rubbed a thumb over her lips and for a moment it was like they were alone in a lovely bubble.

Then Mallory looked up, her eyes red and swollen. 'I knew him.'

Cincinnati, Ohio,
Sunday 20 December, 9.50 P.M.

I knew him. Adam exchanged a shocked look with Meredith at Mallory's whispered words. She hadn't known either.

'You knew the man who tried to abduct you tonight?' he asked carefully.

Mallory nodded, looking so damn weary. Looking years older than eighteen. She hung her head, more out of exhaustion than shame, Adam thought.

'I told you once that I asked a stranger to use her phone,' she whispered. 'While he kept me.' For six years her captor had held her, abusing her on the Internet for millions of pedophiles to see. 'I called the police and told them what he was doing to me. The police came. And one of them recognized me from online. Told *him*, that he wouldn't tell if he could . . . you know.'

'Rape you too,' Meredith said quietly.

Adam *hated* this story. Hated that it was true, that it had happened. That it had happened to Mallory. Hated that they'd found no trace of her call to the police. Hated that they'd found no evidence that any cop had ever investigated her call for help. He hated that she'd been raped by *anyone*, much less by a cop who should have protected her.

Oh my God. His stomach lurched as his brain put the pieces together. She'd known her attacker tonight. It was the same guy. *This is a cop doing this. A cop killing to protect his secrets.* His gaze collided with Meredith's and saw that she'd come to the same conclusion.

He left Meredith's side to crouch next to Mallory so that he could hear every nuance of her answers. 'This was the guy tonight? The cop?'

'No. His friend.'

He kept his voice calm, grateful Mallory trusted him enough to tell him this. He couldn't even imagine how hard it was for her to say. 'The cop brought a friend?'

'Yes. Several.'

He swallowed hard. 'Mallory, I don't know all the details from what happened before, because I wasn't on your case. So can you tell me now about his friends that came with him. Were they cops?'

'I don't know. Some of them? Maybe?'

'Was the guy who grabbed you tonight?'

'I don't know,' she said again, desperately. 'But I knew his voice.' She was shaking. 'He hurt me.' Mallory gripped her hands together so hard her knuckles were white.

'Okay,' he soothed. 'Can you describe any of them?'

'They wore masks. But the cop had a birthmark. Or maybe a scar. It was on his chest. By his heart. His friend . . . I don't know. I only knew his voice.'

'Thank you,' he said softly. 'I hate to ask you all these questions.'

'I understand,' Mallory whispered hoarsely.

'Can you describe the birthmark?'

'It was red. Looked like a burn? It might have been a burn.'

'Dark red? Pink?'

'Medium red.'

'Okay. And the shape?'

'Square, but slanted. Like a diamond, almost.' Her voice had thinned and her body swayed and he worried that she'd collapse where she sat. She had a spine of steel, but at the same time was so very fragile. Brittle. He feared he'd snap her if he pushed too hard.

'All right.' He'd stop for now, resume later if he needed to. 'Thank you.'

Meredith drew a deep breath. Let it out in a weary gust of air. 'What now?'

'We regroup, have another look at the evidence. Come up with a new plan. Because this changes everything.' Especially if they were looking for a goddamn cop.

Cincinnati, Ohio,
Sunday 20 December, 10.20 P.M.

Adam met Deacon as his cousin came through the ER's double doors. 'You needed to see me?' Deacon asked.

Adam motioned to an empty exam room. 'In here.' He met Deacon's worried eyes when he closed the door behind them.

'Hey, you okay?' Deacon asked.

'Yeah. Just . . . I think we might be looking for a cop.'

Deacon's unique eyes, each half brown, half blue, popped wide open. 'Well. Not what I was expecting. Why?'

Adam told him what Mallory had revealed about her attacker today and Deacon slowly sat in a chair.

'Holy God,' he murmured, running his hand through his spiky white hair. 'Do Meredith and Kate know?'

'Meredith does. She was with me when Mallory told us. I haven't seen Kate yet. I thought we could talk to her together. Dani says she's blaming herself.'

'Because that's Kate,' Deacon said with a sigh. 'Any of us would do the same.'

'True enough. What's going on outside? Any sightings of the shooter?' The first responders had put out a BOLO on the shooter who'd escaped on foot from the hospital parking lot. Adam was so relieved that he hadn't confronted Kate in his terror-driven anger. She'd really done an amazing job under the circumstances. 'What about the car he stole?'

The car's owner had run into a convenience store 'for just a second,' leaving the car parked with the motor running. 'He ditched it already. We haven't had any reports of more thefts, so he's either on foot or he hotwired or jacked another car. As for the scene outside, CSU is doing their thing. There's a lot of blood, which you already saw. Quincy got there a few minutes after you came inside. He's like a field marshal out there. 'Do this, do that, get out of our way.' I like him and he's good at his job. He can be brusque, though. Anyway, he's sent the rifle Kate found in the SUV to the lab. The serial number's been filed away, but he thinks they can raise it.'

'Excellent. What about the SUV?'

'He's having it transported to the garage so he can go over it with a fine-toothed comb.' Deacon raked a hand through his hair again, clearly agitated. It had been his habit from the time they'd been small boys. 'A fucking cop?' He sucked in a breath. 'As in maybe the cop that raped her years ago? The one we thought was just posing as a cop?'

'She said he was the cop's friend. It makes sense that they'd want her gone if they think she can identify one or both of them. She was targeted the very first day she left Mariposa House. Up until then she was safe in the mansion.'

'With either Parrish Colby or Kendra Cullen there most of the time.'

Adam nodded. 'A Fed and a cop as bodyguards would be a deterrent. Plus all of us volunteering. And Diesel installed a kickass security system. Nobody's getting in there.'

'So he waited until she was out of Mariposa House.'

Adam nodded again. 'So I've been racking my brain, trying to figure how they found out that Mallory was going to be out *that* day and how they knew she'd be at *that* restaurant. Trip's talked to all of the girls at the house and they all swear they didn't even know where Meredith was taking Mallory, much less tell anyone outside. Wendi gave Trip access to the house's landline call logs. Nothing out of the ordinary there. A few of the girls have cell phones. We can look at those.'

'I hate to do that,' Deacon admitted. 'Each of the girls at Mariposa has had her privacy stolen by her abuser. I hate to violate their privacy too, but we will if we have to. Did Meredith tell anyone where she was taking Mallory?'

'Her friends. Wendi knew. I overheard her talking about it to Kendra when I was doing a repair at Mariposa last week. Someone could have overheard her making the reservation or have access to her calendar. She may remember something today that she was too rattled to tell us yesterday.'

Deacon's laugh was mirthless. 'And she's not rattled today?'

Adam thought about that moment between them, right before Mallory had dropped her bombshell. They'd been cocooned together, gazes locked, her holding their joined hands to her cheek. She'd been . . . at peace.

'I think she'll be able to think more clearly about it now that she knows that she isn't the target,' he murmured.

Deacon gave him a look that was smugly satisfied. 'Took you fucking long enough.'

Adam raised his brows. 'Excuse me?'

'You two have been dancing around each other for a year. More than a year. God. I've been wanting to smack you upside the head and say just get the fuck on with it! Faith kept saying it was none of my business, which is ridiculous.'

Adam stared at him. *I guess I wasn't so discreet after all.* 'Um . . . I'm sorry?'

Deacon snorted, then sobered. 'Let's ask her again. Maybe she'll remember a detail that didn't seem important before.'

His phone started blasting 'Dead Man's Party'. It was Carrie Washington, the ME. He hit ACCEPT. 'I'm with Deacon. Can I put you on speaker?' When she agreed, he put his phone down on the table. 'What can you tell us about Voss?'

'Cause of death, heroin overdose. What was left in the syringe was a potent concentration. He was a long-time user. He may have simply built a tolerance to his old dose and took too much trying to reach the same high. Time of death is three a.m. Sunday, plus or minus four hours. That was harder to pinpoint, with the heat turned up and the fireplace going.'

Adam did the math. 'He died *after* the cops arrived to guard the outside.'

'So it would seem,' she said. 'I may have more by morning. The full set of tox results will be ready by then, plus this is just my preliminary exam.'

'Thanks, Carrie.' Disconnecting, Adam rubbed his temples. 'I need to talk to Quincy, to find out what he got from Voss's house.'

'I already talked to him – while he was driving here from Voss's. He'd found nothing so far. In fact, so much nothing, that it might be something. At first glance, all Voss's computers are wiped clean. Factory resets.'

'Shit,' Adam murmured. He wondered what time Diesel Kennedy had broken into the man's system, because it hadn't been wiped then. 'I know there was data on Voss's hard drives at nine p.m. last night.'

Deacon raised his brows. 'Because your confidential informant told you so?'

'Yes. The computers were wiped clean later. We could be talking murder.'

Deacon nodded. 'Yes, we could. Except that somebody would have had to murder Voss and wipe all of his data, all while CPD sits outside both the front and back gate. How'd that happen?'

'I don't know,' Adam said grimly. 'But we're sure as hell going to find out.'

Cincinnati, Ohio,
Sunday 20 December, 10.40 P.M.

The knock on the door had Meredith looking up as she sat next to Kate's bed in the ER. 'Kate?' she asked. 'Should I see who it is?'

Staring at the opposite wall, Kate shrugged. 'I don't care.'

Meredith sighed. Kate was blaming herself big time. Wouldn't look at any of them. Normally Meredith would have been compassionate and patient, but she was tired and irritable and her own head still hurt. 'Stop it,' she snapped in a quiet voice. 'No one is to blame here, except the asshole who tried to grab Mallory.' The light knock on the door was a welcome relief from Kate's silence.

Meredith peeked out, then opened the door wider for Deacon and Adam. 'Come on in. Did you get my message?' she asked Adam.

He smiled at her and she had to remind herself that things were bleak because her heart soared. 'That Wendi and Colby came for Mallory?' he asked. 'Yes, Colby found us. They're waiting with Mallory in one of the consultation rooms until we sort out getting her protection placement.'

That took Meredith a second but then she blinked. 'Oh. I guess they can't take her back to Mariposa House.' Her cheeks heated with embarrassment. 'That was stupid of me. I just assumed they'd take her home, but that would put the other girls at risk.'

Adam tipped her chin up. 'It was not stupid of you. That old house is about as safe as they come. It's solid rock. But we have to figure out how the shooter knew where you two were going to be yesterday before we can be sure it's safe there for Mallory.'

That should have occurred to her too. 'Because he had to know where we'd be. I don't remember telling anyone except for my friends. I've been racking my brain.'

He kissed the top of her head. 'Regardless of where we place Mallory, I want you to stay at the condo until this is settled. Okay? You may not be a target now, but I still want you safe. Your house isn't secure.'

She wanted to ask if he would stay at the condo with her, but was completely conscious of Deacon standing right next to them. 'I'm not going to fight you on it. Besides, my things are there.'

'Things meaning guns?' Deacon asked. He was studying Kate who lay on the bed, her arm in a sling, her eyes closed.

'Among other things,' Meredith allowed.

Deacon glanced at them, his arched brow a commentary on the

way she and Adam were holding each other, then turned back to his former partner who hadn't stirred. 'How is she?'

'Awake,' Meredith said pointedly, so Kate could hear her. 'Even though she's pretending to be asleep. She's ornery. Feeling guilty. Maybe you two can shake her out of it, because she's not listening to me.'

Adam gestured for Deacon to take the lead. Deacon and Kate had been friends and colleagues for years. None of their group knew Kate as well as Deacon Novak.

Deacon approached the bed, frowning. 'Eighteen stitches? That's all? And you're lying here like a lump?'

'Fuck off, Deacon,' Kate said, very quietly.

'I'd much rather be home doing exactly that with Faith, but that's not the hand we were dealt today.' He took the chair nearest the bed. 'Stop this. You brought an injured person into a hospital. You believed you had backup. And you know what? If you hadn't, we'd all still think that Meredith was the target and Mallory would be walking around unprotected because she wouldn't know the truth. Now we know. Now we know we might be looking for a fucking cop. Now we need your help.'

Kate blinked at that. 'What?'

Adam glanced at Meredith. 'You didn't tell her?'

Meredith shrugged. 'I tried. She told me she'd knit me a ball gag if I didn't shut up.'

Adam swallowed a startled laugh. 'O-kay.'

'I did not,' Kate snapped, then sighed. 'All right. I might have. But the doctor gave me drugs.'

'Not that many drugs,' Meredith said. 'Or not enough.'

Kate glared over her shoulder, then back at Adam and Deacon. 'What's this about a cop?' she demanded, then her face went slack as comprehension dawned. 'Oh God. The cop she was afraid of. The one who raped her.' She struggled to sit up, then fell back against the pillows, eyes clenched, mouth tight with pain. 'We should have looked for him.'

'We did look,' Deacon said firmly.

'We should have looked harder,' Kate said, teeth clenched.

'We investigated, Kate,' Deacon insisted patiently. 'She couldn't describe him except to say he had a birthmark. And there was no record of a police visit to the house where she was being held. We had no leads, Kate. Now we do.'

'A cop,' Kate whispered thinly. 'All this was a cop?'

Deacon gripped her uninjured hand. 'At a minimum, a friend of a cop. I know you've had a helluva night, but we need some information. We know you went looking for Mallory. We know that when the dust settled, we had three injured Feds – you and Agents Helder and Carroll out in the van. We know you got the shooter's gun, his rifle, his knife and his SUV. We know about the eighteen stitches and' – he peered at her head more closely – 'a really bad bruise on your forehead. But there are a few pages missing in the middle.'

Kate sighed. 'I heard Meredith yelling at the shooter, so I doubled back. Mallory was in the SUV, the gunman was standing there, his gun pointed at Meredith, and Meredith was trying to trade herself.' She glanced at Meredith. 'Goddamn idiot,' she said without heat.

'That's been established,' Meredith said dryly. 'Tell us what we don't know.'

'I came up behind the guy, ID'd myself as FBI, had him drop to his knees and drop his gun. I kicked the gun away, Meredith got Mallory out of the van, they started walking. I'd called in for backup and kept hoping it would get there. I didn't know what had happened to Helder and Carroll. What did?'

'One's serious, the other critical,' Deacon told her. 'But they're both alive. So if you had him on his knees and he dropped his gun, how'd he get the upper hand?'

'I'd leaned in to cuff him and he reared back and head-butted my face. Honestly, my attention was split. I was watching Meredith and Mallory out of the corner of my eye because I was afraid he had an accomplice. But it was just him. He had a knife up his sleeve and' – she pointed to her arm – 'he got me with it. I kicked it out of his hand, but he was already going for my gun. We fought for it and I shot him in the chest, but he was wearing a vest. Still had to have hurt him. It was point-blank. He got me by the throat, shoved me into the SUV, backwards, then face first. I . . . I was a bit dizzy.'

'You were curled up on the damn ground,' Meredith challenged. 'I thought . . .' Tears rose in her throat. 'God, Kate, I thought you were dead.'

Kate shrugged. 'I might have been if I hadn't been wearing the wig. He went for the gun again and grabbed at my hair to hold me down. The wig came off, which surprised him so much that he staggered a little. I shoved at him but I was . . . dizzy, so I sat down.'

'Fell down,' Meredith muttered, pushing the tears back.

Kate gave her a dirty look. 'Anyway, I wasn't sure if I could keep the gun away from him. I couldn't get up to run away at that point, so I ejected the clip and threw it as hard as I could, then tossed the gun under the SUV. His was already under there from when I kicked it. He tried to get at both guns, cursed a lot, hit me a few more times, then went running after Meredith. She'd stashed Mallory by this point. She came out with a gun, shot the guy in the chest. He must have been on something because he didn't stop. I mean, yeah, he had on a vest, but that was two direct hits to the chest and he didn't even act like he felt it. She shot his leg and he retreated. I'd gotten to my knees at this point, but I couldn't reach my gun or his. But, hey, it was a black SUV, just like at the restaurant. I figured he might have a rifle in there, since he used it to shoot at Adam and Troy earlier.'

'That was good work, Kate,' Deacon said. 'Where did you find it?'

'Under the driver's seat. I heard four more shots, got close enough to hear Meredith tell him that he'd have to kill her first, that she wouldn't let him have Mallory. Idiot.'

Meredith rolled her eyes, but her voice was soft and non-accusatory when she asked, 'Why did you shoot his arm? Why not his head?'

'You're the best shot of any of us, Kate,' Adam said quietly. 'What happened?'

Kate grimaced. 'I was aiming for his head. My vision was a little blurry.'

Meredith's heart stuttered. Now she understood. This wasn't all Kate being guilty. This was also fear. Kate's head had been hit harder than she wanted to admit and she was scared. *Oh honey*, Meredith wanted to say, but she held the words back, holding Kate's hand instead. Kate tightened her grip, affirmation of just how terrified she was.

Adam let out a quiet breath. 'Is it still blurry?'

'Not as much. They're going to keep me here tonight.' She forced a smile. 'Along with Clarke. Ironic that we brought Mer in for a head injury but we're the ones who have to sleep over. Maybe we can watch movies. Or listen to them. The light kind of hurts my eyes.'

Adam immediately dimmed the overhead light. 'Better?'

'Yeah. Thank you.'

'Why didn't you say something to me?' Meredith asked.

'I didn't want to scare you any more than you already were.'

Meredith scoffed. 'Doofus.'

Kate's lips curved faintly. 'Knitted ball gag threat still in effect.' She sighed. 'Then I shot the SUV's tires. I didn't want him to have an easy getaway. But he got away anyway.'

'We've got half the city out looking for him,' Deacon assured her. 'Where's Cap?'

'One of the hospital volunteers is keeping him right now. I'll have to find someone to keep him until Decker gets home.' Kate swallowed hard. 'He's booked on the first flight out tomorrow.'

'I'll keep Cap,' Meredith said. 'Or, depending on which safe house Mallory's going to, maybe she can keep him. He seems to bring her peace. Or the idea of him does, at least.'

'I'd forgotten about that,' Kate said softly. 'Please, make sure she can pet him.'

Meredith lightly kissed Kate's temple. 'We'll take care of it. I'm going to see Papa for a while, but I'll be back before I have to go. You try to rest.'

Twenty-three

Cincinnati, Ohio,
Sunday 20 December, 11.15 P.M.

'This is a clusterfuck, Adam,' Hanson grumbled as he took a seat at the table in Isenberg's briefing room. He'd made a point of being one of the first ones there.

They were all running on fumes. Especially Quincy, Adam thought, who'd been hopping from scene to scene since yesterday afternoon. Quincy had left other forensic techs at each scene to continue the work, but had continued to revisit each one.

Zimmerman had nearly lost three of his agents tonight, on top of Troy's injury earlier in the day. Kate would recover – although they were all nervous that her vision was still blurry – but the agents who'd been waiting in the van for Kate, Meredith, and Mallory were still unconscious.

Meredith sat in the back of the room, quietly coloring in a new coloring book that Special Agent in Charge Zimmerman's wife had given her when they'd arrived at the hospital to visit Kate and the other two agents. Thoughtful lady, Mrs Z. She'd also brought food for the team, which they'd wolfed down like feral dogs.

Meredith hadn't complained, but Adam knew she was exhausted. He should have asked someone to take her to the condo so that she could sleep, but he found he wasn't quite ready to let her out of his sight. Mallory might have been the target from the beginning, but the shooter at Buon Cibo had fired a second shot at Meredith. Adam wasn't sure he'd ever be ready to let her out of his sight, not ever again.

Standing by the whiteboard, he waited until all the seats were filled. Deacon, Scarlett, Trip, and Nash Currie had joined them, Nash choosing a chair on the opposite side of the table from Hanson. Which seemed to please Hanson a great deal as well.

Adam didn't know what had transpired between the two to make them so contrary, but he was going to find out. He had enough trouble without saber rattling.

Isenberg was the last one in. She glanced at Meredith in the corner of the room, then pulled the door closed behind her. He wasn't worried that she'd disapprove of Meredith's presence. It had actually been Isenberg's suggestion, both to keep his mind free of worry and to get Meredith's take on the case.

They'd come a long way since yesterday afternoon when she'd threatened to pull him from the case if he got too involved.

'Detective,' was all Isenberg said, before sitting at the opposite end of the table. He could feel the weariness pouring off her and wondered when she'd slept last.

'All right,' Adam said. 'Let's get this done so we can grab a few hours' sleep. You've all heard that Mallory Martin identified the man who tried to take her, right? Not by name, but he was one of several men who raped her when she was being held captive.' He was able to deliver the words impersonally, but his stomach still churned at the knowledge.

Heads nodded grimly all around the table.

'So,' he continued, 'we believe that this man was a friend of the cop who blackmailed her captor into allowing him access to her. She didn't see their faces, but recognized this man's voice. The only other thing she remembers was the birthmark or maybe a scar on the chest of the cop.'

Oh. That Voss was being blackmailed suddenly made a lot more sense. Another connection. Two guilty men, both blackmailed by a cop. A glance at Trip showed that he had just put it together too. The rookie was smart. Smart enough to keep Diesel's info on the down-low for a little longer, because Trip gave him an almost imperceptible nod.

'Trip, what did you find at Voss's house?' Adam asked.

'His body,' Trip said. 'We got into his safe, found a little cash, legal papers, normal stuff. Prenup with Mrs Voss, results of a DNA test proving Penny is his daughter, so he obviously had some doubt at some point. Hard to say if he had good reason or because he assumed that Mrs Voss was cattin' around because he was. We found his little black book in which he rated wines, movies, and hookers.'

'You've got to be kidding,' Adam said, wondering why he continued to be surprised.

Trip shook his head. 'Nope. He gave Jolee' – he pointed at the woman's Facebook photo on the whiteboard – 'a solid seven out of ten.' His jaw tightened. 'He had several scores for Linnie. They started high, sevens and eights, then began to decline. He wrote that he wanted his money back after the last entry because she was too bony. His first "grade" for Linnea was six months ago.'

'Voss was a piece of work,' Scarlett said. 'I can't say that I'm sorry he's dead.'

'Neither was Mrs Voss,' Trip added. 'Scarlett and I did the notification.'

'Shit, Trip,' Adam said, wincing. The guy had been destroyed after notifying Kyle Davis of Tiffany's murder. 'Two in twenty-four? That sucks.'

Trip shrugged, the look he gave Adam unhappy. 'Mrs Voss was . . . glad he was dead and I understand why, because the man did horrible things. He assaulted her and endangered her child. But it was almost easier dealing with Kyle's grief.'

Hanson cleared his throat. 'What was the final count on the money in the safe?'

'Three hundred euros,' Scarlett said. 'I expected more.'

'We didn't find any bank records, though,' Nash added. 'We've requested the records from the bank. They've promised them by morning.'

'Would be nice to have them sooner,' Adam said. 'Can you push them?'

'I'll try,' Nash said with a shrug.

'Thanks. Voss's time of death was between eleven last night and seven this morning, meaning he couldn't have committed any of the murders we're investigating. We already knew he had an alibi for the time of Andy Gold's death. If he did pay someone, it was before the fact.'

Dissatisfaction rippled through the group. Everyone but Isenberg and Deacon was hearing this for the first time. Adam and Deacon had informed their bosses.

'How long have you known that?' Scarlett asked.

'Carrie called right before we went to talk to Kate,' Adam told her. 'So forty minutes, tops. Sorry. We were interviewing Kate. It seemed easier to tell you all together.'

Scarlett waved a no-problem hand. 'You were right. And Isenberg did text to tell us that we were looking at cops or friends of cops, which let out Voss anyway. I don't think he considered cops his friends.'

'True enough,' Trip muttered.

Nash frowned. 'What time did you put surveillance outside Voss's house?'

Adam gave him a nod. 'Four detectives, watching front and back, were in place by nine p.m. So, assuming Voss did not inject himself with two to three times his normal hit and that he didn't turn the heat up . . . How did his killer get past the guard?'

'I can answer that,' Isenberg said. 'One of the detectives sitting at the front gate was taking a nap while the other watched. The one awake was approached by a uniform-wearing "cop."' She used air quotes. 'The cop gave the detective a cup of coffee, said he'd been sent by me. Which, of course, he was not.'

Adam blinked at her. 'He believed that?'

Isenberg shrugged. 'The detective questioned it because I'm clearly not known for my hospitality,' she said acidly. 'The cop informed him that even "the bitch has a heart," and didn't want the detective to freeze. The detective was cold and took the coffee and the next thing he knew his partner was waking him up.'

'The coffee was drugged,' Deacon murmured.

Isenberg nodded. 'Yep. The detective swears he was only asleep for a few minutes. His partner couldn't speculate because he had been asleep too. The detective swore that fake cop's badge said Swenson, but the only Swenson on the force was documented to be somewhere else that night. The detective says the fake cop approached him at midnight.'

Nash pinched the bridge of his nose. 'Right after a power outage cut out all the security cameras.'

'You're shitting me,' Hanson said, clearly angry.

'Wish I was,' Nash replied.

'If we knew who'd killed him,' Hanson said, vibrating with the effort of keeping his cool, 'we could crack open this case. Voss had at least two dozen working girls listed in that little black book. And he was obviously buying a lot of drugs, so now we've also lost a tip on the dealers' identities. Are you sure there's no video?'

Nash's lips thinned. 'I said there wasn't.'

Isenberg tapped the table to get their attention. 'Gentlemen? It must have been a very localized power outage. The gate still opened when you all arrived.'

Hanson frowned. 'Your point, Lieutenant?' he asked, far more politely.

'That it wasn't a full outage,' Isenberg said with a patience that not-so-thinly veiled her annoyance. 'Do we know if the cameras ever came back online?'

Nash considered it. 'The DVRs never did. But I don't know about the cameras.'

'I'm still missing the point,' Hanson declared.

'The point,' Nash said with a little grin of excitement, 'is that it depends what was on the circuit that blew. If it was on the DVR only, we wouldn't have saved video but the cameras may still have been streaming to an offsite server. Thank you, Lieutenant.'

Isenberg nodded soberly. 'It might be nothing.'

'But we might get something.' Nash tapped the table nervously, a sure sign that his mind was galloping ahead. 'How did the killer know the code?'

'I wondered that too,' Trip said. 'There was no sign of forced entry. Hell, we would have needed an armored car to break down those gates.'

413

'Maybe Voss was killed by someone who knew him well enough to know his codes,' Adam said. 'The front was 0713 and the back was 0915.'

Hanson pulled out his phone and flipped through some photos. 'Yeah, I thought I remembered the first one. I took photos of the documents we pulled from the safe. Here's a certificate he received the day his company went IPO. September, 2015.' He swiped through his photos. 'And . . . July 1, 2013 is the date his company debuted.'

Scarlett got up from her chair to look over Hanson's shoulder. 'That's worse than my mother's passcodes. At least she picks dates nobody else would know. Anybody with Google could figure out Voss's passcodes.'

Which is probably how Diesel was able to break into his system so easily, Adam thought. And from the look on Trip's face, he was thinking the same thing.

Isenberg's expression grew dark. 'So we've narrowed the suspect pool to anyone with Google. Fabulous. Agent Taylor, did you find any fingerprints that would be helpful?'

Quincy shook his head. 'We found hundreds of prints. It's going to take Latent days to run them all. The man had parties and meetings and hosted company dinners at his home. A seedy hotel room would have fewer prints. But,' he added quickly, 'we do have the rifle now and the SUV, and I think those two things will make a difference.'

'Say more,' Adam requested, relieved when Isenberg settled back to listen.

'Ballistics is finished with the rifle that Kate got from the SUV,' Quincy said. 'It fired the bullet that killed Andy Gold, the bullets that hit your van and Agent Troy, and the bullet that ended Bruiser. And bullets fired during a robbery thirty years ago.'

'Any luck in getting the rifle's serial number?' Adam asked him.

'Not yet, but the lab just received it from Ballistics. You'll know if they're able to lift a serial as soon as I do.' Quincy lifted his brows. 'Now for the second good thing. The SUV the shooter left behind never tried to mask its VIN. The SUV was reported sold last year to a man who's been dead for ten years. The seller on record was Barber Motors in Fairfield.'

Nash sucked in a breath. 'The same used-car place where the three cars belonging to the college prostitute were found.'

Excellent. Adam grinned at Quincy, relieved that at least a few things were coming together. 'Really nice work.'

'Thanks,' Quincy said, his returned smile so big that he popped a dimple, making him look even younger than he usually did. Adam had a few doubts that Deacon was right about Quincy. He'd never seen the hard-faced, order-barking ex-soldier that Deacon claimed was on their crime scene tonight.

'So we pay Barber Motors a visit first thing in the morning,' Adam said. 'Scar? You up for a little SUV shopping?'

Scarlett chuckled. 'I can have any color as long as it's black?'

Adam smiled at her, feeling more light-hearted than he had in months. He'd been Scarlett's partner before Deacon came to Cincinnati and they'd enjoyed this banter every day. Until Adam went off to Personal Crimes and returned a different man.

Maybe he was finally finding his old self. He glanced back at Meredith, who was studying her gel pens. She turned her head and met his eyes with a wink and he knew that she'd been aware he was watching her.

I don't want to be my old self. I want to be a better man.

Adam shifted his attention to Isenberg. 'If we can get a warrant, I'd prefer to bust in without any subterfuge. If not, we can try an undercover op.'

Hanson looked worried at that. 'I don't know, Adam. I'm not sure there's a face in this room that hasn't been on the news. Anybody you send will likely be recognized. Especially Agent Novak.' He looked over to Deacon. 'No offense.'

'None taken,' Deacon said. 'It's true anyway.'

Adam sighed. 'You're probably right, Hanson, but you were on camera tonight too, at the scene of Bruiser's murder. Nash? You wanna buy an SUV?'

Nash nodded thoughtfully. 'Sure. Why not?'

'Only if we don't have a warrant before ten a.m.,' Isenberg

cautioned. 'Plan A is to walk right in and take their files and arrest them if they so much as look at us cross-eyed.'

'Understood,' Nash said.

Adam turned to study the whiteboard, specifically the items they hadn't yet completed. 'The damn hostess,' he muttered. 'We still don't know who paid her to seat Meredith and Mallory by the window.'

'And we can't have her do a voice ID anymore,' Hanson said. 'Voss is dead.'

'You can have her listen to file footage of his shareholder meetings,' Quincy suggested. 'It's not the same but at this point I think we want to rule him out.'

'She still in protective custody?' Adam asked Isenberg.

'Yeah, and a pain in the ass,' Isenberg grumbled.

Adam feigned shock. 'That's a newsflash. Can you have one of your clerks choose some footage of Voss speaking?'

'Yes,' Isenberg said. 'What else?'

Adam's gaze found the photo of the burned-out house. 'The fire that killed the family who lived above Andy Gold's apartment. It wasn't Bruiser, because he was in Chicago at the time. When we catch the SOB who's doing this, I want them charged with four counts of murder for that family too. Do we have the arson investigator's report?'

Trip looked through his file folder. 'I have it. Arson says an accelerant was used. It appears to be gasoline mixed with some kind of soap. I'll meet with the arson guy while you're at the used-car dealer to see what they found at the scene.'

'Thank you,' Adam said. 'Deacon, go with him. I don't want any of us going solo. Not until we stop these assholes.'

'I agree,' Deacon said. 'Tonight's shooter nearly took out three armed federal agents. We need to be on alert.'

Adam clapped his hands once. 'And to do that, we need to recharge. It's almost midnight. Let's go home, get some sleep and meet back here at eight o'clock.'

Everyone filed out until the only people left in the room were Meredith, who was packing up her gel pens, and Nash, who came to stand next to Adam at the whiteboard. He thought Nash would be looking at the photos of the used car lot, but his old friend's gaze was locked on the crime scene photos sent by Reagan and Mitchell in Chicago.

Adam found himself studying the photos for only a few seconds before his attention bounced to something else. Someone else.

Anything else. The Chicago crime scene photos were hard to view.

'What?' Adam asked Nash softly, because Nash was staring at the photo with an intensity that was a little creepy, if Adam was being honest.

'Nothing,' Nash said, breaking his gaze. 'Sleep well, Adam. I'll see you tomorrow.' He waved at Meredith who was all packed up and waiting. 'Good night, Dr Fallon.'

When Nash was gone, Adam put his arm around her shoulders. 'Ready to go?'

'Absolutely,' Meredith said.

Cincinnati, Ohio,
Monday 21 December, 12.45 A.M.

'Took you fucking long enough,' Mike grunted as he emerged from the shadows of the deserted strip mall behind which he'd hidden. He dragged his right leg behind him and his left arm hung uselessly at his side. A deep gash across his cheek still oozed blood.

He leaned heavily against the brick wall of the dry-cleaner located at the end of the strip mall, needing more medical care than he could provide. Although in about a minute, that wouldn't matter anymore.

Because Mike just reached his ex date too. 'What the fuck happened?'

'The women had guns,' Mike said, irritated. 'And knives. They shot me.'

'And stabbed you.'

'Yeah. Bitch. It was the little cunt Mallory that had a knife.'

He drew a deep breath, let it out. 'You were *supposed* to shoot the little cunt through the *head*. With the *rifle*. From *far away*. Why did you drag her to your SUV?'

Mike's jaw cocked, his eyes narrowing defiantly. 'You are not my boss, boy.'

'The hell I'm not! I'm the one taking the risks here.'

Mike approached slowly, a thunderous look on his face. 'You selfish little prick.'

'Me? *I* didn't disobey an order. *I* didn't leave my blood all over the crime scene.'

Mike shrugged. 'Won't help them none. They got nothin' to compare it to. Certainly doesn't connect *us*.'

Because he and Mike didn't share blood. 'But it will connect you to my father.'

Mike rolled his eyes. 'Like anyone's gonna go there. Look, boy, I need you to stitch the leg up. And get me a doctor. I figured you'd bring one with you. Like that pretty one I saw standing outside the shelter last night.' His eyes glittered with lust, surprising considering all his injuries. He should have been half-dead from blood loss alone. Sex should be the last thing on Mike's mind.

Oh. He abruptly halted mid-thought as understanding rushed to fill his mind. The horny little asshole. 'You wanted one last taste of Mallory, didn't you?'

Mike's eyes narrowed. 'Yeah. I did. Sue me.'

Oh, I'll do a lot more than that. 'You risked everything for one last go at that little whore?' He got up in Mike's face. 'Are you fucking insane?'

'No,' Mike said, behind clenched teeth. 'I'm quite sane. And my memory is better than decent. You promised her to me, but it was always your way. Your terms. Your leftovers. I'm fucking *tired* of taking your *leftovers*.'

He lifted his brows, hearing all the things Mike didn't say aloud. Remembering the cash that *hadn't* been found in Voss's safe tonight. 'What other *leftovers* have you taken, Uncle?' As his enforcers, Mike and Butch had collected the blackmail from the victims who'd paid with cash. He'd never stopped to count it, not in a long time. He'd trusted them. 'I know you took cash out of Voss's safe after you killed him.'

Mike's chin lifted. 'I earned it. I took the risk.'

418

'Did you also earn the money you've been skimming from your collections?' Mike's tight jaw told him he'd guessed right. 'Have you been forcing my girls to give you freebies?'

Mike sneered. 'The girls are not *yours*. They're *ours*. I can take what I want.'

He stared at Mike dispassionately. 'Hope if you took what you wanted from Linnea that you used a condom. Turns out that she's HIV positive.'

It was as if Mike's sneer was ripped away by an invisible hand, his eyes widening in shock. 'What?'

'Yep.' Anger churned in his gut, roared through his mind. Because he'd sent Linnea to many, many clients' homes in the last six months. He didn't know at what point she'd become infected, but he could potentially have dozens of infected clients out there. Eventually they'd be diagnosed and eventually there would be a health department investigation because so many corporate icons testing positive wasn't a normal thing. Clients hired his girls because he guaranteed their health.

Because Mike told him they were clean.

He clenched his fists against the wave of fury that made him want to break every bone in Mike's body. 'And how did I not know that, Uncle? You were responsible for having them tested every two weeks. You showed me lab results. Did you not test them?'

'I did. I swear I did.' But Mike's eyes shifted left. His tell.

He'd needed to come here, to confront this situation in person because he'd needed to see that tell. Because he would have wanted to believe his uncle.

Because I fucking trusted him. Sonofabitch.

'You're lying,' he said coldly. 'Why? Why say you did the tests when you didn't? What was worth that risk?'

Mike's eyes glittered, but with hate now. Contempt. 'Do you even know how much those tests cost?'

He stared for a moment, genuinely stunned. 'What? This was about money?'

Mike snarled. 'Everything's about money, boy. Everything. Haven't you been listening all these years?'

'Yeah, I have. And you got plenty of the money. What are you doing with it? Shooting it up your fucking veins?'

Mike's flinch was all the answer he needed.

'You've been using the product? Are you that stupid?' He shook his head when Mike silently glared. 'You *are* that stupid. You dumb fuck. I gave you so much. More than you ever deserved, but it was never enough. You've ruined us. Ruined everything.'

Mike closed his eyes and wearily shifted more of his weight against the brick wall. 'I didn't ruin anything, boy. At least not all by myself. You more than participated.'

His heart was beating fast in his chest. '*I* didn't tap the product.'

'No, you tapped *Mallory*. You just couldn't resist her, could you? All Mr High-And-Mighty who wouldn't touch his own girls got hung up on one who belonged to someone else. And then you left her alive. And then you dragged Linnea into it and that poor friend of hers too. I told you to let me take care of Mallory, but no, you didn't trust me. You had to do it yourself. You had to be the big man. And in the end, *that's* what's ruined us.'

He could barely hear over the rage pulsing in his head. 'You have the nerve to say I should have trusted you? You *lied* to me. You *stole* from me. You have fucked up every job I've given you. Why the hell should I have trusted you? You're fucking lucky you've got a life at all. You were a broken down, sorry excuse for a man. A user. A failure. Everything you have is because of *me*.'

Mike lurched forward, shoving at him with his uninjured right hand. 'You ungrateful little *shit*. I taught you everything you know.'

Yes, Mike had. He'd taught him to never suffer fools, and that fuckups didn't survive.

'I agree,' he said very quietly and Mike, finally reading his mood, took a wary step back. *Not so stupid after all, are you, old man?* 'So you also must know that you are now a liability.' He slid his gun from his shoulder holster.

Mike's good arm lifted as if to stave him off. 'Wait. Don't do thi—'

His uncle dropped to the ground, a single bullet centered in his forehead. The bullet, ironically, came from the very gun Mike had given him for his last birthday.

Goddammit. His legs folded right out from under him, dropping him on his ass. He sat on the concrete next to Mike's body, his breathing fast and shallow.

He'd killed more men than he could remember over the years, but never had it felt like this. Not even his very first, when he'd killed the man with whom he actually had shared blood. Yes, he'd given Mike everything. But Mike had been more than an uncle and more than a business partner.

Mike had been the closest thing he'd ever had to a father. More so than the man who'd adopted him. And a helluva lot more than the man who'd been his real father. Sanctimonious, abusive, preachy SOB that he'd been.

The only good thing his real father had given him was the realization that punching a time clock in the pew every Sunday morning was the best way to hide his sins in plain sight. Mike had taught him almost everything else.

Now Mike was gone. Now it was done. All of it was done. His businesses, so carefully planned and executed . . . all gone. He'd eliminated all the girls that afternoon and the thought of building a new ring of college hookers? Not gonna happen because he couldn't manage them or any of his other endeavors anymore, not without Mike and Butch.

Nor did he want to. They'd built it, together. The three of them.

At least Butch never stole from me. It was a small consolation. Too small.

He stared at Mike's body, his emotions leveling. He shouldn't have been so stunned to learn Mike was skimming. The man *was* a criminal, after all, and he had taught him a lot, but not nearly everything. Mike was a two-bit conman and would have never been more.

Not without me. For now, he had cleanup to do. He'd fully leveled, but he continued to sit on the cold asphalt, regarding Mike. Mike had needed to die, so killing had been right, but he should have done it differently. The bullet was still in Mike's goddamn head.

He made it a point not to leave bullets behind. He'd done so at Buon Cibo because he hadn't had a choice. He hadn't intended to kill Andy with a rifle. He'd intended to blow the poor bastard sky high, along with Mallory and Meredith and anyone else unfortunate enough to have been in the blast zone.

He blinked hard, trying to focus on what needed to be done. Had he fired the gun anywhere that he would have left a bullet in the past? He didn't think so. Mike had sworn that the gun was brand new, never been fired. But Mike was a fucking liar, so who knew?

He let out a heavy sigh. *I'm tired.* He hadn't had a full night's sleep since . . . when? Thursday? He needed to get home. Rita would be wondering why he hadn't called. He didn't have the time or tools to bury Mike and he certainly didn't want the guy's blood – which the cops now had in copious quantities and were testing, for God's sake – anywhere near his own SUV, so he wasn't taking Mike's body anywhere.

But he did *not* want him identified. *Time to go old school.* He had some serious aggression to work through, anyway. He looked behind the strip mall for something that would serve his purposes and found a pile of bricks stacked against the wall. *That'll do.*

Cincinnati, Ohio,
Monday 21 December, 12.50 A.M.

It was quiet. Finally quiet. So quiet that Meredith was almost afraid to breathe as she rode up the elevator to the condo with Adam at her side.

Only Adam. Because they were finally alone.

His arm was around her waist and she leaned her head against his shoulder. And they said nothing, but somehow it wasn't awkward at all.

'It's lovely.' She'd murmured the words aloud without planning to do so.

'Mmm.' He nuzzled his cheek against her hair, the strands catching in his stubble. She liked his stubble. Always had. He reminded her of a pirate. 'You are.'

She hummed softly, her cheeks warming at the praise. 'I meant the quiet. It's nice.'

'I know.'

And of course, now that she'd commented on the quiet, a million nervous words began fluttering in her throat. 'I'm glad everyone is finally settled.'

'Mm-hm,' he said, sounding a little amused. 'Snug as bugs.'

Isenberg had agreed it was a smarter use of resources to house Mallory and Wendi in the hotel room adjoining Shane and the Davises. That way they could increase the protection detail by only one special agent, who'd provide breaks to the other two currently guarding Shane and Kyle.

Parrish Colby would stay with Wendi, but as a civilian. He was technically on vacation, just as Kate had been all day. But knowing Parrish would be there to watch over Wendi and Mallory had left Meredith with one less worry.

She bit her lip. 'It seems . . . decadent to have the condo all to ourselves.'

Adam had offered his friend's condo to Shane and Mallory's group, but moving them seemed more dangerous, especially knowing a cop might be involved. Their location was secret. Other than those being protected and their guards, only Isenberg, Zimmerman, Adam, and Trip knew where they were. Moving them would require resources and planning and a bad cop in the mix jeopardized security. So they stayed put. For now.

'Safer here for you,' he murmured, 'even without the protection detail. Besides, you deserve a little decadence.' His voice deepened to a soft growl that made her shiver.

But her mind would not still. Her grandfather and Kate had both been admitted to the hospital and Bailey had come to watch over them. An RN, Bailey had skills that Meredith did not have.

So now Meredith found herself with no one to take care of but herself. And Adam.

It was a heady sensation. It was what she'd wanted for more than a year. But . . . 'Am I horrible to be relieved not to have to accompany Mallory to the safe house tonight?' she blurted out, realizing this was what she'd really needed to ask.

'No.' Adam kissed her temple. 'What do they say on the plane?

Make sure you put on your own oxygen mask before helping others? You needed not to be needed for just a little while. Let someone else take care of you. Let *me* take care of you.'

He tipped her chin up and took her lips in a kiss that started out chaste and sweet, but quickly became urgent and . . . She shivered. And deliciously carnal. Full of promise.

He abruptly ended the kiss, leaving her blinking at him dazedly until reality seeped through. The elevator doors had opened to the hall and Adam was instantly on alert, looking for threats. Thankfully there were none, because, dammit, he was right. They were due a little respite, decadent or no.

'Why are you smiling?' he asked as he unlocked the door and ushered her inside.

'Just thinking that we deserved the respite and then I heard Kate's voice in my head, asking if that's what we're calling it these days.'

He chuckled, a deep throaty sound that made her shiver again. 'I hope I can make her voice go away.' He closed and locked the door behind them. 'The only one I want you to hear for the next few hours is mine,' he said. 'Stay here. I have to make sure we're clear.'

She said nothing more, allowing him to do his job until he was satisfied the place was safe. He returned to the door where she waited and held out his hand. 'Let's use that tub for something other than to cover up tears, okay?'

A bath sounded heavenly. She was sorer than she'd let on, having hit the asphalt hard when the shooter had tossed her away from Mallory in the parking lot. But she hadn't wanted to be admitted to the hospital, so she'd faked her way through the ER doc's exam.

She'd wanted to be with Adam and now she was. He set the water running and sniffed at the bath bubbles Kate had packed until he found one he liked. 'You have a lot of bubble choices,' he remarked as he studied the label and added exactly the number of capfuls called for. Not more or less.

He was a man who stayed inside the lines. Or tried to. One of these days she wanted to push him outside the lines, just a bit. For now, he drew comfort in routine, just as she did.

He rather formally began removing the scrubs she'd been loaned at the hospital, lifting the top over her head, like he was slowly unwrapping a present. He stood back, taking her in for a moment before gently cupping her breasts in his work-roughened palms. 'You're so damn pretty. You take my breath away.'

He kissed her again, teasing her tongue with his, but not demanding. Just . . . reacquainting them. His fingers pulled at the drawstring on the scrubs and he pulled them down, going down in a crouch as he did. He looked up with a frown. 'You're bruised.' He brushed his fingertips over her hip, his dark eyes flashing with anger. 'He hurt you.'

'It's where I fell in the parking lot. It's fine.'

He looked like he wanted to argue, but thankfully dropped it. 'You're pretty everywhere, you know.' He ghosted a single fingertip up one thigh, stopping just short of where she wanted to be touched, making her knees shake.

'You're a tease, Detective,' she murmured, then surprised him by grabbing his T-shirt in both hands and ripping it over his head. 'That's not very nice.' She kicked away the scrub bottoms and urged him to his feet. 'I should tease you and see how you like it, but I won't.' She angled a smile upward as she pulled his belt from his trousers. 'Because that bath looks amazing and I want in it.' She made quick work of his pants and the tight boxer briefs she had to peel off his body, freeing the very nice erection. *And that I want in me.*

'Come,' she said as she slid into the tub, the word coming out huskier – and sexier – than she'd expected.

He climbed in after her, sinking into the hot water. 'I fully intend to. Several times.' With his back to the tub wall, he held out his hand. 'Come,' he said, his grin wicked.

She laughed. 'You're terrible.' But she took his hand and let him pull her to his lap so that she straddled him.

He ran his hands up and down her sides, teasing her nipples on the way up and between her legs on the way down. 'But you like it.'

She rested her arms on his shoulders. 'I do.' Leaning into him, she covered his mouth with hers and gave him the kiss she'd been thinking about all day. He growled in his throat as he kissed her back, his hips bucking up, splashing water over the tub's edge.

Abruptly he tore his mouth away and disappeared under the water, startling her a few seconds later by surfacing and shaking his wet head. 'I need to get clean because I need to be inside you,' he said and that fast, it was all she wanted too. They washed each other with an urgency that was heightened by the moment, by every brush of his body against hers. Every pass of his cock between her legs, up into her folds.

She locked gazes with him as they teased each other, so she saw his shocked pleasure when he actually slipped inside her. She gasped, her head falling back, because he felt so damn good. So hot. So full. The last time she'd felt a man skin to skin had been . . .

No. Not going there. She wasn't thinking back to the last time she'd been with a man without using a condom.

She stilled and he froze, his only movements the flaring of his nostrils and the throbbing of his cock inside her. 'I'm clean,' he said quietly. 'And before this morning, the last woman I was with was still you, last year.'

'So am I. Clean, I mean. And so were you – my last one. Last year.' She frowned, trying to focus because he felt *so damn good*. 'But I'm not on the pill.' It messed with her hormones, making her super depressed. 'So we can't.'

He let his head fall back with a groan. 'I know. Lift off. Carefully.'

She did and as soon as she was out of the tub he reared up, flooding the floor as he got out, grabbed her around the waist and hiked her up, tucking her legs around his hips. He carried her into the bedroom she'd been given last night, pulled back the sheets she hadn't used and laid her down on the bed she hadn't slept on.

'I'm still wet,' she protested.

'God, I hope so,' he muttered. 'Stay here. I'll get a condom from next door.'

'No.' She opened the nightstand drawer, finding it as full of condoms as the one next to the bed they'd used that morning.

He laughed breathlessly. 'I'm not going to ask. I don't want to know.' He grabbed one, ripped it open, and slid it on. 'Are you still wet?'

Eyes on his, she palmed herself, slipping her longest finger up inside. His eyes blazed, his breaths quickening as he licked his lips. 'God. I want to watch you do that again and again until you make yourself come, but not right now. I need you now.'

She stretched both hands above her head. 'Then do something, for God's sake.'

She didn't need to ask him twice. He crawled between her thighs, sliding his hands under her butt to lift her hips and—

'God.' The gasp was shoved out of her lungs as he entered her in one hard thrust.

Holding himself above her, he dropped his head with a moan she was sure could be heard down in the parking garage. 'I can't go slow this time. Maybe round two.'

Round two? *Yes, please.* 'Then go fast,' she whispered. 'I'll keep up.'

His grin was downright filthy. 'You do that, Dr Fallon.' He began to move in short, hard thrusts, his eyes on hers. 'Show me how you'll keep up.'

She slid one hand between them, mesmerized by him, completely unable to look away. But she didn't need to look. She found her clit and rubbed in time to his thrusts, feeling the tension growing tighter and tighter. But it wasn't until he dropped his gaze to her busy fingers that she couldn't hold back any longer. Head back, she let herself go, let herself fall, conscious that he was right behind her.

He dropped to his elbows, still careful not to put any weight on her ribs and hips. For which – now that they'd burned off some of the need – she was grateful. She hadn't cared about her bruises while they were at it, but once the adrenaline began to fade?

Yeah, she'd feel it then.

He tensed then, surging up into her once more as an aftershock shuddered through him, his gasp followed by another low groan. 'God.' Finally spent, he kissed her shoulder, the side of her neck, the cheek that wasn't scraped up.

'Thank you,' he whispered. 'I needed that. I'll go slower next time.'

'I kind of liked it just like that,' she confessed. 'But I'd be willing to check out the benefits of slow in a little while.'

'I was hoping you'd say that.'

Twenty-four

Adam broke the silence, his voice low in the darkness. 'Meredith?'

He'd turned out the bedroom light and they lay together, legs intertwined. She nuzzled her cheek against his shoulder, her fingers petting the hair on his chest. 'Yeah?' she asked lazily. She sounded relaxed. Replete. Completely sated.

So of course I'm going to dash all that to hell. But he needed answers. 'What happened to you around the holidays?'

Her fingers stilled and he immediately missed the petting. But it was a small price to pay for the truth. As long as she started petting him again. Eventually.

'How much did you overhear yesterday, when Papa and I were talking?'

'I came in when you were telling him that you were okay with how I've dealt with things, so he needed to be too. I heard you ask him to watch videos with you. Of your parents, "On the day." And he said that he'd need me not to be there since he'd need to drink to watch. Which I appreciated, by the way.'

'He's thoughtful that way.'

'Will you tell me what happened?' he asked, and she sighed heavily.

'My parents died in a plane crash three days after Christmas, seven years ago.'

His chest tightened. 'I'm sorry, honey.'

'So am I,' she murmured. 'My parents were . . . simply the best. I

429

see you and Diesel and Kate and Decker and all the other folks in our group that didn't have good childhoods and my heart breaks for you. I miss my mom and dad every day. And that's part of the problem. I miss them and there's still a piece of me that feels like I don't have the right.'

'Why?'

'Because I'm the reason they were on that plane,' she said, with perfect calm. 'I'm the reason they died.'

Stunned, he pressed back into the pillow, angling to better see her face. She appeared serene, her eyes closed, lashes lying thick and dark against her skin. He wanted to shake that serenity off and see her real face, but he didn't. He figured that she needed the zen mask right now and he wasn't going to take that away from her.

He wanted to tell her no, that she wasn't responsible for a plane crash, but she'd uttered the words with such quiet finality that he knew she believed it.

'Why?' he finally asked.

'I was the perfect child,' she said. 'I never rebelled, I got good grades, I was on the track team, I volunteered at the hospital. My parents believed I had my act together.'

'But you didn't.'

'No. I'm good at letting people see what they want to see.' Her petting of his chest resumed and he let out a relieved breath. She was there with him, even if she still hid behind her unyielding composure. 'I was driven. Partly because it's who I was – am. And partly because I hated who I was. Never good enough. Most of my clients have been the victims of some trauma, but not all. Some just don't like who they are. My job with them is to help them see themselves clearly and then to decide – if they still don't like what they see – what will they change and how will they change it.'

'Did anyone do that with you?'

'Yes, but not until it got so bad that I couldn't hide it anymore. My cousin Alex came to live with us when she was fifteen. I was seventeen. I'd been a cutter for years by then. Alex's mom and my mom were twins. We'd always been close, but then Alex's mother was murdered and when we got to Georgia, where they lived, Alex was in the psych ward. They thought she'd tried to kill herself because she'd discovered her mother's body.'

'But she hadn't?'

'Not then. But later? Yeah, she tried. We got her from Georgia to our house here, got her settled in her room, then I set myself up as sentry. Because I'd seen her palm a sleeping pill. I took it away from her and watched her until I was sure she wasn't going to hurt herself.'

'For how long?'

'A few months. Alex went into therapy and got . . . better. I kept the pill.'

Adam sucked in a breath. 'Did you now?' he said with a calm that was pure BS.

The little huff of breath against his chest told him that she knew his BS for what it was. 'I did. And I'd look at it sometimes and think, I could get more and swallow them all and then I'd be done. But I never did. Told myself it was because I was in control.'

'Like an alcoholic who goes to a bar to prove they can say no to booze.'

'Exactly. And down deep, I didn't want to hurt myself. Not then.'

He thought of the scars on her arms. Those from the cutting had nearly faded. The longer, deeper scars just above her wrists signified an act far more drastic. 'When?'

'When I was twenty. There was no single event. No primary trigger. I just woke up one day and knew that I didn't have the energy to do it anymore.'

'Clinical depression,' he murmured.

'Yes. But like I said, I was good at letting people only see what they wanted to see.'

'Who found you?' he asked, because the scars were remnants of an injury so serious that he doubted she could have dealt with it on her own.

'My gran. My parents were traveling. Alex was making friends at university and she . . . didn't really need me anymore. Which makes it sound like I blame her, but I never did. I knew she was doing the healthy thing, experiencing life, while I, Miss Perfect

431

Child, was not. I don't know why I did it that day or why I did it at Gran's, other than I knew she'd check on me. I think she always knew what was wrong. Turns out she'd dealt with depression too, but she didn't tell me until afterward, because people didn't talk about things like that.'

'Still don't.'

'True, but it is getting better. Anyway, my parents found out because I was hospitalized, but I was able to keep it from Alex for years. Partly because as long as it was my secret, I could still be the strong one and she'd be the one who'd palmed a pill.'

'What did she say when you told her?'

'She cried. I cried. We became even closer.'

'When did you tell her?'

'Two years after she met Daniel and decided to stay in Atlanta. They wanted a Christmas wedding and she wanted me to be her maid of honor and I . . . couldn't. It had only been three years since the plane crash. She thought that was the reason and tried to get me to see that it was a tribute to my folks. She'd loved them too, you see, and she really meant that. I told her that I couldn't be in the wedding if it was at Christmas and she knew something had happened. I had to tell her everything. She's um, kind of persuasive.'

'I can't wait to meet her.'

'You'll love her. Everyone does.' She drew a breath, held it for a few seconds then let it out. Adam had learned this meant that he probably wouldn't like what came next. 'She doesn't have to wear a mask for people to love her. She's just herself.'

He'd been right. He didn't like that statement at all. 'Maybe the mask is just an assistive device for you. Like a hearing aid. I learned years ago that Greg uses his hearing aids to control how much of the world he lets in, and that's his choice. The mask is your way of controlling the situation around you, of maintaining calm. You aren't a different person underneath. It's just how much of yourself you allow out on any given day.'

Her fingers faltered for a few seconds before resuming the petting of his chest. 'I hadn't thought of it that way. Maybe you're right. I hope you are.'

'So what happened the Christmas that your parents died?'

'You can't help asking the questions, can you?' she asked dryly.

'Would you want me to?'

'No. I like the man you are. I always knew he was in there.' She kissed his collarbone. 'So. Christmas.' She was quiet for another moment. 'I was married.'

He froze where he lay as the fallout from that little bombshell filtered into his brain. *Okay.* 'Married,' he repeated, just to be sure he'd heard correctly.

'Yes, but not for long.'

Adam felt like he'd been poleaxed, which he did not like. But she'd gone still in his arms and he liked that even less. 'What happened?'

A sigh. 'I had this boyfriend. Chris. He worked in my dad's company. My parents and grandparents weren't crazy about him, and I think I always knew that there was no future for us, but he made me feel not so lonely. One night I drank too much and we forgot protection and I got pregnant. Chris wasn't entirely horrible, and he was raised by a single mom. He said we should get married because he didn't want his kid growing up the same way. So we did. We had a simple service at the end of October and I bought a dress that would camouflage the baby belly. Nobody knew except my parents and grandparents.'

He did not want to think about her with another man. Ever. But she didn't have a child now, so he knew this was important. 'Did Alex know?'

'Not at the time. I was just . . . I didn't want her to know how stupid I'd been.'

End of October. He swallowed a groan, because this was not about him. 'When I came to you that first time and we ended up in bed. That was the end of October.'

'Yeah. I was feeling a little raw myself when you showed up. Don't think you took advantage or anything. I was lonely and needy too. I slept with you because I wanted you and I wanted what we did. I didn't want to be alone and neither did you. So it worked.'

He wanted to argue, but to do so was to imply she hadn't known her own mind, and she definitely did. 'Did he know about the cutting and the suicide attempt?'

'Yes. I mean, he figured it out. The scars were more noticeable then. Anyway, we had Christmas that year and my parents left a few days later to go skiing. Dad had his pilot's license and he'd bought a small plane.'

Oh no. He tipped her chin up so that he could kiss her forehead and then he gently cuddled her close again, ever conscious of the scrape on her cheek. 'I'm so sorry.'

He felt her throat work as she swallowed hard. 'I had my practice by then. Working with children who were depressed like I'd been or, like my cousin Alex, had been traumatized by something horrific. Chris didn't approve. He didn't want me bringing "all that sadness" home. Told me to get a job doing something else, and after the baby was born, I should quit because I was too fragile to handle the stress of being a working mother and that I didn't need the money anyway because my parents were loaded.'

Adam bristled. 'Prince of a guy.'

'True enough. I didn't quit, and Chris and I argued. And then one day, the father of one of my youngest clients got out of jail, immediately hunted down his wife and child, and beat them senseless. The child died and I fell apart. My parents weren't home and Alex was working – she's an ER nurse – and I needed a shoulder. So I told Chris. He wasn't happy with me.'

Adam could feel a growl start at the base of his throat. 'What did he do?'

'He said if I wouldn't quit my job, he was walking. That I was being selfish to keep heaping sadness on his head. That his job was too stressful to be burdened with other people's issues. He wasn't that nice about it, actually. I refused and he slammed the door on the way out.'

'He was looking for a reason to leave.'

'I know that now, but then . . . I was so upset. I actually found a razor. I wasn't going to attempt suicide again, but I was thinking about cutting. I sat there for hours, just looking at that razor. And then I started to bleed and it had nothing to do with the razor.'

'You miscarried.'

'I did.'

'Did you have anyone to call?'

'Wendi,' she said fondly. 'We'd worked together on a few cases. She was a friend. She took me to an ER that wasn't Alex's and called Papa, because she'd met him. Papa called my father and he and Mom dropped everything to come home. Gran had found the razor when she went to get me fresh clothes and she'd told Papa and my parents. They were all worried that I'd try to harm myself again.'

'But the razor was like the pill,' he said, his voice raw because his chest hurt too much to breathe. 'You just wanted to show yourself that you wouldn't.'

She went very still again, then nodded, rubbing her cheek against his chest. 'Nobody got that. Not then and not since. Not until you.'

Hearing that loosened the tightness in his chest enough to let him draw a harsh breath. 'But you didn't harm yourself.'

'No. Although I really wanted to later, because Mom and Dad should never have come when they did. There was a storm. But they were so worried about me. They felt so guilty about missing my depression for so long . . .'

He was unsurprised when his chest grew wet with her tears. 'Their plane crashed,' he said, able to at least say the words so that she wouldn't have to.

'Yes. It was not quick and they did suffer.'

His throat closed on a wave of grief. And anger. 'Who told you that?'

'The state trooper who came by my house later that night to give me the news.'

'Sonofabitch,' he muttered, unable to stop the curse.

'Yeah. That's why when you and Trip lied to Kyle about Tiffany not suffering? I was so on board with that. It wasn't something that I needed to hear when I was in shock and grieving. So, that's the story. Christmas is difficult.'

'Yeah, I can see that.' He kissed her hair. 'What happened to the douchebag?'

Her chuckle was watery. 'Oh, Chris scuttled to his attorney right away to file for divorce. I didn't fight him. I didn't want him by that point. Especially when he blamed me for the miscarriage. I'm not sure who was angrier about that, Papa, Gran, or Wendi. I think he was most afraid of Wendi, to tell you the truth.'

'I believe that. She is fierce when it comes to protecting you. But what she said makes so much sense now. More sense anyway. It made sense when she said it.'

Meredith lifted her head, her eyes wet, her brows scrunched in a frown. 'What do you mean? She promised me she wouldn't say anything to you.'

Adam opened his mouth, then closed it. 'Not going there, Meredith. Wendi scares the bejeezus out of me.'

Meredith's lips twitched, which had been his intent. 'That will make her so happy.'

He lifted his head from the pillow enough to kiss her lips chastely. 'Tell me about the depression. What do I need to know?'

'Not much, really. I have a shrink.'

'I know. I heard you tell your grandfather that too. Do you see Dr Lane?'

'Oh no. She specializes in PTSD and, at least up until yesterday anyway, that wasn't my issue. Dr Lane and I met at a conference a few years ago. I liked her, and everyone I've sent her way likes her too.'

'I'm going to have to check in with her in a few days,' Adam said grimly, because PTSD *was* his issue and this entire weekend had rattled him hard. Which reminded him that he'd promised his sponsor he'd make time for a meeting. He needed to keep that promise. For Meredith. *But mostly for me.* Putting on the oxygen mask first applied to him as well.

'No shame in that, Adam.'

'I know.' He did, but it still rankled from time to time, that he hadn't been able to handle it alone. It rankled worse that he had just heard those words in his father's voice. He shut down the old tapes and refocused on Meredith's needs. 'Meds?'

'Yes. They help. So does yoga and running and playdates with my friends. I nurture myself too. I learned a long time ago to put on my oxygen mask first before helping others. I just needed a refresher tonight. Thank you, by the way. I forgot to say it earlier.'

'When? When I imparted flight attendant wisdom or when you were coming so hard you saw stars?'

Her snorted laugh was the most ladylike he'd ever heard. 'Both.' She sighed. 'I still have bad cycles,' she said, very serious now. 'Sometimes I can pre-plan, like around the holidays. Sometimes they hit me out of the blue and those are the bad times.'

She'd said the words carefully, as if she was afraid they'd make him bolt. 'I'm not afraid of bad times,' he said, trying to put all the honesty he felt into his voice. 'But I'll have them too, so I need to know what you're thinking and I'll do the same. I won't cut you off again, even if I think it's for your own good. From now on, it's full disclosure. Okay?'

'I can live with that. So, in the spirit of that . . . I need you to be careful when you go out to that used-car lot tomorrow. I finally have you. I don't want to lose you.'

'I promise,' he said seriously. 'Because I finally have you too.' He hugged her to him. 'Go to sleep. It'll all be there when we wake up. *I'll* be here when you wake up.'

She burrowed into his chest. 'Good night, Adam.'

He drew in her scent, holding on to the moment. Holding on to her. 'Good night,' he whispered. And for the first time in longer than he could remember, it was.

Cincinnati, Ohio,
Monday 21 December, 2.05 A.M.

He pulled his SUV into his driveway and switched off the ignition. He'd need to get another vehicle. This one had come from Mike's lot and he couldn't have it connected to him. It would be far more difficult to track his vehicles now that he'd burned Mike's used-car lot to the ground, but he wasn't taking any chances, especially with Kimble still alive. The man was sniffing too damn close.

Goddamn him. Except he didn't know who he was cursing more – himself or Adam Kimble or Mike. He was definitely cursing Mike.

For years they'd done so well together. They'd never been a huge enterprise. Never wanted to be. They'd watched others rise higher, only to fall spectacularly over the years.

They'd kept it small, taken advantage of opportunities as they'd come up. Discover a crime in progress? Offer the doer an easy way out – payment in exchange for silence. Sometimes it was a one-time payoff. *Give me the drugs you were about to sell*, he'd say, *and we'll call this whole arrest a misunderstanding*. And then Mike would sell the drugs himself and they'd split the take.

Sometimes the opportunity was too good for a one-time payment. Those were the really juicy crimes, committed by people who had a lot more to lose than a two-bit dealer on the street. Their best clients were the rich elite, with careers, reputations, and fortunes on the line. They were the bread 'n' butter clients who kept paying, year after year.

And sometimes the perfect victim would emerge and be too tempting to pass up.

Voss had been one of those, a man especially vulnerable to blackmail after becoming an overnight millionaire. Especially vulnerable because of his proclivities.

Voss had liked them young.

Which they'd learned after Voss had answered one of their ads, meeting one of their underage girls in a hotel. Of course there'd been cameras. Mike had wanted to blackmail Voss right away within the first moment of seeing the rich man's face on camera. Idiot. They'd had a gold mine in the making and Mike would have blown it as a one-off.

He – not Mike – had been the one to tell Jolee to communicate with the girl while Voss was cleaning up in the bathroom, to tell the girl to offer up her friends for a party. Voss had been greedy, setting the next meet for the following weekend in the same hotel.

Voss never considered he'd been recorded. The following weekend's videos had been the gold mine he'd expected and Voss had been paying through the nose ever since.

Then, no thanks to Mike, he'd tapped the well again. Set up a party with some of his best clients who were not afraid of blackmail.

Provided the entertainment – the drugs and barely-eighteen college hookers that would entice Voss without making him fear further entrapment.

He – not Mike – had made sure Jolee approached Voss that night, selling their services so that they'd become Voss's party service provider of choice. They were milking Voss from the front door and the back, so to speak. Blackmail plus the 'legit' services that were still completely illegal. And the man had no clue that he was paying the same people.

Until Voss got stupid and had a party with his kid at home. Asshole.

If he had to pinpoint the moment when it all began to unravel, that would be it.

Which, of course, was bullshit. He'd played Voss so well because he understood the rich man better than anyone else knew. Anyone else still alive, anyway.

Mike had been right about one thing. He hadn't been able to resist Mallory Martin and he'd never been entirely sure why. Maybe because he'd considered her 'safe.' An asset he hadn't had to personally manage. But more likely because so many on the net had wanted her. *And I'd had her. I'd had something those other losers would never have.*

Having Mallory had made him want a young thing of his own, spurring him to find Paula, and she'd been such a pretty thing. But Kimble had been getting a little too good at his job in Personal Crimes and needed to be taken down a peg or two. Paula had to be sacrificed and he'd been itchy ever since.

And then Mallory had escaped last summer and turned everything upside down.

'I should've let Mike take care of her,' he murmured into the quiet of his SUV. He'd thought himself too smart to fuck it all up. And yet he had.

Now he had to figure out how to fix this mess.

Kimble and the others thought they were looking for a cop. *So give them a cop. And then get rid of Kimble.* The guy was smart. Too smart. Especially now that his brain had dried out from the booze. He was getting too damn close to the truth. Eliminating him would also provide a much-needed distraction. The death of one of their own would demoralize their little joint task force, derailing it long enough to give him time to fix all of Mike's fuckups so that they couldn't be traced back to him.

There was still the issue of Linnea, but she hadn't come forward yet when she could have, nor had she fled town when she should have, so she obviously had an agenda of her own. *Probably wants me*, he thought with a smile. *Little spitfire.* She'd surprised him at every turn. He'd use her single-minded focus to draw her in and end her, permanently.

Maybe he should give her an opportunity she couldn't refuse. *She wants me? Come and get me, little girl. But on* my *terms.*

Cheered by the thought, he turned off the engine and got out of the SUV. Only to be assaulted with the smells and sounds of a barnyard. A peek into his neighbor's backyard revealed a donkey, a cow, and sheep in a pen.

Mr Wainwright had received the permit for his nativity scene. *Wonderful*, he thought acidly. Except it would make Ariel and Mikey happy, so he'd deal as best he could. It was only for a few more days, anyway.

It was almost Christmas. He knew what he wanted from Santa – Mallory, Linnea, and Kimble . . . gone.

Cincinnati, Ohio,
Monday 21 December, 4.45 A.M.

The throbbing in her hip woke her, but the emptiness in her bed had Meredith fully alert. She ran her hand across the sheet next to her, finding it still a little warm. Adam hadn't been awake long. *I'll be here when you wake up*, he'd said, so she knew he was still in the condo somewhere. He wouldn't have left without telling her.

She slipped out of bed with a groan. Her hip was yelling at her for lying to the ER doctors about her parking lot injuries, yet in hindsight she regretted nothing. Yes, she might have a prescription for some nifty painkillers, but she'd have missed the hours in Adam's arms. Totally worth it.

She pulled on the purple PJs he'd pulled off her the day before, sighing contentedly at the feel of silk on her skin. Yes, she was a hedonist and no, she didn't apologize. It was one of the small things she did to keep herself centered. And because it was cold, she layered with the sweatshirt lying on top of Adam's open duffel bag. It hung past her hips and it smelled like him.

She heard the music as soon as she opened the bedroom door, something low and bluesy. He was a jazz fan too, which made her ridiculously happy.

She followed Ella Fitzgerald to the kitchen where she found him at the table, frowning at his laptop. Shirtless, hair tousled, the pair of thin gray sweats he'd worn earlier the only thing covering his skin. *God, he's something.* No, not just something. *Everything.* For a moment, she let herself look. And was then busted when he looked up. His frown softened, becoming worry.

'I didn't mean to wake you up,' he said, closing his laptop and turning down the volume on his phone.

'You didn't. You don't have to turn it down.' She closed the distance between them, dropping a kiss on his upturned face. 'I like this album.'

His slow smile warmed her. 'I'm glad. Ella helps me think.'

'I couldn't sleep,' she said. 'You want some tea?'

He cupped her cheek and pulled her in for a longer kiss that curled her toes. 'Yes, please,' he murmured against her mouth, then released her. 'Tea would be nice.'

I could get used to this, she thought. Being kissed like this in the middle of the night.

'I could get used to this,' he said out loud as she moved about the kitchen, taking comfort from her things. 'Seeing you like this.'

She smiled over at him. 'Making tea while swimming in your clothes?'

The look he shot her was positively molten. 'Doing anything. Wearing anything. Wearing nothing.'

Oh my. A delicious shiver tickled her skin. Then he grinned, his dimple coming out to play, and her heart stuttered in the best of ways. She put the kettle on and took the chair next to his. 'What are you doing up so early?' she asked. 'I thought I'd tired you out.'

His smile faded and her heart sank. 'I couldn't sleep either,' he confessed.

She rested her chin on his hard biceps and looked up at him. *Full disclosure.* 'I couldn't sleep because my hip hurt. I fell harder than I admitted tonight when he threw me off Mallory. Why couldn't you sleep?'

One side of his mouth twitched up. 'Spirit of full disclosure, huh?'

'You're the one who made that rule,' she said lightly.

'Yes, I did. All right then, I had a nightmare. It happens.'

'I figured. Was it Paula?'

He nodded, eyes troubled. 'I dream of her often, usually of the moment she dies. But tonight . . .' He blew out a breath. 'It was her body, laid out on a bed, throat slit. Eviscerated.'

She swallowed hard, needing to comfort but unsure of what to say. So she kissed the tensed muscle of his biceps instead.

'And when I woke up I realized I'd never seen her that way. I know those things happened to her, but I didn't see her body until it turned up in my trunk, burned.'

The thought of him discovering the girl's body that way . . . It hurt. But on this she could give some perspective, at least. 'Our dreams aren't always representative of what we've actually seen.'

'I know. But I realized that I *had* seen that picture. On the whiteboard tonight.'

The photos of Tiffany Curtis and her mother lying dead in their beds. 'I couldn't look at the photos. I'm not that brave.' Then she understood and reared back, staring at him. 'Wait. What?' She shook her head hard, not sure she had actually understood. 'Are you saying that Paula was killed in the same way as Tiffany and her mother?'

He lifted sardonic brows. 'Maybe. Sounds crazy, doesn't it?'

'Yeah, but nothing about this case seems terribly sane, Adam.'

He scrubbed his palms over his face. 'Ain't that the truth.'

The kettle whistled, so she got up to make the tea. Setting it on the table, she tapped his laptop. 'Were you looking at the Chicago crime scene photos?'

He closed his eyes. 'Yes. And the video.'

'The Chicago detectives sent you video?'

'No. I accessed a copy of the recording of Paula's murder.'

Meredith couldn't control the flinch, but stopped herself from completely recoiling from the laptop, knowing that it contained the thing that had nearly crushed Adam. She focused on his word choice instead. '"Accessed"? Does that mean you had permission, got permission, broke into a server, or that you kept it all along?'

'The last one. Kind of. I had a DVD of old case videos in the stuff I'd cleaned out of my desk when I went on mental health leave. One was Paula's murder.'

'But you kept it? Why?'

'It was my pill. My razor.'

Oh, Adam. 'You wanted to know if you could view it without falling apart. Did you?'

He nodded. 'Yeah,' he said gruffly. 'Barely.'

She leaned in to kiss his cheek, his stubble tickling her lips. 'What did you see?'

He swallowed hard. 'I closed my eyes after her attacker slit her throat, you know, the first time. When it really happened. I made myself watch the rest later, but my dream always stops at her throat. I kind of willingly blocked out the rest, I guess.'

'Understandable.' She had to force herself to ask the question. 'Paula was cut open, like Tiffany and her mother?'

'Yeah. It's all there. He held her up for the camera when he did it. He was big enough that he held her like a doll. His body type is the same as Bruiser's. Exactly.'

Meredith sat back in her chair, staring up at his face, stunned. 'I believe you, you know? But I'm having trouble processing all this.'

'Trust me, so am I.'

She reached across him to turn the volume up on his phone and Ella Fitzgerald's voice filled the kitchen. 'So think, Adam. Think and tell me what you see the options to be.'

He set his jaw grimly. 'Well, option one is that Paula and Tiffany were not killed by the same man and it's all a grand coincidence.'

'Possible,' she murmured. 'But not that likely. What else?'

'That the killers were different people, completely unrelated, but that Bruiser knew I was on the case and figured seeing Tiffany's body would freak me out and I'd be too distracted to investigate properly.' He drew a breath. 'Which sounds utterly presumptive and narcissistic of me.'

A shiver clawed across her skin. 'But someone tried to kill you yesterday.'

'I know. That's why I'm sitting here making myself crazy.'

'What are the other options?'

'Just one – that the same man killed Paula and Tiffany and her mother. Which means I'm connected on some level. Which makes sense if we're talking about a cop being responsible. So, I'm leaning toward this last one, as crazy as it sounds.'

'You're saying you know this cop. Or this cop knows you. And wants to hurt you.'

'Well, he wants to hurt Mallory,' he said grimly. 'He just wants to fuck with me.'

She shuddered out a breath. 'It was better when I was the only one in danger.'

He gave her an angry look. 'Not funny.'

'Not trying to be. I'm just being honest.'

He closed his eyes again. 'I'm . . . blown away by this, Meredith. Not gonna lie.'

'How can we know, one way or the other?'

He tapped a beat on his laptop lid, keeping time with the slow ballad coming from his phone. 'We connect Bruiser to the man who hurt you all tonight. And then we check all their connections and find out where they cross paths with the cop who raped Mallory.'

'Okay. That sounds like a place to start.'

His lips curved bitterly. 'Sure. Except we don't know Bruiser's real name, tonight's gunman got away, and all we know about the cop is that he has a birthmark or a scar on his chest.' He frowned. 'And that, if he really is a cop, he had a way to make any records of his interaction with Mallory's captor disappear.' He ran a frustrated hand through his hair. '*And* even if we knew more, we don't know if there are any other players in the mix. What we fucking *know* is a fucking *drop* in the fucking *ocean*.'

Meredith wanted to soothe him. Wanted to assure him it would be all right, but knew that platitudes wouldn't help. Closing her eyes, she let the music fill her mind, brushing all the frustrations into a corner. Humming with 'Sentimental Journey', her thoughts wandered to what she knew, what she had seen and heard, and suddenly little Penny Voss had center stage. Penny's horror, her sadness, and her frustration as she'd smashed the face of her creation because she couldn't replicate a person so sick.

Sick and sad and scared and on the run.

'Linnie knows,' she said quietly. 'Linnie's seen his face.'

A bitter sigh. 'And she's in the wind. She'll never trust us now.'

Meredith opened her eyes, studying his stony profile. 'But she'll trust Shane.'

His black lashes lifted and then he was staring at her with a proud wonder that morphed into intense focus. 'Yeah. She would. I need to get Shane on TV, to get him to make a plea for her to come to us before Andy's killer gets her.'

She smiled at him. 'Then do that.'

He cupped her jaw and roughly pulled her to his mouth, kissing her hard. 'I will.' He let her go and stood up. 'We need to go.'

She blinked at him. 'We do?'

'Yeah. I have to go home and get some clean clothes, drop you . . . where? Where can I take you where you'll be safe? I can't leave you here.'

'I'm not the target,' she reminded him, but he shook his head.

'I don't care. I won't be able to think clearly if I don't know you're safe.'

'Then drop me off at the hospital. I'll sit with Papa.'

'Okay, that's good. Isenberg posted an officer between his room and Kate's. Then I can go into the precinct to—' He cut himself off. 'No, I have something else to do before I set up a TV spot for Shane.' He glanced at her from the corner of his eye. 'Full disclosure? I promised my sponsor I'd hit a meeting this morning. St Agnes's has one at six a.m.'

445

'Then you should. Give me fifteen minutes and I'll be ready to go.' She started for the bedroom, but a thought struck her hard and she turned back to Adam. 'Who knows about that video, Adam? The one of Paula?'

He'd cut the music and had started to dial a number on his phone, but he stopped and frowned at her. 'Wyatt and Nash. They were standing with me when it went down.' He grimaced. 'It was Nash who made me think of this again.'

'He was looking at the photos before we left the briefing room,' she said quietly.

Adam's expression became suddenly unreadable. 'He couldn't be . . . No, Meredith. He can't be involved. Nash's a good man.'

'I'm not saying he's bad. But even if Tiffany and her mother's murders are only related to upset you and throw you off your game, it means *somebody* had to know. You need to find out who's had access to that video. Maybe it was someone you know. Maybe someone you don't.' She grabbed his hand and squeezed it. 'Call your old department. Maybe they'll have records of who's viewed it other than Wyatt and Nash.'

He sank back into the chair, looking like he'd been hit with a mallet. 'Shit.'

'I'm sorry.'

He shook his head. 'No, no. You're right. Of course you're right. But . . . *shit*.' He looked up at her bleakly. 'I'm just . . . Damn, Meredith, who do I trust?'

'Isenberg, Deacon, and Scarlett, for starters.'

He rolled his eyes. 'Well, of course I trust Isenberg, Deacon, and Scarlett.'

Meredith considered carefully. 'And Trip.'

He held her gaze. 'Because your gut says so? I mean, I'm inclined to agree, but I haven't known him long enough to be sure.'

She shrugged. 'It's not just because I like him, even though I do. I trust Trip. But the fact is, the man who raped Mallory was white. The man who attacked us last night was about seven inches shorter and probably a hundred pounds lighter than Trip. And I happen to know he was still training in Quantico around the time Paula was killed.' She rose. 'Call Isenberg. I'll get your things together while you do.' She was halfway to the bedroom when he called to her.

'Meredith? Thank you.'

He looked a little lost, so she retraced her steps to stand behind his chair. Leaning down, she wrapped her arms around his broad, strong shoulders. She pressed her lips to his temple. 'You're welcome,' she murmured in his ear. 'I'm not going to say it'll be okay, but I will remind you that you are *not* alone. Okay?'

'Okay.'

Cincinnati, Ohio,
Monday 21 December, 6.15 A.M.

Linnea woke with a start, mind fuzzy, aware she was in a strange place. She slept under soft blankets and her head rested on one that was folded into a pillow. Her hand covered a gun and her stomach was only a little growly.

The Gruber Academy's little bus. She stretched, wincing when her muscles ached. She'd walked a long way yesterday. But she was still alive and that meant something.

It was dark, so it wasn't seven yet, which was good because parents started dropping off their kids at seven thirty. It had said so on the school's website.

Cautiously, she pushed to her knees and peered out the window, relieved to see the parking lot exactly as it had been the night before. She needed to fold the blankets then find somewhere to freshen up.

She was relieved to see she hadn't bled on their blankets, so Dr Dani's stitches were holding. The woman might be a terrible person, but she was a decent doctor.

Linnea pocketed the gun, wondering exactly what she'd do when she found little Ariel. She wasn't going to shoot the child, that much she knew for sure. And she still wasn't sure that Ariel's daddy was the man she sought.

But this was her best lead and she had to follow it through.

Twenty-five

Cincinnati, Ohio,
Monday 21 December, 7.02 A.M.

Adam drew a deep breath of the cold air as he left St Agnes's after his meeting. Normally the bracing air would smack him into alertness, but he was already too alert, his mind racing with all he'd already accomplished that morning. And all he still had to do.

He'd started before leaving the condo, waking his team – Isenberg, Deacon, Scarlett, and Trip – but they'd all agreed to the significance *if* he was indeed right about the kill styles being duplicated. And they'd also agreed that he wasn't overreacting, given he'd been the target of the gunman the day before.

Which made him feel better, if he were to admit the truth.

He'd sent them the video of Paula's murder that he'd kept on his laptop for nearly a year and a half. They'd review, assess, decide, and then they'd meet thirty minutes earlier than they'd told Nash and Wyatt to arrive.

That gave him time to get Meredith safely into the hospital and up to her grandfather's room and to get to his meeting.

Adam figured with two cops posted at the hospital, it was the safest place for her. One stood guard in the ICU, protecting the two agents who were still unconscious. Nobody knew if they'd seen their assailant's face, but Isenberg and Zimmerman were taking no chances. The other cop was posted outside Kate's room, conveniently placed next to Clarke Fallon's. So Meredith would be covered.

Yes, Adam knew that she hadn't been the original target, but the second shot at Buon Cibo on Saturday had been aimed at *Meredith*. Mallory had already been out of sight.

The second shot might have been fired out of rage because Meredith had convinced Andy to drop his gun or maybe out of frustration that his bomb had not detonated. Either way, Adam was going to make sure she was protected so that he could think, goddammit.

Unless one of the cops was bad, which had him second-guessing himself while standing in her grandfather's hospital room, hesitant to leave her there. She'd clasped his hands in hers and brought their joined hands between her breasts, where something decidedly not soft was nestled. She was armed. Again.

At which point he'd blurted out, 'How many of those things do you have?' making her grandfather choke on a laugh, which in turn made Adam blush like a teenaged boy, because he'd meant guns, but his hands were still nestled between her breasts. But Meredith had laughed and he hadn't cared that he'd looked ridiculous.

Then she'd wrapped her arms around his neck and stood on her toes to whisper in his ear, 'I'm good. Don't worry about me.' She'd kissed him on the mouth, which brought a low whistle and the flash of a camera phone from the open doorway because her cousin Bailey had picked that moment to leave Kate's room to get herself a cup of coffee.

Which meant that the photo of them kissing would be shared with their circle of friends before breakfast. Which didn't make Adam feel ridiculous at all.

Just happy.

Kate had been feeling well enough to hassle him for a status update, but he'd put her off saying he was in a hurry and by that point he had been. He'd made his AA meeting on time, though, and John had been waiting for him, grouchier than normal, but it *had* only been six a.m., and John was *not* a morning person.

The meeting went much as all the others had gone. Adam could never say much. His demons were always someone else's secrets. It was usually after the meeting when he and John grabbed coffee that Adam could unload some of what haunted his nightmares. And his waking hours. John had always understood. He'd been a cop. He knew the drill.

They walked out together, shivering in the pre-dawn darkness. 'You got plans for Christmas, Adam?' John asked as they pulled on gloves and walked toward St Agnes's parking lot. 'Because you're welcome to join my family if you'd like.'

Touched, Adam's heart squeezed a little. 'Thank you, but I do have plans. I'll stop by my folks for a little while, but I'll be spending most of the day with Meredith.' They'd discussed it in the car on the way to the hospital that morning. 'Her cousin's coming in from Georgia and her other cousin's making a feast.'

The cooking was apparently Bailey's forte, but everyone would be pitching in this year. Meredith's little house would be bursting at the seams, which was how she liked it.

John frowned. 'Movin' a little fast, aren't you?'

'Not at all. Making up for lost time. I shouldn't have isolated myself from her all year. It hurt us both.' He said this gently, because it had been at John's insistence that Adam had stayed away. 'At least I should have told her why.'

John huffed out a weary breath. 'I shouldn't have given you the advice that I did.'

'You believed you were doing the right thing. And now I'm going to do the right thing and tell my family what's been going on with me. My mom's got a right to know and my cousins – Deacon, Dani, and Greg – they've been worried about me. They haven't deserved my silence.' He stopped next to his Jeep. 'So, I'm coming up on a year.'

John gave him a 'Duh' look. 'Yeah, I know. And?'

'You said we'd re-evaluate at the end of the first year. Just wondering if you wanted to continue being my sponsor.'

John sucked in a breath, his eyes growing abruptly bright. 'I . . .' He bit his lower lip and shuddered the breath out. 'I-I need to tell you. Why—' His eyes darted to the right, then froze. A second later he was shoving Adam to the ground with all his might. 'Get d—'

The crack of a rifle split the air. From where he'd been knocked to his ass on the pavement, Adam watched in horror as John jerked backward, his head thudding against the roof of his SUV. Someone screamed. Several people screamed. Adam barely heard them.

'John!' Coming up on his knees, Adam grabbed at him, easing him to the pavement between his Jeep and John's SUV.

John's black SUV. John was an ex-cop. Could he be . . .

Adam pushed the thought away. *No. Not now. Focus.* 'John! John!'

But John wasn't answering. Because the side of his head . . .

Adam pivoted on his knees and lost the breakfast he'd eaten on the way to the meeting. *No. God, no.* On his hands and knees, shaking like he had the DTs, Adam hung his head and tried to breathe. John was dead. Just like Andy Gold and Bruiser.

Get a grip. Now.

Adam sucked in air, then shouted to whoever was listening, 'Someone call 911! And stay the hell down!'

'I did!' someone shouted. Sounded like the meeting leader. 'Is everyone okay?'

Shaken *yeses* came from all over the parking lot.

Careful not to disturb John's body, Adam eased over until he sat with his back to his Jeep. He pulled his service weapon from its holster, then took his phone from his pocket. 'Call Isenberg cell,' he commanded, because his hands were shaking too hard to hit the buttons on the screen. Almost too hard to hold the fucking phone to his ear.

'Adam?' Isenberg said, picking up on the first ring. Sounded like she was in her car.

'Lynda.' It was all he could get out. He huffed and huffed, but he couldn't breathe. *Not a panic attack, please. Not now. God, not now.*

'Where are you?' she asked quietly. Competently. No drama. He was so grateful.

'St Agnes's. Parking lot.'

'Breathe. Tell me what happened.'

'911's been called. Sniper.' He clamped his lips shut and breathed through his nose, trying to slow the cannon fire in his chest. His heart beat so hard it hurt. *John. God.*

'Are you hit?' Isenberg asked, still sounding calm.

'No. My sp— My friend. He's dead. Only one shot. Nobody else is hurt.'

'Hold on. I need to make sure the first responders know the situation. Don't hang up.'

'I won't.' He clutched the phone in one hand, his gun in the other, his gloves covered in blood and . . . He grimaced. *Brain matter.* He didn't dare close his eyes. The gunman was out there and there was no guarantee that he wouldn't finish the job up close and personal.

So Adam sat and breathed and waited for Isenberg to come back on the line.

'Are you still there?' she asked.

'Yeah. We'd just exited the church and stopped at our cars and were talking. He saw something right before the shot. Pushed me out of the way.' He coughed, trying to keep the tightness in his chest from suffocating him. 'He said, "I need to tell you why." Then he shoved me and the bullet hit him. He's dead. Like Andy Gold and Bruiser.'

'Where are you now?'

'On the ground. Sitting on the ground.' He clamped his lips together again and breathed through his nose, holding the air in for a few seconds before exhaling slowly. 'I'm sitting between my Jeep and his black SUV.'

'Oh.' The word came out hushed. 'What's your friend's name, Adam?'

'John Kasper. He's a retired cop.' He let out a weary breath. 'He's my sponsor.'

'I figured as much. St Agnes's has hosted AA meetings for thirty years.'

Adam blinked. 'What?' How did she know that? *Why* did she know that? *Wait.* His brain stuttered, unable to keep up. *Lynda's attended meetings?* He shook his head, unable to process that information. Later. He'd think about it later. Because she was talking again.

'Adam,' she said, so gently it almost hurt. 'I would be the last person to judge you. And now that I've seen the video you sent me? Knowing that you saw it happen live? I'll fight to make sure nobody else judges you either. That any of you who saw that girl murdered are still sane is a fucking miracle. And testament to your personal strength.'

He was without words. He struggled, finding two that worked. 'Thank you.'

'No thanks necessary. I'm on my way to St Agnes's. You stay put and I'll take care of everything. I'm going to call Deacon for backup, okay?'

'Um . . .'

'I take it that he doesn't know?'

'No. I was gonna tell him when this was over.'

'Well, Detective, I think your timeline was just taken out of your control. You want me to give him the heads up?'

'No. I'll call him. Right now.'

'All right. I'm about ten minutes out. You should be hearing sirens any second.'

They were faint but audible. 'I do. Thank you, Lynda. I won't mention about you and . . . St Agnes's.'

'I appreciate it. I've been sober for thirteen years. Still hit the meetings from time to time. I'm honestly surprised we haven't run into each other already,' she added wryly.

'Just lucky, I guess.' God. He was lucky. He was alive. But John was not. He leaned his head back against his Jeep. 'I'm gonna go now and call Deacon.'

'All right. Call me back if you need to. Tell Deacon to come to where you are. I've instructed first responders to secure the scene and surround the parking lot, but not to approach you. I'm not taking any chance that our shooter or one of his associates is driving any of the squad cars. You stay put with your head down until either Deacon or I come to get you. Got it?'

'Yes, ma'am.' He ended the call and breathed for a minute, then . . . temporarily detoured. *Full disclosure.* And he needed to hear her voice more than he needed air. 'Call Meredith cell,' he instructed his phone.

'Hey,' she answered warmly when she picked up.

He exhaled in a rush. 'I'm okay,' he said and wondered which of them he was trying to convince. 'I'm okay.'

'Adam?' Her voice pitched a little higher. 'Where are you?'

'Still at St Agnes's. My sponsor is dead. He took a bullet for me. But I'm alive and I wanted you to hear it from me before you heard it on the grapevine.'

For a few seconds all he could hear was her breathing, fast and shallow. 'Okay. Okay.' She made a noise like a choked sob. 'You're sure? You weren't hit?'

'No. Not at all.'

'Are you inside where it's safe?'

He drew a breath. It would be so easy to lie, to tell her what would keep her from worrying. 'Full disclosure? I'm sitting outside in the parking lot, between two large vehicles, next to my sponsor's body.'

'*Adam.*' She packed an astonishing number of emotions into his name. Fear, horror, compassion. Caring. And something else. He hoped. Oh God, how he hoped.

I need to tell her how I feel. I need her to know. But he hadn't wanted to tell her like this. *Not like this.*

'Look, I have to go. Isenberg is coming and I need to call Deacon. I need to tell him why I'm here before he learns the way I don't want him to.'

'Okay. Adam? Not your fault.'

'I know.' He chanced a glance at John. His stomach lurched. *That could have been me. I would have been dead and she'd never know the truth.* 'Meredith?'

'Yeah?' she whispered it into the phone and he could tell that she was crying but didn't want him to know.

She's so damn brave, he thought. *She needs to know. Deserves to know.* 'I know I shouldn't tell you this yet, but . . .' He swallowed hard. 'I've loved you since we colored at your kitchen table. I don't want anything to happen and you not to know that.'

Her sob broke free. 'Adam.'

'Now you know. I need to—'

'Don't you hang up on me yet,' she interrupted in as close to a snarl as he'd ever heard come from her mouth. 'I get to say something too.'

He found his lips curving, despite everything. 'Yeah?'

'Yeah,' she said, the word a sob she couldn't hold back. 'I thought I loved you when you showed up on Saturday with glitter in your hair, just because I said I needed you. Even though I didn't think you felt the same way.'

She thought? he thought, his heart constricting so hard it hurt. But this was Meredith. *She would never hurt me.* 'And then?' he whispered.

'And then you held Kyle when he cried and you held me when I cried and you told Mallory that she was ours – and I knew. No doubts. I love you.' Her voice broke. 'Don't ever think anything different, okay? And come back to me so I can tell you in person.'

Warmth flooded his chest, intense and overwhelming, and he wondered how any human heart contained emotion this powerful because his was pounding to beat all hell.

She loves me. Me. It was too much. *Almost.* 'I'll be back,' he whispered. 'I promise.'

'You'd better.' She was crying in earnest now. 'Dammit, Adam.'

'Hey.' He huffed, trying to distract her so she'd stop crying because it was ripping him apart. 'You *thought* you knew just two days ago? Four months after I knew for sure?'

'What can I say?' Her swallow was audible, but her sobs no longer were. 'I'm a late bloomer.' Her attempt at levity was so forced that it hurt to hear. She was trying so hard to make this bearable and that made him love her even more. 'Besides,' she added tartly. 'I hadn't read the script so I didn't know that you'd already fallen.'

'Fair enough,' he said. 'I gotta go. I'll tell you the right way when I see you.'

'You'd better,' she said, her voice breaking. 'Be careful.'

'I will.' He ended the call and the bubble they'd hidden within popped, letting reality rush back in. *Somebody is trying to kill me. Somebody who knew I'd be here today.*

Somebody who may be a cop.

Unbidden, the memory of his conversation with Quincy rose to the surface. He'd known about his sobriety. Somehow he'd known. *I make it a point to know who I'm working with. Their skills* and *their weaknesses.*

No, he thought. *Not Quincy. Not Nash either.* And Wyatt wasn't even a question. *Hell no.* They'd been through too much together over the years. It had to be someone random.

Someone who knows about Paula, who knew we were in that van en route to the station. Someone who knew Meredith and Mallory were at the restaurant on Saturday and again at the hospital last night. Someone who knew I'd be here this morning.

A random person couldn't know all that. It was an awful truth. *Someone is trying to kill me.* It was too surreal to process.

Someone I know *is trying to kill me.* Adam wished for the numbness of denial, but the body next to him made that impossible.

I need to call Deacon. Prepare him for the whole twelve-step thing. It's only fair.

And that confessing his sins to Deacon was suddenly the preferable task just showed how completely and utterly fucked this entire thing was.

Cincinnati, Ohio,
Monday 21 December, 7.05 A.M.

For a moment he could only stare in disbelief. John was dead. Not Adam Kimble.

Goddamn asshole. Throwing himself into a fucking bullet. Who did that? *Heroes and fools, that's who.* John was definitely among the latter.

Fuck. Fuck John and his last-minute change of heart. Fuck Mike for making me kill him, because I didn't sleep at all last night. Fuck Adam Kimble for making me kill Butch.

Fuck it all. He wanted to scream it, but he couldn't. He had to get away. The police would be coming and he had to get away. He had a rifle to discard. A cop to set up.

A hooker-on-the-run to reel in like a fish on a hook.

Mallory Martin couldn't ID him. If she could have, she would have by now. He was going to have to let her go. For now. *Let things die down. Let her regain her confidence about coming out into public.* Then he'd end her.

And Kimble? He'd be more careful than ever now. And he'd wonder who'd known he'd be at the AA meeting. Kimble had most of the pieces of the puzzle, even if he didn't know it yet. The hero would bring in his traitorous cop. Not the right one, of course, but it would be enough for now. And later? If Kimble kept pushing? Investigating? Trying to find the cop who'd raped little Mallory? He'd have to shut the man up. Permanently.

Cincinnati, Ohio,
Monday 21 December, 7.15 A.M.

'Call Deacon cell,' Adam said, hearing defeat in his own voice. He'd put off this call too long. And with his sponsor's dead body lying next to him, it had suddenly become important that his cousin know the truth. *It could have been me lying there, and I never would have gotten to apologize and make amends.*

Deacon's line rang four times. 'Yeah?' Deacon answered, his voice thick.

God. Deacon either had a cold or he was crying. Adam couldn't deal with any tears right now, not after hearing Meredith's sobs. 'You okay, D?'

'No.'

Yep, Deacon was crying. *Shit.* 'I'm sorry,' he said quietly. 'I should have told you.'

'Told me what?' Deacon demanded.

'Did Isenberg call you?'

'Yes. Told me to head to St Agnes's. That there'd been a shooting.'

Isenberg hadn't told Deacon anything. And the significance of that was not lost on Adam. His boss had trusted that he really would call his cousin. That he'd really come clean. *So man up, Kimble. Do the right thing.*

But his words still hadn't gotten there yet. 'Then why are you upset?' Adam asked.

'You mean why am I crying like a fucking baby?' Deacon snarled.

'Yes,' Adam said slowly. Warily.

'Hell, Adam. I've been a fucking mess since I watched that video.

Faith practically had to scoop me off the floor. *Damn you.* I didn't know *that's* what happened. That *that's* what's been eating at you for the past *year*. Why didn't you tell me? Why did you carry that around inside for a year? *Alone?* Why didn't you let me help you? *Goddammit, Adam.* I thought you *trusted* me more than that.'

'Oh,' Adam breathed. He hadn't truly considered the full impact on the people to whom he'd sent the video of Paula's murder. He'd known they'd be shaken. What human being with a soul could watch that happen and not be shaken?

But not driven to tears. *Those tears are for me. Because I saw it and it messed with my head.* 'I didn't know how to tell you. I didn't want to think about it. It made it not be real if I didn't talk about it. And I should have. But that's not why I'm sorry.'

Deacon grew quiet. 'There's more?'

Oh yeah. 'You might need to pull over for a minute or two.'

'Hold on.' Deacon muttered obscenities at traffic and the universe in general before huffing out a sigh. 'All right. I'm pulled over. Hit me.'

Just get it out. But his brain still wasn't listening, taking the round-about way instead. 'You're coming to St Agnes's for a shooting. I was the target. My . . . friend died instead.'

Careful silence. Because Deacon was no fool. 'Why are you at St Agnes's at seven in the morning? Do they even have Mass that early?'

'No.' Adam sucked in air until he couldn't take in any more. *Do this. Just do it.* He closed his eyes tight and gritted his teeth. Because telling Deacon was somehow harder than telling Meredith. 'I was at an AA meeting,' he said on a rush. 'I'm an alcoholic.'

Silence. Complete and total silence.

'You still there, D?'

'Yes.' The clipped reply emanated waves of anger. 'All this time?'

'Yes.' And then the words came, all tangled and tripping over each other. 'I was ashamed. I wanted one year sober before I told anybody, but then all this happened and I needed to tell you sooner. And I was going to, as soon as we got a second to breathe on this case. But then this happened and my sponsor's dead. Just like Andy Gold and Bruiser.'

'You were the target?' Deacon asked flatly.

'Yes. John – that's my sponsor – I mean he *was* my sponsor, he pushed me out of the way.' He glanced over at John's body, then ripped his gaze away. 'Bullet hit him instead.'

'You're unhurt?'

'Yes. I wanted you to know before you walked on the scene and got surprised. I . . . I've fucked everything up. I've been so damn jealous of what you and Faith have built together. It was hard to watch. And . . . I didn't want you to hate me. But I especially didn't want you to pity me. John thought it would be better not to tell you until I had a year of sobriety under my belt, that it would be easier for me to hold my head up.'

More silence.

'D?'

'I'm thinking,' Deacon snapped. 'Give me a minute. I have to enter traffic.' More muttered obscenities, then a giant sigh. 'I can see St Agnes's steeple from where I am, so I'm close. I've got extra tactical gear in the back of my SUV. I'll bring it to you and we'll secure the scene. Did you give Isenberg all the particulars? Victim's name, et cetera?'

'Yes, she knows.' Somehow this wasn't how Adam had expected his cousin to react. He hadn't expected the anger. Not like this. But Deacon had a right to his feelings and Adam knew that Deacon loved him. So he'd give him time and space.

'Then I'll hang up now,' Deacon said. 'I'll be there in a few minutes.'

Sure enough, two minutes later Deacon's black SUV slowly drove by. Deacon rolled his window down when he saw Adam on the ground, flinching at the sight of John's body beside him. 'I'm going to back up and lift the hatch, so that you can get to the gear without coming out into the open.' He did this, the SUV's hatch slowly rising.

Adam duckwalked to the open cargo area, taking care to avoid his own vomit. *Yay me.* Wasn't he the strong one?

He found a helmet and a flak jacket. He put them on, then grabbed a second set and handed them to Deacon through the window.

'Get in the back seat,' Deacon ordered and when Adam had complied, he drove them to the overhang, where parishioners were dropped off in inclement weather.

Or in the event of a sniper attack.

Deacon turned off the engine and got out of the car. 'Come on,' he barked.

Adam followed him into the church, preparing himself for anything from a cold shoulder to being cursed out.

'Ugh.' It was all he had opportunity to utter before Deacon tackled him in a bear hug so tight Adam feared for his ribs.

'You fucker,' Deacon snarled brokenly, hanging on so tightly a crowbar couldn't have separated them. 'I am so fucking *mad* at you.'

Adam's arms rose uncertainly to hug him back. Deacon tightened his hold convulsively and Adam patted his back. 'I know. You should be.' He hooked his hands over Deacon's massive shoulders and . . . clung to the man who'd been his closest, most supportive family for most of his life. 'I fucked up. I'm sorry. I'm so damn sorry, D.'

'Part of me wants to kick your ass.'

'I know. But you can't reach it like this.'

Deacon's laugh was choked and gruff. 'I think if this had happened yesterday I wouldn't have understood. Not as much. It was the girl, right? Watching her die?'

'Yes. I saw her in my mind all the time. Except when I was completely drunk. It was the only way I could get any sleep at all.'

'I get it. I do. And your dad didn't help. The man's a functional drunk. Always has been. Hell of an example to set for your kid.'

Adam didn't know what to say, so he just hung on. How long had it been since he'd hugged anyone in his family like this? 'I was wrong. I shut you out and I'm sorry.'

'I wish you'd told me. I would've helped. Somehow. I would have.'

'I know. John said—' Adam stopped with a frown.

Deacon stepped back far enough that they could see each other's faces. Deacon's bicolored eyes were rimmed in red. 'John?'

'My sponsor. The guy, you know, out there. He said it would be easier to be proud of myself if I got to a year first.'

'He thought it was a good idea for you to isolate yourself? From your family?'

'Yeah. I guess.'

'No.' Deacon shook his head. 'No. That's not how it's supposed to work. I've not been to AA, but even I know you need support.'

Adam knew it too. Now. He'd kind of known it months ago, but John had seemed so sure. And John had been sober. He'd mastered his demons.

John, who drove a black SUV. John, who'd been ready to confess . . . something. He needed to sort through all of that. Figure it out. But this, this talk with Deacon, came first.

'I didn't want to need it,' he said honestly. And maybe that had made John's advice easier to accept, even if down deep he'd known it was wrong.

'Which is why I wanna kick your ass.' Deacon gripped Adam's face in two big hands, met his eyes squarely. 'I can still love you and support you and want to kick your fucking ass. You understand this, right?'

Adam's lips twitched. 'Yes. I understand.'

'Good, because we're not done with this. But we have a scene to clean up and a body to process. Isenberg and I will take care of notifying his next of kin.'

Adam's heart sank. 'Noreen. John's wife. She's a good person.'

'Most of the people we tell are.' Deacon let him go, giving him a small shove. 'You don't keep shit from me anymore. You got that?'

Adam nodded. 'Yes. I got that.'

'And you keep your ass alive.'

'I will.'

'Good. As long as we're clear. Let's go.'

Feeling lighter than he had in years, Adam followed.

Cincinnati, Ohio,
Monday 21 December, 7.20 A.M.

'Merry, *stop*,' Diesel barked. 'Please. Your pacing is making me fucking nuts.'

Meredith abruptly halted mid-pace, turning to look at Diesel, who'd returned to visit her grandfather shortly before Adam's call. She'd cried a little more after they'd hung up, then, fueled by a surge of energy that burned her nerve endings, she'd started to pace.

Diesel truly appeared ready to come out of his own skin. The big man was pale and jumpy, just as he'd been the night before when he'd spent several hours with Clarke in the ER. Just as he'd been every time she'd seen him in a hospital.

'Are you okay?' she asked him.

'He's obviously not,' Clarke snapped. 'And neither are you. If they'd just let me go the hell home this poor guy wouldn't have to feel obligated to sit in this goddamn hospital with me. And you wouldn't be stuck here with me, either, pacing like a caged panther.'

'I'm not obligated!' Diesel objected. He looked annoyed and maybe hurt.

'You don't wanna be here,' Clarke insisted. 'Do you?'

'Hell no,' Diesel said with a shudder. 'I hate hospitals.'

Meredith had noticed that in the past. Hell, everyone with eyes had noticed that in the past. Any time one of them was hospitalized, Diesel would come and visit and be a friend. But every time he looked like he was about to throw up.

Which is exactly how Meredith felt. The thought of Adam, vulnerable to a bullet that could come from anywhere . . . She'd taken an anti-anxiety pill, but her anxiety levels were still off the charts. *You need to refocus. Think about someone else's misery for a little while.*

Plus, she found herself genuinely curious. 'Then why do you stay?' Meredith asked.

Diesel rubbed the back of his neck. 'I figure the more I do this, the easier it'll be. Like do-it-yourself exposure therapy.'

Meredith smiled at him. 'Somebody's been reading.' Why he'd

want to conquer this particular phobia wasn't hard to parse. Dani worked in a clinic. Diesel wanted Dani.

His blush was visible, even in the dim light. 'Yeah,' he mumbled. 'Stupid fear.'

'So you're really just using me,' Clarke said teasingly.

Diesel's slow grin returned. 'Yep. I figure getting used to all the white' – he gestured to the white walls, white bedding – 'while babysitting an old guy is the least threatening way.' He ducked the tissue box that came sailing at his head. 'Hey. You're not supposed to make any sudden movements. That's what makes you non-threatening.'

Clarke grimaced in pain. 'You're right. That wasn't smart. Damn fucking asshole shooter. What'd he hit me with anyway?'

'Probably the butt of his gun,' Diesel said. 'Or a rock.'

And at the mention of guns, Meredith's anxiety returned. She drew a deep breath, trying to control the rapid beating of her heart. 'Not sure anything else would make a dent in that head of yours, Papa,' she said, but it sounded forced.

She took two paces forward, then stopped herself, fists clenched at her sides. Because all she could see was Adam, hurt. Bleeding. *Stop it!*

'Merry,' Clarke said gently. 'Worrying about Adam isn't helping any of us. What else can you do?'

'I can show you how to knit,' Diesel offered, holding up his knitting bag.

Meredith snorted. The bag said, *You got two eyes, I got two needles. Do NOT fuck with me.* 'Where did you get that?'

Diesel grinned. 'From Decker. He had them made special. He got one for Kate and one for me.' He checked his wristwatch, a big clunky thing that looked like it had been through a war. Maybe it had. 'Decker's on his flight now. He didn't sound so good when I talked to him this morning.'

'He'll feel better when he sees Kate,' Meredith said. 'She's feeling better, but not happy about not being allowed to knit. Eye strain hurts her head.' She turned to Clarke. 'I don't have anything to do. I've colored every picture in the book that Mrs Zimmerman gave

me' – with bold, angry strokes that were not her best work – 'and I
can't run.' Because her own head was still tender. 'I'm ready to find
a waiting room and do some yoga.'

'Then go do that,' Clarke said. 'Because you're driving both of us
crazy.'

'*That* bus's already pulled into Crazytown Station,' Meredith
muttered.

'Well,' Diesel drawled, 'good morning to you too, Dr Insensitive.'

'She'd be yelling at us if we used the term "crazytown,"' Clarke
agreed.

Meredith glared at them. 'I'm afraid to go near any of my clients.
I can't go home. I'm stuck here until Isenberg frees up someone to
come get me. And Adam's . . .'

'*Alive*,' Clarke said. 'He's alive, Merry.'

'But he might not have been!' She blew out an angry breath. 'I
can't help him. I'm stuck here. I get that. I do. But I need to do
something *useful*, for God's sake.'

'Then *figure* it the fuck *out*,' Clarke told her, clearly having lost
his patience. He sighed, then patted the bed next to him. 'Come
here, Merry. Let's figure it out together.'

'No,' Meredith said, pouting now. 'I don't like you.' But she sat
next to him anyway, laying her head on his shoulder. 'I hate feeling
so helpless, Papa.'

'I know, baby,' her grandfather murmured, stroking her hair.

'We're all going stir crazy,' Diesel said. 'I don't even wanna think
about poor Mallory and those Chicago kids. Mallory, having to go
through her story over and over.'

'And Shane and Kyle,' Clarke added. 'Grieving and scared and
stuck in a hotel room. I would have given them my gaming system,
but it's locked up back at the condo.'

Meredith patted his chest, loving that he cared so much for the
boys and that he was so gently bringing her focus back where it
needed to be. 'I spoke to Shane an hour ago. He was awake and
pacing and Parrish let him use his phone to call me.'

'The Feds have secure lines,' Diesel said. 'No way to trace them
to their location.'

'I figured that.' Meredith sighed. 'He's worried about Linnie, all alone out there. He's worried she'll freeze to death, which isn't out of the realm of possibility. He's chomping at the bit to do the interview. Adam had already called him about it.'

'What interview?' Diesel and Clarke asked together.

'Sorry, I forgot you weren't there when we talked about it. Linnie won't trust us to come out of hiding, but she will trust Shane. He's willing to talk to the press, even though it'll put him back in the spotlight. He's still a target too, as long as Linnie's running free. I think Adam's going to have Shane do a video on Colby's phone and ask Marcus if he'll upload it to the *Ledger*'s webpage.'

'I do all the uploading,' Diesel said. 'Marcus isn't bad with systems, but it's not his strongest suit. Next time you talk to your lover boy, tell him I'm happy to help.'

Clarke snickered and held up a fist for Diesel to bump. 'Nice multitasking. You're helping her *and* teasing her all at the same time.'

'I do my best,' Diesel said with mock gravity, then shrugged. 'I have my laptop with me, so I'll be able to do whatever Adam needs done. You know, with respect to the video. I wouldn't presume to offer anything more. Adam might hit me.' He winked at her.

Meredith rolled her eyes. 'You guys are worse than middle schoolers.'

'We *are* middle schoolers,' Clarke and Diesel said together, then bumped fists again.

Meredith rolled her eyes and sighed heavily. 'You guys.'

'Oh, come on,' Clarke said. 'It's part of our charm. Admit it.'

Her lips twitched, because it was true. 'I admit nothing.' Which made her think of Shane again. Her sigh this time was a serious one.

'What was that for?' Clarke asked, jostling her shoulder. 'You got stuff to admit?'

'Not me,' she said. 'I'm back to Shane. He's willing to do the interview or video or whatever, but I think drawing media attention to himself makes him more afraid than drawing the killer's attention.'

'Because of what happened in Indiana,' Clarke said. 'He told me that he lied to the police about what happened in the foster home,'

465

he added when Meredith sat up, eyes wide. 'When you and Kimble were "sleeping" yesterday morning.'

Meredith glared at him. 'We slept.' *Mostly. Okay, a little.*

'Gonna tell me what Shane said?' Diesel asked, eyeing them warily.

Clarke shrugged. 'Andy and Linnie and Shane were friends back in foster care.'

Diesel's expression hardened. 'That can be a decent experience or a shitty one.'

'Theirs was the latter,' Clarke said, then pursed his lips, as if unwilling to say more.

'Andy changed his name when he ran from Indianapolis to Cinci,' Meredith said, because she trusted Diesel. And because an idea had just taken root in her mind, one she'd need Diesel's help to carry out. 'Linnie came with him, because Andy was her protector, but maybe also because she felt guilty too, for what he'd done for her. Linnie was assaulted by the foster father and Andy killed him.'

Diesel's eyes popped wide. 'No shit. Good for him. How?'

'He hit the man with a frying pan. Shane didn't explicitly say this, by the way, but it was heavily implied.'

'Kyle wouldn't let him say when Isenberg and Kimble were questioning him,' Clarke said. 'Kyle's pre-law. He protected Shane.'

Meredith nudged her shoulder into his. 'Adam, Papa. Not Kimble.'

'Fine,' Clarke grunted. 'Adam.'

'Adam and Isenberg didn't use this information against Shane,' Diesel murmured.

'No. Adam wouldn't and Isenberg's not the crusty old hammer that everyone thinks she is. She showed those kids real compassion. To Penny Voss too. I'm an Isenberg fan.'

'Me too,' Diesel said. 'So what happened with Shane and Andy? Andy wasn't sent to prison because he ended up here. Did he run or was he never even charged?'

'The second one,' Meredith said, 'because Shane lied to cover for him. The rapist's wife confronted Linnie later, when Andy had been taken in for questioning and wasn't there to protect her. She accused Linnie of seducing her husband and attacked her with a frying pan. Shane made sure one of the kids was recording it, then stepped in to protect Linnie, but not before the wife got in a few good whacks. Broke Linnie's arm. The wife was charged with the murder and Andy was set free. Wife goes to prison, Andy changes his name, comes here for a fresh start, hopes to have a life with Linnie. Shane goes to Kiesler University on a full scholarship.'

Diesel nodded, his gaze sharp. 'And somewhere in that timeline, Linnie got the attention of whoever killed Andy on Saturday.'

Meredith had always known that Diesel was incredibly perceptive. 'Yes. She was part of his college prostitution ring. Linnie was forced to cooperate.'

Diesel's jaw tightened and he swallowed hard. 'And Shane's afraid the media will latch on to this and find the connection to his murder cover-up.'

Meredith nodded. 'Yes.'

'But *I* am the media and you're telling me.' Diesel lifted a sarcastic brow. 'Why?'

'Oh, I *like* him,' Clarke said to her. 'You sure you don't want him instead?'

Diesel blushed to the tips of his ears. 'Jesus, Clarke.'

She laughed. 'Papa! Don't worry about this busybody, Diesel. You're safe with me.'

'Please continue about *Shane*,' Diesel said firmly. 'Why tell me?'

'Well, Shane didn't tell me as a therapist, so there was no expectation of confidentiality, and he told this guy here.' She tilted her head toward her grandfather. 'So a, I don't feel as if I've violated any confidences and b, I need your help. And c, I trust you.'

Diesel blushed again, but happily. 'Thank you. What do you want me to do?'

Meredith frowned, aligning her thoughts. 'I'm thinking about the connection between Linnie and the killer and also about how to give Shane some breathing room with the media, because it will get out. Especially if the wife serving time starts squawking.' She bit at her lip thoughtfully. 'There was a social worker Shane feared. She had red hair like mine and when Shane first saw the article, he thought she might be me.'

'But the paper listed your name,' Clarke said.

'Andy changed his name,' she said with a shrug. 'I think Shane was afraid the social worker had too. He was relieved when I wasn't her. Whenever the foster kids would complain, they'd be sent to another home and nothing would happen to the foster parents. If it was a sexual assault, like Linnie's, this woman would paint the victim as a slut.'

'Which would go in the record and set the child up for more abuse at the next home unless she's placed in therapeutic foster care or is the only minor in the next home,' Diesel said, his expression hardening again. 'If the kids at the next home find out she was promiscuous, they become predators and she becomes the weakest member of the pack.'

'Exactly.' Meredith sighed. 'Shane believed the social worker and the foster parents were in cahoots.'

Diesel scowled. 'Getting payola from the foster parents to look the other way?'

Meredith nodded. 'Money is the usual reason. How Linnie ended up in the killer's prostitution ring is a big question. Why and how?'

'It could have nothing to do with what happened in Indiana,' Clarke cautioned.

'Except that he'd dug into Linnie's background,' Meredith said. 'He knew that Andy would kill for her and that grabbing Shane would bring Linnie out of hiding.'

'Because she can identify him,' Diesel said.

Meredith nodded. 'I think so.'

Diesel pulled his laptop from its case. 'Where do you want to start?'

Meredith crossed her arms over her chest, the feel of the steel between her breasts grounding her thoughts. 'The social worker,' she decided. 'Because she knew what had been happening in that foster home and she didn't stand up to protect Andy or Linnie. And when the wife was charged, tried, and convicted, she didn't tell the truth then, either.'

Diesel's fingers were poised over his keyboard. 'What's her name?' he asked.

'Bethany Row.' She took her grandfather's hand. 'Thanks, Papa.'

He'd laid back against the pillows, looking suddenly worn and tired. 'For what?'

'For helping me refocus. You've always done that for me.'

He grunted softly. 'Maybe Adam will do it for you now.' One side of his mouth lifted. 'I got me a girlfriend. I need to call her.'

'Oh, Papa, I'm so sorry! I didn't think to call her.'

'S'okay,' he murmured. 'You were a little busy. I called her last night. She's on her way up here. She'll be staying for Christmas.' He opened one eye in challenge. 'She's staying in my room,' he added, like a teenager defying his parent.

Meredith wasn't able to bite back her smile. 'You two have your sexy time, old man. I won't judge, because I'll be having my own.'

Diesel snorted, then paused his typing to hold out his fist for Meredith to bump. 'Doc gets one million points for the win. Game over. *Please*, let it be over.'

Clarke groaned. 'He's right. You win, Merry. I give up.'

She bumped Diesel's fist. 'I accept your capitulation, Papa. Let's get to work.'

Twenty-six

Cincinnati, Ohio,
Monday 21 December, 7.35 A.M.

Linnea stood behind a tree on the edge of the school's property, close enough to hear the parents talking to their children, but far enough away that no one noticed her. They were mostly minivan-driving mommies who appeared frazzled, in a holiday-induced hurry, and annoyed that the school hadn't started winter break the Friday before.

Must be nice if that's the only thing you worry about, Linnea thought sourly.

The moms would park in the lot in front of the school and walk their children inside, their child's hand tightly clasped in their own. Some had babies on one hip. All treated their children like they were precious. Something Linnea had never known.

God, she envied those little kids.

She was so absorbed in wondering what their lives were like that she almost missed the dark-haired lady pulling a toddler out of the car seat in a Toyota minivan.

'Ariel! Sweetheart, don't dawdle. I have errands to run this morning.'

Linnea's gaze jerked to the little family – the mama, the little boy, and the pretty little girl, currently dragging her feet. 'I don't feel good, Mommy. Can we go home?'

The mother hefted the toddler to her hip. 'No. You are going to school, young lady. You've been acting oddly all weekend. What's wrong, honey?'

Even scolding, the woman's concern for her daughter came through. How could this be *his* family? He was cruel and hateful. The mom seemed lovely and sweet.

'Nothing, Mama.' Head hanging, Ariel rounded the van, shuffling her feet.

'Ariel? Does this have anything to do with your performance in math class?'

Ariel's mouth dropped open. 'But how—'

'Miss Abernathy called me on Friday to tell me that you hadn't returned the letter she sent home. I was hoping you'd tell me yourself.'

Ariel's lips quivered. 'I'm sorry, Mama. I can't do that math.'

'Well, we're not going to worry about it today. Maybe we'll ask some of the big kids in church if they'll come help you with your math over the break. What do you say?'

Ariel blinked owlishly from behind her round glasses. 'You're not mad?'

'No. I wasn't very good at math either. And your daddy wasn't mad either. Let's go inside before we turn into popsicles.'

With a giggle, Ariel obeyed, and they walked together, swinging their clasped hands.

Linnea moved as soon as they were out of sight, approaching the minivan with her pilfered antenna, planning to pop the door locks.

But again she didn't have to. The door was unlocked. What was this with suburbanites? It was like they felt insulated from crime.

Linnea climbed behind the back bench seat, crouching so that her head was out of sight. Minutes later, Ariel's mommy came back, toddler still on her hip. She quickly buckled the baby into his car seat, then slid behind the wheel.

Linnea ducked and held her breath, not breathing until the woman had started the engine and they were off.

Now what? She could conceivably crawl toward the front if she could roll over the bench seat without being seen, but that seemed unlikely. Or, she could fold down one of the seats and crawl over if she were very quiet. Or . . . She smiled as Ariel's mommy popped a CD in and choir music exploded from the speakers.

Perfect. Five minutes later, once the woman was on the highway, aggressively singing along, Linnea pulled the release lever for the smaller seat section, caught the seat as it popped forward, and quietly lowered it. Then she slipped from her hiding place, threw herself between the captain seats and grabbed the woman's phone off the center console.

She had the phone pocketed before the woman gasped in fear.

'Don't do anything stupid, ma'am,' Linnea said quietly, showing her the gun. 'I have nothing to lose, but I don't want to hurt you or your little boy.'

'Wh-who are you?' the woman whispered.

'Your husband's worst nightmare. Just drive to your home, ma'am. And don't try anything, please. I don't want to hurt your son, but I will if I must.'

Cincinnati, Ohio,
Monday 21 December, 8.45 A.M.

Adam joined Isenberg, Scarlett, and Trip at the small table in Isenberg's office. He'd showered and changed into yet another clean suit in the locker room while Deacon stood watch outside the door. No one came in or out. Deacon was still pissed at him, but there was no cold shoulder. Deacon wasn't made that way.

Hell, Deacon was actually pleasant to Adam's father who'd made Deacon's life every bit as much a hell as he'd made Adam's, just in very different ways. For now, Deacon was acting as Adam's personal bodyguard, watching everyone who passed by with suspicion.

Deacon closed Isenberg's door and pulled the shades at their boss's request.

'I told Detectives Currie and Hanson to come at nine and nine fifteen respectively,' she said, 'so we have only a few minutes until they arrive.'

'Why?' Trip asked.

'Because we want our ducks in a row before we let those guys in on any more confidential information,' Deacon said grimly.

472

Trip frowned. 'We think they're involved. Really?'

'No,' Adam said. 'I don't think they're involved. I *can't*. But . . . I can't not. Hell, I still can't wrap my mind around the fact that somebody has tried to kill me twice now.'

Trip's eyes narrowed. 'Am *I* a suspect?'

Adam shook his head. 'Mallory's rapist was white. So was the shooter last night.'

Trip's huff was sarcastic. 'So being black saved me? That's ironic.'

Adam winced, wishing he had better words. 'Well, that and the fact that you would have been only nineteen or twenty and away at college when Mallory's assault happened and you were at Quantico when Paula was killed . . .' He blew out a breath. 'I can't see you hurting anyone like that, but I can't see Wyatt and Nash doing it either. I just can't.'

'That's what we're here for,' Scarlett said. 'An objective look at all of this so that we can clear our people and bring them back in.' She drew a breath. 'That was a hard video to watch, Adam.'

'I know,' he said. 'I'm sorry I had to ask you to. All of you.'

Isenberg shrugged. 'At least we were prepared for what was going to happen,' she said briskly. 'In my opinion, the murders of Paula and Tiffany and her mother are linked. Whether it's the same doer or a copycat, I don't know. Even if it is a copycat, that you've had two attempts on your life in as many days tells me that killing Tiffany and her mother in that exact manner was meant to distract you so that you wouldn't properly investigate Andy Gold's murder and link it to Mallory. Who knew about that video?'

'The guys in our unit. I mean, Nash and Wyatt were next to me when it happened, but the other guys in the bullpen heard Paula's scream. Or . . .' He swallowed, his mouth suddenly dry, his hands shaking. 'Or her attempted scream.' It had been a terrible sound.

'Yeah,' Deacon said grimly. 'We know. So the list of people who know about the video doesn't really help narrow things down. Who knew you'd be at St Agnes's?'

After telling Deacon, Adam had let Isenberg tell the others why he'd been there. He felt nothing but support coming from Scarlett and Trip, which was making this moment so much easier than it might have been. 'Meredith and my sponsor. I know she wouldn't have told anyone. I don't know if John did.'

'You said John was saying something in those final seconds,' Isenberg said. 'What was it exactly?'

'He said, "I need to tell you why."'

'He'd told someone where you'd be,' Deacon said grimly. 'Sonofabitch.'

Adam started to deny it, but found he had to agree. 'Looks that way.'

Scarlett's tone was gentle as she asked, 'Did you ask him to be your sponsor or did he approach you?'

'He approached me, about a month in. Said cops had to stick together because nobody else understood. What?' he asked when Scarlett's expression grew sad.

'The black SUV was sold to him by Barber Motors, eleven months ago. For a dollar.'

He flinched, the words like a knife in his gut. It was true then. John had sold him out. For a fucking SUV. 'Same place that last night's shooter bought his SUV.'

Isenberg sighed. 'And the same place that burned to the ground around two a.m.'

Adam slapped his hand on the table. 'You've got to be shitting me. Goddammit.'

Deacon, Scarlett, and Trip let out blistering curses of their own.

'That was my reaction,' Isenberg said. 'Nothing was left. Computers were melted.'

'I bet we wouldn't have found anything on them anyway,' Trip said. 'Voss's computers were wiped clean.' He slid a sheet of paper in front of Adam. 'I dumped the call log from your sponsor's phone. The number I circled is the only one that shows up as untraceable. Several calls and texts were made to and accepted from this number. The last text was sent this morning at four fifty-eight.'

Adam recognized the time and the phone number right away. 'That was the same time that I texted John that I'd meet him at St Agnes's. And that number is the same one that called the Buon Cibo hostess asking her to seat Meredith by the window.' He stared at the piece of paper, trying to make the pieces fit. And then . . . they did.

'Oh my God,' he whispered. He couldn't breathe. 'Oh my God.' He looked at the team, willing words to work themselves past the blockage in his throat. But it wasn't working. The words would not come.

'Adam?' Deacon demanded. 'What is it?'

'*It was me.* I told John where Meredith was going to lunch. I told him that Mallory was leaving the safe house to sign up for GED classes. *I'm the one who set them up.*'

Cincinnati, Ohio,
Monday 21 December, 8.50 A.M.

'Thank you. I really appreciate this information.' Meredith ended her call with a sigh. She and Diesel had set up in the waiting room after Clarke's nurse ran them out of his room. Clarke was appropriately irate at the nurse, but she'd been right. Meredith could see the headache in his eyes, so they'd left him to sleep. 'I suppose it's nice to know that being kind to people pays such dividends, but it makes me feel kind of sleazy.'

Now she and Diesel were working to find out how Linnea had dropped onto a killer's radar. Starting with the social workers she knew in Cincinnati, she'd networked with those she trusted most until she'd landed the name of an Indianapolis social worker who knew Bethany Row, the woman who'd turned a blind eye to Linnea's pain.

Diesel looked up from his laptop, lifting a brow. 'It was definitely educational. I didn't think you had the acting chops, Doc. Kudos.'

'I don't,' she protested, then sighed again. 'Of course I do. Otherwise everyone wouldn't think I have my shit together, because I totally don't.'

Diesel's smile was kind. 'I think we all know you don't, Merry. But whatever it is that helps you cope . . . I don't know. It gives us something too. All of us.'

Meredith's eyes burned. 'You have to stop saying sweet things, Diesel.'

He chuckled. 'Okay, fine. Tell me what you learned from the chatty social worker. That was impressive by the way, the way you leapfrogged from social worker to social worker. You network like a boss. And your use of distraction and disinformation to get to the next name? If you ever decide to quit the psycho biz, you'll make a great PI.'

Meredith gave him a dirty look. 'Nobody can know about any of that. I got a reputation to protect. I'm supposed to be all sweet and kind and serene.'

He smirked. 'Understood. Now dish while this program is running.'

He was working to break into Bethany Row's personal email. He'd already accessed her social media and was now trying every combination of her dog's name, best friend, and boyfriend to determine her password.

'The last social worker, the chatty one, worked with Bethany for a few years and does not like her. At all.' Meredith grimaced. 'That was a *lot* of vitriol right there.'

'I guessed that much. You looked like you were eating a lemon.'

'I bet I did. She said Bethany was fired a few months ago and nobody was shocked.'

'That's interesting.'

'Ain't it, though? Bethany seemed to live well for a single social worker while employed. Some of the staff speculated that she had a sugar daddy, but this woman thought Bethany was on the take and was proven right – she says – when Bethany was fired. She says she was notorious for having to relocate girls who'd claimed assault, which sounds like a more documentable reason for termination, in my opinion. Apparently, she was fired after placing a girl who'd said she was molested into another home. The girl told her school counselor who brought in the police. A detective started asking questions.' She sighed. 'And then the girl committed suicide. It was a big story in Indianapolis a few months ago.'

'You're going to call the cop?'

'Yes. I should probably tell Isenberg first.'

'You probably should.'

'She might tell me not to call the detective in Indianapolis.'

Diesel just looked at her with disappointed disapproval.

Meredith caved. 'Fine. I'll call Isenberg.'

He looked surprised. 'Wow. I have power. That's awesome.'

She smiled at him. 'You do indeed.' She dialed Isenberg's cell and waited. And got voicemail. She ended the call without leaving a message. 'I tried.'

He chuckled. 'You did. I witnessed it.'

She grinned at him cheekily. 'Now I can call that detective with a clear conscience.'

Cincinnati, Ohio,
Monday 21 December, 8.55 A.M.

I did this. I set Meredith and Mallory up to be killed. I did this. The words echoed in Adam's head until they were all he could hear.

'Adam? *Adam?*'

Adam became aware of Deacon's hands gripping his shoulders, tightening his hold past the point of pain. But it was what Adam needed to stop the storm of words in his mind and yank back into himself.

'You good?' Deacon asked, looking him in the eye. He was apparently satisfied with what he saw because he let Adam go, going back into his own chair.

'Yeah.' Adam swallowed. 'I'm good.' He scrubbed his hands over his face. *John. How could you?* 'John and I would go out for coffee after meetings and . . . talk. He'd ask me about my job and I told him . . . you know, what I could. Because . . .' God, this was hard to say. 'Dammit, I isolated myself. I did this to myself.'

'Because he counseled you to break away from your family,' Deacon said, jaw tight. 'God, I wish he wasn't dead because I'd—' He cut himself off. Shook his head. 'Sorry.'

'Don't be.' Adam shoved his knuckles into his temples, needing the quick bite of pain to stay focused as he tried to remember everything he'd told John over the months. 'I told him that I was leaving the condo yesterday to go to the precinct. *That's* how they

477

knew where the van would be. *God.* How could I have been so *stupid*?'

'You weren't,' Isenberg said flatly. 'You were in pain and he took advantage. All right. So we know where the info was coming from. We need to know where it was going.'

Adam forced himself to focus. 'Right. Okay. So . . . John couldn't have been the rapist's friend, the one Mallory heard last night, because that guy was shot in the leg and in the arm. John hadn't been shot.' He had to swallow hard. 'Not until this morning.'

Beside him, Scarlett squeezed his arm sympathetically.

'John also wasn't the raping, murdering cop with a birthmark on his chest,' Adam said. 'I was at his house last summer for a cookout by his pool and saw him without his shirt. He doesn't have a scar or a birthmark.'

'So what else do we know?' Isenberg asked levelly.

Nothing. Adam wanted to scream it, but it wouldn't help, so he clutched onto her calm voice like a lifeline. 'We know that someone knew we were getting a warrant for the used car place because they burned it down. And that somebody knew that Mallory would be at the hospital last night.'

'Did you tell John that Mallory and Meredith had gone to the hospital with Kate?' Isenberg asked.

Adam shook his head. 'No, so John wasn't the only leak.'

'We knew,' Deacon said. 'You told us in the elevator as we were leaving for Voss's house. That was Scarlett, Trip, and me.' He hesitated. 'And Nash.'

No. No, no, no. He trusted Nash. But he'd trusted John too. *I am such a fucking fool.* 'I know,' he murmured.

'Nash also knew the way Paula was murdered,' Trip added quietly.

'But Nash also was the one who led us to the used-car lot,' Scarlett protested, then sighed. 'Which we would have found eventually on our own and didn't really help us until Kate disabled the SUV in the hospital parking lot last night. It was a low-risk breadcrumb to throw in our path.'

Adam shook his head, his gut rejecting the logic his brain was providing. Because . . . Shit. 'Wyatt knew too. I told him when he drove up to Voss's house.' He looked at the worried faces of his boss and his team. 'And yes, he knew about Paula too, but we are not jumping to any conclusions. We need to know for sure before we accuse *anybody*. Hell, last night's guy might have been tipped off by someone in the ER. We don't know.'

'But we'll find out,' Isenberg said as her office phone rang. She picked it up, listened, then thanked the caller before hanging up. 'Let's see what Detective Currie comes up with when presented with all the facts. He's on his way up now. I asked the front desk to call me when he got on the elevator. Come on. Let's go to the briefing room and wait.'

They gathered their things and made the short walk, Deacon's hand gripping the back of Adam's neck in a silent show of support.

He still felt stupid as fuck.

When they got to the briefing room, Adam noted that there were a few new photos on the whiteboard. Stills taken from the video of Paula's murder – her slit throat, her body being gutted – had been placed in line with the stills of Bruiser from the Kiesler University surveillance video, and the photos taken of Tiffany's and her mother's bodies.

'I got the stills of Paula so you wouldn't have to watch it again,' Isenberg said quietly.

Overwhelmed, he could only whisper, 'Thank you.'

She squeezed his arm, led him to the table. 'Have a seat and let's see what happens.'

A minute later, Nash entered the room at a fast walk, but immediately slowed. He looked at the grim faces around the table, then up at the whiteboard. He turned to face Adam, his expression shuttering. 'You figured it out. That Paula was killed the same way as Tiffany and her mother.' He pulled a few sheets from his laptop case and put them on the table. 'I was bringing you the same photo. I didn't want you to have to see it again.'

Adam checked the offering and nodded. 'Thank you.'

Isenberg gestured to a seat and Nash warily took it. 'Where's Hanson?' he asked.

'Arriving in fifteen minutes,' she said. 'We wanted to talk to you separately.'

Nash's eyes narrowed. 'What's going on here? Adam?'

Adam met his old friend's gaze straight on and listed all of the things the killer – or killers – had known. And what had been done with that knowledge. He left the point about knowing that Mallory would be at the hospital last night until the end.

And then he waited, watching as understanding filled Nash's eyes, followed by a flash of fury. 'You're blaming *me*? You really think *I* could be doing this? *Me*?'

Adam shook his head. 'I don't. But I'm not trusting myself at the moment.'

'Which I think has been one of his goals,' Isenberg added. 'Whoever "he" is.'

'Well, *he* is not *me*,' Nash insisted. He shoved back from the table and began pacing the room, then pivoted to face Adam, fists clenched at his sides. 'Do you know why I'm here? I mean, here on this team? On this case?'

'Because you were assigned to take down Voss,' Adam said, wondering if that was really true and hating himself for wondering.

'No. Well, yes, but not first.'

Adam blinked hard. 'You're not making sense.'

'Because I'm so fucking *angry*,' Nash spat, turning to glare at the rest of the team.

'They're being what I can't be right now – objective and professional,' Adam said with a calm he didn't feel. 'They're watching my back.'

'Bull*shit*,' Nash fumed. 'If they'd been watching your back, it never would have come to this.'

'Wait,' Deacon said incredulously. 'What?'

Nash pointed a trembling finger at Deacon. '*You*. You were supposed to care about him, but you let him drift. For months. Didn't you *see* what was happening?'

Deacon's jaw cocked sideways, never a good sign. He slowly, menacingly, came to his feet. 'What are you talking about?'

Nash closed his eyes, then turned to Isenberg. 'You've seen the video? The one that this still came from?' He tapped the photo of Paula's mangled body.

She was considering him carefully. 'Yes. Just this morning.'

'You sent him to us *strong*. He came back to you *broken*. Didn't you wonder why?'

Isenberg didn't blink. 'I did wonder. I don't know why I didn't ask.'

'Bullshit,' Nash said again, but wearily. 'Maybe you knew that you couldn't take it.'

'Maybe,' Isenberg allowed. 'Probably, even. And I was wrong not to ask. But that doesn't explain what's happening right here and right now.'

'And changing the subject does not make you look any less guilty,' Deacon added, but he'd grown significantly less hostile. His arms were crossed over his chest, but his expression had become uncertain. Like maybe Nash's words had hit a nerve.

'No,' Nash agreed. 'But it does explain why I'm *here*. See, I was *there*. I saw what happened to that poor girl.' He swallowed hard. 'And it destroyed me too, to the point that I couldn't see anyone or anything else for weeks. Months. I mean, I saw people. I functioned at my job. Barely. But I didn't *see* them.'

'You were going through the motions,' Adam murmured, understanding.

'Yeah. Exactly. But after some time, and the intervention of people *who loved me*, I resurfaced. I could breathe. And then I really looked around and I saw Adam. Still alone.'

'By choice,' Adam said, but even he didn't believe his own words.

'No,' Isenberg murmured, shocking him. 'He's right. We own some of this too. But, Detective Currie, I have to hurry you along, because Hanson will arrive soon and I want to understand your position before I talk to him.'

'I hope he does,' Nash muttered. 'Arrive soon, I mean. See, when I finally saw what was happening to Adam, I checked in with Hanson. And I didn't like what I saw. He hadn't missed a beat. Hadn't seemed affected at all.'

Adam stared as Nash's meaning sank in. 'That doesn't mean

anything. Everyone responds to stress differently. You don't know what happens when he goes home at night.'

'Yeah, I kind of do,' Nash said quietly. 'Because I started to follow him.'

Adam was stunned. 'What the fuck?'

Nash shrugged. 'At first it was for myself. If he'd managed to sail on undamaged, I wanted to know how. So I watched him. And at first, it all looked good. Family man, all that good stuff. All the *right* stuff. Except for things I couldn't explain. Like how he'd sometimes leave his house late at night.'

'He's a cop,' Adam said, shaking his head. 'That's what we do.'

'Maybe. But I was a little obsessed. And burned out at Personal Crimes. So I asked for a transfer. Into Narcotics.'

'You followed him?' Scarlett asked, intrigued.

'Essentially.' Nash turned back to Isenberg. 'This part you can confirm with my boss, and I hope you do so quickly. The night Hanson showed up here and you thought it was because my boss had sent him? He hadn't.'

Adam looked at Isenberg, confused. 'I thought you said he had.'

She frowned. 'No. I'd made the request. I assumed.' She turned her narrowed gaze on Nash. 'You're saying I shouldn't have.'

'No. Actually, my boss hadn't decided who he'd send. Or if he could even afford to free up anyone. He was a little surprised when you thanked him for sending Hanson.'

Isenberg made a wry face. 'I thought he was surprised because I'd thanked him.'

'Well, that too,' Nash admitted. 'But he went along with it to save face. He didn't want you to think he'd been surprised because he didn't have control over his squad. Wyatt told our boss about talking with you after he left your office that night. He's been looking for more responsibility, because he wants to climb the ladder. Hanson told a group of us that over drinks once or twice. He's ambitious. Even talked about applying for a transfer into your unit, Lieutenant. Anyway, our boss allowed it. He'd already planned to assign someone. Figured it might as well be someone who wanted the task. That's what he told me, anyway, after I heard about it.'

'Wyatt has always been something of an opportunist,' Adam said. 'That he'd totally run with it is completely consistent. But how did you get here?'

'I heard he'd been added to the team and I asked to be added as well. Told my boss that my computer skills might come in handy and that taking down a prostitution ring would look good on all of our resumés. But it didn't hurt that I could keep an eye on Hanson at the same time.'

'You said you followed Hanson,' Scarlett said quietly. 'Where did he go?'

'It was only a few times. Each time he left in the middle of the night and *didn't* go to a recorded crime scene, he went to a garage out in Beechmont. It's owned by a shell corporation. I've been trying to cut through the layers to find a true owner.'

'Did you report this?' Isenberg asked.

'Report what? That Hanson visits a garage? I don't have any evidence that he's done something illegal. Hell, he might even be having an affair.' Nash shook his head. 'But I don't know how he would have known that Mallory was at the hospital last night.'

'He knew too,' Isenberg said. 'Adam told him.'

Looking up from his phone, Trip cleared his throat. 'I have something.' He looked at Adam with a frown. 'Quincy just texted that the lab was able to raise the serial number off that rifle. It was recovered from a robbery thirty years ago, but was stolen from the arresting officers' vehicle. The arresting officers were Dale Hanson and James Kimble.'

Adam gasped, a sick dread spreading within him. 'Wyatt's dad. And mine.'

Cincinnati, Ohio,
Monday 21 December, 9.45 A.M.

'Oh, Shane,' Meredith said softly. She was looking over Diesel's shoulder, watching the video Shane had made to reach out to Linnie. 'He looks so tired.'

Diesel was grim. 'Knowing that this could get him investigated

483

for covering up a murder? He's damn brave. I'm about to upload it to the *Ledger*'s website. It'll get picked up by the rest of the media quickly. I normally wouldn't ask a cop's permission but . . .'

'It's Shane's life we're playing with. I get it. I tried calling Isenberg again, but I keep getting voicemail. I'll try again.' Meredith dialed, surprised when the lieutenant picked up.

'I was about to return your calls,' Isenberg said crisply. 'I was in a meeting. I knew you were wise enough to call 911 if there was an emergency.'

Meredith almost smiled. There had been a compliment in there somewhere. 'Yes, ma'am. I'm here with Diesel Kennedy and we have two questions for you. The—'

'You're still at the hospital, right?' Isenberg interrupted. 'Where the officers I assigned can see you?'

Meredith walked to the door and waved to the officer on duty. He waved back and she returned to the table. 'We are. I just made sure the officer knows we're here in the waiting room. My grandfather's nurse kicked us out, and Decker's here with Kate, so . . .'

'Good. Tell me your questions. I have things to do.'

Meredith did smile then. 'Yes, ma'am. Can I put you on speaker?'

'Do it,' she said, impatience edging the words.

'Okay. Diesel's question first.'

'Oh, okay.' Diesel rubbed his head. 'Adam asked Shane to make a video begging Linnie to contact him and asked the *Ledger* to upload it. You know about this, right?'

'No, but it's a good idea. Please continue.'

'Well, we have the video here. Normally I'd never ask permission, but this is a special case. I want to be sure everyone's still on board. Shane is risking a lot.'

'Hm.' Isenberg paused and Meredith's phone buzzed with an incoming text. 'I just sent Meredith my email. Send it to me right now. I'll look at it before I go into my next meeting. While he's doing that, ask your question, Meredith.'

'Well, it's about Shane.' She told Isenberg what they'd learned from the Indianapolis social worker. 'I've called the detective who appears to be instrumental in Bethany Row getting fired, but I haven't heard back from him.'

'Send me his number. I'll call his CO. It could make a difference.'

'Thank you.' She did as requested. 'I just sent you the detective's info.'

'I just got the video. Give me a minute.' They could hear Shane's voice, tinny on the other end of the line. When the video was over, Isenberg sighed. 'Upload it, Mr Kennedy. Thank you for including me in your decision this time.'

Diesel bit back a smile, because once again there'd been a compliment riding on the barb. 'You're welcome, Lieutenant.'

'Just one thing,' Isenberg said. 'Make sure you have our switchboard number scrolling across the screen. Also to ask for Detective Kimble. Can you do that?'

'Absolutely.'

'Then I'll leave you to it.' She hesitated. 'Stay with Diesel, Meredith.'

Something in her voice had Meredith frowning. 'There's a cop on this hallway.'

'I know. And I hand-picked him. Still, stay with Diesel. It will make Adam feel better. In the future, if you get my voicemail, leave me a message.'

She ended the call, leaving Meredith and Diesel staring at each other.

'That didn't sound good,' Meredith murmured.

'No, it didn't.' Diesel quickly made the changes Isenberg requested then tapped a few more keys. 'It's up. Cross your fingers.'

'I am. I want this to be over.'

'I know. Let's do our part. I'll keep working at Bethany Row's email server and you try the Indy detective again.'

Meredith gave his massive arm a friendly pat. 'Thanks, Diesel. You've been an amazing help the past couple days.'

'You're an amazing help every day, Merry. Least I can do.'

She gave him another pat, then sat down to call the detective again.

Cincinnati, Ohio,
Monday 21 December, 9.45 A.M.

'Pull into the driveway, Rita,' Linnea said quietly, holding the gun at an angle that couldn't be seen by the older man fussing with a string of lights in front of his already over-decorated house. 'Do not stop to talk to him. Just wave like you always do. No more tricks.'

Because Rita had driven around aimlessly for an hour before Linnea grabbed her purse and found her address on her driver's license. Rita lived only minutes from the Gruber Academy, but had apparently been hoping to need to stop for gas – and help. But luckily, the woman had had a full tank. Still, it had taken them another hour to get back.

'How would you know what I always do?' Rita asked angrily.

'Smile, ma'am. Smile like you always do. Now put down the garage door and turn off the engine.' She waited until Rita had obeyed. 'I know you always smile and wave, because you seem nice. I don't know how you can be nice, but I heard you with your daughter this morning. You sounded real. Like you're a good mother.'

'Then why are you doing this?' Rita asked for the twentieth time.

'I'm not sure you'd believe me if I told you. Let's go inside.' She waited until Rita had taken the baby from the car seat before taking him from her arms. 'I'll hold him.' She held up her gun, knowing she'd never hurt the baby with it, but hoping Rita couldn't see that. 'This way you'll think twice before using the phone.'

They walked into the house, a nice two-story, but not grand. Nowhere near the luxury of Voss's home. *Odd that he lives like this*, she thought.

But he did indeed live here. Linnea's heart stuttered when she saw him in the family photo on the bookshelf. *Yes, this is the right place. Keep your cool and get this done.*

And then she saw the next photograph and had to lock her knees to keep them from folding on her. He was wearing a uniform. *A uniform.*

He's a cop. Oh my God. Stunned, she could only stare. *He's a fucking cop.*

Holy shit. Holy fucking shit. Now so many things made sense. He was a cop. He could break the rules without consequences.

I have to be ready to face him. I have to be ready to kill him with the first shot. I have to be ready to be hunted by his policemen friends once I've done the job. I have to be ready to be arrested. Maybe shot on sight.

But she was already ready to die. So nothing had really changed.

Not true. It was even *more* important now that she take him out. It would mean one less cop preying on the helpless and innocent.

Resolutely, she turned to find Rita standing in the middle of the room, hugging herself. 'What are you going to do to us?' Rita asked.

'If you behave yourself, nothing. For now, I'd like you to make me some tea.'

Rita blinked at her. 'Tea?'

'Yes, tea. I like tea. I'm a hooker, not a barbarian.'

Rita nodded stiffly. 'Of course.'

Linnea followed her into the kitchen, watching her every move. Rita did as asked, then she and Linnea sat on their sofa. The toddler squirmed and Linnea tightened her hold.

'Tell him it's okay,' Linnea said quietly. 'Right now. In your nicest, sweetest Mommy voice.'

'Mikey, sit nicely for the lady and Mommy will get you a cookie,' she said brightly, and the boy settled down. 'Why are you doing this?' she asked once again.

'Because your husband murdered my best friend.'

Rita gasped, hand flying to cover her mouth. 'You lying whore.'

'You got the whore part right, but that was because of him too.' Linnea looked down at the toddler sadly. 'I'm not going to say any more because you're too young to know that your daddy is an evil man.'

Rita's chin lifted. 'You lie.'

'No, ma'am.' She shifted the baby to her knee, holding her gun in the same hand. The safety was on, but she hated taking a chance with him. The tea beckoned, though, and Linnea needed something to soothe her stomach. 'When does your husband get home?'

Rita looked away. 'I don't know.'

Linnea sipped the tea, welcoming its warmth. 'It doesn't matter. In a minute I'm going to text him with your phone and ask him to come home. I'll tell him Mikey is sick.'

'And then?'

'And then I'm going to kill him.'

Twenty-seven

Cincinnati, Ohio,
Monday 21 December, 9.45 A.M.

'I don't know,' Deacon murmured as he, Adam, and Scarlett stood in front of the glass in the observation room. 'Your dad's an asshole, Adam, but he's not a criminal.'

Jim Kimble sat on the other side of the glass, ready to blow a gasket. 'Maybe not,' Adam murmured back, 'but Dale Hanson isn't a criminal either – and he's a truly nice man.'

'He was,' Deacon agreed. 'I remember him taking us to your ball games, when you and Hanson were on the team. Then we'd go out for ice cream. I liked him.'

Adam had more than liked him. 'Dale was a much better father to me than my own ever was. I hate that he's been pulled into all this. I mean, did you see him?'

'Of course we did,' Scarlett said gently. 'Deacon and I brought him in.'

Adam cursed silently. He knew that, dammit. He'd seen them escorting Dale into the interview room next door. 'I know,' he said, fighting to keep his frustration out of his voice. Because Scarlett and Deacon didn't deserve it. 'I mean, he's almost blind. Macular degeneration. No way he could have fired a rifle now. Years ago, maybe. He was a crack shot when we were kids.'

'I remember him taking us to the firing range once with Uncle Jim. It was you and me and Dani and Wyatt. We were, what, about sixteen?'

'About that. Dale did tear up the targets that day. Every shot in the kill zone.'

'I remember,' Deacon said, 'because it was the coolest thing ever. Watching that man fire a rifle was almost . . . like music. He was good.'

'But not a killer,' Adam choked out.

Deacon started to argue, but Scarlett gave him a quelling look that had him pursing his lips. 'How long have you known Wyatt and his father?' Scarlett asked.

'His father, a long time,' Adam answered. 'Since I was old enough to remember. He was my father's partner on patrol. We did cookouts and parties and all kinds of things with Dale and his wife, before she died.'

'But not Wyatt?' Scarlett asked.

'Wyatt was adopted when he was about thirteen. His biological father had gone on a shooting rampage. Killed everyone in the house, then turned the gun on himself. Dale found Wyatt hiding in a closet. Took him to social services, then he and his wife fostered him. Ended up keeping him. Dale's a good man.'

'Let's hold to that thought while Isenberg and Trip talk to your dad.' Scarlett bumped shoulders with him encouragingly. 'Maybe there's a good explanation for how that rifle went from their possession to a killer's hands.'

God, I hope so, Adam thought, but his gut was telling him otherwise. And then the familiar voice coming through the speakers had him flinching.

'What the fuck is this all about?' his father demanded as Isenberg and Trip entered the room and took their seats at the table. 'Why did you call me down here?'

Isenberg had decided that she and Trip would conduct the interviews since Deacon and Adam were obviously biased, in different ways. She was saving Scarlett as a pinch hitter should the need arise.

Isenberg had also confirmed Nash's claim that Wyatt hadn't been the Narcotics lieutenant's first choice for her team. She'd asked Nash to wait upstairs in the briefing room in case they needed his help and he'd agreed. She'd informed Wyatt's boss that Wyatt was a 'person of interest' in their investigation and the head of Narcotics cooperated fully because Wyatt had disappeared and wasn't answering anyone's calls.

IA was now involved and that sent Adam's gut on another tortuous roll. Internal Affairs had been anathema in his house. His father and his buddies would actually spit after saying 'IA.'

'We need to ask you a few questions,' Isenberg said. 'I'm—'

'Lieutenant Isenberg,' Jim Kimble interrupted mockingly, his lip curled into a sneer. 'I know who you are. What I want to know is why you've hauled me down here like some common thug.' His eyes narrowed. 'What's that useless son of mine done now?'

Adam winced and Deacon actually growled. Scarlett was visibly taken aback. As was Trip, on the other side of the glass, although he controlled his surprise quickly, his expression flattening to merely bored.

Nicely done, Adam thought. Trip was solid.

'S'okay, D,' he said aloud, giving Deacon's shoulder a pat. 'Not anything I haven't heard before.'

'Nash was right,' Deacon muttered. 'We did abandon you. *I* abandoned you. I let that miserable fuck of a father tell you that you were weak for taking a mental health leave. I let him tell you that you were useless.'

'He would have said those things regardless,' Adam said practically. 'You know it.'

Deacon shook his head hard. 'I should have stopped him.'

'Let it go, D,' Adam murmured. 'You're here right now. And that's everything. Let's listen now, okay?'

Deacon just growled in response, which made Adam want to grin. But he didn't because Isenberg had motioned to Trip, who unzipped the rifle case he'd carried in and put the rifle on the table. It was tagged and unloaded. Trip had made it a point to triple check.

'We have a few questions about this,' Isenberg said, indicating the rifle.

Jim Kimble frowned. 'What? It's not mine. I don't own that model.'

'This isn't just any rifle,' Isenberg said. 'This rifle was used in a robbery thirty years ago. You and your partner, Dale Hanson, stopped the robbery and confiscated this rifle.'

Jim's eyes narrowed. 'It was stolen,' he said curtly. 'Out of our cruiser.'

'Where was it parked when the rifle was stolen?' Trip asked in his deep rumble.

Jim's eyes shifted to the Fed. 'I don't know you.'

'I'm Special Agent Triplett, FBI.'

'And?' Jim asked belligerently. 'Is that supposed to impress me? What does the FBI want from me?'

'The FBI wants you to answer my question,' Trip said levelly. 'Now would be good.'

'The rookie's good,' Deacon murmured.

Yes, he is, Adam thought.

Jim's expression turned stony. 'It was parked in front of the diner where we'd had lunch. Just like the report says.'

'I don't think so,' Trip said. 'Neither did IA when they put you and your partner on unpaid leave to investigate.'

Adam's eyes widened. He hadn't known about that. But then . . . 'I think I remember this. He was home for a long time and there was a lot of yelling. And drinking. My mom cried a lot. I was five.' Which would have been the same year as the rifle went missing.

'The math computes,' Deacon agreed with a nod. 'I didn't know either.'

Jim's face turned red at the mention of IA and their investigation. 'That was bullshit,' he snapped. 'Those IA SOBs never found nothin'.'

'No, they didn't,' Isenberg said. 'But they might reopen the investigation now.'

Jim's eyes bugged in shock and rage. 'What the fuck? It's been thirty years! Why would they open that can of worms again?'

'Because this rifle was found at the scene of a shooting last night,' Isenberg said sharply. 'And it's been used three times in the past two days. Once to target your son.'

Jim straightened in his chair. 'Did he accuse me? That bastard. And you believe him? You'd take the word of a washed-up—'

'Stop right now,' Isenberg said sharply, then drew a breath and let it out. 'Detective Kimble did not accuse you,' she said more calmly.

'Bet he didn't defend me either,' Jim grumbled.

'You'd win that bet,' Adam muttered.

Deacon snorted. 'Once an asshole . . .'

'Shh,' Scarlett scolded. 'I'm trying to listen.' She bumped Adam's shoulder again. 'I wanna hear Isenberg tear him a new one.'

Adam smiled at her reflection in the glass and Scarlett smiled back. But Isenberg had pulled her composure back on like a cape and was coolly regarding his father.

'This rifle,' she said, 'has been used in two murders this weekend alone. Now, I'd like to know where your vehicle was when it was stolen. You're not immune just because you're retired. An investigation could result in the loss of your pension.'

Jim's nostrils flared. 'Bastard kid of mine,' he muttered, but his eyes flicked around nervously. 'I stand by what's in the report.'

'He's lying,' Scarlett murmured.

'Of course he's lying,' Deacon said with an eye roll. 'The question is why?'

Isenberg's eyes narrowed. 'Are you protecting someone?'

Crossing his arms over his chest, Jim stared straight ahead mutinously.

'Well, we have your old partner in the next room. We'll see what he has to say. Whoever tells me the truth first gets my recommendation for leniency with IA. And with the prosecutor.'

'My wife is sick,' Jim said when Isenberg moved to leave the room. 'If I lose my pension, she'll lose her insurance. You'd do that?'

Adam felt the blood drain from his face. His mom had to maintain her insurance. She'd die otherwise. He started for the door, but Deacon and Scarlett each grabbed one of his arms and held him in place.

'Trust her, Adam,' Scarlett said softly. 'Trust Lynda to do the right thing.'

'Okay.' Adam nodded, forced himself to relax. 'You can let go. I'm okay.'

Isenberg appeared unruffled at the prospect of Tammy Kimble

losing her medical care. 'No, Mr Kimble. You'd be doing that.'

Jim looked away, shaking his head. 'You're as big a bitch as everyone says.'

Isenberg actually smiled, but it was her coldest and most ruthless smile. Had Adam not trusted her implicitly, he'd be terrified right now. He just hoped his father was.

'Thank you, Mr Kimble. Are you going to insult me some more or are you going to tell me what I want to know? Because I will follow through.'

'Bitch,' Jim muttered. 'It was parked in Hanson's driveway. He'd gone home to see his wife. She was sick at the time.' Defiantly, he looked at Isenberg then at Trip. 'She had cancer and she'd called him because she needed a doctor. We'd both rushed into the house to help her, and after we called the ambulance, I told Hanson I needed to move the cruiser 'cause we'd get written up if the medics saw it in the driveway, because we were on duty.'

'Surely they would have made an exception for that,' Isenberg said quietly.

'We didn't want to find out for sure. I went out to the cruiser and found the trunk pried open. Looked like a crowbar. The rifle was gone, along with a couple other guns.'

'What did you do?' Isenberg asked.

Jim shrugged. 'Dale was scared for his wife, so I didn't tell him till later. I just returned the car, damaged. Made a big production when I "realized" the rifle was gone.'

'When did you tell your partner?'

'Later that night when his wife was out of the danger zone. She ended up dying, but it took years. Every time she'd call, he'd run to her side.'

'Did he want to tell the truth about the rifle?'

'Hell no.' He rolled his eyes. 'Because we both knew who took the damn rifle.'

'Care to share?' Trip asked sarcastically.

'No, but I'm gonna,' Jim said with a scowl. 'Because I'm not letting him take me down with him for this. Dale has a half-brother. Mike. Always good for nothin'.'

'Can you describe Mike?' Isenberg asked.

'Yeah. About five-ten, used to be skinny. Haven't seen him in years. Dark hair, but it was thinning even then.'

'What about a last name?' Trip asked.

Jim shook his head. 'Never knew. Never wanted to know. Kid was bad news.'

'His size matches with Kate's description of last night's shooter,' Deacon said. 'I wonder if your father knows Bruiser.'

Adam had just been wondering the same thing.

So had Isenberg, apparently, because she put the Kiesler University surveillance photo of Bruiser in front of Jim Kimble. 'Who is this?'

'I dunno,' Jim said. 'I've never seen him. That's the truth. Can I go now?'

'Sure,' Isenberg said. 'But be careful. Whoever's running this show is tying off loose ends. Wouldn't want you to be one of them.'

'Right,' Jim said curtly. 'I told you what you wanted to know. I got no need to worry about IA, do I?'

'I dunno,' Isenberg shot back sarcastically. 'I might ask Detective Kimble what he thinks. After all, he's the only one targeted by this killer who's survived.'

He glared at Isenberg. 'I bet he's sniveling about that too. Son of mine's a disgrace. Goddamn pussy, takin' crazy leave. Cops these days are all gone soft. In my day, we just sucked it up.'

Adam winced, because even though he'd heard it before, it still hurt.

Trip stood, squaring his shoulders in a way that seemed to fill the room. 'That son of yours is a damn good cop,' he said with cold disdain. 'Which I can't say for you.'

That felt good to hear, Adam had to admit. More than balanced out the bad.

Isenberg drew another deep breath and let it out. 'You know, Mr Kimble, my team and I just saw a video of the event that prompted Detective Kimble to take mental health leave. I'd show it to you, just to see if there's any scrap of human decency in you, but I won't use that poor child's death as a weapon. So . . . you're free to go. Watch out for bullets, because there's another rifle out there somewhere. Killed a retired cop just this morning.'

Jim went still. 'I heard about that on the news. John Kasper in the churchyard, right? I was sorry to hear that. He was a good cop.'

'Oh my fucking God,' Deacon growled. 'I want to *kill* that fucker.'

Adam put a hand on Deacon's shoulder. 'Easy. He knows I'm back here. He's just trying to get a rise out of me and I'm not going to give him the satisfaction.'

'Yes,' Isenberg was saying bitterly. 'John Kasper was such a good cop that he sold Detective Kimble out. Told the sniper that my detective was going to be there, in that churchyard. That bullet was not meant for Kasper. It was meant for your son. So by all means, go. And hope that whoever's after Detective Kimble doesn't start worrying about what you've just told us.'

'Wait.' Jim stood up unsteadily. 'You can't just let me go out there unprotected.'

Trip smiled coldly as he stored the rifle and zipped the case. 'If you're *scared*, you can *snivel* about it to the front desk. I'm sure they can help you put in a formal request for police protection. Or you can just suck it up. Have a nice day.'

Cincinnati, Ohio,
Monday 21 December, 10.05 A.M.

The door to the observation room had no sooner closed than Isenberg huffed in irritation. 'Adam, I swear to God,' she said. 'Your father is a—'

'Total dickwad,' Trip interrupted, breathing hard.

Adam chuckled. 'I did try to tell you on Saturday when we were talking about Voss.'

Trip shook his head. 'Man, you said he was an asshole. You didn't say I'd want to punch him in his fucking mouth.' He turned to Isenberg, looking sheepish. 'I'm sorry that I just interrupted you, Lieutenant.'

Isenberg snorted a laugh. 'That's okay. "Dickwad" is a better word than I'd chosen.'

Adam's smile faded. 'Seriously, thank you both. I know I could not have gotten that information from him. And I do remember the time he was suspended. It was not a good time in our house. I remember my mother crying a lot and asking if he cared more about what happened to Mrs Hanson than to us. I didn't understand then.'

'You were a kid,' Isenberg said. 'I guess I understand his reasons, but his behavior was and is not acceptable. God only knows how many people have been killed with that rifle over the years.' She tilted her head. 'Do you remember Dale's half-brother Mike?'

Adam closed his eyes and tried to think back. 'There was one guy that came with us to the target range a few times. His name was Mike, but I don't remember a whole lot about him. Just that he seemed . . . too cool. Like the teacher that wants to be cool for his students. Except Mike was . . . I don't know. I didn't like him. I remember that.'

'When was this?' Deacon asked. 'I don't remember him.'

'Because you were off at college. Wyatt was in the police academy and I was living at home, going to UC.' He bit at his lip. 'It was strange, though, as I recall.'

'Strange how?' Scarlett asked.

'Well, Mike and Wyatt knew each other. Really well. Like they'd spent a lot of time together in the past. I went with the two of them to the shooting range a few times. Mike was good. He gave us pointers. I learned a lot from him.'

'And became a sharpshooter,' Deacon said.

Adam almost smiled at the brotherly pride in Deacon's voice. 'Yeah. So did Wyatt. And then, you know, life happened. He finished the academy and got a job with CPD. Made new friends. I went to school, then the academy. We were partners at the beginning. I learned a lot from him.'

'Whatever he has or has not done has nothing to do with you,' Isenberg said, once again reading his mind.

'I know. But I can't process this. He doesn't live large. Doesn't spend money he shouldn't have. Lives in a normal house, normal neighborhood. He's a husband and father.'

'And a friend,' Isenberg said softly. 'Hopefully he's still all of those things and there is another explanation for all of this.'

'But you don't think so.' Adam's heart physically hurt. 'And neither do I.'

Scarlett made an unhappy sound and looked up from her phone. 'Guys, the owner of Barber Motors is Michael Barber. I mean Michael is a popular enough name, but . . .'

'Goddammit,' Adam whispered. 'If Dale's involved . . . God. I don't know what I'll do. That man was more a father to me than my own for more years than I can count.'

Deacon's hand came up to clamp Adam's neck again. 'Come on. Let's talk to Mr Hanson. See what's what.'

Isenberg was considering him. 'You want to be in there with us?'

Adam sighed, then nodded. 'Yeah. I would. Thanks.'

Cincinnati, Ohio,
Monday 21 December, 10.10 A.M.

He got into his SUV, winded after jogging the half mile from Nash Currie's home in the middle of fucking nowhere. *I need to ramp up my workouts.* Because a half mile shouldn't have winded him. Of course he was running on very little sleep. Hopefully, that would change soon and everything would be back to normal.

He'd stashed the rifle he'd used that morning and the gun he'd used on Mike last night in the shed behind Currie's farmhouse. Emboldened by the fact that the house was a full mile from the nearest neighbor, he'd even set up a 'target range' in the woods behind the shed before hiding the rifle. He'd fired at a tree half a mile away, leaving his casings behind so it would appear that Currie was a respectable shot – one who could have shot at Kimble that morning.

Waiting for his heater to warm up, he checked his phone, frowning at the barrage of new messages and voicemail. A few were from Isenberg, probably because he hadn't shown up at her summons. *Bitch.* A few were from his boss in Narcotics, which made him frown. His boss didn't usually call his cell phone. He normally texted or emailed.

Tension tightened his skin. Something was wrong.

Because the rest of the messages were from numbers he didn't know. He clicked on one of the voicemails.

'This is Lisette Cauldwell from the *Ledger*. We'd like to get a statement on the recent CPD bulletin naming you as a person of interest. Please call me back at 513-555-6220.'

He sat frozen for a moment. *What the fuck? Person of interest? What the fuck?*

He shook himself into action, bringing up the CPD webpage, then stared at his phone screen in shocked disbelief. *I'm done. I'm fucking done.* Because the face staring back from the CPD webpage was his own.

He was a 'person of interest' in his own damn case.

How? How had they gone from 'it's a cop,' to 'it's Wyatt Hanson'?

More importantly, how could he fix this? How could he redirect the attention back to Currie? Or was it too late? *No. Stop it. That's quitter talk. I don't give up. Ever.*

What had he missed? Mallory hadn't described him – he would have known that last night. They hadn't found Linnea. That would have been all over the scanner.

He leaned his head back against the seat, mentally checking the list of everything Adam and his merry band had learned last night. Not Mike's blood. There was nothing to compare it to because Mike had never been arrested, even though he'd deserved it far more times than he could count.

Mike escaped arrest because I saved his ass every single time, the fucker.

There was nothing on file to connect him to Mike. His heart skipped a beat. Except the rifle. The one he'd used to kill Andy Gold and that Mike had used to off Butch. The rifle whose serial number had been filed away by Mike years ago.

Quincy Taylor had been planning to try raising the serial number. He must have succeeded. *I should have gone to the lab last night and sabotaged the rifle.* But dealing with Mike had seemed more pressing. Then wiping out Mike's used car dealership.

His shoulders sagged. The rifle would connect Mike to his father.

And to Adam's father. He wondered if the cops had talked to his father yet and what his father would say.

He took a chance and dialed his father's landline, listening to it ring and ring. And ring. His father wasn't home. His father was always home. He was too blind now to drive himself. Someone had picked him up. Couldn't have been Rita. He'd forbidden her to have anything to do with the old man since they'd had a falling-out. Sanctimonious old prick.

Dale would tell the cops everything he knew, just to get back at him. And the old man probably already had. And then he'd probably told everyone how Adam fucking Kimble would have done everything so much better.

'Fuck you, John,' he snarled aloud. *Fuck you for pushing Adam out of the way. Fuck you for having a conscience at the worst possible time.* But that didn't change reality. Kimble was still alive and probably leading the charge against him.

So what do I do? Cut and run or stay and fight?

He looked at his face on CPD's website once again and had to accept the bitter truth. He wasn't going to be able to pull this one out in the bottom of the ninth like he had before.

He needed to run. Fortunately, he'd been planning for this moment for decades. Living an upstanding life within his police officer means meant he hadn't spent the money he'd been pulling in hand over fist. Not like Mike had, which had kept his uncle cutting corners and skimming to get by.

Fucking Mike. Goddammit.

Focus. He had millions stashed away in his offshore accounts. He needed access to some of that cash. Now. And then he needed to get over the border before his status changed from 'person of interest' to 'wanted for murder.'

He would have loved to hurt Adam Kimble one final time but he couldn't afford the time nor the risk. Once he got away and settled? There were always paid hits.

I can afford it. Because it was no longer about stopping or even distracting an investigation. This was payback. *I have to leave everything behind.* And Kimble got to stay.

Pulling the SUV back onto the country road, he headed for home. His alternate passports were in his home safe. At least Rita wouldn't be home. Today was her weekly appointment with her hairdresser. No answering questions with near-truths and almost-lies. No messy goodbyes.

He'd find a new home and start over.

Cincinnati, Ohio,
Monday 21 December, 10.10 A.M.

Dale Hanson sat up in his chair when Adam came into the interview room. He smelled like a brewery and clearly hadn't slept. He looked sad and a little drunk. A lot guilty and upset. But not at all surprised. More resigned.

'Adam.' He pushed aside a half-drunk cup of coffee. 'I didn't expect to see you. I thought it would be the other two. Deacon and the girl.'

Adam frowned, compelled to demand respect for Scarlett. 'She's not a girl. She's Detective Bishop. And she's a damn good cop.'

'Whatever.' Dale blinked as Isenberg and Trip entered the room. 'Who are they?'

Adam took the chair nearest Dale and wished like hell for a drink. Just the fumes coming off the older man were fucking with his self-control. It was like Dale had bathed in booze with his clothes on.

It occurred to Adam that Deacon and Scarlett had to have known Dale had been drinking. How could they have ridden in the same car and not known? Still, they hadn't said anything. Deacon knew how Adam felt about Dale. Knew he'd need to see it for himself.

'Lieutenant Isenberg and Special Agent Triplett,' Adam said, pointing at each one.

'You don't seem surprised to have been brought downtown, Mr Hanson,' Isenberg remarked. 'Why is that?'

Dale swallowed hard. 'Because I've been expecting you.'

It was like a physical blow. 'Since?' Adam managed to murmur.

'Since yesterday morning when I saw Butch's picture on the

computer. And again last night. Stayed up all night waiting for the knock on the door.'

Adam frowned, startled because they'd brought him in because of the rifle, not because of Butch, whoever he was. 'Who is Butch?'

'Butch Gilbert,' Dale said. 'The guy that got shot downtown last night.'

'Bruiser,' Adam murmured.

Dale laughed again, a jarring, scraping sound. 'That's a good name for him. I didn't know he was still around. Not until I saw the computer. I can't read the paper anymore, but I can blow the print and pictures up on the computer if I use my peripheral. I'm not advanced that far. Yet.'

Adam frowned. 'Wait. You saw him online yesterday morning? We didn't post his photo until the afternoon. The only group posting his photo yesterday morning was Chicago PD, as part of their murder investigation.'

Dale gave a wan smile. 'I watch the reports. Like to keep my mind sharp, even if my eyes are going. I nearly called you. A hundred times.'

'Then why didn't you call me if you knew who he was?'

'I saw Wyatt in the photos with you at the crime scene. I figured he told you.'

Which didn't account for the hours before, when he knew Chicago PD was searching for the man. For *murder*.

'Who is he, Mr Hanson?' Isenberg asked.

'Other than a lying, cheating, and now killing sack of shit on two legs?' Hanson huffed out a harsh breath. 'He was a kid, who I didn't think was so bad. Once.' He rubbed his forehead wearily and glanced at Isenberg. 'You know I adopted Wyatt?'

Isenberg nodded. 'Detective Kimble told us.'

'I found him, you know. Wyatt. Hiding in a closet, a scared little kid. His family was dead. Murder-suicide.' Dale paused, pain skittering across his face. 'Or so I thought.'

Adam frowned. 'Or so you *thought*? What does that mean?'

'My wife always wanted kids and we'd never been able to have any, and we'd been cleared as fosters before her cancer came back, so . . . I thought having someone to mother would make her happy. But she didn't like Wyatt. She was afraid of him from the beginning. And then her cancer came back.' He shook his head with a sigh. 'I needed to take care of him. I guess I needed the control because nothing I'd done could save my wife.'

'Why was your wife afraid of Wyatt?' Trip asked.

'She said he was mean and cruel and . . .' He drew a deep breath and shuddered it out. 'I thought it was her sickness talking. I smoothed it over and I kept Wyatt. Now, looking back, I wonder what he did to her.'

Adam stared. 'What are you talking about? When was Wyatt mean and cruel?'

Another sigh. 'You remember Mrs Hanson's cat?'

Adam nodded warily. He did, but only because of the way it died. 'It was poisoned.' He felt sick. 'You're saying Wyatt did it?'

'I didn't think so at the time, but a few years later it happened to the neighbor's cat too. I searched Wyatt's room and found a box of rat poison.'

Adam drew a long breath, stunned. 'You didn't tell anyone?'

'No. I took him to a counselor at church. Wyatt seemed better, so we stopped.' Dale rubbed his forehead fitfully. 'Do you remember the day you two went to the state championships and you lost?'

'Of course.'

'You remember what *else* you lost that day?'

Adam nodded slowly. 'My baseball glove. My lucky one.' It had been a horrible day. He'd felt so helpless, angry that someone would steal something that wasn't worth that much to anyone but him. 'Are you saying that Wyatt took it?'

'Found it under his bed. I threw it away.'

Adam shook his head. 'Why? Why would he do that?'

'It threw you off your game.'

'But we *all* lost! Even Wyatt.'

'But he looked better than you did that day. Of course, the next year he'd graduated and you played without him. You won. MVP.'

Adam rubbed his mouth with the back of his hand. How had he not known? *How?*

'Who is Butch, exactly?' Isenberg asked, bringing them back on topic. 'And how does he connect to your son?'

'I like helping kids. Like you, Adam. I knew your life at home wasn't great. So I tried to step up. It was the same for Butch. I met him through Wyatt, actually. Butch had been in a fire. A bad one. Left his face so badly scarred that it was really hard to look at him.'

'You took him into your home?' Trip asked.

'No. Wyatt took him into his. This was before he married Rita and the kids came along. You and him had parted ways on the force by then. He'd gone on to Narcotics and one day pulled Butch out of a burning meth house. Butch was, I don't know, maybe sixteen at the time? He spent a lot of time in the hospital after that and Wyatt visited him, almost every day. I did too. He loved baseball. His limbs weren't burned too badly, so we played ball when he got out. Kid had attached himself to Wyatt like a limpet. Wyatt ended up getting him a job in my brother's garage.'

Garage, Adam thought dully. Nash had followed Wyatt to a garage owned by a shell corporation.

'Your half-brother, Michael Barber?' Isenberg asked and Dale looked startled.

'Yeah. Why?' But when no one said anything his face fell. 'Mike's involved too?'

'We think so,' Isenberg said. 'What's the relationship between Mike and your son?'

He shook his head. 'I wish there'd been none. Dammit, you don't know how many times I've wished I'd put my foot down and kicked that sorry sonofabitch out of my home. Out of Wyatt's life. But . . . he was my family, so I didn't. He was always getting into trouble. And I was always getting him out. Risking myself for him.'

'Did you use your authority as a police officer to do so?' Isenberg asked.

Dale shrugged. 'God help me, I did. I thought I was doing the right thing.'

No, Adam thought sadly. He'd known all along he was doing the wrong thing. He'd done it anyway. But challenging an old man's moral compass wasn't going to help anyone now. 'Mike owns a garage and a used car dealership?' he asked instead.

'I didn't know about the car dealership, but that'd be right up his alley. He's a sleazy SOB, but he's always been good with engines and gadgets.'

Trip stilled. 'What kind of gadgets?'

'Appliances, motors, anything you could take apart and put back together.'

'Like clocks and timers and triggers activated by cell phones?' Trip asked.

The bomb. Adam had almost forgotten about it.

Dale closed his eyes. 'You're talking about the device that was strapped to that young man on Saturday at the restaurant.'

'I am,' Trip said. 'Does Mike know explosives?'

'Yes. He used to work road construction, blasting tunnels through mountains. He had his certification in ordnance management. My God. Did he kill that boy?'

'We don't know,' Isenberg said. 'He tried to kill three federal agents and a psychologist, and to abduct a young girl last night, though.'

Dale looked like he'd be sick. Adam brought him a trash can, but he shook his head. 'Not necessary,' he said. 'I . . . don't know what to think. Is Wyatt involved in this?'

'We think so,' Isenberg said. 'But we can't find him. Do you know where he is?'

'No. He doesn't visit me anymore. But there was a pageant at Ariel's school this morning. I saw it on Facebook. He always goes to her school things.'

'Who's Ariel?' Trip asked.

'My granddaughter. She goes to the Gruber Academy. She's seven years old.'

Watching Isenberg text that information to Dispatch, Adam frowned at a sudden thought. 'They have a little boy too,' he said, 'Wyatt and Rita, I mean. About two now? They call him Mikey, don't they?'

Dale's mouth twisted. 'Wyatt's way of saying "fuck you" to his old man.'

'Why?' Isenberg said.

'Because I heard a rumor that the meth house he pulled Butch out of was Wyatt's. I didn't want to believe it, but I asked him. He denied it, but I was never sure. I did know that Butch had been working with meth and shouldn't have been around my grand-children. So I told Rita and she got upset. Told Butch he couldn't be around the kids. That was two years ago and Wyatt hasn't forgiven me. He cut me off from the kids. Named his son after his uncle and not me. I have to sneak around to see my own grandchildren. I can only see Ariel at school, and only because I've made friends with the custodian and he lets me watch her on the playground. And that was only while I could drive myself. I haven't seen either of them in over a year.'

'Did you tell anyone else about the rumor you'd heard about Wyatt and meth?' Isenberg asked, no sign of compassion on her face.

Which was as it should be, Adam thought. He'd always seen Dale Hanson as a father figure, a truly good man. But he hadn't seen him for what he really was – a man who twisted events and truths to make himself feel better about his world.

But that's not me. The thought – and its accompanying relief – hit him squarely in the chest. He wasn't his father and he wasn't Dale Hanson. He was far from perfect, but he'd made himself into a man he could at least look at in the mirror.

A man that Meredith trusted.

Dale was looking to Adam expectantly. 'I couldn't. I couldn't tell on my own son.'

Adam had no compassion for him either. 'Even if your own son was making poison that killed other people's sons?'

Dale's face hardened. 'I thought you'd understand.'

'I don't. I don't understand any of it. I don't understand how you could know your brother stole a rifle from your cruiser and not report it – and him.'

Dale flinched, taken aback. 'What?'

'That's actually why we brought you in,' Isenberg said. 'The rifle stolen from your cruiser thirty years ago has resurfaced. It was

506

found in the SUV that a man matching your half-brother's description was driving. It's been used in two homicides, including Butch's. Why didn't you tell someone thirty years ago that you believed your half-brother had stolen it? That was a felony offense.'

'He's my *brother*,' Dale said, as if daring anyone to call him on it. 'My family.'

'And a killer,' Adam said, losing his patience. 'And if he's not, then Wyatt is. Which it sounds like you suspected already.'

'No. I didn't,' Dale denied.

Adam squinted at him. 'You said you wondered now if the scene in which you found him really was a murder-suicide. You said that.'

'I didn't mean it that way!'

'Then how did you mean it?' Adam demanded. 'And why didn't you call me when you saw Butch's photo in the paper? He killed two innocent women – that we know of – this weekend alone. We don't know what he did in the hours since you first saw his photo.' He thought of the three cars the college prostitutes had driven, all parked in Dale's half-brother's used-car lot. 'He could have killed three more. At least. We could have avoided all of that, if you'd only called me when you first saw his photo. *Dammit.*'

Dale gave him a look of wounded incredulity. 'After all this time, after all I did for you, you talk to me like this? I expected you, of all people, to have my back.'

Adam didn't blink. 'I guess you expected wrong.' As a child, he'd clung to the affection and acceptance Dale had offered. As an adult, he recognized the strings attached that he hadn't even known existed. 'At this point, I'm not sure how we – hell, how *I* – can trust anything you've said. Ever.'

The door opened and Deacon stuck his head in. 'Lieutenant? A word, please?'

It had to be important. Deacon would never interrupt otherwise. Adam waited quietly, emotionally drained and not wanting to waste any more energy on Dale Hanson than he already had. He still had to confront Wyatt.

Wyatt, who he'd thought had been his friend. Had he ever really known him?

Wyatt, who appeared to be involved. Had Wyatt actually killed people?

It was likely that Wyatt's uncle Mike had attempted to abduct Mallory last night and hurt Meredith and Kate when they'd come to Mallory's rescue. Had Mike shot at the van too? Had he shot Bruiser? Andy Gold?

Who had set Andy's house on fire, killing a family of four?

Which of these had Wyatt done?

I knew him. Mallory's whispered words echoed in his mind. She'd known Mike. Wyatt's uncle had raped Mallory repeatedly. God. And Mike had accompanied a cop.

Wyatt. Was he the cop who'd raped Mallory? Who, instead of arresting her captor, had betrayed her when she'd so desperately reached out for help? It hurt to even consider. That the man he'd called friend could have done such a thing. But he had to think about it.

I have to figure this out. Wyatt was linked to Bruiser. *No, Butch.* Butch who'd killed Tiffany and her mother. He sucked in a breath, the truth once again hitting like a sledgehammer. Butch, who'd killed Paula. *While I watched.*

Adam's stomach churned. Wyatt had watched too. Had he known that Paula was going to die? *No, he couldn't have.* But if Butch *had* killed her? Butch, who was Wyatt's friend? Had Wyatt known? *He stood there at my side, watching.*

At a minimum, they knew Butch had killed Tiffany and her mother the exact same way. Butch's prints had been found on Tiffany's clothing. Had Wyatt known he was going to kill the mother and daughter? Adam had to believe it was strongly possible.

'How long has Wyatt hated me?' Adam asked dully, not wanting the answer, but needing it.

Dale huffed bitterly. 'From day one, I think. And you never knew. Hell of a cop you turned out to be.'

Twenty-eight

Hell of a cop you turned out to be. Adam looked away, the barb striking deep.

Trip tapped the table and caught his eye. 'Stop,' he mouthed.

Adam's lips curved, appreciating the intervention. He rubbed his palms over his face. His mouth was so dry and he was starting to ramp up. He'd started visualizing all the liquor stores on his way home, hating himself more with every moment that passed. *Weak. You're goddamn weak.*

So don't be. You don't need the booze. But he did. He needed—

Trip tossed him a pack of gum, his expression knowing. Adam took a piece, ignoring the smug look that crept over Dale's face.

'Always thought so,' Dale remarked lazily. 'You thought you were better than the rest of us. Than your daddy. Than Wyatt. But you're as much a drunk as your daddy is.'

Adam stared at him, genuinely puzzled. *Don't engage. Do not engage.* 'What are you talking about? I never thought I was better.' *Dammit.* He'd engaged.

A shrug. 'MVP of your team, college graduate, detective before you were thirty.'

Adam continued to stare. He'd barely squeaked by in all of his classes. Deacon was the brilliant one. All Adam had been good at back then was hitting a damn ball. 'So was Wyatt. The detective part anyway.' But Wyatt had had a four-year head start. Adam had been fast-tracked. His career had continued on the rise until he'd

509

transferred to Personal Crimes. When everything had gone to shit. When Paula was murdered.

Wyatt had stolen his lucky glove to throw him off a baseball game. Adam had already considered that Tiffany and her mother were killed in that manner to distract him. Had Paula been killed for the same reason? *Oh my God. Oh my God.*

Trip knocked on the table again, this time simply arching an eyebrow.

Right, Adam thought. *Stop it.* He shot Trip a wry smile, earning him a sober nod as Isenberg returned to the table. Deacon waited at the door, arms crossed over his chest, looking pissed off in general.

'Mr Hanson,' Isenberg said formally, 'we may have some bad news for you. A body was just found behind a dry-cleaner about two miles from the hospital where the shootout took place last night. The victim has no ID, but his clothing and the location of his wounds match those of the shooter we confronted in the hospital parking lot.'

Dale sagged into his chair, stricken. 'Mike's dead?'

'We think so. Did he have any tattoos or scars?'

Dale put his right hand over his heart, as if about to recite the pledge of allegiance. 'He had a tattoo here. A Celtic cross in flames.'

Wonderful, Adam thought numbly. *A killer, a rapist, and a white supremacist to boot.*

'Then yes,' Isenberg said, 'the body we recovered is that of your brother. I'm very sorry for your loss.'

Dale just sat there staring at her, hand still on his heart. 'He can't be dead.'

'I'm very sorry, sir,' Isenberg said politely. 'We're done here, so if you'd like, one of my officers can take you either home or to the morgue to do an ID.' Isenberg extended her hand. 'Detective Bishop and I will walk you up front and get you a ride.'

Dale took her hand. 'How did he die?'

'Probably not from the wounds he received during the shootout at the hospital,' Isenberg said, 'but the ME will have to make that determination after the autopsy. Please come with me now.'

Adam wanted to frown, because rushing the next of kin was

pretty ruthless, even for when the victim was a murderer. But he trusted Isenberg, so he kept his mouth shut.

Dale shuffled off with Isenberg, out of the room and out of view. Adam and Trip waited, while Deacon stood at the door, watching Isenberg's progress down the hall. Finally, Deacon entered the room and went straight to the table, pulling a glove on. He picked up the coffee cup that Dale had pushed away and bagged it.

'We're going to need DNA for a definitive ID of the body,' Deacon said. 'Face is bashed in. A bloody brick was found near the body. Dental records would be of no use. Fingers are gone so no prints.'

'And the tat?' Trip asked.

'Cut right out of his skin. But it was over his heart.' He tilted his head. 'Adam?'

Adam blinked up at Deacon, then realized his own hand was over his heart. 'Like the scar Mallory saw,' he said quietly. 'Wyatt had a tattoo, a long time ago. Over his heart. He had it removed when he started the academy.'

'What was it of?' Trip asked in a way that said he already knew.

'Celtic cross in flames. He said that Mike had taken him out drinking for his eighteenth birthday and when he woke the next morning, he had the tattoo. He didn't know it was white supremacist until his father saw it and threw a fit. Wyatt didn't want his application to the academy to be rejected so he had it removed. That's what he told me, anyway. I only saw the tat once and I never knew it scarred. I never thought about how a tattoo would be removed. I didn't even consider he'd have a scar. Hell, I was still in high school and he'd gone off to the academy. I never saw him without a shirt on after he'd graduated high school because we weren't playing ball any longer. He always wore a T-shirt in the precinct locker room.' He closed his eyes. 'Wyatt raped Mallory.' Saying it out loud didn't make it easier to accept. *'Wyatt.* Holy God.'

Deacon gripped his shoulder. 'And we'll make him pay for that, don't worry.'

'He was afraid she could ID his scar,' Trip said. 'And that you could, as well. That must be why you are both targets.'

Adam felt curiously detached. 'I didn't even remember he had one. That was twenty years ago.'

'Sounds like Wyatt's spent more time thinking about you than you have him,' Trip said mildly. 'All that shit coming out of his father's mouth was just that – shit. You know this, right?'

'Yeah. Still stings.'

'I'll bet,' Trip grunted. 'Did you have *anyone* in your life who was nice to you?'

Adam drew a breath because Deacon was still gripping his shoulder. 'Yeah. My mom, when she could be. And Deacon, Dani, and Greg, all of the time.' He patted Deacon's hand awkwardly. 'You can let go now, D. I'm not gonna bolt.'

'Wasn't sure,' Deacon said, dropping his hand. 'You look like you might.'

'It's a lot to take in. And I'm feeling . . . raw,' he confessed. 'I can't believe anyone believed I thought I was superior to anyone. Well, to criminals, sure, but to my family?'

'You are, you know,' Deacon said. 'You could have ended up a mean drunk like your dad, but you're a nice, *recovering* drunk.'

Adam laughed, which he knew was Deacon's intent. 'You asshole.'

Deacon grinned. 'Yeah, well, we all have our special gifts. Come on.'

'Where are we going?' Adam asked.

'Upstairs to strategize.' Deacon held up the bagged coffee cup. 'I'll catch up with you in the briefing room after I drop this sample off at the lab.'

Cincinnati, Ohio,
Monday 21 December, 10.45 A.M.

'Merry, wake up.'

Diesel's voice startled Meredith out of the doze she'd fallen into as she'd watched snow falling outside the waiting room window. She blinked awake, finding Diesel grinning.

'What?' she asked, touching her mouth, hoping she hadn't been drooling.

'You snore.'

'I do not!'

His eyes twinkled at her. 'Yes, you do and it's cute. Ask Adam. He'll tell you.'

She gave him a glare that held no heat. 'Did you wake me up to make fun of me?'

'No. I finally broke into Bethany Row's personal email.'

'Just now?'

'About a half-hour ago.'

'Why didn't you wake me up?'

'Because I wanted to find evidence and you needed to sleep.'

She smiled at him. 'Thank you.' He was a sweet man. For the hundredth time she wondered what Dani Novak was waiting for. Diesel clearly was interested, but Dani didn't seem to be. Which wasn't important now. 'What did you find?'

'Well, several messages from foster parents discussing perks, payments for her looking the other way. Some of the messages come out and say what they'll pay her or what they'll do for her because she's discounted a child's complaint. I imagine that's what's being used in the investigation against her. But I went back farther. She got an email from her bank six months ago saying that ten grand had been wired into her account.'

Meredith stared. 'Ten thousand dollars? From whom?'

'This is the interesting part. The email says the account it was wired *from* is the same account that Broderick Voss was paying *into*.'

Her eyes widened. 'That's amazing.' Then she realized what they had and she groaned. 'And of course we can't talk about it or tell the cops about it because you hacked to learn about it.'

'Which poisons the tree and makes anything the cops learn inadmissible,' he said with a disgusted sigh. 'I like it better when I'm not working with cops. I do what I want with what I find.'

She nodded glumly. 'The Fourth Amendment's a pain in the ass.'

Diesel snorted. 'I'm sure your cop can figure out how to use this info just fine. He can ask the Indy cops for the file on the investigation

513

and this email will pop up. He won't get into any trouble.'

She smiled. *My cop. He is. Mine.* Diesel's expression softened and she tilted her head, studying him. 'What?'

'Your face. You look happy.' He shrugged uncomfortably. 'You deserve to be.'

Her eyes stung. Again. 'You keep making me cry.' She pushed away from the table and was searching the waiting room for a box of tissues when her cell phone rang.

'You should answer that,' Diesel said. 'It's an Indy area code.'

She hurried back to glance at her screen. 'It's the detective.' She hit ACCEPT. 'Hello? This is Meredith Fallon.'

'Good morning, Dr Fallon. This is Detective Santos, Indianapolis PD. I was told by my boss to stop avoiding your calls.'

'Thank you,' she said with a frown. 'That's very polite of you.'

He huffed a laugh. 'I suppose I deserve that. But I haven't been totally ignoring you. I had to go hunting through my personal notes, and given I can't read my own handwriting, that took some time. But I have something for you.'

Cincinnati, Ohio,
Monday 21 December, 10.50 A.M.

Adam and Trip found Scarlett and Nash waiting in the briefing room. Nash was standing at the whiteboard again, once again staring at the photos of Paula and Tiffany.

Adam joined him there and stood silently for a moment. 'I'm sorry, Nash,' he murmured. 'I didn't want to even wonder if you were involved, but I had to.'

Nash angled him a wry smile. 'Hey, it's okay. I might have thought the same in your place.' He returned his gaze to the photos. 'Do you think he had Paula killed? Wyatt?'

'I think it's possible. And that hurts,' Adam confessed. 'So damn much.'

'I know,' Nash said. 'It hurts me and he wasn't my childhood friend. I just can't get over it in my head. How he stood next to us and *watched her die.*'

514

'I know. But, looking back, I'm seeing that Wyatt wasn't really the friend I thought he was. I was only eleven when I met him. I'm remembering a lot of the "pranks" and "teasing" he'd do – stuff that wasn't funny, but I heard a helluva lot worse from my own father, so it didn't register.'

'He also didn't want you to know,' Trip said from behind them. 'Sociopaths are really good at hiding their true nature. Otherwise we'd catch a lot more of them.'

Adam sighed. 'Yeah, I know that. At least some things make sense. Whoever had been hiding Paula knew some sign language. So does Wyatt.'

Nash shook his head. 'But years? He held her for *years*, Adam.'

Adam closed his eyes, unable to look at the photo of Paula's suffering any longer. 'I know. We know he was . . . attracted to Mallory at thirteen and was willing to risk being found out to rape her. Paula wasn't through puberty yet. She was only eleven.' And he'd kept her for years. 'He has a little girl, Nash. She's only seven.'

Nash made a pained noise. 'God, I hope he hasn't touched her.'

Adam wanted to be sick, but he gritted his teeth and forced his stomach to settle. 'Yeah. Hopefully we can save Ariel from what the others went through.'

'If Wyatt was Paula's captor, why didn't she know him the day we watched her die?'

Adam thought back to those few days during which he and Paula had communicated via Skype after she'd reached out to him. 'Because he always stood off-camera. He said that it was "my show" to run. That he'd coach me through it because it was one of my first big cases in Personal Crimes.'

'Which was condescending bullshit,' Nash muttered.

Adam sighed. 'I see that now. We wondered how she'd figured out how to use the Internet and email without raising the notice of her captor right away. Now I'm wondering if Wyatt did this to mess me up. Apparently, he's always hated me.'

Nash was quiet a moment. 'After I came out of my funk? I poked around and found that you paid for her ashes to be buried in a proper grave. Out of your own pocket.'

Adam shrugged, uncomfortable now. 'I couldn't stand the thought of her ending up in some unmarked grave. I didn't know if she had family. Hell, I never even knew her last name. Just . . . for a few days, she was mine to protect.'

Nash's sigh was sad. 'I've been putting flowers there. First Sunday of the month. Maybe next time we can go together. Get some closure.'

Adam's throat thickened. 'I'd like that. Thank you.' He turned away from the photos, just as Deacon came through the door, bigger than life as usual.

But not impervious to hurt, Adam thought. Just like Meredith wasn't as impervious as everyone thought either. *I hurt them both. I hurt a lot of people by closing myself off. Not gonna do that anymore.*

'How long before the lab gets DNA back on Dale Hanson?' he asked Deacon.

'Few hours. They moved it to the top of the priority list. It's so much nicer now with the high-speed methods. Not like the *old days* when we had to wait a whole day or more.'

Nash rolled his eyes. 'I love hearing you young pups talk about the old days. You got no concept about—' He broke himself off, rolling his eyes again. 'God, I'm old.'

Deacon assessed him seriously. 'Maybe. But remember we need to hear from the old guys sometimes.'

Adam knew his cousin wasn't talking about the older detective's methods, but the dressing-down Nash had given them earlier. He was proven right by Deacon's next words.

'Trip, can you drop Adam off at the hospital when we're done here? I think he needs some time to process.'

Trip's brows arched. 'With Meredith?'

Deacon shrugged. 'Adam might need therapy.'

'So that's what you *old guys* are callin' it now?' Trip drawled. 'Therapy?'

'I'm not old,' Deacon protested. 'You're just young.'

Nash chuckled. 'That's what happens when you call someone old, Novak. There's always someone younger to come along and pay the insult forward. And "therapy" is a fine word for it, Agent Triplett. Adam could use it.'

Adam actually felt his cheeks heating. 'Shut up. I'm not going to the hospital for Meredith yet. We are going to find Wyatt Hanson.' He swallowed hard. 'I need to.'

'I know you do,' Deacon said earnestly. 'I get that. But you are his target, Adam. By putting yourself out there, you're putting the rest of us in danger.'

Adam frowned, unimpressed. 'You're resorting to guilt, D? What the hell?'

Scarlett looked up from her phone, her expression a little guarded, making him wonder what else had happened, but she simply agreed. 'It was pretty lame, Deacon.'

Adam gave her a grateful nod, before refocusing on Deacon. 'Besides, it's not your call. Until Isenberg decides otherwise, I'm lead on this case and I'm not going to hide.'

'Isenberg,' Isenberg said as she came through the door, 'has decided otherwise. I'm taking the lead.'

Adam turned his frown in Isenberg's direction. 'Why?'

'Because this case just became a big fucking deal, that's why,' she said cordially, as if they were discussing a sale on chicken at Kroger. 'You do not want to be lead anymore. Hell, *I* don't want to be lead. I'm doing you a favor, Detective.' Then she shocked him by laying her hand on his arm and giving it a squeeze. 'And because,' she added in a murmur, 'you were shot at this morning by someone you trusted and haven't fully processed it.'

Adam wanted to be annoyed, but couldn't find it in him. 'I'm fine.'

'You will be,' she said, gently confident, completely disarming him. 'Let's all sit down. I have information you don't. Let me tell you all and you will be *begging* me to take this off your hands.'

'You might have told him this privately,' Nash said in a loud whisper.

Isenberg rolled her eyes. 'I don't have time for niceties, Detective Currie, and my people are tough enough not to need them.' But she gave Adam a look of apology before continuing. 'I briefed the brass on what you all have put together this morning. Let's just say that the idea that we have a rogue cop out there running prostitution rings and killing innocent people did not go over well. The media haven't sunk their teeth into the story yet, but it's a matter of time. Especially since the video Shane made for Linnie went viral.'

'What video?' Deacon, Nash, and Trip asked all together. Scarlett was oddly silent.

Adam blew out a breath. 'Oh, the video. I'd forgotten all about it.'

'Well, you *have* had a busy morning, Detective,' Isenberg said, her eyes filled with I-told-you-so. 'Tell them now.'

'It was Meredith's idea, actually. We were talking about losing Linnie's trust and how she'd never approach us now, but she might trust Shane. I asked Colby and Wendi to supervise a video of him asking Linnie to come to us, since they're with Mallory in the same hotel as Shane and Kyle. I figured I'd ask the *Ledger* to upload it to their website. But then John . . .' He shrugged. 'I lost the thread in everything that happened next.'

Scarlett blinked at him. 'You did all that *before* your AA meeting?'

He *had* been productive, come to think of it. 'Everything but talking to Marcus. I didn't think he'd be awake at five thirty in the morning.'

'He wasn't,' Scarlett said. Which she'd know because she and the newspaper owner were a couple. 'But you could have asked me.'

Yes, he could have. And should have. Because he recognized the odd expression in her eyes, now. He'd hurt her too. 'I'd planned to after my AA meeting this morning. Honest, Scar. As it turned out, though, Wendi and Parrish Colby were already awake. Mallory wasn't sleeping. Neither were Shane and Kyle. They were all having a *Star Wars* marathon.' He glanced at Isenberg. 'How did it go viral? I never got to ask the *Ledger* for help.'

'Diesel Kennedy took care of uploading it to the *Ledger* homepage,' Isenberg said, then one side of her mouth lifted in a smirk. 'He actually cleared it with me first.'

Scarlett looked surprised to hear that. 'Wow. Diesel's getting downright civilized. Asking permission and everything. I think that scares me.'

'Don't worry,' Isenberg said dryly. 'I don't think he'll be making it a habit. Anyway, the video went viral. Shane said very complimentary things about you, Adam. He told Linnie to trust you, that you wouldn't hurt her. That you're trying to help her. He begged her to come to him, so that they could bury Andy together.'

'No wonder it went viral,' Deacon murmured. 'That's a heartstring tugger.'

'Indeed,' Isenberg said briskly. 'I asked Diesel to put your name, Adam, and the precinct's switchboard number on the video. So far we've gotten a shitload of calls, but none from Linnie. It's only been an hour though. And as far as we know she doesn't have a phone, so she'll have to see it via another medium. Which won't be a problem, because the story's been picked up by every major news outlet in the world.'

Adam stared at her. 'In the *world*?'

'You heard me. A fucking mess is what it is, but that can't be helped. It can't even be contained. We can only try to herd the media in the direction we want them to go.'

'Which is?' Nash asked.

She grimaced. 'Fifteen minutes ago, it was to spin this as a cop suffering from PTSD after too many years on Personal Crimes and ICAC. The mention of cops working Internet crimes against children always makes good press.'

'Except that's not true,' Adam said quietly. 'Especially since he may have been responsible for Paula's murder.'

Isenberg's eyes flashed angrily. 'I told them that. They . . . scoffed.' She drew a breath and regained her composure. 'Initially, anyway. I was able to convince them otherwise. But this is exactly why you do *not* want to be lead on this case anymore, Adam. That a cop's involved in something this huge? It's going to be a political nightmare. I won't let you get dragged into it.'

He was unconvinced. 'And I appreciate that. But I want to bring him down.'

Her expression softened. 'I know,' she said as if they were the only two in the room. 'But you can't. Not anymore. You're personally involved. If you *don't* get him, people will say you protected him because of your friendship and that cops all stick together. If you *do* get him, it'll be portrayed as a vendetta, bad blood between you, bad history because your fathers were complicit in hiding a felony. Either way, it will kill your career.'

Adam knew she was right. He knew it. *But goddamn it.* He needed to see the look in Wyatt's eyes when he realized he was totally screwed with no options left.

She hadn't said another word, just watching him. Waiting for his reply.

Say something. Say anything. Tell her to go to hell. But he couldn't do that. She was trying to save him. Risking herself in the process. Because that was what good bosses did.

Trip spoke into the silence. 'You said that was the spin fifteen minutes ago. What's it now?'

'Right now the department's official position is the truth,' Isenberg said, but she was still watching Adam. 'Thanks to Meredith Fallon.'

Adam's eyes popped wide, then narrowed. 'Meredith? What's she done? If she's left that hospital, I'll—'

'Be sleeping on the couch for the foreseeable future if you continue to speak,' Isenberg said, lips twitching. 'Relax. She's fine. She's exactly where she's supposed to be.'

'Then how?' Adam asked.

Isenberg shrugged. 'Your shrink's been busy. She just got us the missing piece of the puzzle – how Wyatt connects to Andy, Linnie, and Shane.'

'Go, Merry,' Scarlett said with a grin. 'And?'

'She knew the killer had to cross paths with Linnie at some point because he'd hired her for the college prostitution ring.'

Trip nodded. 'Because Penny Voss saw her at one of her father's parties. But we're pretty sure Linnie was coerced. How did Wyatt manage that? What did he have on Linnie?'

Adam could suddenly see the path Meredith's mind must have

taken. Linnie had loved Andy, enough to escape with him when he ran from Indianapolis and changed his name. 'The cover-up of the foster father's murder,' he said quietly. 'Resurrecting the case could have sent Andy to prison and he'd killed for her. Linnie wasn't going to let him suffer for saving her.'

Isenberg nodded sadly. 'That seems to be the right answer. Meredith found out that Linnie's caseworker – the one who was about to move her to a different home because Linnie had reported her rape – has recently been fired because she did the same thing to another girl who ended up committing suicide. The caseworker is under investigation for taking bribes and involuntary manslaughter. Meredith called the detective leading the investigation. He didn't answer her at first, not until I called his CO and requested their cooperation.'

'And?' Scarlett asked. 'What did she find out?'

'Well, she found out that the detective had been quite busy all morning working with the prosecutor who handled Sandra Walton's case. She's the foster mother currently in jail for her husband's murder.'

'The murder Andy Gold actually committed,' Trip said.

Isenberg nodded. 'Mrs Walton's defense attorney requested a new trial. She'd seen the photo of Andy Gold on the news yesterday, and argued it showed he was violent. And if that didn't fly, the defense attorney also offered that Mrs Walton would provide evidence against Ms Row, the caseworker, in exchange for a reduced sentence. The detectives spent the morning pulling together everything they had on the foster mother, the caseworker, and Linnie Holmes. Turns out one of the detectives fielded a request from a Cincinnati Narcotics detective six months ago.'

Adam closed his eyes. 'Wyatt Hanson.'

'Yes. Six months ago, Linnie was caught shoplifting with two other people. Apparently, she'd fallen in with them when they'd shoplifted before and they'd watch out for each other and watch for cops or store security. The other two were known small-time dealers, but with connections to bigger fish that Narcotics had been hoping to bring down.'

'Narcotics thought Linnie also had connections,' Scarlett said. 'But she didn't.'

Isenberg shrugged. 'We don't know if she did or didn't have connections. Hanson was called in to question them because he'd been trying to catch the bigger fish. I don't know if he believed she was connected or not, but he knew Linnie was hiding something.'

'Something he could exploit,' Adam murmured and Isenberg nodded.

'Hanson ran her prints and came up with a match to those lifted from stolen items pawned outside of Indianapolis. That's when Hanson called Indianapolis PD, asking about Linnie's past. The Indy detective sent Hanson his file on Linnie, which contained the report on the stolen items and the complaint she filed against Mrs Walton, the foster mother who beat her with a frying pan. It also had the card of her caseworker, the one under investigation.'

'Did Hanson contact her too?' Nash asked.

Isenberg frowned at him. 'Be patient, Detective Currie. The Indy detective sent me his file and a copy of the caseworker's cell phone log.' She slid a piece of paper, covered in phone numbers, to the middle of the table. Three entries, all the same phone number, were circled.

Adam sucked in a breath. 'The same number that called the hostess at Buon Cibo.'

'And,' Trip added, 'the number that called the bomb's cell phone trigger.'

Isenberg's grin was wolfish. 'And after the second call, Ms Row received an automated email from her bank account stating ten thousand dollars had been deposited. It's circumstantial now, but Indy PD is sending us her bank statements so that we can include them with Broderick Voss's, whenever we receive them.'

'Wyatt paid her for the dirt on Linnie, Andy, and Shane.' Adam was torn between fury at the caseworker and awe at Meredith for putting this together in the few hours since he'd left her that morning. 'He found out that Andy had been arrested for murder.'

Isenberg sighed. 'And probably threatened to tell the Cincinnati cops so that Andy would be extradited. Linnie couldn't let Andy pay for committing murder for her. So she did what Wyatt demanded.'

Trip was shaking his head. 'But why? Why go to all the trouble of setting Linnie up this way? There are, unfortunately, plenty of young women on the street who would've willingly worked for him. Why Linnie?'

'Why Mallory?' Adam asked rigidly. 'Why Paula?'

'Because he can,' Nash murmured. 'He gets off on the power. The thrill of manipulation. Who knows how many other victims he's manipulated?'

'It's all but killed Linnie,' Deacon said, jaw tight. 'Dani was so upset that everything went south at the shelter yesterday. She said she ran tests on the blood samples she took from Linnie and her viral loads are frighteningly high. Her condition has gone untreated. She said that Linnie hadn't eaten in a few days when she saw her at the clinic. She'll never bring her loads down if she's malnourished.'

'I hope she contacts us,' Scarlett said on a sigh. 'But while we're waiting, we need to find the sonofabitch who caused all of this.'

'Wyatt Hanson,' Adam gritted out, the sudden surge of fury a sucker punch to his gut. A clear picture of what he'd do when he found him slammed into his mind and it was not pretty. Isenberg was right. He was in no mental shape to hunt for Wyatt because if he found him, he'd strangle him with his bare hands.

He closed his eyes. 'I think I do need a short break. A few hours, maybe. I'd like to go to the condo with Meredith. Any volunteers to guard my ass on the way?'

He opened his eyes in time to see Deacon close his, uttering a prayer of sincere thanks. 'Took you long enough, you fucker.'

'Yeah, well, when I learn, I learn. You won't have to tell me again.'

'I hope not, Detective.' Isenberg stood, her signal for them to leave. 'Deacon, Scarlett, take Adam to pick up Meredith and make sure they get to the condo safely, then I want you two to go to Wyatt's house. He's not there. My counterpart in Narcotics personally checked out the house this morning when Wyatt didn't show up for his meeting with me. He didn't go inside, because we

523

didn't have a warrant then, but he used a thermal imaging camera. There were no living people in the house at that time. I put a surveillance team on the house as soon as he didn't show for our meeting this morning and he hasn't been home. His wife came home a while ago, but so far no Wyatt. Search the house, question the wife, turn the place upside down.'

'Do we have a warrant now?' Deacon asked.

'You do. For anything and everything. If you find a safe, do what you have to do to open it. Trip, you and Nash go to Mike's garage in Fairfield. It's near the used car place, and – luckily for us – has not been burned down. Find everything you can. Go. Be careful.'

Cincinnati, Ohio,
Monday 21 December, 11.20 A.M.

'I thought you were going to call my husband in "a minute",' Rita said stiffly. 'It's already been over an hour.'

Linnea hadn't yet contacted him, because every time she thought of facing him she wanted to puke. *He's a cop.* But she was not going to give voice to her insecurities, so she shook her head instead.

'He'd know my voice. Either he wouldn't come at all, or he'd take me out with a rifle before I could pull the trigger.'

Rita's chin lifted. 'My husband is a police officer.'

'Yeah. I know.' And Linnea still reeled from the shock. Shifting the toddler to her other shoulder, she continued her gentle swaying. He'd fallen asleep an hour ago, but that wouldn't last forever. She was going to have to make a move soon.

Several short bursts of vibration startled her, followed by another volley of buzzes. Someone was texting Rita's cellphone. A lot. *Maybe it's him. Maybe he knows I'm here.*

Good. Let him come. Although it was likely he'd send his police friends instead. They'd take her into custody because she really wouldn't hurt the little boy. They'd never believe her story. About one of their own? Never. *And then I won't be able to kill him.*

Carefully holding the child and the gun, she slipped Rita's cellphone from the pocket of her coat and glanced at the screen.

Rita. Call me! What's going on? CALL ME!

Followed by: *RITA, r u ok? CALL ME! Wyatt's on the news! Channel 12!*

Linnea's pulse rocketed. 'Please turn on the TV. Channel twelve.' She motioned with the gun when Rita didn't move. 'I said "please," Mrs Hanson.'

Rita reached for the remote in a way that raised Linnea's hackles.

'Don't think about throwing that at me,' Linnea said calmly when Mrs Hanson's arm reared back. 'I don't want to harm your son, but like I said before – I have nothing to lose.'

Rita blinked, sending tears down her face. 'You're vile.'

'Yeah, well, you're right about that. The television, Mrs Hanson. Please.'

Rita switched it on and found the news station. And gasped.

Linnea's eyes widened.

The headline box at the bottom of the screen said: *CPD Detective wanted for questioning in string of recent murders.* The rest of the screen was filled with a photo of Wyatt Hanson. It was the same photo that sat on the family bookshelf.

It must be his department photo, she thought numbly. Then the reality of the words sank in. 'Turn it up,' Linnea demanded. *'Now!'* she added when Rita didn't move.

Rita fumbled with the remote, her hands shaking. 'It's a lie. It's a lie.'

'Turn it up,' Linnea repeated, enunciating each word. 'I'm losing patience.'

The remote was now shaking as Rita gripped it hard but she managed to turn up the volume. The photo of Hanson halved in size and moved to one side of the screen, the other side taken up by a podium, behind which stood a woman in her early fifties with short gray hair. She wore the same uniform that Wyatt wore in the photo. The caption beneath her name identified her as Lieutenant Isenberg.

'It is with great regret,' Isenberg said, the *click-click-click*ing of cameras in the background, 'that we tell you that we are currently searching for one of CPD's own detectives, Detective Wyatt Hanson of the Narcotics division, as a person of interest in the series of slayings that began on Saturday with the murder of Andy Gold.'

The photo of Hanson moved to the far corner of the screen and Andy's face appeared where Wyatt's had been.

Linnea's chest tightened. 'Andy,' she whispered.

'It's not true,' Rita insisted.

Linnea felt the stirrings of pity for the woman. 'I'm sorry, but it is.'

'Since Mr Gold's murder,' Isenberg went on, 'we've seen at least ten more murders, here and in Chicago. These deaths are related.'

'Ten more?' Linnea murmured, stunned. *Who? How?*

'A family of four died in a house fire Saturday night – a fire that was the work of an arsonist. Mr Gold lived in the house's basement apartment. We assume the arsonist meant to destroy evidence that linked Mr Gold to another person of interest, Linnea Holmes. But,' the lieutenant added quickly, 'Miss Holmes is not a suspect. I repeat: she is not a suspect. We believe she has valuable information on the killers' motives. I say "killers" in the plural because we know of two other men who were involved. Mr Butch Gilbert was killed Sunday afternoon and Mr Mike Barber was killed around midnight last night.'

'Mike?' Rita whispered, her face growing deathly pale.

Photographs of the two men popped up on the screen. Linnea's stomach roiled at the sight of the men who'd raped her. Both were dead. *Good*, she thought fiercely. Then she looked at the baby sleeping on her shoulder. Mikey. From the look on Rita's face, she realized the baby must have been named after the man who'd been killed at midnight.

'As I said, there have been ten deaths related to this case. Retired police officer John Kasper became the most recent victim this morning. Two murders were committed in Chicago on Saturday night. Tiffany Curtis and her mother were killed because Tiffany had loaned her car to a friend of Andy Gold and Linnea Holmes.'

'Shane,' Linnea breathed.

'Mr Shane Baird was hunted by Butch Gilbert, who apparently killed the two women in his efforts to ascertain Shane Baird's whereabouts. We are not certain why he was in pursuit of Mr Baird, but we do know that Mr Baird had left for Cincinnati after hearing about Mr Gold's death. He has told us he came to try and find Miss Holmes. In his effort to locate her, he recorded a video this morning, imploring Linnea to contact the police for her own protection, since we have reason to believe that Detective Hanson is still a threat to her. Since its upload to the *Ledger*'s website, the video has been seen over a million times, broadcasted online and over TV airwaves all over the world. We'd like to show the video in the event Linnea is watching this broadcast now.'

The screen then filled with Shane's face and Linnea found herself leaning toward it.

Shane cleared his voice awkwardly. 'Hi, Linnie,' he said with a frighteningly earnest expression. 'It's Shane. I'm here in Cincinnati. I need to see you. I miss you. I want you to stay alive. The police are looking for you – but not to hurt you or put you in a cage. They want to help you. They have been so kind to me and Kyle. Well, you don't know Kyle yet. He's my friend from Chicago, who dropped everything to help me get here on Saturday night.' Shane's eyes clouded with pain. 'The men who hurt you, Linnie, they killed Kyle's girlfriend, Tiffany, and her mother, just because Tiff loaned us her car. They thought they could get her to tell them where I was. They wanted me so they could get to you. I want them to pay for what they did. To you and Tiffany and her mother and Andy, to all the other people they've hurt or killed. Detective Kimble is the lead detective on this case. He has been so *kind*, Linnie. These are good people. So, please, trust them. I know you're scared, but I need you to trust them. For me?' His eyes grew bright with tears. 'Because I have to bury Andy in a few days, Linnie,' he whispered. 'I need you by my side when I do it. I can't do this alone. Please, contact Detective Kimble.' Shane blinked, sending tears down his face. 'I promise the police will do everything they can to help you. I promise. And you know I've never broken my word to you. So do this for me and for Andy.'

The video ended abruptly. Throughout, Detective Adam Kimble's name and the CPD switchboard number had scrolled across the screen. The gray-haired lieutenant reappeared on screen, looking straight at the camera. 'Linnie, if you're listening, you are *not* a suspect in these murders. But we do fear you are in danger. Please call us.' She broke eye contact with the camera, her gaze roaming the gathered reporters. 'I'll take questions now.'

'You can mute it now,' Linnea said quietly.

Rita did so, staring at the television in shock. 'It's not true,' she whispered, but with none of the conviction she'd held earlier. 'It can't be true.'

Linnea stood, the baby still cuddled on her shoulder. With Rita's phone, she dialed the number at the bottom of the screen. She wanted to do the right thing. For Andy, for Shane, for all the other victims.

And for myself.

Twenty-nine

Cincinnati, Ohio,
Monday 21 December, 11.25 A.M.

By the time he'd almost reached his neighborhood, his panic had faded and he was thinking more clearly. Slowing the SUV, he pulled onto the shoulder to consider his next steps. As a person of interest, they'd have his house under surveillance. But he needed to get into his house, dammit. He was not leaving without his passports or the access codes to his offshore accounts.

Only one account had been set up with an easy-to-remember password, because it was the one he used the most, but the other accounts used longer passwords he'd written in the notebook he kept in his safe. Part of him wished he'd kept the records on his phone, that he hadn't been so paranoid about hacking. But it didn't matter anyway. He'd used his alternate identities to open the other accounts, so he needed his other passports.

He needed to get into his house. And out again, otherwise what was the point?

Ah. He had it. Wainwright. He called the man on his cell, hoping he picked up. And that Wainwright had not been watching the news.

'Hanson, this is a surprise,' Wainwright said warmly.

'Oh, geez,' he said, feigning embarrassment. 'I should call you more often to shoot the breeze instead of just when I need something.'

'I hope nothing's wrong. What do you need, son?'

'My SUV broke down. I'm only a mile from home, but it would sure be nice not to have to walk in the snow. I'd call Rita, but I've got

529

her Christmas present in the back. It's a new computer, so it wouldn't be good to leave it in the freezing cold.'

'I'll be there in five minutes,' his neighbor promised. 'Sit tight.'

'Thanks. I'll owe you one.'

'Nonsense. The missus is out with her quilting group and I'm just puttering around the house alone. Besides, what are neighbors for?'

Indeed. He explained where he was, then ended the call and checked his phone for news. And ground his teeth in frustration and impotent rage. A video had gone viral. Shane, pleading with Linnea to turn herself over to the police.

He rolled his eyes. *Oh, for God's sake.* It was even trending on Twitter – under two separate hashtags. At least he wasn't trending. Yet.

He was still 'a person of interest.' They must not have a warrant for his arrest. Yet, anyway. He'd scoff at them from a beach somewhere. For now he had to keep his cool.

Within a few minutes, Wainwright's truck rolled past him, did a U-turn, and parked behind him. He got out, faking a grateful smile. 'I'm sorry to get you out in this weather.'

'No problem!' Wainwright peered into the SUV. 'Where's Rita's present?'

'In the back. I'll show you.'

'Hey, you've got a little company back at your house,' Wainwright offered cheerily. 'A car with two guys sitting out in front. Looked like cops, maybe friends of yours?'

Shit. 'They are. They're waiting for me to get home so we can go out together. I didn't think they'd be there already, though. I hope they haven't been waiting long.'

'Don't know when they arrived. I just saw them out there when I came to get you.'

'Well, as soon as I get this present inside and hidden from Rita, we'll be on our way.'

'Excellent.' The old man grinned. 'I passed two news vans on my way to get you. I think they want to interview me about my nativity scene. I emailed the local affiliates and newspapers this morning.

It'd be better if they came at night to see the lights, but I'm still thrilled!'

News vans? *Shit*. That Wainwright thought they were here for him would have been naively sweet under other circumstances. *They're here for me. Dammit.*

'Congratulations!' he said, then popped the hatch and waited until his neighbor leaned into the cargo area. Then he grabbed his tire iron and swung it down on the old man's head. Wainwright went instantly limp, falling into the SUV. He hefted his body the rest of the way, wincing when his arm twinged. Damn Linnea and her switchblade. Biting his lower lip to manage the pain, he removed the old man's coat and scarf.

He covered the body with a tarp and closed the hatch, then jogged to Wainwright's truck. He put the coat on over his own coat and wrapped the scarf around his neck, jumped into the truck's cab and headed to Wainwright's garage.

He'd slide right in, under their noses.

Cincinnati, Ohio,
Monday 21 December, 11.25 A.M.

'You ready to blow this joint, Doc?'

Meredith spun around at the sound of Adam's voice in the doorway of her grandfather's hospital room. He leaned on the doorframe, his pose casual, but his eyes held such pain. Two steps and a leap and she was in his arms, hers around his neck. Lifting her, he tightened his hold around her back. Her feet dangled, her toes not touching the floor.

But she didn't care.

He's alive. And mine. She buried her face against his neck. 'You're okay.'

'Yeah.' The single syllable was gruff.

She drew a breath, taking him in. Anchoring herself by the feel of his hands on her back, the sound of his harsh breathing in her ear, the smooth skin of his jaw against her temple, his scent that filled her head, all simultaneously grounding her and leaving her lightheaded. 'You smell so good,' she whispered in his ear.

He shuddered. 'I had to shower. After. I was covered in . . . Well, you know.'

'Yes, I know.' He'd been a foot away from a man whose head had blown apart. Just as she'd been with Andy. Except the man he'd seen die wasn't a stranger. He was someone Adam had trusted with his secrets. Turning her head, she kissed his jaw. 'I meant what I said this morning,' she whispered in his ear and felt him shudder again, harder this time.

'So did I.' He swallowed hard. 'God, so did I.'

'I'd like to say it again,' she murmured, suddenly remembering where they were. 'But not here. We kind of have an audience.'

She thought he'd let her go then, but he held on, his face in her hair. 'Deacon was right. I needed this. Needed you.'

'Did you finally tell him?'

'I had to. Had to explain why I was at St Agnes's at seven a.m.'

She had to keep from clenching her jaw in rage, because that wouldn't help him now. But goddammit. He'd been forced to share the secret he'd been terrified to tell his closest friends and family. A killer had stolen that from him too.

The killer who now had a name. Wyatt Hanson. She hated the bastard. *Hated him.*

'I want him to die,' she choked out against Adam's neck. 'I want him to die a thousand painful deaths.'

Adam stilled, then pulled back to kiss her cheek. 'Deacon?'

She snorted a surprised laugh. 'No. Should I hate him too?'

'Nah.' Adam lowered her until her feet were firmly on the floor again. He loosened his hold, but he didn't let her go, just kept staring at her face. 'At first he was hurt and mad that I hadn't told him, but supportive.'

Looking up, she studied his face. 'What else, Adam?'

'I . . .' He drew a huge breath. 'Would you mind if we don't talk about it just yet?'

'Whatever you need.'

His eyes changed then, growing somehow darker. 'Really?' His whisper was like warm velvet brushing her skin.

She shivered. 'Yes. But . . . audience, Adam. Audience.'

He looked behind her, his cheeks reddening. She watched his eyes dart right, then left. Diesel sat in the chair and her grandfather lounged in the bed. Both were knitting.

Adam cleared his throat. 'How are you, Mr Fallon?' he called.

Meredith turned in time to see her grandfather exchange soft amusement for mock ire. 'You planning to actually come into the room, Kimble? Because I won't have you showing up to whisk her away like some teenaged hooligan blowing his car horn outside.'

Meredith rolled her eyes. 'Papa. His name is Adam.'

'I'll stop calling him Kimble when he stops calling me Mr Fallon.'

'Fair enough,' Adam said. Gripping Meredith's hand in his, he went over to the bed and shook her grandfather's hand. 'How are you, Clarke?'

'Better. They say I can go home this afternoon.'

'Maybe,' Diesel grunted. 'They said maybe.'

Adam sat in the other chair and pulled Meredith to sit on his knee. 'I heard you two were busy this morning,' he said. 'You sure you don't secretly want to be a cop, Diesel?'

Diesel's look of horror made them all laugh. 'Hell, no. Stone and I are just getting used to making nice with Scarlett at holidays and family functions. It was hard enough having one cop in our midst. Now we're overrun. The very thought of it . . . No, thank you.'

Adam laughed again, his mood seeming lighter than it had been when he'd first come in. Or maybe Meredith just wanted so badly for him to be happy.

'Seriously, though,' Diesel continued, 'we, uh, found something else we didn't tell your lieutenant about.'

Adam straightened, instantly alert. 'Okay. And?'

Diesel told him about finding the email detailing the ten-thousand-dollar deposit to the former social worker's bank account and Adam grew grimly thoughtful.

'I knew about that, actually. Isenberg said it was in the information

533

she received from that detective in Indianapolis. He also sent her the caseworker's phone logs. Hanson called her just before her bank sent her the email about the deposit.'

Meredith and Diesel exchanged smug glances, telling Adam there was more.

'I don't suppose there's any way you could access the bank account?' Adam asked.

Diesel's brows shot up. 'For what purpose?'

'Not to move funds. I don't want to touch the money. I would like to make it so that he can't access a single penny. Can you find his password, then change it? It's plausible deniability if we're led to the account by another leg of the investigation.'

Diesel grinned. 'Already found his password. Give me two seconds to get in again.' He set his knitting aside and opened his computer, his huge hands flying over the keyboard.

Adam nudged Meredith off his knee so he could look at Diesel's computer, and sucked in a shocked breath. 'Holy God. He's got five million dollars in this account.'

Diesel's expression darkened. 'He may have others. That's the only one I found. What do you want the password changed to?'

'What is it now?'

'KingTriton89.'

Adam frowned, then nodded. 'His daughter is Ariel.'

'I put *The Little Mermaid* into my software as a possible source,' Diesel confirmed.

Jaw tight, Adam turned from the laptop. 'Part of me wants the new password to be a combination of the names of all of his victims, but he might figure that out. So make it completely random. Letters and numbers. I don't want to know what you call it.'

Diesel nodded. 'I can do that. But if you don't know, you can't be sure I'll tell you the new password. I could steal all that money for myself.'

'But you won't. If I've learned anything through this, it's that actions are the real demonstration of truth. Your actions have always been above reproach.'

Diesel did a small double-take, his mouth opening and closing before saying simply, 'Thanks.' And if his eyes got suspiciously bright, nobody mentioned it.

Adam reached for Meredith's hand again. 'Is it okay if I borrow her for a little while, Clarke? I need to . . . process.'

'Sure,' her grandfather said, sounding truly pleased. 'You'll take care of her.'

'With my life.' Adam tugged her hand. 'Come on. I've got Deacon and Scarlett waiting in a van downstairs. They're being extra careful with me today.'

She leaned up on her toes to kiss his cheek. 'Good. It's high time someone was.' Then she kissed her grandfather's cheek and surprised Diesel with a little peck as well. 'I'll be back later, Papa. If they release you, call me right away.'

'I'll make sure he's not alone,' Diesel said.

'I know you will. Thank you, Diesel.'

Clarke waved his hand. 'Go, Merry. Make some merry.' His eyes widened comically. 'No, wait. Nix that. No Merries. Make *no* Merries.'

She and Adam left on a laughing groan, which is what he'd wanted.

They started toward the elevator, then came to a dead stop at the sight of Kate's Decker leaning against the wall outside her door. Every muscle in his face was taut, his head tilted back, eyes closed.

'I just stopped in to check on Kate,' Meredith whispered to Adam. 'She was fine.'

The two of them cautiously approached Special Agent Decker Davenport. 'Decker?' Meredith murmured to the big man who looked so miserable. 'What's happened?'

He didn't startle, because of course he'd known they were there. The man had amazing instincts that had kept him alive during the three years he'd spent working undercover with a dangerous human trafficking gang.

'She's okay,' Decker said in a quiet drawl. 'I just needed a minute. I'm so fucking angry. I want to find the man who hurt her and rip his fucking head off.'

Adam squeezed Decker's arm. 'You don't have to. He's dead.'

Meredith's eyes widened. She hadn't heard this yet and wondered what else had happened that put the sadness in Adam's eyes.

'Did he suffer?' Decker asked gruffly.

'Not enough,' Adam replied. 'He was killed by his partner. Snipping off loose ends.'

Meredith thought of Adam's near miss that morning and her heart stuttered. Adam was *not* a loose end. *He's mine.* Possessiveness welled within her, along with the fierce need to protect this man. She'd keep him safe – his heart and every other part of him. Whatever that took to do.

'Is the partner still alive?' Decker asked, very quietly.

'Yes, but we know who he is now,' Adam said.

Decker's eyes opened, narrowing. 'Who?' The menace in that single word sent chills racing over Meredith's skin.

Adam's gaze flicked away for the briefest of moments, before returning to meet Decker's solidly. 'Wyatt Hanson. My old partner.'

Decker's eyes registered instant understanding. 'Not your fault, Adam. People who live double lives get very good at manipulating what you see.'

'People will still wonder if I knew. Or think I'm stupid because I didn't suspect.'

Meredith wanted to refute this, but she knew he was right. So she slid her arm around his waist and rested her head on his shoulder. It was sympathy and support. And respect. 'Some people are gonna suck, Adam. You can't let their voices into your head.'

He nodded. 'I know. I know. But . . . goddammit.'

Decker pinned him with a hard look. 'Did his bosses in CPD suspect? No. Are they stupid? No. Now, granted, not all of them are as smart as you are,' he added lightly.

Adam chuckled. 'I'm sure they'd disagree with that statement.'

Decker raised a blond brow. 'And they'll take no blame for not seeing it, either.'

Meredith grinned at him. 'Well played, Decker.'

Decker's smile was weary. 'Thanks. Now you guys go. I'm going back in there to tell Kate the fucker's dead so she can stop plotting how to kill him with knitting needles.'

They obeyed, hurrying to the lobby and out into the air, cold but fresh. 'God. I was going so stir crazy in there. I needed some fresh air.'

'Sorry, but you'll have to wait a while longer to enjoy it,' Adam said because the van was pulling up to the overhang. The door slid open, revealing Deacon behind the wheel and Scarlett riding shotgun. Adam helped Meredith into the van, then handed her a flak jacket while the door slid shut. 'Suit up.'

'I'll be so glad when this is over. Tactical wear does not go with my shoes.'

Deacon laughed. 'I can't wait until that's your biggest concern again, Mer.'

Adam put on his own vest then helped her with hers. 'We're going to the condo,' he said. 'Isenberg posted a guard, which I told her was not necessary.'

'Except that someone's tried to kill you twice,' Meredith said tartly. 'Someone only tried to kill me once and I didn't complain about a guard.'

Adam put his arm around her shoulder and pulled her close. 'You're right.'

'Of course I am. Now, it seems a lot's happened since we last spoke. Tell me, please.'

Deacon started driving and Adam started talking and Meredith's heart broke a little more with every revelation. Jim Kimble was an ass. Dale Hanson? Complicit.

But the thought that Wyatt had been involved in the murder of Paula . . . 'Why?' she asked, her voice cracking. 'Why would he do that to you? To Paula?'

Adam shrugged. 'I've been wondering that all morning. I came into Personal Crimes with something of a reputation. A good one.'

'One of the highest percent of closed cases in Homicide,' Scarlett inserted loyally. 'Adam was the homicide department's boy wonder.'

Adam shrugged again, his cheeks growing dark from the praise. 'Apparently, Hanson's hated me since we were kids. I think he wanted to knock me down a few pegs.' Meredith didn't realize her fists were clenched until Adam brought one to his lips and kissed it. 'So I think you know most of it now,' he told her. 'Isenberg's taken over and—' He was interrupted by the Darth Vader ringtone on his phone. 'Speak of the devil.'

Scarlett barked a laugh. 'I thought you changed that.'

'She told me not to. Gives her cachet,' Adam said with a grin, then answered. 'Yeah, boss,' he said. 'We just picked up Meredith. Can I put you on speaker?'

Isenberg must have agreed because he did.

'Linnie called the switchboard,' she said without preamble. 'She saw Shane's video and asked for you. Patching her through now.'

A few seconds passed before Isenberg spoke again. 'Linnie, I've connected you to Detective Kimble. Detective, this is Linnie Holmes.'

'Is Shane really here?' an unsteady voice demanded. 'In Cincinnati?'

She sounds so young, Meredith thought sadly.

'He is,' Adam told her. 'He came from Chicago as soon as he read the news about Andy's death. He's been so worried about you. We all have been. That's why we came to the shelter. We wanted to protect you from the man who hurt you and killed Tiffany and her mother.'

'I don't trust you. I trusted the doctor and she told my secrets.'

'She told us none of your secrets, Linnie. She came to us to defend you because at the time we had a BOLO posted on you. She said you'd been coerced.'

A cleared throat. 'I was. But now I'm doing what I want.'

'Which is?'

'To kill Wyatt fucking Hanson for what he did to Andy.'

Adam grimaced. 'I completely get that goal. I want him to pay too. He's killed more people than Andy, though. Did you know he had Broderick Voss killed too?'

A beat of silence. 'Well, I'd be lying if I said that made me sad.'

'I understand. Voss was a fucker too. My point is that Wyatt fucking Hanson has hurt a lot of people and they deserve their justice too. I get that you want him dead. I want him to spend the rest of his life in a prison cell, worrying about all the people he betrayed who are waiting to kill him. I want him to be afraid every day for the rest of his miserable life. Killing him's too quick.'

Linnie said nothing.

Adam sighed. 'You called me, Linnie. I know you're armed because you shot Butch Gilbert. I know what you want to do to Hanson. Tell me what you want for yourself.'

Her laugh was bitter. 'Nothing. I have nothing left.'

'Not true. You have Shane and you have us. We want to help you. If you kill Wyatt, you can't have a life.'

'I don't have one anyway. Didn't the good doctor tell you? I'm HIV positive.'

'She didn't have to tell us, Linnie. You did, when you called to tell us where to find Hanson's SUV. Because you wanted to do the right thing.'

He pulled up a text screen and sent a quick one to Dani. *Can I tell Linnie you are positive too?*

Meredith watched his phone light up with his cousin's instant response. *Yes. Of course. It's no secret anymore.*

Adam rubbed his face, something he seemed to do to give himself time to think. 'Listen, Linnie, just because you're positive, doesn't mean your life is over. Dr Dani is positive too. She just gave me permission to tell you.'

A sharp intake of breath. 'What? How?'

'That's her business, just like your condition is yours. But your life is not over. You can make it a good one. Just . . . tell me where you are. I'll come get you myself. I promise.'

She was silent longer this time, then spoke quietly. 'I'm sitting in Hanson's living room. His baby is on my lap and I have a gun in my hand. His wife is sitting here, shooting me death glares because she thinks I'm a lying whore.'

Oh God, she's holding a baby hostage, Meredith thought. This had just gotten worse when she hadn't thought it could.

Deacon raised a hand to indicate he'd heard, turned on the van's flashing lights – no siren – and did a quick U-turn.

'We'll deal with Mrs Hanson later,' Adam promised. 'Right now, we want to protect you. I'll be there in . . .' He looked at Deacon who made a sign with his right hand.

'Ten minutes,' Adam finished. 'Hold tight. I'm on my way.'

'Hurry,' Linnie said quietly. 'Please.'

And then she ended the call. Isenberg called Adam right back. 'How old is the baby?'

'About two years old,' Adam told her. 'This just got hairier. Requesting additional backup.'

'Already on the way,' Isenberg said. 'As am I.'

'Thanks.' Adam ended the call and looked at Meredith. 'I'll have someone take you away from the scene when we get there. Until then, you stay down.'

She frowned at him, not liking this at all, but wary of telling him how to do his job. The man had his pride and she wanted to protect that too. But dammit, she wanted him *alive*. 'Adam . . .' She sighed. 'You're putting yourself at risk, getting Linnie out yourself.'

'I know. But I gave her my word. And I need to finish this, Meredith. I *need* to.'

She understood. But still . . . 'What if this is a trap? What if Wyatt Hanson shows up?'

His lips curved grimly. 'We should be so lucky. I hope he *does* show up.'

'Seconded,' Scarlett declared. 'I want to take that sonofabitch down.'

'Thirded,' Deacon chimed in.

Adam took her chin and tugged her face up for a hard kiss. 'You stay down. Got it?'

Meredith nodded. 'Understood.'

Cincinnati, Ohio,
Monday 21 December, 11.40 A.M.

Wainwright had handguns, he remembered as he pulled the man's truck into his garage and closed the door behind him. He knew this because Wainwright had permits for the guns, which he'd looked up when he moved in next to the man.

He wished Wainwright had a rifle, but he didn't. The gun would have to be enough. There were two cops outside his house, just as Wainwright had said. He wouldn't shoot them if he could help it, mainly because it would tip his hand and he wanted to cross over to his own property through the backyard and slip in the back door to get what he needed.

So far, so good, though. No one had come to check out Wainwright's return so soon after leaving. The cops outside weren't very competent. They really deserved anything that he had to dish out.

The news media had been even worse. They were setting up in front of his house. They were going to talk about him. Like they knew anything. But they'd ignored him as he'd driven into Wainwright's garage. As long as he left the same way, he'd be fine.

He found the gun in Wainwright's nightstand drawer, a little surprised it wasn't in a gun safe. But that made things far easier, so he wasn't complaining. In the bedroom closet was enough ammo to survive an apocalypse.

He filled his pockets – or, more accurately, Wainwright's pockets. The old man's coat was a snug fit, but it would keep him warm until he got to his final destination. Which he still hadn't decided on, but it would be somewhere warm and sunny where nobody cared if the girl in your bed was a little young.

Fucking prudes. This whole country was packed with fucking prudes.

Armed and ready to slip next door into his own house like a goddamn thief, he moved to Wainwright's backyard, staying easily hidden behind the eight-foot-tall temporary barn the old man had erected for the animals for his ridiculous nativity scene. Slipping into his own yard was an easy thing. A vault over a standard chain-link fence and he found himself grateful that Rita had nagged him to build the rose trellises that spanned the width of the fence on their property. He was invisible to anyone sitting out front.

It was perfect. Until he paused to check on the cops watching his house.

Goddammit to hell. A van was rolling to a stop, the side door already sliding open. And of course it was Adam Kimble who jumped out the second the van stopped. Fucking Kimble, riding in to save the day like the fucking Lone Ranger.

Hate roared through him like a speeding train and for a moment all he could hear was the pounding of his pulse in his head. He'd pulled the gun from his pocket and aimed before the intention had fully registered in his mind.

Stop. Focus. Focus. If you kill him now, you will never make it out of here alive. Right now, that's more important than revenge or even satisfaction.

The front passenger door opened and Scarlett Bishop got out. They were here. *At my house.* His house that contained his bank codes and passports.

He had to get them. But he had to get away. He wasn't sure how to do both.

Heart pounding, he mentally flipped through his options as Deacon Novak got out of the driver's side of the van and he and Kimble approached the two cops in the unmarked car. Who then pointed to Wainwright's house. *Dammit.* They'd noticed his arrival after all. They'd merely been biding their time, waiting for backup.

In the next ten seconds, two more cruisers rushed up his quiet street, lights flashing, but no sirens. Novak directed them to park across Wainwright's driveway.

SUVs – three from CPD and two black unmarked – pulled up behind the van and Kimble directed the two unmarked to park in his driveway, blocking his own garage.

And that fast he was trapped. No way out. At least not the way he'd come. He cast a look over his shoulder, frowning at the woods at the back of his property that had always been a comforting buffer between his home and the rest of the world. That had given him an illusion of safety, that no one could sneak up on him.

Fat lot of good that does me now. Because, conversely, he couldn't sneak away. At the rear of the property was a thirty-foot drop to Columbia Parkway. He could try it, but there was a good chance he'd break something when he hit.

He couldn't go backward and he couldn't go forward, but he

could go sideways. To the right and he'd be seen by the cops surrounding Wainwright's house. But to the left was the cul-de-sac, six houses down. If he stuck to the backyards, he could get around the cul-de-sac and behind the houses on the other side of the street and find a car to steal.

The five million in his password-accessible account would have to be enough for now and he'd have to buy himself another ID before he got over the border.

Shouldn't have been so greedy. I could have been on my way to Canada by now.

But he'd never been one to dwell on should-haves. He narrowed his eyes and plotted the best way to circle the cul-de-sac.

Cincinnati, Ohio,
Monday 21 December, 12.05 P.M.

Adam wanted to groan when he saw the media setting up in front of Hanson's house, but he wasn't surprised. He was actually more surprised that there weren't more reporters, especially since Isenberg's press conference confirming Hanson's involvement. 'We need them gone,' he said. 'The last thing we need is one of them spooking Linnie into shooting that baby.'

'I'll deal with them,' Scarlett said. She'd gained some experience with dealing with reporters, now that she and *Ledger*-owner Marcus O'Bannion were together. She set a perimeter and directed the crews from two networks to retreat behind it while Adam and Deacon talked to the cops who'd been watching Hanson's house from an unmarked car.

Backup arrived in the form of three CPD SUVs, four cruisers, and two unmarked FBI SUVs. Deacon directed two of the cruisers to park across Wyatt's neighbor's driveway, because the cops out front had seen the neighbor's truck leave and return within a ten-minute time period with a 'different-looking' driver. One of the cops thought he was taller, the other said broader. Either way, the cops were convinced that a different man had returned to the neighbor's house.

Which meant that if it was Wyatt, he'd be able to fire on them at will as long as they moved about the property. They needed cover, so Adam directed the three CPD SUVs to park in a line in Wyatt's driveway, fender to bumper. The cops who'd occupied the SUVs took cover on the passenger side of the vehicles.

He, Deacon, and Scarlett regrouped, using one of the SUVs as cover, just as another black SUV pulled in behind the first two in Hanson's driveway, Trip behind the wheel, Nash riding shotgun. 'We were headed to check out Mike Barber's garages,' Nash said, 'but Isenberg called us back.'

'Good. For now, get out and down,' Adam said, quickly bringing them up to speed when they were shielded by the SUV. 'Deacon, you and Trip and the two other Feds check out the neighbor's house. Make sure we have clearance to go in after Hanson if he's the one in there. I don't want him to slide on any procedural errors on our part. Scarlett and I will approach Linnie, and, as soon as the child and Linnie are safe, you move in on the neighbor's house.' He met Nash's eyes. 'I need to get Meredith somewhere safe. Everyone on Isenberg's team is either in the hospital or here. She'll be safest back in the hospital and I don't trust any of these other cops to take her. I don't know any of them.'

'But you trust me?' Nash asked quietly.

Adam nodded. 'Yes,' he said and meant it. 'I do.'

Emotion flickered in Nash's eyes. 'Thank you. I'll contact you when she's safe.'

Deacon waited until Nash had crossed the street. 'You're sure?' he murmured.

Adam nodded. 'Yes. Plus, I'm sure that I can't have her here and focus at the same time. My gut is telling me that Hanson is around, or will be. I need her somewhere else, because he'd hurt her to get to me. I need you all here, because when I get the kid and Linnie, I'm leaving too.'

'For what it's worth,' Trip said, 'Isenberg said the same thing. I was to stay, Nash was to take Meredith, and you were to leave as soon as the hostage situation was resolved.'

'That's worth a lot,' Adam said. 'Thanks.'

Then, garbed in complete tactical gear, he and Scarlett walked up the driveway, bending at the waist so that the SUVs hid them from view of the neighbor's windows. Once on the porch, Adam knocked on the door. 'This is Detective Kimble. Please open the door.'

It swung open, revealing Linnie holding Mikey on one bony hip. In her opposite hand, she held the gun with which she'd shot Butch Gilbert yesterday. She looked terrified.

Behind her stood Rita Hanson, hands covering her mouth in numb horror.

'Linnie, I'm Detective Kimble. This is my partner Detective Bishop. You called me.'

'I know,' Linnea said, her nostrils flaring with every strained breath she took. 'You said I'm not a suspect, but you brought a SWAT team.'

He'd considered warning her in advance, but hadn't wanted to escalate the situation with her holding a toddler at gunpoint. Nor had he wanted to give Rita Hanson any information in the event she was in any way involved.

'Not because of you,' Adam assured. 'We're worried that Hanson will return.'

Rita made a strangled sound. 'Adam? Why are you doing this?'

He tilted his head to the right, looking around Linnie to a devastated Rita. 'I'm sorry, Rita. I know this is hard for you to believe. It's been hard for me too.' At least he hoped it was hard for her. He hoped she hadn't been in on it. He hoped Wyatt had worked alone. 'But the evidence points strongly to Wyatt's guilt in this. He's done some terrible things. Many of them to Linnie.'

'No.' Rita shook her head desperately. 'It's not true.'

'It is,' Adam said firmly. 'Once we've got Linnie and Mikey safe, Detective Bishop will escort you to your room to collect a few things.'

'Why?' Rita shook her head again, wildly this time. 'I'm not going anywhere.'

'We're putting you into protective custody, ma'am,' Scarlett told her, then gave Linnie a kind look. 'I'll take the baby now.'

Linnie's chin came up, her arms clutching the toddler a little more tightly. 'Where is Shane? I want to talk to him.'

'He's in protective custody,' Adam told her, 'because his life has been threatened twice now. But we can call him and let you talk to him. FaceTime, even. As soon as we get you to a safe place.'

Linnie nodded. 'Please.'

'Rita,' Scarlett barked. 'Freeze.'

Adam tensed, because Rita had crept close enough to grab the baby.

'She has my baby!' Rita screamed. 'She's going to hurt him.'

Mikey reached for his mother, and Linnie's grip on the baby tightened even further, but the gun in her hand stayed pointed at the floor. Mikey squirmed, whimpering, and Linnie began to sway in response, murmuring, 'It's okay,' into his ear.

Scarlett had her hand on her pistol, but hadn't drawn. 'Not if you don't blow this situation up, Mrs Hanson,' she said harshly. 'Which will happen if you try that again. Now, walk into the living room and lie facedown on the floor.'

'But . . . but . . .' Rita spluttered. 'She's the criminal here!'

'She hasn't killed anyone,' Adam said calmly. 'Unlike your husband, I'm sorry to say. Now do as Detective Bishop asks. We want everyone here to stay safe too.'

'I'll have your job, Adam. I promise you,' Rita vowed darkly, but complied. 'And if my baby is hurt – one hair on his head – I'll hunt you down myself.'

Linnie's rocking had quieted the baby, who still whimpered, but no longer tried to jump from her arms. 'Detective Bishop,' Linnie said, as if she'd ignored all of Rita's rant. 'Are you related to the priest? The one whose church is above the shelter?'

'He's my uncle,' Scarlett said. 'He's been worried about you. So have the sisters.'

'They wouldn't let you in,' Linnie said, sounding small and young. 'I saw Sister Jeanette blocking your path. Right before Butch . . . Yeah. Right before he died.'

Scarlett nodded. 'She protected you. And for the record, we were there because we needed your help identifying your attacker. And we were afraid for you.'

'So you always bring a SWAT team for one skinny girl?' Linnie asked sarcastically.

'When a mass killer is involved, then yes. He wants to kill you and we want to stop that from happening.' Adam moved his hand toward his pocket. 'I'm just going for my phone,' he said. Pulling it from his pocket he dialed Parrish Colby's untraceable cell. 'Parrish? Can you put Shane on a FaceTime call? I want him to talk to Linnie. This minute.'

'I'll have him call back on FaceTime,' Parrish promised.

Ten seconds later Adam's phone buzzed with the incoming call. Shane's face filled the screen, his expression full of fear. 'Linnie?'

'She's here,' Adam said, then turned the phone so that Linnie could see. It required her to come a few steps closer, steps Adam was certain she was unaware she'd taken.

Her eyes instantly filled with tears. 'Shane,' she whispered.

Shane's eyes were shadowed with sorrow. 'It's me, Linnie. Where are you?'

'I'm at *his* house.' Her expression hardened. 'The one who killed Andy. A cop.'

She'd tensed as she spoke and, sensing it, the baby began to cry. Immediately she relaxed, swaying again, murmuring the soothing words, but the baby was done.

'Whose baby is that?' Shane asked calmly, but Adam could tell that he already knew.

'His,' Linnie hissed.

Shane drew a breath. 'Give him to Detective Kimble. Please. You don't want to hurt a baby. That's not who you are.'

Linnie started crying then. 'You don't know who I am now. You don't know the things I've done.'

'I know some. I know you've worked the streets. I know you're sick. I know I miss you. I know I love you and I need you with me right now. I can't bury Andy alone.' Shane's voice broke. 'Don't make me do this alone, Linnie. Please. They'll put you in jail if anything happens to that baby and I'll lose you forever. *Please.*'

Linnie had trouble speaking through her tears. 'I'm dead either way. If I give them the baby, they'll take me to jail.' Tears were streaming down her face. 'They all lie. They'll take me away and I won't be able to finish this. And I need to kill him before I die.'

Shane made a choking sound. 'You're not going to die. You can get medicine. Andy's gone. Don't make me live without you too.'

She shook her head. 'He killed Andy. Shot him in the head. I saw him do it.' Guilt lined her face. 'Andy did it for me. He died for me.'

'Because he loved you!' Shane blurted out. 'He always loved you. He . . . he broke rules for you because he wanted you to live. So if you won't live for me, live for *him*.'

Linnie's face twisted then. 'The cop needs to die, Shane.'

'Let Kimble deal with the cop. I trust him. I need you to trust him too.'

'Please, Linnie,' Adam said quietly. 'Give me the gun.'

Thirty

He'd trekked across eleven backyards altogether, going around the cul-de-sac and down five more houses. He now leaned up against the back of the house that sat directly across the street from the home he'd shared with Rita for almost eight years.

He was tired and his arm burned like it was literally on fire. He didn't want to check it. He'd probably popped a stitch or two, with all the vaulting over fences. He'd have to get an antibiotic soon, because it was probably infected. *Fan-fucking-tastic.*

Even worse, not one of his neighbors seemed to be home. There seemed to be no cars to steal in any of the houses all the way to the end of the street. Everyone was out. What busy neighbors he had, he thought bitterly. They were oblivious to the real world around them. Out working or shopping or at school pageants.

He felt a pang. Ariel's Christmas pageant was today. She was going to be one of the reindeer. He'd miss it. He'd miss her. Forever. Because he couldn't take her with him.

He'd had kids with Rita more as a cover than because he'd wanted them. He'd never thought he'd grow so attached to them. But it couldn't be helped. He couldn't take his family with him and he didn't want them visiting him in prison.

There was no choice. *I'll do what I have to do to get out of here.*

He considered breaking into one of the houses and holing up, but that was suicide. Once Novak discovered he wasn't in Wainwright's

549

house, he, Kimble, and Bishop would begin a house-to-house search. He'd rather keep going and take his chances.

He peeked around the corner of the house where he'd stopped to rest and saw the wall of SUVs that Kimble had formed. *In my own driveway, the bastard.*

Yeah, they believed he was in Wainwright's house. *I can't stay here. I can't.*

It was just as well that none of his neighbors were home right now. He'd be stopped before he cleared a stolen car from any of the driveways on his street. Too many fucking cops. He'd keep going, sticking to the backs of the houses until he got to the next block. Besides, nobody home meant no calls to 911 ratting him out.

He'd get to the next block and find a car there, before they realized he was no longer in Wainwright's house. Because then they'd lock the whole neighborhood down.

Cincinnati, Ohio,
Monday 21 December, 12.10 P.M.

Meredith saw the thumbs up Deacon gave her as she was driven away, but Adam was fully engaged in talking to Linnie and he didn't look back. She knew she shouldn't want him to turn to her, because he was focused and doing his job. But she still did.

She'd been instructed to stay in the back and to stay down. Priding herself on not being stupid, she'd obeyed – even as she lost her mind with worry. Adam, out there unprotected save the tactical gear he wore, with a killer who could be hiding anywhere. Every second ticked in her mind like a crashing hammer.

She'd taken her entire daily dose of anti-anxiety medication after Adam's near miss this morning in the church parking lot. And she felt utterly justified having done so.

God, how she wished for a coloring book! The scrap paper in her lap had been an envelope she'd found in her purse, but now it was torn apart, flattened, and covered in the complex designs she'd sketched while waiting. She gripped her pretty pink tactical pen so hard her fingers ached, but she couldn't seem to relax her hold.

'You okay back there?' Nash Currie asked. 'If you're cold I can turn up the heat.'

'No, I'm fine,' she called back. 'Did you draw the short straw?' she added, because he'd been assigned with delivering her back to the hospital safely. AKA, babysitting duty.

He looked into the rear-view with a small smile. 'And if I say yes?'

She made a face. 'Then I'll believe you're not lying.'

He laughed. 'Well played, Dr Fallon.'

'Meredith,' she corrected. 'If Adam is allowing you to drive me, he must trust you a lot, so I think we should cut the formality.'

'Meredith then,' he said, sounding pleased. He was driving slowly and carefully, because the two news vans had been joined by six more in the few minutes she'd sat alone. Reporters had spilled into the street, vying for the best view of Hanson's house. 'You should stay down. These reporters will try to take your photo otherwise.'

Again she complied, folding herself into the tight space on the floor between the rear bench seat and the captain's chair in the middle. 'Done and done.'

He swore again. 'These news vans are blocking the damn road. I'm going to zigzag around them. Hold on.' He made an abrupt left turn and she winced when her head smacked the van's wall. She scooted forward, resting against the chair's arm rest.

'I saw the video of you with the little Voss girl. Penny. I was impressed,' Nash said.

'She wanted to tell. I just smoothed it a little.'

'I worked Personal Crimes for a long time. I was IT. Never led on a case, but I've watched enough victim interviews to recognize someone with a gift for communication.'

'Thank you,' Meredith said soberly. 'You were on the case with Adam. Paula.'

'I was.'

She drew a breath. 'Why do you think Hanson did it?'

There was a long pause and another sharp turn, this time to the right. 'I've been wondering that. And I remembered that right before

551

Paula first made contact with Adam, he'd done this interview for Channel 12. One of those "Heroes Among Us" pieces.'

'Because he'd been coaching the deaf kids. He told me.'

'Yeah. Did he tell you that after the piece ran, he was pursued by all the networks? Even CNN. He has a face for TV, you know.'

Meredith smiled. 'Yeah, I know.'

'He was Mr Popular, but still nice. Never let it swell his head. Even when he was voted Sexiest Cop by a women's magazine.'

'I missed that,' Meredith said dryly. 'But I think I get your point. He was golden and Hanson was jealous. He wanted to pull Adam back. Humble him. Break him, even.'

'Yes. And then Adam did solve a case. A big one. Two teenaged girls being peddled online. A local man was setting appointments and taking payment through a website.'

'I remember that. I didn't know that was Adam's case.'

'ICAC got credit, but Adam did a lot of the footwork. The brass knew. One day our boss kind of joked that Adam should mentor the rest of us. It was light-hearted praise and we all knew it. Except Hanson. He was not pleased.'

'So he set Adam up, then ripped him apart. Adam and you.'

'Yeah,' Nash said gruffly.

'Are you all right, Nash? I'm not asking as a therapist. I'm asking as someone who's grateful you stood up for Adam.'

'I'm okay. I mean . . . it was rough. My marriage couldn't . . . didn't take the strain.'

'I'm so sorry.'

'She couldn't handle my depression. My kids pulled me out. Made me go to counseling. It— *Holy shit*. Hold on. I'm backing up.' The van came to a hard stop, backed up and swerved to the left before coming to another hard stop. 'Stay down.'

He jumped out of the van and Meredith edged back to the driver's side wall, lifting herself enough to peek out the window. They'd stopped for a black SUV pulled onto the shoulder. She heard Nash curse, then he was back in the driver's seat, radioing for help.

'This is Detective Currie. I need backup and an ambulance for—'

The driver's door was yanked open, and Nash was pulled out of

552

the van. Meredith started to move but there was a terrible thud against the side of the van that made the vehicle shudder.

No. No, no, no. Meredith watched in shocked denial as Wyatt Hanson casually set a pistol in the cup holder.

Oh my God. Nash. Did he kill him? If Nash wasn't dead, he was injured. *If he finds me, he'll kill me too.* The thought of it yanked her out of her shock and she pulled her gun from the bra holster. *Not going down without a fight.*

Hanson slammed the van door, gunned the engine, and set off with a squeal of tires. He struck the steering wheel with his fist. 'Motherfucking police van,' he shouted angrily and she cringed until she realized he wasn't talking to her. He was just mad. 'Of all the fucking vans. Goddammit.'

He hadn't intended to steal a police van, she thought. He hadn't known this was a police van. *So he probably doesn't know I'm back here. God, please don't let him know.*

He grabbed the radio. 'This is Detective Currie,' he lied. 'I'm sorry. I don't need those emergency services after all. It was a false alarm.'

Meredith nearly shouted for help, but as soon as he detected her presence she'd be dead. So she kept quiet as he switched off the radio, pulled the handset out of the dashboard, and tossed it to the passenger seat.

Her body jerked when her phone buzzed in her hand with a text from Wendi. *Shane talking to Linnie. Looks hopeful he can get her to surrender the baby. U ok?*

A sob built in her throat and she swallowed it back. *No. No, I'm not okay.* Hands shaking, she replied. **Help. Hanson has me. In the van. Alone. Nash Currie hurt.**

She quickly checked that her phone was on silent. Hanson was driving faster than Nash had been. There was more car noise, so she doubted he'd hear her phone. It was worth the risk. She dialed 911 and slid the phone under the captain's seat that still shielded her from view. She didn't dare speak to the operator, but hopefully they'd be able to track her signal. In case she didn't kill Hanson with the first shot.

She crunched her body close to the wall of the van on the driver's side, stealing a look between the wall and the side of the chair. But her hands were shaking. Just like in the parking lot of the hospital when she'd fired and fired and the man had kept coming. The man. Wyatt Hanson's uncle. Panic clawed at her throat and she dug deep for just a little calm.

Balancing the gun on the armrest of the captain's chair in front of her, she aimed for his neck, the only piece of skin she could see from this angle. *Relax. Pretend you are at the target range with Kate and Scarlett.*

Who I'm never going to see again.

Stop it. Stop. It. Relax. For Adam. Don't make him find your body.

She squeezed the trigger—

She was tossed to the right side when he made an erratic turn, her shot hitting the van's wall. A second shot followed hers by a second. His shot. He'd seen her. *God.*

Fire burned up her right arm and she looked up to see his arm extended back from the seat, the gun still in hand. He'd deliberately swerved to toss her body between the seats.

Move. Get cover. She scrambled behind the captain chair on the right, able to get a better shot now, anyway. Except her arm was shaking. Because she was bleeding. A lot.

She hoped the dispatch operator hadn't believed Hanson's lies of a false alarm. But even if they did believe him, Wendi would have called the police by now and Isenberg's people would be in pursuit. She knew that.

So stop Hanson. Give Adam time to catch up. Don't make him find your body.

Gritting her teeth, she used the uninjured arm to pull herself to a sitting position, gripping the gun in her left hand. Because her right arm wasn't moving. At all.

Closing one eye, she aimed and fired. A sharp cry was her reward. She fired again and the van lurched to the right, throwing her to the floor and sending her gun sliding to the front of the van as they came to an abrupt halt in a cacophony of squealing brakes and crunching metal.

There was quiet then. Absolute quiet for several beats of her heart.

Is he dead? Please, God, let him be dead.

She pulled herself to a sitting position once again. She had to blink hard, unable to see. She wiped her hand over her eyes and it came back red. She was bleeding from her head now. *That sucks.*

An acrid smell burned her nose. *The airbag*, she thought. *Fuck it.* The fucking airbag had probably saved his miserable life.

Then she heard a creak of vinyl a few feet forward. *Sonofabitch.*

He wasn't dead. *Goddammit.* He'd climbed over the center console and was coming for her. His nose was gushing. At least the airbag had broken his nose.

But hell, all that blood . . .

'Hope you didn't have unprotected sex with Linnie,' she found herself saying.

Even through the blood in her eyes, she could see the rage burning in his. 'You fucking cunt.' He spat a mouthful of blood toward her, but it hit the captain's chair in front of her. 'I am going to gut you.'

'Like Butch gutted Paula?' she asked and he grinned, revealing blood-stained teeth.

'Just like her.'

She scrabbled back, frantically searching for something to use in her own defense. *Where are you, Adam?*

'Why?' she asked, running her hand over the floor, finding nothing. 'Why did you kill her?'

'To hurt him, of course.' He loomed, staring down at her. 'Why else?'

'Why?' Her fingers closed over something small, thin, and metal. *Ah!* She recognized it by touch. Smooth, except for brief etchings. They'd be hearts. The pen would be pink. *Thank you, God.* She gripped it in her fist, just as she'd practiced. 'Why torment him?'

He shook his head and reached for her. Grabbing her bulky bulletproof vest in both hands, he dragged her to her feet. 'I'm going to slit your throat and gut you and leave you for him to find.'

No. It will kill him. But she forced herself to smile. 'He's stronger than you think. He's a lot stronger than you are.'

She cried out when his fist connected with her jaw. 'Shut up,' he snarled.

Now. Now. Gripping the pen in her left hand, she arced her arm upward with all the force she could muster. He grabbed her wrist, twisting away before she struck his throat, but his startled yelp told she'd hit something. More blood gushed from his face where the pen had ripped his skin, and he gripped her vest tighter, yanking her to the van door. He tore the pen from her hand, shoved the door open, and dragged her out into the cold air and down an embankment.

They'd gone off the road and hit a tree, the hood of the van crushed and mangled. It could have been worse, because fifty feet ahead was a bridge spanning the valley between two steep hills. If Hanson had been going a little bit faster, if he'd lost control a little bit later, they would have gone off the bridge. They wouldn't have walked away from that.

New panic pushed away any relief when she looked up. The van blocked her view of the road. And, she assumed, blocked anyone's view of her.

Nobody can see me down here. Nobody will know I'm here.

But they'll see the van, she told herself. *They'll be looking for the—*

With a loud growl Hanson tossed her pen aside and dragged her toward the underpass beneath the bridge, then threw her to the ground, her head hitting hard concrete. She blinked up at him, unable to see clearly. There was still too much blood in her eyes. *Stay focused. Keep him talking. Give Adam time to find you.*

'Who was she?' she demanded, scrabbling back. 'Paula? Who was she?'

He advanced toward her and she ran, but tripped and went down. Her shoes came off, the cold concrete burning her stocking-covered feet. He grabbed at her but she rolled away, grabbing for one of her shoes, now covered in mud.

But with a stiletto heel.

'Fucking bitch.' Clutching her vest, he shoved her to her back, his fingers closing over her throat. Panicking, she sliced with one of the shoes.

He yelped and released her.

Yes. She'd caught his broken nose with the heel. But it didn't hurt him enough. He grabbed the shoe and threw it away, then his boot came down on the hand that had wielded the shoe and she cried out in pain.

'Who was she?' she demanded again. If nothing else, she could find this out for Adam. Because he'd be coming for her.

Hanson leaned down, getting in her face. 'She was nobody.'

'*No.* She was a child. Where did she come from?'

His eyes gleamed. 'You'll die wondering.'

He disappeared and she fought to roll over, using her left elbow for leverage because her right arm was numb and her left hand was probably broken. She'd pushed herself to her knees when Hanson grabbed her hair and dragged her to her feet, but she fought, hot tears filling her eyes when her scalp burned.

'It doesn't matter if you fight or not. You'll be just as dead.'

She felt the cold sting of the blade at her throat and knew that Adam would find her this way. *I'm sorry, Adam. I'm so sorry.*

Cincinnati, Ohio,
Monday 21 December, 1.10 P.M.

'Please, Linnie, give me the gun,' Adam repeated and watched all the emotions cross Linnie's face. Fear, hate, sorrow. Hope.

She drew a deep breath and handed Adam her gun, handle first. Then she put Mikey Hanson in Scarlett's arms and Adam's shoulders relaxed. 'Thank you,' he said softly.

Scarlett unhooked the radio handset from her vest. 'Hostage situation neutralized. Child is under our protection. Proceed with next step.'

Which was Deacon and Trip's systematic search of the neighbor's home.

'Are you going to arrest me now?' Linnie asked as a policewoman came through the front door to take the child from Scarlett.

'No,' Adam said quietly. 'You will have to answer for the hostage situation, but we're not putting you under arrest.'

There was movement at the corner of his eye. Rita pushing to her knees. 'The hell you're not! She kidnapped me at *gunpoint*. She held my son at *gunpoint*!'

'Rita, lie down!' Adam barked.

'No! Give me back my son!'

'Not at this time,' Scarlett told her. 'We'll be calling social services for a temporary placement while we figure out how much you know, Mrs Hanson.'

Rita's jaw dropped. 'You can't be serious.'

'On your stomach,' Scarlett commanded, then gestured for another officer to come in. 'Stand next to Mrs Hanson. Make sure she remains face down.'

Adam cleared his throat and gentled his voice as he turned back to Linnie. 'Please stay here with Detective Bishop. The other detectives have to clear the neighborhood because Hanson is out there somewhere.'

'The other detectives?' Linnie asked. 'Not you?'

The girl was perceptive. 'No, not me. I'm no longer on the case. I only came now because you asked me to.'

'Detective Kimble was shot at this morning,' Scarlett explained and Linnie's eyes widened in shock. 'His friend was killed. We believe Detective Hanson was the shooter.'

'*No.*' A sob tore from Rita's throat and she sank back down to the carpet.

Linnie bit at her lip. 'I wounded him. I don't know if it's important, but tell the other detectives that I stabbed him in his left arm. Here.' She pointed to the underside of her upper arm. 'It was enough that he let me go. That's how I got away on Saturday.'

Adam gave her a nod of gratitude. 'Thank you. Detective Bishop will tell them.' He glanced at Scarlett. 'Call me when it's all done.' He left the Hansons' house and ducked so that the line of SUVs in the driveway provided cover. At the bottom of the driveway a sedan waited, tucked behind the SUVs. The window rolled down, revealing Isenberg at the wheel.

'Get in,' she said. She waited until he was buckled in to add, 'Well done. We'll send a secure vehicle for Linnie and the little boy. It's safer for them to stay inside until then.'

He leaned his head back on the headrest. 'I am so tired, Lynda.'

'I know,' she said softly. 'Get some rest. If you need to hit a meeting later, let me know. I'll go with you.'

Adam's throat grew thick. He'd started to say thank you when Isenberg broke into a barrage of cursing, so he chuckled instead. 'What?'

'The fucking reporters. It's like an obstacle course. Slouch forward. I don't want to give them any shots of your face for their rags.'

He complied, pulling his tactical helmet forward. He heard a shout from outside the car, but didn't look up, even when Isenberg cackled quietly.

'I figured they'd move,' she said. 'Those cameras look damn expensive. Wouldn't want them run over because their owners won't get out of the damn road.'

'I'm surprised you didn't want to stick around back there,' Adam said. 'It's just about to get interesting.'

'Nah. I trust Deacon and Scarlett. My job these days is to keep my team healthy. You are a valued member of my team and your career matters to me. Ergo, I'm making sure your ass is as far away from Hanson as I can possibly take it.'

Again his throat grew thick. 'Thank you. For everything. For telling me about your sobriety. Because that shows me that I can still have a career.'

'Yeah,' she said gruffly. 'It's fine. All good.'

It is good, he thought, oddly comfortable with the idea that Scarlett, Deacon, and Trip would be the ones to bring Hanson in. It took Isenberg a few minutes to get past the media, but they were eventually free of the community.

'You can look up now,' Isenberg said. 'No more— What the fuck?'

A black SUV was parked on the other side of the road, a familiar Subaru parked behind it. 'That's Marcus O'Bannion's car. I guess the *Ledger* wants a bite of the story.'

Adam quickly saw what Isenberg meant. The owner of the *Ledger* was standing in the road, waving his arms for them to stop. Isenberg pulled her sedan in behind Marcus's Subaru, then gasped.

'Oh God. Is that Nash Currie?' She jumped out of the sedan and Adam followed, conscious that he was vulnerable to another attack but uncaring.

Because Nash had been driving Meredith. And the van was nowhere to be seen.

Isenberg and Adam hurried to where Nash lay in a dirty snowbank. Stone O'Bannion knelt beside him, fingers on Nash's wrist.

'It is Nash,' Adam said, dread squeezing his heart. 'What happened?'

Stone O'Bannion gently put Nash's arm by his side. 'He's alive, but his pulse is low. I don't know. He's got a huge bruise on his forehead and he's not conscious.'

'Oh my God. Lynda, he was driving Meredith,' Adam said.

Isenberg squeezed his shoulder. 'Keep it together, Adam. Will you stay with Detective Currie?' she asked Stone.

'Of course,' Marcus said from behind them. He was finishing his call to 911. 'Thank you. Yes, I'll hold, but a detective and lieutenant arrived and I'm going to talk to them. I'll put you on speaker.'

Isenberg frowned and quickly walked around the SUV and peered at the back window. 'A bloody handprint.' She huffed out a frustrated breath. 'Because somebody's in there. There's an old man under that tarp. His hand is visible. Marcus, ask for a second ambulance. We have two victims.'

Without hesitation, she opened the driver's door and hit the hatch release. A few seconds later she was leaning into the hatch. 'Caucasian male, in his mid-sixties. His head is bashed in, but he's alive. And conscious. Sir, what is your name?'

She leaned up abruptly and rushed back to Nash. 'That's Hanson's next-door neighbor. Hanson lured him out here, then hit him and left him.'

Nash groaned and Adam, Lynda, and Stone gathered close to him. 'Adam? I'm sorry. He took her. Hanson. I saw the bloody hand.

Stopped. Started to radio location.' Another smaller groan. 'Hanson pulled me out of the van and took off. East.'

Adam ran for the sedan before Nash could say another word, Isenberg at his heels. 'Nash's gun was gone,' Adam said as Isenberg pulled back onto the road like a shot. 'Hanson is armed.' *And he's got Meredith.*

'They can't be that far ahead of us.' Nevertheless, Isenberg punched the gas. This was an old road and curvy as hell. They rounded a bend in the road and there it was. The van had crossed the oncoming lane, gone off the road, and was wrapped around a tree. 'I see the van,' Adam said, his racing heart skipping a beat. 'But I don't see her.' His reflex was to rush in, guns blazing. But that could get Meredith killed.

Think. This is critical.

Isenberg pulled the sedan onto the shoulder and together they made their way down the embankment to the van. Tightening his grip on his service weapon, Adam braced himself for what he'd see.

Don't be hurt. Don't be hurt. God, please don't let her be hurt. He crept up to the van, gun raised.

But the van was empty. Both Meredith and Wyatt had disappeared. *Don't panic.*

The airbag had deployed. On the passenger seat was Nash's service weapon. He reached through the window to scoop up the gun. Quietly he dropped the clip from the magazine. Fully loaded. He pressed the clip back into place, making as little noise as possible, then dropped the gun into his coat pocket.

Isenberg gave him a sharp look. 'Wait for backup,' she mouthed.

But then an echoey voice drifted up from somewhere farther down the embankment.

'It doesn't matter if you fight or not. You'll be just as dead.'

Hanson. Adam's heart stopped. But he forced his feet to keep moving around the van. Oh God. He held back a curse. Because he didn't see her. But he did see a trail of blood in the snow leading to the underpass. Fueled by instinct and sheer terror, he ran down the hill, sliding more than once, picking himself up to run again. And then he saw her.

Knee-buckling relief warred with mind-numbing panic. She was alive, standing on her own two *bare* feet on the icy concrete of the underpass, the flash of relief in her eyes mixed with abject fear. Because Wyatt Hanson stood behind her, the fingers of his right hand wrapped around a handful of her beautiful hair, pulling her head back. With his left hand, he held a knife to her throat.

Her head was bleeding and her right arm hung loosely at her side. Her left hand was bent into a claw. But her chin was steady, as were her eyes as she met Adam's gaze. He wanted to run to her, but he didn't dare.

Wyatt's nose was bleeding, his right sleeve was soaked with blood, and he had an oozing gash in his cheek. With the wound Linnie had made in his left arm, he should be vulnerable.

Except for the knife in his hand. And the mocking smile on his face. 'Detective Kimble,' he said. 'So nice of you to join us.'

Meredith's mouth was moving, but no sound emerged. *I love you. I'm sorry.*

Adam's heart broke into tiny pieces. She thought she was going to die. *And she's apologizing. To me.* He gave her a steady nod, then made his lips curve.

'Me too. And not today,' he told her quietly, ignoring Hanson's barb and hoping she understood.

'How very sweet,' Wyatt drawled. 'You got here in time, Adam. You can watch her die. Just like Paula.' He pressed the sharp blade against Meredith's throat, drawing a thin line of crimson. 'Drop your weapon.'

Meredith was leaning back, trying to get away from the sharp edge of the knife. Adam knew he couldn't shoot Hanson like this – even if he'd been able to draw his weapon fast enough, an instant killshot would cause Hanson's arm to jerk and Meredith could bleed out before help got there. He wondered where Isenberg was. Probably mobilizing a rescue crew. But Adam couldn't have waited. Hanson looked like he'd been ready to kill Meredith right then, whether he'd had an audience or not. *Maybe I can hold him off long enough for Isenberg to save the day.* It was the best plan he had at the moment.

Adam made a show of dropping his weapon to the ground, grateful he'd pocketed the one he'd found in the van. 'There. Let her go. You know it's me that you want.'

'True,' Hanson agreed amicably. 'But I also need to get away and she makes a most excellent hostage. *The* Dr Fallon, admired and respected by all.' He lifted his brows. 'And loved by you?' Adam's composure must have flickered because Wyatt smiled. 'Thought so. I haven't decided if she's more valuable to me as a ticket over the border, or as my last fuck-you to you. What do you think, Adam? Do you think I should kill her now so that you can be a part of it – like sweet little Paula – or should I take her with me and leave you to wonder what I'm doing to her? Because there are so *many* things I'd like to do to her.'

Meredith's eyes slid shut, her throat working as she tried to swallow. Hanson repositioned the knife, drawing another thin ribbon of red just under her chin.

He's baiting you. Don't rise to it. Adam tilted his head, making his expression impassive. He hoped. 'Funny, I thought you only liked them young.'

Hanson laughed. 'Well, I may not enjoy them as much when they get to be as old as your Dr Fallon, but that doesn't keep me from being up to the task. Rita and I have two children, after all.'

'If you kill her, you'll still have to get through a roadblock.'

'True.' He shrugged. 'So I'll take her with me.'

Over Hanson's shoulder, Adam saw Deacon slide down the embankment on the other side of the overpass. He was still thirty yards away – probably the first place he could safely descend.

Deacon began to run. Twenty yards, ten, running fast and soundlessly, slowing to silently approach the mouth of the overpass.

Adam just needed to distract Hanson long enough for one of them to pull the knife from his hand, because shooting him was still out of the question. *I need a distraction. Think.* And then he almost smiled because Deacon stood at the mouth of the overpass now, using sign language to communicate those very words.

I need a distraction. One fucking distraction.

And then Adam knew what to do. *Money.* Wyatt's true love.

'Then what?' he said to Wyatt. 'What's your plan if you manage to get away?' he asked, moving a few steps closer.

Wyatt smiled, revealing a mouthful of bloody teeth. 'I intend to live very well.'

'On what?'

Wyatt's smile faltered for a second before becoming arrogant again. 'I have enough.'

'I'll bet you do. But you have five million less than you think you do.'

Bingo. Yes. Wyatt visibly paled. 'What are you talking about?'

Meredith's gaze flew up to Adam's, her eyes narrowing. Smart, she was. She knew something was coming. And she'd be ready. *Please be ready, baby,* he thought desperately.

He somehow kept the desperation out of his voice. 'I'm sorry to tell you, but an unauthorized person recently changed your password. Your bank should really notify you of things like that.'

Wyatt shook his head. 'You're lying.'

'No, I'm not.' Adam lifted his brows. 'KingTriton89.'

Wyatt's left arm, weakened by Linnie, dropped momentarily in shock. Meredith took that moment to throw herself sideways, but he still had his hand tangled in her hair and she didn't get far. She was on her knees and Wyatt was bent over her.

And raising his knife in the air.

Adam didn't think. He just pulled Nash's weapon from his pocket, aimed at Wyatt's knife arm, pulled the trigger, then launched himself at the man he'd called friend for so many years. Wyatt's scream echoed in the enclosed space, as did the clatter of the knife as he dropped it on the concrete.

Wyatt grunted when Adam's shoulder made contact with his chest, knocking them both to the ground, Meredith's agonized cry slicing through Wyatt's cursing. The fucker had dropped the knife, but *still* had her by the hair.

Adam shoved the barrel of Nash's service weapon up under Wyatt's chin. '*Let her go,*' he growled. '*Now.*'

Wyatt smirked. 'You won't kill me. Not in cold blood like this.'

Adam didn't want to. Not because he thought Wyatt should live, but because he still had too many questions. Mostly why? And why Paula? Where had she come from?

But I'll kill him if I have to. Of that Adam was certain.

Refusing to respond verbally, Adam grabbed Wyatt's upper arm and dug his fingers into the man's flesh. He wasn't sure where the arm was wounded, but the sleeve was soaked in blood so he hoped he was close. Wyatt bucked as his body spasmed, his eyes rolling back in his head. *Yes.* Wyatt's hand opened and Adam freed it from Meredith's hair.

From the corner of his eye he saw Meredith roll free and struggle to stand, but failing, her knees buckling. He opened his mouth to call to Deacon to get her out of there when the flash of silver from the other side of his peripheral vision had him wrenching his full attention back to Wyatt.

But Adam was a blink too late. Hot, searing pain shot through his right leg and he instinctively jerked away, grabbing Wyatt's coat in one hand to keep him from going after Meredith again. He rolled up onto his left knee and tried to put weight on his right, but the pain had him seeing double.

Wyatt had another knife. Which was embedded in Adam's leg. *Son of a fucking bitch.*

Fury had him lashing out, swinging his fist into Wyatt's jaw. Wyatt went down, his head knocking into the concrete with a sick thud. He lay there, blinking and dazed.

Deacon was there, weapon pointed at Wyatt's head. Adam waved him toward Meredith. 'I've got him. You get her out of here. Please. *Please*,' he repeated when Deacon hesitated. 'She's hurt.'

'I'll be right back.' Deacon scooped Meredith in his arms.

His gun pressed to Wyatt's chest, Adam went for his cuffs. He snapped the first on Wyatt's left arm then reached for the right—

Wyatt reared up and knocked his forehead into Adam's. Unprepared, Adam pitched back on his ass, but immediately rocked to his knees and shoved his gun at Wyatt's chest.

But Wyatt rolled to his knees. A split second later, Wyatt was jabbing the barrel of an old Glock between Adam's ribs, his finger on the trigger.

Wyatt was smiling. He'd had another gun too, using the distraction to go for it.

'You won't kill me,' Wyatt said smugly. 'If you'd been capable of doing so, you'd have done it when you had the chance.'

That might have been true a week ago. Even a day ago. But not today. Wyatt had stolen too much from too many people. *He's not stealing Meredith's happiness too. And I am her happiness.*

With no fanfare, Adam pulled the trigger. Wyatt jerked backward, his eyes wide with shock. But he didn't go down. Shock gave way to hate as Wyatt's gun began to lift.

Adam fired once more, the bullet making a neat hole in Wyatt's forehead. Dead center. Wyatt crumpled, dead before he hit the ground.

Just like Andy Gold had. Just like John Kasper had. Vicious satisfaction filled him.

A movement caught his attention and Adam looked up to see Trip walking toward him, holstering his weapons. Trip bent down to pick up the gun that had fallen from Wyatt's hand, only after he was dead.

'You okay?' Trip asked quietly.

Adam looked at Wyatt's face. And nodded. 'Yes. I am.' He really was. He pointed to the gun at Trip's side. 'You were going to shoot, but you didn't. Why?'

'I thought you should do it. But if you couldn't, I was happy to.'

Adam's mouth quirked. 'Thank you.'

'Not a problem. Sorry I got here late to the party. I stopped to check on Nash. Wyatt hit him hard with the butt of his gun. Nash was in some serious pain, but he was mostly worried about Meredith.'

Meredith. 'Where is she?'

'I helped Deacon carry her up the hill. She's in my vehicle, waiting for the EMTs.'

Adam tried to stand, but his leg buckled beneath him. He grunted, pain radiating throughout his whole body. *Fuck.* He'd forgotten about the damn knife. He reached back to pull it out but

Trip stopped him, kneeling beside him to examine the wound.

'Don't touch it, man. The medics are coming. Let them do it. You're not bleeding too much. Yank it out and you might gush like a stuck pig.'

Better do what the rookie says, Adam thought, then blinked a few times to clear his vision when little black dots started to encroach. It wasn't panic this time. Somehow he knew that. It was probably . . . shock?

Holstering Nash's gun, Adam pushed to his knees, rotating a few degrees so that he didn't have to touch Wyatt Hanson's body. He had to close his eyes against another wave of pain. When he opened them, he was surprised to see Isenberg standing just outside the underpass, on the same side Adam had entered.

'She came down the hill at the same time I did, but on the less steep side,' Trip said in a nearly soundless whisper. 'She was ready to shoot him too.'

Isenberg approached, reaching out her hand.

Right. The weapon. He'd fired it. *And I'm not one goddamned bit sorry*. He dropped the clip from the magazine and racked it to be sure there were no bullets chambered. He then placed the gun and clip on her palm. 'Procedure,' he murmured. 'Got it. For the record, I'd do it again in a heartbeat. You can put that in your report.'

Isenberg gave him a look that was equal parts compassion and exasperation. And concern, he thought. A lot of concern.

She dropped the weapon and the clip in her coat pocket. 'It was self-defense, Adam,' she said. 'Trip and I saw it.' She extended her hand again and he realized she'd been trying to help him up.

'Oh,' he said numbly. He gripped her hand, groaning when Trip took his other arm, hefting him to his feet. Reality poured in – the iron smell of blood mixing with the sulfur of fired weapons, the sight of Wyatt's body, the sound of shouting cops and the sirens of approaching emergency vehicles. He hoped at least one was an ambulance. For Meredith.

Now that it was over, he felt the adrenaline crashing and the panic rising. She was hurt and he needed to help her.

'Need to get to Meredith,' he said. He turned too fast and stumbled but Trip held him upright. He tried to yank free, but Trip held firm. 'Let me go, Trip. Please.'

'I don't think so, old man,' Trip said, his rumbly voice soothing in all the chaos. 'Maybe you need to wait for the medics.'

'I think he needs to see Dr Fallon,' Isenberg said quietly, and Adam wanted to thank her. He wanted to weep. He wanted to scream. But he did none of those things.

'Yes,' he gritted out, hanging onto control by a thread. 'Meredith. Please.'

Isenberg squeezed his arm. 'Come on, Adam. Agent Triplett, let's get him up the embankment. And make sure he doesn't fall backward on that fucking knife.'

The two of them kept him steady as he combination hopped/dragged himself around the wrecked van, straight to where Meredith lay in the cargo bay of one of the SUVs. Deacon had begun administering first aid, wrapping a bandage around the arm that still sullenly oozed blood.

'She's lost a lot of blood,' Deacon said quietly and Adam's heart stopped once more.

'How much?'

Deacon's gaze told Adam that it was too serious to say out loud. 'The medics are a minute out. Don't move her other hand. I think it's broken.'

'I can hear you, y'know,' Meredith whispered and opened her eyes. 'You're okay,' she whispered. 'Tell me that you're okay. He stabbed you. I saw him stab you.'

He was lowered to his knees, aware of Isenberg and Trip stepping back to give him some privacy. Leaning into the SUV, he rested against the rear bumper, cupping her non-injured cheek. 'I'm more okay than you are.'

'I'm good,' she said lightly, but it was so forced that it hurt him to hear it. 'The doctors'll stitch me up and send me back into the game.'

Adam brushed a kiss against her temple. 'As long as the game is checkers or dominoes. Nothing more dangerous than that.'

'Deal.' Her eyelids fluttered closed. 'Tell Papa that I'm okay. That I love him.'

Fear speared him. She sounded so weak and her words had slurred. 'You'll tell him yourself,' Adam said firmly. 'Meredith? *Meredith!*'

She wasn't answering. She wasn't conscious. His fear spread and a look up at Deacon told him the feeling was well founded.

'Dani's on her way to the hospital,' Deacon said. 'She'll meet us in the ER and walk us through whatever the doctor says and does.' He gripped Adam's shoulder. 'Meredith's still here. And so am I. Don't forget that.'

A sob rose in his throat and he battled it back. 'I won't.'

Thirty-one

'You need to go home, son, and get some rest.'

Adam didn't look up, didn't look away from Meredith's pale face as her grandfather came into her ICU room and wearily dropped into the plastic chair beside Adam's.

'I'm okay,' Adam said quietly. And he was. The knife had not hit anything major and he had not gushed like a stuck pig when it was removed, contrary to Trip's dire prediction. 'I'll stay until she's awake.'

She had woken once, shortly after her surgery. Her eyes had opened and she'd looked around wildly, only settling when she found Adam in the chair beside her bed. Her dry lips had mouthed 'Love you,' and she'd smiled at him. Then her eyes had closed as she slipped back into unconsciousness.

He gingerly held only the middle and forefingers of her left hand, which bore all the needles and IVs, as well as splints on her ring finger and pinkie. Her right hand was swathed in bandages that continued all the way up to her shoulder.

The bullet Wyatt had fired at her as he'd made his desperate getaway in the van had damaged the tendons in her upper arm, which was why her arm had hung so limply. The surgeon believed he'd repaired the damage, but the recovery would be painful. He had, however, been hopeful that she'd regain full use of the arm. Which was all good news.

That she was *alive* was Adam's main concern. And she was. Her

570

chest raised and lowered with regular, if shallow breaths. The bastard had broken one of her ribs and two of the fingers on her left hand, but she'd fought him hard. She'd shot him twice and slashed his face twice – with her shoe and with her pretty pink tactical pen. With hearts.

Quincy had found the pen in the bloody snow and had brought it to show Adam, tagged in an evidence bag. Adam had seen her coloring with it, but he hadn't known what it was at the time and his eyes had stung brutally when he realized how damn *good* his woman had been at protecting herself. Even though she shouldn't have had to. Ever.

Still, Adam was going to buy her a whole case of pretty pink tactical pens and a closet full of high-heeled shoes when she woke up, because she was who she was, and as long as she helped children in need, she'd make enemies.

Other than that one moment after her surgery, she hadn't woken again. She'd had a steady stream of visitors, because Meredith was well loved by everyone. That had not surprised him.

That they came in one at a time, not one of them disputing his claim on the chair closest to her bedside *had* surprised him. And humbled him.

Clarke resettled his big frame in the small chair. 'You need to eat, boy,' he said gruffly. 'She'll have my hide when she wakes up if you're half dead from hunger.'

Adam's lips curved, visualizing her locking wills with her grandfather. But his smile quickly dimmed. He didn't have the energy to maintain it. 'She told me to tell you that she was okay,' he murmured. 'When we were waiting for the ambulance back at the crime scene. Oh,' he remembered, 'and that she loves you. I'm sorry. I forgot to tell you before.'

The big man beside him shuddered out a breath. 'Thank you,' he said, and there were tears in his voice. And on his face. The old man was crying openly and without apology. And without an iota of shame.

Adam nodded, remaining silent because he was no longer able to trust his own voice. He reached out a hand that trembled and stroked the inside of her left arm, over the faded scars, emotion welling up to choke him. He clenched his jaw against it, clenched every muscle in his body against it.

It always passed, the need to weep. But it wasn't passing this time and he found himself impaled on it, stuck between breaths. Unable to inhale or exhale. And panicking.

A beefy hand thunked him heavily on his back and with a whoosh he expelled the breath that had been stuck in his lungs.

'You gotta breathe, son,' Clarke muttered. 'It's kind of a necessary thing.'

Adam expected the weight on his back to disappear, but it didn't. It gentled, the old man's hand spreading wide and rubbing his back in slow circles. And once again his eyes burned and his breath hitched.

'When's the last time you let it all out, Adam?' Clarke asked in a whisper. 'Let your guard down and just let it all out?'

Adam turned only his head to look at him. 'What?'

Clarke smiled sadly. 'When was the last time you cried, Adam?'

Adam blinked at him, thrown by the question. 'I don't know.'

Clarke sighed. 'That's what I thought. It's okay, you know. To cry.'

Adam shook his head. 'I know that. But . . . not for me.'

The big hand kept making those big, soothing circles on his back and Adam felt his eyes growing heavy. 'I met your father,' Clarke said suddenly and Adam blinked awake.

'When? Where?'

'About an hour ago. And in the waiting room. He's . . . well, he's an asshole, if you don't mind me saying so.'

Adam huffed a shocked laugh. 'No, I don't mind at all. It's true. What did he do?'

'Demanded to see you. All bluster and "me, me, me." He had your mother with him. I think she's the one who wanted to see you, but your dad . . . ? Well, he kind of—'

'Mowed right over her,' Adam supplied sadly. 'I wish I'd known she was there. She doesn't deserve what he does to her, but she doesn't fight back. I don't think she ever could.' He frowned, turning back to the woman who lay in the bed, motionless except for the even rise and fall of her chest. 'She's no Meredith, that's for sure.'

'No, she's not. But she seems to love you. I could see it in her face.' He cleared his throat. 'I offered to bring her back here to see you, but that only two people could be here in ICU and you weren't leaving Merry's side. In actuality, I never would have allowed him to come back here. You understand that, right?'

'Oh, I do. And I agree.'

'Good. Anyway, your father said he wasn't allowing your mom to come back here without him. That you should come see your mom in the waiting room. She backed away from that, said that your place was next to the woman you loved.' Clarke drew a breath and held it for longer than necessary. 'I thought he'd hit her. Does he hit her?'

'She says no,' Adam said uneasily. 'I've never seen him hit her. He never really hit me, even. It was more emotional manipulation. He's good at that. I tried to get my mother to leave, to walk away and come live with me. Well, I used to. I haven't for a year or so.'

And I should have. I'm sorry, Ma.

'Since the girl was killed in front of you,' Clarke said, not mincing words.

Adam's brows lifted. 'How did you know?'

'It's all over the news. The *Ledger* ran a piece on the girl, posted a photo of her taken from one of your Skype sessions. CPD is trying to find out where she came from.'

'Nash wanted to,' Adam remembered. 'Right after it happened. I did too. But Wyatt said the videos had been lost.' He frowned, then closed his eyes on a sigh. 'I found a DVD in a pile of stuff on my kitchen table a few months later. I was drunk that day. Every day back then, actually. I was on mental health leave, but I made a copy and took it to my old boss in Personal Crimes. He promised me that he'd put a team on it. I guess they did for a while, but . . . priorities. They had live kids to save. I should have fought for her, should have asked Isenberg to take the case. But I couldn't. There was this mental block whenever it came to Paula. And then when I got sober? My sponsor said I needed to distance myself. That every time I thought about Paula I was dancing close to the edge, and he was afraid if I fell over again that I'd never find my way back.' He rubbed his temples. 'Now I'll never know if John really believed that or if Wyatt put him up to it.'

'Either way, he may have been right,' Clarke said softly. 'Sometimes you have to walk away and save yourself. Did you wonder where the DVD came from?'

'No. I figured I'd had it all along, that it had gotten mixed up with other stuff.' He winced. 'My place wasn't so clean back then.'

'But it is now,' Clarke said. 'It was military clean when I went with Deacon to get you some clothes,' he added when Adam turned to him, surprised that the old man had gone out of his way. And touched. And feeling his damn eyes burn again. *Goddammit.*

'Thank you,' he managed. 'That was nice of you.'

Clarke studied him. 'I bet your father told you that men don't cry.'

Adam huffed again, this time in frustration. He pivoted in his chair so that he could only see Meredith. Her face was blurry, but he refused to blink. The water in his eyes would drain back into his tear ducts or dry up or whatever it did when this had happened before.

Except he couldn't remember the last time his eyes had blurred with real tears.

'Did he?' Clarke pressed.

Adam clenched his jaw. 'Yes, he did,' he replied with a cold finality that he hoped told the old man to leave it alone. No such luck.

'Adam, he's wrong.' The old man's voice had softened, rumbling between them. 'When I was Shane's age, I was dropped into combat. Korea. I saw my best friend die.' He was quiet a moment. 'He got his head blown off, just like Shane's friend Andy. And your sponsor. Not something a man forgets too easily.'

Adam swallowed hard, not wanting to remember John's head blowing apart all over him. And unable to erase the memory. 'Were you injured?' He meant to ask it confidently, with compassion. But the words came out gravelly and rough.

'Yeah. Nothing permanent, but I needed surgery. I woke up to this beautiful girl. Thought I'd actually died and gone to heaven,' he said fondly. 'It was my Essie. She was an army nurse then. I thought nurses were soft creatures, but I was wrong. She ripped into my hide when I refused to talk about my buddy. When I refused to write home and tell them that I was okay. When I shut down.'

Adam understood. God, he understood. He coughed past the blockage in his throat, keeping his face turned away. Because those tears in his eyes had spilled over to his cheeks. But only two. One on each side. The wetness would dry.

The heavy hand returned to his back and Adam realized he'd hunched over and gripped the bed rails so tightly that his knuckles were white.

'She did not let me get away with any shit. She made me talk about my friend. And when I cried, I tried not to let her see. I turned my face away, but she made me look at her. Made me talk to her. And told me that the tears were good things. I believed her. My pop had cried from time to time. I wasn't personally averse to the notion, you understand. I just didn't want to cry in front of her. Because I was nineteen.'

Adam said nothing, but it didn't seem to matter. The back rub continued, soothing him. The words continued in that soft voice, tearing him apart inside.

'So we got married, Essie and me. Had a good life. I won't say it was perfect. I won't say I was perfect. I still had nightmares, and I still had periods of depression. I'm not saying that letting it all out and crying like a whipped pup was the magical answer that kept me from having the PTSD that a lot of my buddies brought home with them.'

He paused long enough for the silence to become too heavy to bear.

'Then what are you saying?' Adam whispered.

'That it gave me a valve. Gave me a way to deal with my grief. We tried to have a big family, but Essie was only able to carry Merry's father to term. We lost four others. It was ... very hard. Harder to watch her grieve. The first three times I cried on my own. Didn't think she needed to see my grief. But you know? She did. She found me out in the garden one day after we lost the fourth. Weeding and crying. She said it helped, knowing I'd loved them too. So all those years later when my son and my daughter-in-law died? I cried without shame. Essie and I both cried. We held each other and grieved.'

He was quiet longer this time, but the back rub continued. Finally, he shuddered out another breath. 'And when I lost my Essie, I thought my life was over. But I had Merry and Alex and Bailey – all my granddaughters, you see. So I kept going. I cried and didn't care who saw me do it. Didn't care if it made them uncomfortable. Didn't care if they thought I was the biggest wuss on the planet. Because the tears were mine. The grief was mine. And Essie would have haunted me forever if I'd sucked it up and been stoic.'

Clarke cleared his throat loudly. 'Merry is just like her gran. Fearless, even when she's so scared inside that she's about to crack. She deserves a man who's just as fearless. Someone who's not afraid to feel. Someone who's not about to shatter into a million pieces. She's picked you and I can see why. You are brave and you do work through your shit. You protected her with your own life and I am ten kinds of grateful. But I gotta say, son, right now you're looking like you're one breath away from shattering into a million pieces.'

Adam opened his mouth to speak but nothing came out.

The old man kept rubbing his back, seemingly unperturbed by his silence. 'I've watched you sit here, getting more and more tense, more contracted into yourself. That's not so good. Because if you shatter into a million pieces, there won't be anything left to take care of her when she wakes up. Which she will, but on her own time, because Merry always runs a little late,' he said affectionately. 'So what's it gonna be, son? Are you going to sit here and shatter? Or are you gonna let some of that grief go?'

There was something about the cadence of the man's voice and that hand on his back . . . Adam stared at Meredith's face and wanted. He wanted so much to be who she needed. And he was so damn tired. His eyes filled again and this time . . . this time he didn't clench his jaw. He didn't tense his body. He blinked and felt the tears fall.

'Four,' he whispered. 'I was four.'

The hand on his back faltered for a few beats, then resumed the slow circles on his back. 'When you last cried?'

Adam blinked again and more tears fell, landing on his hands that still gripped the bed rail. 'Yes.'

'Then I'd say you were long overdue.' The chair beside him squeaked as Clarke struggled to his feet. 'I'll let you let go in private. This time. But we cry in this family, Adam Kimble. So you better get used to having witnesses.'

It occurred to Adam as he heard the door open and close, that he'd just been called family. He'd think on that later, because he was alone with Meredith. Who he'd almost lost too many times to count. Who'd fought so *fearlessly*. And who'd cried in his arms when her heart couldn't hold any more hurt. Cried for him when he hadn't been able to do so himself.

But what he kept seeing was her face when she'd honestly thought she'd die. *I love you. I'm sorry.* Because she'd known what was going to happen would kill him too.

But she's alive. 'I didn't fuck it up this time,' he whispered.

This time. And somehow those two words pulled the plug on the dam. *This time.* Because all the other times? He hadn't fucked those up either.

Goddammit. All those other times . . . His head was suddenly too heavy to hold upright and he lowered it to his hands, clutching the bed rail like it was his lifeline. The tears Clarke Fallon had urged him to shed came freely. Not as sobs, but as quiet weeping for all the people – the kids – he'd been too late to save. He saw them all. And he cried for them. Cried for himself. Cried for the man who'd spent months drunk and alone, for the man who'd worked feverishly to make amends in the almost-year that followed.

He wept until his head ached, until his eyes were sore and raw. Until no more tears came. And it was then that he realized that he no longer held the rail in a white-knuckled grip. His arms now draped over the rail, pillowing his pounding head.

'They weren't my fault,' he whispered into the quiet. *Goddammit.* All the faces that haunted his dreams at night . . . *He* hadn't failed them. He'd done his job. He'd done everything he could. Every single time.

He closed his eyes, too exhausted to keep them open. *Except for believing in Wyatt Hanson. That was my mistake.*

'Lots of people did.'

Adam blinked drowsily, frowning at the small whisper that seemed like a dream. But then he felt two gentle fingers in his hair and looked up to see Meredith squinting at him. He exhaled in a quiet rush of relief. He took her hand in his and kissed the inside of her wrist, feeling her pulse, so blessedly normal. 'Lots of people did what?' he asked.

She touched his face with her unbroken fingers, caressing his stubbled cheek and dabbing at the corners of his eyes, still damp from the deluge. 'Believed Wyatt Hanson.'

He stared down at her, emptied of anything but sweet gratitude. 'I said that out loud?'

Her nod was slow and shallow. 'You said lots of things out loud. All were true.' One side of her mouth lifted. 'But none of the things were what I was listening for.'

He kissed her hand, then leaned over the rail to kiss her mouth, just a chaste brush of his lips against hers. 'I love you.'

She closed her eyes on a happy little sigh. 'That was the thing.'

He laughed softly. 'You slept a while.'

'I was a little sleep deprived. Can I have some water?' He reached for the cup of ice he'd been smoothing against her lips and she grimaced. 'Ah, the dreaded ice chips,' she grumbled, but sagged back against her pillow when he placed one on her tongue. 'How long before I can go home?'

'Impatient much?'

'Yes. What is today?'

'Tuesday,' he said, and her eyes widened in dismay.

'But Christmas is in three days. I wasn't done shopping yet.'

He couldn't have stopped his grin if he'd tried. 'I'm still stuck on the fact that you're alive. We can do a replay of Christmas once you're able to enjoy it.'

She frowned again. 'This still sucks. But I guess being alive is pretty good under the circumstances.' She studied his face. 'You haven't slept, have you?'

He shrugged. 'A little.'

Her eyes narrowed. 'Full disclosure.'

'Fine. Less than a little.'

'Which means none.'

'I think I should go get your nurse. They need to know you're awake.'

She started to pull on his hand, then winced. 'Stay, please. Another minute.' She glanced down at her bound arm. 'That doesn't look good.'

'It won't be for a while, but eventually you'll regain full use. It'll hurt like a bitch until then, though.'

'It hurts like a bitch right now. You killed him, didn't you?'

'Yes.'

'Good. Asshole.' She frowned again. 'Wait. Was Papa here? Did he call someone an asshole? Did he call you an asshole?'

'Yes, yes, and no. He called my father one.'

'Well, okay. I guess if he's up and about and swearing, then he's feeling better.'

'He'll be better when he knows you're awake.'

'And you'll tell him in a minute. I just . . . I need you a little longer, okay?'

He leaned down to kiss her again. 'Yes. That is more than okay.'

She smiled at him. 'How is Kate? Oh, and Nash? He was hurt too? Wasn't he?'

'Kate is good. Her vision seems to be back to normal. Nash was hurt, yes. Hanson hit him hard, but he was in such a hurry that he didn't knock Nash out completely, luckily for Nash. Stone and Marcus O'Bannion stopped to help him after Hanson drove away with you. Stone did first aid and slowed Nash's bleeding. He'll have a cool scar, but he'll be okay.'

'Oh, good. I was so worried about him. He was so worried about protecting me. Because you'd trusted him again.'

'I know. I've talked about it with him. He and I are good.'

'What about the person he stopped to help?'

'That was Hanson's neighbor, Mr Wainwright. He'll live, although he had a bad head injury. He's been awake enough to tell us that Hanson called him, said his SUV was giving him trouble. Wainwright drove his truck to help him and the next thing he knew, he was waking up in the back of Hanson's SUV with a bloody head and a killer headache. It was his bloody handprints on the SUV's window that got Nash's attention. Hanson had taken Wainwright's truck and drove it into the man's garage, thinking he'd fooled the cops sitting watch outside.'

'Why did he go to Wainwright's house?'

'So that he could cross over their shared fence to get to his own house. Trip found footprints in the snow in their backyards and a safe in Hanson's study. He and Quincy are working on getting it open. Hopefully we'll find out why Hanson felt getting into his house was worth the risk.'

'How did he get from Wainwright's house all the way to where Nash got hurt?'

'He cut through a lot of backyards, left a lot of footprints in the snow.' He stroked her two uninjured fingers. 'On the upside, Mallory is well, as is Agent Troy.'

'Oh, good. Does Troy have someone to take care of him? Kate was going to, but she got hurt too.'

'He does. Faith's stepfather invited Troy to stay with them. Troy and Dr O'Bannion both have ulcers and Dr O'Bannion's husband cooks food for him all the time, so Troy can recover and not starve. The two Feds who were driving your van that night at the hospital were upgraded to stable condition and both look like they'll pull through.'

'Oh good. I was so worried about them.'

'I know, but they'll be fine.' There was more that had been discovered in the last two days, but he didn't think she was ready for any of that.

Her eyes narrowed. 'You're holding out on me.'

He sighed. 'Quincy tracked the past route taken by the SUV left at the hospital's scene.'

'The one that belonged to Wyatt's uncle Mike. And?'

'The SUV went out east, off Nine Mile Road, down by the river. Trip and Deacon checked it out and found six young women buried there. One of them was Jolee.'

Meredith's expression darkened. 'The woman who offered Penny Voss drugs.'

'Yes. Also, Linnie told Scarlett that she was taken to that same area. That's where she stabbed Wyatt in the arm – it was how she got away from him Saturday afternoon. He'd planned to kill her there. We're searching the area for more bodies because a lot of past prostitutes have gone missing. That may have been their burial ground. The ones Wyatt had something to do with, that is.'

Pain flickered in her eyes. 'How is Linnie?' she asked.

'I don't really know. Dani's been with her since she was taken from Wyatt's house. There was no harm done to Mikey and I don't think Linnie will be charged. Scarlett says that Linnie, Shane, and Mallory have hit it off. The three of them went ice skating down at Fountain Square last night. Not far from Buon Cibo.'

Her lips curved. 'Making good memories to cover the bad. I approve.'

'Thought you might. Kyle and his parents left for Chicago as soon as we gave them the all-clear. Shane's planning to return soon, probably after Christmas, after they bury Andy. The university said they'd work with Shane to make up his missed tests. He wants Linnie to go with him. I've been emailing with the CPD homicide detectives we worked with on this case to see if there's a place for Linnie. They're looking into it.'

'That's wonderful. I hope I'll get to say goodbye to Shane and meet Linnie.'

'You should. Shane's been here a few times, hoping you've woken up.'

'He's a good guy. What about Hanson's wife and kids?'

'Rita Hanson's being held in custody until they make sure she really wasn't involved, but at this point it doesn't seem like she was.'

'Who has the children?'

'Social services. Wyatt's dad is their only living relative, but he won't get those kids *ever*. I'll do whatever I have to do to make sure that doesn't happen.' His jaw clenched just thinking about those beautiful children in the hands of a morally bankrupt man like Dale Hanson. 'Rita doesn't have any job skills, but the folks in her church have already set up a fund to help her and the kids.'

She closed her eyes, looking weary. 'How many people did Wyatt hurt or kill?'

This Adam knew off the top of his head, because he'd been thinking about each one. 'All together, seventeen fatalities between Wyatt, Mike, and Butch. Andy, the family who owned the house where he lived, Tiffany and her mother, Broderick Voss, Jolee Cusack and the other five young women we still have to ID, Butch Gilbert, Mike Barber, and John Kasper. Five are still in the hospital – the Feds outside the hospital that night, Hanson's neighbor, Nash, and you.'

'So many.' Two tears streaked down Meredith's face, and Adam brushed them away.

'Too many. And that's enough for now.' He kissed the inside of her wrist. 'I'm going to get the nurse, then I'm going to tell a waiting room full of people that you're awake. Expect a constant parade of people, two at a time, for as long as your nurses allow.'

'As long as you're one of them.'

He smiled as he backed away from the bed. 'Try to keep me away.'

'Adam?' Hand on the doorknob, he turned to her, once again filled with nothing but sweet gratitude. 'I love you too.'

This time when his eyes stung, he didn't fight it. 'I'll be back soon.'

Cincinnati, Ohio,
Tuesday 22 December, 11.00 A.M.

Meredith had her eyes closed when a familiar scent filled the room. Hoping she wasn't dreaming, she opened her eyes to see her cousin Alex standing next to her bed, studying the various monitors, because she was a former ER nurse and knew what she was looking for. Her husband Daniel stood behind her in that quiet way he had and suddenly Meredith was choked up. 'You're here.'

Alex turned a blinding smile her way. 'So are you. We're really happy to know this.'

'We were worried,' Daniel said gruffly. 'You're not supposed to be the one who gets hurt, Mer. So don't do that anymore.'

'I'll do my very best,' she promised.

'You'd better do better than that,' Alex said tartly. 'At least your vitals look good. You, not so much. What were you thinking?'

'That I wanted to stay alive?' Meredith replied dryly.

'And you did.' Daniel gave her a proud nod, then frowned at his wife. 'Sit down. You've been on your feet too much today already.'

Alex rolled her eyes, but took the seat Adam had vacated. 'I can't chase two kids any other way.' She winked at Meredith. 'We were going to save this for Christmas, but Mr GBI-guy here let the cat out of the bag this morning in front of your crowd, so everyone knows.'

Meredith had already figured it out. 'Muffin in the oven?'

'Yep. Due in July.' Alex beamed, as she had through both of her other pregnancies. She was one of those women who looked good while pregnant.

Meredith wondered if she'd ever get to find out how she herself looked in the same state or if Adam even wanted kids. But that was a discussion for a different day.

'We're going to need a godmother and it's way past your turn,' Daniel said.

Meredith just blinked away the tears when they came. Bailey and Daniel's sister were godmothers to Tommy and Mary Katherine respectively. 'I was hoping you'd ask.'

Alex's eyes grew bright as well. 'Pregnancy hormones,' she said, taking several of the tissues from the box next to Meredith's bed. She wiped her own eyes, then Meredith's. 'You're going to need someone to help you with stuff like this when you get home. Eating, drinking, answering the phone. If you were anyone else, I'd be worried, but you've got an army out in the waiting room.'

'A very relieved army,' Daniel added. 'And a very relieved detective.'

Meredith's cheeks heated and she didn't care. 'Did you meet him?'

'We did,' Alex confirmed. 'I hugged him hard and thanked him for saving your life.'

'She mug-hugged him,' Daniel corrected. 'Nearly broke the poor guy's ribs. And bawled all over his shoulder while thanking him.'

'You liked him too,' Alex sniffed. 'When I thanked him, he said you'd saved him first. I thought Daniel was going to shed some tears himself.'

'He said that?' Meredith's lips curved. 'That's so sweet.'

Daniel said, 'Your friends said the same. Apparently, there'd been some doubt.'

Meredith tried to shrug, but the small movement hurt. 'Just a little. I knew whatever doubts they had would be short-lived. So where are the kids?'

'With Hope in the waiting room,' Alex said. 'We found crayons and a few coloring books in your kitchen drawers, so we brought them here and Hope's keeping them busy. We also found lots of finished pictures in the drawer. Who's the artist?'

'Adam,' Meredith said softly. 'It's kind of a long story.'

'Well, you'll have time to tell me *everything*.' Alex settled in the chair. 'We don't have to leave until the thirtieth. Daniel has to be back on duty by New Year's Eve.'

Meredith had always dreaded the time they'd all go home, her grandfather to Florida and Alex to Atlanta, but this year she wouldn't. This year Adam would stay.

For as long as you'll have me, he'd said. Which would be a very long time.

Cincinnati, Ohio,
Tuesday 22 December, 11.15 A.M.

Adam was surrounded by hugging arms and smiling faces – their group of friends and family. He hadn't needed to tell them that Meredith was awake. Apparently, he'd had a sappy grin that had made the announcement for him.

The group had already devised a schedule for visiting her when she woke, rolling dice for position, which made him chuckle. They were pretty amazing, which made him even more grateful they'd welcomed him with open arms and unflinching support for his sobriety. There had been no judgments, no hard feelings. Just open affection.

The first two on the visitor list had already gone back. Alex and Daniel Vartanian, Meredith's cousin and her husband, had arrived from Atlanta in the wee hours of the morning. Everyone agreed to give them the number one slot as they'd come the farthest. Adam had met them only briefly when Alex had hugged him so hard he thought he'd crack, whispering teary thanks for saving Meredith's life.

'She saved mine first,' he'd told her and it was true. It had earned him another hard hug from Alex, a hearty handshake from Daniel, a chorus of awwwws from Meredith's girlfriends – even Kendra, who'd never liked him. And a nod of approval from Clarke Fallon.

Once Alex and Daniel had disappeared into the ICU, Bailey's daughter Hope came up and took Adam by the hand. 'You need to meet people,' she said soberly and led him to a child-sized table where two blond, blue-eyed children were coloring. He'd have been able to tell that they were Daniel and Alex's kids without introduction. Daniel had those same vivid blue eyes.

'These are my cousins,' Hope said. 'Aunt Alex is their mom. This is Mary Katherine. She's four. This is Tommy. He's almost two. I'm their babysitter, because I'm the oldest.' She leaned in to whisper in his ear, as if imparting a great secret. 'Aunt Meredith likes us a lot. If you're going to be her boyfriend, it'd be good if you could like us too.'

Biting back a smile, Adam's answer was equally sober. 'I can. I already like to color.'

Hope brightened. 'You do?'

'Yep. Your aunt keeps some of my pictures on the fridge. Should we make her some to hang in her hospital room?'

Hope nodded. 'That is a very good idea. What should we make?'

He pulled a grownup chair to the small table. 'What do we got?'

'Kistmas books,' Mary Katherine told him, with an adorable lisp. 'I'm doing a tree. Tommy's doing a reindeer.' Then added in a whisper, 'Not very well, but tell him it's good.'

'I will,' Adam said gravely. He chose a gingerbread man and found a bubble of calm in the otherwise noisy room. He was halfway finished when his phone started playing the theme from *Chicago*. 'I need to take this,' he said to Hope. 'It's work. I'll be back later. Promise.' He stepped away from the table, grimacing when his back complained. Too many hours in that plastic chair in ICU. But he wouldn't have traded a single one.

'This is Kimble,' he said, going into the hallway to answer the call.

'It's Mia Mitchell. I'm here with Abe Reagan and a friend of ours. Her name is Dana. We told her about Linnie Holmes coming to Chicago with Shane. She may have a place for Linnie to stay.'

'That's . . .' Adam had to clear his throat. 'That's wonderful.'

'Hi, Detective Kimble.' The voice was throaty and warm. 'My name is Dana Buchanan. I'm on the board of New Start, a halfway house for young women coming out of the sex trade. I believe you have something similar in your town? Mariposa House?'

Adam chuckled. 'We do.' He looked through the doorway at Wendi who perched on Colby's knee, deep in planning with the other women while Colby looked content. 'I'm looking right at the woman who runs it, in fact. I'm in a hospital waiting room filled with nearly all their volunteers. They're Dr Fallon's friends.' And Meredith was their glue. *Mine too.* 'She provides counseling services to Mariposa.' Pro bono, he'd learned.

'We're sorry,' Reagan said. 'We meant to ask how Dr Fallon was doing first, but *somebody* jumped the gun.'

'Sorry,' Mitchell muttered. 'How is she?'

'Awake. She'll be hurting when the meds wear off, but the doctor expects her to make a full recovery.'

'That's good,' Reagan said. 'We've been sending prayers and good thoughts.'

'All appreciated. We'd keep Linnie with us, but she and Shane need each other.'

'And Linnie might need a fresh start,' Dana said.

'That too. What are the housing arrangements and will she have access to counseling?'

'Every resident has their own room. She'll have access to health care – physical and mental health. She can choose to go to college if she wants, but if she doesn't want that, she can train for a variety of different jobs. Is it okay if I send information to your email?'

'Please do. I'll make sure Linnie gets it. When could she move in?'

'We'll have a vacancy after the new year.'

'We appreciate this,' Adam said, not surprised when his voice was gruff. He wasn't going to fight it. 'Linnie deserves a new start.'

'That's why we're here,' Dana said. 'We'll be in touch.'

'Give your LT our regards,' Reagan said. 'And Merry Christmas.'

They ended the call and Adam stood there a moment, feeling happy. Linnie could have a future. And he'd helped.

'Hey, Adam.' Trip's deep rumble pulled him out of his thoughts. Quincy was with him. They looked wary. 'How's the doc?'

'Awake.' Adam had repeated the word a number of times and didn't mind at all. 'What's up?'

Both men relaxed. 'Follow-up,' Quincy said. 'We've found out a few things in the last twenty-four. Can we talk somewhere?'

Adam looked wistfully at the small table with his half-finished picture of a gingerbread man. He'd have to finish it later. He might need to, if he was going to hear difficult news. 'I haven't eaten. You want to walk with me to the cafeteria?'

'I could eat,' Trip said.

'You can *always* eat,' Adam laughed. The three of them got sandwiches and found a table in the corner of the cafeteria, away from prying eyes and ears. 'So hit me.'

'First,' Quincy said, 'we searched Mike's garages – he owns three. His mechanics say they've done a lot of repairs on black SUV's. We found the vehicle used on Saturday. The seats and the back window had been pulled out for replacement.'

'Because Linnie bled on the seats,' Adam said. 'And she said he shot at her as she fled from him Saturday afternoon.'

Quincy nodded. 'Yes. The mechanics said that Wyatt would just change one black SUV for another whenever they needed to be fixed.'

'We also found barrels of peroxide and acetone in the garage's storage area,' Trip said. 'Ingredients for TATP, the same explosive in the bomb Wyatt strapped to Andy Gold. There were triggers, fuses, cans . . . Mike could have made several more bombs. I don't think Wyatt knew about them or he would have burned that garage down too.'

'Good to know,' Adam said. He was about to take a bite of his sandwich, but Trip and Quincy glanced at one another strangely. He put the sandwich down. 'What?'

'We got into Wyatt's safe,' Trip said. 'He had three fake passport – one U.S., one Canadian, and one Bahamian. There was also a list of bank accounts and passwords.'

'How much did he have hidden away?' Adam asked, not really wanting to know.

'Over forty million bucks,' Trip said quietly.

The very number made Adam's stomach churn. 'Enough incentive for him to try to get into his house once more.' Because he'd wondered why Hanson had taken that risk.

'Yes,' Trip agreed simply. 'He also had all kinds of records in there – dirt on a lot of politicians and influential people. He kept a notebook, written in code. Decker translated it.' Because Kate's Decker was good with codes. 'Some of it was potential people he could blackmail later. The Buon Cibo hostess, for example, skated on an arrest for possession. He knew she was desperate for money and he had her phone number because he was the arresting officer. So when he needed a favor from that restaurant, he knew where to go.'

'He had entries about all the neighbors, all his "employees," money and favors he paid out and his "property,"' Quincy said. 'You want the hard stuff first or the harder stuff?'

'Let's work our way up,' Adam said warily.

Trip nodded. 'Okay. Wyatt took in blackmail money from a lot of people, but he paid John Kasper, your sponsor. More specifically, he paid John's wife's doctor bills. She's sick. Cancer. That's why John sold you out.'

Adam drew a breath. 'I guess it's a better reason than a free SUV.'

'Still a betrayal,' Quincy murmured.

'Yeah. How will his wife get her care from here on out?'

The two looked at each other again. 'She's gone too,' Trip said quietly. 'Isenberg and Deacon did the notification and she was found dead the next day. She'd OD'd on painkillers. I don't think she knew her husband had betrayed you.'

'Good,' Adam said. 'I wouldn't want her to suffer any more.'

Trip sighed. 'You're a good man, Adam. Which makes the next thing harder to tell you. So I just will. We found Paula's family. They live in a very rural part of southeastern Ohio. Lots of farms. Paula was playing outside six years ago and disappeared. There was a notation in Wyatt's notebook – a street address and a date. No city or state. It would have taken us a while to search all the addresses against reports of missing children. Her family found me. I put her photo out online yesterday and her family saw it last night.'

'Wyatt just . . . just took her?'

Quincy nodded. 'Looks like it. She'd just come home from the state school for the deaf. It was the first day of summer vacation.'

'You informed her family?' Adam asked, torn between gratitude and irritation.

'We did,' Trip said, his voice heavy with sympathy. 'They'd like to meet you sometime. I told them you were tied up in personal matters now, but you'd be willing to see them when Dr Fallon is out of the woods. They want to thank you. For trying to help their daughter. And for paying to bury her.'

Adam looked away, overcome. 'They want to thank me?' he whispered. He gave up the pretense of control and wiped his eyes on the back of his hand. 'Does Nash know?'

'Not yet,' Quincy said. 'We were going to see him next.'

'He'll want to meet them too. He's been putting flowers on her grave every month.'

Trip hesitated. 'If you two need anyone to go with you when you meet with the family, I'm happy to go too.'

Adam was so finished with trying to go it alone. 'Thanks. I'd like that.'

The three of them sat in heavy silence for a long time. Until the ringing of Adam's cell phone had them all jumping. It was the generic ringtone for people he didn't know. But when Adam saw the caller ID, he blinked. It was Ray, the owner of the condo. The man whose daughter was kidnapped. The case Adam and Wyatt had solved together. Raymond never called him. With growing dread, Adam answered. 'Ray?'

'Adam. Hi. I can't talk long. It's one fifteen here and I have to get to bed, but I needed to call you first.'

'Where are you?' Because their connection crackled.

'Japan. Look, I saw the news out of the States. That Wyatt Hanson was a murderer.'

'That made the news over there?' Adam asked, surprised.

'I have an online subscription to the *Ledger*, just to get news from home. What I needed to tell you is that Skye saw the report and she had a panic attack. It's been years since she had one. She saw Wyatt's picture while I was reading the article. She'd never seen him, you know, after the ordeal. Only you kept up with us. He didn't, except to ask me for stock tips. She said she remembered him. He was one of the men who took her.'

Adam's mouth fell open. 'What? Is she sure?'

'She said she was certain, over and over before we finally got her calmed down enough to go to sleep. It makes a lot of sense. There were no leads, but Hanson spied the car carrying her. Both the men who were trying to get her help were killed.'

'So they couldn't turn on him,' Adam murmured. 'I was shot with one of the men's guns, but Wyatt killed the man right afterward. Said the guy was aiming for my head, so he shot the man first. I wonder now who fired the shot that actually hit my leg.'

'That I don't know. I just wanted you to know about Skye.'

'Thanks, Raymond. Give my best to Skye, okay?'

'You got it. Gotta go. My morning alarm goes off in a few hours.'

The call ended and Adam was left staring at his phone. Numbly he told Trip and Quincy about Skye's kidnapping, finishing with what Raymond had told him.

'Wyatt kidnapped her?' Quincy asked.

'That's what Skye says now.' Adam shook his head, still stunned. 'That means Wyatt was running scams from the very beginning. I was a rookie when that happened. And Skye almost died.'

'But she didn't,' Trip said. 'Because you saved her.'

Adam nodded. 'Yeah. I did, didn't I?'

Trip gripped Adam's arm. 'You gonna be okay, man? You've just been hit with a mountain of shit.'

'Yeah.' Adam nodded again. 'But I did my job and Skye's alive. I did my job and Paula's not. But I did my best. Sometimes that's not going to be good enough.'

And that was the simple truth.

'What happens next?' Trip asked, giving him a cautious look.

'I think I'm going back upstairs to finish coloring my ginger-bread man. Then I'll see Meredith, then I'll go to her house and get it ready for when she comes home. I have to fix the lock on her back door.'

'And then?' Trip pressed and Adam understood.

'I'm not hitting the bar. If I feel the urge, I'll call one of you. How's that?'

'Good,' Quincy said. 'That's what we wanted to hear.'

'I could use an assist, though,' Adam said thoughtfully. 'I'd like to go see my mom, but I always have to listen to my father's shit. If one of you wanted to go with me . . . maybe intimidate him a little?'

Trip looked fiendishly delighted. 'I would be happy to, man. Just name the time.'

'This afternoon? Mom's overdue a visit.'

'We can hit my favorite barbecue place on the way,' Trip promised.

Adam looked at Trip's empty plate and laughed. 'Sounds like a plan.'

Cincinnati, Ohio,
Tuesday 22 December, 6.30 P.M.

It was after sundown before Adam finally returned. Meredith had been moved out of ICU into a private room where she'd been watching for him for hours, through all the visitors she'd had. She sighed with relief when he finally tiptoed in, hands behind his back.

'I'm not asleep,' she said and he relaxed.

'Good. I was hoping it would be my turn again. Your dance card was full today.'

'It was nice to see everyone. But I really just wanted to dance with you.'

He leaned over her bed rail and gave her a sweet kiss. 'Good, because I'm back and you're stuck with me for a few days. I took the rest of the week off. How do you feel?'

'I hurt. So let's talk about something else. What did you bring me?' she asked cheekily. He produced the small Christmas tree from behind his back. It stood about eight inches tall and bore one sad ornament that bowed it over. 'A Charlie Brown tree! I love it.'

He set it on the tray table. 'I figured you would. You're a sucker for the underdog.'

She smiled up at him. 'It's true. I heard you were busy after you left here.'

'It's true,' he said. 'I'll give you the details tomorrow when you're feeling better.'

'I got some of the details from Kate and Wendi. I heard about Linnie's placement. We're all over the moon about that.'

'Me too. Linnie seemed thrilled and Shane is too relieved for words.' Adam sat next to her and held her two unhurt fingers. 'I went to see my mom this afternoon.'

'Yeah, Quincy mentioned that when he visited. He said you had a bodyguard.'

Adam smiled. 'Trip went with me to keep my dad leashed. It was a nice visit.'

'I'm glad.' She was, even though Mrs Kimble didn't deserve a son like Adam.

'She wants to meet you, but I told her that I didn't want my dad around you. She promised she'd come alone. Maybe on Christmas. You should be home by then.'

'I'll be nice,' Meredith promised and hoped she could keep the promise.

'I'd appreciate it.' He kissed her fingers. 'I fixed the lock on your basement door.'

'Thank you.'

He lifted a brow, his expression growing abruptly wicked. 'Oh, I didn't do it for free. Not like all the volunteer work I do all over town. I expect to be paid.'

'With what? Gel pens and colored pencils?'

He leaned in to kiss her again. 'No. Although we could do that after.'

'It's going to be a while before I can do anything, before or after,' she said, grumpy at the thought. The doctor had said six weeks till she was even halfway back to normal.

He waggled his brows. 'I can wait for you. I'll just keep fixing things and adding it to your bill. By the time you *can* again, the rest of your life will be promised to me.'

She closed her eyes, content now that he was here. 'It already is.'

Epilogue

Mount Carmel, Ohio,
Saturday 6 February, 2.00 P.M.

'Oh my gosh. Adam!' Standing in Mariposa House's living room, Meredith turned in a circle, staring in delight. The room was decorated for Christmas, complete with a live tree. All the decorations had been taken down right after New Year's, but someone had put them all back up. Complete with a live, sixteen-foot tree. Adam had promised they'd have a Christmas after she was feeling better and after six weeks of healing and rehab on her repaired arm, she finally was. He'd kept his promise.

She hooked her good arm around his neck, and pulled his head down for a lusty kiss that made her wish they were back at her little house, despite the gorgeous decorations. Because she'd only been cleared for sex a few weeks before, after a long month without.

'How did you do this?'

'I had help,' Adam said, smiling down at her. He often had a smile on his face these days, and that made her even happier. 'I called the guy at the tree farm on Christmas Eve, told him your story, and asked if we could come back and cut another tree now. Diesel went out with me yesterday to pick it up. So you should thank Diesel too. Just not like this,' he teased. He teased more often too. He seemed lighter all the way around.

Meredith found Diesel pretending to be busy in the next room, when he was really giving them privacy. Over the last six weeks he'd become the brother she'd never had and she couldn't imagine a time when he hadn't been there. Now she tugged on the sleeve of

594

his T-shirt until he bent his knees, allowing her to peck his cheek in thanks. 'It's wonderful. Thank you.'

He shrugged it off like it was no big deal. 'You missed Christmas. We wanted to give it to you.'

Adam had followed her into the next room. 'All the girls helped decorate. They'll be disappointed they didn't get to see your reaction.'

Meredith frowned. 'Where are the girls?' She'd run straight into the living room after spying the tree through the window when they'd come through the front gate. She just now realized how quiet it was. The house was never this quiet.

She caught the glint in Diesel's eyes just before Adam turned her around, so that she faced back into the living room, which had suddenly filled with people.

'Merry Christmas!' they all shouted, and that fast she was surrounded by Mallory and all the girls who lived at Mariposa House. Adam rushed to Meredith's right side, making himself a barrier between her and anyone who didn't remember that her arm wasn't completely healed and tried to hug her.

'This is amazing. You girls did a wonderful job!' Meredith sniffed and smelled cookies. 'You guys even baked for me?'

'No,' Mallory said. She'd started GED school right after New Year's and was doing so well. They were all proud of her. Although Meredith still did a double-take whenever she saw her. Inspired by how different she'd looked with a wig, Mallory had dyed her hair and learned valuable makeup skills from Kate. It gave her confidence a boost, made her believe she could walk down a street and not be recognized as who she used to be – a victim.

Which made Meredith so happy she could cry.

'We don't bake,' one of the girls said. 'Miss Wendi always bakes the cookies.'

'Except when I have help,' Wendi called, coming through the kitchen doorway with a big tray of holiday cookies. She was followed by Kendra, Bailey, Scarlett, and Delores, with Faith and Kate bringing up the rear, each carrying a tray of goodies. 'Parrish?'

'We're coming!' Parrish called back from upstairs. He clomped down the stairs, dressed in a Santa suit, with a fake beard and a sack of presents over his shoulder. He was followed by all the partners and husbands, each carrying something useful – another sack of presents, a boombox, a karaoke machine (*um, no*, Meredith thought), a video camera, and . . . a dog?

Stone O'Bannion was carrying a young yellow lab, who looked perfectly at home in his arms.

Meredith recognized the dog right away. 'Mac.' She looked over her shoulder at Adam who was watching the dog happily. 'Are we taking him home today?'

Adam nodded. 'I finished fixing the fence last night. He won't be able to escape.' He'd chosen the dog at Delores's shelter two weeks before – or the dog had chosen him would be more accurate – but the fence around Meredith's backyard hadn't been tended in years and it had had some weak places. Now that the fence was whole, they could take the dog home.

'You named him Mac?' Mallory asked.

'Actually it's Mac-N-Cheese, for the crayon color,' Meredith told her. 'We figure no matter what dogs we get in the future, they'll always have crayon colors to name them.'

'I picked a dog too,' Mallory confided. Meredith knew that she'd been out at Delores's several times a week, scouting all the new arrivals for a good fit. 'She's small, like a toy poodle size, but she's a mutt. Dolores says I can work at the shelter to earn money for her food, and Wendi says she can sleep in my bed if I keep her clean. She's so soft and she cuddled up in my arms and went to sleep. And my new therapist says if I get her certified as a therapy dog, I can bring her to school with me, in case I have a panic attack.'

Meredith gave her a one-armed hug. 'It sounds like you've got a plan. Let's go say hi to everyone.' Because Adam had already hurried over to Stone to claim his dog. The two had bonded from the first moment and it was simply lovely to see.

Dani Novak came in the front door, closing it quickly behind her. 'Sorry I'm late. I got delayed at the clinic.' Mallory took her coat, revealing the delicate lacy shawl draped around Dani's shoulders and Meredith did another double-take. Because she'd seen that shawl before – on Diesel's knitting needles as he'd kept vigil with her and her family during that difficult week after Christmas.

'This is beautiful,' Meredith said, touching the lace after giving Dani a hug. 'Where did you get it?'

'It was the weirdest thing. It was in a wrapped box on my desk chair in the clinic. Had my name on the label, but nothing to say who it was from. It is so soft. And the color is perfect – the black with white streaked through it.' Just like Dani's hair. 'I just love it.'

She should, Meredith thought. Diesel had worked damn hard on the thing. Meredith looked across the room to where Diesel was helping Colby give gifts to the younger girls, who were thrilled to be getting presents for the second time in two months. Diesel met Meredith's eyes, his pleading her to silence and she sighed. Sooner or later something would happen to shove the two together.

Meredith just hoped it wasn't a murder. Or murders. Because Wyatt Hanson had taken nearly twenty lives in a single weekend before Adam had ended his life. God only knew how many others he'd killed over the years. Others like Paula.

'Well, it's a gorgeous shawl,' Meredith told Dani. 'Whoever made it obviously knows you well. Hey, have you heard from Linnie lately?' she asked, because it had looked like Dani wanted to ask what she'd meant by *knows you well*.

Dani's smile lit up her face. 'Linnie is doing well. The folks up in Chicago found her a doctor right away and she's been taking her meds. She's not having any side effects and she's gained a little weight. I don't talk to her, but Shane says she's looking into being a social worker. She wants to do better than the caseworker in Indianapolis who betrayed them.'

'Well, she's set the bar pretty low,' Meredith said wryly. 'I think Linnie can do far better than that. But I'm happy that she's doing so well.' She tucked her arm through Dani's. 'Let's go mingle.'

They found Wendi, who looked pleased as punch at the surprise she'd pulled off. 'I didn't suspect a thing,' Meredith told her. 'How did you manage it?'

'It was mostly Adam,' Wendi said with a smile. 'I didn't know there was such a good guy under all that bitter broodiness.'

Dani sighed. 'I kept telling you. But he had to prove it himself. I'm so glad he did.'

'Me too,' Meredith said. She caught Adam's eye because he'd been watching her, Mac lying peacefully at his feet. She gave him a look that promised future reward, shivering when his eyes darkened. She turned back to her friends, finding them smiling smugly, like they knew exactly what she was thinking. 'I think he's won everyone over,' Meredith said, pretending like they weren't right, and that she wasn't imagining them home in her bed. But they just grinned and she knew she'd been busted. Still she pressed on. 'Bailey and Ryan like him. Alex and Daniel seemed to too, and Papa has adopted him.' Which was a good thing, because Adam's father continued to be horrible and his mother either hadn't tried or hadn't succeeded in getting away to visit her son. Even on Christmas Day. 'I just wish we could have had more time with my family before they all had to go home.'

'You wish that?' Wendi said.

Meredith frowned. 'Of course I do.'

'Good.' Wendi raised a toy horn to her mouth and blew. Everyone went silent, almost as if it were a prearranged signal, Meredith thought suspiciously.

Her suspicions were proven when the kitchen door opened again and Alex, Daniel, and Clarke pushed into the already crowded room. Meredith's mouth fell open and Alex laughed. 'Did you think we could miss your Christmas?' she asked, hugging Meredith's left side as Daniel kissed her cheek.

'You look so much healthier,' Daniel said.

'You got some meat back on your bones,' Clarke said jovially. He looked behind him, stretching out a hand for the tall, slim woman who'd followed him in.

'Sharon,' Meredith said warmly, greeting her grandfather's new girlfriend. 'You two look disgustingly tan.' The Florida sun was good for them. 'How did you all get here?'

'Adam called,' Alex told her. 'He asked us to come.'

'Excuse me,' Meredith told them. 'I'll be right back.' She crossed the room to where Adam stood, his face filled with quiet joy. 'You did this for me?'

'I'd do just about anything for you,' he told her.

Her eyes grew blurry and she blinked at the tears. 'You brought my family and my friends together and all the girls. How do I thank you for this?'

'You bring everyone together, Meredith,' he said seriously. 'I just made a few calls to get them all in one place for you.' He winked at her. 'Besides, I'm not doing this for free.'

She laughed through her tears. 'I thought we tore up my tab for all the home improvements.' She'd never had so much fun working off a debt.

'We did. But if you want to thank me for today, you can wear this tonight.' He gave her a box, wrapped in a silver bow. She lifted one corner of the box to peek inside and felt her cheeks go red.

'There's nothing in this box.'

'I know,' he said wickedly.

Sure that her cheeks were flaming and not caring a whit, she leaned up to kiss him. 'You're lucky that I'd do most anything for you too.'

THRILLINGLY GOOD BOOKS FROM CRIMINALLY GOOD WRITERS

CRIME FILES BRINGS YOU THE LATEST RELEASES FROM TOP CRIME AND THRILLER AUTHORS.

SIGN UP ONLINE FOR OUR MONTHLY NEWSLETTER AND BE THE FIRST TO KNOW ABOUT OUR COMPETITIONS, NEW BOOKS AND MORE.